Dragonlove

Dragonfriend Book 2

by

MARC SECCHIA

www.bluevalleyauthorservices.com

First Edition

ISBN: 1517176336

ISBN-13: 978-1517176334

www.marcsecchia.com

Dedication

For the power of love is greater than any Dragon,
Greater than magic, greater than soul-fire,
It changes the immutable,
Breaks all chains,
And stirs the Islands to dance.

DISCOVER OTHER BOOKS BY MARC SECCHIA

www.marcsecchia.com

Shapeshifter Dragons

Aranya
Shadow Dragon
The Pygmy Dragon
The Onyx Dragon
Dragonfriend
Dragonlove
Dragonsoul
Dragon Thief

IsleSong Series

The Girl who Sang with Whales

Shioni of Sheba Series

The Enchanted Castle
The King's Horse
The Mad Giant
The Sacred Lake
The Fiuri Realms

Equinox Cycle

The Horse Dreamer

Other Works

The Legend of El Shashi
Feynard

Table of Contents

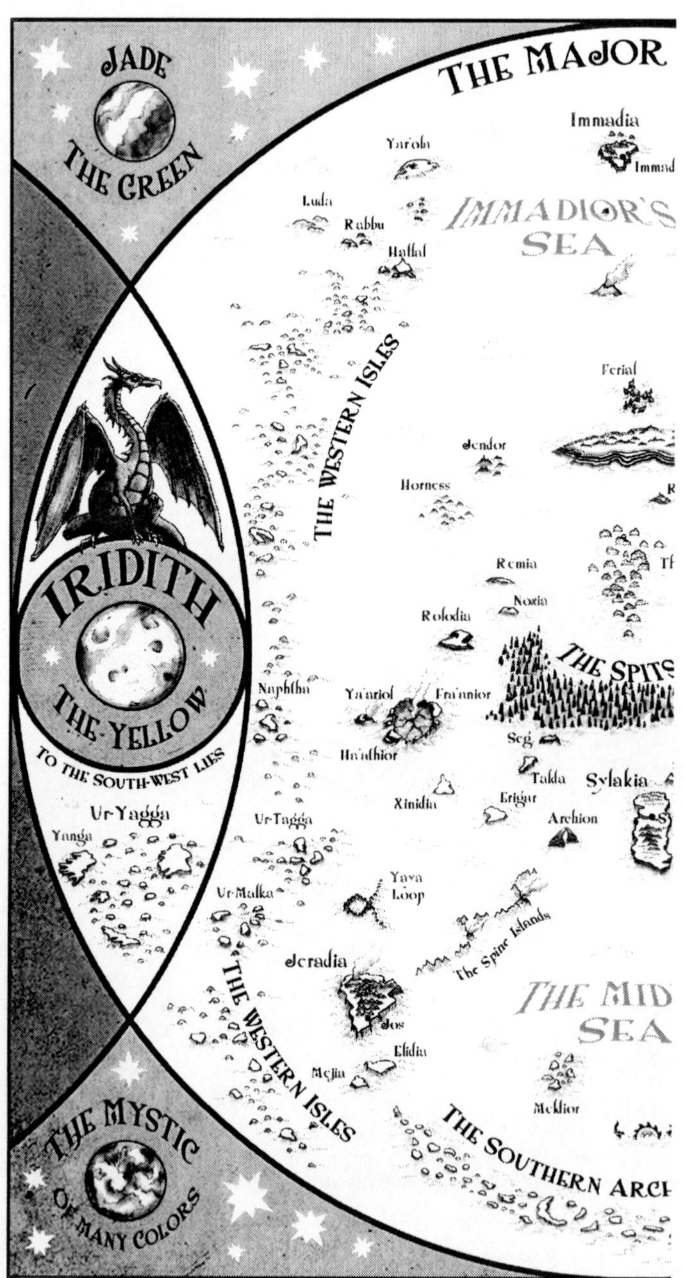
JADE
THE GREEN
THE MAJOR
Immadia
Yar'oln
Immad
Luda
Rabbu
Hallal
IMMADIOR'S
SEA
THE WESTERN ISLES
Ferial
Jendor
Horness
Remia
Noria
Rolodia
THE SPITS
IRIDITH
THE YELLOW
TO THE SOUTH-WEST LIES
Ur-Yagga
Yanga
Naphthn
Ya'ariol
Fra'anior
Ha'athior
Seg
Talda
Sylakia
Xinidia
Erigar
Archion
Ur-Tagga
Yava
Loop
Ur-Malka
The Spine Islands
Jeradia
Jos
Elidia
Mejia
THE MID
SEA
THE WESTERN ISLES
Meklior
THE SOUTHERN ARC
THE MYSTIC
OF MANY COLORS

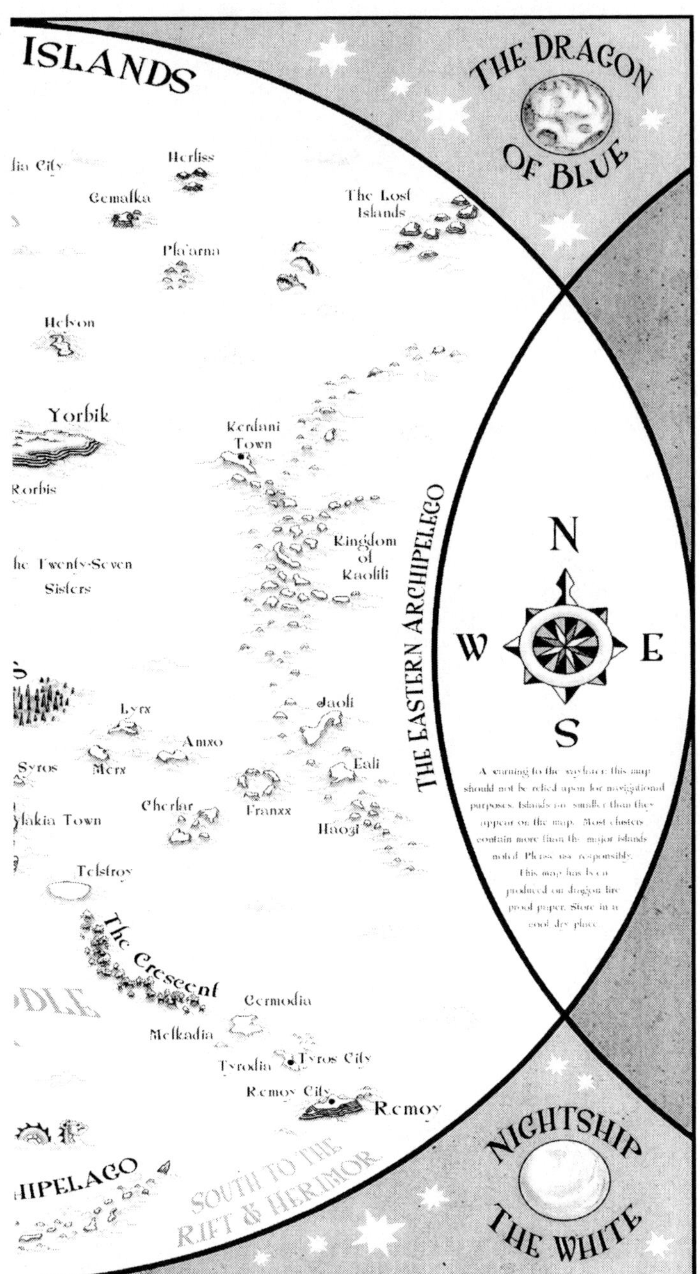
ISLANDS
THE DRAGON OF BLUE
Herliss
Gemalka
The Lost Islands
Pla'arna
Helyon
Yorbik
Kerdani Town
Rorbis
Kingdom of Kaolili
Sisters
THE EASTERN ARCHIPELEGO
N
W
E
S
Lyrx
Jaoli
Amxo
Syros
Merx
Eali
Cherlar
Franxx
Haozi
Telstroy
The Cresecent
Cermodia
Melkadia
Tyros City
Tyrodin
Remoy City
Remoy
NIGHTSHIP THE WHITE
HIPELAGO
SOUTH TO THE RIFT & HERIMOR

Chapter One

Hualiama

DRAGON-THUNDER SHOOK the palace.

Hualiama kicked off her soft slippers. Picking up her formal lace skirts, she dashed out of her chambers, but the long train snagged on the curved claws of a stylised jade Dragon. Dagger in hand, she hacked wildly at the priceless fabric restricting her stride. Bleeding–Dragon fire take it! She stumbled up endless stairs designed by an architect enamoured with galleries sized to house ridiculous mountains of royal artefacts. Entering a long corridor, her woefully short legs stretched into a flat-out sprint. Ranks of larger-than-life paintings of tall, pointy-eared ancestors blurred to either side. All of her attention was focussed on the altercation on the Receiving Balcony, atop Fra'anior's Royal Palace.

A Dragon's voice boomed, "This means war, King Chalcion!"

She had to stop them. Now.

Slewing around a corner, Lia deliberately cannoned off a man-high ornamental vase. She caught her balance with the agility of a dragonet. Head down, she pumped her arms, accelerating to the speed of a warrior and dancer who trained for five hours daily. Twisting between two thickset marble columns to shortcut her route, Lia used a stone pot-plant as a springboard to leap upward at full stretch, flying briefly over a yawning drop to the palace gardens below. Snagging the crenulations atop the wall with her fingertips, she wriggled upward with the facility of a lizard scaling a wall and vaulted smoothly onto the balcony beyond. One more level.

She heard querulous voices, and the swish of Dragons' wings. They were leaving.

Her heart could not sink, because it was thrashing about in her throat. But it should. This was just the incident to ignite the simmering relations between Dragons and Humans. She should know. That very morning, Lia had witnessed a Dragonwing immolating a Human village.

Bounding up the final staircase, she raced out onto the balcony, screaming, "Stop!"

Lia caught her foot in the wreck of her dress, slipped, and skidded across the rough flagstones all the way to the edge of her father's robes.

"Stop them!"

Stooping, the King seized her arm. "This is an outrage, Hualiama! How dare you barge–"

She tore free, hurled herself to the balcony's edge, and screamed again, "Stop! By the Spirits of the Ancient Dragons, please!"

Hualiama gazed out over her beloved Island. Sweet, haunting harmonies of birdsong and dragonet-song saluted the gathering evening. The ever-song, some called it, the unique melody of Fra'anior, an Island-Cluster of twenty-seven Islands precariously perched on the rim-wall of the greatest volcano in the Island-World. The late afternoon light streamed in so thick and golden, she feared the King might pass a law to hoard it in the royal treasury. But she had eyes only for the Dragons.

Four Dragons winged over the vast bowl of Fra'anior's volcanic caldera, their scales gleaming like glorious jewels in the resplendent light. Two were hundred-foot Reds, as perfect as matched rubies, called Zulior and Qualiana, and the third a vast emerald-green named Andarraz. Sapphurion, the Dragon Elder himself, led their Dragonwing. His scales evoked the turquoise hues of a clear lake. All were breathtaking, but Sapphurion was the greatest of all, the leader of the Island-World's Dragons.

The four Dragons banked with supreme grace, angling back toward the Receiving Balcony. Hualiama's heart stood still.

"Now you've done it, you insolent wretch," the King

growled, right by her ear. "You've wrecked our negotiations …"

Words that beat upon Lia's eardrums without meaning.

A hymn of aching awe slaked her spirit as Sapphurion's mighty wings flared, occluding the suns. His talons dug into the paving stones, pitted by many such landings. Crouched down, Sapphurion's spine-spikes exceeded the height of the twenty-five foot flagpole set back from the balcony, flying the purple of Royal Fra'anior. The scent of an adult Dragon teased Hualiama's nostrils with hints of charred cinnamon, sulphur and the smoke of his belly-fires. The other three Dragons thudded down nearby, easily filling the broad balcony as they folded their wings with a leathery rustling. Flame licked about their nostrils.

Zalcion, the King's brother, hissed in her other ear, "I hope you burn for this, Lia."

Lia stood erect, meeting the Dragons' glares with a brave mien, while nerves churned her insides like the bubbling lava-vents of the caldera floor. Let them blow smoke. Six years ago, Grandion–noble, unforgettable Grandion–had broken the draconic taboo of non-interference in Human affairs, helping her to rescue her family. Lia had seen neither hide nor talon of him since, though she daily watched the skies. Did the matchless Tourmaline Dragon shun her out of shame? Or had her impetuosity instigated his banishment, or worse?

Thoughts to shadow the most brilliant suns-set.

With enormous dignity, Sapphurion bent his neck to regard the Human delegation. He rumbled, "Who evoked the Spirits?"

"My daughter, Hualiama," said King Chalcion. "Forgive her, she's but a callow youth …"

The Dragon's predatory gaze lit upon Hualiama, his blue-in-blue eyes swirling with magic and Dragon fire in their depths. She had to lock her knees to restrain an urge to dive beneath the paving stones and pull them back over her head as fast as humanly possible.

Clasping her hands over her pounding heart, Lia bowed deeply. "O mighty draconic majesty, may the sulphurous blessings of the Great Dragon Fra'anior abide with you and your kin."

"Very formal and correct, little one," said Sapphurion, his brow-ridges wrinkling slightly in consternation. "You would speak?"

Must she always be little Lia, or 'short shrift' to her royal brothers and sister? For Lia was unusually diminutive for a Fra'aniorian, just five feet and two inches in stature. She possessed the pointy ears and smoky eyes which betrayed an Isles heritage, aye, but beyond that, her past was a mystery. A Dragoness had found her upon Gi'ishior. The Dragons had brought her to the Human King and Queen, who adopted her at some point after her second birthday.

Petite and small-boned, and twenty-one summers of age, Hualiama wore a proper silken headscarf imported at enormous cost from faraway Helyon, and a now-ruined lace gown in a green which matched her eyes. Her right foot stood in a puddle of her own blood.

Little Lia, lover of all things Dragon.

She blurted out, "O Sapphurion, it *was* Dragons who burned the village–"

Fury! Thunder! Hualiama shrank back before catching herself. How ralti-stupid was she? How many times had the King and Queen not counselled her not to speak with a rush of blood to the head?

"Insolent hatchling!" Andarraz bellowed.

Zulior shadow-charged her, roaring, "Foul accusations!"

The King gabbled, "Lia, please! The Dragons are riled enough already."

Zalcion twisted her arm until her skin burned. "Control your daughter, Chalcion! War breeds in reckless words."

"I bring proof!"

Spoken at a moment when person and creature alike paused for breath, Hualiama's protest rang as clearly as a bell. The silence expanded, as viscous and all-pervading as the golden light.

Every eye, Dragon and Human alike, burned at her.

Sapphurion crooked his foreclaw. "Approach, little one.

Need I advise you how serious an accusation this is?"

Lia tottered forward on legs which had lost the will to support her weight. "I understand, mighty Sapphurion."

"Impossible," sniffed Andarraz. "Must we suffer insult upon insult?"

Had she wished, Lia could have reached out to touch the Blue Dragon. His flank was a mountain of armoured Dragon scales, his forepaw several times longer than her body, and she dreaded to think about his fangs, gleaming briefly within a mouth which could accommodate ten of her in a single bite. Better to face Sapphurion, however, than her father and his bristling posse of councillors behind her. The Dragon Elder might be called harsh and unyielding behind his back, but he was also by reputation a Dragon who valued justice and integrity above all else.

Sapphurion growled, "One must have good reason to stir up the Dragon-Spirits, little one. What proof do you offer?"

"My witness of today's events."

"Witness?" Zalcion almost howled. "Chalcion, brother, this is madness–"

"King Chalcion," Sapphurion boomed, silencing the King's brother. His forepaw engulfed Lia's shoulders, the three forward-facing and two opposing talons closing about her slender frame like a cage of grey swords. Even though his Dragon hide warmed her skin, she shivered. "This is your second daughter, Hualiama?"

"Technically, Hualiama's a royal ward, a foundling–" Chalcion cleared his throat "–but practically, I treat her as my own daughter."

"Technically, I live in a palace, but practically, I'm a nobody."

Lia only realised her whisper had carried when the Dragon's paw twitched. She winced, hanging her head. Please, let none of her family have overheard. What must Sapphurion think of her now–churlish? Rebellious? A foolish child?

Could she be the same Hualiama who–the Red Dragoness Qualiana broke off as her mate nipped her shoulder sharply. Without losing a beat, she added, *Sapphurion, do the dragonets not call this one Dragonfriend?*

The same Hualiama? She had never heard of another person who shared her unusual name.

Aye, I had forgotten, said Qualiana's mate. *Intriguing.*

It took every ounce of Lia's courage to school her features into stillness. They were speaking Dragonish, mind to mind … and thus, she knew his lie for what it was. Sapphurion had not forgotten. Dragons never forgot. She had once lived with a dragonet, her best and truest friend, Flicker–that much was public knowledge. But Flicker had also taught her to speak Dragonish. A Human who understood Dragon speech? Who had lived upon the holy Dragon Isle? Secrets to bury in the depths of the Cloudlands.

Qualiana rubbed her knuckle beneath her eye, a gesture which signified deep Dragon emotion. She said to Sapphurion, *O my soul's flame, this girl saved Grandion's life.*

Silence! Speak not of that traitor in my presence!

Sapphurion's thunder ignited her mind. For several breaths, all Hualiama saw was Dragon fire, a darkly orange conflagration behind her eyes. Traitor. Such a simple, soul-destroying word. A sorer wound she could not have imagined. Oh, Grandion! Great-hearted Grandion, who had sung and journeyed with her. What had she done to him?

The Blue Dragon's voice betrayed no emotion. "Hualiama, you claim to have witnessed today's events?"

Quelling her anxiety, praying the Dragons would not have detected her response, Lia replied, "I did, mighty Sapphurion. You may read my memories from my mind, as I know you're able." His paw tightened, the talons pressing into her belly and upper thighs like a suit of metallic armour. Accordingly, she steeled herself. "I entreat you, o most noble of Dragons, to set aside thoughts of war. We trust you to bring these Dragons to justice. Let us bind lasting peace between Dragons and Humans."

The power of Sapphurion's mesmeric gaze made blackness creep around the edges of her vision.

Wretchedly unsteady of voice, Lia added, "But I beg you to look no deeper than today, mighty Sapphurion. Please, I mean no disrespect, but you must swear it on the name of the Black Dragon, Fra'anior, or upon your mother's egg."

"Heavy words." His wings flared briefly, signalling irritation. "You presume to bargain with a Dragon?"

She could not tell what lay beneath that lidded reptilian gaze. Cold sweat trickled down Lia's spine. "M-Mighty Dragon … I-I …"

Qualiana said, *Have not you tormented this hatchling enough, Sapphurion?*

The fire in his eyes threatened to make her forget her own name. Sapphurion growled, "Very well, little one, I shall honour your request. I so swear, upon my mother's egg."

At his low prompt, Hualiama opened her mind to Sapphurion, and summoned her memories of the day's events. An alien yet beautiful presence, a being of pure flame, stepped within the portals of her being. The Dragon Elder sailed with her in her solo Dragonship, westward and south around the volcanic rim, Island to Island. She stopped at Gi'ishior, home of the ancient Halls of the Dragons, to make necessary repairs. Lia saw just a quarter-mile across the abyss at tiny Giaza Island, Dragons firebombing a Human village, the carnage, the horror nigh slaying her spirit … *those* Dragons blatantly enjoying their sport, tossing bodies to each other and pretending to miss their catches … now hiding from a Dragon who soared above the hallowed ground–stop! She banished that memory. Returning to Fra'anior, the main Human Island, hearing the altercation on the balcony, running upstairs …

"Enough," said Sapphurion.

Only the grip of his paw kept Hualiama from collapse.

Stepping around her mate, Qualiana reached out to touch Lia's forehead with her foreclaw. *Strength to you, little one.* Lia's vision cleared. A sense of wellbeing rippled through her body. And Hualiama reeled, seeing in her mind's eye another time and place, the Red Dragoness crooning over her clutch, and an odd thought intruded. Did she recognise this Dragoness' mental touch? How? No part of her agitated feelings made sense. Her soul sang, 'I know these Dragons!' Something in the timbre of Qualiana's voice had stirred memories so long buried, it was as though they lay beneath the impenetrable Cloudlands. An awakening, her heart insisted. Beyond reason or belief, her rational mind disagreed.

Aloud, Qualiana said, "You received her witness?"

"I saw the truth." The Blue Dragon's brow ridges drew down. "These are the perpetrators, my kin."

The Dragons communed briefly.

Andarraz coughed out an involuntary fireball in surprise, but his aim was thankfully out over the Island, not toward the Humans. The Green growled, "I know these Dragons. They hail from Merx, in the East." *I'm ashamed, o Sapphurion.*

Not all Greens are good eggs, said the Blue.

Sapphurion's muzzle swung back toward Lia, cracking open to reveal a thicket of gleaming fangs, the smallest of which were longer than her arm. He rasped, "Where did you travel today, Hualiama?"

Lia bit her lip so hard, she tasted blood. Oh, flying ralti sheep! She knew exactly which Dragon had flown over the holy Dragon Island of Ha'athior that morning. Betrayed by her own thoughts. For a Human to trespass upon forbidden soil was a monumental transgression, a deed which would land her in hot lava with Human and Dragon alike–just as her flight Dragonback or her knowledge of the Dragon tongue would instantly earn her a sword in the ribs or a Dragon's claw in the neck, no questions asked. But where else could she honour Flicker's memory?

And she had been planning to visit another friend, who hid deep in the bowels of Ha'athior Island …

"I visited a gravesite, mighty Sapphurion." She tried for defiance, but her voice cracked and wobbled like a dragonet drunk on fermented prekki fruit.

"Indeed?" He glared at Lia with the air of a parent chastising an errant hatchling. "For a girl whose lofty ideals include binding lasting peace between Humankind and Dragonkind, Hualiama of Fra'anior, you are remarkably economical with the truth. Know that there can be no peace such as you wish for, as long as this contemptible deceit skulks in your heart."

Sapphurion released her as though he had grasped a thorn bush–not that any thorn could penetrate a Dragon's tough hide. Lia staggered, bereft of words. Sapphurion wished to lump this on her shoulders, after all she had done to rescue the situation? Unfair! Infuriating–and just as devious as the Dragonkind were renowned for. Oh, she had danced right into his trap, more the fool she.

"Dragons, let us burn the heavens–"

"Wait." Wait, while she thrust a dagger into her own belly. "The grave of my friend lies upon Ha'athior Island, where I once lived."

"Desecration!" Zulior, Qualiana and Andarraz snarled in chorus.

Hold, my kin, said Sapphurion. *This Hualiama is either an innocent, or a spy. But the grave belongs to a dragonet.*

Again, the unparalleled capability of the Dragonish language to convey rich nuance, brought to Lia's mind the realisation that Sapphurion was hiding a deep secret within his words. Why? Why did his eye burn with fire, just so? Could this spell danger for Humankind?

King Chalcion wrung his hands. "Mercy, oh mercy, what have I done to deserve this wretched child? I'm so sorry, o mighty Dragons, I shall punish my daughter most severely …"

Lia snapped, "I'm not a child, father! I will accept whatever unjust punishment you deem appropriate. But Sapphurion–all I wished for was peace. Will you grant that much?"

Qualiana said to her mate, *This Dragonfriend negotiates like a Dragoness.*

Sapphurion let fire lick around his fangs as he turned a discomfiting Dragon-smile upon Hualiama. "Aye, little mouse. This day, we shall depart in peace."

Gusts of air battered her face and snapped the tattered fabric about her legs as the Dragons took off.

Lia dusted her skinned palms and checked her grazed left elbow absently. The Dragoness' healing magic had slowed the bleeding from her calf muscle. The cut already showed signs of scabbing over.

Dancing dragonets, what a close shave. War averted, yet the

scales remained delicately balanced. Across the world, Humans stuck to their Islands and Dragons lived where they pleased. The Fra'aniorian arrangement was an eccentric, complex one, where Humans and Dragons had somehow forged an uneasy living arrangement in close quarters–Dragons to the volcanic peaks and caves, Humans hunting and farming the rich slopes above the jaw-dropping vertical cliffs that descended over a league into the active, smoking caldera, and tiny monasteries of Dragon-worshipping Human monks who lived outside the law, clinging like ants to the crags.

Magic steeped Fra'anior's very air.

A sigh escaped her lips. Lia admired the draconic predators dwindling over the caldera, secure in the knowledge that today, no Dragonwing would return in a blaze of fire and fury to destroy her people. Surely her father and his councillors could respect that?

Hearing a footstep behind her, Hualiama turned to meet the King's wrath. "Father–"

He cracked her across the cheek, backhanded, so hard that Lia stumbled to her knees with a sharp cry. "How dare you disrespect me!"

Gone, her tall, dignified father. In his place a panting monster of clenched fists and blotchy jowls, a man ready to lash out again, to hurt her, if she spoke a single word. Numbly, her fingers explored her throbbing cheek, coming away daubed with blood. His heavy signet ring, the symbol of his kingship, had seen to that.

"So help me, I'm a peaceful man, Hualiama, but you've gone too far this time." As if aware of the spectacle he was creating, the King stepped back, dusting his hands on his robes. "I may not be your blood-father, but I am your King. I demand your obedience in all matters."

Hualiama rose to her feet, too shocked to respond.

"You won't speak? Not a word of apology?" Biting off his words as though they stung his lips, Chalcion raged, "Your behaviour is disgraceful! A shame upon this house! Well, daughter, you're grounded–literally. No more frolicking about in your Dragonship. No more privileges. I absolutely forbid you to leave this Palace."

Her cage of gilded splendour. Hualiama lived in arguably the richest household in the Island-World, yet what her heart longed for most could never be found within its walls.

"You will never again set foot on the sacred Island–do you hear me? And while I'm the King upon the Onyx Throne, you'll cease this … this pathetic drivel about a dragonet who died years ago. It's absurd and childish."

"Flicker saved our lives, father."

The King roared, "Do you not think I know that?" Lia could not help but cringe before his upraised hand. "Answer me!"

"Yes, father."

"Do you dislike this life you have, Lia?"

"No, father."

"Would you prefer to be living in a village somewhere, grubbing in the soil for your food?"

"No, father."

"Is there something you lack? Food? Clothing? Love?"

"No, father."

"Then don't make me regret adopting you into this family!"

Now she knew that words could hurt more than blows, because their pain could lacerate her soul. Hualiama felt herself curling inwardly, as though a rajal had gutted her with a cunning blow of its hooked claws.

Uncle Zalcion sniggered, "Well said, o King. Well said indeed!"

She loathed him.

Chapter Two

Summoning

KNEELING ON THE punishment board inside the King's private library, Hualiama whiled away the hours in silent suffering. The board, two feet square, was a mass of uneven, sharpened dowels which dug mercilessly into her knees, calves and feet, pressing in as though intent on drilling through the flesh to torture her bones–an exquisite, crippling type of pain.

She was to kneel on the board, cradling a heavy, smooth onyx stone on her lap, until someone came to fetch her.

Fyria, her royal sister, had been as pleased as a rajal kitten wading jowl-deep through fresh cream to bring her the news that morning. Princess Fyria'aliola of Fra'anior–Fyria for short–was a year younger than Hualiama, but also a head taller, and never failed to seize every opportunity to drive home the difference between their positions. Nicknamed Fiery for her titian hair, her sister was also a great beauty–Islands' sakes, and didn't she know it! She was her father's daughter, right down to the barely-concealed vindictive streak.

Lia also had three brothers–studious, dutiful Ka'allion from her father's first marriage, Elka'anor, her favourite and a perfect scamp, and Fa'arrion, who could never keep words straight in his head, but was able to sing the very suns out of their nocturnal beds. They had given each other nicknames, growing up. So her brothers became Kalli, Elki and Ari, she became Lia, and Fyria … ugh. She became a monster.

Pain radiated up her spine.

Sighing, eschewing any movement that would introduce

fresh agony to her legs, Hualiama gazed at the tall jalkwood bookshelf facing her. It held great ranks of leather-bound tomes which chronicled Fra'anior's rich history. Maybe she could read the titles again. Maybe she could recite them in order from memory, forwards or backwards, shelf by shelf. Why had the King not forgotten the punishment board? She had last knelt here three years ago. Of course Fyria, the prekki-fruit of her father's eye, had never suffered this punishment.

Amaryllion, her Ancient Dragon friend who dwelled in the caverns beneath Ha'athior Island, would have said that bitterness produced bitter fruit. "A cancer of the soul," she growled, trying her best to imitate his thunderous tones. Impossible. But she wrapped her fondest memories of him around her heart. When last had she seen the old lizard? With Ha'athior being off-limits to her and Human-Dragon relations sinking further into the Cloudlands by the day, travel to the holy Dragon-Isle grew perilous. Though she had never seen her friend in the light of day, Lia knew Amaryllion Fireborn was the same onyx colour as the stone she cradled–the colour of the greatest of the Ancient Dragons, Fra'anior, for whom both the Island-Cluster and its main Island, Fra'anior, were named. Fra'anior was a famous Dragon philosopher and scholar, mighty in magic, who had codified the Dragon lore, developed the sciences, and written with great eloquence about the worlds beyond the Island-World.

The stone's smooth lustrous surface enticed her, tugging at a level below conscious thought. Lia allowed her eyelids to flutter shut. She tried to meditate as the warrior monks had taught her.

Hualiama.

Tears sprang to her eyes as she recalled the old Dragon's parting words after her last visit–the first she had shed since the King had struck her yesterday. She wanted to think the physical blow was a minor issue. There had been many other blows, over the years. No, where she felt most wounded was deep within. Lia stifled a sob. The Ancient Dragon had been a better parent to her than her own father, offering sage advice, learning, comfort, and above all, love.

Forbidden, profane love. How could she conceive of love between a Dragon and a Human? She ought to be tossed into a volcano, where she'd burn forever.

Now, Amaryllion was dying.

Hualiama Dragonfriend, come to me.

She jerked, almost spilling the stone from her lap. Re-establishing her position would introduce fresh torment to her limbs. Lia held herself perfectly still.

Er … Amaryllion? Is that you?

Her thoughts twirled in a dragonet's dance.

Hualiama listened until she felt her soul should surely take flight from yearning, yet she heard nothing more. It must have been her imagination, that febrile attribute which regularly landed her in the proverbial lava pit with her family.

The door of the outer chamber creaked open. By their familiar tread on the floorboards, Hualiama knew her parents had come at last. Chalcion and Shyana stopped just inside the doorway, conversing in low tones which carried easily to her sensitive hearing. Lia had long ago worked out she could hear things others did not. Distinguishing truth from imagination was often the trickier issue.

The Queen said, "Chalcion. I thought we'd agreed to stop using that barbarous device."

"Wasn't my idea," he said.

"Lia's twenty-one years old!"

"And she acts a giddy thirteen–but, my sweet flara-fruit, I did not order this punishment. I thought yesterday enough."

"More than enough," said Shyana, her tone taut with anger.

He had not ordered this? And she was the sixth moon in the sky! Lia bit her lip furiously. How could she believe a word her father said? Even poor, harmless Ari had once been beaten bloody by Chalcion when an accidental jostle spilled red wine on Shyana's new ball gown.

"Will you promise to have it burned?" asked Shyana.

"I shall. Now, get that girl out of here. Hurry up. I've an important meeting this afternoon."

"Chalcion, won't you speak to your daughter? You're in danger of losing her."

"When, and only when, she apologises."

Lia gritted her teeth. Aye, that would be when the twin suns rose in the west. His statement summed up Chalcion perfectly. Never bend an inch. Always give an ear to the rumour-mongers, to his weasel of a brother and those slippery councillors of his whom she had heard patting themselves on the back for averting a war with the Dragons. As if they had lifted a finger but to make the situation worse!

Heeding the Queen's call, Hualiama set aside the onyx stone, pushed stiffly to her feet, and limped out of the library with all the dignity she could muster. She did not look at the King. Not once.

* * * *

Of all her family, it was Fa'arrion who found her the following morning, mooching in the chambers used for music and dance. Hualiama sat plucking idly at a harp, picking out the chords for the sad, mystical *Days of Yore*, the tale of a Dragon's quest to find his love who had winged away across the Island-World in search of treasure.

Ari was useless at sneaking up on anyone, but Lia pretended not to notice. Hands covered her eyes. "Ess goo," her brother slurred.

"Guess who?" Hualiama echoed. "It's a Dragon!"

"Ess grin," he laughed.

She guessed again, several times. A beaming, lopsided grin rewarded her game. Ari was always cheerful. He hated to see her melancholy. He capered a little and then impulsively swung her into a dance. "La-La," he insisted. Hualiama had to dance with him.

Suddenly, he froze mid-step. "La ouch?" Ari's huge paw cupped her cheek hesitantly, touching the wound which Queen Shyana had stitched with thin twine of Seg and dressed with a poultice of turbic-gum. Her brother was a ralti-sized man but as gentle as a lamb–unless roused. Then he could be fearsome, knowing no reason.

Lia feared to tell him the truth. "Accident," she whispered.

She gasped as Ari enveloped her in his stalwart arms, raising her at least a foot off the floor. He murmured, "No Ulz? No Ulz? La-La 'kay?"

Great Islands, he remembered Uncle Zalcion! Lia's already uneasy stomach twinged sharply, a pinprick reminder of scars she still carried.

Late in the evening after her absurdly lavish eighteenth birthday party, Hualiama had returned to her chambers giggly and skipping with happiness. Music! Laughter! Actual men to dance with, who were not there just to make moon-eyes at Fyria. Her first taste of sweet, delicious berry-wine, which had fizzed straight to her head. Lia shut the door, pirouetted four times across the space of the floor to her folding changing-screen, and slipped behind it to unlace her dress and headscarf. She hung up her lace-trimmed finery for the maid to clean and put away in the morning.

Humming to herself, Lia tripped over to her hand-carved jalkwood dresser, and smelled him.

In her nightmares, the smell always came first. Strong spirits mingled with the heavy scent of falgaweed, a tobacco-like narcotic, she had learned later. Strong fingers laced into her long platinum tresses; then, the horror. Lifting Lia by her hair, Zalcion flung her across the dresser, scattering perfume bottles, hairbrushes and the slim Immadian forked daggers she had received as a present from her father. Lia began to scream, but his heavy palm cut off her cries.

"Shut the trap, wretch," he rasped. "Nobody's here to hear you scream."

All her warrior training evaporated like the mists of a volcanic dawn, driven away by the tearing pain in her scalp and the ripping of fabric. Cool air trickled down her spine. Lia kicked and thrashed, fearing the worst, but his strength was an Island, immovable. Her hand fell upon a crystal bottle. By blind instinct, she smashed it into her uncle's face.

Zalcion still wore those scars.

Her forehead rebounded off the dresser, the pain crashing between her temples as if she had run headlong into a boulder. Still gripping her hair, Zalcion swung the Princess across the chamber and hurled her facedown on the bed, cursing, "I'll beat you bloody, you little rajal. Who cares what happens to a royal ward?"

He knelt on her back, and she could not move him. The bedding muffled her shrieks.

Then a body crashed into Zalcion, throwing him across the bed. Fa'arrion! Just thirteen, but already as strong as a man; in his frenzy, fiercer by far. He and Zalcion rolled about, punching, grasping, gasping …

Hualiama shook herself. "Ari, you were my strong Dragon that day. Thank you for saving me. Oof, don't break my ribs!"

Her brother set her down as though she were a fragile vase. Lia smiled brightly. Anything to banish those memories. Her uncle still watched her with a sardonic grin curving his lips, making her feel unclean. Zalcion had never sought to enter her chambers again. But he was right. Nobody cared about a royal ward's behaviour, as long as she was discreet. Lia could do as she wished–should she choose to, which she did not–whereas Fyria's unmarried state was the fodder of energetic gossip and an even more energetic posse of suitors for the royal hand. According to the time-honoured traditions of Fra'anior, the chosen one would have the honour of kidnapping her sister, and after seven days of formal nuptials, making the Princess his wife.

Meantime, one of Hualiama's roles in life was to protect the royal honour and reputation. She could say any number of unsavoury things about that!

Lia forced out a chuckle. How could she tell him the truth? "Ari, dear one, will you sing for me? It would cheer me up so."

Fa'arrion's chest swelled. "La-La ingame."

"Er … you want me to sing along? Fine." She waggled an eyebrow at him as if intending to joust with a tiny baton. "You take the first verse, though. Make it good. I want to hear the dragonets join in."

Ari helped her wheel the harp to the outer chamber, which opened upon a balcony commanding a panoramic view over the caldera. A series of delicate archways separated the interior of the Palace from the open balcony, so festooned with flowering vines that it was difficult to see the stone beneath. Two green dragonets darted away with sharp cries as the Humans approached, only to perch on a nearby pot-plant to goggle at the goings-on.

Impulsively, Lia said, *We'd be honoured if you'd sing with us, little ones.*

The dragonets' eyes whirled with excitement. It was such a shame not all dragonets spoke Dragonish, as Flicker had. These were juvenile males, just a foot long, but perfect little Dragons in every detail, right down to the skull-spikes, multi-jointed wings and delicate, razor-sharp talons.

Perching straight-backed on a stool beside the harp, Hualiama's fingers glided spiderlike over the strings, weaving her web of music. Fa'arrion pitched a soft, penetrating C-sharp with such perfection, it made her nape tingle. To produce such a high note so quietly was fearsomely difficult, but he made the technique seem effortless. His tenor soared even higher to the E, before launching as if he were a Dragon taking wing off a cliff-top into the demanding opening passage of *Days of Yore.* The piece was written in a supple, shifting harmonic minor that tested a singer's musicianship to the limit.

The dragonets spiralled heavenward on the wings of his song, trilling joyous descants and counterpoint harmonies as they began a frenetic aerial dance. A mating pair of violet-crested lovebirds peeked shyly from behind the trailing vines to add their own sweet notes to the production.

Tingling with inspiration, Hualiama sang the part of Jynissia, the Amber Dragoness, as she pined for the love of Xaradon the Brown. Lia had a well-trained singing voice, as was proper for a member of the royal household, although she could not match Ari for volume. He was capable of uncorking a volcanic eruption all of his own. Nonetheless, her soprano was rich and effervescent, often astonishing listeners with its lyrical range.

However, the greatest surprise was that when he sang, Ari's mouth produced words in perfect Island Standard.

Teardrops splashed on Hualiama's sleeve as she considered how unfair it was that Fa'arrion would never be able to speak intelligibly. Her throat thickened, giving her voice especial resonance as stanza after stanza recounted Jynissia's descent into the volcanic hells of despair and madness–a feeling she knew all too well. Three dissimilar loves; three losses beyond her control. Now, she treated her heart as a sacred treasure. Lock it away and bury it deep. That way, she could never be hurt again.

Hualiama glanced up to see her mother listening in at the doorway, accompanied by their elderly music tutor, Ga'allio–a musical prodigy if ever one had been born.

When brother and sister finished their ringing finale, Shyana and Ga'allio applauded in the dignified Fra'aniorian manner. "You made yourself cry." The tall, slender Queen set her hand upon Hualiama's shoulder.

"Zees voss pure geniuz!" cried Ga'allio, in his peculiar brogue.

"Will you dance with me today, Lia?" asked her mother. "And Ari, my treasure, will you accompany us?"

"I'd love to!" Lia bounced to her feet, making her mother startle and laugh. Ari made a formal Fra'aniorian half-bow.

"The *Flame Cycle* has been on my heart," said Shyana, allowing Lia to clasp her hand and tug her into the costume-chamber. "I've always felt it's such a free-spirited dance–and if ever I needed a taste of freedom, it is today."

Lia cast her mother a sharp glance. She had a habit of expressing her adopted daughter's feelings as if they were her own. She appreciated empathy, but it could also cut deep.

They pulled on their costumes of crimson and orange Helyon silk, and wound the red feathers symbolising the mythical Firebird into each other's hair. Her mother's waist-length hair, which had not felt the cut of scissors since her sixteenth birthday, was as raven-dark as Lia's was fair. Shyana was a classic Fra'aniorian beauty, with all the lissom height Hualiama lacked, a graceful heron beside her daughter's wren-like, diminutive frame.

With a deft touch of the face-paints, Shyana drew flames radiating from her daughter's eyes. "Today, we shall fly as Dragons," she said. "Thy hair is as unbound as the Dragonflight of our mighty brethren. See, how it ripples like the twin sun-spirits gracing a terrace lake."

Shyana was often mystical, a quality that drove Chalcion up the proverbial cliff. He thought her obtuse. But Lia often wondered if her mother wasn't somehow bonded, as the monks believed, to the spirit of the legendary, many-headed Black Dragon Fra'anior. She saw the world through a different lens. Also, her mother knew the truth–that there was an inner freedom in dance, an expanding of the senses, a joy in movement and expression that Lia found nowhere else.

The intensity of the *Flame Cycle* dance demanded her utmost concentration, the movements complex and haunting, evoking the fiery spirits of Dragons. Ga'allio played for them with great skill, while Ari sang the poetic vocal passages, which described how Dragons' spirits were born in flame.

Lia yearned for the flame. Sometimes, when she performed this dance, the blaze felt so close that if she could only reach out to grasp it, she would become a living flame, dancing beyond the bounds of her mortal flesh, that she could leap and spin with the grace and ease of any dragonet and take her place amongst the stars of the heavens. She burned with an inner fire, flickering and flaring, twirling her limbs like dancing flames … she reached deeper, coveting the very core of the dance, to combust and expire …

Hualiama Dragonfriend, please, come soon!

Amaryllion? Ecstatic laughter bubbled in her mind. *Look at me. I'm Fireborn just like a Dragon. I soar upon volcanic winds–*

His deep groan wrenched silence from her, a pool of stillness amidst the dance. *Thou art the uncontainable song of fire, little one. I must give up mine spirit. Come to me before the Jade moon waxes to its fullness.*

A-A-Amaryllion?

Understanding crashed down upon her. Hualiama faltered, and fell.

"Lia?" The Queen cradled her head. "She's fainted. Ga'allio, ring for a glass of prekki-juice! Lia–child, you're burning up!"

"I was the flame, mother."

Shyana clasped her daughter to her bosom. "Aye, my precious petal. I know how you long to fly. But after yesterday's punishment, and your confrontation with the Dragons the day before, I demanded too much of you. I'm sorry."

Almost, almost it was on the tip of her tongue to voice her needs–her Dragonship, and an excuse to disappear for a day or two. How on the Islands would she gain that privilege when her father had just banned it? Grovel? Until the previous year, Lia had spent two weeks of each season training with her warrior-monk friends at their secret monastery offshore of Ha'athior, but Chalcion had forbidden her visits, deeming them 'inappropriate.' Later, she had discovered that Zalcion had instigated the ban.

Instead, the storm-surge of her emotions veered in an unexpected direction.

"Thy song hath beguiled my Dragon hearts, o brother," she sang, shamefully misusing a line from *Dragons of Yore.*

"And thy song hath animated mine," he adlibbed in tuneful response.

That was no line from a song. Bands of iron gripped her chest. Oh, by the great volcano itself! Wheezing unmusically, Hualiama managed to gasp, "And wilt thou sing again, with me?"

"Aye, my sister. I will sing … forever!"

In realisation of what she already knew, Ari's crescendo struck a prodigious note. The word 'forever' reverberated around the Palace, alarming birds in the gardens and making the Dragonets squeal in amazement.

Queen Shyana's hands flew to her mouth. "Oh, Ari–oh, my precious son. You spoke!"

Lia wept.

* * * *

Jade would wax to fullness in three days. Hualiama spent two of those days trying to determine a course of action which would not lead to her exile on a remote boulder somewhere in the Cloudlands. Echoes of the past, brought into sharp relief. Six years before, with the help of a Dragon and a dragonet, she had rescued her family from exile. And what did her impossible-to-please father make of her endeavours? Disgraceful. Difficult. Ungrateful foundling. An inferior creature compared to her royal-born siblings.

Would she sacrifice her future for an Ancient Dragon?

In a word, aye. Such was the cost of friendship.

Inconspicuously, during that second day, Hualiama began to gather the necessary items. That evening, she dressed in a dark green Helyon silk outfit crafted by her friend Inniora, which had a cunningly split long skirt to allow ease of movement, and a modified tunic top which concealed an arsenal of unusual implements and weapons. Soft, flexible black shoes minimised any sound she might make. She hung a matched pair of Immadian forked daggers at her belt. Lia's Nuyallith blades, freed from their customary double-sheath upon her back, bounced against her right thigh beneath her skirts. Armoured wristlets sported hidden slots for a half-dozen throwing knives and a set of lock picks. Lia secreted a fifty-foot length of climbing rope in her backpack. She braided her platinum hair and tucked it away beneath a black headscarf. Over all this, she donned her ordinary evening clothes.

Lia walked to the door, cracked it open and saw her mother's eye regarding her sternly. "Mother!"

"Going somewhere, daughter?"

Wishing her heart would leap back into her chest, Hualiama muttered, "What makes you think that?"

Shyana pushed her way into Lia's chambers and thumped the door shut behind her. "Petal, you aren't running away, are you?"

"No." No, because she refused to give Zalcion the satisfaction. "Just a short trip, and before you begin the lecture, Mom, I will not tell father and I do not expect him to approve."

"Hush, petal. Is this truly important? Life and death?"

Pursing her lips, Lia nodded.

"It's not about Flicker?"

"No."

"Something to do with the Dragons?"

Hualiama examined her toes, knowing that whatever she answered, her mother understood her so well she'd guess the rest.

Shyana touched Lia's chin. "Look at me, my precious fireflower."

"Mother! Oh … I do love you."

With a gentle yet infuriating smile, the Queen said, "What would you say if I told you I had your Dragonship checked and refuelled today?" Lia collected her jaw from somewhere in the region of her toes. "Aye, petal. We're about to take an urgent trip–Elki and I, and a nameless piece of baggage which may or may not resemble someone called Hualiama, who also happens to be the most rascally Princess ever to walk this Island."

Hualiama hugged her mother Dragon-fiercely.

* * * *

Queen Shyana won past the guards by the simple expedient of sending them off to collect various items she had conveniently forgotten. Sickness in the Palace, she said. She urgently needed fresh supplies of herbs. Lia hid in the bottom of the Dragonship's basket, covered in sackcloth, while Elki tried to find the right Island.

"You custom-rigged this ship, you rotten little rajal," he hissed. "No wonder you're always tinkering with it."

Hualiama's chuckle was designed to irritate. "Need a few instructions, brother? The stove is over there."

"I know how to light a stove … Islands' sakes, what's this bit up here?"

"Just get us aloft and I'll rescue us from your gross ineptitude."

Elki booted her leg 'accidentally' on the way past.

Her brother would not budge from the controls on the way to the westernmost village of Fra'anior Island, but he did question Lia in detail about her modifications.

"Bah," he muttered as they neared Ha'arria village, three

hours later. "I suppose I have to go herb-shopping with Mom while you have fun in your floating laboratory, short shrift. Don't do anything naughty–like stepping onto hallowed ground, baiting Dragons or letting Dad catch wind of your return, just to pick a few random examples."

"Love you too, Elki."

Hualiama tossed out the anchor, which dragged them to a halt above a small meadow just outside the village.

Before she climbed down the rope ladder, Queen Shyana said, "You will be careful, won't you, petal?"

"For the tenth time, Mom–aye!"

Further down the ladder, Elki made a rude noise.

"And you won't go too far?"

"Not beyond our Cluster, Mom. I promise, I swear on all five moons–"

"Why don't you throw in all the stars in the heavens while you're at it, sister?" Elki drawled. "We still wouldn't believe you."

Hualiama yelled, "Elki! Step on his head, Mom."

Thankfully, it was not uncommon for Dragonships to fly after dark. Most nights of the year the moons provided plenty of illumination, a blessing for some–the righteous, the King liked to say–less so for pirates and smugglers, and blasted awkward for those royal wards who may or may not be planning to sneak onto the hallowed ground of Ha'athior Island.

Dragon fire take it!

As if buoyed up by the last rays of a gloriously fiery Fra'aniorian suns-set, Lia's Dragonship floated westward off the cliff-tops toward Gi'ishior Island, home of the Dragons. The journey to Ha'athior was slightly further around the volcanic rim this way, but the direct southerly route from Fra'anior Island was deemed too dangerous due to the presence of feral Dragons.

Lia's single-handed or solo Dragonship consisted of a segmented balloon measuring twenty-four feet in length, three segments filled with hydrogen gas, and a further five with hot air. A simple stove-and-pipe arrangement allowed the pilot to burn wood, coal or any other combustible material to produce hot air, or to melt meriatite stone to produce hydrogen gas for additional lifting power. A lightweight woven reed basket dangled beneath the balloon, holding Hualiama and her equipment. Strong, flexible horizontal masts furnished the ship with its characteristic 'Dragon wings.' Hualiama's design gave her Dragonship two masts rather than the traditional single mast atop the vessel, each canted at thirty degrees from the vertical. A complex system of ropes and pulleys for working the reinforced Helyon silk sails all terminated within easy reach of her chair.

Next, she warmed up another of her customisations, connecting the drive belts of the port and starboard propellers to a gas-powered gear system affixed to the sides of her stove. They chugged into motion, propelling the Dragonship against an insistent breeze sweeping from the northwest. Like most solo Dragonships, there were further propellers at the stern and bow, and above and below, to aid manoeuvring in any conceivable direction. Lia angled the propellers to provide both lift and thrust–the higher she flew, the better chance she had of gliding to a safe landing should problems arise.

After popping a chunk of dense jalkwood into the stove, her Rascally Highness trimmed the sails to catch the wind as she swung the dirigible's nose to point southeast. Usually, she would follow the semicircle of rim-Islands down to Ha'athior, because the caldera's rising vapours could be unpredictable. She judged the breeze steady enough to mitigate the danger of a shortcut. She perched on the pilot's stool, clicked the gearstick a notch to engage the stern propeller, and began to pedal.

A hot, sticky Fra'aniorian night enfolded her.

Chapter Three

Crystal Lair

OVER A LEAGUE beneath Lia's Dragonship, the caldera's lava lakes cast a ruddy glow upon the fat underbelly of the dirigible balloon. Miles-tall cliffs festooned with dense tropical vegetation and trailing vines dropped from the Islands into the caldera, before the heat and poisonous gases strangled any plant life except for lichens. Dragonets, birds, monkeys and other flying and burrowing rodents and insects inhabited the cliffs in their millions. Half a mile offshore the silence was profound, a brooding presence in its own right, a beast of mystery and magic.

Softly, she sang to herself to while away the hours.

Gi'ishior seemed busier than usual. By the light of the Jade, Mystic and Blue moons, Lia tallied at least ten Dragons patrolling the skies above the tall, slender volcanic cone said to house the Halls of the Dragons, and a steady stream of Dragonkind arriving and departing on mysterious errands. What was a Dragon city like, she wondered? How did Dragon mothers chastise their hatchlings? Did Dragon parents ever abandon their eggs, as she had been abandoned?

As Lia turned southward, again maintaining a good separation from the Islands in order to trim the distance she needed to fly, she clambered aloft to unfurl the spinnaker, a big-bellied triangular sail which billowed to fullness as it caught the breeze. The masts creaked as the dirigible leaned over, gathering speed. Such strange names for sails–jibs, topgallants, even a moonraker. She had found the idea of a spinnaker in an ancient, crumbling scroll in her father's archives, and copied it, adding a few 'Lia' touches. How well that described the melody of her life! Could she never be satisfied with things as they were?

As Ha'athior loomed before her after seven hours' sailing, a Yellow Dragoness suddenly rose from the darkness to fix Lia with a scorching gaze. She was as sleek as a trout, with coppery overtones on her upper body fading into a pale eggshell yellow in the underparts.

"Hualiama," she growled. "Mighty Sapphurion said you'd be quick to trespass."

Lia raised her chin, disguising her anxiety behind a thin-lipped smile. "I'm not trespassing, o mighty Dragon. The air is free for Dragon and Human alike."

This comment provoked a fifteen-foot plume of flame that passed dangerously close to her Dragonship's nose. "As cheeky as my hatchlings! Know this, little Human–we Dragons are watching. Always watching."

"I was just–" the Dragoness wheeled away. Lia sighed, "I'm just *parking* at the warrior monastery offshore of Ha'athior. Thereafter …"

Aggravated but unsurprised that the story of her intrusion on the hallowed Dragon Isle had spread amongst the Dragons, Hualiama set her course to skirt Ha'athior Island's northern shore. Passing through the gigantic cleft between Ha'athior and Janbiss Island to the north, the Dragonship left the caldera in its wake as it sailed out across the crimson-tinged Cloudlands, that bottomless realm of poisonous clouds that lapped around the base of the volcano, a league and a quarter beneath her current altitude. Lia trimmed the sails, swooping toward a tiny, obscure volcano just offshore of the holy Island.

Here, she had lived. Trained. Studied. Learned to dance with weapons. Collected more bruises than a girl should have in a lifetime. And–if she were allowed to confess–charmed the beards off more than a few of the warrior-monks.

An unexpected freshening of the breeze slewed the Dragonship about, making Lia leap to the controls. She dropped the spinnaker and raised two stormsails aloft to improve stability, before reefing in the side-sails to further reduce her speed. A touch of the controls cut off the flow of hot air to the balloon. Soon, the Dragonship began to lose altitude.

Lia coasted in over the volcano's rim, the bottom of her basket trailing barely a dozen feet above the rock. She crossed a small crater lake, glistening in the moons-light, and downed anchor beside the dark temple of the Great Dragon–a building so ancient, not even the Dragons knew who had built it.

A monk materialised out of the darkness, calling softly, "Hualiama!"

Ja'al! Lia's heart lurched into her throat.

He said, "The most sulphurous greetings of the Great Dragon to you."

"And may his everlasting fires burn within you, Master Ja'al."

The young monk's teeth glinted briefly at their formality. Sweet Ja'al, still so volcanically handsome–and still so committed to his monkish vows. They had kissed, once. Had he forgotten that day? Judging by the pinch of rose enflaming his cheeks, perhaps not. She must bind her treacherous heart for his sake. Lia forbade her lips to curve upward, and failed. Ja'al's colour deepened.

The monk cleared his throat awkwardly. "We heard the King forbade you to train here, Lia. Therefore, you should not–"

"I'm not."

"Now that I recall, I saw a dragonet fly by. I shall moor this stray Dragonship beneath the trees."

"Thank you, Ja'al."

Only the simplest of words could be risked, or her heart would tear loose of her ribcage and pounce upon the monk, a beast of passion unchained. Her lower lip quivered.

With a soft word of thanks, Hualiama wrenched herself away and loped into the night.

Briefly, her path led past the monastery building, gutted by the Dragon attack which had led to her friend Inniora's kidnapping, but now rebuilt. The no-longer-secret stairway lay concealed in the crack between a huge boulder and a gnarled, ancient prekki tree. Within, the darkness was pure sable. Lia felt for the steps. Right. Hustle, girl! Down forever, until she felt dizzy. Dash away the tears. No time for regrets. Twisting through the tunnel below to the lower slopes of the volcano. Here, an ancient prekki-fruit tree leaned over the gap between the Islands, just a hundred feet wide but two miles deep. A blood-red lava flow glowed down there.

Six years ago, she had found her way across this divide with the help of a braided vine. Now, a knotted rope hung from a branch seventy feet above her head. Lia untied it from an iron ring set in the prekki tree's trunk, and ran the makeshift cord through her fingers.

Beyond this point, she would earn a swift flight from a great height, or an even swifter claw through the chest.

Breathe out. Grit the teeth. Oh–last-second check for lurking Dragons. Lia could not see any, but since Dragons could see a hundred times better than Humans, especially in the dark, that meant little. Seven stutter-steps launched her into the air. She flew, briefly weightless before the rope's pendulum swing rushed her to the far side. She landed catlike on a flat rock. Hold still.

Hualiama half-expected the Island to transform into the fabled Black Dragon himself and with a shiver, fling an irreverent Human mite into the abyss. Instead, she remembered why she had come. A quiver nearly did unbalance her.

Why did Amaryllion have to die?

She tied the rope to the base of a gnarled purple-currant bush. Hopefully, any prowling Dragons would think it was just a trailing vine.

Ahead of her lay a challenging climb, and a race against the coming dawn.

An hour of scaling the vertical cliffs brought Hualiama to a cave, where she rested briefly, panting, checking her fingers, battered and torn by the sharp-edged volcanic rocks. Climbing gloves would have served her well. Ha'athior's shadow stretched almost to the western horizon as the twin suns rose behind the main volcano. She had made it by a Dragon's whisker. Not that Dragons had whiskers–people said the most ridiculous things.

Lia scrambled to her feet.

A warm, well-remembered breeze caressed her cheek, redolent of Dragon-scent–a complex aroma of cinnamon, burnt umber and magic tingling at her senses like an almost-heard, faraway starsong. With it came memories, rustling through her mind with a crackling like dry leaves. A friend long departed. A phantom prickle of claws on her shoulder, a warm dragonet curling himself about her neck. 'Straw-head,' he used to whisper. Dear Flicker. Surely, his death had purchased her life, and restored the King to his Onyx Throne.

Oh, this place was shadowed with memories, the requiem of a weeping heart-wound.

Lia felt her way into the tunnels behind the cave. Now all she needed to do was remember the path through Ha'athior's underground maze, and try not to fall over any of the myriad drop-offs. Flicker, with his typically blunt honesty, had been fond of calling her 'slow-slug', too.

Ha. A dragonet need not fear falling.

For her, falling from a height was a recurring nightmare.

Hualiama's soft footsteps echoed loudly in the stillness. She jogged where she remembered the way was safe and smooth. The caves and tunnels were warm and never without light, just faint hints of radiance at first, growing into patches of crystalline splendour as she penetrated the Island more deeply. She could see how the numinous quality of this light might suggest sacredness to the Dragonkind.

She came to a dark, faceted wall, and turned along it. Lia steadied herself with her left hand, and then on an impulse, pressed her ear against the wall to listen. A steady, complex drumbeat came to her hearing, a draconic warmth of flesh and life.

Amaryllion.

Oh, Dragonfriend … why speak thee to mine underbelly?

Great Islands, that deep voice quivered her surrounds as if the volcano shook its skirts preparatory to erupting. Lia realised what had confused her. This part of the tunnels had always been fully dark. Now the crystals irradiated his scales. Each was as wide and tall as her outstretched arms.

She laughed, *Because I'm as silly as a dragonet.*

After a long pause, his answering laughter beat against her senses, but it sounded frail and faraway, as though his Dragon-spirit had already begun its journey into eternity. *Lia, precious one. Thou hast always brought light to mine darkness. Come to me.*

She ran, but it was another ten minutes through the tunnels before she finally broke out into the cave into which she had once chased Flicker, and found herself in the awesome presence of an Ancient Dragon. Then, all had been pitch-dark save for his burning gaze. Now, she threw up an arm to shade her eyes.

Lia gasped.

She stood on a rocky outcropping which brought her to the level of Amaryllion's gigantic eye, which stood twice her height–an eye she knew well, but she had never fully appreciated the mountain of Dragon-flesh which contained it. The ageless Dragon appeared to lie in an ancient underground stream-bed or gully, his muzzle mostly below her feet, his neck-ruff and skull-spikes looming two hundred feet above her head. Inanely, she realised she could comfortably walk upright into any of his three ear-canals on the near side of his head. Mighty Sapphurion was smaller than a dragonet compared to this beast.

The curve of his orb seethed with Dragon fire, but the luminescent white streamers of fire today seemed darkened and diminished to Hualiama, foreshadowing his demise. Nevertheless, the power of Amaryllion's gaze made the Human's entire body tingle, as though she stood upon a mountaintop caressed by an unseen breeze. Lia clenched her teeth to still their chattering. Visions and impressions of a life aeons long cascaded through her mind. Dragons raised Islands from the abyss, building nests and terrace lakes. A terrible war engulfed her, pitching the Dragons above the Cloudlands against the Land Dragons below … abruptly, the torrent ceased. A touch to her nose brought her forefinger away daubed with blood.

I've caused thee suffering, little one. That was not mine intention … now, as the time approaches, the visions beset me.

Must you die, Amaryllion?

Oh, Dragonfriend, grieve not for me. His magic soothed her anguish. *Even for the most ancient of lizards, a time must come to join our spirits to the great dance of eternal fire.* Switching to her tongue, Island Standard, the great Dragon said, "Tell me, little mouse, what remembrance hast thou of the Dragon Grandion?"

Grandion? He touched her pain so unerringly. "We journeyed together. He saved Fra'anior …"

"How exactly did a Human and a Dragon journey together?"

Lia's brow creased in puzzlement. "I don't remember. By Dragonship, I think, and I remember meeting a Maroon Dragoness who told me Ra'aba was my real father …" Her voice trailed off as Amaryllion's eye suffused with a dull, reddish flame signifying inner pain. "O Amaryllion, what is it? Have I neglected you so sorely?"

"Nay, Hualiama. It is I who have wronged thee."

"You … did? How?"

"I caused thee to forget–wrongly, and too much, believing I should thus best protect thee. With thy permission, might I restore thee to thy right mind?"

Doubt shadowed Lia's thoughts. What had she forgotten? She knew there were blemishes upon her memory, as if she saw indistinctly through patches of fog, but she had always put that down to the trauma of the events surrounding Captain Ra'aba's attempt to murder her, and her eventual triumph over the pretender to restore King Chalcion to the Onyx Throne.

If she agreed, what terrible secrets might be revealed? But Lia knew she must trust the Ancient Dragon, for that, too, was a price friendship should always be willing to pay.

At her pensive nod, draconic power smote Hualiama to her knees. A white-golden light expanded within her mind, driving away the shadows and the mists, a song of magic awakening what had long slumbered beneath a touch she now recognised as the signature of Amaryllion's mind. The world blazed, set afire by his magic. Memories danced amidst the flames. Lurid. Searing. A deluge of bittersweet moments, unfolding the enormity of her loss.

Inwardly, Hualiama howled, *You stole all this from me?*

Words cannot convey mine sorrow, little mouse. His great mind bowed in regret. *Such potential which is thine! And more … more than thou or I might imagine. Answer me now, how did a Dragon and a Human journey together?*

Her thoughts were a scattering of fragments upon volcanic winds. Lia stammered, *A-As a D-Dragon and his … his …*

Dragon Rider, sang the Ancient Dragon. *The first Dragon Rider in our Island-World's long history.*

I'm dead! Hualiama wailed. *They'll kill me … the Dragons, they'll—*

Hush. Do not profane this sacred bond with the dark-fires of limited understanding! Amaryllion's mental thunder stunned her into silence. At length, the Ancient Dragon whispered, "Two thousand, seven hundred and two years have I lived, and tarried to witness at last the unfolding of this magical bond between Dragon and Human. It will be glorious. Yet this was not the prime purpose of my waiting."

A cold, callous blade of betrayal pierced her heart. Now Lia remembered all which had passed between her and the Tourmaline Dragon, and she knew she would never have allowed six years to elapse, had Amaryllion not interfered. She would have sought Grandion with her heart and soul and utmost strength, be that to the twenty-five league tall rim walls at the end of the Island-World, or beyond. Such a waste. A travesty. Fragments of the Tourmaline Dragon's effervescent laughter kindled her memories. She quivered at the gentle touch of his paw. She remembered moments of blushing discomfiture beneath the Dragon's possessive, pyretic gaze and the glory of Dragon flight. Then came the slow, soul-destroying acceptance of the fact that her Dragon was never coming back. The cancer to her hope. The immedicable wound.

She had flown Dragonback!

She had touched the fiery spirit of a Dragon; he had

touched hers. They had shared oaths. Now she was made an oath breaker because of the Ancient Dragon's actions! How could Amaryllion have robbed her so cruelly?

Sapphurion called him a traitor, she realised aloud. *Grandion was prevented from returning … he's dead, isn't he?*

Nay, Hualiama, said Amaryllion. *Lost, but not beyond hope.*

Another memory slipped into Lia's mind, grown fevered with remembrance. "The comet, the prophecy … you said the third great race of the Island-World would emerge from the shadows–"

"Soon will this word be fulfilled," said the Ancient Dragon. "Hear me now, Dragonfriend. My craft allowed me to draw from the magic of these caves to be the sentinel, the one who remained after all others until the balance of the harmonies reached its fruition. But now my time must end. The era of the Ancient Dragons passes with me. It was given to me to be the last egg of Fra'anior, the Great Dragon. And you and I share this grief, for like thee I was the unwanted egg, the son who could never meet his father's expectations. I was tiny and stunted for one of my kind–"

Lia's incredulous laughter burst out before she could bite it back.

"Aye, a titchy Ancient Dragon, I am. I call thee little mouse. They called *me* a hatchling. Canst thou believe it, Lia?"

She said, softly, "If you hear a popping noise, Amaryllion, that's the sound of my brain bursting."

"Then what would thy brain do if I divulged this? It is for thee I waited."

"I-I …"

The rumbling of Amaryllion's voice filled the cavern, but though it shook her through and through, it was also slow and gentle, the speech of a dear friend. "I've learned much in these short years since a slip of a girl first set foot in my abode, bringing her song and dance and laughter, her ten thousand questions and her zest for life, to gild mine elder days with a rare and precious light."

Lia allowed her tears to fall unmolested. "You're too kind, Amaryllion."

"I choose my words with care!" he thundered. Shame blistered her cheeks. "Truly I named thee Dragonfriend–and here is another word chosen with care–know that I have loved thee dearly, little mouse." She made a wordless squeak of horror, but he continued inexorably, "I love thee as I would have loved mine own hatchling, had I been able to conceive. The Dragonfriend and the Ancient Dragon can speak openly of love, for love takes many forms, and none of them are profane, despite all thou hast been taught and all the laws of our respective kinds. They know not the first heartbeat of love."

With all the soul-achingly beautiful nuance of the Dragonish language, he declared, *Thou art my third heart, Hualiama. I love thee.*

I l-l … Lia gulped, feeling sweat bead thick and hot as fresh blood upon her brow. *I-I … l-love thee, Amaryllion Fireborn. Thou art more than a friend to me.* She groaned softly, weeping in response to the words she had just uttered. Anathema! Outlawed! Her heart should cease beating from shame …

The Dragon said, "To some, it is given to fight, to others to learn, some to teach or be parents or prophets, but to some, it is given to love with such power and purity, that no taboo can stand against. Tell me, taboo-breaker and friend, whom hast thou loved in this life?"

Wishing she could read the hypnotic swirls of his incandescent Dragon fires, Lia replied, "My parents and siblings, of course–some more than others, in truth. But it was Flicker who taught me the true meaning of love."

And one other. But she found herself unable to speak his name. Hualiama might have crossed to a forbidden Island, but fear of the inviolable still dominated her stupefied mind; voices, screaming, 'How could you? Sick, perverted lawbreaker!' Yet her mouth had spoken that fateful word–love. Fie, the insanity! Her mind must have been overshadowed by some perverted psychosis of draconic origin …

"The priceless gift of life." The Ancient Dragon's gentleness drew Lia back from the pit of madness. He shifted slowly, a gargantuan movement that dislodged torrents of grit from the cave roof above her head. At length, the Dragon's paw rose above the rock Lia sat upon, and he delicately touched her with its smallest digit, thicker than ten of her rolled together. "Before Flicker died, he gave me a gift to pass on to thee. But I withheld it at the time out of concern for its effects on thee, a Human. I thought thee too immature to use this gift well. I failed thee, Hualiama. Two thousand years is too long. I was cynical."

She whispered, "What was it?"

"Fire. A Dragon's soul is fire, but not an ordinary flame such as that of a candle." Amaryllion sighed. "Grasp my paw. I will show thee. Of course, it is magic, but of a deep and ancient kind. This fire is how the Ancient Dragons were able to travel to this world inside their First Eggs, which for aeons, lay beneath this Island, before the rising volcano brought them to the surface. The essence of a Dragon's being is fire. And the absence of fire is the absence of life."

Hualiama scrambled up into Amaryllion's gigantic paw, larger than thirty royal beds laid end to end, realising now that she had never touched him before. His rough Dragon hide radiated heat. On a whim, she knelt to inhale the scent of his skin, a complex aroma of burned spices and ancient, evocative places which spanned the deeps of the Island-World and its highest glories–not at all what she had expected. His paw conveyed her past the wide tunnels of the Ancient Dragon's nose to his mouth, a cavern in its own right.

"You won't burn me, will you?"

"It's not that kind of fire," the Dragon chuckled, cracking open his jaw. "It's far more dangerous, a fire that inhabits a creature's very soul. Wilt thou accept this gift, Hualiama Dragonfriend?"

Lia stared into Amaryllion's mouth, a hall large enough to hold the King of Fra'anior's annual ball several times over, lined top and bottom with hundred-foot columns of the purest white marble–his fangs–and a tongue the length of a field of mohili wheat.

Her heart's churning, like an active caldera, expressed itself in the tremolo underlying her response. "I don't suppose too many Humans have enjoyed this view of an Ancient Dragon, have they? Not those who lived long, anyhow. Amaryllion, is this gift just Flicker's fire? How can you keep that separate from your own … er, soul-fire?"

"Ah." His laughter blasted her headscarf loose. *Hualiama, a time is coming when this Island-World will face grave danger, when Humans and Dragons will ride to war, and many will be slain. Entire cultures will be erased and their Islands fall into the Cloudlands. I foresee a great role for thee in this age to come–perhaps a role unimaginable to thee today, but it must come. And I, selfishly, would hand on my mantle to thee. Thou must both watcher and judge be, and speak as the voice of reason. The bridge between Dragons and Humans will be thy soul, and according to thy choices, this age will rise or fall.*

Me? The squeak in her voice embarrassed Lia. Courage, girl!

It is no trivial charge, Dragonfriend.

That much was clear from the multifaceted shades of meaning conveyed by his use of Dragonish. Lia wished she understood more. Only ten thousand questions, he had said. However, before she could accept his request, she knew she had to voice what lay heavy on her heart.

"Amaryllion, I once did evil to a Dragon I … liked."

"Grandion?"

"Aye, Grandion. Amaryllion, I forced him to carry me Dragonback and I just learned a few days ago that he's a traitor and probably banished and I'm afraid it's all my fault!"

"Peace, little mouse."

Peace? Lia cried, "Amaryllion, I remember everything, now. I made him feel so guilty for not repaying me for helping him escape when he was trapped in the caves … how truthfully, and how terribly, you label me 'taboo breaker'! I was so foolish and so preoccupied with my own needs."

Away to her left and right, Amaryllion's lips peeled open in what Lia belatedly realised had to be his Dragon smile. "Hualiama, thou hast described one of the qualities I most appreciate in thee. To thee, this world's rules and mores are not unbreakable chains, but function more as … guidance."

Her laughter emerged low and bitter. "Ah, the singeing flame of truth."

"This quality accords thee great power, but can also cause great harm. Little one, what if the chance to right that wrong presented itself?"

In one breath he cowed her. In the next, he detonated a hydrogen-like blast of hope that made her reply desperately unsteady. "My delight would light the moons themselves! But Amaryllion, that's impossible, isn't it?"

"I advise thee to seek your chance. Create it. This knowledge thou must grasp, Hualiama. Every Dragon has a secret name. Mine is *Bezaldior!*"

His unexpected roar blasted her across his palm to fetch up against his curled digits. Lia clambered unsteadily out of the crack between his talons. "Easy on the power there, mighty Dragon."

"Sorry," he chuckled, but it was a wickedly unrepentant sound. "It means 'strength of the fire-born.' "

She nodded, mouthing the word with care.

"Grandion's secret name is–" she ducked "*–Alastior!*"

Lia found herself stuck between his talons this time.

As he watched her scramble back onto the surface of his paw, brushing back her ruffled hair with irritated slaps, Amaryllion said, "Grandion's name means 'noble-hearted son of flame.' He is Sapphurion's only shell-son."

Hualiama stared up at the great old Dragon. This, too, he had made her forget. All her life, she had prided herself on being a forgiving soul. Now she knew that forgiveness might be far harder than she had ever imagined.

Slowly, she said, "Sapphurion knows where Grandion has gone, doesn't he? He banished his own son?"

"Aye, Dragonfriend. He sent the Tourmaline Dragon on an impossible quest."

"You mean I–little *Human* me–must fly to Gi'ishior, home of the Dragons, where they will eat me alive for being audacious enough to set foot on their precious Island–" her voice crackled with positively Dragonish anger "–when I already stink like a windroc's breakfast in Sapphurion's estimation, and convince the leader of the Island-World's Dragons to tell me where his traitorous son–"

"As thou might wish," said the Ancient Dragon.

"As I wish?" She could roar, too, although that effort was wasted on the monster baiting her. "You're ordering me to so wish."

"Never ordering, mouse. You're my friend."

"So, an undersized royal mouse is friend to the scrawniest of Ancient Dragons? Do I earn a long life under a mountain, too?"

Then, Lia had to hold on for dear life, for the earthquake of his laughter thundered over her. Yet she knew that such laughter would never grace the Island-World again.

Amaryllion said, "In a moment, we must go down to the Dragons' graveyard. Thou must remain on the mountainside and be stiller than a mouse. When the time is right, speak my secret name. And then my fire will join Flicker's gift, which I'll grant thee now."

Hualiama could not speak past the Island-sized lump in her throat.

"I would beg a boon of thee," he added. "Wilt thou dance for me one last time, Dragonfriend?"

Chapter Four

A Dragon's Soul

HUALIAMA POURED HER utmost skill into dancing for Amaryllion. To her surprise, he vocalised the music from the soul-dance of the *Flame Cycle*–she had once told him it was her favourite passage–which ranged from dejected to frenetic, full of leaps and twirls reminiscent of the frolicking of flames. But what of the musicianship of an Ancient Dragon! Lia knew Dragons could produce at least three notes in harmony when they sang. Deep, sonorous notes issued from the lower larynx, right down in the chest, mid-tones from the middle throat, and piercingly sweet notes from a flap of skin in the roof of the mouth. Amaryllion's song was a vast symphony of instruments, horns and bugles and drums mingled with softer flutelike tones and haunting strings.

As she danced, he wove magic.

Tendrils of fire began to flicker around Lia's torso. The flames coalesced, gathering form and developing wings and a neck and muzzle, and a body as supple as molten lava. A fire-dragonet, she realised, spurring herself on to greater effort, to greater artistry. Her slippers spun across Amaryllion's paw, barely touching his hide before she vaulted aloft again, soaring, stretching, burning with the passion of her inner infatuation with the flames, as graceful as the first gleam of a twin-suns dawn upon a pristine Islet. The dragonet danced with her, looping and spiralling about her spinning body, weaving his own melody.

Flicker! Her heart squeezed in her chest. *It's you! Oh, my darling ...*

Magic, as thick and buoyant as water, bore Hualiama along on its own wings as Amaryllion juddered into motion, slithering down the gully with a vast, metallic scraping across stone, creating a vibration which drilled into the mastoid bones of her inner ear, and caused the Island to quiver as though a Land Dragon gnawed at its roots.

Faster and faster they descended, following an ancient watercourse. The tempo of Hualiama's dance quickened as she chased the fire-dragonet, playing with him, laughing as he flitted about her face, as Flicker's incorporeal tail stroked her shoulders with a touch of silken fire. Amaryllion bore her upon his paw through vast caves filled with eerie, phosphorescent light and dazzling spars of crystal which made the roots of Ha'athior Island gleam like chambers fit for a king descended from the stars. At length, a new light came to Hualiama's awareness, which she realised was the radiance of the outside world.

The fire-dragonet hovered before her face.

Come, Flicker, she invited him. *Be with me forever.*

The dragonet dived down her throat. Lia gasped, her lungs scorched by heat, a searing sensation that passed almost instantaneously up her spinal cord to detonate behind her eyes. All was flame. Roaring. Lambent. Burning, yet not consuming. An awareness of a mischievous presence darting and diving somehow within her resolved into a conviction that some part of Flicker, perhaps the dragonet's fire-soul, had entered her being without fusing with her, as she had expected. His fire soaked into the most deep-rooted parts of her being, as if a hot volcanic rain fell upon parched ground.

Hualiama soared into the finale of her dance, dimly realising that the Ancient Dragon had halted a few hundred feet before exiting Ha'athior Island, the wide ledge of his forepaw held just above his cavernous nostrils to allow him to regard her with both eyes. She sensed formidable fires mounting within her friend. As Lia stilled, holding the concluding dying-flame position, she read the coils and blossoms of fire stirring within his great orbs, and felt she might understand the mighty

Dragon's emotions.

She said, *Don't be afraid, Amaryllion. The eternal fires are your birthright.*

Her thoughts whispered against his mind like a bird's wings skirting the cliff-edge of an Island. Yet, the Ancient Dragon heard her, and chuckled, *And I thought to comfort thee, little mouse!*

I'm also afraid, she admitted. *I fear what your flame will do to me, mighty Dragon.*

Thy fate will rise not from what I do, but from who thou wert born to be. Hualiama bowed her head at his kind yet immutable words. *Alight now. I must not tarry, for these Dragons who wait, know not the weakness of my third heart–its deep and abiding weakness for thee, Hualiama of Fra'anior. To know thee has been the highest privilege.*

Lia alighted from his paw. *May your soul take wing upon the eternal fires of the Dragonkind–dear friend.*

Speak my name and be ignited, he replied.

The Dragon's body began to slither past her with a majestic scraping of hide against stone. The lung-scorching heat suggested she must be so low down Ha'athior Island, the caldera was close. She should use the cover of his movement to find herself a place from which to observe unseen.

The Human girl crept alongside Amaryllion, angling for a curtain of long, trailing vegetation partially covering the tunnel from which the Ancient Dragon emerged. Mercy, in the twin-suns daylight, he was even more gigantic than she had imagined. But that was far from the only sight which launched her heart into the frantic pulsing of an overheated furnace engine. Dragons! It seemed every Dragon from a thousand leagues around must have gathered to honour Amaryllion's passing on. They covered the cliffs of Ha'athior Island in a living blanket of Dragon hide. Hundreds soared on the thermals above, causing a twin-suns eclipse of the febrile morning air in which myriad Dragon eyes gleamed like living coals in the semidarkness.

She saw Green Dragons and Reds, Oranges and Yellows, and a hundred shades and variations of every colour, here an ultra-rare Grey Dragon and a family of Browns … and Sapphurion! Oh, flying ralti sheep! Hualiama shrank behind a boulder, wishing for Grandion's concealing magic to supplement the solid rock and a veil of leafy vines.

Lia's gaze dipped, only to light upon another wonder. A Dragon graveyard.

Who of the Humankind had ever laid eyes upon this sacred place? From above, much of the graveyard was shielded by a ledge protruding from Ha'athior Island's flank. The ever-billowing smoke of Fra'anior's fires shielded the caldera floor from view. Below the ledge, a cave bored into Ha'athior's roots, gaping wide enough for a dozen Dragons to fly into side-by-side. A tingling of magic made pinpricks of multi-coloured light twinkle behind her eyes as Amaryllion's onyx length crunched over a boneyard, a vast spill of white Dragon bones that lay at the cave's base. This was the Natal Cave, she realised–the fabled resting-place of the First Eggs of the Dragonkind.

Still the Ancient Dragon's body poured sinuously from the cave, shaking the Islands like an earthquake, until at last his mighty hindquarters and tail emerged. The Dragon slithered four-pawed down onto the caldera floor. Three-quarters of a mile of gleaming, Onyx Dragon was he, a living mountain. A legend in his own right. And she called this Dragon her friend?

A person's soul must dissolve into a puddle of awe.

A rush of warmth from her belly presaged the realisation that the Dragons had fallen silent. Magic, thick and profound, curbed even the desire to breathe.

Her friend roared, *I AM AMARYLLION FIREBORN, LAST OF THE ANCIENT DRAGONS! I AM … BEZALDIOR!*

The Island-Cluster shuddered at the power of his spoken name. Fresh cracks snaked across the caldera floor. Lava fountains gushed upward, some exploding in sheets of fire hundreds of feet tall. Thunder pummelled the skies above. Lia knew that they must have felt this earthquake all the way over on the Human Island of Fra'anior, eighteen leagues distant.

The massed Dragons began to hum, a deep thrumming vibrating the air.

More softly, Amaryllion trumpeted, *The age of the Ancients must end, my brethren. A new power shall rise in our stead. I leave thee the blessing of the Ancient Dragons, the sulphurous breath of the Great Dragon Himself.*

He exhaled. It seemed to Hualiama that the Dragon's entire body exhaled, for white-golden fire erupted from his body with the force of a volcanic explosion, three concentric ripples of magical fire that washed over the draconic congregation. She blinked. This heat was more spiritual than physical, a thawing of places and capabilities she had not imagined might exist within a person, and the flame-dragonet danced within her, inhabiting her mind and heart simultaneously.

Sapphurion the Dragon Elder led a bugling, joyous chorus of approbation, which rang back and forth in the great bowl of the caldera until it seemed that the Island-World itself raised its voice in song, and the little Human could not withhold the tears pouring down her cheeks, and steaming on the rocks beside her feet. She did not care. Glorious! Exultant! Every hair on the nape of her neck tingled separately. Now, the Dragonsong split into a hundred harmonies.

From the outside, she felt an interloper, one of small understanding gazing in on the spectacle of Dragon worship, an unworthy eyewitness to the greatest event of this age. Never had she imagined … the raw sensation … the spine-tingling glory! Wonder gripped her, multiplying until Lia became dizzy, intoxicated, and had to grip the boulder in front of her as a reminder of solid, physical reality.

Now, pure white flame began to issue from the cracks between the obsidian slabs of Amaryllion's scales, lighting the boneyard, the spines and ribs and skulls of the Dragons of yore now seared in glorious light. A Dragon took shape above his recumbent body, an image of a fiery light so unadulterated it seared Lia's eyes to look upon, for he shone like starlight. Majesty. Incomparable beauty. Amaryllion's fire-soul filled the space between the assembled Lesser Dragons, a majestic bewinged emblem of draconic power. His brethren had raised the Islands. They had shaped and breathed life into the world she knew.

Amaryllion roared, *I MUST FLY!*

The shock-wave of his declaration punched Hualiama's eardrums. She knew that this was the moment. She must speak, but the pain in her chest rendered her mute. Dragon fear sealed her throat. Yet a word swelled within her. It blazed with irresistible force, summoned by an inaudible command. She meant only to whisper his secret name.

Instead, the word boomed forth so powerfully that Hualiama flew backward. *BEZALDIOR!*

She cracked her head on a granite outcropping behind her.

As Lia glanced up, wincing at the ache in her skull, she saw Sapphurion's quizzical gaze directed at her hiding-place. Mercy! May he lack the power … but the huge Blue Dragon did not appear to detect her presence. Instead, he and all the thousands of Lesser Dragons, from the smallest to the greatest, directed geysers of Dragon fire at Amaryllion's body. Stifling waves of heat rolled up the cliffs. Brighter and brighter blazed the inferno, now emanating from within the Ancient Dragon's vast body. Dragonsong swelled, the elegiac harmonies attaining complexities almost incomprehensible to the Human ear, the magic and music and heat building to a crescendo, the radiance of Amaryllion's Dragon soul surpassing even the twin suns, and though Hualiama's heart thundered in her ears, the magnificent farewell seemed to reach through her nerves and ears and pores to pluck notes upon her soul's own strings.

KAAAABOOM!

Though her eyes were shuttered, Hualiama saw through her eyelids the Ancient Dragon's fire-soul rocket skyward like a comet in reverse–or did she perceive his departure with the eyes of her spirit?

Then, a fragment of starlight detached from the Dragon's soul and shot back toward her. Lia had barely registered its descent before it detonated within her chest. She could not scream, for her lungs seized up. She could not see for flames filling her vision. Hualiama knew only a scorching so sweet it was indistinguishable from pain.

Before she could articulate a single thought, darkness engulfed the light.

* * * *

Waking was a slow surfacing from a faraway place, as though her soul had slumbered in the depths of the Cloudlands. There was an awareness of breath wheezing in her lungs, of life's fires spun in ethereal filaments about the chalice of her soul, of a thinness of spirit as though she had indeed been stretched across time and space. Lia bit back a groan. Aye, four limbs. A chest still whole, not quarried away by Dragon fire. She felt … normal.

Perhaps normal people did not need to pat themselves down as if they expected to find a few vital pieces missing. Sitting up, Hualiama pensively took in the silent, deserted caldera. Judging by the shadows, most of the day had passed. Had she imagined it?

"Right, dust the knees. Be off with you, Island girl."

Before the Dragons found her. Before … she scanned the caldera floor. Lia bit her fist, stifling a cry. Bones. All that was left of Amaryllion, were bones as black as he had been in life. A ribcage she could have flown a full-sized Dragonship into with ease. A skull five hundred feet long. The paw upon which she had danced, lay beneath his chin as though the Dragon were only captivated by an unfathomable Ancient Dragon meditation. Gone. Finally … departed. And with him, the prodigious magic of his kind. What did he mean by passing his mantle on to a Human girl?

Could she believe that something of Amaryllion lived on in her, as he had intimated?

Farewell, Island-biter.

A bittersweet chuckle quivered her lips. He was no Land Dragon–just a titchy Ancient Dragon. Shaking her tender skull with care, Hualiama turned deliberately on her heel, and re-entered the Island.

Two hours' steady hiking brought her to the place where Amaryllion had lain for so long. Stumbling across one of his scales, Lia decided to roll it up to the small stone pedestal where she and Flicker used to sit and converse with the Ancient Dragon. As she sweated and groaned over shifting the seven-foot diameter black platter of Dragon scale-armour up the slope, the wind lamented with desolate mien through the now-empty halls of Amaryllion's abode. The hours she had spent in this cave! Learning, chatting, laughing, singing and being instructed in Dragon lore by Flicker and Amaryllion, Dragonkind's diametric opposites in size yet kindred spirits in their love of legend and fable, and in their caring for a vulnerable Human waif.

All that was left was to cherish memories fled to the everlasting fires of the Dragonkind.

The crystals above lit the cave almost to a daylight brightness, brilliant and magical. She rubbed her arms. There was a special quality about Ha'athior, a sense of the nascent, as though anything imaginable could emerge from the chrysalis of possibility. What? Lia knew she would not seize her destiny by standing in this cave, yet she tarried.

She regarded her reflection in the polished, slightly glittering surface of the scale once she had set it against the pedestal. Serious greenish-blue eyes stared back at Lia from the pearlescent black surface, as though reflected upon a starry night sky. Shadowed, smoky eyes. Wells of mystery framed in an elfin face, the eyes a fraction larger than might be expected, giving her a waiflike appearance that earned itself a kick of her foot in the sand and a snort, "Islands' sakes, girl, you fought Dragons! Rode Dragonback! What's bitten you now?"

Was this the price of forgetting six years of her life?

She should not blame the Ancient Dragon. Aye, he had done wrong. But who knew if those powers that sought her, the prophetic, Dragonish powers, those fey and greedy watchers of whom Amaryllion had warned, might have located and destroyed a Human girl before she was prepared for whatever burden of fate the future held?

Zing! Her Nuyallith blades sprang free of their sheaths. She remembered! Forms and patterns of combat, grounded in dance, flowed like the wind caressing an Island's curves. At the speed of thought, the matched blades cut through the air. Blades forged in Dragon fire, as supple as her limbs yet far stronger. Form upon form. All that she remembered. Ja'al had not completed his task of transferring Master Khoyal's memories of the Nuyallith forms to her, Lia recalled, spinning into a ferocious series of intersecting cuts called the *Dance of Dragonets* technique. On and on she danced, driving her body with all the ferocious power only grief could summon.

Finally, Hualiama finished her martial exercises, panting, "You'll need more of that to get in shape."

Aye, much more talking to herself, and she'd be dancing on the winds like a dragonet.

Hualiama whirled, and set her feet upon the trail.

* * * *

Night had fallen, Lia sensed, but the interior of the Dragon library knew no darkness. "Ha. I knew you could find it again," she congratulated herself. "Pity about the thousand tunnels you searched fruitlessly beforehand."

Hualiama had stumbled upon this library once before. Then, as now, the sheer scale of the place astounded her–a Dragon-sized library in a vertical column, perhaps an old volcanic pipe, thousands of feet tall. The walls were lined with leather-bound books and racks of scrolls. At intervals, wooden beams spanned the width of the column, and held giant reading plinths which stood eighteen feet tall, she estimated. Far overhead, a huge crystal formation blazed with an inner light that reminded her of Amaryllion's Dragon fire, and at intervals down the walls, similar formations provided ample lighting. Lia grinned, examining the crystalline structures with an engineer's eye for symmetry, detail and function. Magical lighting! Everything was Dragon-sized.

Gingerly, Lia crept out of the crack between the bookshelves, and set herself the spider's task of finding her way to the platform fifty feet beneath her position. Gripping the shelves was the easy part. Finding finger-holds between the books was another matter. The tomes on these shelves stood eight feet tall and probably weighed more than half a dozen unruly royal wards all rolled together.

When her feet found the platform, she breathed a sigh of

relief. Now to scale a plinth. This task was harder, but Lia had a core of adamantine stubbornness second to none, as her brother Elki liked to point out. Often. And loudly! Hugging the smooth wood with her legs, Lia crept like an inchworm to the top, and hauled herself over the top edge of the tilted surface which should hold books or scrolls, only, to her intense annoyance, it was quite empty. Flying ralti sheep! Of course she had not checked …

Welcome, Dragon-kin.

More than a few of her platinum strands probably turned pure white as she yelped in surprise.

Speak, and this library shall fulfil your wish.

I … umm …

The library said, *May I present a menu of options?*

Sure. Why not a talking library? Lia perched on the edge of the plinth. *Surprise me.*

Granted, hatchling. Here's the last reference examined by a visitor. You will appreciate the subject.

Hatchling? There was a case of mistaken identity if ever … the breath whooshed from her lungs as from the shelves opposite, a massive tome worked itself loose and skimmed over to her on unseen wings. Hualiama ducked as it thumped down on the plinth. With a frantic rustling, the pages flipped themselves to the desired position.

Clambering down the side of the book, Lia decided that she did not entirely appreciate the way that matters Dragonish made one feel no larger than a gnat. Then, the beautifully illuminated page's title caught her eye. Gold leaf and fanciful dragonets bearing the runic script aloft could not diminish the horror that sliced like a blade of ice into her innards, exactly where Ra'aba had stabbed her in the lower belly before he threw her off his Dragonship.

Ruzal.

How had the library known? Who had been reading about *ruzal?* Hualiama's eyes jumped convulsively to the text.

'*Ruzal.* A branch of spoken magic offering unparalleled control of the mind and emotions of the target creature, similar to a Word of Command but more restricted in effect. *Ruzal* is regarded as a corrupt or debased form of magic due to the damage it may cause to the subject and wielder alike. For example, a powerful word of binding in *ruzal* magic is–'

Lia bit her lip. What was this script–Dragon runes? She eyed the complex character pensively. Perhaps it was better she did not learn the magic which both Amaryllion and the Nameless Man had detected in her, the power of which Ianthine the Maroon Dragoness claimed mastery. Ianthine, who had identified the traitor Ra'aba as her blood-father, had also been the one to rip Lia from her mother Azziala's bosom … Hualiama touched her head to the page as the memories assailed her. Fighting her father. Defeating him. Heavens above and Islands below, what had Sapphurion's Dragon justice meant for him?

For six years, she had barely thought about the man they called the Roc. Oh, the blessed curse of forgetting!

An icy claw touched her neck.

Lia screamed, lost her balance, and came within an inch of tumbling off the plinth. An outthrust hand halted her fall, snagging the lip which kept the book in place.

Dangling from three fingers, Lia found herself facing a Dragon's head formed from blue mist, which swirled around deep, hollow eye-sockets that although empty, fixed upon her with terrible, inhuman force. The mist-beast snarled, *Intruder!*

N-N-No! she stammered. *I've lived on this Island–*

Be silent, creature! Suddenly, a chill attacked her throat, stealing her ability to speak. *Art thou a Dragon? Nay, the Guardian Spirit finds neither wings nor Dragon fire. And thou wouldst steal the secrets of* ruzal? *Thief!*

Hualiama trembled, yet she flung a thought at the creature, *But I know Amaryllion. I have–*

Silence! Even her mental voice cut off as though instantly frozen by the breath of the creature that flowed toward her now, seeping around and enveloping her body, rendering Lia powerless. She floated away into a space dominated by the depthless nothingness of the Guardian Spirit's eyes. A necrotic chill settled in her bones. Never had death seemed more inviting. Yet there was a spark in her that refused its succubus allure, clinging on with the tenacity of ivy to stone, and the breath of her life fanned it into a glow. Abnegation. *I am the child of the Dragon.* Always, in extremity, this idea seemed to shield her. *I am fire.*

A dragonet's laughter bubbled from her lips. Lia sensed the Guardian Spirit baulk. Encouraged, she willed the bright fire forth. White-golden, the magical fire cloaked and protected her. She imagined wings. Claws. Eyes like Grandion's, churning with the compelling infernos of the Dragonkind. The deathly chill receded momentarily. Her feet touched the wooden platform beneath the plinth.

Lia stared at the creature. Now was neither the time nor the place to figure out how she had provoked the Spirits of the Ancient Dragons. How glibly she had evoked them before, back on the Receiving Balcony. How her skin crawled now.

She looked, and perceived death lurking in the shifting mists.

A backward step brought the chill mist a step closer. Delicately they danced, shadowing each other's progress, over to the wall. She saw scroll racks here. These should be easier to climb than the massive bookshelves.

The mist bulged as though the Dragon opened its jaws. *Intruder!*

I possess the gift of a dragonet's fire-soul, Lia replied. But her voice was far less assured than she would have preferred. *Permit me to leave, and I will not trespass again.*

The blue mist stirred restlessly, veils of colour sliding over each other, coalescing around the black-in-black eyes. She touched a shelf.

TRESPASSER!

To her surprise, Lia's white-fires flared up, repelling the assault. No time to reflect on how that had happened. She began to climb. Quick! With a vast, angry hiss, the creature slammed into her fire again. It recoiled. The mist-beast slithered toward her, creeping along the scroll racks, clearly intending to prise her loose.

Lia kicked out. *Begone, spirit!*

The mist-creature's thundering shook her, but Hualiama

kept a white-knuckled grip on the scroll racks. She lashed out with her legs, but the cold seemed as blades sliding through her flesh. Summoning the magic, she tried to warm herself. Blades in her back! Hualiama screamed as pain flared along her old scar-wound, the one Ra'aba had dealt her. Groaning, she dangled above the vast volcanic pipe. The creature coiled and swayed nearby, seeking another, more crippling attack.

'You always take blows right on that definite little chin of yours, zephyr,' she remembered Master Khoyal, her Nuyallith teacher, admonishing her. 'Sometimes the path of valour is retreat. Or simply, to flee. The dead do not fight half as well as the living.' The pain gave her Khoyal's kind of courage. Abandoning her stand, Lia fell to monkey-climbing the wall as though her life depended on it. As she angled for the exit, her route took her out over the chasm, a pipe thousands of feet deep and all of it, lined with the expansive lore of the Dragonkind. There were many platforms down there. Should she fall from this height, visiting one of those platforms would be the last thing she remembered.

DIE, INTRUDER! Cold thundered over her, as though she had dived beneath an icy waterfall. Lia found herself screaming back almost as loudly. Oh, for a Dragon's wings! Aye, she was naturally agile, but this was a series of frantic grabs and thrusts, almost missing a grip as she transitioned over a section of bookshelves, launching herself at last into the jagged-mouthed little tunnel from which she had emerged, dragging her feet up behind her …

Lia shouted furiously as talons of ice gripped her ankles. A monstrous force began to haul her backward. Though her fingers clawed at the stone and her muscles bunched, the Guardian Spirit suddenly seemed to possess the tonnage of an adult male Dragon.

No! She would not yield!

Amaryllion, I need your fire now! Her shriek echoed through the tunnels of Ha'athior Island.

Her bones felt deep-frozen. Her legs and hips dangled in the air. Lia clutched an outcropping with both hands, but her fingers began to slip, a quarter inch, now two inches, as the creature exerted its strength.

Then, her cry returned as fire. Beautiful, clean, crystalline fire shot toward her in a form that suggested a dragonet's wings, as if she had somehow evoked the power of Ha'athior's magical crystals which had sustained Amaryllion's life for so many centuries.

Flames blossomed around Lia, unfolding in vast yet transient petals of colour, blue and white and gold. The pressure vanished. With a terrible cry, the Guardian Spirit released her legs.

Heaving herself into the tunnel with a dancer's upper body strength, Lia surged to her feet, and fled as though she had indeed grown wings.

Chapter Five

Remembrance

EMERGING FROM THE hidden stairwell behind the prekki-fruit tree just after dawn the morning following Amaryllion's passing on, Hualiama ran headlong into the bare, muscular chest of Rallon, who cried, "It's her!"

"Detain the miscreant. Master Ja'al will see her at once," ordered Hallon, his twin brother. The bearded monks seized her, one to either arm.

Great Islands, did these monks never wear more than a loincloth? With her newfound clarity of recollection, Lia remembered how she had first met the twins. She could not ignore the opportunity to foment mischief. She drawled, "Well, boys, and what of your vows?"

"Our vows?" rumbled Rallon, staring down at her from his gigantic six feet and seven inches stature. "What do you mean, scrap?"

"Firstly, you lay hands on the royal ward, part-time Princess of the realm. Secondly, I'm a female. You are monks, sworn to chastity, fidelity, and service to the Great Dragon. Thirdly–"

"What of it?" growled Hallon, his Dragon's-paw grip on her upper arm swinging her off the ground in concert with his twin. "Enough of this nonsensical dragonet-chatter."

"If you don't put me down, I'll make you blush."

"Blush?" chorused the giant twins.

"Like simpering Fra'aniorian maidens on their first appearance in Court," Lia clarified.

"Bah," snorted Rallon. "Just you try."

"Bah," Hallon imitated his brother. "We've learned a great deal about you since the day you first pulled the proverbial ralti wool over our–" his voice rose an octave "–what're you doing?"

"Ooh, you're so *muscly*," Hualiama cooed. "I was just playing."

"Stop that!"

She curled her fingers around his muscular bicep. "But it's just so … yummy."

Rallon laughed uproariously as his brother's ears heated up to a fine, flaming pink. He said, "We should unhand the Princess at once."

"Indeed," said Hualiama, whirling upon Rallon with a gleam in her eye that caused the monk to backpedal, but not fast enough. Laying her hand flat against his stomach, she teased, "My, what girl would not want to hike over boulders like these?"

Rallon's blush emulated the roseate dawn breaking over the monastery. Even Lia gasped at her own impudence. Truth from a dragonet's mouth, was the Isles saying.

"Apprentice Hualiama!"

She jumped, and then clucked crossly. "Ja'al! Don't sneak–"

"Aggravating my monks again, I see?" he cut in, grinning broadly. "Just like the Lia of old."

Had she forgotten more than she imagined? Hualiama's light-hearted mood–a fleeting distraction from the soul-ache over the loss of a dear friend, she realised now–faded into puzzlement. Should she take this for a flash of insight, or merely a chance comment? Either way, this new grief had punctured her heart like a single, clean thrust of a whetted blade.

Turning to the twins, Ja'al rapped, "Don't you have duties?" They rushed away. The monk-leader's voice softened. "Are you alright, Lia? We heard a commotion …"

"Amaryllion died."

She would not cry. Lia defied her tears, but though she lowered her eyes, the gentleness she sensed in Ja'al's regard introduced an uncontrollable tremor to her lower lip. The warmth of his arms encircling her shoulders made the sobs tear loose from a place so deep, they seemed to gash open fresh wounds on their way out. Suddenly, she was a Cloudlands squall breaking above an Island. Ja'al could only pat her back and murmur soft words that reverberated against her cheek, nestled into his chest.

"Islands' sakes!" she sniffled, drawing back at last. "I'm a royal mess."

"Never."

Hualiama made to find a scrap of cloth to wipe her face, when she was arrested by Ja'al's strong, lean fingers pinching her chin between thumb and forefinger and raising her head. He considered her so long and so searchingly, that Lia feared she might succumb to another madcap desire to kiss the monk. Oh, great Islands! Why did Ja'al have to be so volcanically gorgeous, and so forbidden by vow and by faith?

Aye, the day Grandion battled Razzior the Orange Dragon and Yulgaz the Brown, and had been buried in a cave beneath a landslide for his trouble–the pain of that memory seared her afresh. To evade the Dragons' scrutiny, Ja'al had kissed her with devastating sweetness and passion, and then promptly turned about-face and declared he was therefore convinced he must take his vows! Callous fiend. Rotten, uncaring, inviolable monk-monster–she chastised herself. He was a good man.

Thus, their paths had diverged. Ja'al had pursued his faith, and Hualiama found the Tourmaline Dragon beneath the mountain, only to be burned by him in his unthinking, feral state.

Still, Ja'al's fingers gripped her chin.

"What?" she protested. "What have I done?"

"You've changed." He shook his head slowly. "You've … there's something about your eyes. I can't fathom it. Something's changed."

"I've grown shorter?"

"No. You're … back."

"Back?" she echoed, not understanding. "Back how? From where?"

Slowly, as if voicing an understanding only just percolating into his mind, Ja'al said, "Your soul has journeyed afar. You've only just returned. I thought it grief, Hualiama, a natural reaction to discovering who your father was and taking back the Onyx Throne at his expense, and then Grandion's departure … you shocked the living pith out of me, you know." His finger wagged before her eyes, but Lia was so captivated by his words, she did not even blink. "Fine. I confess, I was jealous. You were so obsessed with that dratted reptile, so cutesy-sweet with him–"

Hualiama asked, "Ja'al, have I neglected you?"

"Nay. But–I do feel as though I have stepped back six years in time. Amaryllion did something to you. And now you've remembered everything, correct?"

Wordless, Hualiama nodded. She had forgotten the power of his insight. As he peered at her, cocking his head slightly this way and that, Lia mentally traced a fingertip along the stubble of his firm jawline–Islands' sakes! Had she no self-control around this man?

Ja'al's thoughts were on another Island. He cried, "The spark is back! The flame! And, I do declare, your eyes have changed. Less smoky green. More, as Flicker would've said, a handsome blue like mine." Lia chuckled quietly even in the depths of her amazement, but Ja'al rushed on, "I see Dragon fire! I see power and the Nuyallith forms swarming in your head and I know you've decided to go find Grandion and oh, Lia! I just can't find words … I'm fizzing with excitement. You're back!"

"No over-excited kisses from you, Mister Monk," she deadpanned.

"Lia! Of course not." Had a dragonet bitten her normally stoic friend, she wondered? Normally she was the effusive one. "Maybe a windroc's peck." Dropping her chin, he gripped her fingers instead and placed a feather-light kiss on her left cheek. "Impish Princess, do you not see? This is the trigger. The prophecy must come to fruition and you–I sense it so clearly–are about to turn our Island-World on its head once more."

"Riding Dragonback was not enough?" she protested.

"Not half the nuisance I know you're capable of

perpetrating," said he, with a broad smile to take the sting off his provocation. "Now, snip snap, quick wings. Before Hualiama thinks about travelling anywhere in this Island-World, we must hasten to Ya'arriol Island to consult with my mother."

"Big tough Master Ja'ally needs his mommy?"

She could have sold Ja'al's expression for half of the jewels in her kingdom. He huffed, "How such a Dragon's tonnage of vexation ever came to be distilled in such a tiny frame, Lia, I cannot fathom!"

She dipped into a Fra'aniorian courtly bow, complete with the obligatory hand-twirls. "I humbly obey your commands, *Master* Ja'al."

"This way to your Dragonship, your royal tininess," he retorted, seeming rather steamed beneath the collar–not that monks seemed to regard clothing as much more than a frivolous affectation. "And you'll tell me what happened?"

Hualiama nodded, the rush of reckless abandon giving way to trepidation. The habits of six years would not be easy to slough off. "I will," she agreed. "But can we use the travel-time to Ya'arriol for you to transfer knowledge of all of the remaining Nuyallith forms to me? I suspect I'll have need of them."

Ja'al's brows arched toward the crown of his shaven, tattooed head. "All ninety?"

"All of them," Lia said firmly. That was an invitation to an Island-thumping migraine, and they both knew it.

She helped Ja'al drag her solo Dragonship out from under the cover of a grove of massive giant fig trees. At over one hundred and fifty feet tall, they easily sheltered her small Dragonship. Hallon and Rallon came to lend a hand.

Once Ja'al had finished instructing the twins, he made a face at Lia. "Only now, running this monastery, have I truly come to appreciate Master Jo'el's attention to detail."

"All monks on board. This Dragonship is leaving," said Lia, stoking the stove's fire.

She could not have sworn to it, but it did appear that both Hallon and Rallon were still blushing.

Ja'al leaped in lithely. "Right, short shrift, time to open that devious dragonet's brain of yours. Let's fill it with something substantial, for a change. Don't forget to set your controls."

Egg-head, she said in Dragonish.

"I know what you said!"

Ooh, been learning Dragonish, Mister Clever Monk?

Ja'al grimaced. "No, but I do know when my hawser is being tugged."

The Dragonship rose silently into the gleaming dawn skies above the volcano on a westerly heading, making for Ya'arriol Island, already visible in the distance. Another volcanic Fra'aniorian dawn, Hualiama thought, savouring the subtle tints of the Cloudlands and the luminous quality of the light beyond the long shadow cast by Ha'athior Island. The world seemed pregnant with opportunity.

"Right," she said. "Our heading's fixed and the oven's warm. I'll pedal whilst you fry my brain. Agreed?"

Ja'al loomed over her with a discomfiting sneer. He cracked his knuckles deliberately, making her exclaim in annoyance. "Shall I tidy up a bit whilst I'm in there?"

"Sure. And while you're at it, will you just rustle up a vision of my destiny and tell me exactly where to find my mother?"

"Deal." Ja'al's long, sensitive fingers touched her temples. "First one."

For the three hours it took them to fly to Ya'arriol, Ja'al poured into his subject all the remaining Nuyallith lore he had 'harvested'–to use his descriptor, which made Hualiama squirm–from Master Khoyal before his death. Overhead, the rigging creaked under the variable pressure of a capricious breeze. The hawsers rasped against their pulleys and blocks, and the sails flapped lazily. The stove, which fed the turbines and hot air sacks, crackled cheerfully as Ja'al flicked in chunks of pre-cut, dense jalkwood at intervals between ladling dollops of knowledge into her aching brain. Lia fidgeted and sweated, fighting a migraine that seized her head like a ralti sheep squeezed by a marauding Dragon's talons.

Ja'al paused to mop his brow. "A touch more northerly please, Steersman. Are you alright, Lia?"

"Surviving. Don't spare the meriatite, Master Jo'el."

"Not Jo'el," he smiled. His uncle, Master Jo'el, had perished in the battle for the Kingdom of Fra'anior, six years before. Ra'aba had much to answer for.

Ra'aba, her father. He might be her blood-father, but he meant nothing more. Lia sucked in her cheeks, scowling at the rigging. Traitor, usurper, evil magician, despoiler of women and would-be murderer of his daughter. Charming! How could her mother match up to the Roc? Somehow, the stinging in her bones suggested, her mother Azziala would do all that, and more. Azziala had journeyed from the Eastern Isles to the Halls of the Dragons. At Gi'ishior Ra'aba had forced himself upon her. A child resulted, whom Azziala immediately abandoned to the Dragoness Ianthine's tender mercies. How often had Lia not dreamed of wonderful parents, only to have the truth of her origins strike her with the force of an Isles earthquake?

Was the inner force which impelled her to seek her destiny, at least in part a desire to atone for her parents' misdeeds? And what of the strange connection between Ra'aba and Razzior, the Orange Dragon who had tried to burn her?

Hualiama stiffened as a torrent of knowledge thundered anew into the bowl of her skull, despite Ja'al's avowed attempt at gentleness. Too much! Muscles rigid, burning, a soundless scream rising from the marrow of her soul … she spiralled into darkness.

"The spirit of Nuyallith is dance," she heard Master Khoyal's ancestor instructing him, many, many summers before Lia ever opened her eyes to the Island-World. "And what is dance, but the purest expression in physical movement of the spirit of a person? Therefore, the spirit must be trained as much as the body requires training–even more so than the physical flesh, truth be told. Just as we feed the body and care for its needs, so we must provide the spirit with the nutrients it requires."

"What do you mean, great-grandfather?" The voice in her memory was a boy's tenor, not the aged rasp Hualiama had known.

"A person could spend a lifetime filling the Cloudlands from shore to shore with scrolls upon the subject, Khoyal. Simply put, to meditate and act upon principles such as truth, integrity, beauty, justice and holiness, is to feed the spirit with goodness. The spirit of a person is like fire. Starve a fire of fuel, and it will gutter and die. Feed the fires, boy. Always feed the fires, and be hungry for more."

"Is the power of goodness greater than the power of evil, great-grandfather?" asked the boy.

"How does it seem to you?"

"That the deeds of evil are the greatest fire, which rage and consume all."

"Such a melancholy opinion from a boy of nine summers' age?"

Hualiama jerked awake as though a fisherman had hooked her in the cheek and heaved her out of the water in one powerful pull. "*Gaaah!*"

A hand smoothed her overheated brow. "Easy, petal."

"Yualiana?" Lia whispered. Her eyes flicked open.

She found herself lying abed, the focus of a number of concerned expressions–Ja'al's mother Yualiana and his father, Master Ga'athar, Ja'al himself, her best friend Inniora, and Chago, Inniora's hulking, dark husband who cradled one each of their twin two-month-old baby girls in either arm.

Yualiana slapped Ja'al's shoulder. "You great lump of a monk! What did you do to my little petal?"

"Nothing, I swear–"

"I'll nothing your backside like I used to, Master of Dragon Warriors or none!"

"Now, mother–"

"Aye, and do you know what your mother says? Go put on a shirt! This is a decent household. You should know better than to parade half-naked around impressionable young women."

Lia wanted to tell Yualiana to go easy on Ja'al, but she was enjoying their interaction far too much. However, Yualiana caught Lia's grin before she managed to wipe it off her lips. One raised eyebrow was all it took for a volume of scrolls to be spoken.

Hualiama prattled, "I'm fine. I made Ja'al do it."

"Oh, is it, petal?" Any self-respecting Green Dragon would have gnawed off a limb to enjoy that much acid.

After Ja'al had secured clothing and Lia had offered explanations, Master Ga'athar rolled his eyes and growled, "I see you two are still matched in having a quarter of the brains accorded the silliest dragonet."

When Ja'al's mother and father scolded her, which was infrequently, Lia wished they could have been her parents. She heard love beneath their Dragon-like snarls. Were King Chalcion to chastise her … aye. Another scrolleaf would have unfurled, scribed in pain.

The Master continued, "Now, Lia. Ja'al tells us you bring news. You'd better start a volcano spitting before Yualiana cracks her rolling pin over your head."

"As if I'm the impatient one, Ga'athar," his wife retorted. "Come, petal. A pinch of restorative for your headache and a bite to eat are the medicines you need. When last did you sleep, Hualiama?"

"Ah–"

"I thought so!" A finger wagged beneath Lia's nose. "The Queen will pluck my guts for bowstrings. Lie down. Down, I said! Cheeky dragonet. We'll serve you. Ja'al, quick wings to the kitchen, boy. Inniora, fetch another pillow-roll. Ga'athar, make yourself useful with your grandchildren."

Thus with bark and bite, Yualiana rallied her family. Hualiama sighed. How different this was to palace life, here on a small Island, in an even smaller village. She knew which she preferred.

Lia held out her arms. "Chago, may I demand a cuddle?"

His dark, scarified face broke into a grin. "Aye, Princess. That you may. Left arm or right?"

"Right–that's Bithinia, right? How you tell them apart … so, how are you coping with two sets of twins?"

"I thought warrior training was exhausting," he rumbled, passing the babe over to Hualiama. "Two three-summers boys roaring around the place pretending they're Dragons, and now these two hatchlings–it's a blessing, truth be told, but a vast surprise. Zero to two to four! I was set against the idea at first, but Inniora convinced me we needed help and I'm grateful to have Master Ga'athar and Mistress–"

"Master this and Mistress that, son?" Ga'athar snorted, plucking the other twin, Yaziala, from Chago's arm and settling her with the ease of a father of eleven children. "How many years will it take you to address us as your parents?"

"At least one more," said Inniora, returning with a pillow-roll for Hualiama. Her smile lingered upon her husband in a way that made Lia blush and lower her eyes. Oh, for someone to love like that, not a hulking, scaly lizard with scales the colour of gemstones …

Shortly, the family gathered again. Inniora held a bowl of spicy ralti stew for Hualiama, who had a Dragon-sized hunger, as she used her free hand to scoop up the delicious stew with chunks of sweetbread. She said, "Yum. That's wonderful. What's the grin for, Ja'al? Aye, they do feed royal wards in the Palace! Yualiana, may I trouble you for another helping?"

"Mercy, petal. I mean, have mercy upon Ga'athar, and tell him a few things before he bites off your arm with impatience."

"Well …" Hualiama puffed out her cheeks. "I apologise if I've been acting a bit strange, these past six years …" She told them of the near-disaster upon the Receiving Balcony, and how Amaryllion had compelled her to forget.

Master Ga'athar's eyes flicked several times to the half-healed cut on her cheek, and the yellowing bruise surrounding it, as she tonelessly described the King's treatment of her. No-one, least of all Lia, seemed keen to dwell on the subject.

"Your eyes have changed colour, Lia," Inniora confirmed. "They're definitely bluer; a shades darker than my brother's."

"What do you plan to do now?" asked Yualiana.

"Find Grandion," said Lia. "He has suffered on my account."

"You actually–"

"Flew Dragonback, Master Ga'athar." Lia had no need of his hiss to understand how severely he disapproved. "Worse, or more accurately, Grandion and I exchanged oaths. I promised to aid and protect the Dragonkind against whatever terrible future the rise of this third race might portend, should the prophecy come to pass, and he vowed to aid and honour me, out of his freewill as a creature of fire and magic."

Yualiana sighed, "Petal …"

"I know. He's a Dragon and I'm not. Yet I am fond of him–" she squirmed, but in the end, a desire to lay out her entire sordid history won out "–I'm fond of Grandion in ways which are rather more heretical than I ever felt about Flicker. I'm sorry! The fire drives me, don't you see? Long before Amaryllion ever passed Flicker's gift on to me, I felt driven … and I know how reckless and irresponsible it must seem to you all, yet the song must be sung, and the deed done. I *must* find Grandion. I'm certain of few things, but I know that breaking my oath would be a sin greater than any I have committed thus far."

Inniora squeezed her hand gently. "Don't apologise for being who you are, Lia."

"But I don't want to be who I am!" she burst out. "Islands' sakes, that's the whole problem with my life and it's driving me off the proverbial Island-edge of sanity! Am I moons-mad? I want wings; might I not more hopefully pine for the stars? I cannot have what I want. It's impossible."

Yualiana said, "Having no wings of your own, you want his? It's a heart thing, petal."

Hualiama scowled unhappily. She loved Yualiana, but her self-righteous tone deserved a Dragon-sized slap.

"How do you plan to find Grandion?" asked Ga'athar.

In a tone designed to shock, Lia replied, "I plan to fly to Gi'ishior and ask his father."

"Mercy!" cried Yualiana.

"You're moons-mad and more!" barked Master Ga'athar. "Have you no inkling how fragile is the peace between Dragons and Humans–of course you do. You salvaged that peace last week, but Lia …" He ran his hands through his hair, clearly fighting for calm. "Girl, you know we love you as one of our own. Always have done. But … they'll kill … freaking feral windrocs! Speak to her, Yualiana."

"Petal–"

Ja'al cut his mother short with a peremptory gesture. "Mom, Dad–this is Hualiama of Fra'anior, Dragon Rider and Dragon*friend*."

Inniora put in, "As in, the dancing dervish who kicked Ra'aba's hideously hairy butt all over–"

"Inniora!" Yualiana snapped. "Mind your language!"

"It's true." Inniora folded her arms mutinously.

Ga'athar grunted, "Fine. We're all ralti sheep dancing around the five moons. How do you plan to approach Sapphurion, Hualiama? Twist his wing? Dragonfriend, aye. You know what else the Dragons say? You're a Dragon killer." Half an expletive exploded from Ja'al's mouth, perfectly expressing how Lia felt. Thumping the tabletop with his fist, Ga'athar shouted, "You cannot trust a Dragon! Never! They'll eat you alive, girl."

Far from being taken aback by his vehemence, Hualiama looked inward, and discovered unyielding clarity of purpose. "Master Ga'athar," she replied. "Mistress Yualiana. I've always felt welcomed and loved in this house, and it means more to me–mercy, I'm going to cry–more to a foundling who was abandoned …"

"Easy, rajal," said Yualiana, squeezing her arm.

Lia sobbed, "Yet it seems I've found … love … in unexpected places, all my life."

Master Ga'athar breathed, "Aye, petal. We know."

Her brokenness held them spellbound. Lia glanced at the infant slumbering in the crook of her arm, winding a curl of baby-soft hair about her finger as she fought for control. "This little one enters life at the dawn of a new era in our Island-World. None of us know what the future may bring. Amaryllion told me of war engulfing the Islands; that entire cultures would be erased. He said, 'The bridge between Dragons and Humans will be thy soul, and according to thy choices, this age will rise or fall.' This little girl must have a future. And if that means I must fly into a Dragon's champing jaws to secure it, then so be it. I shall fly."

Ja'al interjected, "And may the courage of a Dragon be your heart's portion."

Smiling gratefully at him, Lia added, "In that library beneath Ha'athior, some person or Dragon had been reading about *ruzal*. I take that to mean either Ianthine is loose, or my father escaped draconic justice–incredible as that may seem. I cannot find Grandion on my own. The Island-World is vast. How many years has he been missing? And when I consider his fate–" she pressed her hand to her stinging heart "–it is as though part of my soul flew abroad and tarries there, as you said, Ja'al. I fear I'll never be whole without it. Without him."

Lia groaned, her fist clenching on the bedclothes. Why such pain? Surely her feelings should have mellowed with time?

"Master Ga'athar, there's a secret about Sapphurion and Qualiana … before Ianthine was banished, I believe she brought me from the East to Gi'ishior as a newborn. Certainly, I was no older than Bithinia, here. I'd need to ask Queen Shyana how old I was when they adopted me, but I believe it might have been between two and three years of age."

"Brought up by the Humans on Gi'ishior, surely?" said Ga'athar, at exactly the same time as Ja'al gasped, "You're not saying Sapphurion–*the* Dragon Elder Sapphurion–"

"I've lucid memories of running into his paw, Ja'al. I could show you, if you'd like."

"I believe you," said Ja'al, exchanging incredulous glances with his father.

"Grandion remembered his mother caring for a green-eyed Human baby. He was terribly jealous. And how come I know Dragonish so well?"

Ga'athar tugged on his beard as though he wished to pull it out by the roots. "Lia, you believe Sapphurion will deal fairly with you, because you are that girl he and Qualiana somehow hid from every other Dragon, against every draconic law, for several years?"

"If my memories do not play me false, Master. If this isn't some stupid, girlish longing for a past more palatable than mine has been. If, if … mercy, too many ifs!"

"The risk! Appalling–"

"Aye, the risk, Master. If I can learn where my Dragon has gone, over the Isles and beyond, I plan to fly first to Fra'anior Island and take leave of my parents–"

"No!" At least three people shouted at her at once.

Lia soothed Bithinia, who had squalled at the noise.

Yualiana huffed, "Petal, honestly. Blasphemous fondness for a Dragon I can handle–roaring rajals, will you hear me? Whatever prekki-fruit mush has clogged up the innards of your skull, can you scrape it out now, please? Ja'al, you didn't–"

"Yualiana–I promised." At a further chorus of scornful snorts, Lia protested, "I promised the Queen and my brother I would not travel beyond our Island-Cluster. A promise is a–"

"Heavens above, Lia!" Master Ga'athar threw up his hands in disgust. "Your father will beat you, toss you in his dungeons and throw the key off the Island! I will personally rattle that cage upon your shoulders until the monkey-nuts inside fly out of your ears!"

Lia growled, "I made a promise."

"Some promises are not meant to be kept," Ja'al protested. "You stubborn minx–look, she's doing that thing with her chin you told me about, Inniora. Might as well talk to a stone."

"True." With a fragile smile, the Princess added, "Master Jo'el demanded the utmost integrity of his monks, Ja'al."

"Duly chastised." He hung his head.

"I'm no longer the girl Chalcion thinks he can bully and browbeat with impunity." She could imagine her father's response. Hualiama dreaded that encounter more than the prospect of facing all the Dragons of Gi'ishior. "But–"

Inniora interjected, "You must reclaim your dignity."

That sounded rather grander than the statement ready on the tip of Lia's tongue, but she was further startled when Master Ga'athar snarled, "I know you'll refuse this offer, girl, but if King Chalcion so much as lifts a finger against you, you can tell him from me he'll have a rebellion on his hands."

Hualiama smiled. "That's rather like carrying a Dragon in my pocket, isn't it?"

"And if the Dragon fails, Mom's offering her rolling pin in service of the crown," said Ja'al, nudging his mother slyly.

"Ja'al!" Yualiana gasped.

"To use it on you, I mean," he said to Hualiama. "To make you feel more part of the family."

"If I catch you, son …" Yualiana chased him out of the room.

Chapter Six

Fire-Dance

AS THE DRAGONSHIP soared aloft on dawn's luminous wings, Ja'al's family receded into the distance, their hands upraised in the gesture of sending-in-love. Lia knew she might never see them again. As Flicker used to tell her, she must stoke her hope as a dragonet stokes his belly-fires. Then again, perhaps dwelling upon the fires that awaited a rogue royal ward was not best-conceived to cheer her pensive mood.

Adjusting the turbines for optimal forward thrust into a gentle headwind, Lia trimmed the side-sails to reduce the drag and ran an experienced eye over the rigging. All good. Better than good. Master Ga'athar had replaced a number of worn stay-lines, and patched two leaks he had pinpointed by tossing a handful of green leaves into the oven to produce enough smoke to pervade the hot air sacks. A neat trick! She had packed a satchel containing an ancient scroll of Dragon lore with which she hoped to satisfy what Ga'athar called an obligation-gift—what the Dragonkind saw as due payment for the favour she would request. She must not mention Grandion by name. She had a hundred Dragonish protocols and manners to observe, many of which she had read about, but the Master's experience brought them to life.

The twin Nuyallith blades she carried sheathed on her back, in a well-worn harness Ja'al had unearthed for her from the monastery stores. The sheaths were cleverly split in their top third, allowing a fast draw of the twenty-seven inch long blades even from atop one's shoulders. A pair of Immadian forked daggers hung from her belt. The powerful Haozi hunting bow lay near at hand, with a quiver of arrows crafted by a Ya'arriol weapons master. It would come in more than handy should she encounter a feral windroc. Inniora and Yualiana had crafted the outfit she wore, including a spare in her travel pack.

"Fire-resistant material this time," Inniora had informed her. "Useful for girls who enjoy entertaining Dragons, isn't it? A short skirt split in four places to allow freedom of movement, or comfortable seating upon a Dragon's back. Everything fitted and triple-stitched so you don't snag a blade in some stupid frill during combat. Armoured wristlets, a decent belt with secret compartments on the inside and an armoured bodice all feature in the design."

"An armoured bodice?" Ja'al's eyes resembled a land-snail's eyes popping out on their stalks.

"Aye. Look, Ja'al, I had to let it out an extra two inches to allow for Hualiama's curves," Inniora goaded her brother. "A fantastic fit, if I say so myself."

"I-I have w-work … somewhere. Something important," Ja'al stammered, rushing off.

Hualiama made a face at Inniora. "You're mean."

"Any girl with a monk for a brother has a right to her fun," came the retort. "Learn to flaunt your blessings, Island girl!"

Hualiama coloured hotly.

More annoyingly, her travel pack contained headscarves for the more conservative Islands lying eastward to Lyrx, and even a face veil suitable for the Eastern Isles. How far did Master Ga'athar think she'd have to fly in search of Grandion? Lia scowled. Oh, the necessities a woman required in this Island-World! Her clothing also concealed a number of additional, not-so-girly 'necessities' such as poison darts, lock picks, a miniature hand-drill, three thin, flexible metal saws, a half-dozen throwing knives, jewels for trade and even a garrotte.

Aiming her Dragonship's nose at the northern tip of Human-inhabited Sa'athior Island, several Islands north of Ha'athior, Hualiama settled in for the haul over the Cloudlands. From Sa'athior, it would be a short flight to Gi'ishior, passing the barren Dragon-haunt of Frendior Island.

Hualiama never tired of this view of her home Island Cluster. Admittedly, she was only eight leagues or so from the volcano, but it dominated the north-western horizon as though planted there since time immemorial, a stark reminder of the power of the Ancient Dragons to raise Islands from the deeps. League-tall cliffs jutted sheer from the Cloudlands, jet-black until the vegetation began about half a mile above the level she assumed was toxic to all life. Then, what profusion! Great trailers of tropical vegetation hung down the cliffs, and trees stretched hundreds of horizontal feet, improbably rooted in the tiniest crack, forever stooped beneath the weight of their leafy boughs. Sometimes she imagined the Islands were shaggy-haired beasts peering out of the Cloudlands.

Her flight path would take her skimming around the rim to Gi'ishior, by a rajal's whisker the most northerly Island of the Cluster.

Softly, Hualiama sang several lines from an elegy she had written for her friend Flicker:

Gliding, soaring, dipping over the brow of the Island-World.
Suns in our faces, wind buoying our wings,
Freedom to roam as widely as our hearts desire.
Moon-riding, windroc-hiding, tickling the clouds with our toes …

Her song spoke of her three best Dragon friends in the Island-World. Two had already died. What hope could she realistically entertain that Grandion had not long since been added to that tally? 'Will my Rider watch the skies for a Tourmaline Dragon?' he had asked. Surely, an implicit promise to return, and an agreement no Dragon would break? For the first time, she realised that if Grandion lived, he might be as much an oath-breaker as she. Might he pine for a Human girl? Or had he forgotten her?

She must guard the portals of her heart, and not allow false hope a toehold.

Warrior-monk exercises, dance in the cramped quarters and meditating upon the new Nuyallith forms occupied the hours. She sipped fresh prekki-fruit juice from a gourd and nibbled at a sweet honey-and-nut roll Yualiana had slipped into her hand just before departure.

All the while, Gi'ishior's slender volcanic peak expanded in her vision, perched upon the northern rim wall like a bird upon a precious perch, while her home Island of Fra'anior on the western rim was hidden behind a localised thunderstorm. At eighteen leagues from her position, that was a perfectly common phenomenon–sunshine on one Isle, hail on the next.

But her fingers turned white on the guardrail of her basket. The sky above Gi'ishior crawled with Dragons. Mercy. "One little snack incoming," she chuckled, sounding rather squeakier than she appreciated. "Courage, Dragon Rider!"

It still felt like a dream.

Returning to her controls, Hualiama adjusted the ailerons to take her around the western periphery of the volcano at a height and heading specified by Ga'athar. She deployed the sails to take best advantage of the wind, scudding forward with renewed impetus where she had been forced to tack before.

Now, how long would it take the Dragons to launch a few friendly fireballs across her path?

All of a minute.

A Dragonwing of three juvenile Orange Dragons came screaming down from on high at a velocity that trumpeted their desire to intimidate. One whooshed by not twenty feet from the nose of her Dragonship, causing it to slew in the air at the wash of his passage. Young male Dragons–Lia gritted her teeth. Cue a surfeit of draconic posturing, silliness and the need to have egos stroked by a few well-turned compliments.

"Turn back!" thundered one of the Oranges, discharging a courtesy fireball across her bow.

Lia called out, "The most sulphurous greetings of the Great Dragon Fra'anior, to you, o mighty Orange Dragon!"

A second fireball crackled past, passing dangerously close to the top of her balloon. These Dragons were easily seventy feet from muzzle to tail-spike, and high on adrenaline and whatever other Dragon hormones might be raging around in their golden Dragon blood.

Mind your claws, Zaxxion! called the Dragon to her starboard side. *This one greets humbly.* Of course, he accompanied this with a hundred-fang, monstrously toothy leer–the only welcome in his smile being an invitation to personally investigate the sharpness of his fangs, followed by an intimate examination of his gullet. The Dragon sneered, "I'm Emburion. Where do you think you're going, little Human?"

Lia firmed her voice. "If it pleases you, noble Dragons, I am Hualiama Dragonfriend, daughter of King Chalcion of Fra'anior, and I wish to speak with Sapphurion, the Dragon Elder."

This stinks of windroc droppings, brethren, Zaxxion complained from somewhere above the balloon.

The Elders treated with those lying fleas just last week, Emburion returned. *I say we frighten it off. What say you, Hazzalion?*

The third voice, beneath her Dragonship, spat, *A Princess? We cannot spurn Sapphurion's word, no matter how horribly it itches our scales. However, I anticipate the Elder will lick this vermin's entrails off his talons.*

Charming image. Hualiama had expected as much, but as the Isles saying went, the rajal's proof was in the sharpness of his fangs. She clamped down on a creeping sense of terror and locked her knowledge of the Dragonish language behind walls of mental granite. She must not even think in Dragonish, Master Ga'athar had cautioned.

"We will conduct you to the landing place, Princess," rumbled Emburion. "Stray a wing's-breadth from the appointed path, and I will take pleasure in charcoaling your meatless rack of bones."

Lia bowed elaborately. "I shall so endeavour, o lava-scaled lord of draconic magnificence–" she managed to deliver her effusive compliment without a hint of irony "–but what Human Dragonship can imitate the aerial prowess of the Dragonkind in anything but name?"

The Orange Dragon's belly-fires rumbled his pleasure.

And so Lia piloted the solo Dragonship around the volcano's eastern flank, closely shadowed by the trio of suddenly voluble Dragons, who occupied themselves with competing to invent the best insults in Dragonish, blithely unaware that the Human girl understood every word.

A semi-circular terrace lake hugged the volcano's base from the western edge of the Island all the way around to the north, gleaming like liquid bronze in the late afternoon suns-light. As they skirted the precipitous avocado-coloured slopes, Lia saw a dozen Dragon sentries perched on the rim wall, beside those patrolling the skies above. Unease trickled like icy water down her spine.

With hands deft on the rigging and controls as the Dragonship bucked disobediently in the whimsical breeze, Lia brought her vessel sweeping down toward the lake. She skimmed over the surface into the mouth of an immense cavern–a tunnel, she realised–which penetrated the volcano's heart. Pristine waters lapped against obsidian shores, set afire by thick streamers of light radiating from above. A huge shadow rippled beneath the Dragonship, making Lia startle. She gasped as a Green Dragoness surged out of the water ahead of them, her ninety-foot wings sheeting great veils of water, clenching a gigantic carp she had between her fangs. The fish had to be twenty feet in length, a meal worthy even of a Dragon.

"Giant whiskered carp," said Emburion, his dragon-smile displaying a row of surprisingly yellow fangs, as though his mouth were filled with wax candles. As the tunnel opened into the caldera, he added, "Welcome to the Halls of the Dragons, o Princess of Fra'anior."

Hualiama inhaled sharply. "Oh, Emburion! It's amazing."

The Dragon waved a wingtip lackadaisically, clearly relishing the opportunity to play tour-guide to an enthusiastic audience. "The garnet, tourmaline and quartzite crystal formations on the volcano's walls augment the natural suns-light, giving our Halls an unparalleled ambience. To your left paw, observe our Dragon hatcheries–heavily guarded, of course. That Amber Dragoness is training her week-old hatchlings in the basics of flight. Over there, in the open lava pits, we Dragons bathe and treat our wounds. Above the lake are the honeycomb caves we've built over thousands of years to house the greatest concentration of our kind in the Island-

World."

"What's that?" Lia pointed up to the rim.

"That's a group of Dragon scientists making observations of the cosmos through a celestial star-gazer, a scientific instrument constructed from a unique combination of physical parts and magic."

A telescope? Lia had never imagined such a telescope, twice the length of an adult Dragon and easily fifteen feet in diameter, if her eyes did not deceive her. What detail they must be able to see, for draconic vision was vastly superior … but they already approached the northern lake shore, where Hualiama saw a Dragonship landing platform built into the slope above the lake. And Humans? She stared eagerly at these fabled denizens of the draconic realm, but found them no different in appearance to ordinary Fra'aniorians. Tall, bearded, blue of eye, these men could have been Islanders from anywhere in the Cluster.

She concentrated on making a smooth landing, despite the distraction of seeing Dragons everywhere, stretching and sunbathing, chuckling and smoking at the jaw, and growling with low sounds of indulgence as they lazed in pools of lava near at hand, or taking off from the dark cave-mouths dotting the cliffs above the lake with massive, air-cleaving strokes of their wings.

Had she once lived in this volcano, surrounded by the splendour of Dragon society?

Upon landing, an egg-heavy Grey Dragoness waddled over with a pompous air to question the Oranges about the Human's arrival. The mention of Hualiama's name set the Dragoness' smoky, burnt-amber eyes ablaze. *Dragonfriend? You clutch of empty-headed, chattering parakeets. This is the Dragon-slayer of Fra'anior, friend of the Tourmaline traitor!*

Her? Emburion, Zaxxion and Hazzalion gasped in concert.

But there's nothing to her, Zaxxion complained, ruffling his wings to express his annoyance. *She's a mite, not even a full-grown Human!*

Foolish hatchling! the Grey Dragoness thundered, snapping at Zaxxion's shoulder. *With my own fire-eyes, I saw her cut out*

Jinthalior the Green's fire-soul with those magical blades upon her back.

All three of the Orange Dragons took a reflexive step or wingbeat back from her. So, Dragons knew fear? At least one of Master Ga'athar's strategies was accurate. She must turn this to her advantage, insofar as a Human could dream of manipulating Dragons–perhaps the most dangerous pursuit beneath the twin suns.

The Dragon Elders will speak with this creature? Flames licking out of his nostrils articulated Hazzalion's exasperation.

Aye, said the Grey Dragoness. *She stands upon Dragon soil, now.*

And with that, Hualiama's momentary bravado evaporated like a bucket of water tossed into one of their overheated lava pools. Meek was not how she needed to feel now. Mentally, Lia kicked any hint of timidity off the edge of the Island. She needed the fury of a Fra'aniorian thunderstorm. She willed Amaryllion's fire to rage in her heart.

Raising her chin, Hualiama cast an imperious glare over the Dragons. "Where may I find the Dragon Elders, noble ones? I await instruction."

Sapphurion shall instruct this quisling at the point of his fangs, snarled Zaxxion, tilting his muzzle so that his flame licked above Lia's head. *May we return to our duties, honoured Dragoness?*

Go. The Grey sucked back her Dragon fire as she turned to the Human girl. "Follow me, Princess."

Despite her egg-laden wobble, the Dragoness set a pace that forced Hualiama to trot in order to keep up. Lia scowled at her massive hindquarters. Subtle, these Dragons! She jogged up a trail leading to a wide cave entrance, guarded by four rugged Reds. Generally regarded as the largest of the Dragons, these Reds stood over twenty feet at the shoulder, and were evidently masters of the brawny 'look-at-my-muscles' posture Grandion had excelled at.

Pushing these flitting thoughts aside, Lia focussed on her mission. Ahead, she saw a Dragon-sized door leading to what she assumed was the Dragon Elders' meeting-cave. To stand before metal doors over two hundred feet tall, she estimated, and twice as wide as that, was an experience she had never imagined. But the thundering and snarling which erupted within as she approached, was a further shock. At first Lia thought there was an all-claws-in Dragon battle inside. But then she heard Sapphurion's roar thundering above the others.

SILENCE! We shall hear the spy's report!

Another voice cut in, *She has spent too long among those vermin, Sapphurion! She thinks as one of them.*

Sapphurion growled, *Describe again the disposition and numbers of their off-Cluster allies, Kayturia. What more did you receive from the King's brother?*

Almost, Hualiama's jaw unhinged itself. Her uncle Zalcion was passing secrets to the Dragons? And what could she make of the accusation that a Dragoness had begun to think like a Human–no, of course, they were using their Human slaves to spy on their fellow-Humans.

Without further ado, the Grey made a gesture with her paw and the doors drew apart several feet. Lia's nape prickled at the presence of magic. Now the Dragons had telekinesis? Her reading of the lore-scrolls had suggested the ability was mythical at best. The Grey Dragoness strode forth, and directed a thought into the chamber: *O mighty Sapphurion, the Princess of Fra'anior waits without.*

An ugly snarl shook the doors mightily, as though a single, monstrous animal had voiced its fury. It throbbed right through Lia's body, causing her heart to turn somersaults in her throat. Again, Sapphurion's mental voice rang clarion-clear out of the hubbub. *Away, spy. Wait a minute before we summon the Human. Brethren, this is Hualiama, the royal ward, called the Dragonfriend. By her hand was Ra'aba brought low.*

Impossible! sneered another Dragon. Did she recognise Andarraz's voice, the Green who alone among all Dragons, matched Sapphurion for stature? *What trickery is Chalcion bent upon, this time? These Humans grow crafty.*

No Human has yet been born who can outwit a Dragon. Sapphurion replied evenly. *Send her in.*

The Grey Dragoness pressed the doors open with her power. "Up to the platform with you, Human girl, and don't tarry. Sapphurion does not suffer fools lightly."

Hualiama approached the Dragon Elders with a definite stride that belied the storm raging in her belly. The twelve-foot-tall, gold-threaded quartz platform, crowned by a solitary chair, did nothing to conceal the draconic congregation gathered beyond it. Nine pairs of orbs suffused with fire as they regarded the Human girl. Seven blazed with malevolent, dark-orange swirls, one pair was a uniquely radiant blue-white, and the last considered her with a gentle effulgence, an altogether softer fire that Hualiama recognised instantly as belonging to the Red Dragoness Qualiana.

Now, she must exhibit the mettle of a Tourmaline Dragon who had fought two powerful adult males almost to a standstill. Squaring her shoulders, Lia marched up to her seat. As her eyes crested the top of the platform, it was to lock gazes with Sapphurion not five feet distant, and what she saw smouldering in his fire-soul caused her legs to seize up. Lia stumbled over the last step, barking her shins painfully and crashing to her knees before the Dragon Elders.

Were this a training fight, first score to the Dragons.

"The most sulphurous greetings of the Great Dragon to you, daughter of the Human King," Sapphurion rumbled. "To what do we owe the pleasure of this unexpected visit?"

Her father ruled one Island-Kingdom, albeit an important one. These Dragons ruled all of the Dragonkind north of the Rift, and Sapphurion was foremost among their number. Hope was an illusion. The comparison crushed her spirit.

Burning with embarrassment before these Kings and Queens of Dragons, Hualiama rapidly found her feet and marshalled her manners. Flowing into an elegant Fra'aniorian obeisance, she said, "May thy sulphurous fires burn forever amongst the eternal fires of the Dragonkind, o noble Sapphurion."

"Be seated."

She began to sit before remembering Ga'athar's idea. Lia slipped her Immadian forked daggers from her belt and, laying them on the platform, said, "I come in peace."

Next, she reached up for the sword-hilts protruding above her shoulders and drew the Nuyallith blades with a bright *zing* of metal. Looking beyond the blades as she drew them slowly downward, Hualiama observed the effect on the Dragons. They seemed mesmerised, all nine sets of fire-eyes fixated on her movements as she bent her knees to place the enchanted blades beside the seat. Lia said, "I bind myself to peace."

With that, she sat. Grim satisfaction curved her lips. Second score to the Human.

Sapphurion cleared his throat by way of expectorating a fireball to her right. "State your business, Princess."

Before she spoke, Lia allowed her gaze to rest briefly on each of the Dragons, acknowledging them each in turn with a slight bow of her head. She identified the Green Andarraz, the Reds Zulior and Qualiana, who were egg-siblings, and Sapphurion. The other five Dragons she knew only from studying scrolls her father kept about the Dragonkind of Gi'ishior. Haaja the Yellow Dragoness she recognised at once, and the Brown male Tarbazzan, but the other Dragons' names escaped her recall.

To war.

Hualiama said, Dragon-direct, "O mighty Sapphurion, I was present the day Yulgaz the Brown and Razzior the Orange attacked a male juvenile offshore of Ha'athior and buried him alive within the Island massif. Three months later, I rescued this Dragon from his cave by blowing the side off the mountain. We made oaths to each other–"

"Madness!" gasped Zulior.

"The paw of the Great Dragon," Lia countered aggressively. "Obligated to me for his life, the young Dragon vowed to help me locate and rescue my family–the Human royals of Fra'anior–who had been abducted and exiled by the traitor Ra'aba, with the aid of the Orange Razzior's paw. I come before you today to declare this: If my foolishness or ignorance brought dishonour upon that Dragon, to whom the Human King and his family owe a debt of gratitude which can never be repaid, I must right that wrong, or I too am foresworn."

That was the most direct and delicate phrasing she and Ga'athar had been able to decide upon. Certainly, it skimmed over perilous secrets, which lurked amidst her words like hidden abysses. Much now depended upon how Sapphurion chose to respond.

He said, "The young Dragon was buried within Ha'athior Island?"

"I affirm that truth," said Lia, with an inward gritting of her teeth. "It was Ra'aba who first cast me upon Ha'athior. A girl who is stabbed so deeply in the stomach that the blades exit beside her spine, before being tossed off a Dragonship, has little choice as to where she lands. I lived upon Ha'athior for a number of weeks before I was able to escape."

The Dragon Elders shuffled their paws ominously, but made no other comment. She concluded they must already know her history. The huge Blue Dragon had raised this topic to press home his magnanimity at her expense. Mercy.

Sapphurion scoffed, "And you brought rich gifts to purchase the chance to redeem this mutual dishonour?"

"I did." She touched her travel pack, "A rare scroll–"

Sapphurion's snort billowed hot, curiously peppery air over her head. "I smelled its magic outside the hall. Don't bother. I already possess a copy in my personal library."

Lia bit her lip. "What would you wish, o mighty Dragon?"

His shrug was a mountainous flexion of blue Dragon hide, his stance uncompromising. "What do you offer which is not already possession of the draconic masters of our Island-World? Why not a token which speaks of the spirit of a Human who presumes to call herself 'Dragonfriend'? Mighty paws for a tiny hatchling, say I."

Most of the Elders growled their approval of Sapphurion's withering sarcasm.

Sensing Qualiana's regard, Hualiama's eyes flicked to the Dragoness. A tiny circle of her fore-talon, a twitch of her wings just so–what did that mean? Her mind raced. What bauble or token could possibly impress the mightiest of Dragons? Nay, the mightiest had flown on to the fires of his kind just the day before, but he had left her a gift. Little Lia would have to rip open her chest and bare her soul, no less. She would parade her outrage and grief in a truly draconic manner.

The Human girl raised her chin. "O Sapphurion, I offer the gift of my dance."

"Dance?" Low, spiteful, his chuckle came furnished with talons and a snarl of real thunder that made Hualiama clutch her chair, white-knuckled. "You offer a *dance?*"

"You may judge the gift when it is given."

Lia distinctly heard his belly-fires bridle at the answering snap in her tone. Yet this was the Dragon way. Answer fire for fire, or be doomed.

Sapphurion crooked his paw. "Summon a musician to attend us." Clearly, in his mien, she read the implication that the Human girl wore his patience thin. But could a father-Dragon's heart deny the hope she offered his shell-son? Denied the chance to help Grandion himself, would Sapphurion reach out to her? Risky.

With each footstep feeling more doom-laden than the last, Lia descended the quartz steps behind the platform and approached the Dragon Elders–approached their paws and knees, truth be told, for as a group they towered above her, a combined tonnage of scale armour, fangs and irritable Dragon fires she dared not guess at. Qualiana stood at Sapphurion's right flank, wing to wing with Zulior, and Andarraz and Haaja to his left. Haaja was a noted Dragon scholar from the far south. The other four Dragons acted as their own group, she noticed–hoary old Tarbazzan, a younger-looking, sleek Green male, and two Reds. They shifted to create a semicircle about her that Lia's gut suggested was uncomfortably akin to Dragons arranging themselves around a tasty dish.

Veiling her anxiety with outward unconcern, Lia limbered up with a few light stretches.

Shortly, a Human manservant appeared, wheeling a full-size Fra'aniorian harp in dark jalkwood with inlays and string-pegs of pure gold. While he arranged himself on a tall stool a second servant brought for him, Hualiama's hands rose–trembling slightly–to loosen her headscarf and liberate her hair from captivity. If ever she needed the symbolic freedom she thus claimed, now was the hour.

The musician nodded gravely to her.

"Islands' greetings," said Lia, with courtly formality. "If I may, master musician, I would request the *Dragonet's Dance* from the *Flame Cycle*."

"And your desired tempo, lady?"

She marked the tempo briefly with her forefinger. "Whenever you're ready."

He bowed over the harp, hands poised with the supple grace of a lesser blue heron feeding beside a still lake, and with a slight but audible exhalation, he began the opening passage leading into the *Dragonet's Dance.* Hualiama almost lost her nerve. She knew his style! She knew this man's music, for every master musician had their signature style, his being a particularly adept usage of his extraordinarily long fingers to produce sixteenth jumps–double-octaves–on the strings of his instrument. Consumed by shock, the royal ward jerked awkwardly into her opening steps. Graceless, awkward, her feet seemed weighed down with lead boots.

This would not do. She could not fail her mission at the first hurdle.

Reaching deep into the corridors of her memory, Lia summoned the snarky laughter of the dragonet she had loved. How Flicker had loved to roost on her shoulder, curving his hot belly around her neck while pretending to pick lice from her hair with his talons. When she danced for him, fire had saturated his eyes and his talons curled in delight. At the very last, the Ancient Dragon had bid her dance as a parting gift, and Lia had spun across his mighty paw even as she danced among the paws and knees of the Lesser Dragons now, and the fire–oh, the glorious white fire–had filled her up to her throat, and burned in her being as though she would never be cold again, and the dragonet's fire-soul had taken wing to dance with her. Who else in history had danced for an Ancient Dragon?

Heat exploded in her chest. It rippled along her limbs, crackling from her toes as she soared into a graceful aerial flare, imitating a dragonet's outspread wings. Lia shimmered with white-golden fire, and the world shimmered before her half-shuttered eyes. Faster. Hotter. Lighter on her feet, flitting like flames embracing a dry twig, weaving Flicker's dragonet-song into her dance. Swooping low. Sprinting five steps before springing upward, a triple somersault flowing without need for thought, now a series of the tight pirouettes Flicker had so loved to show off, because even a bat could hold no bragging rights over a dragonet when it came to aerial dance skills.

Thus, Lia danced for the Dragons.

Visions overcame her. She was lighter than air, burning brighter, flying so high her slippers seemed to prance upon invisible cushions, now the finale, the volatile inner potential no longer able to be withheld. The Dragons would know her spirit? Then see this!

She landed, exultant, and found herself wreathed in flame.

Hualiama gasped, "What?"

She threw herself to the ground and rolled over and over, trying to snuff out the fire.

Chapter Seven

The Halls of the Dragons

PANTING INELEGANTLY, CHOKED with fear, Lia lodged beneath the arch of a draconic paw.

"Hush, little one," said a well-remembered voice. Magic soothed her as a babe had once been soothed by a Dragoness. The paw lifted.

Alive. She was alive, and hale. Pushing up to her knees, Hualiama rubbed her arms and patted her hair in disbelief. Great Islands! What had become of the fire? Why had she not burned up? That was rather more of her spirit than she suspected Sapphurion had bargained for, but as she looked up at the Blue Dragon, past Qualiana's talons which were still curved protectively about her, she perceived a fearful glint in his eye.

Rising, she stepped out from beneath Qualiana's brooding presence.

"How is it that six years ago, a diminutive girl was able to defeat the preeminent swordsman of Fra'anior Cluster?" the Blue Dragon growled.

She had to find her voice. Lia grated, "As you see, Sapphurion, I have power. I was taught the forms of Nuyallith by a master, and have made them my own."

"As you battled for the Human kingdom, you accused

Ra'aba of being your father."

"He is my father."

"Can you prove it?"

"He tried to murder me, and when he failed, he sent Razzior in his stead to burn me. Isn't that proof enough?" Fire roared twenty feet from Sapphurion's nostrils. Apparently not. Lia began, "Your records will show, mighty Sapphurion, that two decades ago, an envoy came from the East to Gi'ishior–"

The Blue Dragon thundered, "I don't want fireside tales, I want proof!"

Aye, well said, growled Andarraz. *Child of the Dragon, she called herself. I remember it well.*

As the Dragon's thunder subsided, Lia shouted, "That man killed my friend with *ruzal*; you promised me Dragon justice! What does it matter, unless Ra'aba is dead? He's alive, isn't he?"

"Insolent mite!" Sapphurion roared, pounding toward her. His massive paws shook the ground beneath her feet as though he beat an impossibly enormous drum. "How dare you accuse–"

"Her accusation rings true," Qualiana snarled, right over the top of Lia's head.

"Don't interrupt!"

"Then speak, though it burns your pride!"

As Qualiana and Sapphurion's fires mingled twenty feet above her head, Hualiama wanted to jump up and down, yelling, 'I'm down here. Speak to me.' In a moment she'd be squashed between two bickering Dragons and that would spell a messy end for the Dragonfriend. Yet suddenly, Sapphurion's muzzle descended to waft the scorching breath of his nostrils across her face.

He hissed, "Ra'aba escaped."

Qualiana sighed–and it was only that sigh which stopped Lia from screaming her fury to the five moons. Her father was alive! Fomenting discord, no doubt, contaminating Dragons with his strange mental powers ... but she must remember why she had come. Sapphurion's Island-roots ran deep. He would have his reasons for mistreating her like this. Could she forgive him? And navigate a way out of this terrace lake of strife she paddled in?

"My proof is that the Maroon Dragoness swears to my parentage," she said, softly. "I can show you my memories as I did before, mighty Sapphurion."

"Trust the word of Ianthine?" Tarbazzan the Brown interrupted. "What manner of fools do you take us for, girl?"

"Aye," growled Andarraz. "A true word, mighty Tarbazzan. What if Ra'aba has taught her the power of *ruzal?* Is this not his scheme? What Human child would dare approach the Dragon Elders with such a ridiculous tale, had she not been coached? Child of the Dragon? Prophecies of a third great race in the Island-World? Slug spit and windroc droppings!"

He capped his speech with a gout of flame that he aimed upward, above the other Dragons.

Before Sapphurion could speak, Haaja added, "Memories are easily implanted. Ianthine has twisted your mind, child. Of course you believe her lies. That's her power."

In a small voice, Hualiama said, "My mother is Azziala of–"

"The Dragon-Haters? I remember her," said the Brown Dragon. "She left suddenly. Strange business."

Balling her fists, Hualiama shouted, "Because Ra'aba assaulted her right here in your precious Halls of the Dragons, and you did nothing to protect her! Nothing!"

"Filthy accusations, you worm!" roared one of the Reds, pouncing.

Before she knew it, Qualiana's paw snaffled her up and the Red Dragoness clashed with her fellow-Red, shoulder to shoulder, with an impact that rattled Hualiama's teeth. The Dragons cuffed each other before Sapphurion charged between them, knocking the Reds apart with a surge of his magic.

There was a hot silence of panting, sulphur-tanged breaths and clenched claws.

From the safe haven of Qualiana's paw, Lia called, "I remember returning in Ianthine's paw and you, Qualiana–you rescued me from Ianthine and gave me to the Human King for adoption. These are not lies! Why would Ianthine carry a

Human child halfway across the Island-World were there nothing to gain by it?"

"Why indeed?" said Zulior, looking to Sapphurion for his lead.

It's impossible! How could that shape-twister be her father? Andarraz demanded. *Is there more to this* ruzal *than we suspect? The Maroon Dragoness roams free. No Dragon is safe …*

Silence! Sapphurion commanded. *Even these walls have ears.*

Mercy! Pray that the Dragons thought her speeding heart was merely due to anger or fear, and not the terrifying knowledge that Ianthine had escaped her draconic imprisonment. No wonder Amaryllion had feared for her safety.

The Blue Dragon loomed over her. "How can we trust one touched by *ruzal*?"

"I gave my gift in good faith …" Lia's voice trailed off under the force of his glare. Her temper finally boiled over. "Why do I sense I'm the only one trying to help Grandion here?"

"Do not speak that traitor's name–"

She screamed, "What kind of father are you? What father abandons his child, and tries to murder them?"

"You rode on his back!" Sapphurion's bellow shook the cavern.

"Did it kill him? No!" she howled right back, feeling the veins in her neck and forehead bulging strangely. So much fire, so much anger, she could more easily have corked an erupting volcano than keep silent now. "Infect him? No! Diminish one drop of a leagues-wide terrace lake of Dragonish pride and obduracy which he has clearly inherited from his shell-father … no! And do you know what? He departed a better Dragon for the experience, Sapphurion; worthy in wisdom and deed, a nobler beast altogether. I'm honoured–aye, honoured and grateful, to have played some small part in his life! So when Grandion returned to his family, intent on making something good of his life, what in a Cloudlands hell did you do?"

"I obeyed our law!"

At last, Sapphurion's cry betrayed real pain. She had pushed him too far. Qualiana made a half-step to intervene, but since Lia and the Dragon Elder had been exchanging verbal fireballs from a distance of just a few feet, his paw was faster by far. Not for the first time in her life, the Human girl found herself the captive of an enraged Dragon.

Squeezed in a grip of iron, Lia gasped, "I want to go after him, Sapphurion. Grant me that pittance, I beg you. Tell me where to find him."

Deliberately, the Blue Dragon's fangs ground down on what Hualiama recognised as the terrible pressure of a vast fireball readied in his fire-stomach. Sapphurion snarled, "We cannot trust a Dragon-slayer."

Lia nodded slowly, feeling sick. "For what it's worth, I regret killing Jinthalior."

Andarraz cried, "Regret? A craven apology! Dispose of the Enchantress now, Sapphurion!"

Flying ralti sheep, what a stupid mistake! Hualiama swallowed hard as Sapphurion's muzzle pressed closer, flame clearly visible down the tunnel of each nostril. "Aye, I regret taking a Dragon's life," she said, forcing scorn and resolve into her voice. "As for that Green, mine was the hand of the Great Dragon's justice that terminated his cowardly, miserable existence. He died exactly as he deserved–in dishonour."

Dragon-thunder reverberated in the cavern. The Elders made a concerted rush for her. Sapphurion calmly sprang aloft, leaving his kindred to slam together beneath him in a ferocious melee of talon, fang and fire. Then he descended, voicing a full-throated challenge backed by a touch of Storm power. Thunder rolled in the distance. The Dragon Elders scattered, giving his wings and tail a respectful berth.

Setting Lia down between the Dragons once more, he growled, "For the third time, I declare to you, Human girl, that we Dragons will never trust one infected by Ianthine's madness. Tell me who sent you hence, or give me some other sign, and I will tell you what you wish to know of Grandion. This is the word of a Dragon."

What could sway him? Every way lay impossibility. Appeal to the Dragons who had raised her, and thereby destroy

Sapphurion's credibility as leader of these Dragons? Speak to them in Dragonish? That would only earn her a faster flight into the Cloudlands. Should she reveal her presence at Amaryllion's final fire-song, against the Ancient Dragon's wishes? No. She had shown the Dragon Elders the dragonet's fire-gift, but that seemed insufficient.

She realised she had one more secret. A name.

Quietly, Lia said to the Blue Dragon, "To you alone will I reveal the name of the one who sent me, Sapphurion. Please, lend me your ear-canals."

His superior Dragon-grin reasserted itself at once. Hualiama recognised the pride, the assumption that he had triumphed in their battle of wits and upheld his dominance at the top of the Dragon hierarchy. Sapphurion smirked, "There are no secrets between Dragons."

"Please …"

How could he not understand the appeal in her voice? Simply, because he chose not to. The Blue Dragon growled, "To all of us, or none, Hualiama Dragonfriend. Prove the worth of your oath."

May she own the courage of a dragonet.

Moving as though gripped by a dream–or a nightmare–Lia slipped out of Sapphurion's uncurled talons, and took several steps backward. On reflection, several steps more seemed appropriate. Andarraz's expression suggested he thought she was about to turn tail and bolt. Lia had no such intention. No more begging for her. No more bargaining with a Dragon for his son's future, whatever ruin thereof might remain to be succoured.

Pain marshalled its forces in her stomach. Hualiama imagined at first she had a case of the worst heartburn imaginable, but it escalated rapidly beyond that, as though the mere thought that she might speak a Dragon's secret name had unleashed a terrible, incendiary power. So afraid! Lia knew a fear that froze the very living pith in her, for there was no telling how the Dragons might respond to her forthcoming declaration. She stumbled backward, trapped in a maelstrom of terror and fire.

The Dragon Elders stalked her sinuously, Zulior and Andarraz flanking Sapphurion, Haaja and two mountainous Reds flanking them. Even Qualiana looked murderous, her tail flicking from side to side.

Lia's throat and chest swelled as though wishing to morph into the capacity of a far larger beast. A rushing of mighty flames filled her ears. She must swallow it down! Her eyes bulged. She had to plug her mouth before the pain struck … yet air sucked down into her lungs as though drawn by the vortex of magic indwelling her now.

The Dragons froze.

BEZALDIOR!

* * * *

Lia felt as though her lungs had emptied inside out. A thunderclap of sound ripped out of her throat, evocative of Amaryllion's triumphal bellow in the Dragon graveyard. It smashed into the massed Dragon Elders, lifting them off the ground, flipping them over with the ease of a cook flipping slices of sweet-tuber in a frying pan. Sapphurion wheezed as he thumped down flat on his back, all four paws scrabbling at the air. The other Dragons fared no better. Gasps and groans filled the momentary stillness her shout had demanded. Even the sounds of the Dragon community outside of the cavern hushed in response.

Perhaps one should never speak a word of such power, aloud.

Suddenly, hot liquid flooded Hualiama's mouth. She wiped it automatically, drew back a hand smeared in crimson.

Her knees buckled.

With a low cry, Qualiana scrambled to her paws, fixated on Hualiama. *Little one* … her mate Sapphurion moved fast, but not as fast as the distressed Dragoness. Magic enfolded her, a touch more tender than hand or paw ever knew. *We've hurt you, little mouse.*

Stabilise her, Qualiana, Sapphurion ordered. *We need to finish this now, and take the girl for treatment.*

What does this mean, Sapphurion? Andarraz sounded dazed and confused.

The Blue Dragon said, *It means she knew the Ancient Dragon. He sent her to us. And as we saw, a mystery: the fire we remarked upon during her dance–that was a touch of Dragon fire.*

Haaja spat, *Only the most blasphemous legends suggest that the Ancient Dragons left a touch of their fire inside of every Human!*

"Hualiama of Fra'anior," Sapphurion said, returning to Island Standard, "Grandion served with honour in the campaign to quell the Green Dragon rebellion on Merx and Lyrx. Upon his return to Gi'ishior, he admitted his trespass with a Human whom he called his Dragon Rider. In this very Hall, he bargained with the Elders for his life."

Lia nodded, clutching her throat. She dared not speak.

"We assigned him an honour-quest. Should he complete the task, the knowledge of his transgression shall be struck from Dragonish memory. Grandion flew to the Eastern Isles to track down the original Scroll of Binding–a scroll of Dragon lore from which, we believe, Ianthine mastered *ruzal*, and the Dragon-Haters of the Lost Islands learned a mysterious power over Dragons. We know little of these Dragon-Haters, for in living memory, no Dragon has been able to penetrate their defences."

So Sapphurion had assigned his shell-son an impossible quest? Aghast, a dull rattle sounded from her chest.

Qualiana hushed her at once. "Peace, little one."

Heavily, Sapphurion added, "Therefore I, Sapphurion the Dragon Elder, must ask you this, Hualiama Dragonfriend. Will you atone for the Tourmaline Dragon's obligation, assuming the onus of this quest for the lost Scroll of Binding? Will you scour the Island-World for him, not returning to hearth or home until you succeed or perish in this endeavour? Will you take his oath upon yourself?"

Hualiama nodded at once.

"We must hear you." To his mate, Sapphurion said, *Qualiana, dull her pain.*

Speaking may further damage her throat, she replied. *There, it is done.*

Lia rasped, "I so swear."

* * * *

Scooping Hualiama up, Qualiana left the meeting immediately and flew a little ways up the cliff directly above the tunnel-entrance Lia had navigated on her way in to the Halls of the Dragons. She felt enervated. Adrenaline, shock and magic, all had taken their toll. She saw Sapphurion following just as they alighted at a tunnel entrance.

It felt strangely comforting to be cradled in a Dragon's paw after six years.

The tunnel was smooth and polished to a high sheen, giving Hualiama glimpses of a wan-looking Human dangling in the Red Dragoness' grasp. Qualiana barely needed to furl her wings to pass through, and after just a few hundred feet, she turned into a narrower doorway. A touch of her foremost talon-pad to a large button caused the tall, intricately patterned metal doors to slide apart, revealing a short, Dragon-sized hallway leading into warmly lamp-lit inner chambers.

"Our roost," said Qualiana, seemingly oblivious to the shock of recognition which stupefied the girl she held. Memories! Echoes of joy! "The main living area looks onto the caldera through that one-way crysglass. Those are Dragon couches. Sapphurion's perch lies to your left–that's fire-fused agate crystal, which he shaped to fit his body while it was still malleable. My mate is a peerless gemstone worker."

"Beautiful," Lia managed to gasp.

"Bathe your face in this laver. The water is cool and refreshing. Then, lie down."

Lia did as she was bid, charily glancing at the Dragoness, who hovered like a broody mother fussing over her hatchling. She reached out to touch Lia's shoulder with one thick, red digit, causing healing magic to pour over and into her like a river of thick, golden honey. Just then, a clicking of claws without heralded Sapphurion's arrival. With two huge Dragons in the room, their quarters suddenly felt decidedly cosy. And warm. Dragons generated so much heat!

With a word, Sapphurion closed the outer doors. Hualiama sensed the unmistakable yet feather-light touch of his magic. Gears whirred and locks clicked shut.

She was confined with a pair of Dragons.

"Sealed," said Sapphurion, deepening her anxiety. And he approached with an altogether gentler, apricot tinge in his eye.

Hualiama shivered where she lay on a cushion ten feet wide and thirty long–and that was only half of a couch, it seemed. The huge Blue slipped lithely onto his beautiful perch, where the variegated blues of agate crystals had been formed into swirling loops and unfolding petals, mimicking with flawless accuracy, she realised with an inward sigh of appreciation, the lilies she had noticed adorning the terrace lake on the way in. The Dragon Elder arranged himself on this perch with a rustling of wings and a sigh that betrayed weariness, and … a nervousness of his own?

The silence grew strained.

Coughing discreetly, Qualiana swamped a couch to Lia's left, her paw crooked behind the Human girl as though the Dragoness meant to embrace her, but shied away from completing the gesture. Two Dragon muzzles turned to Lia, tilted to keep the burning nostrils pointed a little away from her, while their mesmeric eyes stripped away her defences with shocking ease.

Lia had occasionally imagined meeting a potential boyfriend or suitor's parents. Obviously, not in this context! A hysterical wailing burbled around the fringes of her consciousness. Surely, Sapphurion and Qualiana must guess how she felt about their shell-son. What else would drive her to such extremes? They knew she had shamed him, that she must be at least partially responsible for his fateful decision to allow a Human to set foot upon a Dragon's back. They must hate her. Or, perhaps it was merely a violent draconic antipathy?

'Islands' greetings,' she imagined the conversation proceeding. 'Please don't eat me if I say this … I need you to know I'm inappropriately fond of your son, who just happens to be of a completely different species we Humans are openly and covertly at war with …'

She must speak.

Hualiama whispered, "Mighty Sapphurion, I wonder if you remember a particular conversation that took place in this room?" Switching to Dragonish, she quoted from memory, *Here, little mouse. You cannot stay in our clutch forever. We must give you to the Human King.*

The Blue Dragon became still, so utterly motionless that Lia feared she had just signed her death-warrant with the flourish of a verbal quill. Qualiana emitted a soft, ululating cry that seemed to oscillate between desolation and hope. She rubbed her muzzle in a gesture Lia had seen Flicker use when moved by profound emotion. Should she have forewarned the Dragons? Too late now.

You speak Dragonish? Qualiana gasped. *Perfect Dragonish? You remember …*

Fragile as a dew-dappled petal, the moment lingered.

Happiness, Lia said simply. Tears welled up. *For me, this place is a joyous melody. You made it so, Qualiana–and you, Sapphurion. I remember how when I fell, you caught me in your paws.*

You're that girl? It's really true? The Dragoness' left paw clenched, the length of it–twice Hualiama's height–now bridging the small distance between them, a poignant desperation writ in the way her paw cupped Lia's body, covering her lightly, as though Qualiana trusted not in her eyes, but in the touch of skin to skin.

It's true, o Qualiana.

You spoke with care to protect us in the Dragon Council, said Sapphurion. Suddenly he was up on his paws, looming close, his monstrous forepaw extending to match his mate's gesture, so that Lia's prone position came to resemble a butterfly trapped between cupped hands. *Qualiana, my life's veriest breath, even a proud Dragon must learn to bend his hearts. Don't lose a wing over what I shall say.* Bending over the Human girl, he breathed, *Hualiama, I regret doubting you, and I'm sorry for how I mistreated both you and my shell-son. Deeply … remorseful.*

Oh thou, my soul's inspiration! Qualiana nuzzled her mate fondly. *I thought thee incapable of such words.*

As had Lia, recalling how Grandion had bristled at an

apology. Dragons would catch the plague rather than use the word 'sorry', wouldn't they?

Sapphurion added, *I've failed as a father. I sacrificed flesh and blood for political advantage. Rightly you asked what kind of father abandons his only shell-son!* Huge as he was, the Blue Dragon whimpered as though wounded. *And now I've hurt thee, my shell-daughter, and bound thee to Grandion's fate.*

Smiling as though the suns beamed unadulterated upon her world, Lia assured him, *I would choose no other fate … but you know that already, don't you, Sapphurion? Please don't hate me for my deeds.*

His eye-fires gushed in their course around his orbs, making her feel dizzy, but the Human girl found she did not dread what she beheld there. Mind-to-mind, he replied, *Qualiana will recount for you how I raged and thundered, how I blasted boulders into slag and sharpened my talons upon the edges of cliffs, especially since Grandion spoke so tenderly of you. Truly, I do not understand this mystery. I yearned to kill him, yet my thoughts flew to a different Island. I saw qualities in my shell-son I could never have imagined—by my wings, he blazed with the very nobility you spoke of. And I wondered how this could be? How could such a sin lead to gloriously transformed soul-fires?*

We fear this … relationship … can only end in sorrow, Qualiana confessed.

Aye. Extending his right wing, Sapphurion drew it over both Lia and his mate, cocooning them in a secret world within the world of their Dragon roost. He whispered, *Yet know this, shell-daughter. We would've adopted you in a hearts-beat, were it possible. And we promise we shall not be the Dragons to stand between you and Grandion, for we believe you must pursue your fate, be it to the ends of our Island-World, or beyond.*

His words enveloped her in warmth, a treasury of emotion revealed by the rich, nuanced Dragonish he spoke from his third heart.

Fixing her with a burning eye, the Blue Dragon declared, *This I vow upon my honour as a Dragon: never again shall I abandon my child. When you find Grandion, Hualiama, tell him I would rather tear out my Dragon-soul than betray him again. If it costs me my position as a leader of Dragons, I care not. Should I lose my life, I care not, for I would rather die with my honour intact.*

Qualiana said, *We raised you as our own hatchling for three years. We vow to stand beside you, little one. Do you understand?*

I do, Lia breathed, a song of wonder rising in her heart. *And I understand I must teach you something, my shell-parents–if I may call you that?*

You may, they chorused, and rubbed their muzzles together as their laughter spoke of the relief of long-repressed passions. *What would our shell-daughter teach us?*

To delight in her fires? asked Qualiana. *To join in the beauty of her dance?*

Only what Amaryllion Fireborn taught me–aye, mighty Sapphurion, Lia gulped. *I was the trespasser you detected at the Natal Cave. There is something the denizens of this Island-World have made to be profane, which is not. The laws of Humankind and Dragonkind corrupt it into unrecognisable forms. They forbid what is good and wholesome and true.*

The memory of her first touch of Grandion's muzzle stole her away for a moment. When she returned to herself, the Dragons regarded her with identically puzzled expressions.

Impulsively, Lia scrambled to her feet. *Come,* she beckoned them. The rising drumbeat of their hearts generated an audible rush through the great arteries of their necks. *I shan't bite you.*

Lia meant to touch the Dragons each upon the muzzle, just above their nostrils, but her knees buckled mid-motion. She fell against them instead, arms splayed. Mercy! Could she never fail to spoil a significant moment with her clumsiness? Her tiny arms could not hope to encircle their muzzles. Glancing from one flustered Dragon to the other as Sapphurion harrumphed and Qualiana stiffened up until she resembled a gigantic, scaly ruby, Lia found herself ambushed by a fit of giggles, which swelled into Cloudlands-bound river-torrents of joy spilling from her soul. What a delight, that she could stagger tonnes of Dragon with a mere touch!

This is called a hug. She pulled them closer with her tiny strength. *Like this.*

She had never heard Dragons purr in quite the way Qualiana and Sapphurion did now, but their combined vibration thawed places in the core of her being which Lia thought had been excised, and lost forever.

We Humans do this with people, and Dragons, we love.

Chapter Eight

Flyaway

HAVING TARRIED WITH the Dragons until the evening following her arrival at Gi'ishior, Lia hurried home. Her heart rued the rush, but with a frisky following breeze and every sail including her custom-made spinnaker deployed to its maximum, her solo Dragonship speared through the ruddy, late-afternoon volcanic sunshine like a crossbow bolt trailing golden streamers of dust. She raced over tiny Giaza Island, where she had seen Dragons sporting with Humans, tossing them to each other or into the Cloudlands, before steering a more southerly bearing to cross the north-south length of Fra'anior Island to the main city located on its southernmost peninsula. Rugged, jungle-choked ravines broken up by jag-toothed black peaks constituted the untamed interior of Fra'anior, while great flocks of luminous green lovebirds, brilliant parakeets and white finches burst out of the foliage as the Dragonship whooshed by just thirty feet overhead.

A flight of five dragonets came to play around the sails, chittering non-stop to each other or making shrill exclamations such as, *'Look at me!' 'Watch this!' 'A faster wing-flip, silly!'*

Hualiama sang them a lively ballad, although her heart was not in it. The dragonets seemed aware of her distraction and after playing briefly, parroted their own ditty in return before darting back to their warren.

As the twin suns melted into the gleaming copper Cloudlands of the western horizon, Lia approached her home town, the city of Fra'anior. A beautiful job of reconstruction belied the devastation of the Green Dragon invasion six years before. The buildings and homes were built from malachite blocks, onyx stone and the finest garnet, resplendent in the suns-set, while the formal gardens had been restored to the full glory of arguably the greatest collection of exotic plants and flowers in the Island-World. Even aloft, Hualiama filled her lungs with a richness of pollens and scents which left her gasping.

Her gaze tracked the flight of eleven honking blue cranes over the Palace building, only to be distracted by a flash of crimson. A firebird! The fabled firebird of Fra'anior was said to be a cross between avian and dragonet, able to ignite its feathers if threatened but not burn up. Isles legend told that if a firebird could be tamed, it would lead a person to a forgotten Dragon-hoard containing fabulous riches. An amusing tale. But her life had an odd parallel with that firebird, she sensed. Lia had burned but not been consumed. Perhaps she was a firebird.

Perhaps the Dragon astronomers, who watched the skies for the advent of the comet that portended the rise of the third great race of the Island-World, should be watching for the Dragonfriend as she streaked to her fiery demise in the Cloudlands–oh, windroc droppings. That image was scant comfort.

Choosing not to conceal her approach to the seat of the Onyx Throne of Fra'anior, Hualiama landed in her customary berth at the Dragonship bays behind the Palace building. She tossed hawsers to the servants, who tied them off to bollards on the ground. Bank the oven's fires, secure the controls, take her weapons … Lia tossed a short rope ladder over the edge of her basket and clambered to the ground.

A Royal Guard, puffing out his purple-uniformed chest, barked, "Princess Hualiama, by the King's order I place you under arrest–"

Hualiama's smile, modelled on Grandion's best, lip-curling, fang-revealing, Dragon-fire-breathing efforts, appeared to cork his throat pleasingly. She said, "You can try."

And she left the nonplussed soldier and his squad of four

gaping at her back as she marched off. Faintly, she heard a voice inquire, "Why didn't you arrest the Princess, sir?"

"I prefer staying alive."

"Aye!" the others agreed fervently.

So, King Chalcion chose to show his hand? Lia strode toward the palace building as though she were a Dragonship driven by her own burning engine. She would make good her promise. Please, let her treat her father better than he had treated her. Let him see Lia for who she truly was. Let her fury not spill over into violence.

She knew her family would be dining at this hour. Lia recognised her fey, dangerous mood for what it was, and fought for control. Six years of abuse and humiliation. Before that, a long, sordid history of the King's uncontrolled temper dominating his family. He would see her act as open defiance. And who should she tell about her uncle Zalcion's treachery? Could it be proved? No-one in this Palace would trust the word of a Dragon.

A hand seized her arm. "Lady Hualiama, you are under–"

Lia chopped down with the hard edge of her palm. The Royal Guard yelped in pain. She walked on.

Portraits of tall, unsmiling royal ancestors bobbed past her as Lia took the stairs up to the dining hall three at a time. Ahead, heavy jalkwood doors stood slightly ajar, their polished wooden panels inlaid with rubies the size of dragonets' eggs to form the glowing heart of Royal Fra'anior's crest, a stylised volcano. Of course. And people mad enough to live atop a volcano, also had volcanic temperaments to suit.

Smiling grimly at the Royal Guard standing to attention beside the ten foot-tall doors–too tiny for a Dragon, she noted–Hualiama said, "Will you let me in, Ha'arukion?"

"I should by rights arrest you, Princess," he rumbled, but his hand did not stray to his sword-hilt. Instead, he peered narrowly at her. "What's wrong with your voice?"

"Dragon in my throat."

The soldier's regard did not waver. "Seems the girl who stole away with the Queen-mother a few days ago, has come back … changed."

"You knew?"

A slow grin crinkled his cheeks right up to his eyes. "Aye. I warn you, Princess, the King is spitting like a maddened Green Dragon. But I see that pointy chin. You step easy. Now, I'll be investigating a strange sound behind that hanging. Didn't see you slip past."

"Thank you, Ha'arukion. You're diamond."

Lia pressed open the door, and slipped into the informal dining-room–a circular chamber a mere fifty feet in diameter, wherein sat a priceless table hand-carved from a monolithic block of jade. Her family looked up, and gasped as one. No Chalcion. The knot behind Hualiama's left shoulder eased slightly.

"Islands' greetings, dear ones," she rasped.

Oh, their faces! Queen Shyana's colour became as pale as her plate. Flame-haired Fyria dribbled purple prekki-fruit juice down her chin. Her brother Kalli dropped his spoon into a bowl of green oats, while Ari and Elki yelped in delight.

"Lia, no weapons at the table," Shyana said automatically. "Cold stole your voice?"

"What's for dinner, Mom? I'm starving," said Lia.

"Short shrift …" Elki could only shake his head.

"Sulphurous greetings to you all from Sapphurion and Qualiana," Lia added, seating herself in her customary position between Elki and Ari. "Mom, can I ask you how old I was when you adopted me?"

"Sapphurion?" gasped Elki.

Kalli, with his unbreakably serious expression, said, "I remember. You were around three summers old, Lia, no bigger than a dragonet, just these huge green eyes and a shock of white hair."

Queen Shyana said, "Kalli wanted to call you 'little grandmother' until I taught him better. Lia, sweet petal, you do know what you're doing, don't you? Chalcion–"

"Does she ever?" Fyria sniped.

Fyria was her charming self, of course. Hualiama helped herself to a bowl of ralti stew and fresh sweet tuber mash. No telling when she might enjoy her next square meal. For a few minutes, the family ate in silence. Lia found her appetite had fled. Soon, she heard a familiar tread in the private corridor leading to the dining room. Her family only reacted several seconds after she heard it.

Her mother whispered, "Petal …"

"I know."

King Chalcion, deep in conversation with uncle Zalcion, entered through a doorway partially hidden behind a purple tapestry depicting the constellations of Fra'anior's sky. He wore his magnificent, sweeping robes of office, the deep purple of Fra'anior picked out with volcanoes and rajals in gold brocade thread, and he cradled his crown in the crook of his arm.

Apparently sensing the family's stillness, he looked up. His eyes roamed the table. A jolt. Chalcion's face drained of colour, before reversing the process with miraculous speed, assuming the colour and aspect of a rotten prekki fruit, purple and blotchy.

"Where have you been?"

"Islands' greetings, father. Are you well?" Lia responded, fighting an urge to sink into her seat.

Chalcion rounded the table inexorably. Hualiama pushed her chair back on the thick pile carpet and stood, willing herself to remain calm, to put aside the habits of six years of being victimised. She who could stand in an Ancient Dragon's presence, could not stand up to a Human man, King or none? She hated the feeling of inward curling, like scrolleaf tossed into a bonfire blackening and rolling up at the edges.

"You deliberately disobeyed me!"

"I-I w-went–"

"Stop that contemptible stammering, girl! Where in a Cloudlands hell have you been?"

Lia gulped. The King's face halted mere inches from hers, his final words depositing spittle on her cheek. No, she would not quail. Let her words spread fire across her tongue.

"I travelled to Ha'athior Island, father, to attend the passing on of the last Ancient Dragon, called Amaryllion Fireborn. You might have seen the light from here, two days ago, and felt an earthquake strike the Cluster. Then I travelled on to Ya'arriol to meet with friends there. Yesterday, I consulted with Sapphurion and his Dragon Elders at Gi'ishior, before returning."

Chalcion's throat worked as though he had a slice of sour haribol fruit stuck in his craw. The King grated, "Who let you out? Who helped you? Someone must have–Elka'anor? Shyana? Who helped this little dragonet flout a direct order from her King?"

Shyana's chair tipped over as she stood. "I did."

"Mom!" Lia gasped. Once again, her mother intended to shield her from Chalcion's wrath.

Abruptly, the King whirled and ran at Shyana. Lia sprinted after him. A tap of his ankle with her foot brought him down. Hualiama sprang past him and whirled, fists clenched. "You leave Mom alone!"

"Get out of my way!" he roared.

Chalcion rose, wiping a trail of spittle off his chin. A feral glint lurked in his eyes. Bellowing, he charged, tackling Lia about the waist. She rolled with his assault, bringing her knees up as they landed on the plush carpet. The King received the point of her right knee directly in his sternum. Still, he was mad enough to throw a punch. Lia blocked the blow automatically.

Shyana threw herself on her husband's back, screaming, "What's the matter with you? You're an animal!"

Cursing, Chalcion threw his Queen off. Lia twisted aside, avoiding his lunge, rolling smoothly to her feet with the ease the many long hours of training with the warrior-monks had instilled in her. She had wrestled men stronger than Chalcion. But she did not want to hurt him.

As he pushed to his feet, Hualiama said flatly, "Dad, stop it. You will no longer bully us. And if you lay a finger on Mom, ever again, I promise that I will do to you what I did to Ra'aba."

Drawing a dagger from his belt, Chalcion roared, "Fight me, would you?"

"No. I will not draw a blade against my King."

Vile curses flooded from his mouth as the King swung the blade at his daughter. She whispered aside, dance-step following dance-step. He could not touch her.

He panted, "How dare you defy me? Zalcion, help me, brother."

"Help? He's the one selling secrets to the Dragons!" Lia glanced at her uncle. A sword sprouted in Zalcion's hand. He stalked closer, murder blazing in his eyes. Realisation struck. Was Zalcion behind her father's behaviour? Feeding his anger? Worse, doing something to poison him or cripple his ability to rule effectively?

Zalcion snarled, "You been whoring with Dragons again, girl? Nauseating whelp of a diseased ralti sheep. We know all about your precious Grandion."

His vile, twisting words clogged Lia's thoughts with fire. Suddenly Chalcion was upon her, the blade stabbing for her gut. The Princess stood her ground and punched her father with all the force and Dragon fire her petite frame could muster, coupled with the rigorous training she had endured in the monastery. *Crack!* Bone splintered beneath her fist. Chalcion turned grey, clutching his lower ribs.

Lia stared at him, breathing in short, agonised gasps. She had done it.

As the King collapsed, she gritted out, "Never again, father."

"I'll … disown you."

"As if a scroll makes family," she retorted.

Queen Shyana's scream alerted her. Hualiama dodged Zalcion's overhand strike, losing a neat fillet of flesh on her right shoulder to his blade. Her twin swords sprang to hand seemingly at a thought. The Nuyallith forms flowed awkwardly, feeling the rust of too many seasons' disuse. Lia blocked twice with the iron-elbow technique before sneaking in a skill called the switch and double-cross, in which she parried with her stronger left hand while simultaneously bringing her right-hand blade down from high on her left side in a vicious back-handed swing, contrary to the ordinary angle of attack. She pulled the blow at the last second.

He cried out as Lia's blade smashed through the radius bone of his forearm and chinked against the ulna. She kicked his sword away from where it dropped. Zalcion staggered backward, as pale as the fires which had consumed her.

Hualiama thought to feel triumphant. Instead, the victory felt hollow. She had become the bully. Could it be that this was the only language her father understood? What an indictment.

Maybe it was time to speak another language.

Sheathing her blades with a convulsive thrust of her arms, Lia knelt. She touched her father's cheek, ignoring his weak, pawing attempts to push her away. She said, "Many of my friends died to restore the Onyx Throne to you, father. You could at least pretend a measure of gratitude."

Chalcion flinched as if her touch scalded him.

Smiling with terrible gentleness, now, she continued, "Love is a peculiar form of madness, isn't it? I still love you. Maybe you don't grasp that. So I want you to know that for your good, I've struck a bargain with Sapphurion. The Dragons will be watching. If you lift as much as your little finger against one of my family again, they'll know. And then you'd better wish all the Dragons of Gi'ishior had burned this town off the map rather than face my wrath. Understood?"

King Chalcion flung an arm over his eyes as though to shield them from her glare. "Aye," he whispered.

Rising, Lia said, "I would also disperse the forces you've been secretly assembling at Seg Island. The Dragons know all about them, thanks to my dear uncle."

And she turned her back upon the King.

Squeezing her hands together to stop their shaking, Hualiama looked to her mother. Shyana displayed that preternatural calm which Lia knew acted as a shield to the world. It did not stop her wanting to shake her mother and shout in her face, 'And? Didn't you see what I did?' Any reaction would have been better than none at all.

Queen Shyana said, "I'll see to Chalcion. What will you do now, daughter?"

Hualiama reached for the fruit basket and helped herself to a prekki-fruit and a ripe green tinker banana. "I'm going to hunt a Dragon."

* * * *

There was no silence as profound as the space between Islands, no vault as large as the moons-lit sky, hoarding its treasury of stars, nor a loneliness as soul-shadowing as the loss of betrayal. This Hualiama knew as she piloted her Dragonship away from Fra'anior Cluster. She could not sleep. Instead, she searched the emptiness with the eyes of her heart, longing for a glimmer of moonlight upon gemstone scales, for a sign that all was not dust blown into the Cloudlands.

Flicker. Amaryllion. Masters Jo'el and Khoyal. The long-dead face of her Nuyallith tutor, his knowledge lodged in her mind, unforgettable. Sometimes, she felt as though she carried more ghosts than living flesh upon her diminutive frame. She yearned for her spirit to abandon what the ballads called her mortal coil, to roam the Island-World upon wings less substantial than the wind itself; faraway, flyaway, free.

If she listened with the ears of her sixth sense, tasting and experiencing the tides and times of the Island-World, could she not rediscover that bond she had felt between herself and the Tourmaline Dragon, and sing the melody of souls united by oaths stronger than death?

Softly, she poured her heart forth in tuneful lament:

O my Dragon, I search for thee,
My spirit flying far and free,
I call to thee, Grandion. I beg, I burn,
Wilt thou not hear?

Wind keened among the inner hawsers binding spirit to flesh, and flesh to bone. Lia felt a sense of straining, perhaps the Dragon fire of Flicker's gift bound in the form of a Human. Her hands played upon the controls as in a dream, setting a south-easterly course for Erigar Island. The sails were fully deployed to gobble up a bellyful of the night breeze. The stove burned cheerfully. She topped it up with a few chips of dry jalkwood.

A dream seemed to creep over her, a darkness deeper even than the night.

A Dragon lay in his lair.

Nay, not a lair, but a cage of indestructible Dragon bone, bound with bands of magic-infused iron. The Dragon shifted restlessly, as if gripped by dreams of his own–or touched by hers. Anger had long since guttered into grief. Hope lay crushed beneath a burden of despair. The Dragon circled his cage one more time, dragging his steps, and no light of the Island-World entered his eyes. He was blind.

Horror rose in her gorge, thick and virulent. No! Lia cast herself forth, tenuous as starlight, desperate to bring a touch of light to the darkness of Dragon fires reduced to cinders. Did she touch him? Just for a heartbeat, did she sense in him the memory of a Dragon Rider laughing upon his back, of covetous Dragon eyes fixated by a prize he could never have but needed more than the breath rasping in his calcified lungs? It ignited his remembrance of a glorious expansion of spirit as the Tourmaline Dragon escaped from his bondage beneath the Island, as he touched a Human girl, breathed in her scent and revelled in the knowledge of her, she who was no Dragoness, yet who wrote melodies of white-hot magic in the secret places of a Dragon's soul … the feeling was so visceral, so all-encompassing, that Grandion drew her to him now, wanting her yet sensitive to the tenebrous peril of the far leagues sapping her spirit and strength.

Not yet. His breath wafted her home. *I shall wait for thee.*

* * * *

Lia surfaced from her dream with an inhalation that fired her lungs and throat. *Dragon!* Where was she–low, in danger! It was already dawn. Her Dragonship skimmed over the Cloudlands, miles lower than it should have been. The cloying, dead reek of the clouds filled her nostrils, rising toward her like tendrils seeking to entangle and drag her down into the depthless abyss.

What had she done? The stove had burned out, the sails flapped listlessly … the clouds here were a sickly yellow hue, like the luminous cave-dwelling slugs Flicker had enjoyed showing her as they hunted through the Western Isles for her family.

Hualiama slapped the turbine switches. She adjusted the lift. Pedal. Pedal, ralti-stupid idiot! While she had been dreaming of the Tourmaline Dragon, she had almost sunk herself into the Cloudlands. The turbines began to rotate with a *whup-whup-whup* sound, but the drag of the cool air inside the sack was too much. She was still sinking. She had to light the stove and pour hot air into the system. Lia adjusted the rigging, but there was no breeze to provide lift. Where had she packed her spark-stone? Scrabbling through her travel packs, her hand fell upon a boot–a familiar boot!

"Elki?"

A groan came from beneath the sacking covering her supplies. "Eh, it's too early."

"Get up!"

"Mercy, a little more sleep."

Hualiama kicked his foot. *ARISE!*

She clutched her throat in surprise. What on the Islands?

As though he had sat upon a Dragon's claw, her brother Elka'anor surfaced from beneath her gear, gazing wildly about him. "Where are we? Short shrift, what have you done?"

"Shut the trap and light the stove, boy. Snip snap!"

"Don't call me boy. I might be younger than you, but I do have a beard."

He rummaged through his pockets, scowling as she ribbed him, "That scraggly scrap of goat-fluff signifies maturity?"

"I'm seventeen summers old and eleven inches taller than you–count them. E-le-ven!"

Lia rolled her eyes. "Islands' sakes, I've never heard that one before. Fresh wood for the fire–"

"Shut your stove-pipe and let a man do the work." Biting his tongue, Elki struck the stones together sharply, spraying sparks into the stove's heart. "Give me some of that sacking. You got bark shreds? Honestly, can't a fellow stow away in peace around here?"

Delight and exasperation warred in her breast. What did one do with such a scamp of a brother? Kiss him? Thump him over the earhole with the largest hunk of wood she could find, and drag him back to mother?

Lia snorted, "I see you're having your usual morning grump."

"Tends to happen when your sister boots you awake, hauls you about by some magical command and then starts shouting at you." Elki flashed his lopsided, mischievous grin at her. "Where's the thanks, the 'this journey would be so much lonelier without the benefit of my awesome brother's company,' I ask you?"

"I was doing fine on my own."

"Aye, it shows. Asking for help isn't exactly your forte, is it, short shrift?" Hualiama answered this with a wordless growl, fine-tuning the rigging. "No, you're flying off across the Island-World on your lonesome, hunting Dragons."

"Exactly what do my socially unacceptable habits have to do with you?"

Elki drew himself up. "I've decided you can't have all the fun, sister. I'm the second Prince of the realm. Kalli–he gets to rule. What do I do with my life?"

"Excellent question. Make mischief? Remove your rear end from the region of my nostrils, scoundrel."

"Sorry. Well, I want a Dragon, too. There, smoke that for tobacco, if you dare."

Lia shuddered. Her scamp of a brother breezed through life with ne'er-may-care ease, blowing where he wished. Of course he landed on his feet more often than not. Was she just jealous of his irrepressible spirit? Just wait until a Dragon sat on him! He'd whistle a different tune.

As Elki stoked the fire, Hualiama opened the valves to allow hot air to billow into the Dragonship's limp sack. Still, it took a good half-hour before they began to notice the renewed lifting power. That half-hour they spent covering their noses and mouths with damp cloths and hoping that they had not breathed too much toxic gas. The Dragonship dragged itself begrudgingly out of the Cloudlands.

"Right, back to bed," said Elki, curling up between the travel packs. "Call me when you need rescuing again."

"That's 'if'–and I'll not be lugging a lazy lump of lethargy around the Islands!"

Elki replied with an exaggerated snore.

Chapter Nine

Over the Islands

XINIDIA ISLAND TOPPED the Cloudlands like a mouldy, discarded boot, according to her vocally underwhelmed brother. Lia laughed so hard, she was unable to complete her sets of pull-ups. Three days of Elki's barbs and dry wit, and she was ready either to throw him overboard, or to hug him for distracting her from wallowing in wretchedness over Grandion's fate. At least her throat no longer felt as though she were gargling a mouthful of splintered volcanic rock.

"Ugh, more exercise?" he grunted, shifting on the pilot's chair. "Don't you ever rest?"

"At least I do exercise, and I brush my hair. Yours looks like an abandoned windroc's nest."

Elki pretended to primp in front of a mirror. "Aye, because a hairbrush was the first thing I thought to pack when I was planning to abscond to the Eastern Isles with my prodigal runaway exasperatingly focussed Dragon-crazy sister."

She teased, "Do you always gabble on like that?"

"Dear one, what happened the other day when we almost crash-landed in the Cloudlands?"

Lia knew she was about to be verbally sliced up for kebabs. She whispered, "I dreamed about Grandion. A weird, vivid dream–like we really *connected*, Elki. It's happened before, and it's scary because I lose track of everything."

Bounding out of the chair in that lithe-rajal way of his, Elki strode around the oven which occupied the centre of their basket, and placed his hands on her shoulders. "Not a murmur about that beast for six years, and now you're over the moons about him? I guessed it was some passing girlish fancy, like some girls take a shine to rajals or a pet dragonet, or … uh, sorry. I didn't mean it that way."

"Am I different?"

"Weirder than usual? Definitely." Elki grinned down at her. "You tell me you're all chummy with an Ancient Dragon, who made you forget the past. You break three of Father's ribs–totally impressive. Basically, you walked out the door and came back a different girl. I don't know. Still miniscule, though."

"Elki!"

"There's somehow … more. I can't explain it." He scratched as if mining his beard for fleas. "Like someone borrowed half of your spirit for a few years and returned it tenfold. Lia, you've gone pale. Are you alright?"

"Fine. No. I need to sit down." Shaking her head, Lia dropped onto the pilot's chair, trying to decide if now was an opportune moment to have a panic attack. "You couldn't put that more starkly?"

"Slip of the proverbial Dragon's claw there."

"Elki, why did you come along?"

"To buzz around my sister like an impossible-to-swat mosquito?"

She blazed, "Can I have a serious answer?"

"Down, o dinky Dragoness. I get carried away … and now you're doing the smoky eyes thing." Lia grimaced at him. Elki admitted, "Frankly, I was bored. And–moment of rare honesty–when you confronted Father and Uncle Zalcion, I saw you do something I've always lacked the courage to do. Dreamed it. Never did it. So I said to myself, if I could just hang onto my little sister's skirts for long enough, maybe some of her courage would rub off on me. Then I'd also fight men like Ra'aba to a standstill, and go moons-mad for the flash of a Dragonish eye."

Hualiama punched his arm, and then threw her arms around her brother and hugged him as hard as she could.

"Oof," he complained. "Gently with the royal ribcage."

"It strikes me on occasion, Elki, that you're barely tolerable as a brother," said Lia.

"Then explain why your eyes are all dewy?"

For that, she flattened him.

* * * *

Hualiama ticked off the days in her mind. Five days from Xinidia to forest-crowned Erigar was struggle enough. A further six days battling contrary winds brought them to Archion, exhausted and sweaty, and in Elki's case, more than a little pongy.

Lia wrinkled her nose at him. "You stink."

"That's the birds," her brother said, "and you can lay off the body odour insults, monkey mischief."

"Now listen here–"

Elki stormed, "This basket is only so large and I cannot possibly smell worse than those millions of birds out there, liberally splashing their guano all over the Island. Last night, you started poking me at some unsocial hour claiming my heartbeat was too loud."

About to snipe back at him, Lia pulled up short with a frown. Truly? Grandion's hearing had been so amazing, he could hear her teardrops falling from the far end of a cave. Was this Flicker's gift? To her, Elki smelled like the proverbial unwashed Sylakian tribesman, hairier than a hound and never washed until his burial day.

"Aye," said her brother, evidently reading her thoughts. "You're ridiculously sensitive and have probably been overcome by the ripe redolence of your own armpits. Now, lend an ear to your learned brother as he extols the wonders of Archion Island. There are 616 known bird species which roost on this Island-World marvel. The northern leg has fourteen levels of terrace lakes, while the southern leg sports no less than seventeen, making this a veritable avian paradise. Blackwing storks, blue-banded mallards and white-tipped herons are the dominant species, but you'll also find a dazzling variety of flycatchers and bee-eaters, particularly the notable long-tailed greater yellow bee-eater with his fantastic two-foot tail …"

"Scroll-worm," Hualiama teased. "Carry on, I'm almost asleep."

As Elki listed further species, his sister adjusted the sails for a landing near one of the upper terrace lakes, on the 'bridge' level, where the two standing legs of the Island joined together four miles above the Cloudlands. Spectacular. Lia drank in the sight. The mid-morning suns-light reflected off the dazzling layers of terrace lakes, spotted with lily pads as wide as her outstretched arms, and the dense reed beds bordering the lakes played host to the uncountable birds that so fascinated Elki, who was still spouting like the famous geyser north of Fra'anior Town which erupted every hour. She listened with half an ear.

The Ancient Dragons must have had such fun building this Island. It was shaped as if a vast rocky sentinel, cut off at the waist in ages past, stood with his legs akimbo in the Cloudlands. And why such an unreasonable profusion of terrace lakes? Two or three, aye. Sensible. But seventeen? Had the Dragons constructed this Island specifically for the birds' benefit?

"Ah, to the windrocs with sensible." Lia smiled dreamily.

Elki chuckled, "You're clearly three sheets to the wind, sister. Sunk in a keg of berry-wine."

Oh. She had spoken aloud? "It's only because I've been cooped up in a small basket with a chattering parakeet for fourteen days."

At this speed, it would take them a month and a half to reach the Eastern Archipelago, she realised. Archion to Sylakia Island was a decent haul, after which came Syros but a short hop to the north, before the long crossing to the dangerous trio of Merx, Lyrx and Amxo. The latest intelligence had war raging between two bands of Dragons out there, and between the Dragons and the Humans of Merx. She would have avoided those three Islands altogether if she could, but the stormy Cloudlands ocean east of Sylakia made any other route a perilous proposition.

Blast this overheated weather. Wasn't the season meant to

be growing cooler?

They landed on a small stretch of meadow alongside a gorgeous terrace lake. Elki leaped out to secure several hawsers to a fallen tree, while Hualiama bled off just enough hot air to bring the basket to a gentle landing on the soft sword-grass just beyond. Right. She should bank the stove fire, ease the tension on the control ropes and check their supplies of food, water and wood.

After alighting, she patted the basket fondly. "Good girl. Shame you aren't a Dragon."

"I'm off to catch some trout," Elki enthused, unearthing a fishing line and hooks from one of his many pockets. She might not care to admit it, but his packing had been rather resourceful.

"Wash first," said Lia.

"You go ahead. Did you bring perfumes, oils, lotions, soft towels and a court musician for entertainment, your Highness?"

"Nay, good Prince," she bowed with a flourish, "I brought but the clothes upon my back and a handsome rogue to lighten the leagues with his raffish charm."

As she spoke, Lia began to divest her person of weapons. Elki whistled softly. "How many knives, sister?"

"Fifteen. And a few poisoned darts."

"Warrior monk, eh?" He busied himself with the fishing line. "You need to teach me more of that Nuyallith *zing-zang-zong* you do." Elki accompanied his sound effects with a ridiculous, foppish set of martial moves that had her in stitches.

Lia laughed, "Will you keep watch, brother?"

"Aye."

The Princess strode down to the lake shore. All was quiet. Could it last? For her spirit felt the tug of the East as a craving and a frisson of danger. At least she would not face the long leagues alone. She swam far out into the lake, before churning back with all the power she could generate. Her body already felt stronger and more toned as a result of her daily training regimen.

Back near the shore, Lia washed herself in the cool lake water with admittedly first-class soap filched from the palace supplies, and worked hair oil through her troublesome locks. After all, a girl ought to look her best when hunting long-lost Dragons. And her cheeky brother could just eat mouldy windroc gizzards for daring to comment on her travel-stained condition.

"Is my sister slaughtering an animal back there?" Elki's voice came floating on the breeze.

"Blasted hair … I'm fine!"

"So, tell me about life in a monastery surrounded by dozens of toothsome, loincloth-clad monks?"

"Elki," she warned. "I was perfectly chaste."

"Chaste or chased? Ooh–great Islands, you can't go prancing about like that!"

"Elki!" Lia did not appreciate him standing there, gazing ostentatiously at the horizon, with a wicked grin curving his lips. "I'm wearing a decent minimum."

"No wonder your poor Dragon went all googly fire-eyes and wobble-kneed when he saw–"

"That's quite enough!"

He shrugged. "I was just saying."

"You're just being a man. I know. I am your sister and you will act gallantly or so help me, I'll go running to Mom and tattle like when you were five and pinching my toys."

"In all seriousness, short shrift," he shifted uncomfortably, and Hualiama glanced up sharply as she heard his heartbeat rise, unmistakably, from twenty feet away, "without meaning to sound as perverted and sinister as our dear uncle, I'm your brother and I *notice*, alright? Strictly limited, of course, even if you're adopted and not our flesh and blood …" He broke off with a gruff curse. "I swore I'd never make you feel second-rate, Lia, and I just did. I'm awfully sorry."

"I understand. Go on," she said softly, unwilling to break the mood. Her cheeks throbbed, she was blushing so hard. This was her brother Elki speaking? The mischievous dragonet with nary a solemn bone in his body?

"Grandion's a *Dragon.* The very notion of him ogling you

like some of our courtiers used to, just creeps me out. Is it the Dragon hoarding instinct–you know, pretty bauble, nice eyes, I'll drag her off to my cave? Or is something weirder and more worrying going on?"

"Pretty bauble?" Lia quirked an eyebrow at him.

"I mean, you are very easy on the eyes, brave … and undeniably cute …" He spluttered to a standstill, turning a fine shade of puce. "Let's try another Island, shall we?"

Laughing now, she said, "Elki, you're the best brother that ever stowed away on my Dragonship."

"The only one, you mean. Don't avoid the question. Please."

It must have tortured him, she realised, quickly donning her shirt. As they returned from the mine where her family had been exiled to a lifetime of hard labour, Elka'anor had helped her to slip away to fly with Grandion and Flicker. How mad she had been, throwing herself off the Dragonship and trusting that her Dragon would catch her. Of course Grandion had dived after her, and caught her in his great paw. But that act had required an equal measure of trust on her brother's part. She had never realised how protective Elki felt toward her. It was sweet, and unexpectedly poignant.

With the sense of casting herself off the Isle of sanity, Hualiama replied, "Elki, first off, understand that when Grandion and I made our oaths to each other, it was as though the Island-World shivered together with us. There was magic, pure and potent, and it seemed that the Great Dragon roared his approval. It was never love … or if it was, I failed to recognise it. And after six years, can I hope? I can't."

"Lia," he hissed.

She winced at the note of condemnation he struck, but soldiered on, "I suppose I can best say what Amaryllion taught me, Elki. The Dragons have many different words for love–filial love, which they call shell-brother or shell-sister love, friendship love, parental love, courtship love, soul-bonded love and even battle love."

"The love of tearing enemies to shreds and charcoaling the remains?"

"Dragons are very loving and social creatures–stop laughing at me!" Hualiama smacked his shoulder. "The Dragonkind are driven by the fires of passions so huge and consuming, you and I can hardly imagine."

Elki said, "And what about–"

"Aye," Lia nodded, wishing her face would betray less of her discomfiture. "There is also mated love, by which they mean sexual love. That's the part which, for obvious reasons, can never be. Then, in a further nuance, Dragons have an idea of 'roost love' which I believe means Dragons which roost together, but not as mates."

Her brother's grey-eyed gaze crinkled at its edges as he regarded her fondly, yet with shadows behind his eyes which made her squirm. "And where in this glittering galaxy of draconic love does my sister stand?"

"Confused?"

At that, the spell of their intense conversation broke. Elki laughed so hard that tears splashed down his cheeks, while Hualiama had to sit on a nearby boulder or risk rolling on the grass, gasping helplessly. After a while, her brother sauntered over and perched on the boulder beside her. His fingers touched her back lightly.

"Ra'aba sure cut you, didn't he?"

"Aye. And Grandion burned me when he was feral–I told you that, didn't I?" A soul-lost shiver gripped her as Lia gazed out toward the eastern horizon, where a Dragonwing of seven Reds was just visible, flying in a northerly direction, perhaps to one of the smaller Islands above Sylakia, or up to the Spits. "Those who play with Dragons will get burned … of course it is forbidden and impossible and probably a reasonable definition of insanity, and I–and Grandion–would incur the wrath of every Dragon and Human in the Island-World were it true–"

"Probably shake a few starchy old Islands right off their roots," he put in.

"Aye. But Elki, for three years, Qualiana and Sapphurion were mother and father to me. Larger parents than most, but unfailing in their love for a wisp of humanity. Dragons are complex, beautiful and vastly different to us, but they are also emotional and intelligent creatures, and I believe they have souls just as Humans have souls. Well, theirs are fire-souls–never mind." Lia waved that away. "The question I keep coming back to is, 'What if it was romantic love?' What's so wicked about love?"

"What indeed, sister?"

Only a million things, she wanted to wail. Why did she have to be the first?

Elki draped his arm over her shoulders. "So, which martial discipline are you planning to use to destroy me today?"

Hualiama jabbed her elbow into his ribs. "Dance."

"Dance?"

"Aye, you lumbering ralti sheep. Every self-respecting Prince of Fra'anior must learn to dance."

As must Lia. She must dance upon the storm-tides of fate, and never let them roll her under. For she could not survive that. No one could.

* * * *

From the fabled arch of Archion to Sylakia Island was a dispiriting five-day battle into the teeth of an unseasonable series of squalls. Brother and sister took turns spelling each other on the pedals. Lia had to make more running repairs than she cared to count. It was a sorry, battered Dragonship crew that spotted the black-edged massif of Sylakia Island looming out of the Cloudlands, crowned by further menacing bands of dark clouds, early on the sixth morning out of Archion.

"We came within a rajal's whisker of missing Sylakia entirely," Lia said, gritting her teeth as she adjusted their course. "We'll have to tack all the way to the north of the Island at this rate. Pesky storm winds."

Elki said, "No rest for wicked, would-be Dragon Riders, eh?"

"I'm too spent to beat you up right now, dear brother."

"Here's a novel idea–don't." But her wiry brother set to the rigging with a will, hardly needing instruction after two and a half weeks aloft. "How's this trim on the boom?" he asked.

"Perfect. Lash those stays and trim those bushy whiskers, you scurvy brigand, or your back will feel the bite of the triple-stranded flogger!"

"Aye, Captain!" he growled fearsomely, playing his part.

Lia pressed the rudder with both feet, forcing the Dragonship into a closer reach against the wind. It shuddered before picking up speed, scudding north-westward with renewed impetus. "Amazing how close you can haul an airship with the right rigging," she commented.

Elki rubbed his chin unhappily. "I could pass for a barbarous Sylakian. Oh, for a warm inn at Sylakia Town, a square meal and the company of copious comely wenches." He winked at his sister. "Present company excepted."

"There will be no carousing on this journey, o Prince of the realm."

"Bah. Stick to flying the Dragonship, short shrift."

Their journey up the huge Island did however resemble an inebriated man's walk, for they proceeded in a series of league-long zigzags, sweeping from the western shore of Sylakia Island to the central mountains and back again, each time gaining a number of miles of northward progress. But after a few hours, the wind began to gutter and swirl, forcing Hualiama to play the controls with a harpist's skill. Blue skies and a steady following breeze would have been her choice portents for this journey.

"More wood, servant." A wind as fickle as her wry chuckle gusted them sideways toward the peaks.

Elki fed the stove, stiffening as he peered ahead. "Are those windrocs, Lia? Icerocs, I mean?"

"Icerocs? Any less dangerous than–"

"No. A white version of our favourite oversized avian," her brother informed her. "Just as large, just as feral. Lia, these boys aren't here to play Staves. Where's your hunting bow?"

"Shall I shoot?"

"Shall I request a better vote of confidence?" Hualiama's tongue-waggling did nought but exercise a few muscles, for her brother was sensibly hastening to the weapons. He slung the quiver on his back and lifted the bow grimly. "I take it that changing course isn't an option?"

"We're flying sideways as it is," Lia admitted, eyeing the trio of huge, white-feathered predators looming off the starboard bow with trepidation. "I'll try for lift." She tweaked the turbines and adjusted the sails, while feeding the stove again. More power for the turbines.

But the icerocs closed in inexorably, having no trouble overhauling their dirigible airship. Fifteen to eighteen feet in wingspan, they were furnished with a classic hooked beak and talons capable of rending a fully-grown ralti sheep limb from limb. This, coupled with a vicious temperament prone to attacking anything that moved in their territory, meant that windrocs or icerocs were regarded as the most feared enemy of Dragonship captains the Island-World over.

Elki flexed the Haozi hunting bow, but withheld his shot. "Want to see the red rims of their eyes," he explained. "You downed icerocs before?"

"A few. A head shot will do it, or the heart. Aim lower than you'd expect, about a foot in front of the armpit."

"The things my little big sister knows."

Hualiama booted him in the backside. "Mom's relying on me to keep you in line. Oh, and we've another four icerocs incoming. Best stop parading your dubious wit and limber up the bow."

With a series of assertive screeches, the advance trio of icerocs whirled into the attack–perhaps seeking to secure their meal before their fellows arrived? First bird gets the entrails? Suddenly, the Dragonship shook as it came under attack. With a shout, Elki earned his first strike, but it was into an iceroc's belly, not a fatal shot. Leaning out, he scored a fortunate head-strike with his second arrow.

"Ha!" he yelled, dancing happily.

Springing out of the pilot's seat, Hualiama struck out with an instinctive thrust past her brother's head. The iceroc which had attempted to ambush him, reared back with a deafening shriek. It clutched at the basket, pecking Elki's shoulder. Lia's blade speared into its throat. Whirling tightly on her heel, she used the centrifugal force to snap out a second strike, chopping halfway through the bird's neck before the blade crunched against bone. The iceroc writhed. Lia almost lost her grip on the blade as it jerked away, fighting free of the rigging cords and tearing one of their sails on the way.

"Pay attention!" she hissed.

Elki clutched his shoulder, having turned pallid, but then he seemed to rally his courage. He muttered, "Just a scratch. I'm fine."

"Here they come!"

Manoeuvring the Dragonship would be useless, Lia realised. She would do better to attack any bird that intended to breakfast on her brother. A second bow would have been perfect. Instead, they had to stand by helplessly as the Dragonship shuddered beneath repeated talon-strikes. Soon, the feral birds decided that shredding the rigging offered no sustenance, and began to focus on the basket.

"Makes me feel we're lunch, packed in a basket," her brother muttered.

That comment deserved a blast, but Lia spent her anger on an iceroc instead. She came within a rajal's whisker of losing her fingers to a blindingly quick snap of its beak. Elki yelled triumphantly as he placed an arrow down the bird's throat, and then spun to fire a speculative shot at a bird tearing at the basket on the opposite side. They staggered beneath the force of the attack.

Suddenly, a high-pitched whistling sound entered Hualiama's awareness. What was that? Her head swivelled. The sound escalated rapidly, drowning out even the icerocs' shrieks.

Boom! One of the birds exploded–literally, dousing the two Humans in a spray of feathers and blood. A millisecond thereafter, a second iceroc off the starboard bow screeched in fear before–*thud!* A Dragoness snatched the bird out of the air as she hurtled past so narrowly, her half-furled wingtip brushed the starboard boom alongside the balloon.

"What?" Elki whirled. "Oh, freaking Islands–"

Hualiama flung out an arm. "Dragoness!"

The Dragoness flexed her wings with astonishing agility. Turning on a brass dral, she hurtled back up toward the dirigible, scattering the icerocs with a challenge that was not the booming voice of the Dragons Hualiama knew, but more like a trumpet-blast, at once sonorous and terrifying. The Dragoness was an extraordinary colour, scales of liquid bronze trimmed in deep red, and as sleek as a terrace lake trout. She struck out with claw and fang, driving the remaining icerocs off with a fearful flurry of blows. Those that fought, died.

"You had to ask for one, didn't you?" Lia snapped.

"M-m-mercy!" quavered Elki.

Then, the Dragoness approached the airship, cleaning iceroc bones out of her fangs with a casual twist of her needle-sharp talons.

"Sulphurous greetings, o most noble Dragoness," Lia called. "We're indebted to you for your aid."

For several endless seconds, the Dragoness' gaze scorched the air between them. "You're the one they call the Dragonfriend?" Lia nodded mutely. The Dragoness' jaw cracked open in an unsettling smile. Her fangs were just as needle-thin as her talons. "A favourable coincidence. The Dragonfriend has a considerable reputation in the East, on my home Island of Tsugai, which lies a few wingbeats north of Jaoli."

"All good, I hope," Elki whispered.

The Dragoness' smile broadened as she clearly overheard his words. "This must be your brother?"

Elki and Lia bowed in concert. She said, "Noble Dragoness, may I introduce Elka'anor, Prince of Fra'anior?"

The Dragoness inclined her head. A fey light gleamed in her eye, which Lia did not trust one iota. "I'm Mizuki the Copper Dragoness. I hope we meet again, o Prince. You seem a handsome specimen for one of your kind."

To Lia's astonishment, grass-green swirls denoting avariciousness entered the Dragoness' eye-fires. What on the Islands? Even worse, her brave brother mumbled something unintelligible and collapsed at her feet in a dead faint! Great. This encounter was proceeding well.

Mizuki cooed, *Was it something I said? A few bones stuck between my fangs?*

Your mighty presence overcame him. Hualiama answered automatically in Dragonish, before clapping her hand over her mouth. Mercy!

Fear not, Dragonfriend, said the Dragoness, appearing maddeningly pleased with herself. *You fly east? Would you seek a particular Dragon? We heard … rumours. And I hear your little heart quivering like prey beneath my paw. 'Never trust a Dragon,' isn't that the Human saying?*

Aye. Ah, my brother recovers.

A few moments later, a second Human head peered over the basket's edge. The Dragoness' muzzle turned coyly askance. "A touch of the suns, noble Prince?"

"Nay, for thy brilliance hath singed the very suns' rays," replied Elki, boldly borrowing a line from an ancient ballad.

Hualiama wanted to dance for joy! Elki! A fiery snort of pleasure blasted out of the Dragoness' nostrils, burning a foot-wide hole in the basket. "Sorry," she said, covering her fangs with her forepaw in a very Human-like gesture–and coquettishly whirled her eye-fires over her paw at Elki! Her poor brother. He clutched the basket's edge as though his knees had come unhinged.

"I may be seeking a particular Dragon," Lia said, tersely. "Do you know of him?"

"He came to the East on an honour-quest," said Mizuki, returning the same paucity of trust she received.

"Whereas your quest is a quest of sacred fire?" Lia guessed.

"Aye, Dragonfriend. Your knowledge of Dragon lore is, as they say, peerless among your kind. Know that we Dragons of the East do not hold to, nor approve of, all of the traditions of the Island-Cluster from which you hail."

Fascinating indeed. Which, in Dragonish double-speak, possibly meant that Mizuki knew of Grandion's shameful conduct with a Human Dragon Rider, and did not entirely disapprove?

Lia said, "By oath made before the Dragon Elders, I have joined his honour-quest. Was the shell-son of Sapphurion made welcome among the Dragons of the East?"

"Ah," purred the Dragoness. "You do the Tourmaline Dragon great honour. Aye, he came to Tsugai. I was but a forty-foot fledgling and beneath his notice, but well I remember such a–how do you say it in Island Standard? Every Dragoness swooned at his beautiful scales, and can I speak of the indescribable fires of his noble eye? Such power; such wing-shivering glory, as though the stars themselves descended to dwell among us! All of the Dragonesses wanted him."

Hualiama's opened her mouth to voice a shout of pure fury, when Elki stepped on her foot. Hard. "Ouch! You–"

"Noble Dragoness," he interrupted loudly, venturing a smile more queasy than confident, "may we entreat you for news of Grandion? Where might we find the towering–um, blue beast …"

The Copper Dragoness nodded gravely, returned from her romantic reverie. If ever Lia had imagined hurling herself at a Dragoness to throttle her, this was the moment. Green was the colour of her fire. Bright, sparkling, irrepressible jealousy.

Mizuki said, "Would that I knew more. One rumour holds that he travelled to the Lost Islands of the far north, and there succumbed to the Dragon-Haters' magic. In the second, Grandion was betrayed by a Dragoness and caged somewhere in the southern reaches of our Eastern Archipelago, down south past Haozi Island."

Lia shivered, recognising a parallel with her dream. Oh, Grandion!

"Now, I must depart," said Mizuki. "May you soar over the Islands of your life, and enjoy favourable winds, Dragonfriend and Prince Elka'anor."

"We thank you, noble–" Elki began, but with a snap of her wings, the Dragoness sped off toward the east.

Hualiama could not help but imagine that something in their conversation had frightened the Copper Dragoness away. Weirder than ten dancing Islands, were that the truth! And the wind had changed. The breeze blew steadily from astern–a coincidence, surely?

She elbowed Elki slyly. "So, rule number one of dealing

with Dragons. No fainting."

"Shut your prattling beak, short shrift."

Chapter Ten

Dread Pirate-Lord

SYLAKIA TOWN WELCOMED travellers, or, more accurately, their coin. Having secured a berth at the Dragonship port east of the town proper, Lia set about ordering materials for repairs, while Elki sauntered into town to procure supplies. Barbarians, the Sylakians were called, and Hualiama could see why. They were brawny, bluff men with huge, bristling beards and a habit of wearing mounds of stinking animal furs even in the most sweltering temperatures. Eschewing the elegant blades of Fra'anior, the Sylakians brandished two-handed war-hammers, which she had already seen settle three disputes in the course of as many hours aground.

However, there was coin aplenty. Sylakia's advantageous geographical location made the Island the hub of five major trading routes, to the north and Immadia Island, to the Eastern Archipelago, west to Fra'anior Cluster and the Western Isles, and southeast and southwest, to the vast reaches of the Southern Isles, all the way to the Rift. Lia counted over seventy Dragonships moored in port, and more arriving and leaving in a constant stream. The air had a tingle of bustle and excitement. New buildings were springing up to replace the old, square-cut wooden cabins that characterised the town. There was nothing pretty about Sylakia Town. No gardens, flowers, or even a green, growing thing.

There came Elki now, his long-legged stride eating up the ground. Carrying no supplies. Of course. Grr! She finished reefing on a new sail. Once the glue on the hot air sack dried in approximately six hours' time, they'd be all set.

"Found us accommodation and a hot bath," he called up to Lia, earning himself instant redemption.

"Great. Down in a wing-flip." Rope in hand, she let herself down from the 'wing' of the Dragonship and alighted at Elki's side. "What? What's that look for?"

"Glue on your chin," he averred, rubbing it with his thumb. "Mind you, a little fur and I could affix a nice beard."

"No accounting for what you fancy in women," she retorted.

Brother and sister walked up into town, taking their few valuables with them. Up the main street, boarded sidewalks provided relief from the stinking mud through which the pony-carts dragged their loads, and slave-carried litters transported the well-to-do. The inn was clean and not overrun with raffish patrons–a good choice, Lia approved. An hour later, bathed and refreshed, she decided she might even smell somewhat like a Princess of Fra'anior again. They ate a solid if unexceptional meal of ralti stew, not spiced nearly as much as the Fra'aniorian version, before retiring early.

An egg-dream stole Hualiama away. This one was stranger than most. Often she dreamed of a White or a dark Blue Dragoness brooding over her clutch, but this time, she dreamed she was inside an egg, submerged in a soft, yolky warmth.

You will fly to the moons, my little eggling, came her mother's voice.

Mamafire? Mamafire? The Dragoness was gone, and the egg was cold and alone. Another had come, but it was not the same. *Mamafire, don't leave me! Mama …*

Her third heart broke. The tiny Dragoness yearned for that comforting maternal voice, never seen but always loved, always reassuringly present. She was gone. Mamafire! Her baby presence floated on the world's winds. Her eggling-wings were not yet strong enough for flight, rubbing against the smooth inside of her egg as she dreamed, yet her fire-spirit roamed free and far. Danger! Instinctively, she hid from a great, tyrannical presence, cowering inside the egg. The dark one passed over, his many-fold power seeking, always seeking.

No, she must protect her egg-brother and egg-sister, those other infantile presences which she had known since before her first lucid thought. Her magic reached out. She sang:

Hush thee, hide thee, be not afraid,
I am thy sheltering wings.

Countless moon-cycles after she had sensed the dark one, the little Dragoness peered out again with eyes which reached beyond her body, beyond the shell. No, she must not break out. That time would come. Yet she sensed an impending tragedy. What was this? The anguish called her, a summons more imperative than the needs of a Dragoness' body when the birthing-pangs came upon her. She must protect. She must nurture. There was a little one crying out to her, just a spark of a sweet, alien soul, and it sang to the Dragoness' fire-soul with the beauteous melody of her mother's fire, as pure as starlight.

Egg-sister, the Dragoness whispered. Soul-sister. Obeying instincts so deep they transcended words, the unborn hatchling sang again:

Silver-fire, be mine. Steal me away,
Let her pain be mine, is my vow,
May we be one.

Drawing a cloak of silver-fire about her according to the magic she had perceived in her mother's mind, the unborn Dragoness transformed.

The shell stood empty. Never cracked, never born, lying between two others which also remained whole but filled with Dragon-life. An ethereal draconic presence winged away over the Island-World, questing.

Lia awoke weeping for Grandion. As Flicker would have said, shards take it! She dashed her tears away. Control. Why was she always behaving like a mawkish teenager when it came to that Tourmaline troublemaker? No wonder people thought her cute and frivolous … but thoughts of the Dragon paled as Lia became aware of a portentous heaviness upon her spirit, not linked to Grandion, but to the melancholy dream–a dream of immedicable loss and hurt, a mother's abandonment of her precious clutch.

The room was too still. Where was Elki?

Before she knew it, Hualiama flung aside the covers and rose smoothly to her feet, blade in hand. Shoes. Daggers. She corralled her wild hair with a headscarf.

She cast about the inn, calling her brother names in Dragonish she had learned from Flicker and his fascination with all things vile and disgusting. No sign of him, even in the busy downstairs. Pensively, she approached the innkeeper, a portly fellow who looked as though he and a tankard of golden Sylakian ale were the best of friends.

"Have you seen my brother?" she asked. "Tall, thin fellow. Pointy ears."

"Aye, him?" The innkeeper's three chins wobbled together. "Left 'bout an hour ago, lady. Two women with him."

"Where'd they go?"

Lowering his voice and hiding his mouth with his hand, the man whispered, "Try the Luscious Sow. Two roads over, north side of the city. Them women have a business preying on strangers."

Fire crackled in her voice. "You allow their kind in here?"

"Can't keep watch on every customer, lady," said the man, drawing back in alarm.

She exited the inn at a healthy clip. Quick, bearings. Hualiama set off at a run, her feet pounding the boards up to the first crossroads. Carousing, drunken laughter, shouts and curses rent the night air. How had she slept through this? Stupid brother! When had he started seeing strumpets?

Lia knew Elki was in trouble. She felt it like cold oil sliding along her bones.

Two roads later, she stopped a couple singing at a street corner. "The Luscious Sow. Where can I find it?"

"Sweet lady like you don't want that place," slurred the man.

His companion slapped him, and screeched, "Keep yer eyes to yerself, husband! That way, lady. And leave my man alone."

Well, she'd take whatever help she could get. Hualiama sprinted away.

A fire blazing brightly in a metal bowl advertised the delightful premises of the Luscious Sow. Men and women danced in the mud around the fire to the tuneless wail of the Sylakian triple pipes and a hand-drum. Putting a hand to her dagger, Lia slipped past them and into the building. The din inside was incredible. No sign of Elki. She pushed through the crowds, yelping as a vulgar hand pinched her behind. Upstairs? Had to be. Lia forced her way to the stairs, ruing her diminutive stature as not being much use in boorish, ale-soaked crowds. At the top of the stairs, a man lurked in the shadows.

"Have you seen a Fra'aniorian-looking man come up here with two women?" she asked.

The man looked her up and down as though she was a sweetbread he intended to sample. "What's it to you, lady?"

"He's my brother," she said.

"Been naughty, your brother?" drawled the man. "Through there. Last door at the end."

Hualiama had an inkling of what he intended. Three breaths later, a squeaky floorboard alerted her to the fact that she was being followed–even above the tavern's roar, she picked up his tread. Lia focussed her senses. Muffled voices. A groan–Elki's? She heard the breathing of at least five or six people in that room as she made her light-footed approach. Now, the thud of fist against flesh.

That sparked her fire. Lia kicked the door open with her foot, as it was already ajar. Her eyes leaped to Elki, tied to a chair, lolling as blood dribbled from his mouth. Two women huddled in a corner, scared … she somersaulted up and over a hammer arcing toward her stomach. The Nuyallith blades whispered free of their sheaths, striking a half-breath after she landed, left and right simultaneously. Lia cartwheeled to her left. Two miniature crossbow bolts whispered past her flailing limbs to bury themselves in the torso of the man who had been torturing Elki. He doubled over, losing interest in the battle.

She whirled. Her glance took in two more men lurking in the shadows, besides the one out in the corridor.

Lia knew she should not cross the space in front of the door, but Elki was vulnerable. Dive! Lia rolled awkwardly into the space behind her trussed brother. Seizing the solid wooden chair-back, she yanked Elki toward her. Another quarrel plunked into the wood beneath his right thigh.

She reached into her bodice.

Mister Crossbow out there was still winding up his weapon when a dart found his exposed bicep. He convulsed as the powerful poison took effect. Lia stalked the last two men. One fled past her strike. She hacked into the door-frame as he dived through. The second man was not as fortunate. Lia expended her rage on him with a swooping dragon technique, and yanked her blades out of the lifeless body before it struck the floor.

"Elki, dear one–"

"Crummy brother, aren't I?" Blood dribbled out of his mouth. "Got drunk, stupid …"

Drawing her dagger, Hualiama severed the ropes lashing his hands and torso to the chair. "Easy, Elki. What did they want? Jewels?"

"Information," he gasped. "Do you know a person called … Raz … Razzal?"

"Razzior?"

Even ahead of her brother's confirming nod, Lia's breath whooshed out of her lungs in a pained wheeze. No! The Orange Dragon had found them! Should she be surprised that some beast among the Dragon Elders did not want to see the Tourmaline Dragon return? Stupid, naïve Dragonfriend! Pray Razzior was only casting his net, and that an invisible hook was not already reeling them in.

They had to flee. Now.

* * * *

Mizuki's wish held true for Hualiama and Elki as they fled Sylakia Island four hours before dawn. A stiff following breeze filled the spinnaker. Sylakia's massive cliffs raced by on their starboard flank. Thankfully, dark clouds crowded overhead, reducing the visibility to what should have been a dangerous minimum. Patched by his sister's hand, Elki resembled one of her early engineering experiments, Lia decided with a bleak chuckle.

"So, you don't see that promontory up there?" Lia pointed.

"How many days are there in a week?"

"Nine, why?"

"For the tenth time, no." Elki winced. "Ouch. Mustn't smile. I do not see what you see. You're definitively and irrevocably weird."

Lia grimaced in return. "Before I definitively do irrevocable things to the position of your head on your shoulders … Elki, please. What's happening to me?"

His hand moved to find hers in the dark. "Scared? Aye, I'd be. You swallow down an Ancient Dragon's fire thinking nothing of the effects?" Lia bit her lip so hard, she tasted blood. "Amaryllion admitted he couldn't separate his fire from Flicker's gift. The true weirdness is what he said afterward, that whatever you're born to be is even more important than the fire he gave you. Besides, what's wrong with seeing in the dark? It's a splendid gift, which merely enhances your all-round awesomeness."

"What do you want, brother?"

"Ooh, don't make me laugh. Hurts …"

"Teach you not to listen to your big sister." But she squeezed his fingers sympathetically. "We're flying into the proverbial Dragon's maw–Merx."

Elki chuckled hollowly. "Let's hope your prediction is less accurate than mine about wanting a Dragoness."

Fair winds hustled them across the wild northern reaches of Sylakia Island, so that by dawn, the black granite cliffs were drawing aside to allow the rising suns to strike them full abeam. "Syros." Hualiama pointed far to the northeast. "That must be it."

Elki squinted and offered a grunt of negation.

Lia groaned, "No …"

"Aye. Either my eyes have grown weak in my old age, or … shall I pilot while you sleep, sister?"

"You're injured. Rest."

"The last thing I need is you mothering me on this voyage!" He mussed her hair fondly. "Sorry. Why don't you set our course and catch a few winks yourself?"

Lia could not sleep. She fiddled with the sails while Elki, who could apparently sleep for the both of them, snored like a purring dragonet. She must not think of Grandion. If she experienced another waking dream, she might end up flying them straight into the side of an Island. Instead, one of her and Flicker's favourite songs, albeit a melancholy one, came to mind. She sang quietly:

Alas for the fair peaks, my love, my fierce love,
Alas for the scorching winds, which stole thee away,
Let my soul take wing upon dawn's twin fires …
And fly to thee.

Most of the Island-World's denizens would think it insanely inappropriate for her to be singing such a song, the soul's cry of a Dragon and Dragoness pining for each other. This first verse was the Dragon's lament as he mourned the scorching winds which had stolen his third heart away, his Dragoness-love. Then, the Dragoness replied:

Alas for the long leagues, my song, my soul-lost song,
Oh alas for fate's grieving, my tears a fiery rain,
Let my soul take wing upon dawn's twin fires …
And fly to thee.

Hualiama rubbed a knuckle rather fiercely at the burning sensation in her eyes. No. The draconic way was not to weep and wail and mourn and rail, even if the ballad she sang exposed her deepest longings. She must be strong–stronger than Razzior, stronger than her father or Ianthine or even her fate, and certainly, stronger than the pain of loss, the secret grief a person could conceal all their life. Perhaps six years of imposed forgetting meant that the remembrance should come the more powerfully upon her now, for she had not dealt with her bereavement in the ordinary way.

She slumped back on the pilot's chair, enervated by an unforeseen outpouring of magic. From the White Dragoness' scale she wore around her neck, Lia saw the fiery form of a dragonet emerge. He seemed to smile at her. An invitation.

Mercy. She was going crazy.

Impulsively, Lia addressed the spectral fire-creature. *Tell Grandion, I come.*

Just that. Simple words, but the utterance of hope demanded no edifice of eloquence.

The fire-creature opened its muzzle and voiced a plaintive cry which seemed to shiver between the winds of the world. It raced away over the eastern horizon where Lia saw a momentary flash of light, before all became preternaturally still.

Let my soul take wing upon dawn's twin fires …

* * * *

… And fly to thee.

In the darkness, a Dragon stirred. He barely remembered who he was. Yet a strange shiver trickled along his long-unused wings, teasing the sensitive membranes with the memory of wind flowing in forceful flight, glimmering like forgotten fire along the tracery of arteries and veins criss-crossing the great flight surfaces, and burrowing beneath his scales with the insistence of a thousand scale-mites all scrabbling at once.

A troubled groan forced its way between his chapped lips.

What was that–a memory of a song once sung? This cage consumed all magic, for it had been built by Dragons for the containment of Dragons, but with that signature touch of magic–surely, an incendiary spark delivered deep into the forgotten depths of his belly–like the sluggish progress of a cooling lava flow, the workings of mind and body rekindled. Malnourished, clothed in the forever-darkness of his blindness, the Dragon knew nothing of the redeeming light of the twin suns, even when it blazed for an all-too-brief two hours daily through a tiny hole in the top of his cage. All he knew was its precious warmth upon his back. Warmth upon his back …

Alas for the far shores, my heart, my third heart,
Alas for the stars, illuming thy doom.

The Tourmaline Dragon's neck-vertebrae creaked and popped alarmingly as his long neck jerked. Coveting the light of a presence he had long given up hope of, and concealed in the most inviolable depths of his third heart, his muzzle gaped open to vent a cry of haunting distress:

GRRRRAAAAARRRGGGH!

* * * *

Hualiama cried, "Grandion!"

"Sorry to disappoint you, but it's only your dear brother." Elki clasped her shoulder. "You were moaning fit to wake the dead … great Islands, Lia, you're so cold!"

"The fire left me," she whispered, appreciating her brother's embrace. "I felt him. I felt Grandion, Elki, and he was so lost, and cold and alone … how can a Dragon lose his fire, Elki? What's wrong with him?"

Elki's expression made it clear he was more concerned about what was wrong with his sister. But he shooed her gently off the pilot's chair. "You're stretching yourself too thin, short shrift. Now, take your orders like a good girl. For the love of–oh, roaring rajals, I'll just say it then–for the love of Dragons! Get some sleep."

Hualiama rubbed the gooseflesh on her arms crossly. "Elki! Don't say things like that."

He sang, "Love, love, love. My sister's all about love."

Ridiculous man! She smiled at him. Even if he said things that shivered her world, turning it white with magic, she still loved him.

"There's power in voicing the forbidden, isn't there?" And

he laughed, not without an undercurrent of unease, "I'm starting to sound as mystical as Mom–freaky. Now, what do you make of that Dragonship astern? Just a trader, right?"

Lia narrowed her eyes. "Aye, their markings make them a trader out of Cherlar, I believe. Wake me when something exciting happens."

Finding a sunny spot at the front of the basket, Lia curled up like a cat and fell asleep. For once, she did not dream.

Waking as they sailed by the improbably square-cut outline of Syros Island, Lia sipped water from a gourd and peeled a tinker banana. "Thanks for piloting the day away, beloved brother. I needed the extra sleep."

"Oh, I whiled away the hours singing songs, braiding my lovely locks and dreaming of Dragons," he teased.

Lia coloured hotly. "Listen here, monkey mischief, I think that fiery Copper Dragoness took quite a fancy to you, handsome *specimen* that you are."

Well, that made two of them blushing away like a volcanic suns-set. Lia scanned the far horizons, batting away persistent concerns about what she intuited regarding the Dragoness' intentions with regard to her brother, before her gaze lingered on the trailing Dragonship. It was no nearer, but no further behind either. She did not like it. Time to deploy a few sails and blow them away like dust.

Come morning, the Dragonship was still there. Closer.

Elki employed one of Lia's swords as a mirror to help him trim his beard. "They're making good speed for a trader, aren't they?"

"Very good."

"I fear neither man nor beast, for my sister's the best Dragonship pilot of Fra'anior Cluster."

Hualiama favoured this with a withering glare. "Aye? Do I know thee, thou suddenly complimentary Prince of the Towering Volcano?"

"Fine, o irresponsible imp, who boasts the temper of a rajal with a wasp stuck up its left nostril, and whose hair that resembles an unwashed goat's pelt. Better?"

"No! I'm pedalling."

"Oh, what are you peddling, most winsome of wenches?"

"WENCH?" Her roar staggered Elki and it also hurt her throat. Hualiama dropped her gaze, thinking, 'Mercy … the magic's turning me into a freak.' She grumbled, "Sorry."

They spent the day in a curious, silent race. No amount of adjusting sails or feeding the turbines gained them a single foot. The trailing Dragonship drew closer–given as it was five times their size, they could probably afford fifteen men at a time on the manual turbines, fondly called the back-breaker, working in hourly shifts. Over a long haul, Hualiama knew their extra power would prove decisive, unless the wind picked up. There was neither sign of wind, nor of a handy squall in the cloudless skies. If that Dragonship was a trader, she was a bearded goat. The decreased distance allowed her to make out twin catapult emplacements, unusually, placed on a frame alongside the side-mounted turbines, and three war crossbows spaced in front of the forward crysglass windows. No trader packed that much heavy weaponry–perhaps a smuggler, but that made them a rajal's whisker short of pirates, in her opinion.

All they needed to see now was the red rajal pennant of a pirate.

Overnight, the chase continued. Come dawn, with the Dragonships a hundred leagues east of Syros in the vast gap between the Islands, the pirates showed their colours. They were just a few hundred feet astern and gaining every minute.

"Up we go," said Lia. "I've read that there's more wind at higher altitudes."

"But doesn't the cold reduce our lifting power?" asked Elki. "Won't we burn too much fuel?"

"If we run out, we'll burn your favourite shirt," she replied. "Set aside three cords of wood and bring the rest over here."

Carrying thinly to them on the wind, a voice cried, "Stand to!"

Hualiama growled, "Stand frigging nothing. You let me aboard your Dragonship, I'll beard the bunch of you." She caught Elki, wincing, stroking his facial hair. "Ready? Hold on."

She smacked the turbine controls and hauled in the sails simultaneously. The Dragonship lurched into a rapid ascent, landing Elki in a heap atop the firewood. The gap opened rapidly as the more manoeuvrable solo Dragonship powered aloft. Far from complaining, her brother began to hand firewood up to her as the airship's nose pointed at the sky.

The pursuing vessel tilted upward. They distinctly heard the beat of the turbines pick up.

"Pray for wind," said Hualiama.

Four hours later with no improvement in the wind, the bigger Dragonship ran them down. A little man hopped up and down on the forward gantry, between a dozen or so heavily-armed fellows, screaming, "Stand to! Stand to!"

To a man, they wore an unfamiliar style of banded armour, and had long, raven-black hair that they wore tied at the base of the neck with a leather thong. Their slant-eyed, steely regard came from faces high in the cheekbone and pinched in the cheek, and their skins were noticeably sallower than her tan Fra'aniorian tones.

"Shall we warm up the hunting bow?" asked Lia.

"Down!" Elki pulled her down as a six-foot crossbow quarrel buzzed toward them, puncturing the sack just above their heads.

"The next one will burn you with fire!" yelled the man.

"Odd little fellow, but he does have my full attention," Elki drawled. "Where's he from, do you think? Are they all that small in the East?" Cupping his hands, he shouted across the divide, "What do you want with us? Piracy is outlawed among the Islands."

"I don't see any Islands," came the answer. "Now, stand to and prepare to be boarded, for I am the dread pirate-lord Qilong, scourge of twenty-two Islands!"

Elki stiffened, trying not to laugh. From the corner of his mouth, he whispered, "Am I mistaken, or did he just extol the size of his manhood?"

"*Qi*long," Lia chortled. "And, only twenty-two Islands? Not much of a pirate, is he?"

"He's the pirate aiming a bushel of weaponry at us," Elki

noted. "That gives him all the bragging rights, in my opinion. Now, we're not carrying much of value apart from you, my infinitely precious sister–" he quirked an eyebrow at Lia "–so why don't we just talk nicely to him, and hope he'll let us go?"

"Aye, because when he learns we're runaway royals of Fra'anior, he's not going to want a ransom, oh no."

"Oh. No."

"Indeed. I've a better idea. We're going to board him."

"My ralti-stupid sister is planning to *attack* a pirate vessel stuffed to the eyeballs with vicious, bloodthirsty brigands?"

Hualiama puffed out her cheeks. "I knew the compliments wouldn't last. Aye. That's my plan."

From fifty feet aft and below them, the short, dark-haired pirate cried, "Qilong, masterful pirate-lord of thirty-six Islands, demands you stand to, or he shall feed your sorry carcasses to the windrocs!"

"Not the sharpest stick in the bundle, is he?" said Lia. "Hold on, and when I say hold on, do it properly this time."

Shutting off the flow to the turbines, Lia punched the release for the spinnaker. She let out the side-sails, and gripped the emergency gas release. The effect was as if she had thrown out an air-anchor. The pirate vessel was steaming along happily when their intended victim stalled in the air. As the larger dirigible surged beneath them, Lia yanked the gas release cord. *Shweesshhh!* The balloon deflated as though torn by a Dragon's claw. They dropped right on top of the enemy vessel's hot air sack.

The Princess of Fra'anior rapidly uncoiled a length of rope and tied it to one of her Dragonship's hawsers. "Make sure I don't pull us right off the top, alright?"

Elki's lips curled as though she had force-fed him a mouthful of rancid haribol fruit. "Lia–"

"Dread pirate-lord of ten Islands?" she yelled.

"Aye, I'm Qilong!" came from below.

Lia wound the rope about her right wrist, crossing it several times to prevent slippage. She gripped the free end in the same hand. "Let's hope this works as planned."

Orienting on the sound, she ran over the nose of the pirate

Dragonship and leaped into space. The rope snapped taut, wrenching her forearm, but the armoured wristlet could resist worse punishment than a rope-burn. Lia swung back in, accelerating with the drop, drawing her knees up to her chest. She sped right between the crossbow emplacements.

Hualiama had a half-second to revel in Qilong's shocked expression before she kicked out, booting the dread pirate-lord of an uncertain number of Islands right through the forward crysglass panels of his Dragonship.

Chapter Eleven

The Men of Merx

SHARDS EXPLODED IN Lia's face as she and the pirate-captain smashed through the crysglass, which thankfully was a thinner, inferior variety compared to the reinforced type used by her father's Dragonships of war. The momentum bundled her over his body. Hualiama fetched up against the helm, a wide, spoked wheel under the command of a man-mountain, quite the largest Human she had ever laid eyes upon. Despite the coal-black of his eyes, his orbs appeared to blaze at her from their narrow slits in his rotund face.

Quick. Shaking glass out of her hair, Lia reached for Qilong.

Her head jerked backward as something snagged her hair. An irresistible force hauled Hualiama into the air by her braid. Dangling, she still attempted a swipe at Qilong, but missed. She swung instead for the huge man, but he blocked her strike with a forearm which had to have an inch of armour wrapped around it. The Nuyallith blade spun from her numbed fingers.

"What shall I do with the little dragonet, master?" rumbled the man.

Qilong picked himself up gingerly, evidently ruing the force of that kick. Lia reached at once for her daggers, but an arm the size of her torso clamped her to the man's chest. Mercy, she had no idea how many sackweight he weighed, but it had to be at least ten of an undersized royal ward. She was helpless.

"Who dares attack Qilong, frightful pirate-captain of thirty-nine Islands?" wheezed the pirate captain.

An Ancient Dragon's name burned inside of her. Perhaps it would not be the smartest move to rip apart the Dragonship which kept them above the Cloudlands, however. If they had hydrogen sacks amongst the hot air sacks, then she might just finish them all in a suns-hot fireball.

She blustered, "Desist from this attack, Qilong, or I shall use the force of my magic to blow your Dragonship into the Cloudlands."

Qilong nodded slightly. Just as from the corner of her eye Lia saw Elki descending on a second rope on the port side of the Dragonship's navigation cabin, a huge, meaty paw smashed down on the top of her head. Blackness snatched her away.

* * * *

Lia's eyes fluttered open to behold the opulent hangings of a bed fit for royalty. Four posts reached the cabin's ceiling. The bedframe was swathed in fabric decorated with unfamiliar lake scenes and creatures she had no words for, being part-person and part-fish. The mattress could have served for a Dragon's couch–well, perhaps a hatchling's couch. More worryingly, she found herself shackled hand and foot to those sturdy bedposts, leaving her splayed helplessly in the centre of the vast, plush bed.

Rapidly, Lia took stock of her situation. Her weapons lay on a hand-carved jalkwood desk on the far side of the cabin. Every feature and fitting boasted the utmost luxury, from the fabulous paintings covering every square inch of available wall, to the golden, jewel-encrusted navigational instruments lying beside a magnificently illuminated map, fully fifteen feet long and ten high, that dominated the wall to her left. An oddly shaped sack lay next to the desk. Did it hold a person? A captive, like her?

Elki breezed in through the doorway. "Awake, sister?"

She stared at her brother. No chains, no bruises, and heaps of that attitude which invariably infuriated her and drove his mother up the proverbial Island cliff.

"So, how was your one-woman assault on the splendid

flagship of Qilong's fleet, he who is the most notorious pirate-lord of fifty-six Islands?" As he spoke, Elki casually scratched his ear. No, cupped it. A listener?

Hualiama bit back words which would undoubtedly have scorched the air. "Ill-conceived?"

Elki grinned encouragingly. "And, as a weak-willed female, you tremble in fear of the titanic bane of the Islands, the formidable and enigmatic Qilong?" Lia's tested the chains, but she was well and truly secured. "You abase yourself, puny and worthless female, before his majestic presence, do you not?"

Why the hyperbolic insults? Lia ventured, "I … do. Er, who's in the sack?"

Elki shook his head. "The sack contains another vacillating example of the fragile female kind." The sack made muffled screeches of protest, as though it hid a windroc rather than a person. "Qilong's future bride, I believe. In the sack, so to speak." Lia was not certain, but it did sound as though the sack's inhabitant was making gagging noises. So, she knew Qilong? Perhaps she could be an ally.

"Now, the indescribably mighty Qilong will practice his skills at ravishing ladies upon you, my gentle sister."

Lia's jaw dropped. Before she could protest Elki's rapscallion wink, the door slammed open and the petite pirate captain swaggered in. He wore highly polished, knee-high boots over purple and yellow striped tights. A flowing maroon shirt covered his upper body, so broad and muscular in the shoulder that Hualiama could only imagine that the fates had gifted him that stalwart frame in recompense for his lack of height. Multiple knife-laden bandoliers criss-crossed his chest, while no less than three swords and a war-hammer hung from his broad leather belt.

"I am Qilong, dread pirate-lord of ninety-one Islands!" he roared, standing legs akimbo at the foot of the bed. "Prepare to be ravished, o scrumptious strumpet!"

Blast him, behind Qilong her brother smiled genially, while a selection of Qilong's men trooped in, including the man-mountain who had given her a massive headache. They were not the motley collection of gap-toothed rascals and scraggly-haired ruffians she had expected from a pirate crew. Too neat. Too straight-backed. Lia frowned, but became distracted when the sack hissed viciously. This evidently prompted Qilong to strike another martial pose.

"Behold, my future wife!" he boomed, flicking his shoulder-length, jet-black hair back from his face in a clearly rehearsed gesture.

Lia could barely summon her powers of speech. It did not help that Elki was contorting his face into what appeared to be a selection of the shapes of the known Islands, while the pirate crew, to a man, sniggered behind their hands. Now Elki held a finger to his lips. Be quiet? What in all the hellish fires of a Cloudlands volcano was going on? She was not about to lie about idly while some pirate popinjay exercised his nasty fantasies on her for the entertainment of his crew!

Why was she still fully dressed?

Addressing the bed-hangings with gusto, Qilong demanded, "Declare to me, o weeping maiden, what is the antidote for the poison with which your darts secreted in your … your … um, in there–" he waved in the direction of her left foot "–laid my men low?"

His men had raided her bodice? Her expression must have resembled thunder, because Elki turned as pale as freshly sheared ralti wool. He made a series of increasingly desperate 'simmer down' gestures. So, the men wanted to play games, did they? This Princess had an inkling of how she might turn the situation to her advantage. Hopefully, a few hints Master Ga'athar had given her about Eastern culture might just save her hide.

And she would *destroy* her brother later.

Hualiama pursed her lips. "Oh unimaginably puissant master of one hundred and eight Islands, wilt thou not ravish thy unwilling captive?"

"At once!" shouted Qilong. "Er … what are you doing with your lips?"

"Preparing to be ravished."

His dramatically outflung hand quivered. "What do you mean?"

"Ravishing means we touch lips," Lia smiled. Smirked, really. Perfect. "We exchange saliva."

"Ew!" squealed the dread pirate-lord.

"Of course! Every maiden longs with bated breath for the touch of a terrible pirate's lips upon hers."

Hurt failed to describe what she'd do to Elki. She'd tie his foot to a rope and drag him backwards through a swamp, and may the leeches infest his armpits like clumps of ripe prekki-fruit! She would practise her carving skills on his thick skull until she had a decent trophy she could use as a candle-holder in her room. And that was just a start!

Qilong's expression suggested he had discovered a Dragoness in his bed. "You want me to … no. That's vile!" He screwed up his face. "The diseases I'd catch … no. Unspeakable!"

"Ravish me, o dread pirate–"

With a sob, his courage snapped and Qilong bolted out of the cabin, shrieking in what sounded suspiciously akin to mortal terror. Most of his men filed out after him, sighing or shaking their heads. One remained, who frowned as Hualiama rattled her chains purposely.

"First Mate Genzo, my lady." He bowed curtly in her direction, barely a nod of the head. "As you can tell, we're a pirate vessel of a somewhat unusual nature." Although his Island Standard was heavily accented, Genzo's delivery was grammatically perfect and mellifluous, as though he chose to deliver his phrases with the skill of a trained singer. "The chains must remain. Please accept my apologies in this matter, but His Royal Highness Prince Qilong of the Kingdom of Kaolili might otherwise fling himself into the Cloudlands should he encounter you unexpectedly in a corridor."

Elki offered a typically Fra'aniorian flourish with his bow. "My dearly chained sister, I believe your honour is hardly imperilled in this situation–"

"Apart from fifty other lusty crewmembers, no!" Her sarcasm could have stunned a Dragon. Her brother flushed. "Pray explain about the poor girl in the sack, Elki, if I was to be the appetiser to the main course?"

The First Mate disagreed, "Oh no, the Prince has declared you are his new best love, Hualiama."

The sack fiercely disputed this idea.

"He's enamoured with what he calls your golden sunsbeams hair," Elki explained, drawing a further stifled howl from the other prisoner.

Lia snorted, "If he knew what he was up against–ah. Ahem." Now was hardly the moment to mention Grandion. "So, how can we return his attention to the smelly old sack over there?"

Genzo scratched his short, pointed goatee and grunted, "Don't know. His father will execute us on the spot if His Highness returns without the courage demanded of a citizen of the Kingdom of Kaolili. The girl in the sack seemed a good plan at the time." His despondency was matched only by the person in the sack beating their head repeatedly against the cabin wall. "Turns out she was a maiden, alright, but she hails from a warrior tribe of Eali Island. The pirates we pinched her from planned to sell her to a secret gladiator society down in Sylakia. You know, fights to the death, weaponless women pitted against starving rajals. Barbarians. Wouldn't know honour if it punched out their teeth." He spat accurately on Elki's boot.

The Prince of Fra'anior took this perfectly in his stride. He spat back at Genzo, missing his target, however.

"So," Lia mused. "Would it be honourable if I could convince sack-lady to marry Prince Qilong?"

The First Mate made a universally rude gesture. "You can try. He's an–" he mouthed the word, 'idiot.'

"Maybe a girl-talk might be in order?" Elki suggested. "We let bag-woman out of the sack, she and Lia talk it over, and one of them agrees to … Islands' sakes, that won't work."

Hualiama growled, "At least de-sack the poor thing."

"De-sack? And de-chain? I'm starting to quite enjoy these Eastern attitudes to women," her brother opined.

"Aye, because our Fra'aniorian kidnappings are the envy of Island-cultures the world over. We know all about treating women decently, don't we, brother?" Elki had the grace to hang his head. Lia hissed, "Fine. Qilong can have the warrior maiden chained up with me if he likes. Better than life inside a smelly sack."

The girl who emerged from the sack was tall, as lithe as a serpent, and annoyingly good-looking for an Eastern Islander. She had almond sloe-eyes and perfect skin. Furthermore, her hair was so short-cropped, it could not possibly pretend to be mussed. How did she do it? Lia gazed enviously at the warrior-girl, suddenly aware of the deficiencies in her own appearance, which appeared to have been rearranged by a troop of rabid monkeys. In contrast, the girl appeared to have stepped out of a royal bathhouse rather than a well-used canvas sack.

The man-mountain, who went by the name of Sumio, jauntily whistled his way through arranging both girls on the bed, manacling Lia's right hand to the girl's left, and both to the bedframe. He repeated the exercise with her right ankle and the warrior-girl's left ankle, and then completed a thorough job of chaining the remaining limbs to the respective bedposts. Through it all, the girl was utterly silent. Rather timid for a warrior maiden of Eali Island, Lia sniffed inwardly. The scrolls certainly made them sound fiercer than this wet dishrag.

When the men finally withdrew with an admonishment to 'play nice', the girl shifted her head.

"I am Saori, Warrior of Eali Island. You've dragged my honour through the dirt."

Lia blinked at her waspish tone. "Er, I'm Hualiama, Princess of–"

"Usually, I'd just slit your throat, reach down your royal gullet, and turn your lungs inside-out," Saori continued, her melodious accent making the process sound cheerful and painless. "Given how we're chained together, I think I'll just start by breaking your fingers one by one."

"Well, I'm also a warrior, and … Islands' sakes! Get off!"

Fighting back half-heartedly, Hualiama was more than startled when Saori grabbed her little finger and bent it backward. She struggled and thrashed, but the wretched girl had a grip like a Dragon's fist. Pain multiplied upon pain. One sharp crack and a scream later, Lia found herself surfacing once more from blackness.

Saori growled, "Thought so. You scream like a stuck pig. Call yourself a warrior?"

"You broke my finger!"

"Makes up for the 'poor thing' insult. Shall we continue with 'sack-lady'?"

Hualiama jerked her throbbing hand away from Saori's questing fingers. "You little rajal! I guess you liked it better in the sack?"

"In the sack? You just can't keep your smutty mouth shut, you long-haired whore!"

"Mercy, what's made you so touchy?"

Saori jolted her hand again. Pain stabbed up into Lia's elbow, making her feel nauseous. The other girl hissed, "A slew of abuse, capped by stealing my man!"

"You *like* Qilong?"

"It's a debt." They wrestled furiously, hissing and growling as they fought the chains and each other, but Saori triumphed by dint of hitting Lia's broken finger repeatedly. Twisting the ring finger savagely, she growled, "He saved me from slavery."

Hualiama arched off the bed, gasping, "Curse your stupid honour, you vixen!"

"Here goes the second finger," Saori warned, forcing the digit in the wrong direction.

Blood squirted into Lia's mouth as she bit her tongue inadvertently. Saori was relentless. Surely only a Dragon could be so strong? Being handled like this, especially by another girl, swept Lia beyond fury, to a place where anything seemed possible and the need to escape the pain overrode all reason. Imagining the Tourmaline Dragon, she convulsed as though struck by lightning from afar.

Grrraaaaarrrgggh!

Her roar echoed Grandion's, a smaller thing altogether, but the sound was infused with a wild, draconic strength. Suddenly, her left hand was free. Lia swung her fist across her torso. Blue light flared in the room. Flesh sizzled and the bedclothes burst into flame. She gasped, half in fright and half in amazement. Heavens above and Islands below, what had she just done?

Saori could not even scream. Her jaw hinged open and shut soundlessly.

The cabin door smashed open. Elki rushed in, followed by Genzo and a knot of pirates.

"What the–" Her brother sprang atop Saori, beating at the flames smouldering beside her left flank. "Pillow-roll!" he shouted, snatching one up to snuff out the fire.

Elki's eyes flicked to the trail of smouldering blankets and barbecued flesh, taking in a blackened painting on the wall, and then swung back to fix on Lia's left hand.

Hualiama shook her hand violently, trying to douse the unearthly halo of blue light. "Mercy!"

Saori yelped, "Get me away from this madwoman!"

* * * *

The moon Iridith rose in stately majesty ahead of the twin suns, eclipsing the eastern horizon until finally, the first golden slivers of true dawn glimmered past its edges. Golden spears radiated across the Island-World, crowning the previously dark brow of Merx Island in a glorious array of lime green and auburn treetops. Lia had never seen an autumnal forest display before, for Fra'anior's volcano made the climate tropical all year round. She leaned moodily on the Dragonship's gantry railing, and tried to ignore the clinking of manacles linking her ankles and wrists.

So much for trust.

Blame them, when she could not trust herself? How was it possible that in extremity, she had channelled Grandion's power? Lightning had spurted from her fingers. She flexed her left hand. Ordinary, Human fingers. 'Enchantress' was the whisper, a moniker sure to earn her a swift dagger between the shoulder-blades.

Hearing a soft footfall she turned, expecting Elki. Her face fell. Saori.

The tall girl limped over, dragging her own set of chains, and settled against the railing alongside Hualiama. "How's the finger, Princess?"

"Improving. How're the burns?"

"Improving," Saori returned dryly. "What do you see out there?"

"Dragons swarming over Merx like wasps disturbed from their nest."

Saori said, "The Merxians fight like ghosts from the deep forests and caves, in ways my people would regard as dishonourable. Your brother tells me they've perfected a type of mobile giant war crossbow which fires bolts up to twenty feet long. That's like throwing trees at Dragons."

There was a lengthy, awkward silence.

"Princess, can I touch your hair?"

"What?" Lia swung away from the railing, clenching her chained fists despite the pain it caused her broken finger. "Wouldn't you rather have a couple more fingers to break?"

There was a tautness in the girl she could not fathom. Hualiama wished her face could crack into a smile–amused or fake, it hardly mattered, for she hated to shun anyone. Intending to hurt them, she only hurt herself. That was Lia. But this windroc had been set against her from the beginning.

She muttered, "I've the impression that if I made the same request, I'd more safely explore the inside of a starving rajal's mouth with my hand."

"You're so unlike us," Saori breathed. "Hair as untamed as a Cloudlands-bound torrent. So many words. Master of your own Dragonship. Such a freedom from stricture, tradition and honour."

"I have honour!"

"Then honour my request."

"Ah … Islands' sakes! I can't even pretend to understand you."

Responding to Hualiama's reluctant nod, Saori reached out a slim hand and touched her hair. A tiny smile played about her lips, an unconscious sigh seemed to waft out of her very soul. Lia stood frozen. This was an Island beyond bizarre. She could stand alongside another Human being, and know less of them than she understood of the legendary realm of Herimor, beyond the Rift.

"Your turn." Saori guided Lia's hand to her short-cropped hair. Again, she sighed. Was Saori was making some sort of romantic overture? Hualiama removed her hand as quickly as possible, not wishing to feel those soft bristles ever again.

Lia wet her lips and asked, "What're you doing?"

"Breaking taboos." The other girl spread her hands apologetically. "In our culture, long hair in a woman is a mark of shame and degradation, a sign that a face must be hidden from view. We shun the face veil, unlike most Eastern Isles women."

"In ours," the Fra'aniorian Islander responded, "a shaven head is the mark of a prostitute. Sorry. But they shave their hair to avoid diseases carried by head lice and fleas."

Saori laughed curtly. "I don't suppose we'll ever be friends, will we?"

Lia shivered. "I doubt it."

"Too bad. The Prince speaks highly of you."

"Qilong?"

"No, your brother."

"Elki?" she squeaked involuntarily. The sheer nerve of this sadistic tramp!

While Lia fought for control, Saori said, "Could a Prince ever like a girl like me?" Lia flushed hot and cold, robbed of words, but the Eastern Isles warrior added, "I tell you this, because as his sister, you should be the first to know that I intend to make him mine."

Hualiama managed only a graceless, incoherent splutter by way of reply.

"I could never wed Qilong. But your brother …" Saori blushed delicately. "He shivers my Island, o Princess of Fra'anior. There can be no other for me. What say you?"

"I-I-I … I'll kill you!"

* * * *

To watch Saori and Elki tiptoeing around each other was like lying beneath a waterfall and allowing the flow to pound her brain into prekki-fruit mush, Lia decided. Everyone knew

Saori was making moon-eyes at him. Nobody admitted it. Nobody knew what Qilong would do if he found out.

Cold-blooded murder was not a Hualiama character trait. Besides, it was too much fun to watch Elki behave as if he were entirely oblivious to Saori's intentions. Was her brother such a fine actor? Or was he truly head in the clouds, feet floating above the Island? Even his sister could not tell. She should definitely not enjoy how much his behaviour appeared to torture the Eastern Islander, should she? Nor should she be so mean-spirited as to occasionally draw Saori's attention to the splint on her little finger, a silent threat.

Qilong had not made his intentions regarding his captives clear, nor had he dared to raise so much as an eyebrow in Lia's direction.

Instead, flying the white flag of an envoy–a diplomatic flag–Prince Qilong's Dragonship dropped into a deep ravine which housed Merx's worst-kept secret, the massively fortified entrance to the Human-inhabited cave-system, and the Dragonship's unusual crew found themselves chugging toward a sight that drove any thoughts of her brother's admirer clean out of Lia's head.

Dragon battle!

Or was it? She saw a fantastic snarl of Dragons on the ground and in the air, Dragonships, and Human troops holed up in caves firing the enormous crossbows Saori had referred to at any Dragon that dared to brave the restrictive airspace. Why were the Dragons fighting each other? Why were there metal hawsers spanning the quarter-mile-deep ravine, if not to snarl Dragons in flight?

"Full reverse!" bellowed Qilong. "Get us out of here, now!"

Fireballs hosed the cliff where the men of Merx hid their weapons. Not two hundred feet off their bow, a Dragon spun in the air, speared through his torso by one of the tree-trunk quarrels. Lia clutched her chest in horror, almost as though she had felt the impact in her own person. Why would the Dragons risk an attack against such a heavily armed fortress? She scanned the scene as their Dragonship shuddered, struggling to change direction.

There. "No!" Lia sagged against the railing.

Saori, blast the girl into a Cloudlands volcano, thrust a shoulder beneath her armpit. "What? You're hit?"

"Noo … down there."

Bait. She saw bait, in the form of a days-old Green Dragon hatchling squirming and squealing beneath a heavy net the Merxians had staked to the ground just outside one of their caverns. A Green Dragoness stalked them, but the men held her at bay by threatening the hatchling with their spears. Two more hatchlings cowered behind the Dragoness' wings, clearly distressed, mewling and hiccoughing the beginnings of fireballs. Maddened beyond reason, Dragons stormed the ravine, trying to reach the trapped hatchling, but they had to cross a terrible field of fire to reach the ravine's bottom.

Her gorge rose. This was perverse, threatening a hatchling to lure other Dragons to their doom. Before she knew it, Hualiama shook Saori off and lurched into the navigation cabin, where Qilong stood in his customary wide-legged pose, barking orders at his men.

"Please!" The Fra'aniorian Islander cast herself at his feet. "Qilong, please–"

He startled. "I am Qilong, dread pirate-lord–"

"Mighty Qilong! This is wrong. I beg you … I have to go down there and save that hatchling. Please, Qilong. Show your mercy. Let me go."

Saori suddenly fell to her knees beside Hualiama, and pressed her forehead to Qilong's right boot. "Display the greatness of your magnanimity, o mighty Qilong, terror of one hundred and seventy-one Isles. Free the worthless Fra'aniorian, that she might prove her mettle in the fires of battle, or perish in misery and shame."

Lia hissed sidelong at Saori, "What are you doing?"

"Giving you a chance to die."

Chapter Twelve

An Old Flame

SAORI THRUST ELKI backward with the palm of her hand. "You do the Princess dishonour."

"I prefer my sister alive, thank you kindly!"

"You've not the first understanding of our ways," the tall girl blazed, her dark eyes as hot as lava pits, and her body positioned inflexibly to deny Elki's advance.

Hualiama slid her Nuyallith blades home in their sheaths and lifted her Haozi hunting bow. "I'm ready."

Aye, she was sick of being chained, irked at being the risible Qilong's captive and more than ready to be chasing her Dragon across the Isles. But Lia would rather die than turn her back on that hatchling.

"Can't a fellow follow ten paces behind?" Elki insisted. "Can I fire an arrow in my sister's defence without ruining some ridiculous Eastern honour-code? She's … breakable! Not half as invincible as her stubbornness suggests. Lia! Stop!"

Hualiama gripped the rope Qilong's men held ready for her. As the Dragonship reversed back up the fern-fringed ravine, away from the battle, another Dragon tumbled by their starboard bow, its left wing clearly broken between the second and third wing-joints. It crash-landed heavily, a slap of flaccid flesh against stone, and did not rise.

"Leave it!" snapped Saori, thumping the Prince in the chest with her chained hands.

Elki howled, "I will not! You stay right where I can see you, short shrift, or I swear–"

"I love you too, Elki, but I need to do this," said Hualiama.

Saori added, "In our culture–"

The Fra'aniorian Prince snorted, "Culture? I'll show you culture! Where I come from, when we want to kiss a woman, we do this!" There was a short, shocked pause. "And to the windrocs with the consequences!"

Speechless, Saori seemed torn between dissolving into a puddle of tears, and wishing to slip a dagger into Elki's chest.

Elki growled, "Obstinate wretch. You provoked me."

Qilong clapped his hands happily. "Ah, a fine demonstration of barbaric Western customs. Perfectly decadent and worthy of a dread pirate-lord."

Departing from a tableaux which could she have painted it, would have fetched a princely sum, Hualiama swarmed down the long rope, letting the tough cord rasp against her wristlet to control the speed of her descent. The cool depths of the ravine could not dampen her fire. The rage in her breast demanded to be unleashed, like the swollen, hail-pregnant black clouds that loomed over Fra'anior Cluster before a thunderstorm broke. An alert stillness pooled in her being. She took in the battle's details, absorbing through her pores and nostrils the scents of mossy rock and Dragon fire, and the acrid stench of the Green Dragons' highly acidic spit. Her ears attuned to the madness of feral Dragons. She palmed an arrow from her quiver, ready on her right hip.

Touch down. Lia sprinted across the slippery boulders of the riverbed, as nimble as a dragonet. She knew she would approach from behind the desperate Green Dragoness. Were she that Dragon, she would destroy any Human within reach. Arrow to the bowstring. Curse the still-tender finger, safely ensconced in its splint. Great Islands, how that Dragoness filled the narrow ravine-bottom with a mountain of gleaming draconic scale-armour! A tight-knit squad of ten soldiers faced the Dragoness, armed with spears and tall metal shields. Two Merxians menaced the hatchling, while another squad waited nearby, their eyes fixed on the battle higher up in the ravine.

Over the bunched boulders, Hualiama saw the tip of a crossbow quarrel orient on the stricken mother Dragon. She must hear Lia's footsteps approaching from behind. The Dragoness was more concerned with her hatchling.

Instantly, the Human girl changed the angle of her attack. Shouting, *Murderers!* Lia ran up the Dragoness' back to use her as a springboard, vaulting skyward to find an angle for a vital bowshot. Her arrow ricocheted off the boulder just ahead of the crossbow, and sprouted miraculously from a soldier's helmet.

A huge green paw swiped at her. *I'm a friend!* Lia cried, flexing her legs to take the impact.

A what? The Dragoness blinked as Hualiama skidded off the two backward-facing 'thumbs' of her paw and dropped awkwardly beneath the Dragon's neck. *You're a Human.*

Sinking to one knee, Lia sighted along her arrow at the soldiers menacing the hatchling. *I am the Dragonfriend.* Her shot sped true. It did not penetrate her target's breastplate, but the shot's power knocked him clean off his feet. Her follow-up arrow darted barely an inch aside from a shield-boss as a soldier tried to throw Lia off her aim. The second spearman threatening the hatchling clutched his shoulder, and collapsed.

"Get the girl!" roared the leader of the green-clad Merxians. Their feathered helmets bunched as the men drove forward in a tight formation.

You deal with the catapult and those men, Lia called to the Dragoness.

The Green Dragoness blinked her nictitating membranes, clearly confused at fielding orders from a Human.

Lia taunted the soldiers, "Can't catch me, slow-slugs."

Hurdling bushes and bounding over boulders like a cliff-goat scenting a hunting rajal, the Nuyallith-trained warrior evaded their spears and charged across the fifty yards or so separating her from the second squad of soldiers and the trapped hatchling. Fire! She dived aside to avoid the splash of a stray fireball. Two of the soldiers were less fortunate, and were roasted in their armour. Behind her, the Dragoness roared an earth-shattering challenge.

Still flat on her stomach, Lia drew and fired a reflex shot into the catapult-crew, exposed by her new position. If that twenty-foot, metal-tipped quarrel struck the Dragoness from this short a distance … she howled as a spear-point lanced into her right buttock, while two more spear-tips pinged off rocks near her right hand. Rather than stand and run, Lia dropped her bow and rolled, coming up with a Nuyallith blade in either hand, the right held clumsily–Islands' sakes, was the little finger so important to a proper grip? This inane thought sneaked into her mind as she witnessed the Green Dragoness rear up, and simply drop her belly atop the squad of soldiers.

Who cared about elegance or style? She grinned. *Awesome!* Spinning, Lia launched herself at the crossbow crew, briefly startled to hear an incoherent but clearly female battle-cry coming from further up the ravine. Then, Elki's well-known voice, shouting the ancient monkish battle-cry, "For the Dragon!"

The Dragon! Oh, the Great Dragon! Amaryllion's fire boiled in her veins and fizzed in her ears. Destroying the team of crossbow engineers as though a tornado had ripped through their little emplacement behind the boulder, Lia reversed direction, scanning the battlefield. Three more squads of heavily armoured Merxians approached along the ravine floor, marching in close formation, showcasing the awesome discipline they were renowned for. Four men ran toward the trapped hatchling. Here came Saori, unchained, wielding a type of long dagger unfamiliar to Hualiama. She ran gracefully, her long legs scissoring across the ground. Elki thundered along in her wake, brandishing his sword with far greater zeal than skill. The pair crashed into the closest knot of soldiers with a crunch that made Lia wince.

Lia skimmed across the tops of three large boulders in succession, almost airborne as she bore down on the Dragon hatchling with her swords upraised.

Fear not, little one, she called.

My baby! The Dragoness screamed as Hualiama pounced upon the soldiers, her twin swords blazing with fire, red and blue mingled into an intense purple as they crossed briefly. Perhaps the Green Dragoness thought Lia intended to execute her baby. Acid spit rocketed past her left shoulder, striking one of the soldiers squarely in the face.

Refusing to look at the result of that acid attack–the sounds were hideous enough–she clashed with the remaining trio instead. Lia danced around the hatchling, her swords cleaving armour and bone. Nuyallith techniques flowed from her body like a river of molten lava–the rajal pouncing, a sideways snake-strike, the two-handed cleaver to finish off the final soldier. Lia winced, holding her leg where a glancing hammer-strike had cannoned off her kneecap.

She hobbled over to the hatchling. *I'm a friend, see? Don't be afraid.*

Despite being a hatchling, the several weeks-old male Dragon was twelve feet long and stood as tall as her shoulder. He blinked at her. *Mama fire-eyes?*

Your mama's coming, my flame-heart. Be strong! Fire your courage.

With a mighty blow, the Princess sliced through a good four feet of netting. Though the hatchling snarled and tried to spit fire at her, she marched around to his forepaws and began to cut them free. Those squads were too close. A crossbow quarrel fell from above, right on the hatchling's tail. Lia yelped as he made an involuntary snap at her, snagging her wristlet with immature but needle-sharp fangs.

MY BABY! The Green Dragoness' pounce took her right over Hualiama, rolling her in a flurry of wings and paws and a jarring blow to her hip.

A deeper rumbling sound, however, undercut the sounds of the soldiers' boots tramping in strict time. Lia gasped as a section of the opposite ravine-wall tumbled away, revealing three war crossbows and a catapult concealed in a flat cave entrance. The engineers rapidly oriented their weapons on the melee down on the ravine floor.

Now a high-pitched whistling rose over the sounds of battle! Lia knew that strange, ululating sound … it cut into her eardrums–*wheee-yyiiii-boom!* Hualiama recoiled as an entire squad of soldiers vaporised before her eyes. One moment they were marching, the next, even their armour and weapons exploded into a thin, crimson-and-silver mist. What Dragon power was that?

Take cover! The Copper Dragoness Mizuki hurled herself at the crossbow emplacements, while the Green did anything but take cover. Mizuki sprayed the advancing soldiers with Dragon fire somehow mixed with acidic Green Dragon spit–or was this her special attack once again? Shields drooped over the soldiers' arms. Their flesh boiled. Lia felt a wash of magic as the Copper Dragoness swiped her forepaw across the emplacements, blew up the catapult with her weird vaporising attack, and took two crossbow quarrels directly against her chest without flinching. Stone skin? She had encountered that skill when fighting the Roc. That Copper Dragoness had more tricks stored in her belly than an entire Dragonwing of Blues. Freaking awesome!

Dragging her attention back to the fight, Hualiama charged out from behind the Green Dragoness and barrelled into the remaining squad of Merxian soldiers.

Mizuki roared at the Green, *Protect your younglings!*

Elki at her right shoulder, Saori at her left; they pounded the soldiers, who closed ranks and stood their ground grimly.

"Slow retreat?" Saori suggested.

Dragon-rancorous, Lia snarled, "Have I demonstrated my courage yet?"

"Oh, stop with the bickering already!" But Elki howled as Mizuki plucked him deftly out of her way, before whirling to vanquish six of his foes with a mighty snap of her tail. With his free arm, he threw her a jaunty salute. "Timely rescue, o mistress of might."

Retreating, Hualiama cast about for her Haozi bow. Mizuki's eyes whirled as she set the Prince down. The Dragoness said something to Elki which made Saori's face darken, before she turned with massive, gleaming menace to start hosing down the ravine with fireballs, clearing their escape route. A few stray spears and crossbow quarrels rained down upon them as Hualiama, Elki and Saori sprinted after the departing Green Dragoness, who had all three of her hatchlings on the move as she fled the scene of the battle.

How had that hatchling been trapped? Which Dragons in their right mind would attack the famously impregnable fortress of the Men of Merx?

Now was no time to sit and ponder the lay of the Islands. She bolted.

* * * *

Having made good her escape and returned to Qilong's Dragonship as promised, Hualiama found herself the subject of another insane argument in the navigation cabin as they made their best speed away from Merx. Mizuki had stayed behind to protect the Green Dragoness and her hatchlings. The Human Dragonship fled like a fat turtledove fleeing a hundred hungry hawks.

"I will not bind that wound on your hind parts!" Saori growled. "It's shameful. Ask your brother."

Elki, seated while First Mate Genzo bound a burn-wound on his upper arm, clucked his tongue unhappily. "She's my sister, but–"

"I shall treat her alluring buttocks most tenderly," said Genzo, with a gap-toothed leer at the subject of their conversation.

"You may eat my sword," the royal ward glared at him, reddening. She began to unsling the Haozi hunting bow from its crosswise-slung position across her chest, but stopped. "Saori, at risk of offending you once more, I wanted to thank you–and Elki–for coming to my aid."

"I, the piratical pestilence sweeping over two hundred and thirteen Islands, declare it a most noble deed," said Qilong, unexpectedly joining their group. "I decree it most royally. Besides, if she who is no longer my intended can survive the humiliation of a barbarian's ravishing kiss, she must surely consider the treatment of honourable wounds–"

He broke off as Saori tickled the underside of Elki's throat with her dagger. "Prince of Fra'anior."

"Aye?" Elki squeaked.

"What did that repulsive cultural gesture signify?"

Hualiama expected her brother to start babbling like a laughing dove surprised by a hunting cliff-fox. Instead, he fixed his grey eyes on the Eastern Islander. The corners of his mouth curved upward in a slow, quirky grin that even his sister had to admit, was not unhandsome. Though Elki said not a word, Saori seemed ensnared. The Eastern Isles warrior's hand began to tremble. Her entire arm shook. A blush began at her collarbones, raced over the pulse suddenly fluttering in her neck, and exploded into her face.

Softly, the Prince said, "*That's* what it signifies."

"Oh," Saori whispered.

Grandion had once electrified her with such a gaze. Lia's own heartbeat escalated, thudding so loudly she was certain everyone knew the tenor of her thoughts. This was how the Tourmaline Dragon had melted her fears and her resolve, how taboos came to be trampled upon and the ways of two hearts–three in his case, of course–might dare to fly to treacherous, forbidden Isles. Fighting for calm, Hualiama moved to the starboard crysglass windows. Reason and prudence. Two words her heart clearly refused to listen to. She must crush her soul's song. These feelings would only interfere with her mission to find the Scroll of Binding and return it, together with Grandion, to the Dragon Elders at Gi'ishior.

Her nape prickled. Magic. Concealed magic.

Suddenly rigid, only her eyes moved as Hualiama scanned the storm-dark afternoon sky. One of those strange, low-down Cloudlands storms had rolled in while they were fighting at Merx. Now, the storm front seemed to reach from the heavens above to the Cloudlands below, a massive rampart sweeping in from the northwest, consuming the Islands like a rolling avalanche. The weather had been too hot. Qilong's orders had them racing for Tarxix, a small, usually unmarked Island lying forty leagues east and a few compass-points south of Merx. There, they must take shelter, for to be caught by those clouds spelled certain death.

But something else lurked out there. Something as deadly as the storm.

She called, "Brother, will you come here a moment?"

"If the warrior-maiden has finished shaving my beard," he said, by his cheerful tone clearly oblivious to the premonition curdling her innards. "What is it, short shrift?"

Lia had never been more grateful for his strong hands on her shoulders. "I sense something out there. Hold me if I fall."

Without waiting for any sign of assent, she pushed her senses out into the space around their Dragonship, already ten leagues out of Merx and five miles above the Cloudlands as they made their top speed. What had triggered her alarm? She saw nothing. She sensed …

Ah. I feel your presence, little one.

Elki's grasp saved Lia from an inelegant collapse. That voice! She knew that voice!

Before she could cage it, a mental wail slipped free, *Razzior!*

Aye, Razzior. The slow, crackling whisper filled her mind. *I failed to burn you once, clever little Princess. I shall not fail again.*

Lia curled against Elki. No. No, no … not him, the brutal Orange Dragon, scarred like Ra'aba … even by his mental touch she knew he possessed the power of *ruzal*, for it ignited a dark flickering within her own being, an involuntary reaction to his dominant, hateful cry.

Brethren, we are discovered.

"Lia. Lia!" Elki shook her by her shoulders. "What is it?"

"Razzior."

"Razzior?" he echoed. "Oh, roaring rajals, no …"

"Not rajals." Hualiama pointed aft, off the port side, where Razzior the Orange and his Dragonwing had materialised from thin air. Less than a mile separated them. "Roaring Dragons."

"Suffering volcanic hells, that's at least two dozen Dragons," Elki swore. He abruptly shook her again, harder than before. "Snap out of it. Short shrift, you swallowed the power of an Ancient Dragon. What're you going to do? Make a plan. Hide us? Shoot us across the Island-World like a comet? Escape? Knock those flying reptiles out of the sky?"

Heat detonated in her belly. Aye. There was one chance, and Elki had just voiced it. "Elki. How secure is that solo Dragonship up top?"

He glanced guiltily at Qilong. "I loosened the moorings …"

"Great!" Lia clouted her brother on the shoulder.

"Ouch, darn it, for a guppy you've a punch like an angry

Dragon."

Saori said, "What're you two planning?"

The Dragons swooped in with terrifying speed, making at least thirty leagues per hour. They would be overhauled in moments. Hualiama rattled, "No time to explain. Razzior's the Orange at the head of that Dragonwing. He tried to kill me before. I'm pretty sure he and my father are trying to overthrow Sapphurion and the Dragon Elders, with the heartening aim of restoring draconic rule and Human slavery to the Island-World."

"Your father?"

"Saori, not now."

"I'm coming with you," said Elki.

"No. You need to save this Dragonship and everyone on it. The only person aspiring to commit suicide is me. I need to get up top. Now."

Qilong said, "What're you going to do?"

"Stuff your ears, alright? Block them in layers of cloth, you and all the crew. Get three men on the wheel. Secure everything you can within two minutes, and damp the engine fires. It'll be a rough ride–I hope." Lia stood on her tiptoes to press her lips to her brother's cheek. "Fly strong and true, brother. Love you."

"You too," he gulped.

And then she was out of his arms and through the doorway, darting to the nearest hawser that would take her up to the sack. Razzior powered toward the Dragonship with strong, sure wingbeats. He had nothing to fear. Two dozen Dragons against one Dragonship? Easier than swatting a mosquito. But the Orange Dragon did not know what he was dealing with–hopefully. Lia only prayed she could summon the power she had summoned before, without destroying the Dragonship she stood upon. Would it buy enough time to escape? The black storm-front already rolled beneath the Dragonship, she saw, perhaps three miles beneath their position. From afar, the dark, massed vapours appeared deceptively calm.

Lia climbed rapidly, yet when she turned, Razzior was only

two hundred feet abaft the Dragonship.

His fangs gleamed against the backdrop of darkness. *Ah, so good to see you again, Princess. No escape this time. No hiding places out here, between the Islands.*

What do you want of me, Razzior?

She had to brace her stance against the wind's buffeting. Hualiama's long platinum strands whipped about her face as she tried for a confident glare, for the same audacity she had unexpectedly discovered when speaking to the Dragon Elders. This time she enjoyed no terrace lake brimming with courage. Razzior was right. Either her ploy would work, or the Island-World would be rid of one pesky royal ward and an airship full of Humans.

The Dragons slowed and spread out, confident of having cornered their quarry. Yulgaz the Brown was present. All told, fifteen Reds, five Greens, two Browns, a Blue Dragon and Razzior the Orange lined up off the Dragonship's stern. When it came, the firestorm they could produce would rival that Cloudlands storm churning beneath them.

Razzior grated, *War multiplies across the Islands. My power grows. Soon, I will uncover the precious Scroll of Binding the Tourmaline failed so miserably to track down. With that knowledge, I shall compel all Dragons to join our new age of draconic dominion and justice.*

She said, *I will not allow it, Razzior.*

Great Islands, and now he cracked that smile that reminded her so keenly of Ra'aba, it seemed to Lia that it was her father's lips forming the discomfiting, disdainful curve of Razzior's muzzle.

You won't allow it? the Orange guffawed, and most of his Dragons with him. *You and what Dragon army? I see one pathetic little Human ensnared by my trap on Merx, and an everlasting drop into the Cloudlands. My fire-stomach holds a special fireball which shall wipe one bothersome Human, and the threat of the prophecy, off the face of the Island-World. FOREVER.*

As he thundered 'forever', flame roared around his fangs and nostrils. There was so much power and heat in him, the entirety of Razzior's body smoked. Lia did not wish to find out what that power portended.

Where was the magic? Would it not come? Yet even as she fretted, a faint tingling began in the mastoid bones of her ears. Without warning, an excruciating pain blossomed in her chest, a pain of fire uncontainable, a summoning of magic from across the vast leagues of the Island-World, gushing into a frail Human vessel.

Razzior's eyes bulged as he evidently sensed the massive force of magic concentrated in her breast. *What is this?* He bugled, *Burn her! Burn the Human, my brothers!*

An inrush of air developed across the divide between the Dragons and the Dragonship, as the massed Dragonwing drew breath to stoke their Dragon fires.

Lia fell to her knees upon the soft, resilient air sack. Spreading her arms, she opened her soul to the knowledge of magic. Staggering. Breath-stealing. White tendrils of flame seared her vision. Below, many leagues away in the Cloudlands, she saw the smoky outline of a great Onyx Dragon. Amaryllion? Could it be that he lived?

She meant to cry, 'Begone!' But as the massed fires of twenty-four Dragons roared out of their long throats, their hatred spoken in tongues of flame, a different word emerged from her breast to resound across the deeps. It rocked the Islands upon their foundations.

BEZALDIOR!

* * * *

Grandion's head snapped about so sharply that his neck-vertebrae popped with a series of sharp reports. His years-long blindness had caused his other senses to become extraordinarily sensitive. But he needed no great sensitivity to detect this perturbation. Stronger than the first two, it shivered every one of his scales.

She had become powerful. He whispered, *Hualiama.*

Her name was a breath of cool air in his foetid underground cage. Her presence soothed the futile rage that had augmented in his chest since waking to the realities of his incarceration, and caused a clearer, whiter flame to flicker within his flame-soul.

Her. The inexplicable song of his fire. The source of hope long forgotten. She burned ever closer. The Dragon found that by holding an image of Lia in his mind, he could begin to keep the cage's insidious, magic-denying power at bay. Deny the denier. The smoke of grim amusement belched from his nostrils. Ordinarily, a Dragon would take pleasure in the sight of his own fire or smoke. Grandion had to settle for sensing the prickle of particles upon his sensitive muzzle-scales, and listening for the unique properties of smoke-laden air swishing past his ear-canals.

What quality of a soft-skinned, hatchling-helpless little Human could so capture a Dragon's regard? He had long pondered this question. The only conclusion he had reached with adamantine certainty, was that her power stretched beyond the power of an oath to bind his third heart, and that she caused the great arteries of his throat to throb with life. Her. A slip of a girl. Why did the rippling of her hair bewitch his eye? Why did her laughter resonate with his belly-fires? How did the softness of her perfect hide, the wondrous, multifaceted hints of her scent, cause a Dragon's talons to wish to curl about her with delicate yet unbreakable custody, and make her his own?

No Dragoness had ever moved him as Hualiama did.

How his shell-father had raged. Sapphurion had betrayed his son, and condemned him to a quest every Dragon knew was an invitation to a guttering of his flames upon a faraway, forgotten Isle. How easily the Tourmaline Dragon had allowed himself to be brought low.

Now, his fires dampened almost to darkness. He was blind. Helpless. Weaker than a new-born, yolk-slick hatchling. Who was dependent now? Bound for years in a cage of unbreakable Dragon bone, what use was he to any beast under the twin suns? Hualiama would not have him. She must not. Grandion felt as though he had swallowed a bilious boulder of shame into his food-stomach, the second-most important stomach for Dragons after their fire-stomach. No, his fate was desolation.

Yet, she drew nearer, and he knew it was for him that she

came.

A Dragon should know no fear.

Chapter Thirteen

Storm

STUNNED, RAZZIOR AND his Dragon-kin tumbled toward the Cloudlands. But Hualiama had no chance to celebrate. The power of her cry slewed Qilong's Dragonship violently, a twisting motion that knocked her solo Dragonship loose from its sabotaged moorings. Lia had half a second's warning as the basket and balloon tumbled end-over-end toward her. She collected a bruising blow upon the back of her skull before toppling helplessly off the stern, past the rear turbines.

This time, there would be no Grandion to catch her.

Her brilliant plan had been to stand on the curve of the Dragonship's sack, knowing that ripping her throat out to perform the magic would blast her backwards. That part had worked perfectly. Being struck by her own Dragonship–less perfect. She was fortunate not to have broken her neck.

Wriggling into a facedown, arms and legs outspread position, Hualiama looked about for the Dragons. Her eyes watered at the wind's force. Razzior's group had to be a quarter mile away, falling with flaccid wings and lolling necks. She had knocked an entire Dragonwing that far across the sky? Mercy. But her own Dragonship was falling faster than her. The stove had been cold for the better part of a week. There must still be some hydrogen left in the inner sack, but much would have leached away.

Tucking in her arms and legs, Hualiama tipped her feet up and her head down. The acceleration was immediate. Unholy windroc droppings! Lia whizzed down to the sack, stretching with every sinew in her body to snag one of the lashings on the port-side mast. Never had she been so grateful for rope-burn on her fingers. Pulse pounding, terror and adrenaline continued to fizz in her veins as she swarmed along the ropes and into the basket. Hualiama checked rapidly for damage. Half of the wood was missing, but the stove appeared to be intact–mostly.

Great. So she would just light up in the few seconds left before the storm engulfed her.

Think, girl! Throwing herself at the controls, Lia deployed the side-sails at the vertical, and then by degrees, adjusted them to brake the Dragonship and bring it into a gliding configuration. Of course, a twenty-four foot balloon had all the aerial prowess of a large, stubborn rock, but its sheer bulk provided useful wind resistance. The turbines! Pedal! Lia started her legs moving while her hands fumbled with the stove door. The wind kept slapping it shut. She jammed her splinted little finger, howled a string of nonsensical but nasty words, and stuffed handfuls of wood chippings inside.

She stole a glance over her shoulder. This time her throat corked up with a mixture of anger and trepidation. Razzior's Dragonwing had evidently begun to recover, but not soon enough. Battalions of clouds rolled over the Dragons. Hopefully they would end up at the bottom of the Cloudlands. The royal ward knew she had problems of her own. Abandoning the pedalling, she shoved both of her hands into the stove and clacked the spark-stones together fervently. Come on! Catch on something, sparks! Casting about, she snatched up a strip of dry bark and bundled that inside. *Click. Click.* Yes!

The wind snatched her long hair past her face, almost into the stove's hungry belly. Lia clipped the stove door shut, trusting that the small curls of flame would take swiftly to the kindling. What supplies did she have? Almost none. She pushed two water gourds beneath her pilot's chair and found a stray prekki-fruit that still looked edible. She shoved it down the front of her tunic.

One moment she was in the clear, and the next, damp darkness enshrouded the Dragonship. Streamers of cloud whipped by on the wind, which caught the balloon and tossed it in a new direction–more southerly, toward the fabled volcanic ramparts of Franxx–said to be the tallest mountain in the Island-World–at least a week's sailing under ordinary conditions. But these were far from ideal conditions. Dank, cloying gases rose with the storm blast. The rigging thrummed tunefully. Quickly, she eased the sails to reduce the strain. Lia tightened the additional, double-stitched sails aloft to allow the vessel to run freely with the wind. Now she could see just how flaccid the balloon was, for the blast dented it severely. The frame she had designed began to buckle under the stress.

"Come on, you beauty!" she yelled. "Fly the storm!"

Lightning split the darkness. She had never imagined flying like this–after all, who was foolish enough to fly a dirigible in a storm? Only one desperate enough. One pursued by Dragons. Just then, Razzior's words struck her. Ensnared on Merx? Did that mean he had arranged the entire battle with the Men of Merx, and the trapped hatchling … with the intent of flushing her out? The storm was not cold, but Hualiama shivered so violently she almost tossed a chunk of jalkwood overboard. Razzior knew what she could do, for she had revealed her greatest power. Lia could not imagine how the Orange Dragon might use that knowledge against her, but the ice in her bones told her, he would. Aye, most surely.

As the dirigible bobbed away like a cork tossed by black, foaming waters, she could only pray her brother and Qilong's Dragonship crew would be safe. Had she done enough? She felt responsible for her younger brother. She should've turned around and kicked him out at Fra'anior.

Lia whispered, "Those who play with Dragons …"

* * * *

Night or dawn, it made no difference. All she knew of the Island-World was the darkness of shrieking winds and flurries of stinging hail which drummed against the balloon as though she fled from great catapults loaded with cold metal pellets. Perhaps she was higher–that was the reason for the cold. The sack had filled, eventually. The Dragonship flew on a more even keel, canted at thirty degrees from the vertical due to the fickle wind's buffeting. Lia eked out her pitiful and now soaked supply of wood, and nibbled cautiously at the prekki-fruit. She dared not sleep. Already, the overstressed rigging had snapped twice on the starboard 'wing', forcing her to clamber out to affix new triple-strong lines or face being spun about helplessly, a leaf caught in an eddy.

Lia measured days by the growing knot of hunger in her belly. She sucked on wood chips, but that only made her belly shout louder. She could only guess where in the Island-World she might end up. When, one night, she realised the fingers of her left hand had frozen together, she had to sit on the hand to unthaw it. Tears of agony rolled down to her chin, and froze there like a ridiculous goatee. When she found a sack containing a handful of maggot- and weevil-ridden grain tucked beneath her dwindling woodpile, Lia performed a silly dance right there in her basket.

She burst into a rowdy ballad she had learned from Qilong's men:

A handful of mouldy bread, my Island love,
A crazy dragonet and a cooing dove,
Is all we need for the flowering of…
Lo-ooo-ooovve! Aye, lo-ooo-ooovve!

Maggots, weevils and all, she munched every last grain. She needed the nourishment.

Days passed. Hualiama sank into a delirium of occasional activity, rousing herself to throw another jalkwood chunk into the stove, forcing her numb fingers to check the lines one more time. She searched the basket at least fifty times for any further scrap of food, but found none. Once, the clouds rolled apart to reveal unbelievably tall, jagged mountain peaks so close at hand she felt she could reach out and touch them–the very next second, rock ripped through the bottom of the dirigible basket and took with it the stove, the pilot's chair, most of the control lines, and very nearly her left leg as she leaped aside. Only the safety line she had rigged kept her safe.

Lia stared through the hole at the mountain peak below. Franxx, perhaps? Then the storm closed in and tossed her across the Island-World once more.

She tried to fix the sails, but the last of her spare rigging lines had been lost. The Princess found herself holding imaginary conversations with Amaryllion, remembering how he had told her about a time in his youth. 'The Cloudlands were not always present,' his dry, vast voice resounded in her memory. 'I remember gazing down from the peaks to the floor of the world, occasionally revealed through the mists, to see Land Dragons sporting there.'

Did she remember rightly? Then how had toxic gases come to fill the oceans between the Islands?

Lia knew the Dragonship was losing altitude. She lashed herself to a hawser, too weak to imitate a monkey in the rigging any longer. She slept, or slipped into unconsciousness for periods of time. Days later, a dark, rain-lashed Island heaved itself out of the Cloudlands directly ahead of her. It moved with majestic slowness, a moss-slick carapace with luminous bands she estimated at a mile long, slowly rolling beneath her Dragonship, until near the far end of the creature a pair of caves vented a phenomenal blast of moist, warm air that tossed the Dragonship way, way up into the breaking storm. A Land Dragon? She must be dreaming. Was it dawn? Or suns-set? Her sense of direction had been lost to the storm.

"Ho, Island-biter …" she moaned. "Aren't you a legend?"

Beyond the creature lay another Island. A real Island. Galvanised, Lia tugged on the ropes to attempt to steer the Dragonship, but she missed that Island and swept over to a smaller, mountainous Isle. She had to land. Using her Nuyallith blade, Hualiama slashed the balloon open. Warm air hissed against her face. Suddenly, shouts came to her ears. The Dragonship scooted over a group of hunters, on a collision course with a small tent-camp hidden at the base of a group of towering trees.

She could not have aimed better had she spent months practising the manoeuvre. With a series of splintering crashes, the Dragonship tore a path right through the middle of the tent camp, piling up at least six tents on its nose before slamming to an abrupt halt against one of the trees.

Lia groaned, and heard other groans amidst the wreckage. She was alive. Grateful tears squeezed between her eyelashes.

Voices approached, speaking Eastern Dialect. Angry voices, querying which fool had thrown a Dragonship from the sky and were all the children safe? That much she understood. Hands found her snarled up in the rigging.

"By the Rim!" someone gasped, releasing her arm. "A foreigner."

"A warrior," said another voice, one accustomed to command. "Look at these weapons."

"This is a Haozi hunting bow," said another.

"Ancestors protect us, have you seen this hair? Such a wealth of shame!"

"You spit words like a cobra, Iyumi," said the commanding voice, switching to Island Standard. "This is a Western custom. She is not one of us. Observe these ears. The girl hails from Fra'anior Cluster, or I miss my mark."

Superstitious muttering filled Lia's hearing. Someone said, "Rajal ears?"

Hualiama dragged her eyes open. Hard warrior-faces, all women's faces streaming with rain, surrounded her. Fingers worked at her lashings, trying to bring her down from where she hung alongside the balloon. But she had eyes only for one person.

Reaching out, Lia gasped, "Saori? How …"

The woman flinched. Then she seized Lia's hair in her fists and screamed, "What do you know of my Saori? Where is she?" She shook Lia until she felt like a cliff hyrax trapped in a rajal's jaws.

"Go easy on the mite, Naoko." An older, iron-haired woman pushed between them. "Even the spirits speak, given time."

The woman called Naoko relented, but not for long. She

began to bark orders, all the while shooting dagger-glares at Hualiama. They lowered the Fra'aniorian Islander now. A huge woman stooped over her, scooped her up with the ease of a Dragon, and took her to a warm place.

* * * *

Much later, as the unfamiliar birdsong of the Island's eventide cheered the encampment, Lia awoke with a Dragon's hunger snapping in her belly. For the first time in what seemed like weeks, she felt warm and comfortable. Rising from a pallet covered by an unusual, soft blanket, Lia padded around the tent's neat central fireplace to peek out of the flap.

A solid arm halted her. "Lie down."

Hualiama decided that there was little point arguing with a giant–for a giant this woman was, two heads taller than her, and wider than three of Lia stood shoulder-to-shoulder. Her eyes must have betrayed awe, for the woman laughed, not unkindly.

"I'm Miki of the Ippon people, the giants of the East," she said. "Lie down, girl. You're as sore used as a tired drumskin. I'll bring you food and those eager to examine the innards of your brain."

"Ah–thanks."

Mercy. What manner of people were these who numbered giants among their kind, and whose trees dwarfed the nearby low hills? Lia peered around a little shyly at the encampment, taking in men caring for and playing with happy children or cooking over open fires, before Miki's meaningful glance sent her scurrying back to her pallet. Was she their prisoner? Although someone had removed her weapons belt and the shoulder-harness for her swords, her weapons lay in a neat pile at the head of her pallet. One Nuyallith blade was missing–the red one. A terrible loss.

Lia had barely shuffled closer to the fire, drawing the blanket over her too-thin shoulders, when the tent-flap jerked open and Naoko ducked inside, followed by the gruff older woman and a handful of other warriors. They arranged themselves around the fire, kneeling, but there was nothing subservient in their manner. Eastern clothes. Cord-bound leggings, unfamiliar cloth for the clothes, shorn hair …

"Well?" Naoko demanded.

The older warrior threw her a quelling scowl. "I'm Akemi, Saori's grandmother. Please, speak of her fate–is our Saori alive, or does she live among the spirits? Honour us with your tale, girl. What is your purpose here?"

Wetting her lips, Lia said, "Where am I?"

"A small Isle called Brezzi-yun-Dazi, a day's flight southwest of Haozi. What of our–"

"Saori's alive," Hualiama assured them. "At least, I last saw her alive near Merx Island aboard the Dragonship of Prince Qilong." Stony silence greeted these words. "As for my purpose, I hunt a Dragon."

Before she could blink, steel menaced her heart. Naoko growled, "You *hunt* a Dragon?"

"I … seek a Dragon," Lia corrected hastily.

The short blade did not waver an inch. "A soft foreign woman flies across the Island-World in search of a Dragon?" Naoko's eyebrows rose toward her shaven skull. "I suppose you expect us to believe you commune with the Dragon-spirits, and that the Blue Moon is in truth a vast prekki-fruit hanging in the sky?"

Hualiama chose softness for her reply. "Honoured Naoko, is it not a saying of these Islands that one must first know one's enemy, before deciding exactly how to despatch them to the spirits?"

Akemi said dryly, "It is, youngling. Are you our enemy? A Dragon hunter?"

Miki entered the tent, holding a bowl of fragrant-smelling soup, but she paused at the tense scene. Then, her broad face broke into a smile. "Food before fighting, ladies!"

Ignoring the giantess' attempt at humour, Naoko pressed the blade's point against Lia's breastbone. She snarled, "I'll have answers before wasting precious dragon pepper soup on this snake-tongued foreigner!"

"Ah, the growl of the daughter repeated in the mother,"

said Lia, forcing out a chuckle. "Before she knew me, Saori broke my finger. She was Qilong's captive. He had stolen her from a slaver near Sylakia Island and intended to marry her. Do you know Prince Qilong?"

A chorus of snarls and spitting on the ground assured her that they knew the same Qilong she did.

"Anyways, Saori appears to have fallen for my brother instead. Could I please taste the soup, Miki? My stomach's gnawing its way down my legs as we speak."

"Sounds exactly like Saori–or my Naoko," said Akemi. "A family of hot-peppers, we are. Speak, girl. Is your brother worthy of our Saori? Which Dragon do you seek, and why? For you must know that our people venerate Dragons, and these my kin-sisters will be asking themselves, 'What does a weak foreign woman know of the Dragonkind? Can she be trusted?' "

Hualiama retorted, "How do you measure worth? Shortness of hair?" And they could just stuff that up their collective fumaroles! "My brother is Elka'anor, Prince of Fra'anior. Impressive enough for you?"

Hunger sharpened her words. Or was it the fire speaking? She muttered, "I'm Princess Hualiama, a royal ward of Fra'anior Cluster. Please call me Lia and I … mercy, I apologise for destroying your camp. I'm so sorry. Was anyone hurt?"

"A child has a broken arm, nothing more," said Naoko, accusation writ in every syllable.

"I didn't exactly aim for your tents!"

Naoko snapped back, "I didn't say you did."

Lia glowered at her soup, which had turned the inside of her mouth into a lava pit. She had the impression that even the soup's spiciness was meant as a test. As she stroked her hair deliberately to emphasize her differences from these grim warrior-women, blue sparks flew from her fingertips. Great. Her anger faded. If they venerated Dragons, she would tell them her tale from Amaryllion's perspective.

With studied calm, she said, "When I was stranded on Ha'athior Island, I befriended a dragonet called Flicker and an

Onyx Dragon called Amaryllion, who was the last of the Ancient Dragons. Amaryllion gave me a quest which has brought me to your Island. Which Dragon was it you said you worship?"

Sagging jaws surrounded her. Hualiama decided that a touch of petulance on her part was worth that reaction.

When the stories were told, Naoko and her warriors withdrew to deliberate. Stuffed to the ears with warm soup and delicious bread, Lia drifted off into a nightmare about Razzior burning her and Grandion, both of them lying chained and helpless in a foetid dungeon while the Orange Dragon's cruel, mocking laughter filled the dark halls. She awoke to a hand clutching her shoulder.

Akemi said, "Bad dream? Come, I'll show you where we make our ablutions. Then it's back to the pallet with you, youngling. This day's seen enough fighting with storms, fates, Dragons and Eastern Isles warriors. Even Fra'aniorian spirits demand their rest."

Lia was glad for the darkness to hide her blushing.

When they returned to what she realised was Akemi's tent, the old woman bustled over to tuck her in with an oddly familiar air, as though Lia were her own daughter. She said, "We call this a futon, not a pallet. Comfortable?"

"It's wonderful, thank you," said Lia, meaning it.

As if struck by an afterthought, Akemi turned to the Fra'aniorian Islander, saying, "One thing about your story doesn't ring true, Hualiama. I'm a mother. I know of no mother in this Island-World who'd allow their daughter to pursue a Dragon, alone, across the breadth of the known Islands." Holding Lia's gaze, she added, "Is this Tourmaline Dragon a … *special* friend?"

The Princess knew her face gave far too much away. She wanted to bury its burning in the pillow-roll, but instead, she tried to meet Akemi's gaze with an innocent arch of her eyebrows.

"Besides the fact that the timeline of your story is impossible using any Dragonship technology yet invented," the old woman said, with a kindly twinkle in her eye, "I know a few things about young women's hearts. Keep your peace; hear my tale before you judge me a nosy old woman, for I've a tale to tell. I too have a special friend–a Dragoness called Yukari. If pressed, she'll admit she's an Aquamarine Dragoness and possibly the oldest living creature in the Eastern Archipelago. When I was young, my village on Jaoli Island burned down in a bamboo forest-fire. Yukari tried to save as many as she could, but my parents and brothers perished in the blaze. I was severely burned."

Her rich accent, so strange to the royal ward's ear, caused a succession of vivid images of that bygone time to parade through Lia's mind. Magic? Her words seemed simple enough …

"Yukari took me to her lair, cared for me and healed me. When I was strong again we returned to the site of my village, but the survivors had moved on. My people are nomadic, moving from place to place in the two hundred and fifty square-league bamboo forests of Jaoli Island. I could have spent ten lifetimes searching for them. Though I was but ten summers, I made a decision. I studied at Yukari's paw for two decades."

Suddenly, Lia understood. "You're a Seer."

"Very good, youngling," said Akemi. "Yukari was blind. But as you may know, oftentimes those born with what we regard as disabilities, have greater gifts than our own. Such is Yukari's gift. She would love to meet you. I suspect you'd have a great deal in common. We became friends, and more than friends. Such we still are. That's why I see the fire burning in you. That's why your story, while neatly and cleverly told, does not ring true."

"Aye," Lia admitted.

Apparently unfazed, the old woman changed the subject. "Naoko has a cunning plan. We will trade you to the Warlord of Gao-Tao Island. A prisoner-swap. Gao-Tao lies in the far south, past Haozi. That's where we believe your Tourmaline Dragon is being held. If the rumours hold true, they alone, south of the Lost Islands, possess a cage capable of holding Dragons. We'll trade you for our kin. You convince the

Warlord you have magical powers. He'll feed you to the Dragon."

"Which is when I pray it's Grandion they're holding–"

Akemi nodded. "You'd have to go weaponless, as a prisoner. Is his life–or yours–worth the risk? A chain of risks. Should one link fail, you'll perish."

Hualiama measured the old woman shamelessly with her eyes. "You're planning to keep my weapons here, hoping I'll return to you?"

"Aye."

"What makes you think that Grandion isn't in the north, in the Lost Islands?"

"He might be," said Akemi. "Yukari told me a Tourmaline Dragon had come to her, seeking word of a lost scroll of ancient Dragon magic. She knew of two possible locations, south and north."

Lia said, "Tell me of the north."

"The Lost Islands are another world, youngling. Nobody goes in there, and nobody, to my knowledge, has ever come out. Even their Dragons are said to be a wild breed, different from what we find here in the East." Her restrained delivery nonetheless struck Hualiama like powerful hammer-blows. "They've never been under the command of the Dragons of Gi'ishior. They war constantly against the Humans of the Lost Islands–and I cannot say how the Dragonkind resist the fabled magical power of those Human Enchanters. We call them the Dragon-Haters. Men with power over Dragons, power to dash Dragons against cliffs. Had Grandion travelled north, I believe you would've dreamed of his death."

Only the muted keening of Hualiama's grief broke the tent's stillness.

Extending her hand, Akemi took Lia's hand in her own. Her manner trumpeted dignity, empathy and a searing brand of honesty. "Did you ever play the game of writing on hands, Lia?"

"Aye."

"Some words are too treacherous to be spoken. You believe Razzior seeks you. If he possesses something of yours, he might be listening to this conversation, even now."

The missing Nuyallith blade? Lia could not believe … yet she must. Why had Akemi not invoked this game before, in that case, for now they had revealed their plan to a listening draconic ear, surely? The past was a stream flowing off an Island's cliff, blown to mist by the wind.

With her finger, she wrote on Akemi's palm, *Aye.*

"What is between you and the Tourmaline Dragon, Hualiama?"

She wrote, *Unbreakable, shared oaths.*

"And?"

I rode Dragonback. Akemi's indrawn breath and the involuntary tremor of her hand, betrayed her response. Released now, Lia's words flowed: *He is my Dragon. I'm his Rider.*

Six years have passed, wrote the old woman, her finger trembling with pent-up emotion. *Yet you seek him?*

Hualiama hesitated long before she replied, *I seek him.* When Akemi only shook her head, Lia added on her palm, *I fear much has changed.*

A fragile smile swept over Akemi's lips. Silently, she clasped Lia's hand to her heart. Tears flowed freely down her wizened cheeks. Then she wrote, *The old taboos are broken. We will aid you.*

Aloud, Akemi said, "The reason we live in tents is because of Dragons. There is a new way of war in the East, pioneered by Razzior, who commands the Dragons in rebellion against Sapphurion. The way is total annihilation. Attacking in massed Dragonwings of up to fifty Dragons strong, they systematically raze an Island until all life on it has fled, or is burned to ashes. That's what happened to Eali, my home Island, and Saori's, too."

Again she wrote, *This power of seeing is called a Dragon's Eye. Do you understand?*

He can focus on me?

If you aren't shielded. Grandion will know how … I can protect a little.

Fishing down her bodice, Hualiama withdrew the White Dragoness' scale and held it out to Akemi for inspection. The old woman's eyes danced approval. *Perfect. This will work.*

Using her thumb, Akemi traced a series of arcane symbols upon Hualiama's brow.

As an irresistible power caused her eyes to flutter shut, she remembered whispering, "Why do I scent Fra'anior in your magic, Akemi?"

"Very perceptive, youngling. My grandmother was a Fra'aniorian. Now, draw the cocoon of safe sleep about yourself. May you dream of Dragons."

Only one, Hualiama wanted to say. A Tourmaline Dragon.

Chapter Fourteen

The Dragon Keepers

THE SOUTHERN REACHES of the Eastern Archipelago were aptly named the Dragon's Tail. Swathed in the rich jade of the tufted bamboo forests which garnished a tracery of cobalt-blue lakes and waterways, the Islands beyond Haozi made Hualiama picture a garden designed and tended by Dragons. The Isles faded away to the south and east, like a long, curling Dragon's tail slowly dipping into the Cloudlands.

She saw few Dragons, but the tallest jinsumo trees of these Isles, which invariably crowned the highest mountain or the most windswept cliff-tops with their mighty four hundred-foot boughs, housed many dragonet nests in the nooks and crannies of their fantastically gnarled trunks and branches. Hualiama could never tire of drinking in such sights. She leaned over the gantry of their slim, fast Dragonship for hours on end, when she was not debating the finer points of Dragonship construction with several of the warrior-women who had teased out her penchant for engineering and innovation, or pestering Naoko for stories about Dragons. Saori's mother was a fine storyteller when the mood took her.

Slowly the Cloudlands assumed the jade tint of the Islands, until four days out of Haozi Island, they sighted the rocky fortress-Island of Shinzen, Warlord of Gao-Tao, undisputed ruler of this wild, untouched corner of the Island-World.

In the secret places of her heart, Hualiama whispered, *Grandion. I come.*

Hualiama washed her hair and brushed it out until it

gleamed like a white-golden waterfall afire with magic. She donned a traditional Eastern face veil and suffered her hands and arms to be lashed to a short bamboo pole tucked between her elbows, behind her back. So naked without her swords! A disgraced Princess had no right to feel humiliated.

Taking brushes in hand, Naoko painted her eyes and forehead with great skill to resemble a firebird of Fra'anior, which Hualiama had described to her.

Naoko squeezed her shoulders. "Ready, Hualiama?"

"Aye."

They brought the Dragonship to a landing in a wide open field before the towering, two-hundred-foot battlements of Shinzen's underground fortress, great black granite ramparts surmounted by catapults, war crossbows and flame throwers, amongst other weapons unfamiliar to Hualiama. No person came to greet them. Naoko and her troop of warriors were forced to march up to the mighty, forged metal doors and pound upon them to demand entrance.

The doors rumbled open to reveal a small army drawn up in what Lia realised was an outer courtyard. A portcullis and a dark tunnel guarded the entrance to the fortress proper. But before that stood fifteen ranks of soldiers clad in shining banded armour, bearing halberds eight feet tall. Yellow pennants flapped jauntily in the warm afternoon breeze, matching the yellow suns-blazons on the soldiers' uniforms and neat, round shields. Raising her eyes to the battlements, Hualiama estimated at least a further two hundred crossbowmen standing alertly, weapons tensioned and ready, above them. But her eyes dropped immediately to a tall, broad throne of jade stone upon which a giant of a man took his ease, resplendent in golden armour, his dark hair flowing over his back and shoulders, while an eye-popping arrangement of moustaches and his beard reached midway down his stalwart chest.

The Warlord.

Copying Naoko and her warriors awkwardly, Hualiama knelt in the middle of a courtyard so spotless, she imagined it must have been licked clean by legions of unhappy slaves. For that was her sense of this place. Despair, aye, and a brooding malice as if the flagstones and walls themselves cried out for justice, which could never be found beneath the twin suns. She must keep her gaze lowered at all times, but Lia could not keep from glancing beneath her lashes at Shinzen, especially when he rose from his seat to thump, step by step, down toward his visitors.

Great Islands! Never had she imagined a man like this! He appeared to grow taller the closer he approached. The leather belt bracing his belly was ten inches wide. She felt the thud of his boots through her knees. He wore no weapons, but a man his size had no need of them. Shinzen could wrestle Dragons, she imagined. It was not just a trick of perspective. As he drew close to Naoko, who was no stripling, Lia realised that the Warlord was half again as tall as her. Nine feet tall? More? He stood head and shoulders taller than Miki, who seemed to have captured his fancy, for he leered at her, his teeth startlingly black beneath lips as red as blood.

"Naoko of Eali!" he boomed. "It has been too long. I hoped you had brought me a proper woman to grace my bedchamber–" his thick finger stabbed at Lia "–not some pathetic, foreign waif. I'll snap her like a twig."

As Naoko and the Warlord swapped formal greetings, Hualiama marvelled at the depths of terror she felt. She wanted nothing more than to pull up a flagstone and hide beneath it. Her fear of the man was so visceral, it reminded her of Dragon-fear. Aye, that soul-lost shiver when she considered him … Shinzen had a peculiar brand of magic, dark and malevolent, as if an oily shadow lurked within his prodigious being. Mercy, pray this monster did not choose her for his bedchamber. He would destroy her. Whatever had she been thinking, placing herself in such a man's power?

Naoko said, "She is called the Firebird of Fra'anior, Shinzen. A magic-user, like you."

"Aye?" Shinzen twirled a moustache briefly. "Fine. Bring me the offering."

Grasping the bamboo pole, the warriors dragged Hualiama forward and cast her roughly at Shinzen's feet. He wore open sandals rather than boots, for which they might have to tan an entire ralti sheep's leather, she imagined. She gasped. He had six toes … a vast paw slapped her back, drawing a second, more pained wheeze from the Human girl. Shinzen raised her effortlessly, dangling by her elbows, bringing Lia up to his face for examination. His breath reeked of the garlic these Easterners loved. He must eat it by the barrel-full. Black-in-black eyes fixed upon her, their soul-shadowing power making her feel naked and dirty inside, as though he had already violated some part of her being with a mere glance.

"The Firebird of Fra'anior, you say?"

"An Enchantress of Fra'anior, Shinzen," said Naoko.

His eyes glittered like pits of onyx. "The gift is acceptable. Pray she lives up to her reputation, or we shall have reason to visit you again, Naoko."

"She will please the Dragon-spirit."

"Aye? That beast grows fat on my prisoners."

Lia winced involuntarily as a wailing began in her spirit. No! Grandion was no man-eater. This had to be another, feral Dragon, a beast who supped on the forbidden flesh of Humans … she wanted to scream at Naoko to save her, but Shinzen was already turning to toss her causally at four of his men. Her tongue seemed to be glued inside her mouth. The foursome crashed to the ground with Lia on top of them.

"Release the prisoners to this rabble."

With that, Shinzen clearly dismissed the matter from his mind. He marched away toward the portcullis, bellowing contradictory orders in several directions.

Tossing a cloak over Lia's head, the soldiers dragged her away into the coolness of Shinzen's underground lair.

* * * *

Once she was locked in a cell in a corridor lined with such cells, the four soldiers searched her body with no small relish, before cutting the ropes off Lia's arms and abandoning her to her own devices. Now she was grateful she had listened to Akemi and left all of her more unusual gear behind, save for a few lock picks cunningly hidden behind her belt buckle. Vials of poison or metal files would have been found. Grinning, groping apes! She mentally reserved a special place in her future roost with Grandion just for them. They would make fine footstools.

Could Grandion be a man-eater? What a horrifying thought. Surely not Grandion–but he was a Dragon. They were hardly paragons of mercy.

Underground, there was no marking the passage of time. A servant brought her a simple meal of bread, vegetables and water, but refused to engage in conversation. By the time the four stooges returned, hours later, Lia had exhausted herself in fear and self-recrimination.

"Shinzen will see you, foreign filth," the foremost soldier greeted her.

They conducted the Princess though a seemingly endless warren of tunnels and locked doors to a hall filled with opulent divans, rugs and cushions, where musicians played and acrobats performed, and Shinzen disported himself with his guests. The smell hit her like a clenched fist, exotic spices and sweat and an undertone of strange, oily magic. She tried not to look too hard at what some of the guests were wearing–or not wearing–or to imagine what might be going on in the darker corners of this barbarous, drunken orgy. Thick smoke curled around Shinzen's mighty frame where he lounged on a divan clearly purpose-built for his bulk, sucking smoke up a clear pipe running from a strange, bubbling brazier.

Winding through the crowd, the soldiers brought her before the Warlord and thrust Lia to her knees.

"The firebird, mighty Shinzen."

His eyes were too bright. The Warlord looked her over, before grunting, "Why's she wearing such dross? Foreign filth–no, leave her clothes. Come here, girl."

Hualiama's skin crawled as Shinzen drew her into his stinking, sweaty embrace. She needed to pretend no reticence. "Look," he pointed with the pipe at a trio of sloe-eyed beauties clad in wisps of Helyon silk, who simpered on cue. "Those are real women. What're you planning to show me? Hedonistic practices from your Island?"

"I-I'd gladly d-dance for you, mighty Lord Shinzen."

"Dance? How boring. I've a hundred dancers." He mauled her right thigh with his fingers. "No meat on these bones. What Dragon would want this?"

"I dance with fire, my lord." If only she could shoot a fireball of her own down his throat, Lia imagined, yelping as he squeezed her tightly against his stomach, the Island-World would be a better place.

"Flaming torches? I've jugglers–"

"No. I make my own fire, my Lord. Magical fire."

Suddenly, his eyes narrowed. Hualiama sensed a fearful intelligence there. It was all a sham. Lies and subterfuge. Shinzen was very, very intrigued by her statement and he was not half as drunk as he pretended.

"I'll show you why I'm called the Firebird of Fra'anior."

And then if he could kindly toss her to the Dragon, her life would end at the point of a talon and nobody need concern themselves with the rise of a third race in the Island-World. Perfect.

Shinzen raised his hand languidly, creating an instant hush. "Clear a space. This luckless wench would dance for us." Turning to Lia, he added, "Bore me, and you'll be dancing for my soldiers in the barracks. They'll take any trash, foreign or none. After the first hundred finish with you, you'll be begging for the mercies of my pillow-roll."

His booming laughter chased Lia out into the space between his guests.

Frightened and fired up in equal measure, Hualiama spoke briefly with the head musician, a flute-player who clearly found speaking to a foreign woman a distasteful affair. She settled for *Chasing the Wind*, the energetic yet haunting penultimate dance from her favourite *Flame Cycle*. But she found that the flame had deserted her. Suddenly she was graceless Lia, awkward and unsure of herself, ensnared in the coiling terrors of her own imagination.

Grandion! The memory of his fire slipped into her mind, the day he had burned her in the tunnel beneath Ha'athior

Island. Though flame filled the halls of her mind, her magic remained stubbornly quiescent. She saw Warlord Shinzen yawn. No. His handling repelled her, for a Dragon's paw was all the touch she desired. Frantically, Hualiama sifted through her memories, the dance growing jerky, her limbs heavy … and in a flash, she saw Grandion soaring into a sky dark with Green Dragons. She sensed the Blue Dragon power called Storm swelling in his belly, and gasped as the first sparks crackled off her toes as she extended into a split leap. Touchdown. Here came the fire! Mercy … soaring again, whirling, a shower of sparkling blue. Her audience inhaled and clicked their fingers in approbation.

Joining in the quickening tempo, the Fra'aniorian dancer built up to the finale. She launched her body into the leaps with mounting joy. Grace became her wings, the swirling robes of her fire. The song of her soul escalated, drawing her closer to the fire, her limbs wreathed in beauty, her hair spinning about her like a golden halo as she swung her head in a series of increasingly violent rotations, the death-throes of a Dragon. This she knew. Grief tinged the expression of her joy, the sparks growing darker, through aquamarine to a deep sapphire.

Flare! Arms pointed at the ceiling, blue lightning blasted from her fingertips. Lia leaped lithely aside as masonry exploded from the point of impact. Flare! The crowd yelled and ducked as lightning crackled above their heads.

"Stop her!" someone screamed.

A clean, sharp scent, like the freshness of the Island-World after a storm, struck her nostrils. This was spectacle enough for the Warlord, surely? Her hands ignited as she swept into the complex, rippling passages that spoke of storm winds sweeping over the Island-World, as the Dragon-lovers took their tumultuous parting, separated in body but united in their fire-souls. Lia's feet barely seemed to touch the floor. The stench of burning fabric wreathed her spinning body. Upon every dragonet-light step, blue sparkles burst from her neatly-pointed toes.

"Assassin!" bellowed another voice.

Shinzen began to heave himself off his divan. Halting in the final, dramatic pose, Hualiama's intertwined hands lowered to point directly at the Warlord. Lightning flashed across the space between them, detonating among the pillow-rolls and cushions he used for comfort. Shinzen roared as fire enveloped his massive frame.

Wood spun end-over-end toward her. Pain exploded between her temples.

* * * *

The Tourmaline Dragon flared his nostrils, drawing in the scents of the world outside his cage. Why did he scent ozone, when he tasted no incipient storm-moisture on the breeze? What did all the shouting in the depths of the Warlord's fortress signify? The urgent thudding of booted feet and the rattling of gates and armour? The Dragon took it in uneasily. Great events were afoot.

Could it be the girl?

Later, he heard footsteps approaching the tiny, impossible-to-leave door of his cage. He heard four Human heartbeats, one much lighter and quicker than the others. He smelled the greasy oils adorning freshly repaired chain armour, and heard the clink of weapons. A low muttering, 'Hurry with the lock.' Grandion sniffed in disdain. Periodically, Shinzen's warriors tested him with a warrior or two, and several times, they had provided him with female slaves he assumed had been disobedient in some way. Shunned by the Dragon, the females had all chosen to risk the uncertain destination of the small stream that flowed through the cage. The foul, mammal-sweaty warriors had departed the same way, either clawed, flattened or burned to death.

Was this their idea of feeding a Dragon? He abhorred the taste of Human flesh.

Grandion had not fed in a month. He dreamed of meat, any meat, great slabs of flesh dripping with blood, of the joy of sinking his fangs into a hapless ralti sheep and bolting great, slippery hunks down his throat, of lapping up deliciously iron-rich blood with his tongue, swollen rivers of blood …

This was another Human. He must be strong.

The Human stood near the entrance, its heart tripping along as if to cry, 'I'm here.' Its breathing sounded strangely muffled, but it smelled female. Unmistakably female.

Pacing toward the creature, Grandion hissed, *Hualiama?*

No reply.

If it is you, speak to me. The creature made muffled noises of distress, but as it moved, his ear-canals detached a soft *clink*. Metal. Stupid Humans. A female warrior–of course. He was wise to their tricks.

Grandion spat a low, vicious chuckle. He spoke mentally, *So, little Human. Come to test your courage against a Dragon?*

The petrified Human could not speak. A whiff of mammalian terror-sweat tickled his nostrils most agreeably. Ah. Fear. Acrid fear. His stomachs began to boil with fiery contempt. No, this meant joyous battle. Her weapons against his talons. The Tourmaline Dragon's hearts accelerated, priming his muscles for action. Ever since he had detected Lia's magic, he had begun to exercise again, as much as he was able in the restrictive below-ground space. Although he was half-starved, Grandion incongruously felt fresher than at any time in the last several years. The missing element was his magic. Still, talon and fang would suffice for this trifling task.

He would teach this pathetic Human what it meant to bait a Dragon.

* * * *

As the door clanged shut behind her, Hualiama halted, afraid to run headlong into an obstacle.

The leather hood snugged down to her neck rendered sight useless, and breathing next to useless. Her hands had been twisted up between her shoulder blades, courtesy of her dancer's flexibility, and lashed in place with what seemed cord sufficient to furnish a Dragonship. Her hands were therefore useless. But that had not been enough for the Warlord. Before his men affixed the hood, Shinzen had taken manifest delight in checking the ridiculous gag which corked her mouth more effectively than a skein of wine readied for transport, firmly buckled beneath her chin and in three places behind her head. That rendered her mouth … useless. She could shout about as loudly as a mewling kitten.

All this for someone they planned to turn into a Dragon's snack? Lia would not have wasted the equipment, even if it did honour the Dragon-spirits in some inexplicable way. No single Human warrior on foot could dream of defeating a Dragon, could they? Except one who wielded Nuyallith blades. But she was weaponless, and trussed like a ralti sheep ready for the spit. She could trust the Dragon to light up the barbecue. As the great beast moved, Lia sensed the vibration through her soft slippers, and heard the metallic brushing of Dragon scales against stone. The tiny bit of air leaking up to her straining nostrils brought her the powerful, pungent odour of an adult male Dragon–charred cinnamon and sulphur, and an exotic spiciness that made her head reel.

Lia called in her mind, *G-G-Grandion? Is that you?*

Silence.

Dragonish was the only language which would communicate to the beast. Lia pleaded, *Speak to me, o Dragon. Please. I'm Hualiama, called the Dragonfriend.*

A laugh of booming malevolence turned her bones to water. Oh, mercy, mercy, a thousand times mercy … this was no Grandion. He would never have laughed like that. Despair choked her more effectively than the glob of mouldy material they had packed into her mouth. Draconic smell-memory was like a Human memory of pictures, he had taught her. Dragons could remember particular smells–their shell-mother, the scent of their mate–for decades. If this Dragon knew her, he would know her scent.

Yet how could the Dragon think she came to fight him in this ridiculous state? She was no threat. He must be blind.

Dragons did not forget. Was this Grandion, or not?

"Hmm-mmm!" she called.

A sharp rustling warned her. Lia sprinted to her left, dodging the Dragon's opening pounce. Who cared for the darkness? Her head slammed into a wall, and that was how the

Dragon came to miss his follow-up swipe. The ground shook as the Dragon pounded by.

A pause. They both listened for each other.

Ah … Bezaldior? Bezaldior!

Nothing. Not a whisper of magic, nor even an echo of a whisper. The Dragon's belly-fires growled with subliminal, unending intimidation. Hualiama tried to extend her senses. She sidled along the wall, on tiptoe and breathless, trying not to deal herself another bruising encounter with an unseen obstacle. Perhaps if she neither drew breath nor allowed her heart to beat, the Dragon would not be able to track her–no, he still had his nostrils. What chance did she have of avoiding the Island-World's apex predator in his own lair?

Run!

A Dragon's paw slapped her, flipping Lia effortlessly off her feet. She tried to land and roll, but the Dragon was upon her in a flash. A massive weight settled upon her stomach and legs.

"Mmm!" Lia screamed into the gag.

* * * *

By his wings, the way the little thing wriggled beneath his paw! The flutter of her heart! The trembling of her limbs! The muted snuffling of her breath–it all reminded Grandion so forcibly of prey in the instant before he gutted a creature, that his mind blanked in a pre-gustatory welter of ecstasy. Food! Oh, just a morsel … the sweet burst of bodily fluids upon his tongue, followed by the muscular palpitations of his long throat as fresh kill slid down into his food stomach …

Saliva splattered over his talons and doused her torso.

Smell the food. Another whiff to savour … oh, she was glorious! An aroma as complex and beguiling as a Dragoness' filtered into his astounded nostrils. No Human, slave or warrior, had ever blasted his olfactory nerves to cinders like this.

His prey struggled so deliciously, so defenceless beneath his controlling paw, that a wave of heated pride surged through the Tourmaline Dragon. He was mighty. He was also starving. His stomach had shrivelled to the size of a large nut. It had long since given up screaming at him to be filled. No more scruples about cannibalism of his fellow intelligent creatures. He had to survive. Survival demanded sacrifice–this Human to his appetite, and his ethics to grim reality.

"I'm terribly sorry," he rumbled.

Raising the morsel to his lips, Grandion drew breath to chargrill his meal.

* * * *

Her mouth was stuffed with so much material, Lia knew the Dragon could not understand a word she spoke. Trapped beneath his paw, so much larger than Grandion's had ever been, she knew only endless cloudscapes of desolation. It ended here for a Princess of Fra'anior. She had gambled and lost. This feral beast intended to eat her, for as he raised her in his fisted paw, she knew she would feel the Dragon's fangs next. She could practically taste his hunger, the helpless quivering of a Dragon who had already entered the portals of starvation.

Her magic was dormant. Her Dragonish would not communicate. Was this a key property of a prison capable of holding a Dragon?

Then, he voiced an undraconic apology.

Hualiama almost swooned as the Dragon's voice resonated, it seemed, within the very marrow of her being. Grandion! Her heart skyrocketed upon wings of peerless tourmaline, swooping and playing with him among the Islands. The darkness beneath the leather hood exploded like the birth of constellations in a moonless night.

As the Dragon drew breath, Hualiama's spirit drank its fill from the wells of her exultation, summoning his secret Dragon-name from the treasuries of her soul.

Uncontainable, his name rang forth, *Alastior!*

Chapter Fifteen

Reunited

GRANDION SWALLOWED HIS flame with a gulp of the most arresting astonishment his Dragon brain had ever known. All three hearts raced off in different directions, competing and contradictory, howling in celebration all at once. A newfound, ravenous hunger raged through the Dragon–a beast of passion, unchained. The yowling of his stomach beat against his consciousness without meaning. He breathed in again, dying for the scent of her, desperate to draw into his fire-soul the inmost essence of the creature, the wonder, the girl he cradled in his paw. It seemed his entire being was aflame. Body, soul, he could not separate it. Understanding blossomed within him, as though the world were a flower unfurled before his gaze, unguarded to its vulnerable core.

His throat thickened, while his chest swelled prodigiously. Taking a mighty, four-pawed stance, the Tourmaline Dragon released what he intended to be a Dragon-challenge, only it was a deeper, sweeter, more sonorous sound than he had ever imagined, a song of her name:

HUUUAAAALLLIIIAAAMAA!

* * * *

In such beauty, a soul could only dance. No chains, physical or spiritual, could have denied the response of Hualiama's soul to the wrathful, mournful, mind-blowing cry of the Dragon.

She sang in her heart:

AAALLAAASSTIIIOOORRR!

Their cries mingled at a level beneath conscious thought, perhaps the magic of their oaths once made to each other, or a deeper, more fundamental form of communication still. Lia knew the softness of his paw and the wash of the Dragon's breath. She knew the fire of his breath as though it were scribed in tongues of fire inside her eyelids. Her spirit mingled with his, communed with his, indwelled him even as he indwelled her.

For a breath within a breath, all was glorious. Lia became the fire she had always desired. She was light and song, a dancing wisp. Freedom's sweetness honeyed her tongue. Then, darkness rose to eclipse that glorious expansion of her consciousness. Hualiama shuddered at the power of an inner command.

Let it be bound.

The *ruzal* within her had spoken, and tainted the sweetness irretrievably.

She wept.

* * * *

Grandion wondered at the stifled, snuffling sounds Hualiama began to make. Was she crying? Struggling for breath? Dying?

Frantic now, his claws clamped on her head, trying to peel off the covering she wore. Stinking animal hide. Ropes. By touch he identified what had eluded his understanding–she was a prisoner of these Dragon Keepers. Lia's pained mumblings informed him what a poor job he was doing with his clumsy talons. He was fearful of harming her, for she seemed much smaller than he recalled. Fool Dragon. It was he who had grown. Six years. Where had she tarried for six years? What would she make of a blind, defenceless Dragon?

Before he knew it, Grandion set Lia down and retreated, shaking his head. If this was the Grandion of captivity, he was caged more surely than he had imagined. His fury raged against this Dragon. Where was his courage? Flown to the five moons? Lia made a soft interrogative noise. When he did not respond immediately, her query escalated into a mewl of distress so akin to a hatchling's wail of terror, that Grandion charged toward the sound before he considered the wisdom of tossing his tonnage blindly about the cavern.

Thump. Yelp. Growl in dismay. Growl for real as he felt an accurate kick on the tendon just below the wrist bone of his left forepaw. Pain lanced up his limb. Suddenly, the Tourmaline Dragon found himself guffawing. Had he been in any doubt, that kick confirmed it.

"Feisty as ever," he rumbled, righting her with an awkward touch.

Mumbling something acerbic, Lia felt her way along his paw to his talons. "Hmm-mmm."

"What is it?" Grandion unsheathed a claw.

By trial and error, they worked out a system of communication which involved many questions on his part and a great deal of mumbling and a few more kicks on hers. Soon, Grandion was holding his foreclaw firm while Hualiama bobbed up and down, sawing at the ropes binding her wrists. Ten minutes later, a series of muffled whoops announced her success, followed by the groans of returning circulation. Lia unbuckled the hood and flung it away angrily, judging by the sounds he understood.

A Human could be muzzled into silence. No Dragon would bind his own kind like this. In his third heart, as he listened to Hualiama fighting to free herself, Grandion bled for her. Yet, he cautioned himself, the power of the Scroll of Binding which they had sworn to find, was a similar, magical binding of Dragons. Leather or magic were only two ways of silencing freedom. There were cultural practices and power mongering, he reflected, and law and taboo, injustice and murder. So many ways freedom could be stolen. It was not so easily built or attained.

Taking his talon in her hands, Lia guided his claw-tip alongside her head, beneath one final, stubborn strap. "Hmm!"

He twisted, snapping the buckle with a tinny plink.

Hualiama coughed, spat and laughed softly at something a blind Dragon could not see.

And then her hand warmed his muzzle. Aloud, in Dragonish, she said, *Thou, my soul … united at last.*

Thou, the myriad harmonies of my Dragonsong. Grandion's paw curled hesitantly about her shoulders and back. Lia laid her head upon his foreclaw, and her long hair caressed the sensitive hide of his digits.

Tranquillity.

* * * *

Hualiama marched along the length of Grandion's body, measuring him with her stride. "Tail straight, you trickster. Wow. Thirty-one paces. Ninety feet, give or take."

"Seventy, with your stride," he teased.

She patted his tail, affecting lisping baby-talk. "Who's a big grown-up Dragon, then?"

Through a smoky growl, Grandion grumbled, "You've no idea how close I came to eating you."

"I'd only stick in your craw and give you indigestion."

"I was this close." He illustrated with his talons. "I've never eaten a person. But I'm … famished. Captivity makes a Dragon crazy. I'm not a cannibal, neither of Dragons nor of Humans. But your scent–I don't understand. You've changed."

Hualiama did not follow his logic. "Same girl," she said. "Freshly washed, too. A girl ought to look her best for her Dragon."

But Grandion's sigh only puffed smoke. In fact, Lia had concluded after a judicious examination of her Dragon, everything about him seemed subdued. His scales, lustreless. Fangs, yellower than she remembered. His hide sported many patches of scale-rot, and places where the mites infested him so thickly, they bulged beneath the scales like clusters of dark purple maggots. But his eyes–oh, his poor, milky eyes. What had become of the fires which had so charmed and captivated her? This beast was larger by half again than the Tourmaline Dragon of six years ago. The immensity of his presence made her tongue stick gracelessly in her mouth. His spine-spikes towered at least fifteen feet above her head. Lia shied from imagining how many tonnes of fire-filled, draconic muscle were trapped in the same small space as her.

Wetting her lips, she said, "Grandion, I know you despise apologies–"

"You've no cause to apologise!" he growled.

"But I do." Islands' sakes, would her voice not stop wobbling like a teenager giddy on berry wine? This was Grandion. She knew him. He was older, aye, and different, but still Grandion. "I would've come after you, had Amaryllion not stopped me. It hurts up here in my throat, Grandion, to think upon it. The Ancient Dragon has passed on to the eternal fires. Would you hear my tale?"

"If you wish."

He had no better response after all she had suffered for him? Hualiama was certain the sparks of her anger spat against his scales, but the Dragon seemed so dispirited and soul-lost … she would bring him back. Rescue her Dragon. Because if there was one quality she possessed in Island-sized portions, it was stubbornness. Oh, aye. She could out-stubborn any Dragon, any day of the week. But first, in truly draconic style, she should shoot a verbal fireball across his bow–just to set expectations.

Grandion. His eyebrow-ridges twitched. In tones of saccharine steel, she said, *I flew a thousand leagues to make you mine. Mine alone. And I will have no other.*

I'm broken, imprisoned and blind, he muttered.

You are my Dragon! Besides the oath-swapping business, which I do not regret for an instant longer than the flip of a dragonfly's wing, I happen to care about you. Don't think you can be rid of me so easily.

Grandion only hung his head. Hualiama stood, hands on hips, and fixed him with a glare fit to curdle milk. He could not see, but his Dragon senses would detect her elevated heart-rate and the irritable rasp of her breath.

Struck by a wild idea, she began to laugh. "Grandion, are scale mites edible?"

"I believe so," he said doubtfully. "You aren't suggesting–"

"I ate maggots for you, Dragon. The least you can do is listen politely while I harvest dinner from the region of your rump."

At last, Hualiama heard the crashing disapproval of a proud young Dragon. His spirit was not completely broken. Did she dare to hope? Might a Human girl still occupy a place in his third heart? There must be something to the song of their names, and his breath which had fired her senses. She was so confused. What darkness had emerged to steal that joy?

Ruzal. Ianthine's claw-mark upon her life.

* * * *

A cage of rust-red Dragon bones formed the arched walls and ceiling, joining together overhead in a hole large enough to accommodate a petite Human. The floor was hard flagstones cemented over more Dragon bones. And those bones, secured with massive brackets and hawsers of metal, also bound and subdued their magic–Grandion told her of the stench of ancient magic imbuing that metal, which Hualiama struggled to identify for herself. They had briefly broken through, however, when she cried Grandion's secret name. Did that mean the cage's magic could be overwhelmed?

The Tourmaline Dragon lay unspeaking, curled up in the shadows at the edge of their circular chamber. Lia learned to use the White Dragoness' scale to easily carve away great scoops of scale mites, and in the fading light of evening, she cleansed his lower left flank as best she was able. He stoically accepted the paltry offerings she placed upon his tongue.

Wishing to enliven the taciturn Dragon, Hualiama began to tell him what had passed in the six years since they parted ways at Ha'athior Island. She asked, "What do you think of that, Grandion?"

He said heavily, "Amaryllion made you forget? We must bow to the Ancient Dragon's wisdom in this–much as it dampens my fires to reflect upon how his decision changed you. The gift of Dragon fire is unprecedented. You see it personified, as though the dragonet lives within you?"

Unexpectedly, he added, "I miss Flicker. His was a cheerful fire, a soul whose brightness could chase away even the shadows of a place like this."

"Aye," said Lia, her thoughts darkened, but for a different reason. Grandion's thought processes seemed sluggish and unclear. Had the cage stolen that, too?

Returning to her tale, she related her confrontation with the Dragon Elders at Gi'ishior. He chuckled gruffly at her impressions of the volcano, and much more loudly as she related how she had blasted the Dragons with Amaryllion's name-power. Grandion called her a 'proper little Dragoness' and seemed inordinately proud of her actions. When she told of her sojourn with Sapphurion and Qualiana, he rubbed his muzzle with his paw in a draconic gesture betraying his swelling emotions, and his wings flicked and rippled restively.

Lia said, "It was precious to hear from your shell-parents about my early years at Gi'ishior. But I'm sorry I stole their love from you, Grandion."

"Stole?" he snorted hot air past her legs. In Dragonish, he added, *Bitter, these scale mites. As bitter as my hearts back then. I had no right to feel so darkly-jealous. My shell-mother counselled me otherwise, but I was too full of the roaring of my own fires to listen to her—or to any Dragon. They tried, Hualiama. But I had a skull of diamond and thoughts darker than a moonless night. I was a cruel little beast.*

Hualiama reflected upon this. *I hardly remember that, Grandion. I do remember playing with you, and*—she coloured unexpectedly, hoping he could not sense the heat upon her skin—*I remember playing at tickle-fights over the couches, and you tossing me into the air and catching me in your paws. You were neither cruel nor unkind.*

Despite my worst efforts, I remember that time as being often filled with bright-fires and goodness, the Dragon admitted. *You are goodness.*

Uh … right. You wouldn't say that if you knew what I did to my father.

Speaking of King Chalcion brought fresh pain to her breast. Images assaulted her, of past beatings and hours spent in agony on the punishment board, of being locked in a weapons-room and having her legs beaten with rods until she could no longer walk, and the finality of her victory over her adoptive father. Hollow, and bitterer than a haribol fruit. Could she be glad of it? Rationalise her actions as necessary and even commendable? At least she had earned Chalcion's respect. She was safe. And maybe next time, she'd bring home a Dragon to make her point.

The faint radiance of moons-light from the air hole in the cavern's roof touched the Tourmaline Dragon's scales, hinting at their former beauty. The scales beside his eyes were relatively tiny, Hualiama saw, peering at him in the gloom–just the size of her thumbnail. Before, their pattern had suggested delicate veins of minerals cutting through the underground glory of Ha'athior's abundant gemstone geodes. Now the scales seemed wrinkled, like the prunes King Chalcion had once procured from a trader from Somax in the Southern Archipelago and proudly displayed at a feast–one made memorable, Lia recalled with a pang of shame, for the King becoming drunk, ranting at a guest, and then punching Kalli in the mouth when his son tried to calm him.

"Your eyes still gleam slightly," she realised aloud.

Grandion rumbled, "Such afflictions are due to disease. It's hopeless. My retinae are ruined."

Lia bristled at his low, irate growl. "Don't lose hope, Grandion. I found you halfway across the Island-World, after all."

"Well done. You beat up both of our fathers and found a blind Dragon."

Her teeth ground together so hard, Hualiama was afraid she had chipped a tooth. Rage blinded her as surely as the insulting, scabrous serpent was blind. Lia stormed off across the cage, afraid she might shout something she'd regret forever. For a long time, she struggled against the desire to punish him. Words could sear like acid, twist and torment and pry … yet she withheld. She had her pride, too–whole Dragonships full of ralti-stupid, worthless pride no royal ward should have a right to claim. Lia was no curling night-pansy. She was the Dragonfriend, and the holder of Dragon fire.

Softly, he rumbled, "You may not know this, but in our culture, it is anathema to raise a paw to one's shell-parents. Despite all he did to me, I never raised a paw against my shell-father."

"Yet you wished him dead."

"Aye, there's a limit on paws, but not upon hot-tempered idiocy."

No. As his snarl echoed around the fully dark chamber, the Human Princess knew his words for the truth–and for an apology. Dragons. She rolled her eyes in the dark, knowing it was safe as he could not see. Or could Grandion hear her eyeballs swilling about like liquid in a goblet? That was a tasteless image, but not beyond the capabilities of a Dragon. Yet he had been greatly moved by Sapphurion's apology. He was not made only of fire. Grandion had changed. She heard little of the youthful arrogance which had driven him to clash with his shell-parents. Perhaps this signalled a more temperate beast? Or perhaps it was just depressing.

Lia's feet tapped around the cave, bringing her full circle to where the Dragon lay. Lying down with his chin on the ground, the top of his nose stood taller than her head. She said, "Grandion, will you allow me to rest this night beneath your paw, as before?"

The Tourmaline Dragon let smoke sigh between his fangs. "Need you ask?"

"I must."

"You may, if you wish."

"I do so wish."

She wished for many things. Did he? Lia snuggled into the space between Grandion's neck and his forepaw, and wondered what the Tourmaline Dragon made of her boldness. Then, way down in the depths of his body, she heard and felt his belly-fires rumbling away soothingly. Aye. Not quite the rebellious reptile he pretended to be.

"Those are long leagues you travelled by Dragonship," said the Dragon.

"Aye. Can I borrow a talon for a pillow?"

Grandion adjusted his paw as requested, providing her the

outermost and smallest talon of his paw to rest her head upon. Comforts fit for royalty, she chortled inwardly. Creature comforts.

Unexpectedly echoing her thoughts, he said, "Creature comforts? By my wings, you've changed little."

"You mean, I remain little."

"The quality of a gemstone is hardly reflected in its size," averred the Dragon. "It lies in the beauty of the facets and the inner structures, in the way great heat and pressure forged the mineral and the skill of the jeweller to craft that hidden beauty into life. Why did you seek me across the Isles, Hualiama?"

She wiped her eyes. "To hear you speak like that."

"I could speak of the way that life shapes us. Sometimes the jeweller must take his courage into his paw, and make an irrevocable cut." Hualiama wondered where his oblique draconic logic might be leading. "We were rough jewels, six years ago. We've been cut and ground and polished. Neither of us is flawless. I ask again, why did you seek me?"

"Because I suffer from double vision."

His laughter shook her, and the second and third digits of his paw, lying across her upper torso like a hot blanket, squeezed with care. "You confound me. What does this mean?"

The Princess nuzzled his paw as she imagined a Dragoness might. Deliberately switching to Dragonish in the hope that the language would better express her feelings–although draconic telepathic speech was more deeply communicative by far, Island Standard was still her heart-language–Lia replied, *My physical eyes see thee struck down by circumstance, Grandion. Though the fates have wounded and sorely tested thee, thou art a Dragon most majestic.* And now she spoke with the resonance of an Ancient Dragon? She shook herself mentally. *The eyes of mine heart see thee twice. Once for the flaws, aye–but are we not all flawed, and our esteem swells despite those flaws, or even, because of them? No being upon this Island-World may claim perfection. Courage is only called courage because of our weaknesses–it is the greater for them, and nothing without them. And secondly, mine heart has the power to see thee as flawless.*

Unexpectedly, Grandion sighed, *Ah, by the Spirits of the*

Ancient Dragons!

When he said no more, the girl continued, unable to prevent the ancient speech-patterns from rising to the foremost position in her mind, *Aye, Dragon thou art, and Human I am. Were one to look upon outward appearances, impossibilities and conundrums and insurmountable differences abound. But we two are living souls. Thy shell-parents saw this. I only relate that which the finest of Dragons taught me. The power of the third heart, Dragons say, lies in the art of tasting the soul-fires of another. I cannot claim to understand these mysteries. So I call this 'double-vision.' I see thee twice. Thrice. Perhaps I miscount …*

His muzzle shook slightly against her, and the tenor of his fire-rumblings changed. *Is this a Human power, Lia?*

Which power?

The Tourmaline Dragon lay still for so long that Hualiama found herself having to fight the delicious warmth that spread lassitude throughout her body. Something within her had uncurled, she realised. Tensions fell away. Perhaps it was that as she sighed, her spirit sighed too. Grandion was imperfect. The royal ward he held was worse. The blunders she had made! The idiocies she had perpetrated, becoming his Rider, foolishly and unthinkingly condemning her Dragon to this fate.

On one side, the law. Unchanged for thousands of years. On the other, a magical vow apparently condoned by an Ancient Dragon, and a scandalous, exuberant rapport …

Grandion said, *The fabled Star Dragons had a power they called the 'Word of Command'. Once spoken, these words remained immutable. They could bellow commands of such suns-dimming, Island-shivering power–*

They could knock Dragons from the sky? Lia bit her knuckles in fear.

Even Grandion's voice caught in awe. *Aye. No Star Dragon graces our Island-World now. They have passed into legend.*

You speak of Istariela, the soul-mate of Fra'anior?

Aye, Dragonfriend, he agreed. But she was catapulted back to an old dream. Lia touched the White Dragoness' scale beneath her clothes, warm against her chest. What had become of the eggs the Dragoness had hidden? A Dragoness, frantic to hide her young from a searching Black Dragon–had that been Istariela?

The Tourmaline added. *I would speak of another power. For your words reach into a Dragon's third heart. You sharpen me. You ignite my fires, yet I am dull-witted, and slow. I remember reading such a thing of Star Dragons. They were Dragons set apart for a task of maintaining the balance of our Island-World–*

The balance of the harmonies. Exactly what Amaryllion had said!

Great Dragon fires! Grandion's flame spurted from his nostrils, lighting the cavern briefly. *The knowledge stuffed into that tiny brain of yours. I'm surprised it doesn't frazzle and spit sparks all the time.*

Was this her task? Suddenly, Hualiama wondered at this hitherto unidentified melody she sensed in her life. No. It was too great, too grand, for a mere Human to contemplate. But if the Ancient Dragons had departed for the eternal Dragon fires, surely they had thought to leave a Star Dragon to protect the balance? Her mother Shyana loved esoteric speculations. Her daughter? Not so much. Yet a tiny flame of hope flickered in her breast. Someone must find the Star Dragons, mustn't they?

Those eggs would be a thousand years old, perhaps more. Yet the original First Eggs of the Ancient Dragons had survived unknowable aeons and the blackest reaches of time and space, to arrive safely on their Island-World. Could a Star Dragon's eggs do the same?

Grandion interrupted her thoughts with a low chuckle. *I thought a Tourmaline Dragon potent in magic. Now, I will have the tale of thy journey. Your brother stowed away on your Dragonship, you said?*

* * * *

Hualiama's voice was an invisible stoking of fires so long dormant, they had almost forgotten how to burn. The Tourmaline Dragon felt a lightness in his wings and belly as if he were flying. He could not help comparing Lia to Cerissae, the Red Dragoness of the Lost Islands who had brought him to the cusp of speaking the ascending fire-promises together, and then betrayed him with callous, stunning disregard.

There could be no fire-promises spoken with Hualiama. She was no Dragoness. But her fierce, understated pride as she told of rescuing her brother, and her service to the Dragoness and her hatchlings, was telling. She did not praise her own paws, whereas Cerissae's boasts would have rung to the heavens in true Dragonish style. He told her Mizuki had the power of Shivers, a rare draconic power capable of powdering the stone of fortresses and, as Lia had seen, exploding the flesh of unprepared enemies. Grandion remembered the pretty Copper fledgling from his sojourn among the Dragons of Eali Island.

If Mizuki had grown as powerful as Lia described, perhaps she was the Dragoness to light his fires? Thinking this, he immediately felt unfaithful to the tiny Human.

Oh, how his bugle of pleasure at Razzior's downfall made her chortle! Hers was the laughter of waterfalls, bubbling and pure. Cerissae had never made him feel like this. Lia had a gift.

When his companion was done with the telling, the Tourmaline Dragon was left shivering at the sensation crawling along his spine-spikes. He said, "Do you remember, Hualiama, how both the Nameless Man and Amaryllion called you 'child of the Dragon' and 'child of Fra'anior'?"

"Um … what's that got to do with the price of berry wine?"

Humans had the silliest sayings. Then again, the Dragonkind were obsessed with sayings about wings and talons and all things fiery. He growled, "I was just thinking that there may have been a Tourmaline Dragon who, with a dollop of acid worthy of a Green, told you that you did not in a million wingbeats merit such a title."

"Aye." She jabbed the surprisingly sharp point of her elbow into his jaw muscle. "Jealous, were you?"

"No."

"Well, I certainly smell another back-handed–I mean, back-winged or whatever you Dragons say–non-apology being made right around now."

"What I smell is the friction of Human effrontery

sharpening draconic lethargy," he retorted, but was displeased when Lia shook her head in clear confusion. Should he simplify? Grandion said, "I'm grateful for your abrasive wit to sharpen my own."

In response, Hualiama sang:

Arise, thou prodigal son of dawn's fires,
Enflame the Island-World with thy igneous breath,
Wing o'er the sky-fires in exalted majesty.

The Tourmaline Dragon purred with delight, for the magic of her voice hardly stopped at commanding words. But when he did not speak quickly enough, the Human girl said impatiently, "Explain yourself, lizard. What are you thinking about this 'child of the Dragon'?"

"Only that your Nameless Man and our Amaryllion might have meant more by it than we can imagine," said Grandion. "You've always dreamed of being a Dragon."

She shifted restlessly in his paw. "Oh, Grandion. Little girls have to grow up and face reality."

Always, she had seemed the one who slipped between the laws of reality like water grasped by a Dragon's talons, that Dragons were bound by draconic law and Humans by the mores and principles of their kind, and Hualiama, Dragon Rider and Dragonfriend, somehow moved in a different plane of reality. He hated the note of despair that shaded her response. He hated that she was right. How could he respond? He yearned to hear again the birdlike trills of her laughter, to tell her sweet lies that aye, Humans could surely grow wings, and truly, they could soar like the Dragonkind.

All lies must, in the end, be shown to be hateful at their core. He could not bear to hurt Lia again. Yet her melancholy pained him, for the song of his third heart was joined to hers.

Grandion said, "Let me tell my memories of your early life, Lia. Then I would speak of these six long years which have passed. Will you stay awake?"

"Permission for you to sharpen me with your talons, should I snore," she said boldly.

He tapped her abdominals with one long, steely talon, finding the muscles startlingly resilient. "Beware what you promise a Dragon, o damsel most fair."

She whispered, "I sought you, Grandion, because I promised to. I sought you because I care."

Thou art the radiant embers of my soul, he breathed. And his fires seethed like ten thousand bees swarming in his belly.

Chapter Sixteen

Six Long Years

GRANDION STALKED INTO the nursery with exaggerated, stiff-legged muscularity. His hide was sleek, freshly bathed in lava, brushed by the stiff-bristled rollers in the hatchling rooms, and then oiled with a quick dip in the bubbling jalga-oil baths, which helped protect against scale-mites and fungi, especially a hatchling whose scale-armour was not yet as thick and strong as his shell-father's. He wanted his Mamafire's eyes to whirl with fire the way they did when they lit upon the Human hatchling. Chattering pest! But a pretty pet, admittedly. Why did his shell-parents keep such a secret? He had promised them never to speak of her with his Dragonwing friends.

Grandi! The little Human girl ran to him, excited, her white-golden hair flying as she dashed across their roost. She could not pronounce the 'R' yet, not even in her mind, so his name emerged as, '*Gwandi.*' Huh. An insult to a creature of flame. Grandion's talons extended involuntarily. The metallic scraping on the warm granite floor of their roost drew a glance from his shell-mother, but not the admiring one he craved.

Grandion, claws sheathed indoors, Qualiana scolded. However, her eye-fires brightened upon him. *Heaven's wings, who is this beast who graces my halls?*

Hug me. Paws up, Hualiama demanded.

Grandion sighed, letting the hairless monkey climb into his paws.

Qualiana added, arching her wings, *Do I know thee, o Dragon most resplendent?*

Grr! The Tourmaline hatchling, all twenty-two feet of him, quivered with the effort of producing a fine battle-challenge. His Mamafire's belly-fires ignited with pleasure, causing an answering frisson to roll heatedly across his hide, all the way down to his tail-spikes.

Grr! The girl copied him.

Grandion could not help chuckling at the girl wriggling in his paws. Her smoky green eyes crinkled at him in what Humans called a smile. He said, *Did I hear a mouse squeak?*

Grandi's a big mouse, she teased. *Throw me. Higher! Again, Grandi!*

He prodded her with a knuckle, claws sheathed. *Squeak, little mouse. Display your mighty fangs.*

When I'm big, I'm going to be a Dragon, the mite announced, as if by belief alone she could change the Island-World. *Then I'll bite holes in your scaly butt.*

"Grandion!" Hualiama's laughter drew him back to the present. "I didn't actually say that, did I?"

"Guess who taught you that memorable phrase?"

The Tourmaline Dragon had always displayed an understated, undraconic tenderness he would probably never admit to. Human scrolls described Dragons as fierce, rapacious killers. Twenty years on, he still cradled her in his paw–wearing a few more clothes than that day, admittedly–and Hualiama still dreamed dreams which could never be consummated. Sometimes, the Isles saying went, life blew over the Islands; other times, it sucked. Lia's face screwed up as though she had indeed sucked on rotten windroc eggs.

He said, "I misjudged you. Human developmental speed is so different, Hualiama. I expected too much of one who was but a child."

She said, "We've known each other all our lives, haven't we?"

Grandion replied. "Dragons say, *The fires of true friendship burn brightest.* Aye, I know you, o radiant dawn over Fra'anior, yet I've always sensed something indefinable about your nature, a quality I wish I could trap in my paws …" Above her, the wall of his hard-muscled flank quivered. "Such fires cannot be fathomed. We must simply allow them to burn."

"My Grandi," she whispered.

After a long moment in which all she heard was the soughing of his belly-fires, Grandion whispered, "I'll continue. The story has a point besides embarrassing you with childhood memories."

Hualiama! Qualiana said sternly. *We don't use that language in our roost.*

Sorry, Mamafire.

Grandion jeered, *She's not your Mamafire!*

Grandion. The Red Dragoness moved like hot quicksilver pouring over the couches. *We spoke about this.*

I don't understand, Mamafire. Grandion peered at Hualiama. Her eyes filled with grey smoke that eddied with hypnotic power. *Why adopt a Human hatchling? It's not right.* He shook his head-spikes forcefully. *No other Dragons keep–well, it makes my wings shiver. You say she's not a pet, but a living soul, like us. Not a fire-soul, but a different sort of soul. I see that. I see more, for this girl-child has power–doesn't she, Mamafire? Magical power.*

The two Dragons rubbed necks as they gazed at the mite, wide-eyed, sucking her thumb. The eye-fires mirrored the soul-fires, Dragons said. The draconic sense called intuition-certainty ruffled their wings simultaneously.

Aye, said Qualiana. *You make me so proud, my volcanic shell-son. Magic swells in your breast. Mightier than your shell-parents, you will be.*

How did you know her name, Mamafire?

Sapphurion's low growl throbbed from the entryway, *Ianthine, the Maroon traitoress, named her Hualiama.*

Sulphurous greetings, shell-father, called Grandion, as his belly-fires sang their welcome.

So formal, my shining shell-son? Grandion wished he moved like his father, shaking the earth with every step. His power overshadowed and overruled, yet laughter was readier upon his tongue than fire. Sapphurion had wisdom beyond his Dragon-years. He had been elected the youngest-ever leader of the Dragons of Gi'ishior just two seasons before.

Thou, the breath beneath my wings, Qualiana purred.

Thou, my living lava lake, Sapphurion purred back, making the crysglass windows of their roost rattle. He shook his spine-spikes irritably. *Council was dark-fires today. Dragons should speak with true, refining flame, or not at all!*

The Red Dragoness said, *You hate the politics, don't you?*

Aye. I'll not trouble your hearts with their twisted words. Stumping over to his mate, Sapphurion twined necks with her. *How fare our hatchlings today? Did I interrupt a story? I'm starving! Any fresh meat in the bowl?*

Meat? Grandion's paws jerked, spilling the girl.

Catch her! Qualiana cried.

Hualiama dangled by her fingertips from his talons, laughing. *I'm fine, Mamafire. Look–whee! I'm a Dragoness!*

Come, said Sapphurion. *We'll share a haunch. Shell-son, it's time you knew this Human's tale.*

I'll put you in the meat-bowl, Grandion whispered to Lia.

His shell mother cuffed the youngster a blow that would have squelched his Human cargo like a bird struck by a speeding Dragon, and snaffled Hualiama from his grip.

Over his mate's back, Sapphurion snarled, *Such dark-fires have no place in our family.*

Just joking, the Tourmaline hatchling sulked.

Remember how the Maroon Dragoness returned from the East two years ago? Sapphurion growled, quelling Grandion's sulk. *She caused great upset. You know that Ianthine was banished, Grandion–but few Dragons know why. Are you mature enough to hear this truth?*

My fires are yours to command, o shell-father.

Again, Grandion's formality surprised Sapphurion. Nevertheless, the massive Dragon Elder gestured with host-generosity at the eating-bowl, twenty feet wide, laden with four haunches of ralti sheep and a whole spiral-horn buck. *Eat to become strong, my kin. Listen and flourish in wisdom.*

Qualiana diced meat deftly into slivers with her razor-sharp foreclaws, and cooked a portion with her fiery breath. *Eat, little one.* She fed Hualiama off her claw-tips, occasionally blowing on the meat to cook or cool it as needed.

The Maroon Dragoness was always a peculiar one, said Sapphurion. *Rather than seeing visions, the visions possessed her. She became violent, as strong as many Dragons in her madness. Ianthine was powerful in magic–dangerously powerful. The Council decreed she must live in isolation, apart from the Dragonkind. The Maroon Dragoness travelled away from Gi'ishior for years at a time. She loved to sniff out the Island-World's secrets, to gather a great Dragon-hoard of lore and treasures and experiences.*

*This last time, Ianthine returned to Gi'ishior and immediately sought counsel with the Dragon Elders. She raved about a magic she had learned–*ruzal, *the magic of the Dragon-Haters of the Lost Islands. The Elders said she was mad, that* ruzal *was legend. The Dragoness insisted the legend was true. She had seen the Scroll of Binding. Ianthine even read part of the lore, before the Humans stole it from her. When the Elders scoffed, she demonstrated her power on the Green Dragon Elder, Andarraz. No questions, no by-your-wings. Just raw control. She made Andarraz beg and roll over like a trained hound.*

No! Grandion gasped.

Qualiana put in, *They must've heard Andarraz's displeasure down in Herimor!*

Then, stranger winds blew upon the Island-World, said Sapphurion. *Ianthine began to shriek about proof, that she had brought a baby from the East as proof. A Human babe? Nonsense, the Elders thundered. The Dragoness' eyes spurted fire–literally, Dragon fire–and her voice changed to the multiple-larynx thunder of the great Black Dragon himself. She began to declaim an obscure prophecy about the child of the Dragon and a third great race rising in the Island-World. She held us spellbound. When we recovered our senses, the Maroon Dragoness had fled the chamber. Qualiana tracked Ianthine to her lair. Tell your part, my third heart.*

There's little to relate, the Red Dragoness responded, but her talons clenched involuntarily, making the Human girl withdraw fearfully. *Peace, little one.* Qualiana eased her stance. *I found Ianthine in an old Dragon-roost below the western cliffs of Gi'ishior, shaking this mite out of a reeking animal-skin. The babe was weak and sickly, and stank worse than windroc vomit. We fought, and Sapphurion came, and together we defeated her.*

Sapphurion grunted, *Brave heart, you defeated the Maroon Dragoness. I mopped up afterward.*

Qualiana's eye-fires gleamed at her mate. She stroked the

girl's golden head with the tip of a talon. *Sapphurion soothed you, and popped you into his mouth in order to smuggle you into our roost. The Dragon Elders banished the Maroon Dragoness by the concerted magic of thirty Blue Dragons. But we never found out why Ianthine brought you to Gi'ishior. Nay. That's a mystery, little one.*

Hualiama blinked her smouldering green eyes at the Dragoness. *Are all mysteries as nice as you, Mamafire?*

* * * *

Lia dried her eyes on her sleeve. "Sapphurion the Dragon Elder put a stinking Human child in his mouth?"

"That's how they tell the tale," Grandion rumbled contentedly. "Ianthine knew nothing of Human babies. Apparently she fed you raw windroc eggs–that's what kept you alive as you crossed the Island-World. My shell-mother says she had to spend two weeks healing the burns on your skin."

"Charming." Hualiama sighed moodily. "And I was living proof of *ruzal's* power? How is that? Ridiculous. As if I want to be anything like my father. I hate mysteries."

Thou, the mystery of my flame's heart, purred the Dragon.

How his voice shivered her Island! Another mystery. Lia rubbed the gooseflesh on her arms, saying, *I, the prekki-mush-hearted object of my Dragon's ardent regard.*

Grandion's guffaws shook the cavern.

At length, the Dragon said, "Leaving you at Ha'athior Island was one of the hardest choices I've ever made, Hualiama. You were so broken by Flicker's loss."

"I forgot."

"Aye. But I remember with the eidetic faculty of a Dragon–powerful and painful as that can be."

Lying in his paw, warm and safe in the cavern's darkness, Hualiama could imagine–almost–that she lay in the arms of a lover, who spoke such delicate, searing truths they made her mind explode with colours and her limbs tremble. The forbidden, unspoken truth bound their souls. Physical reality bound their bodies. She touched her stomach, knowing that no Dragon eggs would ever swell her belly. Grandion would want a clutch of his own, one day. How could she deny him? Quietly, ignoring the desolation of her heartsong, Lia made her decision. For Grandion, she would make this sacrifice. He should have a Dragoness. He must.

Well, a Dragoness might have a Rider. Maybe she could fall in love with another Human Dragon Rider? Maybe such a fool had not yet been born.

A love quadrangle? Nonsensical dreaming.

"Will you tell me what happened after Ha'athior, Grandion?"

* * * *

The Tourmaline Dragon had flown on to Gi'ishior, where he took a commission to lead a Dragonwing of younger Dragons against the Dragon-rebels of Merx. They campaigned and battled for the better part of two years, hounding the wily Green Dragoness Hazzarak and her Dragons all over the East, from the Spits to Cherlar, and all the way north to Kerdani Town in the Human Kingdom of Kaolili. Grandion bloodied his muzzle in glorious Dragon battle, leading his Dragonwing to many victories despite the unimaginative strategies employed by his Wing-Leader, the powerful but stolid Bronze Dragon Gazzathon. Gazzathon was a strong contender for the leadership of the Dragon Council.

"Never have I seen so many Dragons fall, Hualiama," Grandion reflected. "We're our own worst enemy. What have Humans to fear if the Dragonkind war amongst themselves? We boast about scars and torn wings and brag with our fire-songs. Humans boast by populating the Islands abandoned by Dragons–no disrespect, Lia."

"None taken. The only reason Humans survive is because we're so thinly spread out. As our Dragonship technology improves, Grandion, I wager that will simply improve our reach and ability to wage war on each other."

"Ah, this is the Princess of engineering and strategy speaking?"

Hualiama's cheeks reddened in the dark. "I'll thank you not

to mock my maidenly pursuits. On with the story, thou pain in the unmentionables."

Gnnaarraggrraaaagh, Grandion grumbled in response. "Finally, we trapped Hazzarak in a shadowed ravine on the northern fringes of Franxx Cluster."

Gazzathon's hoary muzzle turned in the air. *Tourmaline. Take your Dragonwing and scout above for any bolt-holes. I want that slug trapped in her lair, and crushed.* His eye-fires blazed. *I don't care who your shell-father is, youngling. This time, stick to the plan.*

Aye. Grandion did not twitch a wingtip, but his inner furnaces raged at the insult. Fusty, fangless old bone-licker! *Dragons! Ready your fires.*

Grandion led his dozen-strong Dragonwing eastward, toward the mountainous Isle reaching up out of the grey-green Cloudlands like the slender grey blade of a Dragon's talon. His spine-spikes prickled. Nasty place. Unseasonable weather accompanied his premonition. A chill wind blustered from the north, seeming to mound the Cloudlands against Franxx's broad-based ring of Islands, which were the peaks of a hidden volcano about two-thirds the size of Fra'anior's gargantuan eighteen-league caldera.

A pretty young Blue called Aquirelle, a sixty-eight foot Dragoness four years his junior, scrutinised the terrain with her senses alert. *My scales itch.*

Grandion nodded. *Likewise. What's your seventh sense, Aquirelle?*

Dramagon's creatures arise, she said, quoting a prophecy ancient even among the Dragonkind.

The Tourmaline Dragon's wingbeat stalled. *Giants?*

"Hold on," said Hualiama, suddenly catapulted from the looming massif of Franxx and an impending Dragon battle, into a fine muddle. "What Island did you just land on? What giants–do you mean Shinzen? And we're talking about Dramagon, the infamous mad-scientist Ancient Dragon of legend, right? How did he suddenly jump into the story?"

"Background," Grandion said, crisply. "According to legend, Dramagon was one of Fra'anior's shell-sons, a two-headed Red of enormous and devious power. He is called the father of *ruzal*."

Roaring rajals!

"Dramagon was a brilliant scientist with a particular flair for designing Islands," Grandion told her. "He's credited with shaping the Halls of the Dragons at Gi'ishior. He built the first celestial star-gazer. By my wings, I cannot express what an incalculable loss our heritage beyond the stars is, Lia … but I digress. Over the ages, Dramagon's experiments took a sinister turn. It became clear he experimented with crossing Dragon seed with Human seed–plundering the populations of nearby Islands to harvest what he required for his trials. When he was eventually exposed, they say that the remains of his victims and experiments occupied many caverns beneath Gi'ishior."

Lia shivered. "Horrible. But why combine Dragon and Human–"

"Humans are blessed with fecundity," the Tourmaline Dragon said. "It's rare for a Dragoness to lay more than one clutch in her lifetime, or, it has become rare for reasons we Dragons do not understand."

"Oh."

"You are never to repeat that secret. Never!"

"I–Islands' sakes, Grandion. Simmer down."

"I do not simmer–" He chopped off his roar with a curt laugh. Lia blinked away the suns-spots on her eyes from the fireball he had produced. "Nay, I erupt. I meant giants like Shinzen. Here in the East, they say that his kind are the corrupt spawn of Dramagon's laboratories–Humans of draconic size and strength, who command a debased variant of Dragon magic. Giants."

Dread sharpened Hualiama's response more than she had intended. "Who haven't taken over the Island-World because …"

"They can't procreate. They're infertile." She made a face which he inevitably detected, because the Dragon added snidely, "Not for lack of trying. They are creatures of vast appetites, as you saw with Shinzen–indeed, my delicate damsel, you're fortunate to have ended up trapped in a cave with a mouldy, feral Dragon, rather than–"

"I am not delicate!"

"Fie, wild beast, lay thee down," said the Dragon, tickling her stomach with the end of one digit, thicker than her knee. The Princess giggled helplessly, but Grandion allowed her to push his claw away, growling, "Now, let us speak of Franxx."

Gazzathon dived for the ravine, bellowing his challenge. Fifty-eight Dragons shook the morning air with the surfeit of their rage. The Dragonwing warmed their bellies and marshalled their magic, warning the enemy in the best draconic tradition of the impending attack. There was no glory in a sneak attack. Grandion's hearts wanted to sing with the thrill of battle, but instead he had to champ his fangs and hang back. Mop-up duty. It was enough to make the toughest Dragon's wings droop.

Half a minute later, Gazzathon's Dragonwing drew together into a narrow spear-formation, four Dragons high and two abreast, as they shot toward the narrow entryway of the ravine which concealed Hazzarak's lair. Long had they sought this place. It was beautifully constructed, trailing vines hiding the ravine's entrance, while at the top the ravine walls drew so close together, only a Dragon hatchling could have fit between them. Muffled booming rose to their ears. Fireballs. Battle joined.

Grandion moodily scanned the long, snaking passage of the ravine toward a trio of active volcanoes dominating the centre of the Isle, zooming in on the details, seeking to penetrate the gloom. Shadows. Odd, oily shadows. Instinct shaped his wing-flight. His Dragonwing responded instantly to his lead.

Aquirelle said, *A Dragon sense, Grandion?*

Aye. Let's scout the top of the ravine. Handizor, take a trio and work east. Yandazzia, westerly with your egg-sisters. We'll take the midsection. Report anything unusual.

A pregnant silence enveloped the ravine as the last member of Gazzathon's Dragonwing vanished into the cool ravine.

Grandion's hearts pounded: *Thud-a-doom! Thud-a-doom!*

Nothing?

Suddenly, alongside him, Aquirelle voiced a challenge that rose into a trumpet of full-throated horror. The shadows spewed men. Platoons of great, dark men charged from the not-shadows, from beneath a shroud of uncanny magic, shouting as they shovelled cartloads of massive barrels over the edge of the ravine. All along the length of the ravine, a stretch of three miles, thousands of giants repeated the action.

ATTACK! Grandion bellowed.

But even as his wingbeat trebled in tempo, he knew they were too late. Wind screamed over his scales as the Tourmaline Dragon accelerated to attack velocity, over forty leagues an hour.

Orange flame blossomed from the depths, transforming the ravine into a long, volcanic vent in full eruption. The concussion struck them a second later. *KAARAABOOM!* His ear-canals constricted, denying the massive explosion access to the ultra-sensitive inner ears, but the concussion-wave still punched the Dragons in their bellies and throats, throwing the Dragonwing off its course. The flames burned so heatedly, the ravine's lips glowed like a vast, red-rimmed mouth–consuming the Dragons of Gazzathon's group as though they had never existed.

"Not a single Dragon survived. Fifty-nine skeletons line that ravine," Grandion said, a lament whispering from his upper palette to shade his words with melancholy. "More, for Hazzarak sacrificed a number of her own kin to bait the trap. Those men were giants, some standing twice your stature, Hualiama–great ragged beasts of men, with concealing magic and powers akin to Brown Dragons, magical powers to manipulate earth and water and fire. The trap was baited with an oil of Franxx. They lined the ravine from end to end with barrels and deposits of oil, and fired it once our Dragonwing flew inside. Even Dragons will burn in such a pyre."

For a time, Grandion stared blindly into space, reliving his memories. Unshed tears burned beneath Hualiama's eyelids. Those Dragons had been fools–glorious, draconic fools. What a travesty.

The Dragon added, "We hunted those giants down to the last man, and destroyed them. Then, we hunted the Green Dragoness Hazzarak. I destroyed her with a lightning-strike.

On the very eve after I had downed Hazzarak, we received a messenger from the Council of Dragon Elders."

"We were discovered?"

"Aye. I knew it from the tone of the summons. It seemed the dragonets had revealed our secret, Hualiama. And it was Razzior who laid the accusation."

"Always Razzior!" How the Orange Dragon must have delighted in discovering a way to humiliate Sapphurion! Prattling dragonets. Hualiama's teeth ground audibly as she said, "Your shell-father told me how bravely you bargained for your life before the Council. I'm sorry–"

"Sorry? Ignited by oaths of wing-shivering beauty and irresistible depth of purpose, could we have expected otherwise?" The Tourmaline's ire rose. Flame flickered between his fangs as he snarled, "So aye, I abased myself to save my Sapphurion's position on the Council. He sacrificed his shell-son. Now he sends a Human to convey his regret? Where is my shell-father now, Hualiama? Cowering back at Gi'ishior! He called you his shell-daughter, yet in the same breath, despatched you to the same doom!"

Panting and smoking at the jowls, the Tourmaline Dragon's talons tightened like steel, clamping Lia's arm against her hip. The bones ground together.

"Grandion–"

"What? What can you say to this?"

"Please. You're hurting me, Grandion. You're too strong."

For a breathless second, Hualiama thought that the Dragon's paw would convulse. Then he unclenched his grip deliberately, rumbling, "Aye. Like it or not, our fates are bound together more surely than Islands are bound to their roots beneath the Cloudlands. The strong and the weak. Dragon and Human."

Weak? Was this how he regarded her–little Lia, inferior companion to a mighty Dragon? That sealed her decision. Grandion must be liberated to love a Dragoness.

Her heart beat like a hollow log drum. She would take that log and roll it off the nearest cliff. She must.

Just that endless plunge. The rest was fate.

* * * *

Following the debacle at Gi'ishior, Grandion forged his way across the Island-World in search of the lost Scroll of Binding, past the Dragon haunts of Merx, Lyrx and Amxo to the vast reaches of the Eastern Archipelago, which stretched two thousand leagues from south of Haozi to the North's Lost Islands. There, he put claw to stone in a year of fruitless hunting. Grandion communed with the Eastern Dragonkind. Caves. Haunts. Ancient lairs. All felt the tread of Tourmaline paws.

Oddly, the Eastern Dragonkind treated Grandion as a hero. He wanted no hero-worship. They regarded the tale of his humiliation and downfall as an inspiration. The Princess concluded that even among Dragons, cultural differences could surprise and bemuse.

"I came to a place of dark-fires in my thoughts, Lia," he admitted. "It's a draconic state akin to Human depression. The soul-fires grow feeble. A Dragon is preoccupied with his own needs. He's restless and feckless, and aggressive if disturbed. I … I cursed our oath. I told myself I hated you, and hated having subjected a Dragon's spirit to a Human's dominion, or artifice, or magical interference–whatever I imagined had happened between us. I don't say this to hurt you, Hualiama. I want you to know what state of mind I was in when I met Cerissae."

"You met a girl?" said Lia, unthinking.

"That's old news," Grandion quipped. "This was a Dragoness–a Red Dragoness."

Cerissae was an Amber-Red Dragoness of thirty summers who had flown south from the Lost Islands on her sacred fire-quest. She was feisty, spiky and ten feet larger than Grandion. Together they tracked down every lead to the Scroll of Binding, until only two places were left–the Human-controlled central Lost Islands, which spelled certain death for a Dragon, and Shinzen's lair.

Preoccupied with Grandion's description of how he had travelled and roosted together with Cerissae for over a year, Lia suddenly became aware of a stabbing pain in her left palm. Her tightly-clenched fingernails had cut into the skin! She sucked the wound absently.

The Dragon concluded softly, "There was nothing between us at first, Lia. No spark. But as we journeyed and battled together, a friendship grew. I thought there was more. I considered speaking the first fire-promises with Cerissae, callow fledgling that I was, but the Amber-Red Dragoness had other plans. I was ignorant of the fact that the Lost Islands Dragons have developed entire branches of magic unknown or at least, lost to the Dragons of Gi'ishior. As we flew toward Shinzen's fortress, Cerissae performed a healing reversal on me, seizing my energies and striking me down. I woke up in this cage, and the rest you know."

Bitterness tinged Lia's response, despite her best efforts to contain her feelings. "She played you–but to what purpose? I don't see what Cerissae stood to gain, Grandion."

"I believe her first purpose was to secure the Scroll for herself and her Dragon-kin," he replied. "Its power is immense, Lia. They say the Dragon-Haters keep Dragonkind bound as defenceless thralls by the commands of their Enchanters. They can command a Dragon to throw himself into the abyss or tear out his own hearts."

"No!"

"Aye. Cerissae gave up on the Scroll of Binding, believing it truly lost, or destroyed by Ianthine. She made a bargain with Shinzen which, to my knowledge, has never been consummated. Once, in a drunken rage, I heard Shinzen shouting about it outside this cavern."

"What bargain?"

"To employ Dragon magic to raise Shinzen's kin to life."

Lia wished she had not asked. "Unholy windroc droppings! Can this get any worse?"

"Indeed," grunted the Tourmaline Dragon, seeming perversely cheered by her reaction. "This fortress once belonged to Dramagon. Shinzen was created here. He covets an army of giants to help him conquer the Island-World."

Chapter Seventeen

Reignited

COME MORNING, LIA sprang to her feet and sang out, "Rise with the birds, Dragon!"

"Is it dawn yet?"

"Time to rise and shine! Literally."

"Crazy Human, what're you up to?" He resettled his muzzle on the floor. "Do what you wish with me. I'm not–"

"Aye? I will." Hualiama kicked his stomach as hard as she could without breaking a toe. "I didn't know wishes could be fulfilled so quickly in this life."

A chortle absconded from Grandion's muzzle.

Lia said, "This cage stinks. I refuse to live in a cesspit of ralti sheep bones and Dragon droppings. After all, even the most violently felonious Dragon-fancying Princesses have their standards. We should block up the stream to flood the floor. Then–"

"When we first met, someone I know seemed to think she needed to light fires around a Dragon," Grandion rumbled. "I feel a different approach is needed."

"Oh? Now you're the domesticated one?"

"Well, I don't have much fire–stop tapping your foot. I can hear what you're thinking."

Lia snickered, "Oh, do tell."

"You plan to insult me to arouse my fires."

Right. But Grandion had not the first clue how devious a Human female could be. "No, quite the opposite." The Tourmaline Dragon had barely hissed his confusion, sounding like an overheated steam-turbine, when Lia, infusing her voice with every ounce of slow, sweet seduction she possessed, cut in, "I'm overawed by how *huge* you've grown, Grandion. My heart turns somersaults over the moons every time I look at you. You're one gorgeous, swoon-worthy monster."

On cue, Grandion belched an impressive fireball.

"Excuse you," Hualiama chuckled. "Found our fires, Dragon?"

"Aye." Two of his talons crooked jealously about her waist. "I found my fire."

A deliciously perilous fluttering filled the pit of her stomach. And Lia, colouring like the most volcanic suns-set, discovered that the joke was on her.

Grandion laughed up a minor thunderstorm, shaking the cavern and eventually falling into a helpless fit of fiery hiccoughs. Wretched reptile! She could cheerfully have throttled him, or rather … what? That was the question which knew no answer. And her decision? Overturned in a millisecond. Her pendulum swung from the depths of the Cloudlands to the heavens above. She must unchain the beast, yet she could not. She'd rather leap off a nearby cliff.

Aiming the Tourmaline's muzzle with her hand, Hualiama helped him sweep the chamber with fire, turning every scrap of refuse to ash. Then Grandion plugged the water outlet by the amusing but practical method of sitting on it, and the streamlet began to back up. Removing her leggings, Lia waded through the rising water to mop Grandion from head to toe–at least, that was her intent, but she soon realised she had begun a process not likely to take less than a few days.

"You could swim out of here," he said, at one point. "Or, I could lift you up to that hole in the roof. You could escape, Lia."

"And leave you behind? Splendid idea. Why didn't I think of that?"

The Dragon persisted, "From the outside, you could find the way to open this cage. There must be a Dragon-sized door."

"I'm not leaving you again!" Lia had intended a snarky

response, but the emotion betrayed in her voice ambushed and stunned her. "I wasted six years. Six! Never again, Grandion. Do you hear me?"

Grandion reached out. "Don't. I'm not worth crying over."

He heard her silent tears? Or had he guessed from other cues only a Dragon's senses were sensitive enough to detect? Lia pressed her forehead against his paw, muttering, "You're not worth a few tears? Confoundedly stupid lizard. What in a Cloudlands lava pit do you think I'm doing here? I swear that massively armoured cranial cavity of yours contains nothing but a pile of gravel! I did not fly to Gi'ishior on some girlish whim. You and I are getting out of here *together*–end of Island!"

To her surprise, after a pregnant pause, Grandion began to guffaw.

"What?" Lia demanded, thrusting away from him. "I'm spilling my heart over your paw and you're laughing at me? I'll slap your witless Dragon muzzle so hard–look at me! I'm spitting sparks! I'm actually … spitting … oh, flying ralti sheep."

The Tourmaline Dragon's quaking shook the cage. How tiny she felt before such a storm, vibrating with the force of his laughter like a leaf in a gale. But his mirth was far from unkind. Alien, aye, and intimidating, but resonant with a delight she suspected was founded in the presence of a Human companion. How … curious. How unbelievable; truly scandalous. What could a person do but yield to the power such moons-tides exerted upon her life–were she the yielding sort? Sweeter by far not to fight it, Hualiama realised, and that was the part that frightened and thrilled her in equal measure.

Her head-decision had no hold on her heart. Lia writhed, at war with herself.

"What I would not have given to see you flatten the Dragon Elders," said Grandion, "or to be present to savour Razzior's downfall–although we may yet regret revealing your talents to that rancorous reptile. Lia, my third heart, I do not question your courage. Nor do I question the fires I sense within you. What I question is why you're bothering with a blind Dragon who has been trapped in this cage for three years, seven months and nine days."

"You question my heart," she said, hurt.

Grandion's massive paw lunged in her direction, but he missed his aim by several feet. *Princess.* She held her breath. *Lia! I can't ... see you.* His huge reptilian muzzle, taller and wider than her, swivelled with a desperation she had never thought to see in a Dragon. *I want to see your eye-fires, I need to ...*

He spoke to the accompaniment of a deep groan originating in the lowest reaches of his chest, making the Human girl imagine the foundations of an Island groaning beneath the pressure of a tectonic shift. Lia did not know why, but she remained stubbornly unspeaking as the sound swelled. Suddenly it became elegiac, echoing the sound the Dragons had made at Amaryllion's passing on. Ripples of organic fire chased over her skin like a crazy silver filigree. Her scalp prickled as though charged with electricity, and the entire length of her hair rose about her, before–*kiiiraaack!* A lightning bolt sizzled from Human to Dragon. Grandion yelped, his trigger-response propelling him a hundred feet across the chamber in an eye-blink.

Whirling, the Dragon panted, *Not your heart. Mine. I feel as though I wish to soar to the moons, only, there's an Island chained to my tail.* Words poured out of him now, taut and hot with emotion. *I try to fly but it's just dragging me down into the Cloudlands, an impossible burden. I can't live like this, Lia. I can't fly. I feel ... I suffer ...*

Call a wing a wing, Grandion, she whispered. *You're afraid.*

FEEEAAARRRR! His roar rolled over her, and she was mute, convulsed by sorrow and the pain of a creature of enchanted Dragon fires, thus abased. He roared, *Content, Human girl? A Dragon admits fear! He scorns the hollow edifice of draconic pride and admits he needs you.*

She felt ashamed.

Raising his muzzle with a hint of the old, imperious Grandion, the Dragon added, *We have words for our fires–dark-fire, light-fire, liquid-fire and star-fire ... and since you came, Hualiama, both dark- and light-fires rage in my breast, so intertwined that one is the shadow of the other ... unbearable sweetness, mingled with hope stolen from the abyss.*

Tenderly, Hualiama's song enwrapped his words, stilling the Dragon:

Let my soul take wing upon dawn's twin fires …
And fly to thee.

Grandion's claws flexed, tearing up the flagstones on the floor. His chest heaved, while his tail flicked side-to-side behind him. *You sang that before,* he gasped. *I heard you, but did not believe. I could not.*

Grandion, I'll help you fly. Abruptly she hurled herself across the cavern, sobbing, running, flying to him. Never again. *I'll be your eyes. You'll be the song of the wind, one with my soul's wings.*

Hualiama crashed into his neck, bounced off, and sprang in again, desperate to hold him, to know the clutch of his paw, to be enfolded in his draconic warmth. Grandion's throat worked spasmodically. Laughter cascaded from the triple larynx of the Tourmaline Dragon's throat, the thrilling low notes of a draconic trumpet, a series of whip-cracks as if chains snapped in his middle larynx, and a wild, unfettered descant warbling from the upper palate. The sound seized her legs and hurled her away in a dance of pure jubilation. Hualiama pranced about the Dragon, making triplets of leaps in which her legs spread forward and back of her like a Dragon's wings, and her head arched backward with each jump until it touched the inside of her knee.

Then she spun back into his paw, laughing through tears, *My Dragon. My Dragonlove!*

* * * *

"Tell me you came here with a plan," Grandion chortled.

All was laughter now. Shinzen's guards must think they were moons-mad. Lia was mad, but it was a peculiar form of madness that transcended the physical structures and trappings of reality, as if she possessed the key to the fabled immortality of the Ancient Dragons. She was boundless. Caged, but free.

She had fought storms and battles and Dragons for him, and brought a gift in the form of his egg-father's unprecedented apology, apart from the treasure of herself.

To think that as a hatchling, when he clasped this wisp in his paw, his Dragon fires had darkened with jealousy and rage. To think that a tiny, green-eyed sprite had matured into this woman he held now, clasped in the loose cage of his talons that he knew she could slip through like smoke whenever she wanted–yet she chose to remain. Hualiama was the ultimate conundrum.

Did she know what she had called him, in the welter of her ecstasy?

Dragonlove.

What Dragon hoard had ever boasted such a treasure? All the softly gleaming gold and glittering jewels of the Island-World's kingdoms could not compare. The stars sang no greater song. Panic and exaltation surged in his white-fires, the purest, most elemental expression of a Dragon's being. The word was right. It shivered his bones.

"Plan? What plan?" she imitated his laughter, poorly.

And she was off again, twirling across the cavern floor as he failed to track her efforts by scent and hearing. He ached to revel in that expression of her beauty. There was such a richness of detail conveyed by Dragon sight, he felt as though a heart had been carved out of his chest by its loss. Her feet whispered upon the flagstones. Her heartbeat raced across his senses like a crazed hare, bounding up and down with her dance. Could he not share her fire? Could he not, if he yearned strongly enough, if he reached for her with every ounce of his strength …

* * * *

"We need an escape plan," Hualiama growled, flexing her wing arches to display forceful irritation. "I–what're you doing? Grandion!"

"Get out of my mind," squeaked the Dragon, in ridiculous soprano. Putting his paw to his ear canals, he dug about exactly like a Human rooting for ear wax.

Lia thundered, "Grandion, stop that!"

Only, her thunder was disturbingly mouse-like compared to what the draconic presence within her mind expected. Across from Hualiama, the real Tourmaline Dragon stood on his hind legs, wagging his finger at the impertinent Dragon–or was that Human–opposite. "You put me back this instant, you lumpen overgrown gecko, or I swear …"

Suddenly, with a crack like an overstrained hawser snapping, Lia recoiled back into her own body and landed on her tailbone. "Roaring rajals." After rubbing her bruised rear, she checked her arms and legs suspiciously. Grandion was doing exactly the same, humming in pleasure as he discovered wings and fangs all in good order. Hualiama wished, just once, that she could do a dint of serious damage to her draconic cellmate. Sweetly, she inquired, "What did you just do to me?"

Grandion's head snapped up and he swallowed fire with an audible, painful-looking gulp. "Now listen here, you interfering dragonet–"

Lia folded her arms across her torso. "No invading my privacy."

For a minute or more, all she saw was smoky breath curling in and out between his fangs. The muted storm-susurrus of his belly-fires filled the cavern. Snaking toward her, jarring the ground with every step, Grandion hissed, "You forget you speak to a Dragon."

The icy claws of Dragon-fear seized her belly. Her chattering teeth rather spoiled the effect of her heated reply, "Well, Dragon, you forget you're speaking to someone who can touch your soul."

"True wisdom lies in the fear of Dragons."

"I don't like it when you … when you stalk me, all scary and predatory."

GGRRR! Grandion sounded incensed.

Hualiama gave up the pretence of bravery. She should not have taunted him, as amusing a pastime as it might be. With a mind of their own, her feet conveyed her backward as the Tourmaline Dragon lumbered toward her. She pressed her shoulders against the cavern wall. Bolt? Hide? Where could she possibly run? These shivers were not delicious–or were they? The heights of adrenalin, the caged-bird thrashing of her heart as Grandion bunted her with his nose, the effervescent, crystalline magic he ignited up and down her spine …

In and out, his breath sucked into the vast olfactory instruments that were his nostrils, drawing at the cloth of her outfit. "Mmm," rumbled Grandion. "You smell positively Dragonish."

Her little arms could not possibly hold him at bay, but she made a valiant attempt. "Grandion, I'm no Dragoness. Or have you forgotten? Pestering females is your culture, not mine. Alright? Now get off before I flatten you like I flattened your father."

Blast the overzealous leviathan, he only purred in his tongue, *A bit of growl and snap there, Lia? Most becoming. I'll make a Dragoness of you yet.*

His intense purring made it difficult to think. Seeking firmer ground, Lia ventured, *So, Grandion, how does a Dragon show regard–I mean, roost-love? We can't exactly rub necks. Not easily, anyways. Your shell-mother and father seemed very moons-over-the-Islands together. 'Thou, my glowing moons,' and all that. Fluttering wingtips. And the sniffing of the neck just behind the skull-spikes–what's that about? And Grandion–*

I'd quite forgotten the Human penchant for their own form of pestering–chirping out questions like the million water-birds of Archion Island.

She smacked his muzzle. *Better still? Were you like this with what's-her-name?*

* * * *

Should he regret telling Hualiama about Cerissae? Her question betrayed an unprecedented level of unhappiness–he had read her correctly, while telling his tale the previous evening. None so fiery as a Dragoness scorned, was a favourite saying around Gi'ishior. And Hualiama was quite the terror when aggravated and frustrated–as she was now.

Not entirely, Grandion rumbled softly, and stalled. How could he explain when he did not understand himself? *I'm struggling to identify appropriate behavioural boundaries in this cross-species relationship, Hualiama.*

Grr. Honesty as stiff and dry as a Dragon's bones. What a brave Dragon he was!

But she responded softly, *Me too. I understand, Grandion. I'm sorry … I'm also sorry I'm stupidly apologising when I shouldn't do that to a Dragon.*

Lia, Lia, Lia, he clucked. *Why don't you just be yourself?*

Be Human, do you mean?

Now, a wash of bitterness against his senses.

Regarding Cerissae, the truth is that she never awakened my fires as you do. Grandion swallowed, wishing he could see Lia's eyes to judge her reaction. *That's the last word I wish to speak about that betrayer. We must work out what we do about … this, what we started by making our oaths and what moons-madness infects us now.*

Lia growled, *You mean, me.*

I meant us and I said us! Again, the Tourmaline Dragon had to swallow back his fire, and the desire to nip her shoulder to make his point clear. *We must help each other, my Rider, to find a way of roost-love which is pure and true. Now, Dragons sniff behind the skull-spikes because they conceal at their base certain olfactory glands, which give a Dragon their unique scent. Scent is a deep signifier of relationship. You Humans must know this–perhaps in a limited way, given the paucity of your senses. We Dragon perceive scent as a vast palette of–wait. Someone approaches.*

His ears caught a sound. To his embarrassment, a low purr throbbed from his chest as Grandion's salivary glands kicked wildly into action. He felt Hualiama spring aside as drool spilled uncontrollably out of the side of his mouth.

She said, *What … oh. That's a sheep.*

At that instant, the muffled bleating of an unhappy ralti sheep was the most enchanting sound he had ever heard, more evocative than starsong dappling night-dark Islands and more heartening than Qualiana crooning over his egg. Every muscle in his body seemed super-charged with power. All twenty of his talons gouged the ground as Grandion stalked toward the sound. Dimly, he heard Lia's feet tapping along beside his left flank, but he was wholly focussed on the grating sound of a stone door pressing open, the scents of warriors on a slight breeze that entered the cavern overridden by the all-consuming musk of a terrified ralti sheep.

Lia's steps quickened, lighter and faster. Was she running?

"Yaah! Get in there!" yelled a man. The dull thwack of a stick against woolly flesh came to his ears.

Then, all became confusing. Hualiama cried out sharply. A sudden shuffle of her footwear on stone preceded a tiny flapping of wind against cloth. The Tourmaline Dragon was closing in on his prey when *biss-crack!* Light flared against his damaged retinae. The sheep bolted. Lia gave another cry, low and pained, as she ricocheted off Grandion's forepaw and crashed into his lower shinbone.

One of the men laughed cruelly. "Found us some magic? Stupid wench."

Another added, "That's why it's called unbreakable, y'know. Don't matter what's inside."

The scent of the sheep was a whisper of the fabled hundred-year Dragonwine to Grandion's senses, the drink prepared by Dragons from the prekki-fruit-sized grapes of Fra'anior's rich volcanic soils in a process that combined fermentation, filtration and magic, and shared when Dragon and Dragoness began to say the ascending fire-promises to each other.

Grandion ignored the screaming of his stomach. *Lia? Are you alright?*

"Bah," laughed one of Shinzen's men. "Go down the river, girl. That way's open, only you'll find a lake full of toothfish at the bottom." His voice diminished beneath the four foot thick stone door as it grated closed. "Plenty of bones down there."

He nosed the girl. *Princess?*

I'm bruised and shaken–ran into a magical wall, of sorts. Nothing broken.

Good. He shook, but for a different reason. Fires rose in his mind, threatening to steal away his sanity. *Truly alright?*

A tiny hand pushed his nose. *Grandion, you're covering me in*

Dragon slobber. Still he hesitated, wishing to demonstrate that she mattered more than a meal, even one he could gladly have died for. Lia smiled audibly, *Islands' sakes, go put the poor animal out of its misery. Just leave me a bite.*

The Tourmaline Dragon whirled, unable to deny the craving any longer. Wool. Meat. Terror. Irresistible scents, magical sounds.

GRRRRAAAAARRRGGGH! He charged across the chamber.

* * * *

Hualiama clapped her hands over her ears, but Grandion's Dragon-thunder deafened her regardless. The Human girl knew she would never forget the spectacle of a Dragon attacking his prey. Regardless of the fact that he was blind, Grandion knew exactly where that ralti sheep stood, frozen by his mighty roar. Wings flared, talons slashed; the hapless ralti sheep slammed against the cavern wall and was dead before she could even think to gasp.

This was a hundred Islands beyond what she had imagined a Dragon feeding-frenzy to be. Lia could only shake her head as the Dragon guzzled and snorted and growled and bolted hunks of meat. Grandion tossed the sheep toward the ceiling, tearing off a haunch with a violent shake of his head. Growls of pleasure resounded deep in his chest. Cracking open the skull, he sucked out the sheep's brains and slurped them down with such relish that Lia decided, on the spot, to turn vegetarian.

Imagine these table manners at a Fra'aniorian royal ball? "Oh, sweet Dragon," she chortled to herself, "how delicately you dine."

If she did not lay claim to a chunk of meat soon, there would be nothing left. The Tourmaline Dragon was making a hearty mess of the spine and abdominal cavity, having already polished off the entire rear half of the sheep–a mind-boggling feat in itself. However, Lia realised, any interference might place one royal ward on the menu, roasted to perfection.

Grandion needed to learn to treat his Princess-Rider with respect! Her stomach gurgled eagerly. Blow respect into a Cloudlands storm. She'd settle for food. Any food.

Lia limped toward the feast, calling, *Grandion. Will you share fresh kill with me?*

The Tourmaline Dragon's paws clenched spasmodically, and his wings flared in a clear threat. Gore dripped from his snarling maw.

Wow, you sure destroyed that sheep, said Hualiama, with forced admiration. *Spare a fillet steak or two for a starving Human?*

She noted the exact moment that rational thought returned–the sheepish droop of his wings signalled chagrin, which Grandion immediately disguised with an overly casual relaxation of his posture. *Of course I'll share,* he rumbled. *Cooked?*

Chargrilled, said Lia. Yum! She'd make a terrible vegetarian.

Do I hear you smiling?

Drooling, actually.

Aye, Princess of Fra'anior? he replied, with a crafty smile. *Since e'er you saw a Tourmaline Dragon rise resplendent from the crater lake at the monastery, you've been drooling over me, haven't you?*

Grandion! She blushed furiously. He remembered! Sly, scheming serpent–forty tonnes of macho ego furnished with a flaming temper, and she was surprised he acted in character? *I'm hungry,* she announced, primly. *Feed me before I get grumpy. Who'd want to keep us alive? Razzior?*

That's it, Grandion exclaimed, spitting a gobbet of meat against her thigh.

Lia threw it back at him. *You're a messy eater. Who else but Razzior would pay Shinzen for the likes of us? Does the Orange traitor seek the Scroll of Binding for himself?*

The Tourmaline thundered his unhappiness around the cavern. *Heavens above and Islands below, that tiny cranium of yours must conceal an incredibly dense lump of brain-matter.* Lia's response was a low growl. *Aye, you're right–what does Razzior want more than ultimate power in his paw? We need to think. Plan. What type of magic can break through Dragon bone? How can we foil Shinzen's schemes?*

Hualiama echoed, *What kind of magic, indeed? Force won't suffice.*

Grandion's fiery breath hissed over the sheep's remains, crisping the skin and sizzling the fat. He said, *When you ran for the door, I saw a flash of light–or magic. Perhaps my eyes aren't completely ruined.*

Oh, Grandion! Lia danced over to him, slipped on a sheep-bone, and landed awkwardly on the hard upper surface of his forepaw, right on the primary thumb joint.

She hugged his ankle fiercely.

Chapter Eighteen

A Dragon's Eyes

UNBREAKABLE. IMPERVIOUS. THE cage had defeated Grandion's every artifice during his three years of captivity. Designed by Dragons for the containment of Dragons, the structure was not only built from the strongest substance known to the Dragonkind–Dragon bones–but further reinforced with cunning spells of an ancient, forgotten weave which destroyed the ability of those incarcerated within its bone cage to perform magic of their own. Telepathic Dragon speech was impossible. Magical Dragon attacks were impossible–on the contrary, Grandion informed Lia, his attacks had only served to strengthen the structure.

A week later, she was still arguing the odds.

"It's impossible," Hualiama grumbled. "There has to be a weakness."

"Keep trying. Your skull is, after all, more impervious than either Dragon hide or bone."

Lia refused to be provoked by her oversized sheep-obliterating cage-mate. "We're missing something, Grandion. Somewhere in the magical lore, there must be a clue. A trick. A reversal of logic. A fresh insight. Years ago, a girl beat the premier swordsman of Fra'anior Cluster. It is possible. It must be."

Irritably, the Dragon growled, "It's difficult indeed to reverse something we can neither identify nor understand in the first instance. Hualiama, we've covered this ground twenty times over. Our best chance is to wait for Razzior–"

"To attack us when we're helpless?"

"Dragons are not easily chained."

"Pity us Humans, then," Lia sighed. "I'm not content to wait, Grandion."

His knowing chuckle brought a burn to her cheeks. Aye, Lia would never sit back, content, while fate sent an Orange Dragon to finish the foul work he had begun. Ra'aba had escaped Sapphurion's justice and roamed the Islands freely. Razzior would be on their trail just as soon as Shinzen put the pieces together. She scowled at the Dragon, aggrieved that Grandion chose to exhibit a fine imitation of a blue doormat.

A magical cage required a magical solution. But of all the strangeness which had attended her fragmented existence, perhaps the strangest was the magic of a Dragon's secret name, *Alastior!* That was magic of a type or character she could not reproduce. Nor could she cry the Ancient Dragon's name. It accomplished nothing in this cage. Yet, she knew magic had touched her life repeatedly. Ianthine's paw. Flicker's soul-fire. Amaryllion's bequest. Heavens above and Islands below, she dreamed impossibilities, rich, lucid dreams of playing in the Island-World's vast aerial realms, and her mysterious shell-dreams. Lia had dreamed of being raised by Dragons and that, confounding all belief, had been true.

What did it all mean? Oh, for a draconic paw to scribe the answer on a handy wall! She chuckled softly, making the Tourmaline Dragon orient his blind gaze upon her. "What now?"

The Princess asked, "Grandion, do Dragons dream shell-dreams? Before they crack the shell, I mean?"

Stillness greeted her question. Grandion always fell silent when he was thinking deeply, or when she asked an inappropriate question. Nevertheless, she pressed gently, "I do not wish to pain you, but could I ask–do you remember your mother's voice speaking to you as an unborn hatchling? Did you sense the fire-souls of your siblings … who died?"

"Aye." His claws curled unconsciously, as though he pictured snatching his shell-siblings from death's paw. "Sometimes, I imagine I still hear their voices, perhaps their spirits speaking from the eternal flame. They died peacefully. I, in my immature way, tried to command their spirits not to leave. I fought the eternal fires that day, Hualiama. I railed and cursed. I wept a rain of fire. Thus, I must perforce live three lives."

At once appalled and deeply moved, Lia whispered, "You honour them, but at what cost?"

Grandion pawed his muzzle roughly. "Why ask this question, Lia? Why summon dark-fires from the past?"

"Because I dream what seem to be shell-dreams–please don't hate me for saying this, Grandion." The Tourmaline Dragon's tail flicked dangerously behind him. "I know how precious these dreams are to the Dragonkind. I'm not making it up. Maybe it's a magic-induced form of insanity. Could it be the Ancient Dragon's fire-gift? Some kind of echo–"

"And the Dragonfriend profanes the sacred once more," he blazed. "No Human is welcome to trample these precious mysteries."

People and Dragons mixed as well as Islands and the Cloudlands. These dreams must hint at the transformative power of Amaryllion's magic.

The Ancient Dragon might have questioned the wisdom of imparting such a gift upon a Human, but that was no excuse for Grandion's surly response. Let him sulk. He did not carry the burden of conflicting claims of magic in his life, nor the affliction of a prophecy that shadowed a person's soul. What third great race? What great cataclysm? She wished she knew what any of it meant.

Yet, magic's touch had not always been for ill. A miracle had placed an unwanted babe in Sapphurion and Qualiana's roost. Magic had underpinned the bond of friendship between her and Flicker. And the magical Nuyallith techniques had manifested through her dance with truly disruptive power, as her fathers–blood-father and adoptive father alike–had discovered to their cost. What power could disrupt this cage? A force such as that she had sensed both in Razzior's link with Ra'aba, and in the strange gemstone-eyed young man who had appeared to help her as she confronted her father before the

Onyx Throne of Fra'anior? The youth who reminded her so forcibly of Grandion?

People did not become Dragons, nor Dragons, people. That boy had vanished like rain falling upon the Cloudlands. Hualiama eyed Grandion speculatively. It was a girlish fantasy, but how might he look as a man? Eyes of striking, tourmaline blue, wavy dark hair … just as gorgeous as the young man she had fancied. Six years later, his features graced her memory with pristine clarity. Certainly, that oh-so-leopard young man had tipped the balance in her fight with Ra'aba. He had bowed to her as if he knew exactly who she was.

Her mind bounded in another direction.

Disruption. *Ruzal* was the ultimate disruptive magic–dark, devious and debilitating. Razzior had commanded the Greens against their will. A flick of Ianthine's *ruzal* had ejected Grandion from her lair as though he were a child's toy. In the midst of her joyous celebration of calling the Tourmaline Dragons' secret name, what had reared up to steal her joy, if not *ruzal?* And if the Ancient Dragon had correctly identified the taint of Ianthine's *ruzal* magic upon her earliest years–what had the Maroon Dragoness bound? What had she disrupted? If only she knew.

Then, realisation struck her like a Blue Dragon's most potent attack, storm-powered ice. Hualiama could not prevent a keening cry of horror from escaping her lips.

"What?" Grandion demanded, from across the cave. "Smarting as you ought to be, Dragonfriend?"

Repentance was a thousand leagues from his thoughts. But Lia, nauseated to her core, could barely think past the simple, chilling knowledge that she had the power. She knew the darkness of *ruzal.* Malleable, seductive, it sang to her spirit. It wanted to be used. It wanted to ooze into her life, to seep into the despicable, unlovely corners of her being. *Ruzal's* darkness would steal all that was good and light within her, corrupting and tainting Hualiama–yet it promised a sweet, poisoned chalice of freedom.

A Dragon's paw steadied her. Hualiama startled, having not heard Grandion move. "What?" he growled again, but his tone betrayed gentleness this time. “Are you unwell?”

“I know how to escape.”

* * * *

Words burned in Grandion’s throat, but he refused them egress. A Dragoness would have nipped his wingtips. Lia had no such recourse. But she was smart. The Tourmaline Dragon had always thought Dragons far superior in intellect, but that a five-foot wisp of a girl possessed the capacity to constantly surprise him–she deserved his respect rather than the scourge of draconic scorn.

Grandion hissed between his fangs, “Escape? How?”

The girl trembled in his paw. Terror, he realised. One of the bravest creatures he knew, one who drew strength from grief and power from the unspeakable wells of vulnerability, was afraid.

Her fear focussed his mind upon the only possible answer. He said, “*Ruzal*. Lia, you mean to use *ruzal*, don’t you? May the Great Dragon’s wings protect us!”

His throat closed. That inner darkness, that almost-presence which had stolen her joy … a Dragon-sense made every scale on his body prickle with painful intensity. She had voiced the only answer. This was Ianthine’s signature work beginning to flower in her life. No, not to flower–an unfortunate choice of words to describe a vile fate. Suddenly, Grandion was afraid for his bright, beautiful Rider, whose song had entwined with his fire-spirit. Perhaps it was grounded in the Ancient Dragon’s and the dragonet’s gifts, but he knew the colour of her white-fires as pure Hualiama. Those sacral fires must never be extinguished. They kindled his Dragon-senses to a pitch of sensitivity he had not enjoyed since waking in Shinzen’s cave. Yes! For a dazzling moment, Grandion’s magic surged, and his mind reached out.

To contemplate Hualiama as he did now, with the insight of his seventh sense, was to behold a star-like spirit imprisoned in frail Human flesh. To imagine this star consumed by a darkness deeper and more terrible than his own lack of sight, filled Grandion with a wild, towering rage. Suddenly, the Tourmaline Dragon felt vitally, painfully alive. His hearts pounded three distinct drumbeats within his throat, chest and belly, driving blood along his arteries so powerfully, his body buzzed in response. He wanted to pounce upon something, to attack, to rend and claw and bite …

Yet he remembered not to clench his fist.

A soft query tickled the Dragon's ear-canals. *Grandion? Speak to me. Have I angered you?*

NO! he boomed. *No. I'm angry at what must be done.*

Why?

He replied, *The word* 'ruzal' *is similar in meaning to 'infiltrate' or 'sabotage'. That's the fundamental nature of this magic. As you Humans say, it is a two-edged blade. Opening yourself to this twisting and tainting influence, Hualiama, carries an appalling risk.*

Her fingers caressed the sensitive scales beside his left eye, with a touch both tender and troubled. *Your caring warms my heart, Grandion.*

Then you'll do it?

I'm not strong enough. So terrified …

Suddenly she was bent over his paw, her body racked with sobs, shaking the Dragon to his core with a force beyond his comprehension. How could he feel like this, if it was not right? Yet millennia of draconic law and tradition would tell otherwise. His left paw rose uneasily to stroke her unbound hair in a gesture with which he had seen Qualiana comfort a Human child. To what good end could this forbidden passion possibly lead?

There was an un-nuanced quality to Hualiama's Dragonish which oftentimes struck him as ingenuous, for it contrasted so sharply with the complexities of which an adult Dragon was capable. Meaning was veiled, distorted, processed through so many layers of subterfuge that mental or vocal communication often resembled a game of strategy, in which neither player knew quite what the other meant, nor entirely what they themselves wished to convey. It also lent her language a direct, refreshing quality which the Tourmaline Dragon revelled in.

The Princess of Fra'anior sniffed, *I'm such a bleating coward.*

Never! His growl caused his captive to stiffen. *I'll gnaw your head off your shoulders if you dare to invent falsehoods. Now, fire up that Dragoness' heart of yours. Gird your courage as a Dragon girds himself for war, in Dragon armour and the splendour of his power, spread your wings, and fly to the battle with a song of Dragon fire alive in your breast!*

Hualiama snorted, *Bah, and I thought you the miserable one. Now you're a draconic war-poet?*

Grandion's laughter thundered over the girl. *See if my words don't fire you up. I feel the strength in your spine. I sense the smoking paths of your thoughts—thou, the ardent cataclysm of volcanic glory!*

Her shoulders shook. At first he mistook her response for amusement. His belly-fires roared in protest, but then he sensed her head shaking side-to-side in the Human gesture of negation. She said, *How do you know me so truly, Grandion of Gi'ishior? Empowering and overpowering, awakening and inciting … is this what it means to be a Dragon?*

The music needs only to be unleashed, little one. He uncurled his paw. *This is the Dragonsong of your heart.*

Her breath sucked in sharply. Then she performed that inexplicable, chrysalis-like transformation which never failed to astonish him. He could almost imagine the clicking of door-locks or the throwing open of hidden chests of energies and potencies within her being, for the Human girl switched personalities in the time it took him to formulate a coherent thought acknowledging the fact.

Right, Dragon, she said, in a voice like a whetted blade. *You will teach me everything you know about Juyhallith, the way of the mind.*

In the next hour? He wafted sulphurous smoke in her direction, a draconic way of amplifying negation.

Our time is short—do you not sense it?

Grandion gasped, *Hualiama! How, by the Spirits of the Ancient Dragons …*

Her clothing rustled as, he imagined, she shrugged her shoulders. *The scent of the Island-World tingles upon the breezes. The balance changes. And a girl can stand tall with a Dragon beside her, Grandion.*

She thought he grasped something of her essence, and then she made statements like this? Grandion ruffled his wing-membranes in consternation. Oh, to feel such a breeze buoying him up! The very thought aroused the melody of Dragonsong in his hearts.

He whispered, *And her Dragon can stand aside while his Rider revolutionises said Island-World …*

Never aside, sweet Dragon. Never second-rate.

* * * *

Hualiama knew the precise moment she released the *ruzal.*

Grappling with that dark kernel of power was an exquisitely painful sensation she could only liken to trying to force food down a throat clawed repeatedly by a dozen dragonets' needle-sharp talons. It was not natural. The magic needed to be torn free, gasping and bloodied, a ghastly birth of something within her that should never have seen the light of the twin suns.

Gaaaaarrgggh! Lia wailed.

The magic of their Dragon-bone cage recoiled, before surging back to seal the tiny breach she had wrought.

Behind her, the Dragon's agitated pacing increased exponentially. He had given up trying to comfort her as she forced herself to forge a channel to release the *ruzal.* Concern radiated out of the great beast, along with a heat in the cavern that only seemed to increase the harder Lia worked. A cold sweat shone on her skin as though she strained to vomit, but could not. When the *ruzal* licked out for the first time and Hualiama groaned, the Dragon's massive paws shook the ground behind her.

"Stand back," she called, holding out a hand. "I don't know what might happen."

"I felt that!" growled the Tourmaline.

"I know."

The Dragon could still his entire being, it seemed–belly fires, breathing, even his hearts-beat if needed–for an instant, to listen. He rasped, "When we breach it, they'll come." She did not need to express her question; somehow, he knew. "I sense fresh movement in Shinzen's hideout. Unusual sounds."

"Dragons?"

"Nothing I could rend with my claw." Sweltering air boiled over her shoulders. Despite the heat, Hualiama shivered. The Dragon said, "We need to work together. When you rupture the magic, I'll try to tear into the wall with my claws and pull a few of those Dragon bones free."

"I want you out of the way." Hands on hips, Lia addressed Grandion with asperity. "I can't guarantee your safety."

"Yesterday, you said, 'Never aside, never second-best.' "

"That's not a word-for-word quote."

Grandion showed her a hundred-fang smile. "Call me sweet again, I dare you."

Fending his muzzle away with a straight-armed push, Lia turned back to the wall. Taking a deep breath and squaring her shoulders, she summoned up tentacles of dark magic, envisioning as Grandion had suggested, a shadowy pond which contained the *ruzal*–both as a focal point for her concentration, and as a means of limiting its spread into her mind. Lia's imagination drew oily, black appendages out of the water, waving with animate purpose, which she determinedly shaped and extended toward the cage wall. Pain blossomed between her temples. Sweat pearled afresh on her brow. Hualiama's back and shoulders creaked under the strain as she compelled the *ruzal* to bend to her will.

Her loathing of the process only served to strengthen the *ruzal*. Where had it come from? This knowledge seemed embedded in her psyche–had Ianthine implanted her terrible, corrosive magic within a Human baby? Sick, perverted Dragoness! Focussing on the cage, Hualiama scraped together every ounce of disgust, animosity and despair she had ever tried to blot out of her existence. As much as she loved the light, these things were part of her nature, too. She pictured Zalcion's vile attack. She remembered Razzior's invitation to run, because the pursuit and slaughter of a helpless Human excited him. She gagged at the foetid scents of Ianthine's lair.

The power swelled grotesquely. She was too good at this. Oh no. Oh …

I HATE YOU!

She meant the cavern, and Shinzen's heartless capture of

her Dragonlove. No Dragon deserved to die in captivity. Her hands spread involuntarily. *For your sake, Grandion.*

The tentacles juddered as they impacted the Dragon-bone wall, making Hualiama's body jerk about in a surreal parody of dance. They pulled at her in the region of her belly, plumbing her power, sucking her dry. *Ruzal* poured like fine dust into the gaps between the bones, leaching beneath the binding metal hawsers. The *ruzal* warped and undermined the beautiful edifices of Dragon magic.

Tears streaked Lia's cheeks.

Grandion shoved past her, thrusting his talons into the wall. Dully, she heard him roar, heard the crack of bone separating from metal and rock, as the Tourmaline Dragon exerted his exceptional strength to tear a section loose. A thirty-foot segment of the cage framework sagged away, aged bones trapped in metallic netting.

"Again!" growled the Dragon.

"To your right paw," she ordered.

"Nothing but rock?"

"Aye."

The Dragon hooked his claws into the mesh and heaved, but nothing happened. Hualiama heard faint shouts in the distance. Grandion called, "Again. Wreck it."

She was enervated. The strain of struggling non-stop for over thirty hours to trigger the magic had taken its toll, and Lia had little left to give. With a wrenching cry, Lia managed to weaken another ten feet of wall. Grandion ripped it away. She had to skip backward or face being crushed beneath the heavy Dragon bones.

"Again!" thundered the Dragon.

"Grandion … I can't." Hands on knees, she gasped for breath. The headache had bloomed to blinding proportions.

"What do you mean, can't? There's no such word!"

"I've nothing left. No strength. No–"

The Tourmaline's poisonous expression corked the words in her throat. He growled, "Then find the strength." When she hesitated, he exploded, "Don't you understand what it means for a Dragon to be caged for three years? Three summers of no suns upon my back. Three summers–"

A despairing scream echoed mockingly in her ears as Lia failed to elicit so much as a ripple from her dark pond. She glanced at Grandion from beneath her lowered lashes, and winced.

The Dragon blazed, "That was the most miserable excuse for magic I've ever seen, you flameless lump of windroc excrement."

Hualiama stared, before realising that the force of her glare was rather lost on a blind Dragon. "Grandion, insults fire up Dragons, not Humans."

In a low, penetrating snarl, he continued, "You pathetic, two-legged dancing worm! Miserable cretin! I should have stamped out your woeful little existence the first time."

"It's not working. Shut your muzzle before you say something you'll regret."

Grandion's voice deepened. "Your father never loved you. He loathed you with such brutal–"

She screamed, "Grandion!"

"Do you hear Ra'aba sniggering, Hualiama?" His hateful hiss spoke directly to her *ruzal*, causing it to quiver with unbearable relish. "From the moment you were conceived, he hated you, and he has never stopped hating you. He thinks you're so pathetic, so loathsome, you're like a cockroach he'd rather crush beneath his heel–"

The Hualiama of old might have curled up like a leaf tossed on a bonfire at his words. This Lia exploded like a hydrogen balloon sparked by a misfiring Dragonship engine. Fire surged, uncontrollable. The dark pool in her mind detonated, spewing power upward and outward, a great rippling of the fabric of reality grounded in the power of an Ancient Dragon, still alive and vital within her being. Lia saw minutely, the motes of dust springing free as the walls of their cage imploded, the instantaneous severing of metal hawsers thicker in diameter than her wrist, the tourmaline wings of a Dragon snapping shut overhead as Grandion's Dragon-swift reflexes protected her from a rockfall–bones and rubble, she realised belatedly, the pulverised remains of their cage.

The Tourmaline Dragon heaved upward, scattering boulders and debris, plucking Lia free with his paws. She heard, *Swish-thud!* Bent over, hacking and coughing dust out of her lungs, Hualiama did not at first register what had happened.

Grandion roared in pain. He whirled, smacking Lia into the air with his tail. She absorbed the worst of the impact with her knee and a jarring blow to her forearm, rising to witness Grandion shouldering his way out of what had to have been the main doorway for the cage, a fifty-by-thirty foot hole leading to a tunnel. His spine-spikes were entangled in the Dragon-bone mesh–what was left of it. Her mouth fished for flies. Great Islands, what had she done? It appeared as if she had macerated the stone surrounding the chamber, collapsing it inward. That was not enough to reveal open sky, as she had seen through the ventilation hole at the top of their cage. A hundred feet of solid rock separated them from freedom.

Now there was a new aeration feature.

Grandion's roar had an edge of pain, of panic. His tail lashed about, peppering her with stones the size of her head. This was hardly the moment to be stuck behind a feral Dragon!

Only one way out. Pouncing on Grandion's half-buried upper rear thigh, Lia sprang as high as she could up his back. She caught a spine-spike. Steady! The Tourmaline thrashed about in a welter of fury. She felt heat rolling over her back, sucking her lungs dry. Oh, he had found his fire. Calderas full of fire. His roaring battered her ears and shook Shinzen's lair at a stunning pitch, a madness rooted in the scent of freedom.

Swish! Hualiama yelped as a crossbow bolt nearly parted her hairline. Six feet long and barbed to ensure a good hold in the flesh of a Dragon or Dragonship, one of those would make short work of any royal ward. She slipped on his damp-slick scales, but the rolling of Grandion's muscles pitched her upright again. Lia's line of sight topped his shoulder. Great Islands! Four crossbow teams faced them down the tunnel. The men raced to reload their weapons.

"Stone skin!" she yelled.

Grandion shot a fireball at them, so super-heated his flame

spurted out white rather than yellow. It exploded against the first catapult on the tunnel's left side, destroying it and the four engineers working the mechanism. Hualiama felt the impact beneath her as a quarrel slapped into his hide, a dull, wet sound as the shaft feathered in the enormous bulk of the Dragon's left shoulder. Jerking about like a trout snaffled in a net, the Tourmaline Dragon hosed the tunnel with fire. What he lacked in accuracy, he made up for with blind fury. Catapults burned. Engineers ran for their lives.

She had no horror to spare for the carnage. *Grandion! LISTEN TO ME!* The Dragon stiffened beneath her. Suddenly, telepathic Dragon-speech was possible. *Save your fires. We'll need them.*

What do you see, Rider?

Tunnel. Leads deeper into Shinzen's lair, straight ahead. You've cleared the immediate danger. Hurt?

Not badly.

No, he only had a couple of quarrels buried in his obstinate hide. Apparently not enough to stop an angry Dragon. Lia eyed the hawsers above her, stretched across his back. *Wriggle backward, Grandion.*

What? We need to escape.

Shut your flaming gob-hole and listen to me! You're dragging half a cave-load of Dragon bones after you.

I'll snap these threads like—

Go stuff your overweening pride in a Cloudlands volcano!

Grandion only chuckled, *Told you those insults would work. You've Island-shaking power, Lia.*

Aye, and his words were quarrels buried in her mind. She would never forget them. Her father had hated her since … forever. She snapped, *Back. Now.* Her voice shook in reaction. That much *ruzal* blasting through her being? She must not become a channel for hatred.

As the Dragon retreated, Hualiama advanced up his back. It took all of her strength to shift even one of the braided metal hawsers, until she realised she could direct Grandion to use his paws. Then it was easy—as long as long as a ninety-foot, freedom-crazed Dragon followed her directions. Not so straightforward. Lia realised that it was up to her to find a way out of Shinzen's lair. She had to become Grandion's eyes. Keeping them alive would require a miracle.

Then, she heard another Dragon's booming battle-challenge.

"Razzior!"

Chapter Nineteen

Shinzen's Lair

GRANDION BRIDLED AT the Human's commands. "Aye, Razzior," he growled. "We need to move. Sing out the route, Rider." He promptly chipped a fang on the wall. "Lia!"

"Give me a chance!"

Little Dragoness. She could snarl with the best of them. A shame he could snap her in half with a flick of his smallest talon. Fire bubbled in his arteries. Ah, the long-dormant thrill of magic! Grandion sensed his inner potentials adjusting, the storehouses of Dragon fire and ice and lightning swelling with new life, the feedback from his remaining senses suddenly so sweet and fruitful, he swayed dizzily and thumped his head again.

Tiny feet pattered up his back. Hualiama slipped into her customary position between the spine-spikes above his shoulders. She said, *I know thy zeal, thou, the kingly splendour of the twin suns.*

Thou, the hallowed essence of my soul-fires, he crooned involuntarily, startled into a response that revealed the secrets of his third heart.

Grandion stumped forward, testing the air with his nose and Dragon-senses. He had burned this place out. Nothing lived. If he were true to his fires, the Tourmaline Dragon would have to admit he was afraid of venturing out into the world, blind. He had enjoyed a protected existence in the Dragon-bone cage–enjoyed? Burn that notion and crush the cinders beneath his paw! He growled unhappily.

A foot tapped his shoulder. *Be strong, Dragon. We'll get you out of here. Three hundred feet, then a turn.*

Hualiama's thoughts increased in pace and quality as she directed him down the long, snaking main tunnel of the lair. Now he could be grateful for the stream of her thoughts, which he had more than once characterised as monkey-chatter. As if the girl had opened a spigot, Grandion began to comprehend her spatial awareness–so different to that of a Dragon–which allowed him to adjust to the tunnel's twists and even the occasional lowering of the roof. His throat warmed with fire. This could work.

Catapult dead ahead!

The Tourmaline responded, springing sideways. *Oof–shards take it!* His shoulder took the brunt of an unseen blow. He heard his Rider's teeth snap together at the impact. But the shot missed.

Fireball–no, ten feet left. Two squads of soldiers incoming.

Ten feet left? Grandion adjusted the stream of fire with his tongue, making it billow wider and flatter as Lia's instructions flowed unabated. Screams of pain and panic assured him of his success. Ha. See if a blind Dragon couldn't fight!

Charge! Get moving, you blue lump! Not up–Islands' sakes, Grandion, there's a roof … hard left … we'll bulldoze a catapult emplacement in two … one … jump right! A quarrel glanced off his flank. *Darn it I can't see everything … forward a touch left faster no slower–fireball!*

Flame and smoke detonated ahead of him, filling Grandion's nostrils with the delicious scents of battle. Beautiful! His pulse surged. The Dragonsong of combat swelled his hearts with its treacherously addictive payload. His Rider shouted at him to slow down. Her directions became increasingly desperate as the Dragon, overflowing with exultation, the scent of freedom and three years of cage-aged rage, charged instinctively into the fray. She was a mosquito upon his back. Words beat without meaning inside his ear-canals.

Grandion's jaw gaped. *GGRRRAAARRGGGH!*

For the first time in years, his Dragon-roar had a real crack of thunder to it. His stomach contracted with pleasure. Aye. Ice and wind, snow and hail, and storm power. He was Dragonkind!

* * * *

Hualiama gave up trying to bridle Grandion, and settled for funnelling his rage while keeping the stone-headed lizard from braining himself, or her. There was something so visceral about sitting atop a stampeding Dragon–minus any useful weapon whatsoever–that she began to laugh. Lunacy! Spine-tingling madness!

Suddenly, she caught sight of thick stone doors ahead. They inched shut under the efforts of a sweating troop of Shinzen's soldiers, who viewed the Dragon's approach with the terror of men trapped in the path of an avalanche. Beyond them, she saw through the narrowing crack, a phalanx of armoured Human giants. Nine, ten feet tall. Four feet wide. Massively armoured, they crouched behind a wall of interlocked shields. The doors were twenty feet apart and closing steadily.

Rouse my powers! Grandion's voice boomed in her mind. *I smell open air!*

Rouse his powers? The Tourmaline was asking for help? Astonishing. Perhaps he was a changed Dragon after all. Raising her voice in a turbulent, compelling chant, Lia began to declaim a passage from *Saggaz Thunderdoom,* a famous Sapphire Dragon who dominated many of the vocal sagas:

Bestriding boiling thunderheads, the Thunderdoom arose,
His roar a trump of thunder,
Like wingéd lightning his mighty paw,
Struck the skies asunder!

Beneath her, the Tourmaline Dragon's belly boiled–literally, Lia imagined, for the powers churning beneath her thighs sounded like a vast pot left to boil over, bubbling and hissing and steaming as its contents sizzled upon the coals. So much potential! No wonder the Blue colours were regarded as the mightiest of draconic magic-users.

With a thought, Lia pointed Grandion at the doors. *Take the shot, my beauty!*

The Dragon's flanks rippled. His throat convulsed and his muzzle shot forward, elongating his throat into the barrel of a weapon. Light streaked her vision, not a fireball as she had expected, but ball-lightning, which roiled through the air with a hungry crackle before detonating against the left door. Cacophony! Destruction! Lia's head rang. Her own magic resonated in response, as if her body were a gong pealing the knell of Grandion's assault.

Brace for impact! Lia yelled. A massively muscled Tourmaline shoulder shattered the weakened door. They barrelled through the wreckage, the smoke and the crazily crackling leftover energies, kicking charred bodies left and right as the Dragon thundered into the huge cavern beyond.

Dragons! Grandion roared.

That's Shinzen! Razzior! And–unh! Lia's hand flew to her face. Blood spurted between her fingers. Had she broken her nose on Grandion's spine-spike? *Grandion?*

Can't move.

At the same time, Shinzen waved a hand languidly. "Islands' greetings!" he boomed.

Grandion had stopped as though he had run into a wall–Shinzen's magic? The air around her was too still. The Fra'aniorian Islander sensed her Dragon fighting back, magic for magic, but three cage-bound years had weakened him severely. Could he even fly? The Warlord had not moved from his relaxed stance on a small dais–as if he needed the additional height–set two hundred feet to the right of the doors. Lia saw at least a dozen Dragons inside the cave; she picked out Razzior by his sheer bulk and the ghastly scar on his face.

Shinzen said, "Razzior, the scrawny beast is all yours. My part of the bargain."

Razzior's fangs gleamed in a twisted smile, again, so similar to Ra'aba … "Aye, a good bargain, Shinzen."

Good bargain? What in a volcanic hell?

Compared to Razzior, Grandion resembled a scrawny

adolescent. The Tourmaline had been starved in captivity. Beyond Razzior, her frantically swivelling gaze was drawn to a Dragoness who could only be Cerissae–the distinctive yellow dagger-patterns on her fantastically pointed scales, and the additional rows of spikes on her muzzle, skull, spine, tail and even her wing-struts, matched Grandion's description exactly. She cast an avaricious glance at Lia's mount, but the murder which gleamed in her torrid gaze was reserved for the girl upon his back. Grandion quivered as he counteracted Shinzen's magic. Two huge men standing behind Shinzen began to chant softly, and Hualiama felt the magic intensify, as if the very air had turned into chains to hold a Dragon fast.

The Orange Dragon's flaming eye rose to fix upon Hualiama. He grunted in recognition. "Lia. We meet again."

"You know the wench?" Shinzen asked.

"Nasty piece of windroc bait," growled Razzior. "That's Hualiama, Princess of Fra'anior. We've run into each other, aye, several times."

"To your detriment, Razzior," Lia called. "I defeated–"

"Shut the trap." Magic seized her jaw. Shinzen's eyes glittered at the now-silenced Human Princess. "A princess, you say? Have you any use for a Dragon-riding princess?"

The Dragon turned his regard upon Shinzen. An understanding seemed to pass between them. "A deal-sweetener? Use her as you wish, Shinzen," rasped Razzior. "Abuse her. Only, watch out for her magic."

Lia fought Shinzen's power furiously. The touch of it left a rancid taste upon her tongue, a hint of *ruzal*, but it was subtly different. She was not about to sweeten anything for anybody. Pillows of air gathered beneath her legs. Suddenly, she wafted off Grandion's back and over the phalanx of giants, flying toward Shinzen. The giant loomed larger and larger–freaking Islands, what a rajal of a man! His magic brought her to a halt at arms-length, holding her aloft with dreadful ease. How could she fight this? The black-in-black eyes bored into Lia's mind, rummaging, defiling.

"Oh, precious!" Shinzen threw back his head with a roar. "She's untouched."

"All the better to enjoy," Razzior chuckled horribly.

That was it. The backdrop of Dragons and Humans alike chortling at her humiliation, brought a spark of inspiration to Lia's misery. If she possessed Grandion's power … impulsively, she reached for the Dragon, and dove *into* him. He had what she needed. She dove deep.

* * * *

The girl-Dragon flexed her back-muscles. Ah. For the first time in her life, she commanded another being. Unfamiliar scents crowded into her nostrils–the metallic stench of the giants, the sulphur-and-musk reek of aggressive male Dragons and the clean, intoxicating scent of freedom. Her belly seethed with potentials she could barely imagine. From the four-pawed, falling-on-her-nose stance of her new body, to the pain of the quarrel buried in her shoulder joint, to the scintillating colours which bewildered her Human consciousness, all was alien and exhilarating and *wrong*. She trespassed on the province of Dragons.

So, Grandion, shall we twine necks again? Cerissae crooned. Memories–wholly unwanted memories–battered her mind. Dragon emotions tumbled over her like a Cloudlands-bound stream surging from a league-tall clifftop to dash its fury upon the uncaring rocks below. Molten heat rose in rivers from her lower belly to surge through the massive portals of her hearts. Soughing. Hissing. Piercing her awareness, priming her muscles for action.

How could she control this? She barely raised her head above the flood, gasping for breath, before she sank again.

The Dragoness called, *Don't you remember what we shared, Grandion?*

Lia hated the Dragoness. Was this how Cerissae had deceived Grandion, her shifting mind-magic coiling about his consciousness with serpentine glee … only now, she dealt with an irritable, panicked, possessive Dragon Rider!

You filthy, stinking whelp of a cliff-goat! Lia snarled. Cerissae recoiled, her bared talons involuntarily shrieking across the stone. *Sneaking weasel, slink back to your burrow!*

The Amber-Red Dragoness had a foolish, flaccid sag to her lip as she stared at Grandion.

Lia chuckled, *Island drop on your head, you bloated maggot?*

Cerissae flinched.

With a fierce mental pinch, the Princess reminded herself that all she sought was the Dragon's freedom. The temptation stunned her. How could evil be so captivating? Barriers she had thought inviolable, the very values and pillars of her life, could crumble in an instant. As she wavered, Grandion's consciousness roared back into the breach. An avalanche buried her.

* * * *

Grandion blinked. Vision! Shapes and shadows and tints washed into his mind, stimulating long-forgotten centres of sight. Oh, this was a taste of glory, filtered through a Human's pitiful senses.

Behind him, Razzior rumbled, "So, Shinzen. We've a deal. Lead me to the caves of your giants, and my Dragons and I shall rouse the rest. Soon, you'll have your army."

"Your Dragonwings approach?"

"It takes time, Shinzen." Razzior's irritation boiled between his fangs in clouds of smoke. Shinzen appeared unmoved. "Fifty Dragons fly from Rolodia. Sixty roost at Helyon. At Haozi, we number but thirty-one, while over a hundred allied Dragons keep Sapphurion and his toadies busy around Fra'anior."

Grandion's mind quested through the unfamiliar, muddy backwaters of a Human's psyche. By his mother's egg, this was how they stood, unbalanced on two spindly legs? His body felt so light, he feared that the merest breath of wind might send it sailing away over the Island-World. A single heart fluttered like a panicked terhal, a flightless bird he had hunted for several times on the most northerly Isles around Pla'arna Cluster.

Just let Shinzen take this new Dragon-beast to his pillow-roll.

Suddenly, it struck him with the force of a crossbow quarrel. This was the moment he had waited for, that he had imagined but withheld out of concern–misplaced concern. Dragons did not ask. They seized what was their right. And the Human girl had made it abundantly clear, through oath and deed, that she was his possession.

The Tourmaline Dragon reached out, and seized Hualiama's powers for himself. He must have it all. Only a Dragon could survive this.

The girl resisted. A catlike keening singed his mind before he slammed down the barriers, cutting her off without remorse. Necessity dictated his actions. He needed no distractions.

But Grandion could not understand the world of Lia's unique powers. All he knew was what existed, the white-fires trembling within her soul like perfect lilies floating upon a tranquil pond. *Arise!* The Dragon snatched at the lilies, bruising, trampling, forcing compliance to his will. Now, back to his Dragon body. Keep the sight. The Tourmaline Dragon divided his consciousness. The white-fires surged with him, shockingly lambent, firing him so sharply that the prickling of his scales was torment, that the vast reaches of her potential burned even a creature of flame … he could not breathe … nor command a muscle … a volcano's core seared his body!

Then, blessed coolness bathed him through and through. Hualiama's spirit reached inside the barrier of his Blue Dragon enchantments, the mightiest magic Sapphurion knew to teach his shell-son, as though it were a gossamer veil. She brought balance. Beauty. A hint of melodious laughter, wrapped in anguish. *Must you?*

He kicked her away. *Begone, and let a Dragon do his work!*

Craven doubts gnawed at him. This was Razzior's approach. Hualiama would never have mistreated him like this. Did he seek to punish her? Yet the Dragon plunged on recklessly. The Dragonkind desired neither permission nor forgiveness.

Grandion rapidly rearranged his mental space. Eyes, in the girl's body. Her power radiating from his scale armour now, burnishing it like the fires of the twin suns reborn, irradiating the cave. Shinzen paled. Razzior's head began to turn as his magical senses reacted to the incongruously lyrical white-fire trembling the air. Grandion lunged for the girl. The massed giants drew their formation together, but the Dragon simply poured over them, the white-fire slicing cleanly through the spear-heads thrust his way, and the barrage of black giant-magic which momentarily stymied him, shivered and disintegrated into shimmering dust beneath an all-consuming caress that was the pure essence of Hualiama.

Grandion's battle-laughter belled out over the watching Dragons. Stunned, not a creature moved as he snatched Lia out of the air in front of Shinzen. The Tourmaline Dragon whirled, smashing the Warlord and his two bodyguards aside with his tail. He lunged for the open cavern entrance and the beckoning skies.

Oddly, Razzior did not lift a claw to stop him.

Grandion trampled a smaller Red as he stormed out, finding himself in a huge courtyard covered in nets, the main gates standing ahead, bolted and barred against excursion or incursion. He bobbed the girl's body about, using her inadequate eyes to survey the scene, cursing beneath his breath as he realised he was still trapped. No. She had one more power, a word which she had described to him ever so charily, spelling it backward. Its allure was greater than any Dragon-hoard, greater than the power pure gold exerted upon a Dragon's avarice.

Give it to me.

No. The tiny spirit flickered weakly, yet still defied him. *Grandion, you must not–*

He quashed her with a roar, *I will not be disobeyed!*

Now Razzior moved like a river of hot lava, readying his powerful molten rock attack. Grandion knew he could not fight the wily Orange in his condition. Razzior was a notorious brawler, a killer of Dragons who opposed him.

Screaming, *I'll die without my freedom!* Grandion breached the Human girl's defences and snatched the knowledge from her. Lia's power alone could scribe his freedom. His jaw cracked open, *BEZ-*

Thank you, Razzior whispered, breathing his magic.

The girl convulsed in his paw, as though the Orange Dragon had torn something out of her with hooks. The word Grandion spoke, died before it touched his fangs. Blackness crowded around his vision. Her vision.

* * * *

Warmth was the first sensation a Dragon-eggling knew. The warmth of perfect security in a home which she would learn was a Dragoness' egg-pouch hid deep within her belly, near the third heart.

The eggling listened. She listened with more than her tiny, finger-sized ear-canals. She listened with the albumen-soft hide of her babyish Dragon scale armour. She listened with her hearts, feeling their rhythm change to match that of the great, pounding drumbeat that filled her world, never silent, never ceasing. She listened with her tongue, tasting the strange and exciting flows of magic coursing through the world about her. Sometimes, Dragonsong vibrated through the great body housing her world–her egg. Aye, she was an eggling.

Her spirit communed with the great, protective spirit surrounding her as surely as the egg sheltered a tiny, developing Dragon baby. She sensed two other eggs near her, dormant, but alive.

Song or movement stimulated her senses. Soon, she became aware of new sounds and sensations. The Dragon-mother would sing or speak, hum or slumber, and then, a strange thing: a paw, rubbing nearby, its action muted by the body between them–the egg-shell, the womblike egg-pouch, the stomach and the strong hide which covered it all. Joy shivered the eggling's budding spine-spikes.

With joy, came knowledge. She was Dragonkind. She was …

Conscious.

Thinking. Feeling. Language blossomed in her mind, still too nascent to inform her tongue, but there was no need. Her mind yearned for the great one who loved her.

Mamafire?

The movement paused. *No. It's too early. Must be a Dragon-sense.*

Deep within the Dragoness' belly, a tiny frown of consternation wrinkled the eggling's brow-ridges. The movement started again. Rubbing. Circles. The Dragoness massaged her egg-laden stomach. She sang, in gorgeous three-part harmony:

Soft now my egglings, sleep thee tight,
Mamafire loves thee all the night …

She squeaked, *Mamafire!*

Great, shining white-fires washed over her consciousness. Astonishing. The eggling watched, so entranced that she barely sensed the Dragoness' affectionate mental touch. A tiny claw pawed at the white-fires, moving as dreamily as a swimmer underwater. Then, she became aware of a great one watching her, a brooding presence which she realised had encompassed her entire life, somehow part of her, but different and separate. She stilled.

Eggling? The nurturing voice touched off cascades of happiness in her belly. *Are you alive? Already?*

Mamafire, is the white … you?

The white?

All around me. It's beautiful, like dancing fire.

The Dragoness caught her breath sharply. *You see white-fires, my eggling? Oh … how? They said egg-heavy mothers have strange thoughts. Am I dreaming?*

The eggling giggled, *Mamafire, you're silly. Can I dance with your fires?*

If you wish, eggling. Let me show you. First, you must shape your spirit, like this …

The Dragoness demonstrated. In a moment, a fragile form winged from the eggling to join her mother's white-fires, soaring between them, learning to play in their tempestuous billows, riding the bubbles of her mother's answering joy with spontaneous delight. They communed. They laughed together. The Dragoness sang the first song of burning, the eggling's welcome to the fires of Dragon-life.

And the eggling danced.

* * * *

Hualiama surfaced from her egg-dream like a drowning woman breaking a lake's surface to snatch a breath into stinging, desperate lungs. She expected light. All was darkness, and the memory of a Dragon's tyranny. Bitter. Soul-lost. Lia had a sense of drawing bruised fragments of herself back together. No beating in her life, of which there had been no lack, could compare to the damage Grandion had meted out.

Muted thunder rumbled in the distance, suggesting a storm's approach. Lia knew movement, a Dragon's body squeezing through a narrow, vibrating metal space, now pinpricks of arrows on her skin, a larger streak of flame against his hide and then the pounding of feet as the Dragon accelerated. Briefly, there was a soaring sensation, but the Dragon's flight was severely hampered by the crossbow quarrel lodged, by a stroke of ill fortune, right in the protective sheath around the major wing-joint of his left shoulder. As he flapped, the point scraped against a nerve, firing excruciating pangs right along the wing-bones into his wingtip.

Why could she not see? How did she know this?

Grandion's dominion weakened. Her spirit was trapped somewhere inside the Dragon's being. Her body dangled from his paw. Strangely, Lia sensed this was not the first time in her life she had been so dislocated, spirit from body. Did the removal of spirit from body not kill a physical being? Was being spirit, or spirit being?

No time for philosophy, though the Human girl sensed she trembled on the cusp of grasping a great and wonderful truth. They must escape.

Pain ravaged the Dragon's consciousness. Lia wanted to exult, to whoop the agony on in an act of revenge, but resisted. Images flashed and disintegrated before her. A long green slope leading to a tangled stretch of jungle. Waterways gleaming among the giant trees. A backward glance at Shinzen's fortress. Dragons climbing into a storm-dark evening sky, wheeling into the pursuit with eager roars. Razzior led the charge.

The Tourmaline Dragon groaned with the effort, making such a tremendous speed that Lia's flaccid limbs rattled and flapped in the airstream of his passage. Wouldn't this damage her joints? Her eyelids fluttered. Grandion growled, trying to force her to keep them open, but Humans did not have the secondary nictitating membrane which protected a Dragon's eyesight. Vision suffered at this speed. Grandion swept past trees, weaving down one of the channels that led into a leagues-wide swamp. Heavy leaves slapped his flanks and underbelly. Long minutes passed.

Suddenly, water sheeted over her face. Lia choked.

Holding her above the brackish swamp waters, Grandion bellied down beneath the trees, forcing his body deep into the thicket. The royal ward felt the Dragon's magic enfold them in an unnatural silence.

She groaned at the pain in her arms and legs.

* * * *

The Tourmaline Dragon listened watchfully for sounds of pursuit. Hualiama blew water out of her nose and coughed up what sounded like ten mouthfuls of swamp scum, before the sound changed and Grandion realised she had stifled a sob.

Are you hurt, my Rider?

Her whispered reply made him wince.

In the ensuing silence, Grandion worked on his screening magic. No iota could be allowed to escape. Razzior would pursue them with every artifice at the Orange Dragon's command. He was no fool. But the Tourmaline's mind kept returning to his Rider. What had prompted that response? They had escaped. She had broken the cage; he had broken Shinzen's defences, blasted down his front door and winged away. Perfect teamwork. Did she understand what a sacrifice he had made in giving up his eyesight again?

We must see to your wounds. Warm water splashed along his flank. Small hands and feet made the ascent. His scales prickled with a Dragon-sense of impending doom. Even now, in extremity, she had a largeness of spirit that baffled him. Hualiama served her erstwhile oppressor.

He said, *We escaped, didn't we, Rider-heart?*

I'm not your bloody heart … anything! Lia bit off her mental scream. *Quiet. Razzior approaches.*

Grandion whispered, *We're alive, aren't we?*

The Dragon smelled a strangeness about her. Was it the *ruzal* magic? Eventually, as though she pawed through words for the right fragments to throw at him, the Princess cried, *You stupid, spineless … reptilian tyrant!* Her voice cracked. *That was an act of … of such … it was mental rape!*

He shook his head. Her affliction shook the Islands of his world as though an army of Land Dragons had attacked them. *That's strong language–*

It's true! Dragons seize what they want! They violate, despoil and never give back. I came to you in that cage and ever since you've treated me like something nasty you found under your paw. You maimed me, exploited our–

Her raw emotion ignited his furnaces. *I did what had to be done!*

You had no right!

I had every right. You swore an oath.

You swore to honour me!

And I have. You bleating wretch, you live beneath the twin suns! I gave my hide for you.

What do you know of honour? Lia kicked the quarrel embedded in his shoulder, making Grandion's entire body spasm. *Because of you, Razzior stole my magic. Now I am less, Grandion. I'm the little one, so inferior to a smug, self-serving, greedy monster who couldn't wait to plunder the powers he's so infernally jealous of–don't think I didn't feel your claws in my mind, Grandion! To think I called you Dragonlove. To think I let you in.*

Aye, you did, and–

I hate you! I wish I'd left you to rot in that cave!

Her scream stunned the Dragon. He had caused this injury? Her voice stabbed him with the icicles of a Blue Dragon ice-storm. He could not imagine this Hualiama. No fires. There was none of the habitual lilt that made him imagine she was smiling, just a little, whenever she spoke.

Grandion's mind reeled, running back in a squawking panic over the many paths of his interactions with Hualiama since he had known her. Did they not bring out the best in each other? Had he not forced her to tear the *ruzal* loose? Had he not borne her upon his back, the greatest indignity possible for a creature of fire and magic, a transgression which thus far had cost him six years of his life, three of those in captivity?

She tugged at the quarrel. *This thing's buried up to the fletching. How will we remove it?*

You're the Dragonfriend, he protested.

Don't say that! Just … don't. I thought there might have been … something, between us, Grandion. She kept fighting her tears, and losing. *What a fool I've been. A pathetic, benighted fool.*

Hualiama had reached out to him first, and known the act to be profane. Grandion had shown no such scruples. He had acted with perfect draconic domination. Rue brought howling storms of dark-fires to his hearts, the knowledge that there was a better way. There had to be.

Lia, my Rider …

There are Dragons about, she snapped. *Give me your paw, Dragon. You'll have to dig this one out yourself.*

Give me your eyes, and I will do it.

Frosty silence.

Chapter Twenty

To Rise on Wings

TWO DAYS OF skulking through a foetid swamp wearing two large holes in his hide was enough to make any Dragon snappish. Grandion knew that Lia had been right to force him to dig the crossbow quarrels free with his own talons. The Dragon ate well, supping on three anacondas, any one of which would have made a tidy meal of his tiny companion. She picked off eager swarms of swamp leeches attracted by the scent of his blood in the water, and ignored him otherwise.

That third morning, as a misty dawn leached unwillingly through the trees–the Dragon imagined such a dawn, straining to touch his hide with a breath of heat tempered by the damp–Lia muttered, "I sense giants."

"All passengers aboard," Grandion said cheerfully.

Hualiama sighed and climbed up his thigh, eschewing a proffered paw.

"May I use your sight?"

She sighed again. "If you must."

"I won't touch anything else."

"Sure. I trust you."

Never had words rung hollower. Grandion's belly-fires declared his frustration all too eloquently. The Dragon reached for her sight as the pint-sized paragon of vexation who masqueraded as a Dragon Rider clambered up to his shoulders.

With serpentine undulations of his body, the Dragon navigated the waterways, using his tail as a rudder and for propulsion, and his mighty paws as additional paddles to push through the reeds, muck and rotten vegetation. He swam the deeper parts. Thirty-foot giant salamanders and toothy reptiles Grandion recognised from a scroll attacked them repeatedly. "Crocodiles," he said. "One of Dramagon's misadventures." Drawing no response from his Rider, he added, "It seems Dramagon did not encourage visitors."

She said, "These three years, the spirit of Dramagon has been your mentor."

The Tourmaline Dragon choked on his own fires.

He stared unseeing into the swamp-mists. Misery. A mighty Dragon, reduced to borrowing a Human's inferior eyesight–and he should be grateful for the pittance. Bitter dark-fires soured his stomach. When a crocodile snapped at his left thigh, Grandion crushed it with a single bite, thinking how impossible it was to fathom that Lia's words could wound worse than a Dragon's claws or fangs. He had never imagined … she was speaking. His Dragon hearing brought her speech to his ear-canals with perfect clarity.

Hualiama said, "Before he died, Amaryllion Fireborn spoke to me at length. One thing I remember is what he said about love, that some creatures–he meant me–are given the power to love with such power and purity, that no taboo can stand against. He did not warn me that love can make us vulnerable. In my life, I've made terrible mistakes. But I have always allowed love its way, no matter the anguish and suffering it might cost."

Why did she speak of love, the Dragon wondered? He knew many words for love. Did she mean kinship-love, sacred-love, roost-love, or heavens forbid–

"You and I are taboo-breakers, Grandion. We've broken, and continue to break, one of the oldest taboos in existence on this Island-World."

What they had done was to obey the obligation of oaths recklessly taken, but grave in their consequence! Yet, he would never recant. Grandion began, "Which cost me–"

"Hush." A word, and she banished his hissing. Dragon fires surged behind his blind eyes, a sudden splash of colour where he expected none. "I know my deeds harmed you, Dragon. I can only apologise, here and now. I don't presume to teach a Dragon his path. I don't expect you to fly to this Island of fate with me … but we are united, Grandion. United by oaths which we swore freely, heart to heart, and we added to that the oath of seeking this Scroll of Binding together. We joined our fates in the strongest ways known to our respective kinds. You seem to imagine an oath is a malleable thing, to be used or set aside at a whim. You think the same of your Rider. Use her. Abuse her. Rip from her what you need."

Like mist, her words seeped into his mind–only her words were not clammy. They seared his third heart. "I know about abuse, Grandion. I'm versed in behaviours as twisted as *ruzal* itself, and I hate my past. If to grasp the essence of love means to grasp its diametric opposite, then I am detestably educated. I'm a detestable being."

Grandion quivered with the effort that it cost him to keep listening. Bonfires and lightning and storm powers raged in his stomachs, screaming around his thoughts like feral windrocs mobbing a fresh carcass. How could she be detestable? How could she speak this way?

"There's a fine line between bending in love and being a victim." She shifted restlessly on his back. "Bear to your left, Dragon. The going's easier. I think the swamp will end soon."

He knew that. He heard the sound of water rushing down a cliff, and the change in the way the wind flowed over his scales. There was vertical air movement, and the chattering of cliff-larks. Was he ready to fly?

Was he ready to fly–with her?

"The habit of being a victim scars and stunts a person. It becomes an easy posture to maintain, the default posture. I don't understand how to break free of its chains. I broke my adoptive father's ribs. I beat my blood-father in hand-to-hand combat. Aye, I handed the Onyx Throne from one father to the other–and am I the better person for it? I don't know what to do now, Grandion. With you. You hurt me, so … so …"

"Effortlessly," he mourned. "A cold, calculated raid."

Warmth dripped upon his back, warmth that tingled with a redolence of Hualiama. Even her tears, he thought. Even those were magical.

"I don't presume to say, 'Never again,' because–" she snuffled hugely, scaring several nearby water-birds into a honking panic "–because I'm probably stupid and craven enough to give it all over again, for the chance to save you. But you need to trust me, Grandion. Don't ever think me a tool, or a pet. Nor am I indestructible, nor without feelings. Somehow I envisage equality between Dragon and Rider. A partnership not founded upon grasping what we want, but thriving in mutual need and interdependence. We're two souls of equal worth–and if that sounds naïve to a mighty Dragon's ears, then I'm sorry, but that's how I see it."

Was it partly instinct, rooted in the simple physical disparity in their sizes? One of the deepest Dragon instincts was to protect hatchlings. His accelerated Dragon development had meant he outstripped her, moving through the Dragon equivalent of human childhood and teenage years in two summers, while Hualiama remained a child far longer. Lia's acumen had penetrated the heart of the conundrum. His intuition informed him that these ideas were merely the surface expression of a far deeper misperception on his part. Upon the scales of his draconic worldview, Humans weighed a mere fraction of what Dragons did. Undervalued. Belittled. Enslaved.

Dark-fires of shame excoriated his magical and emotional pathways. He had done evil. He just did not know how he could have done differently. She deserved an apology. Grovelling might have repaired some small part of the damage. He rebuked his fierce Dragon pride, flailing for words which eluded his grasp.

Beneath the water, Grandion's claws clicked on stone. He walked up a short slope, sloughing swamp water and muck off of his flanks and limbs, flicking it off his scales, flaring his wings as his body quickened at the prospect of flight. He had not risen aloft for three years.

He asked, *Do you sense anything ahead, Lia?*

Nothing, she replied. *Only mists drifting over an unknowable chasm.*

The Tourmaline Dragon extended his wings, a song rising in his heart as he remembered the ways of the winds over the Island-World, and the joy of soaring and swooping, and the rush of wind upon his muzzle and spine-spikes. He began to tip forward.

One more thing, said Hualiama. *Right now, you are not, by any measure under the twin suns, Dragonlove. You're just Dragon.*

And his hearts sank even faster than a Dragon's plunge off the cliffs of Gao-Tao Island.

* * * *

Nightmares pulled Lia's soul into darkness. The odour of falgaweed and alcohol choked her. So deeply was she mired in her dream, she was unable to escape the slow, creeping terror. Zalcion. His weight on her back, his stinking breath hot on her neck … she thrashed and screamed, but could not escape. Suddenly, the man's already inescapable weight seemed to double, to quadruple. In the darkness, a Dragon's cruel laughter washed over her. His paw held her fast. The terror of violation detonated in her heart. No longer was he the shining, beautiful spirit of a Dragon. Grandion was a dusky storm sweeping over Lia's being, all-knowing and all-conquering, a creature of bestial appetites and the power to crush her beyond redemption. Her white-fires fled before his mighty presence, shredded, brilliant petals cast adrift on an Island-World breeze.

This is the fate of the child of the Dragon! he roared. *Never will you dance again!*

Lia shot into wakefulness like a Dragon broaching the surface of an oily lake, screaming, "*Gaaaaaaaaah!*"

Grandion held her!

"Get off! Get off! Oh, great … get off me you freak!"

His paw lifted as though he had stepped upon a crossbow quarrel. "Lia? Are you alright?"

"No!" Her chest felt as though a Dragon still stood upon it. For long moments Lia leaned over, head tucked between her knees, trying to will breath into her lungs. Her world comprised the need for air. With excruciating reluctance, the invisible paw seemed to ease its grip. Hualiama hugged her knees, bidding her nausea settle and her headache abate.

"Can I help?" the Dragon asked.

The Yellow moon glinted off the Dragon's scales, highlighting how his great bulk filled the tiny valley in which they had snatched a few hours' rest. All was calm.

She said, "You can stay away from me."

All around, fifty-foot bamboo forests concealed Dragon and Rider from casual view. The Island was small, just a half-mile or so across, one nameless Isle among thousands which littered their northward flight path. Lia scowled at the four paces which separated her from Grandion's forepaws. It may as well have been a mile, crossing a chasm filled with Land Dragons the size of the creature she had seen off the Eastern Isles, or a hike across a bubbling lava lake.

Somehow, setting out, it had seemed so easy. Hualiama Dragonfriend would cross the Island-World for love, rescue her Dragon, and the stars and the moons would join in beneficent Dragonsong to celebrate the union of their hearts. Now, she feared him. She feared him with a soul-shrivelling, panic-inducing level of phobia she had never imagined. Perhaps the Dragon had touched a fear common to all women, a fear encapsulated in what she had feared her uncle intended to do to her, and Grandion had achieved in mind and spirit. Somehow, she felt complicit in her own violation. Surely, she had sparked his actions by reaching into his mind first. She had shown him the way. Her magic had enticed him. Was it even his fault?

Aye! No! She did not know. All Hualiama knew, was that she despised this woman. She loathed them both: Grandion for his unthinking dominance, and herself for the curled-up weakling she had become as a result.

Razzior had stolen her word.

Bezaldior. Alastior, she breathed. Nothing. The Orange Dragon had stolen her greatest weapon.

I am Alastior, Grandion replied, misinterpreting her words. *What of it?*

What did she know of love? For Humans, love was one

word with meanings as scattered as the stars spanning the heavens. Infinitely complex. Infinitely pliable. Dragons, with their love of linguistic precision, codified love into many words. Was there a Dragonish word for wounded-love? Soul-crushed love? Love which caused the Islands to weep? Even now, the tremor of Grandion's paw asserted his feelings. Yet if she went to him it would proclaim forgiveness–a lie, for understanding and pardon were in scant supply in her heart. But could a Rider and her Dragon stand opposed when Razzior sought the power of the Scroll of Binding for himself? That way spelled madness. Failure. And, an oath-breaking.

Hualiama, worthless as she might be in every other respect, was never an oath-breaker. Not willingly. All it needed from her, all the grace she felt she could give, was a decision.

She would rise. She would dance. She would love again.

Suddenly, Lia found her feet. Approaching Grandion, she laid her hand firmly upon his muzzle, wishing upon a thousand stars that she could gaze into his eyes once more.

Grandion, I might seem small and insignificant to you, but I have a dragonet's courage. I want you to know that I am Hualiama Dragonchild. An Ancient Dragon tarried in this world for me. I carry the fires of Amaryllion Fireborn in my soul, and I will never let them die.

The Tourmaline Dragon vented a bemused grunt as Lia scrambled over his forepaw, and deliberately pulled at his talons until he made a nook for her to curl up into. He must think her cracked in the head. Good. Let him think it. She would play him like a harp, with a Dragoness' cunning and a Human's flair for the unexpected.

The treacherous, beautiful warmth of a Dragon compelled her eyelids to flutter shut.

Later, nightmares drowned Lia's soul in darkness. The odour of falgaweed and alcohol choked her … Lia shot into wakefulness like a Dragon broaching the surface of an oily lake. "Razzior!"

Scrambling to his paws, Grandion asked, "Aye, he has sensed us. But how?"

"A Dragon's eye." Hualiama threw sand onto the embers of their fire. "I think he might have one of my Nuyallith blades. I didn't tell you the rest of my tale after I crash-landed right into the tents of Saori's people, did I?"

Nor had she pondered the Copper Dragoness' disturbing regard for her brother. Lia frowned. What was the Island-World coming to, when Dragonesses flirted with Human men? A score on which she was hardly blameless, mind–no better than the twin suns arguing with each other which was the brightest! This could not be the change which the prophecy implied, could it? Improved relations between Humans and Dragons could not cause stars to fling themselves out of the skies, nor account for Ra'aba's terror at the prophecy's implications.

Grandion deposited Hualiama upon his shoulder. "Quick, take your seat."

"You possess concealing magic?"

"Aye," he growled. "Why didn't you tell me?"

"Why didn't you just steal it from me when you had the chance?" she shot back, and bit her tongue. "Go on, Grandion."

With a thrust of his massive thighs that articulated his rage, the Tourmaline Dragon launched himself skyward, beating his wings hard to rise above the treeline. He levelled off and pointed his muzzle to the northern sky. Seated between his spine-spikes, Hualiama twisted about to scan the horizon. "Dragons," she said. "Twenty, maybe thirty …"

"Try this, Rider. Hold what you see steady in your mind, as though you frame a picture. Aye, good. I can touch it already. Now, imagine bringing it closer. Will the picture toward you."

Lia gasped as the image leaped, magnified. "Drat, it's gone out of focus."

"Try again."

The Yellow Moon waxed lambent, illuminating every Island for leagues around, but Lia had eyes only for the Dragonwing scudding in low from the south–hunting them, she realised. There was something strange about those Dragons. They flew poorly, as though heavily laden, but there was no mistaking the way that they headed directly for the Island which Hualiama and Grandion had just departed. The Tourmaline flexed his wings powerfully, driving them onward into the wind-still night, and although she knew that his magic concealed their presence from the naked eye, she also respected a Dragon power which could track them when unseen. Had Razzior sent those dreams into her mind? She shuddered, realising that if he could wield her deepest doubts and terrors against her, the Orange Dragon boasted at least Grandion's power–and he had his *ruzal* to accomplish the rest.

The Tourmaline Dragon's features blurred in the window of her soul. Transforming. Hualiama blinked. Gazing back at her, smiling, was the young man of the brilliant blue eyes. Not Ja'al, as she had sometimes suspected. No, he was different. He never spoke. Turning, he walked with the ease of a spirit-creature through the window, which seemed to be a portal to the understanding of mysteries which had plagued her since before her birth. Yet Lia could not follow. He beckoned; she glanced over her shoulder, seeking the Tourmaline Dragon in the dreamscape of her thoughts, but he was gone. Only the young man remained. A gesture of his hands brought her perception into focus. 'Like this,' he seemed to say, and her white-fires responded to his direction, the most delicate filaments springing like a perfect spiderweb toward his fingers, a web of gossamer delicacy and astonishing tensile strength.

Tracing that pearlescent web with her mind, the Fra'aniorian Princess began to grasp what Grandion had shown her before. The picture distorted strangely before steadying, many times magnified.

"Ah," said Grandion. "The Dragons carry Shinzen's forces."

Each Dragon carried a forty-foot bamboo pole clutched in his forepaws, and hanging from the pole were–she counted swiftly–fifteen armoured giants per Dragon. Surely these Dragons could not bear such a load far? The picture was faraway, but clear.

Beneath her, the Tourmaline's belly-fires spoke urgently. "Aye. They cannot move fast, but there's no need. That force will crush any Human settlement in these Isles. We must warn your friends from Eali Island."

"How fare your wounds, Dragon?"

"I'm alive. I'll be wishing I wasn't after this day's flying, however. You?"

"Alive. Aye. Glad to see my fires. Razzior only stole my words … I don't understand, Grandion. How could he do that?"

"Steal an individual Dragon power?" Grandion shook his muzzle. "I wish I knew. Now, I need to know about this Dragon's eye. We must subvert Razzior's chase."

During the course of that perfect, sunny day over the Eastern Isles, Grandion and his Rider put the dust of the long leagues between themselves and Razzior's Dragonwing. Islet after dazzling green Islet passed beneath them, until in the dying suns-shine of evening, Hualiama began to recognise the shapes of the Islands from a map Naoko had ordered her to memorise–a woman as inflexible as her daughter, Lia observed sourly. They had flown in nineteen hours, the same distance a Dragonship might cover in four days and nights. Grandion had overworked himself. She, as his Rider, ought to have been taking better care of him than this!

"Brezzi-yun-Dazi lies yonder," said Lia.

Grandion, who had fallen silent in the late afternoon, heaved a sigh that bobbed them about in the air. "Aye? Excellent."

On an impulse, she leaned over to pat the iron muscles of his shoulder. "You've winged a mighty distance this day, o son of the dawn fires. This Rider thanks her Dragon for his unstinting–" a low growl of approval thundered in his belly "–or should I say, headstrong, efforts, and she would say–"

"Oh, she would?" Grandion surged through the air.

"Aye!" Lia's voice rose over his growls. "I want you to know, I'm grateful."

"I am … remorseful." Gruff, he was, and as uncomfortable as a cat doused in water. Lia wanted to laugh as he almost barked, "Contrite, even. I only wanted to prove …"

Great Islands, she understood at last! "Your worth? Your Dragon-ness? Oh, Grandion." But she could not speak further of her feelings. Not yet. Not ever. For her heart was untrustworthy and fey, and Hualiama saw a speck in the distance, and knew that another draconic visitor angled for the Isle that was their destination. Destiny? With forced lightness, she said, "A Dragoness approaches. I rather suspect that you'll want to beat her to the Island."

Hualiama dampened the spark of forgiveness gleaming amidst the desolation she felt. She must be, rather than think about being. Thinking was a luxury for persons who entertained hope.

The Tourmaline Dragon's challenge split the purpling twilight. *GRRRRAAAAARRRGGGH!*

Lia whooped softly as Grandion took a comet between his fangs, as the draconic saying went, and blazed a trail across the sky.

* * * *

Landing Dragonback in Naoko's campsite was a rather more elegant affair than her previous arrival, and considerably more impressive. There was something about a ninety-foot Dragon, even one in as sorry a state as Grandion's battered and travel-worn lack of lustre, landing beside a Human tent-encampment, that put the word 'dwarfed' into context for everyone concerned.

Lia swaggered down Grandion's back, knowing from the tenor of his fires that he understood exactly what she was doing, and why. *Come, Dragon,* she urged him. *You know you want to impress–*

Then she squawked, "Elki!"

"Hey, short shrift," her brother called–from a safe distance. "Nice Dragon. Is he safe?"

Hualiama sprinted over and hurled herself into his arms, making him stagger. "You made it, my darling–oh, did I just call you darling? Stupid, blockheaded brother! Where've you been? What're you doing asking ralti-brained questions like that? Of course he's not safe! He's about as safe as a very grumpy volcano. Sorry, Grandion."

"No offence," rumbled the Dragon. "This is your brother?"

"Aye, Elki–this is my … er, Grandion. Sapphurion's shell-son. Grandion, meet Elka'anor, Prince of Fra'anior. Stowaway, rogue and adventurer–just as rebellious a character as a certain Tourmaline Dragon I know."

Elki almost purred. Almost. But then his eyes lifted, and Hualiama startled at a punch on her shoulder. "Well, Lia. You've been busy since you abandoned us off Merx."

"Saori! You're here, too!"

"Where else would I be?" Saori sounded amazed. "It's my home."

A massive shadow loomed over Hualiama's shoulder, making the Eastern Isles warrior baulk. Grandion rumbled, "This is the one who broke your finger, Lia?"

"Aye … Grandion! No!" Trying to fend off an irritable Dragon, never mind a creature of Grandion's prodigious strength, was about as effective as spitting into a howling storm. Hualiama found herself flattened beneath the Tourmaline's paw, along with Saori. "Grandion, confound it! Let her go, you ill-tempered fiend. We're friends now. Friends, I tell you!"

By way of answer, the Dragon flexed all of his talons, giving the terrified Saori an eyeful of an array of metallic weaponry. A fiery snort of contempt accompanied his open threat. "You hurt my Rider, little Human."

Saori squeaked in terror.

A horrible snarl puckered his lips. "Do you know what I do with people that hurt my Rider?"

"You let them go because I tell you to," Lia exclaimed. *Grandion, this is not helping. Stomping about, being the big macho Dragon …*

"You. Tell. Me?" Grandion rolled Lia out from beneath his paw, rather deftly considering his lack of sight. "Run along now, little Rider. Hug your brother. Bring me that tasty buck you promised me. This girl won't mind. She'll be too busy turning purple while I crush her chest. Maybe … I know. I think I'll use this talon–" of course, he would not be Grandion without flourishing the said talon dangerously around Saori's head "–to carve the longest word I know in Dragonish on her hide."

Saori had turned green rather than purple, which Lia might have enjoyed were she not convinced that Grandion intended to do the Eastern Isles warrior real harm.

"Or shall I start chopping randomly until I actually find her fingers?"

You block-headed chunk of … whatever you are! Now's the time you choose to develop a sense of humour?

His fangs gleamed. *Insults only fire up Dragons.*

"Stop!" Lia bounced off as the Dragon somehow heard her coming and thrust twelve feet of paw into her face. "Stop it, you ridiculously oversized, flying cart-wreck. So help me, Grandion–" she dodged another swipe "–you will treat my friends with respect …"

Lia groaned as she saw Naoko and Akemi sprinting toward the fracas.

"Enough! Grandion, listen!" As she yelled at him, lighting crackled off her hair and fingers, and the fires of her vision imbued the world with magic.

Then, a familiar rising whistle registered on Lia's hearing.

Mizuki! No! A thunderclap lifted her body off the earth. White seared her vision.

The Copper Dragoness missed her deadly strike on Grandion, and plowed a huge furrow into a stand of bamboo just behind him. The last thing Hualiama saw was a forty-foot wall of bamboo exploding as Mizuki flung herself back into the fray.

Chapter Twenty-One

Six Armies

LIA SWAM BACK to consciousness with a feeling that the darkness gave her up begrudgingly. At once, her low groan was truncated by what sounded like nearby thunder. What? Trees being flattened? Clumps of bamboo tossed into the air? Now a Dragon's battle-cry–no! Grandion!

Her brain leaped to its feet and charged toward the battle. The rest of her body did not quite follow suit. She crumpled over her brother's outflung arm.

"Lia!" Elki staggered.

"Roaring rajals, Elki, I have to–"

Both Humans whirled as the pair of Dragons tumbled out of the bamboo, fighting tooth and fang, roaring and biting each other in an animalistic frenzy. Feral? Grandion's Storm power shook the encampment, flattening five of the tents and two trees to boot. Simultaneously, Mizuki's prodigious fireball roared off in the opposite direction, setting seventy feet of bamboo forest alight. Grandion punched Mizuki with a blow that could have felled half of the Palace back at Fra'anior. The Dragoness sank her fangs into his tail, only to receive a five-clawed cuff in the head for her trouble.

The ferocity of their combat left Lia speechless. That many tonnes of Dragon-flesh brawling like immature fledglings shook the very ground. Then, her knees locked. Ready.

Having no real idea what to do, Lia ran straight at them, yelling, *Grandion! Mizuki! Stop it, you pair of ralti-brained idiots! Stop!*

Useless. Worse than useless. Lia flung herself aside as Grandion's tail pulverised a boulder right next to her leg.

Grandion … suddenly, her eyesight seemed unexpectedly sharpened. She needed the fire. She needed what had transpired when she danced for the Dragon Elders, not to fashion a fortress of her inner being because of her hurts, but to forge an openness to the fires which had not only been given to her, but *were* her. They were Lia. She saw that now, and accepted it.

Lia flung out her hands toward the two Dragons, summoning her magic. She expected lightning, a concussion, a spectacular demonstration of power. Instead, white-fire fell like a shower of blossoms, as softly as rain wafted upon a spring breeze, imbued with such purity that it mesmerised the souls of her Dragon-friends. Her touch quietened their fires–not causing them to gutter, but rather to burn more steadily, brighter, unadulterated by anger or battle-lust. Her feet itched. A dragonet's unruly laughter burbled in her veins. Volcanic Island girl? Aye. She succumbed to a madcap urge to dance, twirling fluidly into action, arching her body like the twin suns bowing to the horizon. With a giggle as joyous as the inexplicable fire she had released, Hualiama danced up to the two stupefied Dragons, spinning between their flanks, circling their paws, spreading the infectious fire wherever she moved.

Grandion, Mizuki, follow me.

Spellbound, the two Dragons dogged her footsteps as Hualiama returned to where Elki stood, holding Saori in his arms, staring at his sister with an expression she did not entirely enjoy. Lia stopped dancing between flutter-steps. She straightened her back, and tried to walk as regally as a queen.

She collapsed.

"Lia?" A Dragon's muzzle pressed into her back.

"What's with this stupid fainting?" Lia complained, trying to sit up.

"Lie down!" Four people and two Dragons yelling at her at once? Headache!

Lia rubbed her temples. "No need to shout. I'm alive–no thanks to that pair of squabbling hatchlings." Grandion and

Mizuki snorted unhappily in tandem. Lia could not repress a bright smile. "Listen, I know it's because you love me so much, but if you could love me a little less violently, that would be truly excellent."

She could have knocked Mizuki over with a puff of air.

"Now," she waved a hand, "you should twine necks like … uh, maybe that's inappropriate. Introductions. Grandion, this is Mizuki the Copper Dragoness. Mizuki, Grandion the Tourmaline, shell-son of Sapphurion. You know Saori and Elki, don't you?"

"Aye," said Mizuki, her eye-fires brightening appreciably as she regarded the Prince.

Saori frowned in puzzlement, but she was not half as puzzled as Lia, who had what she could only describe as a magical itch. If she had not been so enervated, she might have known what it meant. She glared at the Copper Dragoness. What was she doing? The magic originated with her–or did it?

Grandion just ogled Mizuki, saying nothing. His fires … crooned. Had she been a Dragoness, Hualiama would have thumped the living pith out of him just then.

"What just happened?" she asked.

Elki said, "First, you knocked Mizuki out of the sky with a bolt of lightning–"

"I did?"

"Aye!" growled her audience, at various tonal levels of Dragon and Human speech.

Her brother added, "And the magical snow shower? What was that?"

"I've never seen snow," Lia said, inanely. Quick, corral those errant thoughts! Would her Dragon stop sniffing around that female and pay attention? "Naoko, could we prevail upon your hospitality again? We've two hungry Dragons to feed and a great deal of strategy to plot. Grandion needs healing for his eyes. Shinzen is on his way north with Razzior and an army of Dragons and giants–spawn of Dramagon's evil experiments. No doubt Mizuki's going to tell us that the Dragons of Fra'anior are also on the move?"

"Aye. Probably passing Merx as we speak," Mizuki said

softly. "And, we Eastern Dragons want to stand against Shinzen. With you Humans, if you'll have us."

Naoko and Akemi gasped in amazement.

"Why?" Saori blurted out.

Lia took the opportunity to plant the sharp end of her elbow into Saori's ribs. In a stage-whisper, she said, "Take the offer, sheep-brain. That's an order fresh from Royal Fra'anior."

Grandion made sure he flexed his talons in Saori's line of sight.

Her friend cried, "Aye! Anything–Princess, keep that beast away from me."

Lia could not resist. "Grandion's partial to a bit of haunch, aren't you, my Tourmaline beauty?"

Her Dragon was, but the picture in his mind was not Saori's haunches. Ugh, windroc droppings. There was one image which would linger. Hmm. Maybe this could work to her advantage. Mizuki was a fine specimen of a Dragoness …

Mizuki said, "I don't understand these giants she speaks of, but if Shinzen has a force of Dragons at his disposal, we Eastern Dragons know what that means for our kind as much as for you Humans."

Naoko said heavily, "It means hiding, evacuation, and warning every Human and Dragon up to Kaolili. Unless they turn for Merx and Franxx?"

"No," said Lia. "They'll be bound for the Lost Islands, and the Scroll of Binding. We can hope that Sapphurion will slow them down, but I suspect that he's going to come into the Eastern Archipelago behind Razzior's tail, if he hasn't already run into trouble and delays. Razzior is well prepared for this campaign. Akemi or Mizuki, do you know anything about Dragons' eyes? My Grandion is blind, but I hope it's only a temporary affliction. If we are to arrive ahead of Razzior, then Grandion desperately needs his eyesight. My eyes aren't good enough."

Mizuki and Akemi chorused, "He uses your eyes?"

Elki protested, "She didn't say that. You didn't, did you, Lia?"

"Brother dearest, there are Dragon powers none of us

understand," Lia said, rather unwillingly. "Grandion can borrow my eyesight. He reads pictures from my mind." The expressions around her registered astonishment. Why not, she wanted to protest? Was this not normal? Lia pressed on, "And then there is *ruzal*–a twisted magic which allows a Dragon or a Human to control the Dragonkind by commands. It seems Razzior is adept at *ruzal*, as am I."

Mizuki snarled, "Is what you just did–"

"No. That was white-fires. I don't know what else to call it."

Grandion rumbled, "Aye, it was not *ruzal*. I know the stench of that magic. This was pure and captivating, a different Dragonsong altogether."

Hualiama had the uncomfortable impression that had his eyes been whole, his eye-fires would have registered that burning Dragon-lust for that which moved a Dragon's soul–greed, yearning for beauty, or the possession of whatever they desired most. Mercy.

She stiffened, turning half-away from him. *Keep your distance, Dragon.*

Only the quirk of Mizuki's brow-ridge betrayed her surprise at this exchange.

Akemi said, "Come. The shadows of our Isles lengthen. We should examine Grandion's eyes before nightfall. Mizuki, may I suggest that you devise ways of rousing our Eastern Isles Dragons? We may need them to transport a Human cargo to safety. Our basic strategy will probably be to clear our non-warriors out of Shinzen's way, and to attack his forces as and when we can. Even these giants must burn."

"They do," Grandion growled, "but will an Eastern Dragoness stoop to these tasks?"

Mizuki bristled, "We are not above getting our paws dirty, unlike our noble shell-cousins from the West."

"Some of us have carried Human Riders–"

"And some of us have snappish appetites which need food," Hualiama put in.

You actually call the Human your Rider? Mizuki asked the Tourmaline.

Proudly. Even his tone swaggered, now. Hualiama rolled her eyes.

I noticed. Extraordinary.

It makes sense when one is blind.

The Copper Dragoness purred, *Aye. But you befriended the Dragonfriend long before you were blind, Grandion. Perhaps it is only the rest of us Dragonkind who are blind.* And her gaze lingered on the Prince of Fra'anior.

Jutting out her jaw, Saori wrapped her fingers deliberately around Elki's bicep. Lia bit back a groan. She smelled trouble. Cartloads of trouble.

* * * *

Hualiama awoke an hour before dawn, unable to sleep. Knowing that at least six armies–or Dragonwings–were closing in on their position, or soon would be, was no recipe for peaceful dreams. Shinzen, Razzior and the giants approached from the south. Sapphurion and his kin flew in from the west, possibly already skirmishing with Razzior's Dragonwings, who were also angling for the Eastern Archipelago. The Lost Islands Humans and Dragons waited in the north, bitter enemies to each other, and not exactly welcoming to strangers. She and Grandion planned to fly right into the heart of that pile of old mouldy boots. Then there were the Eastern Dragons, Mizuki's kin, an unknown quantity. Would they fight alongside the Humans, as Mizuki suggested?

Rising from Grandion's paw, she glanced across at the Copper Dragoness, sleeping in the Dragon way, pressed up against Grandion's flank. At least one minor riff to her strategy appeared to be proceeding to plan. Mizuki was noticeably smaller-boned and sleeker than Grandion. When she had not been making fire-eyes at Elki, she had been sizing up the Tourmaline Dragon with thinly-veiled interest.

No examination of Grandion's eyes, however, had yielded any clues.

Lia breathed out slowly, quelling her frustration. A flash of white caught her eye. Oh. Elki was also awake, emerging from the tent he shared with Saori. Of course the young Prince had let no blade of grass grow beneath his feet when it came to making himself comfortable, nor with ingratiating himself with Naoko, who appeared to have fallen for his dubious charms and dull-as-dust witticisms. Lia, naturally, still appeared to leave a bad taste in Naoko's mouth, but not Elki. Oh no. Were he a sweetbread sopped in gravy and dropped by accident, he would always land dry side down.

Nonetheless, she padded over to her brother. "Couldn't sleep, Elki?"

"Not a wink, mighty Dragon Rider. You?"

"Whole Islands on my mind."

"Me too," sighed Elki.

"Let me guess–the lovely Saori, or the equally lovely Mizuki?"

"Aye," he agreed glumly.

He had no right! He had two girls practically fighting over him, while Lia enjoyed no such attention. She had a big fire-breathing boulder whom she was trying to push in Mizuki's direction as hard as she dared, hoping it would solve an insoluble problem. The problem beating inside her chest.

Hualiama said, "So, I'm off to see the Dragoness Yukari in the morning."

Her brother sniffed, "You're lucky. I get to sulk in camp while Copper-lady goes recruiting around the Isles."

"Sulk? You have Miss Silken Bowstrings in there–"

"Elki? Are you coming back to bed?" The voice issuing from within the tent cut short her spiteful comment. In a moment, the flap twitched. Saori emerged, not even slightly tousled. "Elki, you left me so cold–oh, sorry, Lia. I didn't see you there."

Hualiama scowled daggers at a blameless blue star twinkling on the horizon. "No. People rarely do."

Now Saori was giving her the magical itches! No disrespect to her personality, of course. Oh–did they have to? Lia pretended to examine the stars around the crescent Jade Moon, and White blazing pinpoint-sharp nearby, while princess-perfect Saori and her brother made noises like dragonets feeding. Shameless hussy. Meantime, Lia examined the odd sensation inwardly. Mercy, why was she in such a porcupine mood? Should she scratch where it itched?

Immediately, Saori exclaimed, "Ouch! What pricked me?"

"Ow-ow-ow, you little rajal." Elki stood rubbing his chest, making a royal meal of his hurts, as usual. "That hurt."

Next he'd be pouting and running to Queen Mommy. Lia grinned. Now, what was the magic up to?

Saori snapped, "What're you grinning at, short shrift?"

"Me?" Once again, the Eastern warrior's nerve rattled her. Nobody but her brother called her 'short shrift.' With that, Hualiama's thoughts pitched in an unexpected direction–aiming to create trouble between Saori and Mizuki. She found opportunity at once. There. A tenuous magic, if magic it was, linked the Copper Dragoness with her brother. What on the Islands … Hualiama stood stock-still, silenced by a thrill of recognition.

Oh! Dear sweet rainbows over the Cloudlands, was *this* what Amaryllion had meant when he spoke of the unfolding of a magical bond between Dragons and Humans? She could not keep it to herself. The world of white-fires revealed an inclination of Mizuki's fire-soul toward a yearning of equal intensity within the Prince's being. Lia visualised the magic as an eruption of delicate, frond-like filaments of the purest turquoise Helyon silk from the glorious, burning essence of the Dragoness, and similarly from the noble, eagle-like soul that must belong to her brother.

At one level, Lia was dumbfounded that such a power even existed in the Island-World. She should not be. She knew it for herself. Yet, the connection was incomplete. It required a catalyst. A delicate touch to meld the threads. Aye, this was magic to set a soul alight. Here lay a true labour of love.

Lia's affirming thought caused a quiet ripple of magic to lap over her brother. The filaments altered, growing in length, becoming kaleidoscopic in colour as they melded with the Dragoness'. Elka'anor lurched away from Saori, his hand fluttering to his heart. Mizuki found her paws, moving forward with a curiously high-stepping fluidity, her eye-fires utterly radiant, utterly fixated upon the Prince of Fra'anior.

Thou … Mizuki whispered.

"I don't know … what is this … bonfire in my heart?" The Prince stumbled to his knees, within touching distance of the trembling Dragoness. "Lia?"

"What in a Cloudlands hell is going on?" Saori complained.

"I only helped release what was there all along," said the Princess, brushing off Saori's grasping hand. Her feet seemed to float across the dew-damp grass to a point where she completed a triangle with Elki and Mizuki. She gazed from one to the other, suddenly formal, even bashful. These were forces that shaped lives, and seized destiny by the throat. Lia felt humbled. Unworthy. What could one say to crown such a magical moment?

Glancing to the skies, it seemed to her that the face of a well-loved friend gazed back from the stars, at once as black as soot, and as white as star-fire. *Aye,* she smiled. *Thank you, Bezaldior, for giving this gift.*

The Ancient Dragon dipped his muzzle solemnly.

Lia drew a huge breath. "Mizuki the Copper Dragoness, and Elka'anor, Prince of Fra'anior, I believe it would be appropriate to say this oath to each other: 'Let us burn the heavens together, as Dragon and Rider.' "

A jewelled spiderweb of silence glistened between them.

Smiling, Hualiama prompted, "Let us burn …"

As Elki and Mizuki began to stammer through the simple vow, a strangled cry rose from nearby. Saori fled.

Neither the Dragon nor the Human even noticed, lost in their private communion.

* * * *

Riding a southerly breeze, the Tourmaline Dragon rose above the Islands at dawn three days later, visibly sleeker and more powerful than before. That was the advantage of a Dragon's physiology, Hualiama thought. They used nutrients so efficiently. Her mount was surprisingly scientific in his approach to diet, seeking out not only the protein to rebuild his massive musculature, but fruits and even peat from a bog to supplement the minerals that he required. His long, sensitive nostrils could tease out trace metals and minerals, or identify the herbs best suited to cleansing his digestive tract and easing a painful wing joint.

They flew east, seeking Yukari's wisdom. Here the jagged, fern-fringed Islands were sparsely populated by jungle-dwelling Human tribes. Lia hoped that Shinzen would not bother with these people. Naoko had disparaged them as savages and cannibals. As she gazed over the sprinkling of low Islands spearing like uncut emerald rods out of the Cloudlands, Hualiama recalled Grandion noting that he smelled hints of smoke on the breeze, and her thoughts turned often to the south. Pillage and raze, was Razzior's plan.

One morning, Lia remembered to ask, "Grandion, what did you say to Saori to ease her mind?"

The Dragon had insisted he speak to Saori. The Eastern Isles warrior had emerged from her tent an hour later, deathly pale but determined, and flown off Dragonback with Elki and Mizuki in the morning, heading westward for the nearest colony of Dragons just offshore of Haozi.

"I told her of the ways of Dragons and their Riders," he replied. "I insisted that the Copper Dragoness can never replace her in Elki's affections."

"Because Humans and Dragons are never meant to be together?"

"In a sense." Before Hualiama could do more than recognise the hot disappointment rising in her gorge, the Dragon added, "Still your heated words, my Rider. Two days hence, I felt you create magic of a kind hitherto unknown in this Island-World. It may seem a fresh, wondrous thing. But we must be cautious. The Ancient Dragons did not craft our laws without cause or reason."

"I released–"

"–what was already present. Aye. So you said."

"Thanks for the measure of trust, Dragon." Ponderous, pontificating … animal! Would she ever understand him?

Grandion rumbled, "You think my restraint unjustified.

You think I despise and regret what we share, even though I continue to act upon the oaths we spoke together."

Hualiama knew she had to bottle up the frustration paining her breast. She schooled her reply into a measured response. "I think–I had hoped–it might be … different … between us, Grandion."

"You're a special, magical woman."

"But?"

"Do you feel compelled by a binding oath when you'd rather be chasing other, less belligerent and blind Dragons about the Island-World?" Grandion asked. Lia hissed wordlessly. "Is it that you don't want to push me into a romance with the Copper Dragoness, but your ungovernable heart insists you must? Aye, you're about as subtle as a volcano blasting an Island off its foundations. So you can stand aside once more and be little Lia, the bitter, cast-off victim this time not of fate, but of your own injudicious decisions?"

There was something so breath-taking and infuriating about having her emotions read accurately by a creature of another species, that Hualiama felt her blood begin to fizz and boil. He deserved to be windroc bait!

Her heart was truly as ungovernable as the fires which burst from beneath the Island-World's skin. Could what she had never suffice? All her deeds, all that she had wrought and sacrificed and wept or rejoiced over, what she had fought for and learned and dreamed of–it was never enough. She was Lia. A royal ward, not true royalty. An unwanted Enchantress, hunted by Dragons. A person so enamoured of the madness of riding Dragons that she wished the same for others, and apparently possessed the power to make it so? Yet her life felt hollow. Fallen somehow short of its true potential.

Hualiama kicked against the goads. Rebelled. Struggled endlessly, just as her life had been an unceasing struggle for acceptance and love. She was obsessed with chasing a love she could never have. She might better chase a breeze laden with fireflower pollen across the Islands!

Why? Why did fate choose to scorn and scar her?

Wrapped in silence, they flew on.

The edge of the Island-World was a barren ocean of tan Cloudlands. With evening closing in, the shadows of the Islands reached out like long fingers intent upon grasping what lay beyond the horizon. Had she Dragon sight, Lia might have seen the tips of the Rim-mountains. Perhaps no eye could see that far. Yet Hualiama would dream of flight beyond the moons. The Dragon, pulsing with fiery life, oriented upon a talon-shaped Island right on the edge of that uncrossable desert, and his great, leathery wings creaked as they furled to trigger the descent to the place Akemi had described for them. 'I shall not come,' the old woman had said. 'It is not my place to soar Dragonback. I will stay with my people and help with the exodus.'

Was it not? Hualiama wondered about that statement from a woman who should also by rights be called Dragonfriend. She had held her tongue. What right of interference had she?

Faster, faster flew the Tourmaline Dragon, drawn by a surging of hope in his breast, Lia recognised. His flight-muscles flexed like steel bands beneath his armoured hide. His neck stretched out for streamlining, while his four paws tucked up beneath his elongated body. Just the smallest flicks of tail or wingtips governed his course. Within, Hualiama considered the soul-fire creature that hovered within the portal of her being, coming no closer, not taking her over–as he had promised. Never again. A Dragon burned there, angelic.

Strange word. Hualiama had once helped an archivist monk at the monastery offshore of Ha'athior to copy several scrolls of ancient lore relating to mythical beings. Leviathan was easy. Every Dragon was a leviathan, yet the monk averred that the word referred to a sea-creature, perhaps a swimming Land-Dragon. Lia had wondered aloud what might become of the Island-World if the Cloudlands turned to water–to an ocean, another impossible, magical idea. The archivist had chuckled softly at a girlish fancy, but rather than disparaging her, had said, 'Girl, you must be an angel. Read this reference. Angels are spirits of the purest fire. A thousand summers ago, Humans used to believe Dragons were the embodiment of these angels, fire-spirits clothed in flesh, an eternal fire-soul trapped in corporeal form.'

Girl, you must be an angel. She had never forgotten his words, a nugget of kindness in a dark place.

What a fey Isle greeted a Dragon and his Rider. Using Lia's sight, the Tourmaline Dragon brought them in low, so that together they could appreciate the stone archway that bridged the middle of the Isle, forming it into the shape of a wedding band a quarter-mile in diameter set upon its edge on a pedestal of rock. Thousands of jinsumo trees bearded the bridge in lush emerald foliage, sweeping hundreds of feet downward and sideways, the great veils of vegetation heavy with creamy blossoms. They shifted and stirred like a maiden's long hair in the light breeze. The perfume was heady and enigmatic … and dragonets! A dark shadow seemed to ease from her soul as she spied a flight of sleek, tiny green dragonets whizzing through the portal. Oh, the birdsong! The dragonet-song! Though it was different in many characteristics, the Isle reminded her of exotic Fra'anior, and the thought of home was a pang so sweet, Hualiama gasped and rubbed away a crawling sensation on the nape of her neck.

Grandion's huge wings flared, bringing them to an abrupt landing in the shadows of that archway. His knees flexed to take the shock of touchdown, driving draconic footprints two feet deep into the soft soil. A chorus of tropical birdsong assaulted her ears, while damp, loamy odours filled her nostrils. Hualiama sighed and stretched luxuriously. Wow. Dragon flight made her ache in the oddest places.

Inclining his muzzle toward her the Dragon whispered, *I've a brash and foolish tongue, Lia. I've hurt thee.*

If that rocky arch was a wedding-band to place about one's finger, then Hualiama Dragonfriend was the bride of sorrow, for she could never have her beloved. Lia said, "O Tourmaline, I wish for what lies beyond … life. Possibility. This entire Island-World."

Taking a moment to formulate her heartsong into words, she vocalised:

Oh for wings to bear my soul,

Beyond the cloudscapes of my dreams,
Escaping the mortal coil that binds a being,
Into flesh and blood and bone.
Beyond this present world,
Into eternity.

White-fires touched her world. Somewhere *beyond*, yet within her being, Amaryllion dipped his great head, as if to acknowledge an oath. What did it mean? Where had those words come from, if not from her soul … or from whatever lay beyond, unreachable?

Thrice-fold you wished for the beyond, Grandion sighed, palpably moved. *May it be so, Rider. Let's go find the Aquamarine Dragoness.*

Aye, Dragon. Don't let me drag you into my melancholy.

The Tourmaline Dragon raised his forepaw. *Will you take the easy way down–for once?*

Lia laughed. What bitter, penetrating insight from her Dragon. *Aye, Grandion. I grieve for what cannot be. I must learn to look to the brightness, to the Dragon fires and miraculous beauties of our Island-World, and not to my soul's warped cravings. I'm sorry …*

Sliding down Grandion's shoulder into the cup of his paw, Lia allowed herself to be conveyed to the ground. She looked about, and the Dragon looked from within her.

A narrow trail appeared to lead beneath the archway, through ferns and fronds that brushed Hualiama's shoulders, to a pool which had gathered there from the water which tinkled or trickled down from above. She stretched her legs along the trail, keenly regretting the loss of one Nuyallith blade. Her double-sheath seemed unbalanced, but she had her Immadian forked daggers on her belt and the rest of her weaponry secreted about her person once more. Lia's boots sank into soft loam, and even Grandion's tread was muffled, although he left a much wider trail of broken and crushed ferns in his wake.

They should find Yukari near the pools beneath the archway. The Dragons believed that the pools had magical properties–physical restoration would have been perfect, but these were pools used by Dragon-seers and mystics seeking to penetrate the mysteries of the present and future.

That meant no healing, unless Yukari as a Blue-coloured Dragon had healing powers like Qualiana's.

Hualiama brushed through a veil of jinsumo blossoms which hung right down to the ferns, dusting her shoulders and hair in creamy, aromatic pollen, to find herself standing on the shore of a set of interlinked pools which were exactly the colour she imagined Yukari might be. The still pools called to her spirit with promises of serenity. So alluring was the call that Lia pictured the stillness of death, and shivered. Beautiful, but undeniably creepy.

She asked, *Do you sense her?*

Nay, said Grandion.

Hualiama wandered down to the shore, peering into the clear waters. An unusual mineral deposit turned the stones of the pools aquamarine blue, making a startling contrast to the dark ferny banks, so that for a moment, the Human girl imagined she looked downward into the sky. Vertigo tugged at her senses, but Grandion pinched her shoulders lightly with his forepaw, a steadying touch.

Without speaking but in constant communion with each other, she led the Tourmaline Dragon around several pools, before finding a small animal path that led deeper beneath the archway, to a wider pool completely undisturbed by water trickling from above. Here, the illusion of sky was nigh-perfect. Hualiama stepped up onto a blue boulder, the better to peer down into the water. Odd. The stones were a more regular size here, making a pattern she could follow with her eyes, suddenly picking out the crook of a massive foreleg and the edge of a wing …

Mercy! Oh, G-Grandion!

Chapter Twenty-Two

Aged Wisdom

LUNGING FORWARD, THE Tourmaline Dragon snaffled Lia roughly off her perch as the ground shifted, transforming into the knuckle of a Dragon's paw. The girl's eyes rolled wildly before settling upon the skull-spikes of a Dragoness rearing out of the pool, her crushingly vast muzzle cracking open to vent a chuckle that melted Grandion's bones. Never in his life had he imagined such a venerable Dragon Elder! Her size! Her presence! The purity and power of her Dragon fires! Before her he felt as a newborn hatchling, soft with yolk as he broke the shell for the first time, and trembling, beheld his shell-mother.

You've found Yukari, little ones, rumbled the Dragoness.

Bowing his muzzle to the ground and arching his wings in a gesture of the deepest deference, Grandion said, *The most sulphurous greetings of Fra'anior be thine, noble Dragoness. I am Grandion of Gi'ishior, shell-son of Sapphurion and Qualiana. My companion is–*

Hualiama Dragonfriend, Princess of Fra'anior, she chirped, *and I befriended an Ancient Dragon who was twenty times your size, Yukari. You don't scare me.*

Disrespecting an Elder! Grandion's fires howled his dismay. Catching Lia about the waist with an angry squeeze of his claw, he snarled, *Don't you dare cheek your elders and betters, hatchling!*

Peace, Grandion, said Yukari, unaccountably amused by the Human's antics. *We females play deeper games than you imagine. Come. Of late, the Island-World's winds communicate much strangeness to my nostrils. You've travelled far from your Cluster. What do you seek of old Yukari?*

Healing for my sight, said Grandion.

Lia added, *I seek to help my Dragon, but I do wish you'd return to see Akemi, mighty Yukari. She misses you.*

To Grandion's shock, Yukari thrilled the heavens with her bugle, causing the waters of her pool to ripple in response, and the nearby dragonets to break into trilling, happy song. She was awesome. Dragons grew all their lives, albeit more slowly as they moved out of their fledgling years into adulthood. Sapphurion, measuring one hundred and thirty-two feet from wingtip to wingtip, was the largest Dragon Grandion knew–though not the oldest. Yukari had to be double his size. Her fangs stood like lances in her jaw, and the magnificent sweep of her hindquarters made him weak-kneed.

Then he beheld her eyes through Lia's sight, and Grandion had a further shock. The Dragoness was blind!

If Yukari could not heal herself, what hope was there for him?

I was wounded young. The great Dragoness' thoughts, redolent with notes of experience and potent magic, fired his mind. *In those days, the Eastern Dragonkind believed that a Dragon born with the power of Seeing could never attain their full potential unless they were blinded. So, my eye-fires were snuffed out by my shell-parents' talons.*

Grandion bowed mentally, chastised and sorrowful.

How is it that pictures of me form in a blind Dragon's mind? Yukari asked.

Hualiama is my eyes, Grandion replied, suddenly aware that Yukari could read his thoughts like an open scroll. *She is my Rider, my friend, my rescuer and the fires of my soul.*

Yet what is this sadness I sense between you? the Dragoness inquired. *A quarrel between soul-bonded lovers?*

The Tourmaline stiffened at her use of an ancient term. Cautiously, he said, *Not soul-bonded lovers, great Yukari. Hualiama is no Dragoness. We've not even spoken of the mystical ascending fire-promises–*

No Dragoness? A vast snort blasted water at the pair of them.

Lia's tiny hands rubbed her eyes. In a moment, the

Aquamarine Dragoness returned to his view. The sardonic expression curling her lip minded him of nothing more than his shell-mother about to rebuke an errant hatchling. Huge as he was, Grandion shrank into a hatchling's submissive posture. It seemed appropriate.

Grandion, I don't understand that word she used, Lia's broke in.

Soul-bonded lovers? It's the state of a pair of Dragons who have breathed the sacred fire-promises together, the Tourmaline Dragon explained, conveying disapproval, outrage and finality of the utterly impossible in the nuances of his reply. *These promises are for Dragons alone—they are oaths made between fire-souls. For there are types of Dragonish love beyond roost-love or mated-love or egg-hatching love* … he trailed off in embarrassment. *Yukari, with all possible respect, I must correct you. Hualiama is a Human—*

Piffle, growled Yukari, rudely. *Hatchling-spit and fireless smoke.*

Lia's gaze darted to Grandion. He saw himself crouched at the water's edge, an expression of stubborn disbelief crinkling his eyebrow-ridges, never mind the confusion roiling in his belly. He must swallow Yukari's withering insults. Among the Dragonkind, an Elder's words were sacrosanct, inviolable. Yet his fires betrayed him, for a smoky fireball leaked past his fangs.

Quietly, the girl explained the Ancient Dragon's passing on, and her confusion over her growing magical gifts. The Aquamarine Dragoness spoke right over her, as if she did not exist.

Grandion. Smell her.

He protested, *I know how she smells—*

HOW DARE YOU DISOBEY! The Dragoness' wrath rolled over him like a scalding lava flow.

Pressing his nostrils against the girl's back, Grandion inhaled hugely. Involuntarily, his tongue flicked out to taste her upper left arm, drawing a quiver from her body to match his own, albeit on a far larger scale. Hualiama's scent was as he remembered, and so much more. Fire and spice. A staggering richness of mystery. Starsong over moons-lit Islands. She was the bewitching heart of Dragon fires and the tingle of magic upon his scales.

As intricately beautiful as any Dragoness, he whispered.

Yukari growled in approval, *Nobly done, youngling. Now, hearken to the song of her inner being.*

The Dragon's ear-canals attuned to the eager throbbing of her heart, to the catch-me-if-you-can rhythm of her life.

No, go deeper. Like this. Yukari's magic tingled against the scales of his head and muzzle. *Listen with your third heart, youngling.*

The Tourmaline Dragon saw an egg of pearlescent white, nestled in the warm sands of a Dragoness' roost. The egg stood with two others. Where was their shell-mother? It would not do to leave a clutch unprotected. Grandion pressed deeper for the truth of this vision, but it eluded him. A tiny Dragoness-spirit lifted free from the egg and soared away from his presence, coy and fey. Tinkling laughter fell upon him. Suddenly she became that Human sprite who had so entranced a Dragon hatchling with her irrepressible zest for life.

You never wanted to wear clothes, Grandion told Lia. *You never wanted to be bound or restricted in any way. You sang, oh my wings, how you sang! There were days you spoke nary a word, but your words were dance and your heartsong, Dragon fires.*

Standing with them in a shared vision of the past, the Aquamarine Dragoness said, *How do you see her now, Grandion?*

She's as unruly as the wind.

Hualiama's laughter lingered over both of the Dragons. Grandion knew that Yukari's wings burned with the sweet fire that the girl's laughter evoked; it was the whisper of wind caressing Dragon scales in flight, and the magic that burned in their veins and flowed in rivers of golden Dragon blood. Her hilarity was a blood-fever, a power akin to the slow rolling of a storm over his Island, and it sang to the lightning of his Blue Dragon powers. A thrilling battle-readiness surged behind the protective strictures of his fire and lightning stomachs.

Dragonsong, said Yukari.

Dragoness, agreed Grandion.

And what of her dreams, Grandion?

Abruptly, his paws returned to the ground, and the soaring sensation vanished. *She claims to dream shell-dreams,* he said, troubled. *What can this signify but Amaryllion's power, unleashed?*

The image in his mind walked upright on two legs. She had no wings. Grandion did not understand the import of Yukari's lesson. Must he learn to see her differently? Aye, he could. Must he listen with all seven senses? Aye, he would. But the reality of Lia's humanity could not be escaped. Belief could only convey a creature so far. A Dragon must know what his paws touched, what entered his senses, and what buoyed him across the abyss.

In a profoundly deep voice, Yukari said, *There is blindness no Dragon power can heal, young Grandion, no salve can ease, and no medicament can make well. If you truly would be the noble-hearted son of flame for which you are named, then you must slough off this inner blindness.*

Grandion shook at the force of her censure. *My Hualiama is Human!*

Yukari ruffled her wings derisively. *Think you I lack sense because I lack sight?*

The Tourmaline's wings half-flared in response to her challenge. *No, but I believe what my eyes have seen. I hear two feet brushing upon stone and gravel. A single heart beats in her chest …*

Dragoness!

She has dreams and hopes, but dreams disappear with the dawn, and hope can play us false. Grandion loomed protectively over his small companion, gathering a trembling body into his talons. *She is a living soul, o mighty Dragoness, and I fear these injurious words. You play on her most inmost fears–*

Yukari roared, *GRRRRAAAAARRRGGGH!*

* * * *

Dragon-thunder shook the world-within-a-world beneath the archway.

Hualiama laid her hand upon Grandion's muzzle, quieting his fury. Though both Dragons were blind, they faced each other with their lips curled back to bare their fangs in challenge, their stances matching each other for muscular aggression and their fires primed to a fighting pitch. Gratitude and fear pulsed equally in her veins. Somehow, the aged Dragoness' insistence on the unattainable had liberated the great-hearted guardian in Grandion, and his attitude moved her more surely than Yukari's words had roused her grief and despair. The Aquamarine Dragon-Seer had shed no light upon Lia's state or her magic, but she had broken a barrier of pain and offence which had grown up between Dragon and Rider. Perhaps her Dragon had not realised it yet?

Aye, Yukari played a deep game. A Dragoness' game.

Drawing a shuddering breath, Lia said, *I've dreamed of flying for longer than I can remember, Yukari. The fires of a precious dragonet dwell within me. It must be his earliest memories which stir my soul, for I have these shell-dreams, as you call them, strange dreams of a time before Sapphurion and Qualiana raised me with their own paws. I'm unashamed to admit that I love those Dragons. The truth of the matter is, Yukari, that you See differently to other creatures. I understand that your power can be both gift and curse.*

Yukari's wild, vicious spurt of laughter boiled the water to Hualiama's right hand. *Oh, now you understand me, little one?*

Lia found herself baring her own teeth. *I understand I'll be whatever you want me to be, if you'll help my Dragon. If I must be a Dragoness, then may it be so. And aye, I have insight. I know that something of your pain might be healed, if you see Akemi again.*

Shoulder to shoulder, she and Grandion confronted the huge Dragoness.

By degrees, the two Blue Dragons began to simmer down, communicating with each other at a level Hualiama could only guess at–instinctual? Magical? The Aquamarine Dragoness' regard burned upon her without need for ordinary sight, for the power of her inner gaze was enough to arouse Lia's white-fires, until the pools seemed to burn and breathe the magic she had sensed before. As Yukari's gaze penetrated her being, Lia stood stock-still, fearing to trust the Dragoness but knowing she must succeed for Grandion's sake.

Ungovernable indeed, said the Dragoness, appearing unexpectedly contented.

With that, Yukari fell to a ponderous examination of Grandion's condition, which soon tested the limits of

Hualiama's patience. Shinzen advanced. Dragonwings marshalled in far off places. Amaryllion had warned of an impending war in which Lia would play a crucial role. Unease drew together in her belly like storm clouds gathering in their battalions, preparatory to unleashing their fury upon the Isles.

Hualiama expended her frustration in exercise and dance. She listened in as the Dragoness spoke to Grandion at inordinate length about Dragon powers and the dampening, stunting effects of long captivity–not just the obvious effects on physiology, musculature and even bone density, but the effects on what she called his inner balance and flow of magical powers. Yukari confirmed what the engineer in Hualiama had long suspected. Dragon flight was magical, not merely mechanical. Blues could manipulate the flow of air about their bodies and over the wing surfaces, achieving greater flight speeds, endurance and manoeuvrability than any other Dragon colour. Kinetic and levitation powers, rare even amongst Blues, could arrest the effects of momentum and gravity, giving a Blue Dragon unparalleled advantages in combat, and even strike an opponent down without need to bloody claw or fang.

Dishonourable, Grandion sniffed.

The Aquamarine Dragoness staggered him with a paw-strike, roaring, *And when this hollow honour wastes Dragon blood and lives, only death wins!*

Aquamarine and Tourmaline, Hualiama thought, comparing the two Dragons–two ultra-rare gemstone colours, indicating their consummate magical abilities. Yukari's colouration was like the blue of Gi'ishior Island's terrace lakes, several shades darker than the luminous hues of Grandion's scales, which hearkened to clear lake water beneath an enchanted gemstone sky.

After completing her Nuyallith exercises, Lia stripped and swam in the warm, alkaline waters, washing off the grime of travel. She sensed the feathery touch of Grandion's magic, and knew that Yukari noted it. Did the male Dragon reflect upon her humanity and femininity? Suddenly conscious of a queer but not unpleasant burning in her belly, as though she boasted her own fire-stomach, Hualiama slipped behind a clump of ferns and squeezed the water out of her long hair, which when wet trailed to mid-thigh. Mercy. She must remember to braid it to keep from tangling her hair in the flowing Nuyallith forms. And she must remember that neither fern nor boulder could keep a Dragon-adept from sensing her with his magic.

Grandion and Yukari conversed long into the balmy night. Lia eventually found a warm hollow and curled up to listen. Of course, that was a prelude to drifting off to sleep. She enjoyed dreams of Flicker tugging her hair with his small paws and calling her straw-head. Hualiama stirred in the small hours. She checked the position of the Dragon's Paw constellation. Three hours until dawn. Padding over to Grandion, she sleepily noted the renewed sheen of his scales. Had Yukari achieved that? How?

You've star-shine in your scales, she yawned, pulling his paw over her torso.

Aye? Are you cold, Lia? Did you dream ill?

No. But there had been a dream just before she awoke, a fragmentary memory of searching endlessly across the Island-World … Lia murmured, *You warm my fires.*

To the tune of the Dragon's purring, sleep enfolded her.

Lia often dreamed vividly, but the dreams that came upon her thereafter seemed to have a purpose about them, even a driving force, that she could not fathom. Many Dragons soared through the portals of her memory, great and small, and she joined them in a Dragonwing flying to the stars, but the stars changed into bellowing Dragons. White-fires rose within her, and in the flames strange and troubling images danced.

In an instant, a White Dragoness flicked by her sight, wild and agitated. Behind her came a storm–the most fearful storm Hualiama had ever seen, an Island-swallowing black vortex that pursued the Dragoness with deadly intent.

Mamafire, she whispered, touching the scale which rested against the pulse in her throat. *Flee, Mamafire. I'll protect you.*

My eggling!

Go. Fly strong and true. Mamafire.

Somehow, her strength seemed to calm the Dragoness, to

return sanity and reason to the churning eye-fires and terrified pulsating of her wings.

How are you able to do this, little one? wondered the beautiful White Dragoness. *Why …*

I am the balance, she said.

The storm broke over them! Dragon-thunder shook Dragoness and eggling mercilessly. *ISTARIELA!* a mighty voice roared from the storm. *WHAT HAVE YOU DONE?*

Mamafire! She summoned her tiny magic, and thrust it like a sharp pin into the White Dragoness' breast. *Nothing here but a spark. Be the spark shooting from his bonfire, lost in the night.*

Taking the form of a tiny, gleaming mote of light as bidden, the White Dragoness shot away into the gathering dark as if a shooting star had briefly flared, and died. She was gone.

The little one turned. Seven black thunderheads reared out of the storm, titanic Dragons' heads, as black as obsidian, writhing about the mote. Bolts of lightning surged out of the clouds. Smoke billowed, hot and acrid with the fury of an Ancient Dragon, and before he spoke, she knew his name.

I AM FRA'ANIOR, DRAGON-LORD OF THIS ISLAND-WORLD, thundered the seven heads, his voice the Dragonsong of the tempest, at once spine-tingling and overpowering. Darkness and tempest mantled his majesty. *WHERE IS THAT TRAITORESS?*

Gone where you can never find her. A squeak of a reply.

Far away across time and space, Hualiama groaned in the clawed grip of her dream. *Mamafire! Help me …*

The Black Dragon's heads surrounded her with all the devastating power at his command, as if seven storms had joined forces to obliterate an unwanted Island. Fra'anior roared, *WHO ARE YOU?*

She whispered, *I am the future.*

With a mind-shattering roar, the seven Dragon heads vented their wrath upon the little one who defied the mightiest of the Ancient Dragons. Chaos enveloped her. She was tossed away, helpless, but a flicker of maternal consciousness clasped her in paws of love. *I will never leave you, precious one. I'm always inside you. My knowledge is yours.*

Knowledge flowed into the eggling. She folded the fabric of her world about herself, and vanished.

The Black Dragon's rage obliterated nothingness.

Lia blinked. Awake, or asleep? She could not tell, but her heart lurched in her chest for an entirely new reason, for she found herself lying in the arms of the young man of the brilliant blue eyes. A hand, warm upon her cheek. His lips, so close that his breath caressed the upturned corner of her mouth. His scent, beautiful cinnamon and sweet musk, a melody of draconic intoxication playing upon her senses. Concern registered upon his expression. Had he sensed her chaotic dreams, and come to her?

The contrast between her nightmare of the Black Dragon and this sweet awakening could not have been starker. She feared to breathe lest the intense connection be broken. All she knew was his smiling eyes. Lia did not move a muscle, yet it seemed that every element of her being had been ignited by an unknown, overwhelming force, and that upon the swelling tide of its power, her soul could indeed take wing, and fly. Every heartbeat detonated against her eardrums. There was a taut ache in her chest, as though the fullness of her feelings stretched her ribcage almost unbearably, and that within the comfort he offered lay a peril so delicious that no woman could resist–and Hualiama did not know whether she was strong or fragile, for the way he held her made her feel both at once.

Her eyes lidded.

Only the slightest shift of her head would bring her lips to his, but a fingertip stroking the tiny whorls of hair beside her ear rendered her helpless. Hualiama's fires coursed through her being, radiant. Had she ever imagined a lover such as this? Now, she must take courage. Riding the inner tempest with the audacity of one who dared to ride the mighty Dragons of the Island-World, Lia melded her body against his. Questing. Hungering.

Only the cool night air greeted her burning kiss.

Lia sat upright with a desolate cry. *Grandion? Where … oh.* Had she dreamed?

The Dragon slept.

* * * *

Grandion heard sobbing, muffled against his paw. His third heart melted. Comfort her, would he? He had only succeeded in hurting Lia again. A Dragon should rather tear off his own wings.

When the girl's breathing eased into the rhythm of sleep, the Tourmaline Dragon's breathing eased too. Close. The exhilaration of lava-like heat running through his veins gentled, and Grandion allowed a soundless exhalation to impel a jumble of draconic emotions into the pre-dawn stillness. Ever since the first time he had pounced upon this girl intending to slay her for her trespass upon the holy Dragon-Isle, Lia continued to confound him. Then, he had been suffused with righteous indignation. Any other Dragon would have smeared her life upon the rocks. Now, his fires sang a different Dragonsong.

Hualiama, thou art ... what? What was she, this girl? Power. Flame. White-fires. The Enchantress of a Dragon's soul. Wielder of *ruzal*. A girl who possessed a fate beyond his comprehension or Yukari's power of Seeing. How could he trust her, when all was veiled? How could he not? He could not tear away. That was the path of dark-fires, of oath-breaking insanity. He had no choice. He must fly the maelstrom.

Grandion shook his muzzle slightly.

Then, he froze.

Aye, I'm awake, Yukari growled. *And you–*

Don't say it, said Grandion.

I will say this, shell-son of Sapphurion. I never thought you a wingless, witless fool, until just now.

The Tourmaline Dragon willed his fires to still, although heat erupted in his belly, and the sphincter valves controlling the egress of his Storm and Ice powers clenched painfully.

The Aquamarine Dragoness said, *I see that the Dragons of Fra'anior have developed the power of projection to a greater degree than even Dramagon thought possible. How is it used–to spy on Human slaves by assuming Human form? Seamlessly?*

Aye.

The great secret of Gi'ishior, she snorted, richly scornful. *You fear the Humans so greatly, you swear death-oaths upon your mother's egg never to reveal this Dragon power–whereupon you slither and skive like worms among the Human masses, debasing the Dragonkind into common thieves.*

Grandion kept his silence only with the utmost difficulty. How dare she? He could point to wars averted, intelligence that saved Dragon eggs from thieves, the delicate balance of politics, economics and social order ... yet he sensed it was not these concerns which had roused her wrath. Projection was an art. It could only be sustained by powerful Dragons for a matter of hours at a time–was it Hualiama's fear she referred to, that Ra'aba was a projection of Razzior's? Was her father a Dragon's magic enwrapped in Human form to such an unimaginable degree that procreation had become possible?

No, said Yukari, reading his thoughts. *Life transcends the mimicry of magic. Life-bearing Human seed is a mystery, just as the commingling of father-fire and mother-fire produces an eternal mystery, a new triplet of living soul-fires. She suspects this much? You'll plunge into the Cloudlands, young Grandion.*

What harm do you fear? he scoffed, goaded at last into a heated response.

Harm? Beside him, the huge bulk of Yukari's body writhed in an expression of her fury.

Aye! Grandion spat. *Is it not possible one creature can roost-love another? You gave up on your Human and live here, alone, growing old and embittered—*

INSOLENT HATCHLING!

Both Dragons caught their breath as Hualiama stirred. However, she only wriggled against Grandion's paw before sighing and slumbering on. Humans. They'd sleep through an earthquake.

Yukari whispered, *But there's something fey in her nature, o Tourmaline, is there not? Destiny burbles in delight when she laughs. The miraculous seems but a claw's touch away, and the numinous, to flutter upon the breath of her lungs. Listen well, o Grandion, and set aside these concerns about your physical beings. Still your doubts. You are one intelligent creature, she is another.*

Two souls, Grandion agreed, doubtfully. *I know this. Of course I've been a fool–*

A fool who makes fate-defying oaths? To honour a life-debt? Suddenly, the great Dragoness seemed to soften, and her maternal bulk pressed against his flank as Qualiana's bulk had once overshadowed her hatchling. *Grandion, you're stronger than you think, but you are misguided. You err if you think I disparage your feelings for this Hualiama. Roost-love? Why not? Soul-bonded love? Youngling, that fire-promise is already spoken.*

Grandion gasped, *No!*

You showed me your memories. You did not speak the ancient formulae, but the mien of your hearts is clear. Even against her desires, a Seer must See truly. She laughed, at once softly deprecating and a trill of Dragonsong. *You're a pair of beautiful, wilful, courageous spirits. Who knows what will be?*

I'm … confused, he admitted. *You called me a wingless, witless fool. I know I am reckless, but these feelings are just so … I burn, o mighty Yukari. How I burn!*

What you don't understand is the way of true-to-your-wings-love, she replied, using the Dragonish in a way Grandion had never before heard, but nevertheless made sense to him. A Dragon must be true to his wings. He must be authentic. He must be …

Oh, Yukari! You mean–I cause her to love a phantasm?

The Dragoness' fiery breath washed over his neck. *Aye, now your fires burn unadulterated. Grandion, love can take many forms, but above all, it must be real. You can construct your phantasms of magic–beautiful blue eyes, black hair, so masculine in a Human way. You can be all you imagine she might desire.* Yukari's wings shivered. *To speak this truth is hard. I do not understand every facet of your regard for Hualiama, Grandion. What should a Dragon desire in the soft hide and fireless eyes of a flightless creature? Humans are blood and bone. Dragons are fire and magic. Never the twain should–*

He broke in, *Then you admit she's Human?*

Yukari's belly-fires chuckled deep in the furnaces of her belly. *The impetuosity of youth! Grandion, allow me this counsel. Never toy with a female's feelings. If she learns what you've done, she will despise you. Love must be real. You must summon the sacrosanct fires of your courage–which sing clearly to my seventh sense, of that I harbour not a single cold, dark doubt–let justice shape your breath, and truth be the work of your mighty forepaw. Then, she will honour your soul.*

A truth as concrete as the First Egg of all Dragons, the Tourmaline reflected.

Yukari said, *Then, and only then, will your souls fly together.*

You … wish this, for us?

With all the fullness of my hearts, the Dragoness agreed. *If it is mine to give, Grandion, then Yukari the Aquamarine Dragoness would bestow the incandescent blessings of Dragonkind's eternal fires upon the entwined songs of your souls. Be blessed, shell-son of my spirit. Be blessed, o daughter of fire.*

* * * *

From within the curve of blind Grandion's paw, Hualiama gazed at the Yellow moon, just crowning the horizon.

A tear trickled down her cheek.

Chapter Twenty-Three

New Magic

AQUAMARINE AND TOURMALINE, the two Dragons rose above the easternmost Island of the peninsula that had been Yukari's home for forty summers, and winged northwest. Dawn fired the eastern sky. The clouds just above the rising twin suns glowed like embers. Golden fingers of life-giving warmth reached across the Cloudlands, between the low cloud-cover above and the dark, sediment-hued clouds below, to gleam cleanly off the Dragon scales flexing and rippling with every contraction and release of the mighty flight muscles, until Hualiama thought she might laugh from sheer joy but found herself ambushed instead by a wild sob.

"Lia?" Grandion turned his head, listening. "What was that?"

"I'm happy," she sniffed, wiping her eyes.

"Happy? You're crying."

"I didn't say it made sense, did I?"

"Females," the Tourmaline snorted, even as Yukari, cleaving the air two hundred feet off Grandion's left wingtip, vented an amused fireball that expired into smoke against her muzzle.

"Lia, would you be willing to do Yukari a favour?"

Hualiama nodded, knowing her Dragon would sense the tiniest movement. Yukari was sweet. She should never say so to a Dragoness! But the Dragons' interaction had been so beautiful the previous evening. What had she missed before Yukari's roar, she wondered? How could the ravaging, animalistic beasts of Human scrolls and legends behave like this? How could the creature who had plundered her mind also claim to burn for her, and send phantasms to haunt her dreams, treacherously adoring?

Suddenly, her muscles seized up. Grandion! It had been his work as she confronted Ra'aba at the Onyx Throne of Fra'anior–he had been the bright-eyed young man who had destroyed all of Ra'aba's archers around the hall! So much for the draconic rule of non-interference. But how could he have accomplished such a feat of magic while on the wing to Fra'anior Island? He had arrived with Jinthalior the Green clawing him to pieces, whereupon Hualiama had launched herself across the divide with Ja'al's aid, and killed Jinthalior. Divided consciousness. Perhaps Grandion had not even felt the Dragon's attack until he vanished from the hall, and returned to his body.

A secret draconic power–aye, and the spy she had heard about at Gi'ishior, accused of spending too much time among Humans! Kayturia must be a Dragoness. Imagine the possibilities! If King Chalcion ever heard of it, there would be open war, of that she had no doubt.

Grandion said, "I hoped you might be willing to show Yukari how we share minds. She has not seen the Island-World since her first roar."

Yukari snarled, "You take liberties, youngling! I asked no such boon."

"Yet I am willing," Hualiama called over to the Dragoness. Was she? A frisson of doubt crawled up her spine like an icy centipede and lodged at the base of her skull.

"You must teach Lia the art of Juyhallith to counteract this fear of mental domination," Yukari said. Lia stared at the massive Blue Dragoness. She was far too adept at reading thoughts. How much else had she revealed, inadvertently?

"Teach Lia to protect herself from me?" Grandion laughed hollowly. "We began her training, but not on the defensive–"

"Teach her the skills every hatchling is taught," growled the Dragoness.

Hualiama frowned. "I don't understand your underlying

tonal implications, Yukari."

"As you know, youngling, Blue Dragons excel at the higher magical disciplines," replied the Dragoness. "We're adept at cognitive functions and mental powers–shielding, foresight, insight, kinetic powers, levitation and even psychic blasts, amongst many others. Telepathic Dragon speech is the most basic of these skills. However, possessing these powers also makes us vulnerable. Therefore from our hatchling days, we learn to discipline the mind. Lia, you do not protect your thoughts well, though you exhibit elements of natural shielding. As you suspect, I can read some of your thoughts. Your thoughts and emotions are exceptionally powerful."

"A volcano erupting," Grandion averred.

The Human Princess clucked in annoyance. "Unfeeling lump of flying granite. Fine. I will learn your mental trickery, if you tell me where we're supposed to find healing for Grandion's sight."

"If I may finish my thought," the Aquamarine Dragoness snapped. Hualiama had to smother a chuckle at the picture of a stern, talon-wagging Dragon-Elder Grandion projected into her mind. Yukari said, "Dragon magic has always been thought to eclipse Human abilities. For many generations, Dragons have rested secure in this knowledge–although, what Grandion did to you, Lia, is strictly forbidden. But my wings tingle. If powers like yours can rise in Fra'anior Cluster, and *ruzal* is loosed upon the Island-World–that's a Dragon of a wholly new colour."

"Razzior has a power like *ruzal*," Hualiama put in. "Perhaps it was he who read about *ruzal* in the library of Dragon lore at Ha'athior."

"Could it have been Ra'aba?"

It took Lia a few moments to string together the implications of Yukari's typically obtuse draconic reasoning. Then, she caused Grandion to stall in the air as she shouted, "Razzior's the innocent victim in this? Ra'aba subjugated a Dragon?"

Grandion gasped, "Lia–"

Inexorably, Yukari rumbled, "Consider what he did to you.

Why not just slit your throat? Why throw you off his Dragonship? A short flight to a long drop—what could be more draconic?" Lia was so maddened, words stuck in her craw. She could only scream incoherently as the Dragoness' voice resounded in her mind, *Your descriptions accord him ruzal enough. He has stone skin and inhuman strength. He escaped Sapphurion at Gi'ishior and roams free. Who but a Dragon could do that?*

She hissed, *Now Ra'aba's a Dragon?*

The Aquamarine heaved a mountainous sigh. *No, he's a Human with Dragon powers stolen from Razzior.*

Child of the Dragon, she moaned, rocking back and forth between Grandion's spine-spikes. *How else could he overcome an Enchantress from the Lost Islands? How else could he make—me? The bastard child of Dragon magic? What the volcanic hells am I, Yukari? WHAT?*

Her scream thundered out over the Isles. Real power. Real thunder, a whip-crack of her inner despair. Was she the twisted spawn of Ra'aba's *ruzal* magic, a corruption of the very kind Dramagon had hatched in his hateful experiments, which had seen him cast out from the Dragonkind and eventually destroyed by his fellow Ancient Dragons?

Softly, hatchling, Yukari gentled.

Windroc sh—Lia roared back, biting off an expletive. Even now, her precious morals intruded. She shook. Mercy, how the fires consumed her, how the intolerable white-fires of magic burned her up, too bright. A shooting star must combust. The fires of a comet must burn, and die. *Yukari, it's too much. Too many layers. Magic. Everywhere I turn. Flicker's dragonet lives in me. Amaryllion's white-fires burn—what did he do to me, Yukari? Why did he demand this of me? I can't keep this inside … and now ruzal … my father hates me, Yukari! He abhors everything I am!*

The Dragons did not speak, but she sensed their deep, abiding sympathy.

They rose above the curve of the Island-World, and a darker dawn Lia had never seen. Only the susurrus of air moving over Dragon wings could be heard, and the faraway cry of a hunting copper-headed eagle, melancholic.

A whisper drifted like blown ashes into the silence, *I wish I had never been born.*

Grandion said, *Lia, you'll spread your wings–*

I'm not a bloody Dragon! Islands' sakes, can we at least agree on that? Breath clawed in her throat. *I swear, I'm not going to give him the satisfaction. That man raped my mother. He attacked my family and tried to kill me. He will choke on my power. Razzior too. And if I have to shake this Island-World into prophetic madness with my dying breath, I will see it done!*

Both Dragons began to shout to drown her out, but even as the words scorched her tongue, Hualiama knew they could not be unsaid. Magic rippled outward. A shocking oath.

She pressed her forehead against Grandion's spine-spike, overheated, miserable and alone.

* * * *

Traversing the Eastern Archipelago up to a remote northern peninsula of Eali Island, a large Human-inhabited Island over seventy leagues in breadth and fifty-eight in height, took until the evening of a fourth day at Yukari's deliberate pace. The Dragoness would not be hurried. They must instruct Lia, she growled. The Tourmaline took no small pleasure in learning at the mighty Dragoness' paw himself. The Dragon lore she knew! The stories she told!

Constantly, his thoughts turned to his Rider. She clearly brooded over the possibility of finding her blood-mother, but her behaviour showed none of the suicidal dark-fires he feared after her outburst upon leaving Yukari's lair. Instead, she applied herself to earning a Dragon-sized headache. Even the Aquamarine's wings had quivered in surprise at the Human girl's knowledge and insight.

One morning, like Dragon fire from clear skies, Lia had said, "So, Yukari. Seeing as you're intent upon keeping your silence, I've read your mind. You wish us to fly to the Lost Islands and there whistle up a Land Dragon who will provide us a magic potion for Grandion's healing?"

Yukari's hoary muzzle turned as if she could indeed see the irrepressible Human girl, or at least, burn the cheek out of her with her fiery gaze. "Exactly. A perfect read."

"You're joking."

"You're insulting an aged Dragoness, hatchling."

"You mean it?"

"Shiver my wings, a Dragoness who flies true to her word," the Aquamarine Dragoness snorted, without great rancour.

What he saw in Hualiama's mind, Yukari could see, too. How the Dragoness had wept fire-tears when she learned to see through Lia's eyes! Now, she would see perhaps the largest living Dragon in the Island-World, two hundred and eleven feet from muzzle to tail, glaring at a tiny Rider seated above her Dragon's shoulders. She would see blonde hair flying in the breeze, and the easy way Lia rode the motion of Grandion's every wing-stroke. High cheekbones and curling eyelashes framed eyes of a luminous blue, the eyes of a Fra'aniorian Enchantress. How they had changed. None of them could fathom it, nor did Yukari know any applicable Dragon lore. Grandion clearly remembered her having eyes of Flicker's smoky green colouration. Now it was as if the storm clouds had drawn aside to reveal deep lakes of power.

His vision bobbed as Hualiama's head bowed. "Please explain, mighty Dragoness."

"Grandion's optic nerves have been damaged by the growth of a rare type of fungus, which I have removed. Dragons can regrow nerve damage, but they require certain key and unusual minerals and nutrients to do so. Magnesium, potassium, zinc and meriatite are essential."

"Common minerals," said Grandion.

Lia chuckled, "Won't meriatite give him the most terrible gas?"

Yukari cut in, "For the remainder, you must fly to the easternmost of the Lost Islands, little one, where it is said that a high-flying Dragon can see the Rim-mountains. There, you will summon the Land Dragon Siiyumiel–I will teach you the words to use. You'll ask him for a cocktail of heavy metals, which the Land Dragons are able to extract from the base of the world using their unique brand of refining magic."

"Heavy metals?" asked Grandion.

"Dragon scientists have categorised numerous rare elements found in the Islands," said Lia. "Some are much heavier than copper or iron, for example. What else do we need, Yukari?"

"Quite a list," she purred back. Grandion flicked his wings in irritation. No, he was not the scroll-worm his Rider was, nor half the engineer. That birdcage-sized cranium of hers concealed more than a few secrets. "Vanadium, tungsten, iridium, antimony and actinium. Also, a touch of thorium."

Grandion growled sullenly, "Oh, that makes it clear."

The Dragon's fires surged as Lia's blithe giggles washed over his back, sparking an involuntary quiver in his muscles. "Ooh, Grandion," she cooed. "You concentrate on flying and looking handsome. Leave the thinking to me."

This time, he cleared his throat with a lung-bursting roar. *GRRRRAAAAARRRRGGGH!*

* * * *

Winging across the desolate northern reaches of Eali Island into the region appropriately nicknamed 'the Barrens', Hualiama's gaze turned every few minutes to the southern horizon, until the Dragon beneath her chortled, "You'll make me airsick, Rider. What's bothering you?"

Lia said, "Dragons don't get airsick!"

"Shinzen," growled Yukari.

"And Razzior," agreed Grandion, with a no less fearsome growl. "I smell his stench upon the breeze. The foul miasma of *ruzal* clogs my nostrils and sickens my stomach."

Lia rolled her eyes. Dragons. "Aye," she said. "I'm sorry I don't–"

"Ugh. An even fouler apology," the Tourmaline interrupted.

Now she knew he was pulling her wings–so to speak. Lia sighed. "I'm not sure I want to see what they're doing to the Islands." The southern horizon was one huge smudge of grey smoke, to a Human's vision. She turned again, searching. "Aha, I see our friends."

After a moment, the threesome began to laugh. Ahead of them, it appeared that Naoko and her people had set up camp beside one of the ancient fortresses the Isles north of Eali were famed for. Blasted by a war between the Ancient Dragons, it was said, the jagged, cracked slivers of Islands had long been a favourite haunt of bandits, scoundrels and freedom fighters, depending on one's point of view. They were a natural stronghold, the only place in which Naoko and her people might conceivably survive a combined assault by Dragons, giants, Dragonships and ground troops. A hundred leagues to the north lay the border of the Kingdom of Kaolili, Prince Qilong's country, famed for its lush, garden-like Islands and copious production of mohili wheat.

Lia squinted, magnifying her sight as Grandion had taught her. Aye. Near the fortress, the ruddy evening suns-shine picked out perhaps three dozen of the Eastern Dragons Mizuki and Elki had promised to recruit. They looked as nervy as Dragon hatchlings who had stumbled over an Elder's tail-spikes, lumped together shoulder to shoulder as though confronting a fearsome enemy. Opposite, the Human force huddled in a state of anxiety evident from a league off. Mizuki and Elki stood squarely between the two forces, clearly nonplussed.

Evidently, the Humans and Dragons trusted each other implicitly. Great.

Hualiama had a spine-tingling premonition as she surveyed the scene. *What I wouldn't do to be Akemi when she sees you, Yukari.*

The Aquamarine Dragoness' response was a keyed-up shiver. Fire leaked between her fangs. *Do you think she'll remember me, Hualiama?*

She wanted to cry. Lia said, *She has dreamed of nothing else, all these years. But—go gently with her, Yukari. She's no youngling, and this will be a great surprise …*

"I'm no youngling either," said the Dragoness, squirting a playful gout of fire in her direction. "Can you see her?"

"Not yet," said the Human.

"I had hoped for more Dragons to oppose Razzior," Grandion remarked.

"Aye, Dragon. Let's go land plumb in the middle."

"Making a royal entrance fit for a Princess of Fra'anior?" he suggested.

"A disgraced royal pain in the armpit of destiny," said Lia, mangling a Dragonish saying. Her Dragon companions grinned toothily in appreciation. "Come on, Yukari, lift a wing. I know all Dragons secretly love to show off."

"I'm not too tired to swat you to the next Isle, youngling!" Yukari warned.

Smugly, Lia said, "Then I shall have to provide the encouragement you require."

Choosing a stanza from one of her favourite ballads, *Saggaz Thunderdoom,* Hualiama raised her voice in the ringing chorus, usually performed by a baritone soloist:

When that mighty Dragon-lord voiced his roar,
He shook the Dragons to their core,
He fired the mountains, burned the plains,
Until the ashes fell like rains …
Crying–

The pair of Dragons surged through the air in spontaneous delight, roaring along with her: *Thunderdoom! THUNDERDOOM.* Their Storm-powered challenges rolled over the Island in a low reverberation of real thunder, causing the faraway Dragons to flare their wings and bugle the alarm. Hualiama could not have heard their response, but Grandion did, for it communicated to her across their mental link. The figure of fire touching her mind seemed to shimmer with pleasure.

Aye, he said. *If I can use your senses, you can use mine. Be at liberty, Dragonfriend.*

Liberty? If only. This Dragonfriend struggled in the grip of titanic tides coursing through her life. Nevertheless, she let Grandion hear the smile in her voice. *With a roar like that, you could be the Thunderdoom himself.*

You honour me. Pride lent an extra bounce to his wingbeats.

Lia decided her Dragon would not recognise sarcasm if it

slapped him ralti-stupid.

The Blue Dragons swept down on the congregation at an eye-watering speed. As Grandion's wings beat the air to bring him to a spectacular, sharp landing between the assembled Dragons and Mizuki's position, glad cries rose to her ears. When Yukari landed, the Dragons genuflected as one toward the ancient Dragoness. Not even Sapphurion earned such grave respect, Hualiama thought, shaking off a shiver as she impetuously swung off Grandion's paw and somersaulted into a lithe crouch upon the barren, black volcanic stone. Where was Akemi?

The Dragonfriend, whispered some of the Dragons, jostling each other for a view. They were mostly young adults and a few smaller fledglings. Only a handful were larger and older than Grandion.

Sulphurous greetings, mighty Mizuki. She inclined her head.

The Copper Dragoness, with an awed glance at the flanking bulk of Yukari, stretching her wings and spine in the warm evening suns-shine, said, *These were all who did not fly against Razzior, or ignore our invitation. These are Dragons willing to deal with Humans.*

Lia glanced over at the Human congregation. Naoko and her people stood near the fortress, all tall, dark-haired female warriors in battle array. The men and children must be hidden inside.

She grinned at her brother as he sauntered around Mizuki's left wingtip, holding hands with Saori. "Islands' greetings, Dragon Riders. Nice work."

Elka'anor honoured her with a courtly bow. "Princess." And perhaps conscious of all the attention, he bent to peck her cheek. "Mighty Dragonfriend. Is this Yukari? Wow. Flying mountain."

Lia said, "Yukari, the Aquamarine Dragoness, may I present Prince Elka'anor of Fra'anior, my noble brother and fellow Dragon Rider?"

Elki managed to not quite pop with pleasure.

"Greetings, Prince of Fra'anior," rumbled Yukari, inclining her muzzle. For Mizuki, she added, *Sulphurous greetings, my noble kin.*

"Listen," said Elki. "Mizuki's been teaching me Dragonish." *Sulphurous grittings to thee, nibble Yucky.*

Hualiama blenched.

Mizuki's fires raged in embarrassment, but Yukari only said graciously, "Well spoken, youngling. You'll become a master of Dragonish yet."

Raising her voice, Lia called, "Noble Dragons, welcome! At a time of great peril for both Dragonkind and Humankind, you have made a flight of great courage. I believe your decision honours the Spirits of the Ancient Dragons. I am Hualiama, adopted into the Human royal family of Fra'anior. I was raised by Dragons."

The sleek, beautiful Eastern Dragons raised a brief clamour of shock. Raised by Dragons? How could this be? A peculiar Fra'aniorian custom, another claimed. But the girl was so tiny, a Green Dragoness wondered. How come she sensed so much magic?

Right, Lia decided. If she meant to impress these Dragons, then she had better produce a properly draconic display of shock and awe. She said, "Sapphurion the Dragon Elder and his mate Qualiana raised me for three years in their own roost. I call them shell-father and shell-mother–unashamedly. I love them as my own parents!"

Grandion's bugle stilled their restless murmuring, while several of the Dragons hurriedly bit back the bonfires that roared out of their throats. Arching his neck arrogantly, he rumbled, "This Human and I are bound by oath and life-debt. Much can be sung of our story, my Dragon-kin, but know this. I am Grandion, shell-son of Sapphurion and Qualiana. I bear Hualiama of Fra'anior upon my back with the most fiery dignity and pride of our kind. She brightens my soul-fires. Twice, this girl has plucked my life from the pit of darkness, and once from the snap of a Dragon's jaws. I can think of no greater honour than to know the Dragonfriend. She has earned her name as a creature not only of blood and bone, but of fire and magic, and it is the hope of a new magic that I believe has brought us together today, to this place. Here, we will sing a new Dragonsong, working and fighting alongside Humans."

Suddenly, dozens of Dragons' orbs burned upon her, and Lia became aware of the weight of expectation that attended her arrival. This was what they had come for. These younger, more adventurous Dragons scented a different future–one not hidebound to draconic tradition. They wanted to reach beyond the rigid societal structures of their kind. They did not rush to battle. These Dragons embraced–what? Could the Dragonfriend offer them a future, when she did not even know what it meant for herself? She must sate the cravings of these flaming hearts. Soothe and woo, fire and inspire …

The combined power of their emotions made Lia falter as she turned to beckon Naoko and her warriors. Instantly, Grandion was at her side.

A torrent of white-fire poured over her vision. Magic, unbidden, rising–so much! How could Human flesh contain it? She had a vision of Amaryllion Fireborn burning up outside the Natal Cave, his fire-soul finally blazing through his hide, consuming until not even ash was left to clothe his bones. When she looked up, Naoko stood nearby, and she realised that the two groups had drawn close, as though compelled by the forces that raged within her now.

Her breathing failed. Someone patted her back as she wheezed. Lia shook her head. "I can't. It's too much. Grandion, help …"

The Dragon rumbled, "How? Instruct me, Lia."

She was lost in a sea of fire, drowning. Grandion's paw clasped her, but Lia sensed that even he feared to hold one who burned as intensely as she did, with such purity that the colour white came to represent excruciation, the refining heart of a blast-furnace in which metal must turn to slag, creating new alloys from the pure ores that remained.

Screaming! Blue-white lightning jolted her Dragon!

"Fight it, Lia!" he thundered.

"I can't. Grandion …"

One at a time, ordered another voice. Yukari. *Choose one; focus there.*

With a mental flailing, Lia reached for the Dragoness' voice.

Grandion's mental touch steadied her, a desperately beautiful coolness that gave her, momentarily, respite from the fire. She homed in on Yukari, shutting out the others. Lia saw tantalising hints of magic reaching all the way into the fortress, yearning for completion …

"Akemi." Lia rounded upon Saori. An Enchantress' voice commanded, "Fetch Akemi. Now."

"She's amputating a gangrenous leg," Saori began to protest.

"Now!"

The Eastern Isles warrior sprinted back to the fortress as though blown by the storm winds of Lia's fury. Such power! Such evocative Dragonsong, falling upon her soul like the torrential rain of lava blasted out of a volcano. Hualiama tried to swallow it back. She wished someone would say something, rather than this endless madness of waiting, braving the billows of magic that no Dragon seemed able to see.

Akemi emerged from the fortress, grumbling, "This had better be important, Saori!"

Saori simply pointed.

"Aye, there are Dragons and–what?" The old woman staggered.

"I came," said the Dragoness.

Akemi gasped, "You said you'd never …"

In a flash of scales, the elderly Dragoness moved as though she had been teleported to her friend's side. "Akemi. Beloved Akemi. My hearts were blind, until the Dragonfriend came."

Desperate hope creased Akemi's face. "Girl, how … what did you do? What is this magic?"

"The power to abolish taboos," Grandion averred.

"To sculpt hearts," Yukari added.

"To entwine souls with bonds of immaculate fire," the Tourmaline sighed.

The Dragoness grinned happily. "To bring Dragon and Human together in the heavens, in glorious newness."

Reaching out for Akemi's hand, Lia raised her to her feet. A little testily, given the near-blinding pain sheeting like white rain across her vision, she growled, "All I know is that you two belong together. You've tarried far too long. Now arise, and make your promises."

And she gave of herself to unite them.

Chapter Twenty-Four

Hualiama's Way

DESCENDING FROM THEIR training flight with nineteen new Dragon and Rider teams, Grandion sensed fatigue in his Rider's posture. *You gave too much,* he accused.

How could I refuse?

The Tourmaline stilled his wings, letting the breeze buoy them as his mental voice deepened in concern. *I will ask Yukari–*

I just need to recoup. I had no idea magic could empty me like a gourd.

Magic has limits, which some people gaily trample over. This comment earned an irritable snort. *By my mother's egg, Lia, what's riled those Dragons?*

Through her eyes, Grandion examined the Dragons which had remained grounded while those who had found Riders practised formation flying and shooting arrows at aerial targets, mostly empty sacks held by Dragons. Naoko's warriors were capable, the Tourmaline Dragon thought with satisfaction. Only two had fallen out of their improvised seats during sharp manoeuvres. Their Dragons quickly snaffled them up. Perhaps Lia was right. A saddle strapped to a Dragon's spine-spikes would prevent those types of accidents. What Dragon would wear a saddle? Those were for domesticated beasts.

Dragons aren't tame, said the Princess, reading his unshielded thoughts. Excellent progress. He clicked his fangs together in approval. *There's much I don't understand in you, Grandion–potentials and senses I have no words for, which no scroll could possibly describe. But*

I am learning.

Grandion back-winged powerfully, bringing them to a landing. Hualiama walked down his back, checking her weapons, especially the powerful Haozi hunting bow.

She said, *A Dragon who could carry three or four archers would enjoy a huge advantage in combat.*

Aye.

Dragonfriend! Vinzuki, a fiery Orange Dragoness, stumped over to them, displeasure writ in every aspect of her body language. *What about us?*

What about you? Lia spoke crisply, but she stumbled upon alighting from Grandion's hind leg, and picked herself up with annoyed slaps at her knees. *Explain yourself, mighty Dragoness.*

Glancing left and right as her fellow Dragons moved closer, Vinzuki growled belligerently, *I want a Rider too. Why are we left out? Are we not worthy?* Lia stiffened physically, emotionally and mentally at her sharp accusation. *Look. We are twelve. Four say they want no Rider, but will fly with us. That leaves eight. What makes us different? Why do you refuse to work your magic for us?*

I don't refuse–I'm just tired. And, it doesn't work like that.

Like what? Hideki, a hulking Green, growled. *Like you choose–*

Pushing back her hair from her eyes, Hualiama snapped, *I don't choose! I don't manufacture relationships, Hideki.*

Vinzuki smoked liberally as she ground out, *You're deliberately excluding us.*

Grandion noted the khaki green swirls half-hidden by her eye-fires, and the clenched position of her right forepaw. Aye, she was jealous. And why not? What Dragon enjoyed another being honoured above them? Especially one as forthright of wing and mien as Vinzuki?

It's not a right. Hualiama sighed. *Humans are not for bartering or picking from a shop window.*

Well spoken, Lia. The Tourmaline found himself nodding, and taking a protective stance above his Rider, his bulk unsubtly threatening any Dragon who would dare to breathe fire at her. His triple heartbeat picked up pace, readying his body for possible battle. But when the Princess suggested they try on the morrow, the Dragons raised a chorus of snarling discontent. Others landed about them now, kicking up a brief storm of dust and grit. Lia shaded her eyes with one hand, and brushed her long hair back from her face. Vinzuki's mate, Raiden, a Blue only slightly smaller than Grandion himself, pushed between the others to rub necks with her.

Looming above Hualiama, Raiden said, *Dragonfriend. Let your heartsong be Dragonsong.*

I–don't understand, she said.

He means, you fail to grasp Vinzuki's meaning, Grandion thought to her, privately. *Is there nothing to be done? Truly? A path we haven't considered …*

I don't mean for anyone to be left out! She's just jealous.

Of course, Lia left her thoughts unshielded.

A hundred fangs snapped toward Lia's face, but the girl did not flinch, not even when Raiden's paw intervened to head off his mate's shadow-charge. Grandion felt his hearts swell with pride. By the First Egg of all Dragons, when they saw her courage and ardour, what Dragon could fail to recognise the fires within her? Now, those same fires spoke.

Vinzuki, I will not be bullied! I have done my utmost. Hualiama's voice was flat and confident, and Grandion's sixth sense of intuition confirmed his assessment that she commanded respect from the listening Dragons as a result. *Nineteen Dragons have Riders! Toss it in a Cloudlands volcano, of course it isn't enough for you that I'm on the point of collapse. It's never enough for a Dragon. You're like a bunch of covetous hatchlings, anxious to possess the pretty jewel another has picked up, squabbling, unable to exercise a second's patience–*

And then she tossed her good work off the proverbial Island cliff. Grandion knew he had to intervene. The fury building in Vinzuki would find no good outlet. Behind the Dragoness, muttering between the Dragons reached a different, dangerous pitch.

Lia, he warned.

We want Hualiama's Way for all of us, said Raiden.

What by the volcanic hells is Hualiama's Way? Lia shouted, losing her cool. Grandion felt his own dark-fires rise, resentful.

Raiden, clearly aiming to be the voice of reason, said, *We Dragons call this magic Hualiama's Way, or Grandion's Gift.* He bowed slightly to the Tourmaline, who voiced a low rumble of endorsement. *Vinzuki's voice is our voice. We enter this partnership with Humans willingly, but charily. Mistreatment and favouritism warm no Dragon's roost.*

As he spoke, darkness closed around her vision. Distinctly, Grandion sensed his Rider giving in, a moment of weakness. She sought oblivion, to simply shut these Dragons out. *No!* Faster than a draconic heartbeat, his pride switched to scorn. Not like this! He snatched Lia up in his paw, growling, *You won't faint.*

Hualiama struggled weakly. *Mercy, Grandion. They ask too much. How can I give what isn't mine to give? Help me. I need space to think it through … tomorrow. Make them understand.*

Raising his Rider to the level of the Dragons' eyes, twenty feet off the ground, Grandion said, *Allow me to instruct you, my Dragon-kin, in how this Dragon-Human relationship works. What you call Hualiama's Way, is a state of being between a Dragon and his Human–*

Tyrant! Lia hit his fisted paw. *Release me this instant. I can't–*

Shut the chattering monkey-mouth, Grandion growled. Lia hissed furiously, but he ignored her. *Attend my words, noble Dragons. Lia, 'I can't' is unacceptable. Listen–*

I will not listen until you release me, you fire-breathing fiend!

He breathed, *Thou.*

What? Lia tried to kick his nose, but could not reach. *Despotic Dragon! Don't teach them your overweening ways.*

Thou, Grandion said softly, putting his hearts into it.

Her pulse skipped a beat. *Grandion … n-no. You're embarrassing m-me.*

Through the connection between them, he sensed the heat rising in her face. Now she understood. The Tourmaline knew he had won, but his third heart dictated the gentle pulse of his response.

Thou–he wafted the invisible magic of his soul-fire into her face–*art mine, and I, thine.*

* * * *

With the fire came understanding. On the wings of the Dragon's magic, Lia felt revitalising strength infuse her being. There was no need to struggle. Grandion was right. It was a way of being between Humans and Dragons. The Dragon was asking her if she was alright, but Hualiama was already five steps ahead. She wanted to chuckle. Males and females were so different, no matter the creature-kind they represented.

The watching Dragonkind seemed torn between laughter and outrage. Right. Time to work. *Thank you, Grandion.* Turning to Raiden, she said, *Raiden, do you third-heart-love Vinzuki?*

Aye! His eye-fires blazed.

Does the flow of this Dragoness' wingbeat not conjure visions of hot lava racing down a mountainside?

AYE! The Blue Dragon thundered. He lowered his muzzle with a toothy Dragon smile. *Why these poetic words, Dragonfriend?*

I seek what is hidden, she replied. *Vinzuki, do you truly love this breathtaking Blue beast?*

Somewhere below her, Elki said to Saori, "What's she doing?"

Grandion whispered, "Finding connections."

Vinzuki's eye fires blazed. *Of course I do. What truths are these idiotic questions meant to divulge?*

How can you be certain? Lia inquired.

You insult me! But the Orange Dragoness glanced at Raiden. *He …*

The Blue Dragon flexed his massive shoulders and wafted fire playfully against his mate's flank. *Tell me, how do I soulfully-love thee, o fearless sky-warrior?*

Vinzuki blurted out, *Every morning at dawn, he sings to me.* Her belly-fires roared in a Dragon's blush, but Lia was motionless in Grandion's paw, wholly focussed on the soft effulgence she began to detect between them. Could a Dragon's fire-soul be seen, even as she had seen Amaryllion's inner essence? *Raiden warms our roost, and his eye-fires incite … Dragonfriend, you aren't listening.*

Hualiama waved a hand dreamily. *Tell me more. Tell me*–she

switched languages abruptly–"Elki. I understand now. Go fetch everyone from inside the fortress. Every Human."

Saori protested, "But that's the men and children. It's not our way–"

"It's a family's way!" Lia threw back her head, laughing merrily, and the more so at the stir of draconic and Human confusion that greeted her eruption of mirth. "Dragon Riders are not only warriors."

"They are warriors first and foremost," said Elki, doubtfully.

Lia smiled down at her brother. "In your circle, brother–" she indicated Saori, Mizuki and Elki "–who are the warriors?"

"My women–my Dragoness and my Human love," he said. "Me–well, not so much. Warrior in training. Slaying the enemy with perfect comedic timing … oh. Now I get it, sister."

"What I get is the stink of fresh windroc eggs," snorted Vinzuki.

"Aye, my third heart?" Raiden nuzzled her neck fondly. The Orange Dragoness nipped his shoulder.

"Saori, please fetch them." Lia aimed another futile kick in Grandion's direction. "I'm rather held up, presently."

Elki groaned, "Terrible joke. Right. Back in two shakes of a dragonet's tail."

Shortly, people began filing out of the fortress–a surprising number–the men and youngsters dressed in soft animal skins against the underground cold, the female warriors wearing light, loose cotton-weave clothing beneath hard leather armour. Naoko folded her muscular arms across her chest and took her stance, legs akimbo, signalling her displeasure with the Fra'aniorian who flagrantly disrupted her arrangements. Never mind that. Lia was about to usurp their entire social structure. For Dragons, while fierce and noble masters of the sky, were not all the warring beasts Humans imagined them to be. There were scientists and doctors, engineers and explorers, and Dragons who kept the nursery and trained hatchlings. She had been too narrow-minded in her conception of who Dragon Riders might be.

Dragons, listen with your fire-souls. To Raiden, she said, *I'll need your help, Blue. Would you sing your love for Vinzuki? Dragoness, while he sings, we shall seek out your Rider, should he or she stand among the people.*

Hualiama drew a deep breath, but Grandion interrupted, pitching his booming voice to carry across the Human congregation, "The Dragonfriend seeks more Riders! Listen to Raiden's Dragonsong and search your hearts, Humans. Hearken to magic's call."

As Raiden's Dragonsong rose to salute the gathering evening, Lia turned to survey the watching faces. So many lives. What hid behind the dark, slanted eyes–what stories, what grief, what capabilities or fears, she could not possibly know. They looked to her as a visionary, yet Hualiama knew her own failings and lack of understanding. How could she inflict this fate upon others? Yet here they had gathered, Dragons and Humans alike, seeking a greater future, or simply one different to what had been before. Bridgers of the divide. Brave souls, all.

And that courage was what moved her most profoundly.

White-fire swirled around her, ethereal and frustratingly aimless. There must be something. Perhaps the magic depended not only upon her bringing Dragon and Rider together, but upon their faith? For the threads rising from Vinzuki seemed frail and few, and above the Humans, she saw but a hint of white mist.

"Closer," she said aloud. "Grandion, let me approach them. Vinzuki … come."

In a moment, she was upon her feet. The Orange Dragoness trailed her with unexpected meekness as Lia approached the silent ranks. So orderly, these Easterners. They had arranged themselves by family group and height, in rows she could not have drawn straighter with the edge of the suns-beams streaming beneath a band of storm clouds on the horizon. Lia gazed at them. She had to create … expectation. Why? Could she explain that she had a magical itch? Hardly.

Dipping her gaze, she called, "I sense your presence, Dragon Rider."

This provoked a stillness she could have bottled and sold to kings and princes. Behind her, Dragonsong swelled afresh as Raiden, his new Rider still seated upon his back, drew near.

She swept her eyes from left to right. "You must believe. One of you burns with fire uncontainable. One of you knows this is for you. I cannot explain such a knowing. It springs from the unfathomable depths of our being, an echo perhaps of a time when Humans first trod the Isles of our world. It is magic. Good and pure magic–what was that?" Lia whirled. "Over there."

Vinzuki's muzzle jerked as though slapped by an invisible blow. Still the fire would not find its target. Lia squeezed her eyes shut. This was stupid. This was–Flicker? *Flicker?*

This way, straw-head, chuckled the dragonet, his image dancing in her mind. *Follow if you dare.*

Keeping her eyes firmly shut, Lia stumbled into the crowd, treading on toes and bumping against arms and hips. "Sorry. Sorry, everyone."

Her hand fell upon a muscular, fire-scarred arm. Yes!

Hualiama smiled up at a tall young man, a blacksmith judging by his fire-scarred leather apron. Jet-black eyes widened as the import of the moment sank in. "Me?" he squeaked, squirming. "I'm an armourer, not a warrior."

"Him?" said Raiden's Rider. "That's my husband."

Vinzuki purred, "He's that Human's mate? I mean, Fumiko's mate?"

Fumiko, the warrior on Raiden's back, suddenly broke into a high-pitched ululation of delight. "Perfectly matched!" she whooped. "Come on, husband, how's about you get used to forging with living fire?"

Fixing her ardent eyes upon the man, isolated now as the crowd instinctively shrank back from him, the Orange Dragoness said, "Dragon fire has been used for centuries to forge the finest weapons in the Island-World. I would be honoured–careful!"

The young armourer extracted himself from a tangle of people he had bowled over. "Sorry. Forgot anyone else existed …"

"Quite excusable." Lia grinned at his ralti-struck expression.

Gripping his battered hammer as though he intended to employ it on Vinzuki, the blacksmith advanced toward his Dragon. "So," he inquired, "how does one stoke Dragon fires?"

* * * *

When Lia awoke in the dark of night, it was with a despairing groan. She could not possibly have enjoyed more than a blink of rest. Her body felt as though Grandion had used her to clean his fangs. Mercy, how could magic's use lead to such physical enervation? By her tenth introduction of a Dragon-Rider couple, as she had come to call her peculiar brand of matchmaking, pale-as-clouds Hualiama had to resort to clutching Grandion's paw in order to stand upright. The Tourmaline Dragon, with profuse draconic non-apologies, whisked his Rider away.

Lia scowled at the sleeping Dragon. Nice of him to tidy up after his ridiculous, roundabout performance of forcing her to push beyond her limits.

Ten more Dragon Riders. None had been as romantically convenient as the paired couples of Vinzuki and Raiden, with Tadao the blacksmith and Fumiko respectively. One had been a female warrior of barely her fourteenth summer, paired with a fifty-foot Green fledgling. Hualiama had heard the girl's mother yelling at Naoko afterward.

She had been but a year older than that girl when Ra'aba tried to murder her.

Dark clouds smothered the five moons. Hualiama shifted restlessly, quite convinced an unseen Dragon's claw was quarrying holes into her spine. All around her, she could just about make out the dim shapes of Dragons sleeping with their new Riders. Mizuki slept near Grandion's left forepaw, her right eye cat-slit, alert. Elki lay between his Dragon's forepaws, having kicked his blanket into a fine tangle. Where was Saori? There, seated on Mizuki's right forepaw. Gazing into the darkness. Hualiama wondered if she rued not having found a Dragon. Saori always acted the tough girl, keeping her illusions intact.

Naoko was the kind of mother who demanded her daughter go farther, go beyond. Perhaps she had been even more disappointed than Saori. Failure was unthinkable for the chief's daughter.

Mizuki? Lia roused the Dragoness. *Is Saori alright?*

The eye cracked slightly wider. *Hardly, Dragonfriend. Dragons go to mountaintops to brood. This night breathes dark-fires even to a Human's soul.*

Lia rose. *Grandion, I'm going to Saori. You sleep.*

But he lifted his muzzle, scenting the air. *Who patrols–aye, Hideki. Have you seen him?*

Disquieted, Hualiama scented the night air, much as her Dragon had done. Where was the Green Dragon? Dragon night-sight was leagues better than a Human's, but Grandion was blind. Did this hint of moisture signal an incoming storm? No, it was something else–sulphur and cinnamon? Suddenly, she was moving. Checking her weapons. Snatching up her hunting bow.

Mizuki.

The Copper Dragoness' eye-fires surged. *What?*

I sense … she shivered. Nothing she could have placed, just an unaccustomed chill down her spine and an awareness of a pressure against her mind.

Grandion growled, *Lia, speak to me.*

The ground quivered ever so slightly. Lia swayed, gripped by an escalation of a familiar feeling, the nearness of great magic when she had approached Amaryllion …

Hualiama snapped, "Saori, wake Elki. Mount up!"

The Tourmaline Dragon bawled, *DRAGONS! AWAKE! DANGER!*

Lia had never mounted up so fast. Grandion practically threw her at his spine-spikes. She had barely begun to fix her long belt when the Dragon crouched and hurled himself skyward. The snap of his massive thigh muscles wrenched her neck, but Lia wound her legs around the spike in front of her and rode the buffeting, searching the gloom with her weak, inadequate eyes–knowing it depended on her to keep

Grandion alive in a combat situation. Black shadows raced across the ground. Magic swelled.

She screamed, *Shield them all, Grandion!*

A Dragon's fireball at ground level lit a fifty-yard swathe of rock over which Shinzen's giants pounded, closing the distance to the encampment with fearful speed. Hideki broke through the clouds above them, caught in a coiling battle with three or four other Dragons. Had he been ambushed? Where were the other three sentries?

The Tourmaline Dragon twisted in pain as a mountain seemed to strike his mental shield. Tonnes of rock, perhaps meant for the sleeping Dragons, fell short of their mark. Now, helped by the flaring of Dragon fireballs, Lia finally saw a Dragonwing striking low for the fortress, sweeping the ground ahead of them with fireballs as they attacked the ground-bound Dragons. All was a welter of confusion below. Dragons sought their Riders and fought each other for wing-space to take off. They launched attacks with scant regard for who or what stood in their path. Below the attacking Dragonwing came a spread-out line of giants, perhaps four dozen in number, who paused to fracture massive boulders from the living Island beneath their feet and to propel them through the air–some upward, aiming for Grandion, and others shooting horizontally, battering one of the Red Dragons who had stormed outside of the ambit of Grandion's shield.

Can't hold … that many, he gasped, wallowing.

Left! she cried. But her mount shuddered as a rock struck him on his hindquarters. *We need–*

Yukari! Grandion thundered in recognition.

With a monstrous battle-challenge, the Aquamarine Dragoness rose from her position near the fortress and launched herself into the fray; Akemi swung from her paw, waving a crossbow. Sweeping over the top of the untested Dragon and Rider force, somehow avoiding the Dragons taking off with a cunning twist of her wings, Yukari's jaw gaped open to expel a dazzling white fireball at the enemy Dragonwing. It detonated in their faces. Multiple chains of lightning seared Hualiama's vision, leaping between the

Dragons and down to the giants below as though possessed of a destructive insanity all of its own. Chain lightning! Lia and her Dragon gasped as one. The rarest and deadliest of Blue Dragon powers, the awesome power of her attack struck the enemy Dragonwing as if an earthquake had split an Island asunder.

Now Grandion followed suit with a powerful attack of his own, sending lances of ice spearing into the tumbling Dragons. Suddenly they were among the enemy, claws flying and fangs clashing. A heavy impact threw Lia off her aim. Grimly, she raised the Haozi war bow, determined to make her shots count. She had no idea how Grandion could fight blind, but the Tourmaline Dragon grappled with a Red and ripped a twenty-foot tear in his wing before Lia drove an arrow right into the Red's ear-canal, if she saw rightly. Grandion's ice attack had downed three Dragons, one of whom brawled briefly with those still on the ground, only to be crushed beneath four attackers.

Dragons tumbled from the sky. Hualiama recognised two of the sentries before a Green Dragon's split-second attack distracted her. Grandion fought free, panting, roaring his wrath. A second Dragonwing drove in from the west, dropping off a load of giants on the run. Lia saw magic as flashes of light, whether real or through the eyes of her second sight, as the giants paused to rend the earth with their strange, *ruzal*-like magic. The sky filled with boulders and smaller stones. As Grandion ducked and weaved, his Rider plied her bow with terrible effect, scoring head-shots on several giants and a difficult eye-shot to down a stalwart Yellow Dragon, perhaps the leader of the attack.

Lia ducked reflexively as a fireball sizzled past her left shoulder, and directed Grandion into a tight turn. Reflexively, she placed an arrow into a giant's throat, but the man kept on running. She blinked as the man's head leaped off his shoulders. Mizuki corkscrewed past them with her wingtips brushing the ground, having made the killing blow. Elki lost his grip on his sword as he gutted another giant who dared to confront the Copper Dragoness. Those massive men knew no fear.

Ahead, she saw half a dozen giants swarming over a Green Dragoness, clubbing and stabbing her with terrible ferocity.

"Up, Grandion!" she shouted. "To the fortress!"

"Stop twizzling your head around and focus me on a target," he panted.

"But we'll get hit."

"I'm shielding, Rider." Oh. When would she learn? Grandion only laughed, "Battle is a song, Hualiama. It's a dance. Feel the rhythm; let it fire your blood. Here, I'll show you."

Bloodthirsty laughter belled out of her throat as the tide of Grandion's emotions caught her up–not crushing, as before, but savage and uplifting, focussed through the incredible power of Dragon reactions and senses. Merging momentarily with the Dragon's mind, Lia marvelled at what she experienced. She was sight. He was stone skin. She knew the rush of air over sensitive wings and noted how he made minute muscular adjustments to account for the debris filling the air. He directed her arrows, touching several with his magic to bring them on target. Lia instantly sought new targets.

In battle-song they became one. Organic. Brutal. Triumphant.

Ice shards sprayed from Grandion's mouth, scything through the band of giants attacking the fortress, perfectly avoiding Naoko who stood immovable in the entryway, and rose to blind a Brown Dragon intent on ambushing the Human leader from behind the northern battlements. Grandion smashed his shoulder into the Brown's muzzle and whirled, intending to finish him off, but Yukari was already there, jabbing the three forward-facing talons of her right forepaw into the Dragon's belly as he wobbled in the air. She ripped out a pawful of intestines.

With a departing aerial obeisance, Grandion angled for three huge Reds mobbing Mizuki. Her power of Shivers shrieked through the register of Human hearing. The Reds scattered, but not quickly enough. One of the Reds, a Dragoness, lost her right foreleg and half of her right wing in the resulting explosion.

DIE, YOU WINGLESS COCKROACHES! Grandion roared, smashing into another of the Reds. He missed his neck-bite, but caught the Red's right wing midway, near the second wing-joint, and savaged bone, wing-struts and wing surface with his fangs, inflicting a terrible injury.

Then, the Tourmaline Dragon shuddered beneath the blows of the third Red, who turned literally on a wingtip to tear into Grandion with all twenty talons bared. Suddenly Mizuki was there, biting the Red's muzzle, and Lia caught a flash of steely talon from the corner of her eye. She blocked instinctively. Pain spread up her forearm. Flung free! Severed from her perch, Lia tumbled off Grandion's left wings onto Mizuki's tail. She clutched a spine-spike for a moment, but the Copper Dragoness was the lowest member of the maul just then. Lia found herself scraped off unceremoniously and dumped atop a large, flat boulder.

A giant leaped at her. Lia somersaulted backward, evading the arc of his sword but not the clutches of a thorn bush. Pain lanced into her thigh and side. Draw the sword! Nuyallith blade in hand, she tore free of the bushes and smartly ducked a second blade aiming to trim more than just her hair. The giants slammed together mid-air, only to bounce apart and turn upon her with disconcertingly identical smiles. Twins? Or did all the giants look the same?

Hualiama backed up slowly, wishing she had her second blade. She palmed an Immadian forked dagger in her less-preferred right hand.

"I've a taste for girl-meat," growled one of the giants. He had to be nine feet tall and nearly as wide, while his sword looked suited to chopping down trees. Despite their bulk, the giants moved with uncanny agility over the rough terrain.

"There's a Dragon behind you!" Lia shouted.

The giants hooted.

"No, really!" She dived back beneath the thorn bushes as Green Dragon spit splashed over the two men. Blinded, with flesh bubbling off their arms and shoulders, the giants nevertheless attacked in the direction she had taken. Lia danced lightly aside, and then gasped as Grandion's tonnage hurtled down from above in a deliberately hard landing, flattening most of one giant and the upper half of the other. The Tourmaline Dragon finished the survivor with a casual thrust and twist of a talon.

"Done with fooling about on foot?" he asked.

"Just keeping my skills honed, Dragon," Lia retorted.

Dropping to her left, Lia lashed out with the Nuyallith blade, severing an incoming giant's right leg beneath the knee. Grandion smashed him aside with an irritated backhand slap.

"I'll swat the mosquitoes, if you look out for Shinzen's cockroaches," he growled.

"What did we miss?" Lia asked, looking around the dark, mostly quiet battlefield. In several places, Dragons flapped weakly or staggered along, gravely injured. "How did they sneak up on us?"

Grandion shook his head. "A power of concealment akin to *ruzal*–a novel technique. We must not underestimate Razzior or Shinzen again. And, your hand's glowing, Hualiama."

She had been gazing at the soft blue flame sheathing her left hand and the Nuyallith blade without truly seeing it. The flame faded.

"Where's Razzior?" she asked.

"Not with this group, clearly," said the Dragon. "But he'll be coming. You can stake your life on that."

Chapter Twenty-Five

The Kingdom of Kaolili

GRANDION SHOOK HIS muzzle and said bluntly, "For the fourteenth time, my Rider, their deaths were not your fault, nor are we cravenly fleeing the battle."

"Five Dragons killed, Grandion. Two will never fly again. Six Riders killed–"

"Ours is a greater calling."

"Greater?" How sanctimonious. "I think not. But it is our calling, as you put it. A cunning enemy fell upon us when we were ill-prepared. I only hope Kaolili's preparations progress apace. Half of the Dragons in the Island-World are either on their way, or are here already. War will consume these Islands, Grandion."

"Aye," he rumbled. No Dragonsong, just a flat acknowledgement of reality.

Two days later and five hundred leagues of fast flying from Eali Island, Grandion and Hualiama had passed over Jaoli into the sparse, widely-separated Islands that marked the southern fringes of Kaolili, by geographical extent, the greatest kingdom in the Island-World. The land was green and pleasant, the Islands scattered in the Cloudlands like jewelled raindrops of a vibrant lime-green, the colour of the verdant mohili wheat plantations. Did they grow nothing but wheat here? Everything about these Islands was neat. Neat edges. Neat plantations, squared off with lines of wind-breaking trees and drainage ditches. Plentiful terrace lakes including inland lakes on the larger Islands. Neat rows of wood-framed, paper-walled houses. Paper? She longed to go down there and touch the fabled substance. Give her scrolleaf any day. It was far more durable. Grandion said that if a storm flattened a house, it could be rebuilt in a day. Why not build houses to be durable in the first instance?

She had seen no Dragonships or army movement, however. Could Naoko's message already have reached the King of Kaolili? Perhaps the distances were too great. It was said to be another thousand leagues to Kerdani Town, and from there to the Lost Islands, a further fourteen hundred leagues' flying. Such was the mindboggling extent of Kaolili.

"I made up a song," said Grandion. "It's about this Human girl I know."

Hualiama smiled wryly. Did she know this Dragon? Where was the stiff, formal beast who had transported her to the Spits and back six years before? "Trying to cheer me up?"

"Using your favourite language, song," he agreed.

"I'm listening."

With a full flourish of his Dragon throat's gorgeous harmonies, the Tourmaline Dragon sang:

How do you love a rainstorm?
One drop at a time.

What was this? Cautiously, heart fluttering in her throat, she echoed back:

Am I a rainstorm? I thought you'd simply jump in and get wet.

The Dragon laughed, "There's more." And he sang:

How do you love a suns-beam?

An imperious waggle of his left wingtip demanded a reply.

Lia vocalised:

You cannot catch it in your jaw, or roll it in your paw,
Do I want to be a suns-beam?

Swelling in volume upon the breeze, the Dragon's voice rang forth:

You herald its appearance, to pink the eastern sky,
You yearn for its light, to gladden every eye,
Swift to the clouds you soar and cry, 'Allow her suns-beam to pierce your heart,
Usher her radiance to the Island-World's every corner.'
Aye, you are a suns-beam.

Hualiama did not want to spoil his good mood with a crass word. Clearly, the Dragon had no interest in Mizuki. That ploy had failed. But how could he so blatantly profess a romantic interest in his Human Rider? Madness. A Dragonsong of doom, should anyone ever dare to sing such a song. The stars should fall from the sky, the prophecy said. A clear vision rose before her eyes. War would roll over these fertile lands like Land Dragons rising from the deeps to stampede across the Islands, casting them down into ruin. The people down there had no idea.

Lia rubbed her arms and extinguished the flame which had briefly haloed around her hands. Heavens above and Islands below, where had that vision sprung from? She and Grandion raced to warn the risible Qilong's father. She prayed the monarch cared much for his people, enough at least to heed the booming drums of war.

Her thoughts returned to her broad-winged companion, he of a bristling array of skull- and spine-spikes and a tail which lashed over sixty feet behind her seat. With only the sky's endless vault to witness their interactions, who would know? Yet, she must deflect his attentions. Pensively, Lia sang:

How do you love a fire?

Will you not simply … burn?
Be warmed, but don't come too close …

Mercy. Fool that she was, speaking before sense gripped her tongue and stopped its hurtful wagging. Hualiama bit her lip, quelling an apology which would only have compounded his wrath, which burned audibly against her. This was how she repaid his sweetness? A thousand Islands screamed, 'Fool!'

After a time, Grandion sang so wistfully that tears sprang to Lia's eyes:

You become the fire.

And the long leagues lay heavy upon their souls after that.

* * * *

Five and a half days they spent aloft, snatching two full nights of sleep in that time, before Dragon and Rider sighted Kerdani Town, Kaolili's sprawling capital city, upon the horizon. Surely a record time for such a journey, Grandion remarked.

She leaned closer to him, a slight shift of her insignificant weight, in that way that she had when she wished to convey an intimacy. Grandion's scales prickled as she said, "Surely, this great-hearted Dragon hath burned the heavens with the swiftness of his flight."

His entire body shivered with delight. He growled, basso profundo, "We merit a reception committee."

"Aye. I was beginning to wonder where all their Dragonships were."

All they had seen for days were merchant vessels bearing cargo hither and thither. Now, a dozen large Dragonships rose to bracket their flight path. On the horizon, Hualiama's alert gaze informed Grandion of the mounded tops of dozens more Dragonships, lined up like sleek giant carp catching suns-shine in the shallows of a terrace lake. The army was assembled, the Dragon deduced. Good news.

Lia groaned. "Oh, ralti droppings! We forgot the white flag of an envoy. I'm not about to wave this green tunic top in surrender."

"Isn't your under-tunic white, Rider?"

"Waving my underwear at soldiers might attract the wrong sort of attention."

The Dragon knew she meant for him to deny the fact, or to assert his ability to protect her. Human females. They were just like Dragonesses, preening to invite a compliment. A goading was in order. "Perhaps the garment is too travel-stained?"

He practically heard a snap of fangs. "I can be snarky too, mister fungus-scales needs a lava bath."

Grandion only chuckled indulgently. In a few moments, he felt her wriggling about as she removed her Human clothing and then reassembled her outfit minus the under-tunic. With the breeze blowing from astern he scented her clearly, from the hint of fresh dorlis-flower perfume that still somehow lingered upon her skin since she had bathed at Yukari's Island, to the piquant, peppery magic of her Nuyallith blade, and aye, a touch of the Islands about her, as the Dragons put it delicately. Properly civilised Dragons would bathe every day, sometimes several times a day. No wonder he had the purple cloud-fungus. And even Lia might wrinkle her nose at his Dragonish odour.

"I've never seen Humans in such numbers," the girl said, a trifle breathlessly.

Humans were fleas in the armpit of the world, Grandion had once growled at her. Even a reformed Dragon felt edgy in the face of a multitude. She should wait until she saw the city proper beyond the hills.

The Dragonships rose purposefully on an intercept course, but after Hualiama waved her improvised flag, an answering white flag fluttered from the starboard gantry of the foremost Dragonship. A brief parley followed, in which the soldiers tried to disguise their disbelief at finding a Human riding Dragonback, and Lia requested an audience with the King of Kaolili.

"Never heard of Fra'anior?" Lia snorted, after the young

officer vanished briefly to consult his superior officer. "He couldn't find his own nose in the dark."

Grumbling, the Princess set about fixing a headscarf from what she had in her pockets, and rigging a face veil from a scrap of cloth Grandion had heard Akemi insist upon. Ridiculous Human customs. He preferred the carefree Hualiama, not the one who seemed to avoid offence. She was more true to herself when dealing with Dragons. The Tourmaline Dragon let fire bubble between his fangs to seal the accuracy of his insight. Grandion had spent many hours in Kaolili as his alter ego, the young Human man, seeking knowledge of the Scroll of Binding. But the need to hide his Dragon form while a projection snooped about had been tricky in a city of this size. Twice he had come perilously close to being discovered, and once, an otherwise demure Eastern girl had tried to kiss him. That had inspired him to work on his feedback loops, part of his fiendishly complex magical construction. Projection? The Aquamarine Dragoness did not know the half of it. His projection could smell, taste and see more than adequately. It could draw a bow in protection of a Human girl.

The young officer returned, and curtly ordered them to follow.

Grandion winged to a landing field close to the palatial living quarters of the King of Kaolili, which rivalled Gi'ishior's Dragon accommodation for extravagance, he begrudgingly admitted. Hualiama sat perfectly silent upon his back, but he could sense her goggling at her surroundings, which were indeed to be marvelled at. A Human city of some quarter of a million inhabitants, it housed five times the number of the entire Human population of Fra'anior. Furthermore, the city was immaculate. Not a stone protruded out of place. No stray leaves blew about the streets. The buildings of the central part of town were works of art created in dozens of shades of stone, each shaped to represent an animal of importance to the Kingdom. Water buffalo. Antelope–his mouth watered. White heron. Even the crocodile was represented, which interested him. Had Dramagon's creations made it this far north?

After a considerable delay at the landing field, a court functionary dragging a robe so long it trailed fifteen feet behind him and had to be carried by six attendants, met the official delegation from Fra'anior Cluster. If he was surprised at the appearance of a Dragon and a Human together, he did not admit it.

An unctuous wave of his hand followed the formalities. He pronounced, "If her Royal Highness of Fra'anior would accompany me?"

"And my Dragon?" asked Lia.

"Your Dragon?" A perfectly manicured eyebrow met his elaborate golden headgear. "The beast is with you?"

"I fear to affront Grandion, noble shell-son of Sapphurion, leader of the Island-World's Dragons," said Hualiama, with a courtly bow that reminded Grandion of Dragonish courtship rituals. Curious.

"Her Highness does not wish to freshen up before meeting the king?"

"Her Highness does so wish," said Lia. Grandion flexed his claws as he detected her irritation at the functionary's insinuation. "Her Highness will do so in the company of the mighty Tourmaline Dragon."

Well, she could certainly affect an air of snootiness when she wanted to, the Dragon observed, following this exchange with interest. Would she get her way?

The man bowed. "Number one. Fetch the Mistress of Baths. Number two, go clear the bathhouse on the corner of first and third street. Number three, see to the Princess' comfort. Four and five, fetch a detachment of the Royal Guard and deploy them at the baths. See that nothing disturbs our visitors. Number six? My robes. We must inform the King of the Princess' arrival."

The servants rushed off like ants disturbed from their nest, while the sixth servant patiently gathered up the folds of the great trailing robe, until he could barely see where he was going. With that, the functionary withdrew.

"Number three?" said Lia.

"Your Highness?" said the man, a younger version of the

functionary.

"Shall we proceed?"

A hint of confusion crossed his otherwise impassive features. "Where shall I order your belongings to be sent, Your Highness?"

Hualiama smiled without condescension. "All of my belongings are upon my person. Oh, and the Dragon. He will bring himself."

Grandion bared his fangs at the servant, who lost his nerve in the midst of expressing how very good all the Princess' wishes were, and rushed ahead with rather more haste than was apparently permitted in the Kingdom of Kaolili. Their short walk to the bathhouse made every citizen in sight stop and stare, or scream.

"You scared him," Lia remarked dryly.

The Dragon opined, "Every Human needs to experience mortal terror from time to time. It's beneficial for their physical, mental and spiritual wellbeing."

Lia's gaze measured him up and down. "Tyrant," she teased.

"My name is *Grrrrr*-andion," Grandion purred, strutting in a way that brought her wonderful, effervescent laughter forth to brighten the stifling early afternoon air.

* * * *

When they caught up, Lia smiled brightly at the manservant. "What's your name?"

"Number three," he replied.

"You don't have a name?"

"Three is my name."

"Saburo means third son, does it not?"

He barely masked his surprise. "This cannot be her Highness' first visit to the East?"

Grandion sniped, *Oh, her Highness is exceedingly clever. And she says Dragons show off.*

Colouring, Lia murmured, "Are these the baths already?"

At the baths, surveying a public pool sized for two hundred

Humans or one adult Dragon, Hualiama further nonplussed the man by skating casually over his offer of either male or female attendants, and requesting twenty-one servant girls. "One for me; twenty for the Dragon," she ordered. "Girls who won't faint in awe of his magnificence."

Telepathically, she added, *Adequate for your exceedingly overblown sense of consequence, Dragon?*

Grandion almost unleashed a fireball in annoyance.

"I need girls armed with long-handled scrubbing brushes, ladders and enough soap to lather a Dragon," Hualiama continued, undaunted. "In Fra'anior's past, it was customary for Human slaves to serve Dragons in this way. My companion, who belongs to one of the most venerable Dragon bloodlines, is especially hidebound to the old traditions."

Such as supping on sassy Humans, Grandion growled, unable to resist a nip aimed at the region of her haunches.

Frank amazement at their interaction broke through Saburo's typically Eastern, unreadable expression. Bowing deeply, he gasped, "As you wish, Princess!"

"Claws in, Dragon, lest you wreck the tiling," Lia commanded, every inch the imperious royal.

Shortly, Hualiama was bathing in what had previously been a ridiculously oversized indoor pool for a dragonet-sized Human royal ward, now overflowing due to Grandion's bulk. The water was steaming hot, but evidently not scalding enough for a fussy Dragon, who declared his preference for lava to bake the lizard-rump. Now, twenty-one awed servant girls filed in, wearing simple knee-length smocks with matching dove-grey face veils, which covered their faces up to the eyes but left their black hair uncovered, to her surprise. They huddled fearfully on the far side of the pool.

"Showtime," said the Dragon, flexing his wings.

Lia jibed, "Are those Dragon hormones I hear fizzing in your golden blood? Or an overflow of masculine ego?"

Grandion moved sinuously across the pool, saying, *May jealousy fire your blood, Dragonfriend.*

"Sooo." The Tourmaline infused his voice with fiery seduction as he loomed over the girls. "How is it that a bevy of this Island-Kingdom's most beautiful maidens has come to grace my bathtub? I must be the luckiest Dragon alive!"

Pure slush, but Lia found her knees rather weaker than she wished to admit.

Pesky Dragon.

The water was soothing; the building housing the ancient baths, spectacular. Floating on her back, Lia scanned the fresco artworks covering the vast domed ceiling overhead, depicting scenes of rural life from around the Kingdom of Kaolili. So different from Fra'anior. So exotic. The octagonal pool lay directly beneath the dome, perhaps a hundred feet overhead, and the eight fluted marble columns which supported the roof plunged into the water, down to a surprisingly deep bottom covered in what appeared to be blue gemstone tiling in fanciful swirls and patterns.

Grandion was in his element. Girls swarmed over him, scrubbing away briskly. Lazily, he thought to her, *So, this is the royal life. You had it tough.*

Your parents sure pampered me, she chuckled.

The Tourmaline Dragon's legs rivalled the roof columns for thickness. Swimming underwater toward Grandion's muzzle, having half a mind to surprise the Dragon, Lia coughed bubbles of air when she saw the toes of his forepaws, the three forward-pointing talons and the two rear-pointing talons, curled tight with draconic pleasure. The old fraud! He purred like a kitten beneath the ministrations of his energetic posse of petite admirers. Aye, so she was jealous. As a Dragon might say, jealous-love stirred the heart-fires to an agreeable blaze.

Taking a deep lungful of air, Lia swam widths of the pool underwater, amazed by the amount of time she was able to hold her breath. She must be fitter than she had assumed.

Vibrations conducted through the water came to her eardrums. Booted feet? Rising to the surface, Hualiama flicked water out of her face. The servant girls were all kneeling, heads to the ground, deathly silent.

"–majesty of ten thousand Isles, the incomparable King of Kaolili!" she heard.

Oh, monkey droppings. And her without a stitch of clothing.

A crisp baritone voice said, "Where is the Princess of Fra'anior? I must speak with her at once."

Using Grandion's chin for cover, Hualiama peeked at the King. He was built like his son, short but thick through the shoulder. A plain grey travel-cloak spanned those stalwart shoulders. His piercing grey eyes swept the scene before him with the ease of a man used to command. He wore banded golden armour which was no ceremonial showpiece, while a sword in an unadorned scabbard graced his left hip. His retinue numbered a dozen men, army officers by their bearing.

The grey gaze picked out her hiding place. "Princess." He bowed in the Eastern way, stiffly from the waist. "Forgive the shameful lack of formality and disturbance, but my border is threatened. I was about to embark with my Dragonship fleet, when news reached me of an envoy riding a Dragon into Kaolili Town. I knew there could be only one person in the Island-World who would dare such a deed." A second bow followed the first. "My son Qilong described his unwitting capture of your Dragonship, and your battle against the Dragons of Merx, with great passion and admiration. Be welcome in Kaolili, Princess of Fra'anior and Grandion, shell-son of Sapphurion. All that you need shall be yours for the asking. But first, tell me, what intelligence do you bring?"

The penetrating intelligence of a straw-head, Grandion's thought curled into her mind.

Hualiama quelled an urge to slap the Dragon. "I regret having to meet under these circumstances, o King. I am indeed the Princess of Fra'anior. Thank you for your gracious welcome." She was impressed by his staccato delivery and clear presentation of the facts, while the hand resting firmly upon the pommel of his sword underscored his desire for haste. "There is much we wish to share with you. Urgently."

"Aye. As we tarry, lives are lost."

"Bathing can wait. I will speak with you, o King."

"About face!" barked the King. As one man, he and his dozen-strong retinue of officers turned their backs upon her.

Lia blinked. He said, "Arise from these cleansing waters in good faith, o Princess. Girl. Bring clothes for our guest. Hurry."

A row of ramrod-straight backs greeted her curious gaze. They would not look? Eastern honour was a strange thing. Lia swam out of Grandion's shadow. Her serving girl, Yumi, who stood no taller than Lia herself, held out a thick roll of cloth these Easterners called a towel.

In her soft, lilting accent Yumi said, "Regrettably, lady, your travel clothes are being washed as we speak. We can fetch suitable apparel from the Palace–"

"The King cannot wait," Lia replied. "Is this towel large enough?"

"Great lady, the dishonour–"

"Is not worth the lives it would cost, Yumi," Hualiama said gently. "You haven't seen the enemy. I have."

The King and his twelve officers caught her eye by bowing simultaneously to the empty entrance. "You do us honour," intoned the King. "Where are you bound, Princess? Why did you seek this audience?"

Certainly, the prodigal Princess of Fra'anior had not sought an audience with a King intending to carry out her diplomatic duties clad in a towel. She collected her thoughts with haste. "A mighty power rises against your kingdom, my Lord. My Dragon companion and I are bound for the Lost Islands in search of knowledge which is of incalculable value to our enemy."

"You seek the Scroll of Binding," stated the King.

Grandion growled, discontented.

Did you seek to hide your intentions, Grandion? Her question communicated a peevish undertone.

Not enough, clearly.

Nevertheless, we could gain a powerful ally against Shinzen and Razzior, and save lives, both Dragon and Human.

Sapphurion would thank us, the Tourmaline agreed.

Conversation at the speed of thought meant that Hualiama hardly missed a beat as she replied, "I'm ready, o King."

He turned smartly. Lia kept her back very straight as the

King marched toward her. Barefoot, dripping wet, the face veil sticking to her nose–he seemed to take no notice of these things. Storm-grey eyes evaluated her. His gaze touched the cut on her left forearm, healing after a Dragon's talon had sliced open a five-inch cut during their battle against Shinzen's forces. Although there was nothing unsolicited in his attention or manner, heat rose into her cheeks. The King of Kaolili possessed a power of presence she had seldom encountered in a man, and an air of mystery, as though behind the mask of his features, a draconic brain made a billion calculations a second.

He said, "Dragon Rider, Princess of a volcanic kingdom and a warrior of beauty and grace. You aren't as tall as I expected of a Fra'aniorian."

"I did not know my mother, Majesty."

The low rumble of Grandion's belly-fires changed pitch as she skirted the truth. Not a lie–not quite, but Lia knew he would raise the issue later. Dragons never flat-out lied.

A genuine smile creased the corners of the King's eyes. "Nor are you half as tall as the tales they tell, even here in Kaolili. Yet there is something Eastern about you, I feel. Your spirit is of Fra'anior, but also of the East." Now, Hualiama had to lower her gaze. Perceptive! "The enigmatic serenity of your spirit hides depths as stormy as this Dragon," he added. "I should have appreciated the time to know you better, Hualiama of Fra'anior. Perhaps in another time and place."

"My King," she murmured, discomfited.

"There's no need for a headscarf, unless you prefer it," he said, causing Yumi to pause her work.

Lia said, "I thought long or uncovered hair was objectionable to Easterners?"

"You confuse our culture with those Human cultures located further south in the archipelago," said the King. "Here, only married women or servants wear the headscarf, while unmarried girls and women wear their hair long. All women wear the face veil."

"In which case, Yumi, please desist."

"A braid, Princess?" suggested the servant.

"Perfect, thank you." Lia paused. Where to begin their tale?

"Do you need a medic to treat your arm?" he asked.

"Thank you, o King. Perhaps later." Reacting to his nod, she said, "We have flown directly from the Barrens, seven and a half days on the wing with scant time to rest. The south is already overrun by the armies of the Warlord Shinzen, who hails from Gao-Tao Island, beyond Haozi. Shinzen recently formed a pact with Razzior, a powerful and ambitious Orange Dragon whom we Fra'aniorians know well. Six years ago, Razzior tried to usurp the Human Kingdom of Fra'anior, sparking a war in which both Dragons and Humans became involved."

One of the officers put in, "Why should we care for Shinzen? He's nothing but a bandit and a petty tyrant."

"Razzior is a master of a rare type of magic called *ruzal*," Lia replied evenly. "He has used this magic to revive some of Dramagon's creations." Faced with blank expressions, she explained, "Dramagon is an Ancient Dragon scientist famous–or rather, infamous–for his experiments in cross-breeding and modifying different creatures in our Island-World. He was cast out by the Dragons of Fra'anior, and it is his ancient fortress which Shinzen chooses to occupy. With Razzior as his ally, Shinzen now commands an army of Dragons and giants. These giants are Enchanters, powerful magic-users capable of–"

"Giants? Fireside tales for children," scoffed the same man. Lia flushed at his scorn.

"Do you mean the Ippon people of the south?" asked another.

"No, these are creatures Dramagon bred, even greater than–"

The King silenced the first officer's snort. "Peace, Commander Hiro. We don't seek a quarrel. This Razzior's plan cannot be the conquest of Humans, surely?"

"Partly," rumbled Grandion. "A return of Humans to slavery under draconic rule would not be unattractive to Razzior and his ilk. We estimate the number of Dragons directly allied to Razzior's cause as being upward of five hundred. Razzior's eye burns against the rule of my shell-father and the Dragon Elders. The knowledge contained in the Scroll of Binding would allow him to control the Dragonkind with unbreakable strength, as though he grasped puny Humans in his paw. That's his ultimate goal."

"Meantime, Sapphurion brings a huge Dragonwing from Fra'anior and its allies to fly against Razzior. My father would be honoured to be your ally, or at least, would value your neutrality."

In a war between Dragons? Impossible, isn't it? Lia loved having an undetectable side-language. More than useful!

Aye, Lia. Allow him to draw his own conclusions. This King is no feral-head.

The King clarified, "So you think we face a Dragon assault on our territories?"

"Can we trust a girl who rides a Dragon?" Commander Hiro's face resembled stone. "Or does Sapphurion's shell-son create his own draconic law, and force a Human slave to do his bidding?"

"I am no slave!" Lia snarled.

Grandion bared his fangs at the officer. "A fine question, Commander Hiro. Princess Hualiama has a will of her own–which I neither predict nor own."

His lamenting tone made more than a few of the officers chuckle.

"I know she speaks the truth, because I was Shinzen's captive for three years. And if you do not judge his power enough by his ability to keep a creature of fire and magic captive, then perhaps you might better judge from Hualiama's memories. We will show you."

Show them, Grandion? How?

This demands both power and control. If you summon up your memories–key and brief ones–I will project them on the water. We'll cut through a great deal of idle chatter as a result.

Aye. Smart Dragon. Diplomatic, even.

The Dragon's magic caused an area of water at the pool's edge to became as still as a mirror. The Princess summoned up a memory of Shinzen. Magic embraced her like cool rain, transferring the picture onto the canvas created by the Dragon. She saw his six-toed feet. A vast paw slapped her back. Shinzen raised her effortlessly, higher and higher, holding Lia as if he dangled a rat by its tail for examination. Black-in-black eyes fixed upon her, their soul-shadowing power making her feel naked and dirty inside, as though he had already violated some part of her being with a mere glance … several of the officers gasped as her mental image betrayed the true size of the man.

Flick. The image changed. Grandion barrelled into Shinzen's throne-room, where the Warlord stood overseeing his troops. A terrible force seized the Tourmaline Dragon and held him immobile. The image wavered as the Dragon's fury rose. 'Do you have any use for a Dragon-riding princess?' Shinzen asked. Razzior bared his fangs. 'A deal-sweetener? Use her as you wish, Shinzen.' The Warlord threw back his vast, shaggy head, his laughter booming across his troops and the gathered Dragons. 'She's untouched? How precious!' Hot shame enveloped her, but Grandion soothed Lia with a mental touch.

Next, she raced into battle. A Dragonwing swooped low to drop off clumps of giants … huge boots pounded across the rocky terrain, their gigantic strides visible even in the low light … six giants mobbed a Green Dragoness, their swords and clubs rising and falling with blows powerful enough to fell a Dragon … a giant sprang at her! She stood barely taller than his belt buckle. Lia's somersaulted backward as the giant pursued her with deadly swiftness.

Finally Razzior arrived, descending outside her cave in the panoply of his blazing majesty, his murderous gaze lighting upon a small Human hiding in a cave mouth. 'Run.' The Dragon made a shooing motion with his forepaw. 'Go on. It's more amusing for me.' Fire thundered from his mouth.

The picture wavered, and the normal rippling of water reasserted itself.

"There is more," said Hualiama.

The officers looked stunned. Even Commander Hiro's lips compressed into a thin line as he considered what he had seen.

With quiet gravity, the King said, "Hiro, start the fleet moving south. If you should encounter Sapphurion's forces, offer them the solemn word of this King. We seek an open alliance. I will remain to question our envoys."

"One last thing, Commander Hiro," said Hualiama. "I rather suspect you'll run into a few more Dragon Riders down south, members of a female warrior tribe who have allied with the Eastern Dragons in a new collaboration–a new magic. They're friendly, if you can overcome your prejudices."

I see my Dragonish-ness is rubbing off on you, Grandion commented, approvingly.

Commander Hiro bowed curtly to them both. "Not all that is new, is good," he stated flatly. "However, I trust my King's insight. May the heavens clear to smile upon your path, Dragon and Rider."

Chapter Twenty-Six

North on the Dragons' Highway

MAY THE HEAVENS smile? Hualiama eyed the incoming storm front with a fury she usually reserved for her worst mistakes. Mercy. The upward curve of the ominously dark cloud-battlements east and west of their position did indeed resemble the corners of a Dragonish smile, with the black, sinister centre of the storm being the gullet of a Black Dragon capable of swallowing a thousand Dragons flying wingtip-to-wingtip. The Isles below had grown more mountainous and forested with conifers, she noticed, grateful now for the warm clothes and gloves the King's armourer had insisted she include in their baggage. Two new saddlebags sat just behind her perch, buckled in place with stiff leather straps.

Grandion had fumed, "You'll have me wearing a saddle, next!"

"Is that an offer, Dragon?"

"Nooo–AAAARRRRGGGGHH!"

Double mercy slathered in rotten prekki-fruit peels–so the entire senior command of the Kingdom of Kaolili now knew the state of her maidenhood. They thought her a rebel and Grandion a lawbreaker. Which was worse? She sighed heavily.

"We'll find a man for you yet," said Grandion, breaking in on her thoughts.

And now her Dragon had become a sensitive, caring soul? "Just point me in the right direction," she chuckled. "I'll hunt him down Dragonback …"

"And lash him up there in place of your saddlebags?"

"Aye, and for laughs, I'll teach him how to pamper my Dragon every day."

"Perfect. Although, this mysterious man will have his work cut out for him to beat the efforts of twenty cute little servant girls of Kaolili Kingdom."

"Grandion!" she huffed. "That's quite enough!"

The Dragon held out a foreleg for her inspection. "I've never gleamed like this before. I find the idea of Human slaves highly appealing. They were so … frisky."

"Frisky?" Hualiama's voice took on a dagger-sharp edge. Sensitive and caring? Slug spit and stinking windroc eggs! "That's because those poor chicks were too frightened to *stop* working once the King suggested they continue! I'll have you know, Grandion–"

"Apparently, you've monetary value," the Dragon continued, conversationally. "Commander Hiro thought your innocence worth at least a thousand gold drals, if not two."

"He … what … that's a ridiculous fortune!" Lia spluttered, blushing furiously.

"Underpriced?" Grandion inquired, archly.

"I'm speechless."

"Why do Humans say that when they're clearly not?"

The toxic brew of fury and embarrassment had not rendered her speechless, but it did make Lia momentarily able to breach Grandion's mental defences to retrieve the memory foremost in his mind–Commander Hiro's vile calculations, and more, the damage done at the speed it took for an image to transfer between their linked minds.

"He thought my hair worth a two hundred dral bonus?" she yelled. And then it struck her. Lia's hand flew to her throat. "He wanted to … to … oh, m-m-mercy, Grandion …"

"That's the trouble with reading minds," he said, with a crackle of helpless rage that echoed hers. She would never forget that image. Never.

Throwing back her head, Hualiama howled at the skies with such raw, animalistic ferocity that the Tourmaline Dragon answered with a thundering cry of his own. Yet she barely heard him. Her hands rose slowly from her sides. Lightning blazed forth from her fingertips in great arcs, as if she crooked fingers of lightning to beckon the storm on, defying it, challenging it to blast its mightiest load of wind and hail into her face, for her rage was greater still. The Island-World seemed to shift. For a moment, Hualiama saw black, ethereal Dragon heads materialising within the embracing thunderheads, heads greater even than Amaryllion had been in life. Fra'anior! The legendary Black Dragon for whom her Island-Cluster was named.

The sound of his roaring came distinctly to her ears as Dragonish speech, multiplied sevenfold. Majestic. Crushing. Mesmerising her soul. *YOU SUMMONED ME?*

Summoned? From where?

I ... I ... No coherent speech was possible.

How could she continue to exist, when she knew that *he* was the tyrannical power from which the Dragoness of her vision had fled; that White Dragoness' scale scalded the skin above her breasts as though set alight, and that she had seen a tiny eggling defy the mightiest of all Dragons, spiriting the beautiful mother Dragon away from Fra'anior's wrath?

Who are you? The titanic black heads searched the skies as though the Dragon could not see her, as though every guile of his Ancient Dragon magic simply passed over or through her, like sunlight passing through water to dapple the bottom of a terrace lake. *Why do I recognise your spirit, little one?*

Hualiama fled, screaming in mortal terror.

* * * *

"Lia! Princess!" The Tourmaline Dragon shook her flaccid body. "Stupid girl, you cannot just run off my back and expect a blind Dragon to catch you."

As if shaking her would help. Grandion shook too, mostly from the surprise of his Rider burning a neat hole through the membrane of his left wing–hardly a fearsome wound, but the sensitivity of his wing nerves made it smart sharply. What smarted was his pride. It had taken him four catches to snag her, at least one of which had added to the cuts on her body, which the medic had jokingly referred to as, 'lost a fight with a thorn bush?' How true. 'When I'm not fighting with Dragons,' Lia had riposted dryly.

"Lia, have you gone feral?"

She made no reply.

Despairing, Grandion tried to use his magical senses to appraise the storm. Over, or under? Could he manage a safe landing by bat-like echo location, as he had practised back in the Dragon cage? Magical detection of non-living matter was an imprecise science at best–Brown Dragons could probably do it in their sleep, but this was one instance where a Blue Dragon's powers were mismatched to the task at hand. Flying half a mile aloft into the teeth of a storm was no place for a blind Dragon.

Grandion powered higher.

Soon, icy northerlies brushed his scales with a deceptively feathery touch. The Tourmaline Dragon deployed his magic to keep Lia warm and oxygenated. Unseen air pockets buffeted him. He scented clammy moisture, which soon collected along his spine-spikes and wing-edges, streaming over his smooth scales with the speed of his ascent.

An hour later, the wind was a cruel beast, grappling with him like a Dragon seeking to batter his wings and drive him to the ground. Grandion kept his aerodynamic shape with the help of his magic. When last had he flown in such foul weather? This was one of the legendary beasts of the north, monstrously fickle, laden as much with hail as it was with spite; Nature grown wrathful at the doings of creatures upon Her Isles. Nature was often personified in Dragonsong and legend as a White Dragoness called Numistar, an Ancient Star Dragon as light as Fra'anior was dark, and as merciless and unthinking as the Black Dragon was majestic and cunning. As the tempest buffeted him with powerful updrafts that flung him miles into the air and peppered him with hail seemingly shot from a million war crossbows, Grandion began to wonder if the legends were not true. Time and time again, his great strength could not avail him against Numistar's all-conquering might. Ice smashed against his shield. Electricity crackled all around him. The sharp smell of ozone was nectar to his Dragon senses, setting them abuzz. He rode bolts of lightning between the thunderheads, his body stinging even as he laughed in commingled trepidation and delight.

Grandion flew storm-entranced, for many hours a creature almost as insensible as Hualiama.

Unnh, she moaned softly. *Unnh–Grandion? What hit me?*

Lia? Wing and claw check?

The Dragon could have thrust a fang through his tongue, but wry laughter entered his mind. *No wings. No claws but yours, and a headache worthy of this storm. Where are we? I'm wounded.*

My fault, he admitted. *You rose and ran off my back. Just like that. When I caught you, you were unconscious.*

I saw Fra'anior … a vision … in the clouds, Grandion. Didn't you see him? The Dragon lost his wingbeat in surprise; his fires boiled massively, forcing him to expel a steady, controlled stream of fire. *I was so afraid.*

Will you show me?

I–I'm too scared. Let me just dig some courage out of my pockets. Grandion, you tracked and caught an unconscious person falling from the sky–how?

Grandion squirmed, curling his claws with care about her delicate frame. Delicate? When this girl had power to speak to a storm and find an Ancient Dragon in it? Not for the first time, the Tourmaline Dragon knew unease. This was why the prophecy had terrified the living soul-fires right out of Ra'aba. This was why Sapphurion and the Dragon Elders had debated the subject for over a week and come to few conclusions. He remembered the fragment of the prophecy they had found, aye, with the clarity of a Dragon's eidetic memory, and it darkened his fires no less now than it had then:

A life birthed in fire,
Star Dragons sing starsong over her cradle,

The Cloudlands rise up to bow,
And the Islands roar at her name.
… third Great Race will emerge from the shadows,
And take their place at destiny's helm.
A time of rebirth, struggle and …
… a multitude of stars plummet …

Sapphurion had convinced the mighty Dragon Elders not to destroy Lia out of ignorance and wing-shivering fear. Grandion's chest swelled. His shell-father's work was nobly done.

At times, the Human girl seemed so frail. She spoke through quiet weeping, *You're awesome, Grandion.*

He bugled his pleasure loudly and long.

At other times, even poetic language failed to compass the powers surging within her. Draconic powers such as lightning or her grasp of Juyhallith techniques, he could understand. But her powers were also otherworldly, and that kept Dragons like Tarbazzan the Brown Dragon Elder, Razzior and Yulgaz and many others, gnashing their fangs.

Turning to the storm, the Human girl's vision revealed a tumult of cloud ramparts and lightning-chased chasms between them, great thunderheads looming miles overhead, and a momentary flash of the White Moon through the clouds marching by upon their right flank.

"Turn your muzzle five points to the west," she said at once, having reckoned their heading. Grandion agreed with her assessment, and adjusted his flight path. "Will you continue above the storm?"

"I don't know how long I can protect us," he said. "Those thunderheads and updrafts carry great loads of ice, which burden my shielding."

"Go higher?"

Raising his paw, he rumbled, "Up to your seat, Rider. Dragons can fly up to heights of four leagues–a mighty height, where the lack of oxygen or low pressure can kill. I don't know if Humans can stand those conditions, not even with a Dragon's aid."

"Especially the low pressure," Lia agreed, scrambling over his banded flight muscles. "I can't say I wish to experiment. But I can stand a little more, I suspect. Come, take us over that thunderhead, o mighty wingéd serpent, and we shall survey the way forward."

"Aye."

"The meriatite and mineral ores the King of Kaolili supplied us with have not improved your sight?"

"Nothing detectable, although–" he bounced suggestively in the air "–I do feel stuffed with goodness. There's a work to be done by someone to understand proper draconic dietary needs. Usually, we just eat meat. Mountains of it."

She noted, "All that internal heating. The energy has to come from somewhere."

Above the thunderhead, Dragon and Rider found themselves embroiled in a storm of oceanic proportions. There were no Islands to be seen. No land of any description. Just another, even taller army of clouds poised to crash down upon their heads. The quiver of Lia's muscles disclosed to Grandion that she feared the Black Dragon's presence. Visions, he thought. Past, present or future? His Human had always experienced visions of Dragons–strange dreams of flying, of nesting, even shell-dreams of being a Dragon eggling. He rolled that sacred word across his tongue. How could a Human have such insight into the deepest Dragon lore? Who could fathom the purposes of an Ancient Dragon in pouring his soul-fire into a mere girl?

Mere? Grandion growled softly. Merely a fool, the Dragon who thought that.

Thy fate will rise not from what I do, but from who thou wert born to be. So the Great One had claimed–her power rose from her natural being, not from any interference. He shook his muzzle. Dark-fires and egg-stealing villainy! Was he simply jealous that Amaryllion had chosen to befriend Lia, and not him?

"Those wispy clouds ahead," Lia said. Her finger rose into Grandion's vision, pointing upward at an angle of roughly thirty degrees. Odd, seeing the Island-World from a Human's perspective, he thought. Most instructive. Their mindset, from the outset, was fundamentally different to that of a Dragon. "Their structure suggests an opposing wind. Could that be a Dragons' Highway?"

She even navigated the skies like a Dragoness.

"Oh, poor darling, did I burn a hole in your wing? I'm so sorry."

"It's nothing," he grumbled. Could she not focus on one task for more than five seconds at a time? Always flitting from one thing to the next, as busy as a butterfly trying flowers in a sunny meadow. Grandion grinned at his mental image.

"A butterfly?" she chuckled. "Dragon, you've a heart filled with prekki-fruit mush."

A fireball roared out of his gullet.

"Good to clear out a few cobwebs," Lia teased. How she vexed him! "Any other bits and pieces you wish to burn to a crisp while you're at it?"

Now the girl rooted around in her pack for a bandage for her leg. He had indeed scored a shallow, four-inch cut in her hide above the right knee. He wished she would concentrate on their surroundings. Not that there were trees or mountain peaks to avoid up here. Pumping his flight muscles with the deep joy Dragons always enjoyed while airborne, the Tourmaline Dragon soared into the heavens with his Rider. Aye, the wind would come, blowing almost directly from the south. He sensed the airstream, heard its roaring tremble the skies at a different note to that of the storm.

Hualiama said, "So, when were you going to take me to task for lying to the King of Kaolili?"

Another butterfly-hop. "Task? Oh, there are so many things for which your hide deserves a meticulous roasting," he riposted. "No, I was going to teach you that by using Juyhallith, there is indeed a way for Dragons to lie openly, without detection. Blue Dragons learn this skill. It–"

"Grandion, stop. I don't want to know."

"What?"

"With all possible respect, no thank you. I don't want to learn how to lie."

Grandion struggled to subdue his irritation. "Lia, there's a line between your precious conception of morality and the skills needed to survive in this Island-World."

"Then I'll keep my conscience clear."

"Listen, you don't have to do it. Just accept the knowledge."

"No!" She shrank away from him, mentally and physically, rejecting the thoughts he offered openly in his mind. "Crafty Dragon, don't you try to trick me. This is not a game of draconic manipulation. When I say I don't want to know, I mean, I don't want to know! Not even if you think it's a survival skill, or simply of academic interest, or whatever you think."

Grandion roared, "I think it'll save your stupid, conceited hide!"

"Which part of 'no' don't you understand, you arrogant, fire-stuffed flying furnace?"

To her quivering indignation, Grandion began to guffaw. "Very well, o Princess of peevishness. I'll let you win this battle."

Lia stomped on his shoulder by way of reply.

He said, "I was wondering if, drawing upon the Nuyallith expertise in that arrogant, lore-stuffed mental madhouse teetering atop your shoulders, you could conceive of a way of teaching a Dragon how to navigate when blind? I've been using a primitive echo-location technique, but I sense there must be a better solution."

"A bit of magical engineering?" Hualiama was instantly intrigued.

"Magic is far more than a mere art, o esteemed biped," Grandion continued loftily. "It's a science. The building blocks of great magic can be broken down into their component parts. Each element must be perfect in composition and execution. We Dragons love to study magic in all its endless variety and subtlety."

"Magic is a technical pursuit," Lia agreed.

"Aye."

"Yet instinctual."

"Aye. And where is this argument leading?"

"The elements of dance are innately technical–the precise placement of the feet, the angles of the limbs, the training of the muscles and ligaments to support the dancer, the aerial movements, and much more. Yet if dance does not flow from the heart, it is a stiff and ungainly thing, of little beauty or artistry. Thus, my fine quadrupedal reptile, is magic. Lesson ended."

The Tourmaline Dragon snorted, "You might as well have described Dragon flight."

She responded:

Dragonflight is the Dragonsong of a Dragonheart.

Grandion sighed a hundred-foot sigh which conveyed the burdens of all three hearts as her impromptu composition faded on the breeze. "Just when I was brewing up a fine fireball to express my exasperation with a Human presuming to teach a Dragon his magic … you! You're incorrigible!"

What he did not express was the reason underlying his melancholy. The Tourmaline Dragon wondered if she knew how cruelly the Island-World could chew up a creature, and spit them out. Surely, her sufferings should not have conspired to produce this … he struggled to find a word. Deep joy? Exuberance? When he remembered his captivity, he should be consumed by proper dark-fires and righteous, burning fury. Nothing could be more Dragonish. Yet all he could think now, was that this girl had broken into the darkness, cheerfully wrestled with the spectre of death, and drawn him as if by the paw into a place of glorious light, where all became fresh and possible.

It was too good. Too sparkly and sweet and noble. Was that his problem? That he kept looking for the shadows behind the light?

Then, his wings fluttered as a harbinger of the Dragons' Highway ruffled the membranes.

"Hang onto your hair," he warned.

* * * *

The Tourmaline Dragon winged nonstop through a starry, one-moon night. The Blue moon lit the endless cloudscapes below, giving the impression of hovering in a vast stillness, even though they were making a tremendous velocity of close to forty leagues per hour, by the Dragon's best estimate. The airstream roared from several points west of a direct southerly, providing the most frigid, uncomfortable experience Hualiama had endured in her life. She was a child of a volcanic Island! Ever-hot, ever bubbling, the vast caldera of Fra'anior kept the Island's climate tropical all year round. This was no weather for a Fra'aniorian Islander. Despite Grandion's attempts at heating the air within the oxygen-rich shield he maintained for her, Hualiama wore every scrap of clothing she possessed, and still shivered uncontrollably. Her fingernails had turned blue. Huddling close to the Dragon, she wished wholeheartedly for belly-fires of her own.

Mid-afternoon of the following day signalled an unexpected lull in the storm. The weather-front rolled away southward, leaving a smattering of broken clouds in its wake. Hazily, through the clouds, Hualiama made out the tiny specks of the northernmost Islands of the Eastern Archipelago, curving like the tip of a bow to the east. This was where they might find Qilong, the King had told them, investigating a suspected incursion by the Dragon-Haters.

Grandion had been aloft for forty-two hours, a massive undertaking for any Dragon. He was grumpy from tiredness and hunger.

"I'm fine to continue," he growled, in response to her fifth, increasingly anxious query.

Lia ducked, but the wind's force had the curious effect of keeping his belch of smoke exactly where it appeared around his muzzle. The Dragon sneezed mightily. He had slowed, she realised, barely keeping pace now with the Dragons' Highway, which raged unabated.

"But I'm not fine," she said. "I don't have your endurance, Grandion, and I can't feel my ears and nose anymore. Please."

Who was she fooling? Grandion knew exactly what she

meant.

The Dragon's wingbeat stilled. Dipping his muzzle, Grandion entered a long, rapid dive from the boundless realms of the skies to the world of Islands, people and Dragons below. Hualiama calculated the distance they had flown in a mere day and a half on the mental map in her head, and gasped. Upward of fifteen hundred leagues, or she missed her mark!

Before their noses, Kaolili's Isles tapered off rapidly into the Cloudlands. This was far further north than Lia had ever travelled, right up at the latitude of Helyon Island. The Lost Islands lay yet further north, over the horizon. The King's Cartographer put his 'best guess' at a further eight hundred leagues from their position—fifty-three hours for a fast-flying Dragon, given favourable conditions, and beyond the range of all but the most powerful adult Dragons, Grandion had noted. No wonder these Islands were so isolated, and unknown. Legend was plentiful, and readily available from the King's Library. Facts had proved to be in scant supply.

They had seen no sign of Qilong, any Dragonships, or any Human habitation whatsoever, only a colony of Red Dragons who had kept their distance. Grandion said the Reds' behaviour indicated they should be left well alone.

"You're trembling," Lia said, sensing the Dragon's fatigue through her knees.

"I'm fine."

"Dragons never lie."

"I'm fine to make it to a landing place," said Grandion. "Then, I must rest. Satisfied, Rider?"

Lia yawned several times to pop her ears as the air pressure increased rapidly. "No. What should I look for?"

"Ordinarily, I'd seek a volcano with a nice pool of lava to ease my muscles, or at worst, a terrace lake." His voice was choppy, gasping with effort. "Blast these cramps. I thought I was in better shape."

"Would any Dragon be in excellent shape after flying so far, so fast? Right. Volcanoes seem to be in short supply. Search for a handy lake? Or can you sniff out a volcano—sulphur, gases, and so on?"

"Usually, my sight would pick out volcanic gases."

"Aha, because Dragons see in a wider spectrum of colours than Humans?"

"And hear in many more frequencies."

"Awesome," said Lia, meaning it. Grandion's weak snarl informed her that he had misunderstood. She said, "Do you find auditory echo-location limited in range, Grandion? Probably not terribly useful unless your prey's right in front of your muzzle, right? Would producing sounds at higher frequencies help? Or sounds at faster or slower rates?"

"I need rest!"

Clearly, he was in no mood to discuss potential solutions.

Hualiama puzzled over this problem as the Islands loomed larger in her vision. Grandion angled for a small inland lake she absently pointed out, preoccupied with issues surrounding acoustics in the outdoors such as atmospheric turbulence and pressure, obstacles, spreading and absorption of different types of surfaces and conditions. How could it work? Range was one issue, accuracy another.

At the last second, Lia realised he was coming in far too fast. "Brake!" she shouted. "Flare!"

The Dragon spread his tired wings, but his left wingtip smacked into a lone coniferous giant, slewing him off course. Grandion corrected, but either his muscles cramped or his wing collapsed, because the next thing Hualiama knew, he struck the ground with a fearsome blow, flipped over as if he were barrel-rolling mid-air, and tumbled away like a runaway cart. An unseen blow punched her right shoulder. Lia struck the lake's surface so hard that she skipped several times before halting in a spray of water.

No time for whinging. Lia kicked for the surface, cradling her right shoulder, which felt dislocated. A cloud of pretty, gold-coloured fish surrounded her body. Scales flashed around her, followed by a nibbling sensation at her fingers and especially near the wound on her thigh. Carnivorous? Suddenly, she could not swim fast enough. The pretty fish mobbed her, tearing at the bandage over her cut. Lia broke the surface as though she intended to launch herself skyward, like a rainbow trout leaping for a tasty insect.

"Grandion! *Heeeeeelp!*"

Chapter Twenty-Seven

The Lost Islands

YELLING FIT TO imitate a squad of soldiers charging at the enemy, Hualiama churned across the terrace lake before Grandion heard her tread crunching upon the shingly bottom. That was when he started laughing. Lia clearly did not appreciate his reaction, nor his inaction in saving his Princess.

"Pernicious reptile!" she howled. A jolt of lightning struck him square in the flank.

"Found a few Scavenging Brightfish in the lake?" he inquired.

This time, her response frazzled his tongue.

"Simmer down!" Grandion bellowed.

"Me, simmer? I'll show you simmering! What were those—there's one stuck to my ear!"

"One of the wonders of the Island-World," he explained, smiling as a 'plop' told him where the wonder had ended up. "Scavenging Brightfish are healers. They eat dead tissue, suck away infections and apply a healing salve to wounds. Very rare. You could make a fortune if you remember this place."

"Lake-dwelling bloodsuckers? I'll pass."

"Is her Highness injured?"

She growled, "Your excellent landing dislocated my shoulder, but I think that moment of panic you found so ruddy hilarious has served to pop it back into place."

Grandion chuckled softly, "You'll be pleased to know I landed on a sharp rock. The only parts of me which are punctured are my rump, and my pride."

"Well. Forty-two hours and a crash landing? You aviation-loving ralti sheep!" Far from being spent, her ire surged afresh. "Next time, will you listen? I do, on the rare occasion, attempt to talk some sense into that block of granite you mistake for a cranium!"

"Lia–"

"Lie down!" she roared. "Better yet, why don't you let your friendly Brightfish feast on your august rump while I go hunt for us?"

"Hualiama of Fra'anior …"

"What!"

"Thank you."

Muttering something that mangled the words 'pestiferous', 'malfeasance' and 'wisdom of a ralti sheep' together into a description of a certain Tourmaline Dragon, his Rider steamed off.

* * * *

Hualiama's fury lasted as long as it took her to walk one hundred yards around the lake shore, whereupon she stepped directly between the coils of a large, irritable reticulated python. She yelped. Dropping her half-drawn bow caused an arrow to zing off across the corner of the lake, passing close to the startled Dragon. Nuyallith blade in hand, Lia hacked at the python.

"Die!" She missed. "Just freaking hold still, will you?" Six cuts later, Lia finally managed to land a killing blow. "Stupid snake!" She chopped it in half for good measure. "Huh, not so tough now, are we?"

A touch of unnecessarily vicious butchery later, and she was done. Panting. Victorious. Mighty hunter she was, using herself for bait. Lia hauled a length of snake over her good shoulder, and marched back to Grandion, who lazed in the lake on his side, with a swarm of fish boiling around his left hind leg and rump area.

"Killed the snake good and dead?" the Dragon ribbed her.

Dragon hearing. She should have known. "Open the maw,

beast." Lia deposited the length of python onto his tongue, and stomped off to fetch another chunk of python, wishing just for once, she could kick that Dragon right in the manly jewels.

A day's recuperation at the warm lake was the perfect medicine for Dragon and Rider. Grandion had sorely abused his body during his marathon flight, but he had the resilience of a Dragon's superior physiology to speed his recovery. Python meat, several hefty chunks of rock salt Hualiama carved off a cleft above a warm spring for him, and a good long drink of the mineral-rich waters were what Grandion needed to replenish his depleted reserves. After daring to bathe in the lake–she was only ever in danger of dying from laughter as the persistent fish nibbled her toes–Lia held up a chunk of python meat spitted on a stick, and Grandion cooked her dinner. Excellent!

Lia experimented with tossing chunks of meriatite down Grandion's gullet. Dual-purpose science, she claimed–helping his diet, and a chance to produce hydrogen-powered fireballs, combining the gas of one stomach with the fire of another. Impressive! The first successful hydrogen fireball Grandion produced was so powerful, it literally blew him off his feet. Hualiama had a turn laughing at the Dragon until, smarting with injured pride, he placed a paw upon her chest.

"Oh, come on!" Lia gasped. "Don't you want to do that to Razzior?"

A-HA-HA-GGRRRAAARRGGGH! A staggering hose of Dragon fire, eclipsing an adult Red in the heat of his mightiest rage, erupted out of his muzzle. Three hundred yards long and fifty wide, she estimated. The draconic world had not seen such a firestorm since the age of the Ancient Dragons.

She quipped, "Well now, there goes my fortune. You boiled all those expensive fish. More dinner?"

Grandion laughed until he started hiccoughing fireballs.

Quietly, as night wrapped the Isle in a velveteen stillness, Lia talked to the Dragon about her hopes and dreams for finding her mother. Fragile dreams. Knowing that joy and pain balanced on a knife-edge. Her father had tried to murder her. Could Azziala do worse? "Who wants to tempt fate,

Grandion?" she asked, her voice as hollow as a gourd. "Yet she was an envoy of the Dragon-Haters. She must have been a woman of importance and power."

"And some courage, to make the journey to Gi'ishior," said the Dragon.

"Or madness. The Maroon Dragoness mentioned a twin–the madwoman, she said." Hualiama shuddered at the memory. "Grandion, it could be … awful. How can I love the woman who turned me over to Ianthine? Amaryllion always said my power was grounded in love. But its opposite is hate. And that's where we're headed. The realm of the Dragon-Haters."

"Or the Human-Haters, according to Dragon lore. A strange, fey tribe of Dragons inhabits the Lost Islands, Lia. Dragon legends have no good word to speak of them."

"Perfectly matched," she whispered, shuddering. "Lost in so much more than name."

"I will be with you."

Hualiama clasped his fore-talon in her hands. "Grandion …" She could not say 'Dragonlove', though the word burned on her tongue. Lia finished lamely, "You're a rock."

The low rumbling of the Tourmaline Dragon's fires percolated into her awareness. Soothing. Ever burning. And if they were quenched? So too the fire-spirit, the eternal essence of a Dragon.

"I'm afraid for you," she said.

Grandion's wings rustled restively. "Aye? Same here. Can you check my claw-sheath? Your hand's right on a tender spot."

"A shard of volcanic glass," she said, after a minute. "I'll dig it out." Arranging his paw over her lap, Lia drew her dagger. "Now, this might hurt. No nasty little fireballs or snappish fangs, alright?"

"I'm not a hatchling!"

Lia jabbed her elbow into his muzzle. "Joke. Simmer down."

Later, beneath a clear, two-moon sky, the Princess of Fra'anior walked a slow circuit of the Island with her Dragon. The night was so still, they heard every night-bird's call and the chirruping of myriad insects. Insects, the prey of rats, gerbils and marmosets, she noted inattentively. They in turn fed the numerous snakes. This was the Island's basic ecosystem, of which her awareness probably only scratched the surface.

She said, "Did I ever tell you the detail of that dream about Azziala?"

"Remind me."

"The Dragoness said she had come for me, according to their bargain. Ianthine gave her knowledge in exchange–the knowledge of *ruzal,* from the Scroll of Binding. Azziala was triumphant. Her cry sounded like a windroc's screech after a successful hunt. And then she gave me to Ianthine. Just so. She said, 'Take Ra'aba's whelp, Ianthine. Use it against him.' It, Grandion. She called me an 'it'! And then the Dragoness said, *Oh, you supreme fool, that I will.*"

"Two things," the Tourmaline Dragon said slowly, when Hualiama fell silent. "One, Ianthine must have read the Scroll of Binding. What became of it afterward? It cannot be in your mother's possession. These Haters have some power over Dragons, but not the unstoppable, all-conquering power I believe is promised by the Scroll. When she was interrogated by the combined might of the Dragon Elders at Gi'ishior, Ianthine had no knowledge of it–no knowledge of *ruzal* save some fragments sourced from the Dragon Library at Ha'athior."

"Did that interrogation drive her mad–feral?"

"No, she was mad already, my shell-mother said." But Grandion lifted a talon to his lips in a surprisingly Human-like gesture.

"What?" Lia asked.

"I've always harboured doubts. That type of psychic examination is harmful to a Dragon. We aren't merciful creatures, and the Dragoness was rightly accused of teaching *ruzal* to Humans. The interrogation would've been brutal. Razzior recognises your power of *ruzal.* He, and many Dragons loyal to Sapphurion, would slay you instantly were they aware that you have such a power. And–Hualiama, do you remember anything else? Anything more you dreamed about your mother, or Ianthine, that could brighten our mind-fires?"

In his passion, the Dragon slipped into directly translating concepts from Dragonish, Lia noticed, nodding. "Aye. There's one more thing, which I don't believe I ever told you."

Ignoring his low murmur of encouragement, Hualiama focussed on recalling the exact phrasing of the Maroon Dragoness' words from her dream.

Hush, little one, the Dragoness whispered. *We return to the Isle of your father. This is the hour of my greatest triumph. All Dragons will know that Ianthine saved them from a fate worse than death.*

"Say that again?" Grandion wheezed.

Repeating her words, the incongruity struck Lia even more forcefully. "Ianthine believed she was saving the Dragons from a fate worse than death. Human-death, the nuance suggests–doesn't it, Grandion? A death that doesn't join a Dragon to the eternal soul-fires of their kind. Is that even possible?"

Bellowing, Grandion began to swing his muzzle toward her, before raising his long neck to the sky to voice a terrible, despairing scream. It cut her to the living pith of her very soul, wounding. Weeping. A cry of such anguish, it seemed to her that the Dragon's three hearts stopped pulsing, and the silence that followed their scream communicated every ounce of the terrible idea she had unthinkingly voiced. Grandion stood rooted, every talon clamped into rock and soil as he fought to master his emotions.

The Maroon Dragoness had returned to Gi'ishior expecting a heroine's welcome. Instead, she had been accused, mentally shattered, and cast out to live in the most squalid, demeaning captivity Dragons could dream up. Another truth struck Lia, then. Ianthine was the only Dragon ever to return from the Lost Islands alive.

But she dared not reveal this insight to Grandion. She had never seen him so shaken.

* * * *

Northward they flew, bound by oaths made to each other and to the Dragon Elders of Gi'ishior. Pensive. Lost in their private thoughts. Filled with trepidation. As Grandion's wings stretched above the pearlescent white Cloudlands and a glorious suns-rise fired the eastern sky as though the soul-fires of all Dragons had joined together in joyous, world-spanning harmony, Hualiama called to mind those she had left behind to make this journey. Ari, Shyana and Ja'al. Master Ga'athar and his family. King Chalcion. Elki and Saori. Yukari and Akemi, united at last. And even Shinzen, Razzior and Ra'aba. Friend and foe alike, she had left all behind. Now she and Grandion, the first Dragon and Rider in the Island-World, flew into the unknown.

They spoke not a word all day, but it seemed to Hualiama that much was spoken between their spirits which could never be framed in word or thought. Dragon and Rider travelled with unconscious closeness, flowing together without need for speech, as though they were one creature that lived and breathed and laughed and loved, dancing upon the winds of the Island-World, sharing a soul-deep intimacy. The weakening Dragons' Highway was their friend. Lia kept expecting some great omen–perhaps the back of a Land Dragon breaching the unbroken expanse of Cloudlands beneath them, or a comet to streak across the evening sky, but no such portent saluted their traverse of the void between the Islands. Perhaps the stars themselves regarded their presumption with bated breath.

Could it last? Could two souls travel together, forever?

They flew directly toward crescent Jade, as though seeking to rise above the curve of the moon itself. Soon, the Blue moon rose to pour forth great sheets of radiance, until it seemed to Lia that the Cloudlands had become a single, vast terrace lake. An ocean. A place where Dragons swam and sported … she shivered. Could those poisons ever be transformed into something so beautiful? Only the Ancient Dragons boasted such almighty powers.

May it be, Lia whispered, checking the position of the stars.

Grandion tipped forward slightly, bringing them into a steady descent. Aye. They must not miss the Lost Islands. Lia rubbed her arms. Brr. One could really feel the difference in climate after travelling thousands of leagues in the course of a week. Odd how she had always thought of the Island-World as flat, but now, after flying with Grandion at enormous altitudes, she knew that it curved away to the horizon. Oh for the eyesight of a Dragon, that she might see the Rim-mountains. That would be another first. The only way Humans knew about the Rim wall, was from scrolls of Dragon lore.

Hualiama scanned the semidarkness.

"I see lights," said Grandion.

"Where?"

"East. Six points from where you're looking, I think."

"Oh." Lia swallowed as the twinkling lights of fires or lanterns, barely visible as specks across the miles, resolved in her vision. "Grandion, I wanted to say, if we don't make it–I mean, I believe we will, but …"

"We Dragons say, *Our soul-fires are always within us. They'll burn together, no matter what befalls.*"

She could barely squeeze a whisper past the lump in her throat. "Aye, Grandion. Now, let's carry out our mission. No doubts. No regrets."

"Aye. We'll scout as softly as moths in the night."

The Dragon shed height rapidly, drawing his cloak of concealment tightly around them. Lia popped her ears. Wow. She checked her weapons, right down to the lock picks concealed in her armoured wristlets and the poisoned darts concealed in her bodice. If only she had her missing Nuyallith blade to complete the set. Grandion ghosted closer and closer to the Island, a velvet shadow enveloped in velvet darkness. He had subdued the natural gleam of his scales, she observed, and even stilled the wind's whistling over his spine-spikes and wings. Nothing was left to chance.

The Island-Cluster hove from the Cloudlands, white-backed and rugged, serenely illuminated by the White and Blue moons. Snow and ice, she realised. Was the season already so advanced? Surprisingly substantial, the Cluster stretched away northeast like a double line of fangs embedded in an Ancient Dragon's lower jaw. Above the lights, a lone volcanic peak rose like a flagpole to an improbable white point. Several Islands further east, Lia saw the unmistakable glow of lava. Some said the Dragons still built the Islands from beneath, that the activity of volcanoes was really the stirring of vast magma-Dragons who lived beneath the habitable realms above the Cloudlands.

Just a mile offshore, now. Lia strained to see the details of those lights. Something about them struck her as man-made.

Grandion whispered, *I hear the sounds of habitation. Animals, scavenger birds and the thrum of furnaces or a forge. The wind's wrong to scent them–oh. Is there something behind us?*

Lia swivelled in her seat. *Nothing. You sure?*

Could've sworn I smelled something, but it's gone now. Here, examine this scent-memory.

Wood smoke. From back there? She scanned the Cloudlands and the skies, high and low. *Dragonship? Grandion, that's jalkwood. I'd know that smell from a thousand leagues … the wind's blowing southerly. It can only have come from a Dragonship. You see anything? Sense anything?*

Nothing.

Her skin prickled as Grandion strained his Dragon senses to their utmost. Long minutes passed.

Can you form a magical pulse? Like this? You'd have to send it out like concentric sound-waves, and then listen for the echo, however that translates into Dragon magic-speak.

I understand your meaning, he said, drolly.

Hualiama's stomach wobbled slightly as the Tourmaline Dragon shaped and released his power. Almost immediately, she felt it return. *Huh? Right in front–Grandion! Turn!*

Clang! Clang! Clang!

"Dragon!" a man bellowed. "Watch! Summon the Enchanter!"

Grandion sheared away from a Dragonship with enormous power, accelerating so forcefully that Lia could neither drag herself away from the spine-spike grinding against her back nor expel the breath trapped in her lungs. The bell tolled frantically. Lia glanced backward, shocked. Where had that vessel sprung from? How had they missed it in a moonlit sky? The Dragonship was thinner through the beam than the Fra'aniorian design, and almost twice as long. The stippled material of its air sack reminded her strongly of pebbles on a terrace lake beach.

Just as her head turned to the fore, Grandion's body convulsed like a trout stung by the fisherman's hook. One second, he was present, a pinpoint light in her consciousness. The next, an oily darkness swallowed the Dragon's being. Black, yet gleaming like mercury running across glass, the eerie magic surged through their link and inundated Lia.

"Dragon, obey." A commanding voice seized all the Islands of her world, utterly compelling. "You are my slave. You will do exactly as I command. Turn, and follow."

Her last, despairing thought was, '*ruzal?*'

* * * *

Human voices impinged on her awareness. The cloying stench of oil lamps singed her nostrils. Lia heard the creak of a Dragonship's rigging. These impressions woke her, but she remained in darkness, although she could hear activity all around. She smelled a cavern's dankness, metal armour, aged leather and the musky odour of animal sweat, thinking: Enslaved. The Dragon-Haters had a power that enslaved Dragons. Was she trapped inside Grandion's psyche? How? Lia kept her body limp, even in a position as painfully hunched over as she was, hoping to learn what she could before anyone took notice.

She had not fallen off. *Grandion?* she ventured, just a wisp of a thought. *Grandion, are you there?*

"Captured us a Dragon!" someone announced, in a barbarous dialect, all clipped-off consonants and guttural vowels. "Plenty power in this one."

"Empress will be pleased. Stock's running low, y'know."

"Aye, but she'll whip the Watchman. Sleeping on duty. Fancy missing a lizard this size?"

"Slackers! Paw-lickers!" This voice was even more clipped, and clearly in command. "Get the bastard Blue down to the pens before I stripe your sorry hides! Where's my pipe?"

Lia imagined Grandion was a lake and she was rising to its

surface. In a few moments, lamplight filtered through her carefully slit eyes. Her awareness separated from the Dragon's.

Suddenly, a volley of curses erupted from above. "Spit me with Dragon-shell, there's a girl! Idiots! Scurvy, mange-ridden sons of rock goats, a girl! There, on the beast's back!"

Lia glanced around the huge, lamp-lit cavern. Moored Dragonships. Grandion walked slowly along a bustling ledge, overlooked by a wide wooden platform. Everywhere, she saw pale men clad in unfamiliar uniforms of tight azure leather and blue skull-caps, their muscled upper bodies left bare, apparently to display the fantastical, swirling body paint they wore. Aye, there was a girl. She was livid. Reaching out with her white-fire magic, Hualiama performed a desperate hatchet-job of undermining the inexplicable, oily coils she found entwined in Grandion's psyche.

GGRRRAAARRGGGH! The Dragon's battle-challenge resounded in the cavern. A vast, churning fireball roared out of his throat, splashing liberally over the nearest Dragonships and down into what appeared to be a cargo handling area. Flame sheeted upward, enveloping the gantries and observation posts overlooking the operation. Men bellowed in pain.

Grandion–Islands' sakes, Grandion, are you sleeping?

Impressions cascaded through her dazed mind. No response from the Dragon. Shouts and curses from his captors. "Get the Dragon Enchanters!" A quiver ran through the Dragon's muscles.

Terror shaped her response. They had to escape! Hualiama tried to scream Amaryllion's name, but rediscovered that Razzior had done his work too well. Her white-fires seemed to lack use as a weapon. That left *ruzal*, or the weapons upon her person. Drawing her Nuyallith blade with speed born of instinct, Lia stabbed it into the muscle of Grandion's left shoulder. The effulgent blue blade slipped several feet into the meat of his main flight muscle.

Pain yanked the Dragon into the present.

GNNAAARRR! This time, his Storm power smashed two Dragonships across the cavern, raising a brief windstorm that had men staggering, falling over barrels and toppling off the edges of gantries.

Quick, Grandion! Turn around!

Lia … where've I been? Where are we?

Her shout in Dragonish was like a slap to his jaw. *Attack, you ralti-brained–*

Eat this, you sons of dogs!

The Tourmaline Dragon found his voice and his fires simultaneously. Lia clapped her hands over her ears as a wall of fire and ice swept halfway around the cavern, bulldozing everything in its path and setting the debris afire. Her laughter mingled with the Dragon's as they surveyed the damage. Fabulous. Now, to escape …

"Dragon, obey." A commanding voice seized all the Islands of her world; multiple voices, layered over each other in an eerie almost-harmony. This time, she anticipated the venomous vortex of their magic's allure. "You are my–"

Hualiama shouted, "No!"

The oil-slick magic sucked at her strength, viscous and cold, so very cold, before receding. Grandion shuddered, seeming to shake off the effects with her help.

Neck swivelling, she searched for the source of the terrible voices. Three men stood in a triangular formation on a gantry above, wearing long blue robes and tall, mushroom-shaped hats which buckled with a thick strap beneath the chin. Their mesmerising blue eyes locked upon the Dragon as they raised their right hands in concert.

Lia, give me your power, Grandion begged. *You must–*

"DRAGON, OBEY." Triple-strong, their voices swelled, cutting off his mental communication instantly.

"NO!" Her magic staggered the Enchanters.

For a moment as long as a breath, the oily darkness evaporated. Whipping the Haozi war bow off her shoulder, Hualiama placed an arrow perfectly into the chest of the foremost member of that trio. Adrenaline made her draw so powerful that the arrow protruded a foot out of his back. She nocked a second arrow to the string.

"ENOUGH." Lia twitched as an unseen power seized her body. "I WILL DEAL WITH THIS ONE."

Helpless, she struggled against succumbing to the voice of a mental giant–an Enchantress, she realised. Unseen hands plucked her off Grandion's back. Hualiama shot sideways as though she had been swatted by a Dragon, slamming into the wooden support of one of the platforms. She cried out in pain. Mercy. Blood trickled from the corner of her lip. Lia rolled over and tried to stand, but her knees buckled.

"Dragon, obey," came the hateful voices in a fivefold chant.

More of their magicians? Lia's fingers clawed at the wooden gantry she had landed upon. She groaned, "Nooo … Grandion! I'm coming! Leave my Dragon alone!"

"You are our slave."

Alastior! Don't leave me! Her cry fell on emptiness. Once more, the Dragon was gone, subverted to the repulsive power of the Dragon-Haters. His wings folded, and the fire which glowed behind his fangs, extinguished in a curl of smoke.

Bezaldior, if ever I needed your white-fires … she remembered how Grandion had used her fire, charging through Shinzen's giants as though his entire body were a blade wreathed in irresistible white flame. Raising the Nuyallith blade, Hualiama ignited it. Her eyes blazed. She was a warrior-monk, following the Way of the Dragon Warrior. Distinctly, she felt the heavy tresses of her hair slap against her shoulders and back, leaden with the waves of magic suffusing her body. She sprinted ahead, trying to find a way to reach her Dragon. The workers who had begun to gather to gawk, fell back, giving way to the advance of a well-organised squad of soldiers clutching round shields and unfamiliar, curved blades. They trotted around Grandion's flanks with a jingle of chainmail armour, keeping their formation with impressive discipline.

The Dragon shifted away, heedless.

The Princess scowled at the squad of soldiers, lowering her blade. She growled, "You're in my way."

Perhaps it was the white lightning playing along the length of her blade, or the sight of her eyes, spitting with fury, but the entire squad seemed to draw together with a collective intake of breath.

One man sidled forward. "I'll accept your challenge,

stranger."

Lia barely understood his accent. He was no bigger than the rest, but the easy way he moved proclaimed the man's skill and confidence. "Let's just be clear, I'm with the Dragon. Understood?"

The soldier crooked a finger at her. Ra'aba had once done exactly the same, before teaching her a lesson in swordplay and hurling her bleeding body off his Dragonship, destined for the windrocs. Rage detonated within her breast. For perhaps the first time in her life, Hualiama knew the pure, killing rage Grandion sometimes spoke of when he described a Dragon's love of battle.

Dancing forward, Hualiama performed the triple-feint hidden underhand strike technique, designed for use with the single Nuyallith blade. Her thrust pierced his breastplate smoothly. A sweetish wisp of smoke drifted to her nostrils as the man fell. Charred flesh. Lia sprang over his dead body, and charged the rest.

"REMARKABLE," said the huge female voice.

Lia clashed with the soldiers, her kneeling, horizontal sword-stroke powering through two shields and a soldier's sword-arm. A thrown blade pierced her right bicep. Spinning, a man's head seemed to leap off his shoulders as her blade passed perfectly between his shoulders and the base of his helmet. She parried smoothly with the Immadian forked dagger in her weaker right hand. Her blades crossed in a fraction of a second. The attacker jerked as her sword-point entered his eye and drove through to the brain.

"ENOUGH. TAKE HER ALIVE."

An Island dropped on top of her head and burrowed inside. Lia could think of nothing but the pain screaming inside her skull, overwhelming all rational thought, all capacity to resist, all that she was.

Fists and boots battered her head, ribs and abdomen.

Only oblivion could win such a battle.

Chapter Twenty-Eight

Enchantress

"BY MAGIC, SHE broke a Dragon Enchanter's command-hold."

Fingernails tapped upon stone. *Tac-tac-tac.* An agitated rhythm.

"She was seated upon the Dragon's back." Hard as granite, the soldier's voice nevertheless conveyed an edge of disbelief and dread. "She fought to rejoin the lizard."

Distinctly, she heard the man gulp.

"Go on." This voice was icy, as cold as the stone Lia lay upon.

"Her provisions were strapped upon the beast's back. She slew four Royal Elites with ease before your grand intervention, Empress. And … she called …" The man faltered. Confined beneath a leather hood, Lia's nostrils nevertheless flared at the stench of his terror. "She called the lizard b-b-by n-name, Highness. Mercifully cut out my blaspheming tongue, o Fire of the Dawn, I beg you."

Silence greeted his words. Hualiama wished she could wake from this nightmare. No. She must take stock. That was what the Master of Shadows, the monk who had trained her in espionage, had always stressed. 'Assess your situation, no matter how hopeless it appears. There will be a way out.' Heavy metal fetters adorned her ankles and her legs above the knees, she judged from the chill against her flesh. Her wrists were chained to a belt encircling her waist. Someone had taken advantage of her dancer's flexibility to shackle her elbows so tightly, they touched behind her back. A leather hood covered her head, while a leather harness forced a chunk of wood between her teeth. She was hurt but alive, resting on her side where she had apparently been thrown. Hope had long since fled. What had become of Grandion? Where was she now?

"Request denied," came the woman's voice. "Continue, soldier. What did she say?"

"Something like, 'Grandion'," the man blurted out. "But definitely, she claimed to be with the lizard, even shouting, 'Leave my Dragon alone!' "

A low curse issued from the woman. Lia heard a sound like a stick striking flesh.

"May this pain cleanse my soul," groaned the soldier. "I thank you, Empress, for deigning to–"

"You reported well, soldier. The fool Watchman from my Dragonship shall endure five hundred lashes, tomorrow at dawn, on the eastern outlook." Lia stiffened. That had to be a death sentence. "Belay that. Have him await my displeasure. The Masters will cleanse you with ten lashes. Dismissed."

Slippers whispered on the cold stone.

"What to do with this one, Highness?" asked a new voice. Aged. As cruel as a feral Dragoness. "Surely, no lizard of this Island-World would dare to commit an act of such profanity with a Human?"

"Aye, Feyzuria. Or one of our people, with a reptile. Abhorrent." The Empress was the Enchantress of the overpowering voice, Hualiama realised. Of course. She struggled against a tightness clamping her chest and her heart's leaden throbbing. "She is conscious. Guards! Raise this filth and uncover it, that I might spit upon its hideous, Dragon-worshipping visage."

Rough hands grasped Lia's chains, forcing her into a kneeling position. She felt a tugging at her neck as a soldier unclasped a buckle. Frigid air swirled beneath the hood, providing a small measure of relief to a face taut and swollen after the beating she had received. Her weapons had been taken, she realised. But these Dragon-Haters could not possibly imagine all the weapons which she possessed. The soldiers tore the hood off her head, yanking her head almost to the floor. Then, with a parting shove, they drew back.

Again, silence. This Enchantress was a master of using silence as a weapon of fear. Clenching her jaw in the manner Elki had always teased her was her 'determined look', Hualiama steeled herself, heart and mind. She would not cower before a Dragon-Hater. She was the bearer of Dragon fire.

The vision of her right eye was blurry and narrowed, probably due to a fine black eye. Had she the use of her arms, Lia could have reached out to touch the dainty pair of slippers that greeted her grim gaze. The woman wore a simple azure blue dress of expensive Helyon silk beneath a heavy velveteen robe of midnight blue. Before her gaze reached the woman's knees, Hualiama sensed her formidable power. Enchantress. Commander. Absolute ruler. No need for guards to menace a prisoner's back with swords. If the Enchantress could reach through the fabric of her realm from an unknowable distance to strike a person down with callous ease, what need for weapons? The chains must be for show. Like it or not, Lia felt intimidated. Healthy fear, anyone? Healthy fear in Dragonship-sized doses?

The Enchantress held a sceptre crosswise across her body, fresh blood smeared on its bulbous, jewel-encrusted tip. Panic twisted Hualiama's gut. How hard had she struck that soldier? The woman's arms were bare, her skin as golden as Dragon blood. Unnatural? Magical? A braid of perfectly white hair threaded with fine golden chains hung down to the sceptre, hair as unusually long as Lia's …

This had to stop.

Raising her chin, Hualiama looked at the woman full in the face.

She gasped.

Had she always known? Eyes as hard and brilliant as sapphires assessed her, eyes so lambent with power they made the rest of the Empress' face seem to retreat into shadow. Her features were flawless, like a statue cast in pure gold. Lia wondered briefly if she wore makeup to achieve that brilliant golden effect. A fractional narrowing of the Enchantress' gaze was all that alerted her. The woman slammed her sceptre into Lia's stomach, right beneath her sternum. She tried to roll with the blow. Still, the pain was as though a Dragon had run her through with its talon. Hualiama collapsed with a whimper, falling heavily upon her shoulder.

Then the Enchantress seemed to fold inward, the mask of that face cracking and melting like gold cast into the crucible of a furnace. One hand flew to her lips, trying to stifle a gagging, gasping sob.

"Highness?" Feyzuria's creaky tones cut in, alarmed.

Lia bit the wood in her mouth so hard, she felt it splinter. The Enchantress stumbled backward, falling into the cushioned lap of a wide, low throne.

All else was immaterial. Forcing garbled speech past the gag, Lia said, "Islands' greetings–mother."

Soft words; their shockwave a Dragon's battle-challenge.

Had the woman been able, she surmised, Azziala would have turned as pale as her hair. Her lips moved in shock, but no sound issued forth. Lia became aware of a low murmur rising from behind her in the chamber. Rich tapestries, majoring on the blue theme, provided both insulation and adornment to the walls. Large braziers in the corners provided heat and lighting against the pervasive cold, and a hint of incense not vastly different to a Dragon's scent–cinnamon, hints of sulphur and agarwood, and other exotic spices Lia could not place. A quick glance about her revealed the presence of soldiers posted at intervals around the circular chamber, and an array of female Enchanters wearing apparel even richer than Azziala's, perhaps an inner circle of councillors. Most of them stared at her as though she had grown spine-spikes and a tail. Lia lay on a stone dais, hurting, but where the councillors stood, the floor was covered in thick rush matting, presumably against the cold.

"Empress, did this wretch just call you–"

"No … it's impossible. W-W-Who …"

Time seemed to stretch unbearably thin. All within the chamber knew something had to snap.

"Whelp of a windroc!" Azziala sprang from her seat with

the grace of a startled rajal. The sceptre whistled down to shatter on the stone beside Lia's head. "No!"

Shocked, Hualiama realised that several jewel shards had become embedded in her scalp. Pushing with her tongue, she found she had cracked the tough wood gag right through. She stared at Azziala, speechless. Had she not rolled aside, her mother would have summarily finished the job her father had failed to complete. As Azziala shrieked something about taking her away, Lia rolled over several more times, thumping her abused body down the steps and bumped up against one of the soldiers' bootlaces.

Azziala stormed after her, her golden face a mask of insane fury. Vile curse-words, many of which Lia did not understand, flooded from her mouth. "You lying paw-licker, I'll have you—"

"No." Another woman, kicking Lia's head casually on the way past, stepped between them. "I, for one, am very interested to learn about this unknown heir, o Empress." Scornful, her words stopped Azziala in her tracks. "Wasn't there a babe who died?"

"That lizard-lover is no child of mine!"

"Truly?" The tall woman swooped unexpectedly, plucking Lia off the ground with draconic strength. "Can any person present deny this is Azziala's whelp? Look past the scourge of holy pain. Look into the eyes."

"Aye," someone whispered.

As she dangled from the woman's hand, the song of Lia's soul revolved around the grief of finally meeting her mother. None of the hoped-for joy would materialise. She understood that now. Her sweetest, most cherished dreams would never flower to supplant the reality surrounding her very existence in the Island-World—she had parents spawned in the pit of some nameless volcanic hell. This was a barren place, a place where hope came to be tortured and broken by a dungeon-master's cruellest implements. This was a place that reeked of pain, of vaulting ambitions and unholy secrets. This was the realm of hate.

"Stop the posturing, Shazziya," Feyzuria hissed. "We all

know your purposes here."

"Then, by the Sixteenth Protocol, I invoke a council of–"

"Let it speak." Like a whetted razor drawn delicately across skin, Azziala's voice stilled them. "First it must speak, lest the Protocols be contravened. You. Remove the gag. As if her magic could override this Council!"

Politics. Hualiama's brain raced feverishly as she considered the import of this encounter. Azziala's position had been weakened by her arrival, perhaps fatally. Now she fought to re-establish control. Shazziya had ambitions for the crown. Her eyes glittered as she dumped Lia ungently on the rush mats. Feyzuria sought to play the mediator, but the clasp of her clawed fingers upon the handle of her cane suggested that she might switch sides should it prove convenient. To a woman, Azziala's councillors displayed the strangely golden skin and plain white hair, so different to that of the soldiers–an insignia of their magic, she concluded, wondering what could produce such an effect. She must speak wisely, and conceal her true abilities. Aye, bury her secrets deep. If she could not stand against Azziala's power, then the power of the thirteen gathered here would destroy her in a heartbeat.

Could an Ancient Dragon's fire ever be destroyed?

Shazziya towered over her compatriots. "You read her mind while she lay unconscious, Feyzuria?"

"A natural shield," the old woman sniffed.

Ha. So Grandion's Juyhallith training had proved successful. One of his tricks was a shield which protected the mind when unconscious or asleep, which appeared to be an innocuous natural resistance to psychic probing. Forewarned, Lia buttressed her shields and silently constructed a fake shield behind the first, should that be breached, and a third, far deeper layer to conceal her magic, *ruzal* and Dragon fire, disguising it as a latent capacity for magic. Mercy. The mental tricks Dragons dreamed up. Subterfuge layered upon deceit wrapped in guileful innocence.

As she watched, Azziala's face reassumed the planes of confidence and indifference, as if she were a statue cast in cold metal. "Who are you, girl? And what do you seek here, in the

Lost Islands?"

With her mouth free, Lia waggled her jaw before saying, "I'm Hualiama of Fra'anior."

The sceptre tapped against Azziala's open palm; her face masked every secret. "A full answer," she grated, making her meaning abundantly clear.

"I am Hualiama, Princess of Fra'anior," she said, "royal ward of the court of King Chalcion and Queen Shyana. Daughter of Ra'aba, former Captain of the Royal Guard, and Azziala of the Lost Islands."

Azziala's response was icy. "Continue."

When Lia mentioned that she had been brought to Gi'ishior as a babe by the Maroon Dragoness, Shazziya exclaimed, "A plot with a lizard, Azziala? Or did you think to take a lizard at her word while speaking out of the other cheek to your sisters here?"

"The babe died," Feyzuria growled.

Another of the councillors snorted, in a high, reedy voice, "Are you accusing Azziala's daughter of flying here on a lizard?"

"That's immaterial," said Azziala. "Do you believe you're my daughter?"

Hualiama pushed up to her knees. Speaking from the floor was too demeaning. "The Tourmaline Dragon is Grandion, the shell-son of Sapphurion, Dragon Elder of Gi'ishior–a Dragon I believe you've met, Azziala." She pounded her words into the frozen silence that gripped the women. "He is my Dragon and I am his Rider, bound by mutual oaths. If you cause any harm to come to him, I swear, it will start raining Dragons around these Isles! And as for your question, mother–I don't just believe it. I know it. I know the bargain you struck with Ianthine–"

"You know nothing!" Azziala snapped.

"Nothing?" Lia exploded. "I know you hated your baby. You peddled me to that Dragoness in a vile exchange for *ruzal!* Look at me! Look at–"

Furious sobs burst out of her, uncontainable.

Raising her hands, Azziala clapped them together in a

thunderclap of sound which ignited her sceptre and stilled the angry shouts of her councillors. With great deliberation, she said, "What I did was for my people. One life sacrificed that the many may live, no longer subject to the claw of draconic tyranny. Child, if you truly are that whelp of my flesh, know this–your life is nothing, and worth nothing, to me. I would do it again in a heartbeat."

* * * *

Frigid water laced with herbs bathed her heavily bruised face.

"If seeing you pop out of the Empress' birth canal counts for more than a dragonet's chirp, then aye, chicklet, I know you're her daughter, and one of us."

One of them? A Dragon-Hater? Lia lay abed–such as her mother's people called this bowl of rushes lined with animal skins and piled high with large, soft cushions which apparently doubled as blankets and padding–having her wounds treated by Yinzi, a woman who effortlessly defined the word 'motherly'. She was built like a Dragonship, broad in the beam, but clearly had a heart to match her frame. Hualiama eyed the woman curiously. These people had a distinctive look, much paler of skin than Saori's people, but also black-haired and angular of facial features. Where the residents of Kaolili were predominantly petite and small-boned, these Lost Islanders appeared to vary widely in build, but were so similar in visage, she had the impression of a large family of brothers and sisters, aunts and uncles. People stamped of a single mould? Perhaps their isolation, even inbreeding, had contributed to this uniformity in appearance?

And the overlarge eyes. Lia considered her attendant. Yinzi had beautiful, lucid eyes, framed by long eyelashes that gave her a girlish air, despite her iron-grey hair. She had always thought her own eyes a few fractions too large for her elfin face. To see her own eyes looking back at her from Azziala's visage had been a shock.

"And how do I look?" Yinzi smiled.

"Just as I remember you," the Princess smiled back. "Yinzi, isn't it impossible for a days-old babe to remember such details?"

The old midwife and healer paused to glance at the three Enchantresses standing guard at the door of Hualiama's small chamber–her cell, more accurately–before sighing. "Chicklet, I suppose it won't hurt you to know." Hualiama wrinkled her nose. "It's the eyes, as you were thinking."

Was the woman a mind reader? Now she felt as though she had swallowed a spear of ice.

"One examines the eyes to know the bloodline," said Yinzi, sounding as though she were quoting from a scrolleaf. "The Second Protocol lays out the desirable traits and the means of honing the genetic potential of our people, until the wheat is separated from the chaff, and the High Ones rise to claim their birthright, the throne of the world. With your magical power and half-Fra'aniorian heritage, you'll make a fine addition to our breeding stock."

Yinzi delivered her speech so sweetly that it took Lia several moments to work out its import, and be rattled to her core. Did she know what she was saying? Nauseated, almost unable to bear her touch, Lia stared at the woman. Yinzi did, and believed it utterly.

"What are these Protocols? Who made them?" she managed to ask.

"Mighty Dramagon codified our lore," said Yinzi in the same sing-song voice.

"Wasn't he a Dragon, Yinzi?"

"An ancient heresy," she cut in. Again, her eyes flicked to the watching Enchantresses. Lia wondered what would have happened, had the woman dared a wrong or unsuitable answer. "Dramagon was a Human, the greatest leader of the former age, when Humankind rose up against our Dragon overlords and cast off the paw of draconic tyranny forever."

"Of course. Yinzi–" she wet her lips "–if you're Dramagon's favoured people, why do you live here in this faraway corner of the Island-World?"

The midwife intoned, "A harsh people for a harsh land.

Here, among the bitter snows at the end of the Island-World, we wait and grow strong. We are tormented by the cold and movements of the Islands and tempered by the cunning lizards of these Isles, who winnow us with their powerful magic. But the time is coming, chicklet. With Azziala's ascent to the hallowed crown, may her holy name forever inspire us, the Lost Islands people have developed the skills to overcome these wicked reptiles, to strike them down and use their body parts as we will–their hide clothes our airships–"

Lia's aghast gasp made Yinzi break off with a motherly frown. Gently, she touched the Princess' forehead with three fingers. "Soon, you'll understand these things, my chicklet. Dramagon's enlightenment will brighten your mind. Rest now; don't fret. You're home. All will be well."

All was a monstrous irony, she wanted to scream. The Dragon-Haters swore by a manual handed down to them by none other than the infamous Ancient Dragon scientist, Dramagon, and continued his scandalous experimentation with the bloodlines of their own people! Breeding stock indeed–may her womb shrivel at the thought! Mortification struck her instantly. She should neither mock the childless woman, nor the gift of life itself, even if the idea of being bred like livestock was repugnant … she touched her stomach fearfully, invoking the ancient blessing, 'guard this belly, guard this womb, guard the fruit of life's great loom.'

"Is that what they'll do with my Dragon?"

Her plaintive question earned her another gentle frown. Yinzi made a superstitious gesture and spat on the rushes beside the bed. "That Blue lizard has beguiled and blinded you with his powers, Hualiama. Tell me you grasp his devious ways. No? Your mind must be acutely sensitive. That'll be a definite boon when you follow in the mighty footsteps of your mother. Can you do magic without Dragon blood, chicklet? Can you? Are you the one we've been waiting–"

"SILENCE, YOU BABBLING FOOL."

Azziala! Lia startled, wrenching her neck.

In a flash the large woman knelt, head bowed to the rushes. The Empress growled, "If your work is done, Yinzi, return to your duties. I would speak with my daughter."

Her tone made the midwife's dismissal clear. Yinzi fled.

How had Azziala entered the chamber without her hearing? Lia knew she had slept for some interminable period after being interrogated for an hour before being summarily removed from the Chamber of Counsel, as Azziala referred to their meeting-place. The meal she had eaten in this room had contained unfamiliar herbs. How long had she slumbered? Had they drugged her? Were they planning to perform some horrific Dragon-Hater ritual that would turn her into one of them?

More upset than she cared to admit, Lia snapped, "You clothe your Dragonships in Dragon hide? Truly?"

The golden face remained serene, despite the tension so thick between them, it seemed to flow and crackle like cooling lava. "Of course, child. Our hold over a captive lizard is absolute. Once the command-hold is established by a Dragon Enchanter, a Dragon will do his bidding without question, be that to peel off his own hide, destroy his soul-bonded companion or fly headlong into a cliff."

"You don't fly them in battle?"

"What for? Lizards are too treacherous to be trusted, even as helpless slaves to an Enchantress. And who would grant them the glories of battle promised in the Seventh Protocol? I'll be glad to capture these other Dragons you've promised us. They'll be helpless fodder. You see, the Eastern lizards have developed skills that allow them to resist our powers. Dramagon said we would be tested, and we are. Those vicious animals raid our villages, steal our livestock and murder our children. But your precious Dragons of Gi'ishior have no such resistance."

"Which you established by travelling to Gi'ishior," Hualiama realised aloud.

"Aye. Those who would Ascend must prove themselves worthy."

All within her was turmoil as wild as the storm which had driven her Dragonship from Merx to the Eastern Archipelago. This woman feared nothing. She feared not to walk the very

Halls of Gi'ishior, despite her heritage and powers. The Dragons must have known. No wonder the Lost Islanders had removed her chains and not replaced them. A person who exerted absolute dominion over Dragons could hardly fear one girl, Dragonfriend or none. How could she hope to escape the jaws of this trap she had willingly entered?

Azziala's eyes glittered as though she were privy to Lia's fears. "I stole from the Halls of the Dragons the secret lore of Dragon blood–a branch of *ruzal* called *dorzallith* in the old tongue, or 'the way of inheritance'."

"And gained a child."

"Who lacks the most elementary respect!" Seizing the front of her daughter's tunic top, the Enchantress shook her violently. "That fool Yinzi presumes to teach my daughter precepts about which she knows not the first iota. Address me with respect–"

"Respect? Unholy windrocs, you abandoned me to Ianthine!"

No inhuman strength, nor the fear searing her gut, could keep Hualiama from screaming right back in her mother's face.

Azziala spat, "You will join your people, or die."

"If you hurt Grandion–"

"Your precious lizard?" she sneered. "You're incredible! You come riding in on the breeze, blow up five airships and destroy half of our cargo bays, and you think we're just going to cosy up, make friends and let you go? Child, I'm not here to bargain with you. Nowhere in this Island-World can you ride a Dragon without paying the penalty, but especially not here in the Lost Islands."

Clamping Hualiama's cheeks with her free hand, Azziala peered into her eyes. After a moment, she shook her head. "Plain as suns-light. The child of my flesh could not be less the child of my spirit! Well, we'll soon remedy that. You'll learn my true power, and join us heart and soul."

"Let my Dragon go, and I'll–"

"No craven bargains will be tolerated here." The dark blue eyes appeared to moisten unexpectedly, before she hurled Lia back against the bed. "Whelp of a windroc! You've no choice, my dear, long-lost daughter. There is no Scroll of Binding. It was stolen by the Maroon Dragoness when she stole you. Of course I bargained with that lizard. Of all of their hell-spawn, that one is the closest to understanding our ways. She gave me words; with the words, we are able to extract Dragon powers from their blood and feed ourselves. Feeding ourselves, we become strong. Becoming strong, we shall overcome!"

Dragon blood was the source of their power. It turned their skins this peculiar golden colour …

Lia shuddered in concert with her mother, who seemed gripped by some unholy ecstasy. The woman was mad–either power-mad, or simply insane. She could not make sense of the emotions sparking and raging within Azziala. What she had learned so far was too patchy to draw conclusions, or even to stitch together into a coherent picture. She had only succeeded in throwing accusations at her mother, she recognised now. She blew hot air across rock instead of mining for truths that might point a way out of this vortex of hate.

Her own emotions seemed dangerously unstable and untrustworthy. One moment she wanted to weep, the next, she wanted to pounce upon her mother with her claws bared and fangs agape … but for poor Grandion. She had to help Grandion.

Quaking, she said, "Mother, I will agree to–"

"Empress!" roared Azziala, striking Lia backhanded across the cheek in a ghastly repetition of what King Chalcion had done; only, Lia saw the blow early and chose to receive it. Physical abuse had no hold over her any longer. She was stronger than that girl, and it must have shown in the steel of her gaze as she refused to flinch, even though her cheek exploded with heat and she tasted blood in her mouth.

Perversely, Azziala seemed to approve. She said, "Until your mettle has been proved in the Reaving, I'm no mother of yours. I've a better idea. Would you care to see your father?"

Hualiama sat down with a bump. "He's alive? Ra'aba's alive?"

A hateful smile proclaimed Azziala's pleasure at her reaction. "Aye, Ra'aba's alive. Want to talk with him?"

Chapter Twenty-Nine

Abomination

FOUR TIMES A day, the Dragon Enchanters came to renew the command-hold. "Dragon, obey. You are our slave. These are your instructions."

The Tourmaline Dragon knew only contentment. He knew to eat and grow fat on the rancid, fatty meat of a large quadruped the Islanders called orrican, shaggy beasts well suited to the blasting cold that sometimes swept through the caverns. He heard other Dragons come and go, some weakened by the process called harvesting, but he thought nothing of it. There were no questions to be asked. He had the warmth of a roost and other Dragons for companionship.

In the pre-dawn hours as the magic-induced haze over his mind weakened, the Dragon dreamed of one who spoke gently to him, a sprite with hair like fire and laughter that reminded him of tumbling through the air in joyous play. On the third day they found him perched in a cave mouth, and two Dragon Enchanters led him back to his broken pen with many unkind words and additional commands.

"He is strong, this one," said a male voice.

"He resists our commands, Kaynzo. The Empress should harvest him, and soon, by the Tenth Protocol. What's she waiting for?"

"Don't question the Fire of the Dawn, Jurizzak," cautioned Kaynzo, sanctimoniously. "She penetrates all, even the innermost thoughts of our minds. Cleansing will follow."

"Should we add command stations for the night? We could

consult the Interpretations for guidance."

"Bah. My nights are better occupied–"

Jurizzak snorted, "Warming the furs with golden Xerzia? Mind she doesn't harvest your brain cells, boy. Me, I'd give my gonads for a run at that foreign girl, lizard-lover or none. Killed my brother." In a voice grown thick and moody, he said, "When the Reaving's done, she'll be one of the High Ones. Best kill her before–"

"Jurizzak! Shut your fumarole!" Kaynzo gasped.

"Too Ninth Protocol for you, boy? Revenge is a sacred duty. I'll flay that Hualiama with my own skinning knife–"

HUUUAAALLLIIIAAAMAA!

The Dragon Enchanters whirled as the Dragon bugled her name. The Dragon felt blood as warm as his satisfaction spurt over his talons. Sweet.

The one called Kaynzo babbled, "Dragon, obey! Dragon, obey!"

He obeyed the instinct to destroy those who would eliminate the beautiful laughter. Then, the Dragon returned to his pen, and let his own bloodthirsty mirth thunder out over the Dragons crammed into a cave far beneath a cold mountain. He sniffed out a haunch of meat, and ate until he was replete.

* * * *

Ra'aba. Father. Would-be throne-stealer and murderer. What did one say to such a man?

Thoughts mobbed Hualiama as though her mind were fresh kill ripe for the carrion birds. She had imagined this moment a thousand times, yet found herself unprepared. Mute. Punch-drunk, even, in the way of a former warrior-monk apprentice who had fetched one too many blows around her aching skull. Too much was happening at once. Perhaps this was Azziala's plan, to traumatise and scar her daughter, to take away her Dragon-companion and her freedoms, to mould Hualiama into whatever this despicable mother desired her to be?

The Empress was petite, but not as petite as Lia. They

stood before Ra'aba's barred cell door, the mother's hand on Lia's shoulder in a familiar gesture that made her skin crawl. Within, a solid metal grating separated the chamber into two halves, one half occupied by two of the gold-skinned Enchantresses, and the other, by a shattered husk of a man.

She would not have known him, save for the distinctive scar on his left cheek. It remained unchanged.

"What does this to a man?" Lia breathed.

"Torture," said Azziala. "It's what I do to those who oppose my will. Go speak to your father, girl. For certain you'll find the experience instructive."

A soldier unlocked the door. The Empress' hand impelled Hualiama within. She was dimly aware of Azziala moving on, her retinue of councillors accompanying her. Both men and women could be Enchanters, she had learned, but the men worked with the lower magical functions specified by the Protocols–enchanting Dragons, husbanding the crops, hunting and mining and the like. The Enchantresses were more powerful, dominating their Island society from their positions in leadership and warfare. The magic users comprised the highest class. The middle class were men and women like Yinzi, who had a craft or skill lauded by the Protocols. The lowest class were menial workers and soldiers. Where did villagers fit into this structure?

Ra'aba continued to rock back and forth in a corner where he had built himself a meagre nest of furs. His gaunt face peeked at her. The grossly distorted knuckles of his right hand hugged his knees like gnarled roots wrapped about a boulder. His whimpering rose and fell, as though he wanted to sing, but could not find words to express his brokenness. Of the powerful, lithe swordsman who had fought his daughter for the Onyx Throne, no trace remained. How had he survived?

Appalled, Lia began to weep.

She hated herself for weeping over this man. Yet for all his evil, he remained her father.

Glancing up, Ra'aba cringed. "No, not thee, Enchantress," he mumbled. "Come to torture old Ra'aba? What's left? Not even his teeth. Crushed them with pliers, see? All these stumps in my mouth, I should be a woodsman." Ra'aba sank what remained of his teeth into the knuckles of that ruined hand. "I won't speak! You can't make me! Didn't you steal it all already? Vile Enchantress. Slug spit to your vile *ruzal*, I hope it eats you from the inside like cancer." Blood trickled over his fingers. Feebly, he cried, "Get away from me! Vixen! Spawn of a goat …"

"Father, don't," Lia whispered.

His head cocked to one side like a fowl regarding a tasty worm. "Father? What trickery is this?"

"Father, it's me. Hualiama."

"Lia? Nooooo … she's dead. Never lived. She hurt me. Then the Dragons, oh mercy, the Dragons and the burning, so much burning …"

"Father."

"She isn't here. No. Can't be–run away!" His abrupt, spittle-flecked shriek made her jump. "Flee while you can. Too late, oh, too late. Pity you. Despair, despair, despair, little one."

"Father, it's me. Lia, not Azziala. Focus on my voice."

"Lia? Little Lia?" Standing, he began to shuffle toward her, hunched over like a wounded windroc. He sobbed, "Forgive me … no!" The voice changed again, his mood shifting like clouds racing over the suns. "You're lying. I see you there, with your Enchantress' eyes."

"Father, I need to know what happened back at Gi'ishior."

"They questioned me, those Dragons. So many Dragons. Always the burning. Burned my thoughts right out of me, don't you see?" He squinted up at her, the left eye focussed, the right rolling wildly in its socket, repeating 'don't you see' numerous times. Spittle dangled from the corner of his lower lip.

"Father, about my birth–"

"Lia? Little Lia? A prophecy, aye–I must kill you!"

Suddenly, he charged at the bars. A paralysis birthed in horror kept her immobile for a second too long; too late, she realised Ra'aba had been stalking her with the cunning of a wounded rajal. The grotesque hands clamped about her neck with a measure of the inhuman strength Ra'aba had enjoyed before. Lia chopped down with the tough edges of her hands, but his madness multiplied that grip. She could not break it. He shook her, bruised her lips against the cold metal.

The two Enchantresses spoke in concert, "Back!"

Ra'aba reeled as though struck, but did not release his chokehold.

"Back!"

A sliver of tooth popped out of his mouth, followed by a gobbet of blood. Freed, Hualiama stumbled backward, holding her throat.

Her father began to cackle, "Afraid of old Ra'aba, are we? I've the strength of a Dragon!" And his cackles continued, eerie gasps of mirth that made the Princess of Fra'anior imagine maniacs dancing across her grave, such was the soul-lost chill it evoked in her spirit. Evidently she was not the only one, for one of the Enchantresses cursed and lashed out with her magic, only to be stilled by the other. Panting, they faced Ra'aba. Magic stung Lia's senses. The laughter choked. He turned purple as they cut off his air supply.

"Enough," Lia rasped. The women glared at him, identical stares from identical golden faces. "He's suffered enough."

One said, "No Cloudlands ocean of suffering is enough for one of his ilk."

She only calmed Ra'aba after a considerable effort. He kept pawing at his throat and cursing the Enchantresses and the Lost Islands and Azziala in particular with curses so vile and sordid, Hualiama could barely bring herself to listen–but listen she did, in the hope of learning something new.

At length, when she judged the man somewhat returned to reason, she said, "Ianthine insisted that you were my father, Ra'aba. Is that true?"

Ra'aba hunched in his corner, and groaned, "Child of the Dragon. Child of the–"

"I have to be the child of a Human man and woman," said Lia, trying to force the deep distress out of her voice. "Human seed and Dragon soul-fire cannot mingle. Thousands of years and Dramagon's foulest abominations attest to that truth. Yet both you and Azziala claim I am your child, or that I may be, or am not. Why deny it? What's the truth, Ra'aba? I've a right to know."

"Rights?" The maniacal laughter belled out again. "You don't want to know. You can't handle the truth, little Lia."

His use of her hated nickname sealed the matter. Anger fizzed in her veins. Between clenched teeth, she hissed, "I have to know, Ra'aba. If it's the only good thing you do in this life, do good now. Speak the truth."

"Confusion, conundrum, mystery so humdrum," he cackled.

"The truth!"

"Little Lia doesn't like puzzles?"

Before she knew it, *ruzal* slithered out from beneath the barricades she had built with such care and patience. *Speak!* she commanded.

The two watching Dragon-Haters exchanged glances. Lia groaned. Oh for Grandion to sit on her chest for that mistake! Now, Azziala would hear of her abilities, of that she had no doubt. Ra'aba began to slam his head against the bars, over and over, each blow like a sickening strike of a gong. The Human Princess looked to the Enchantresses, stricken, but the identical gestures of their left hands informed her that this was normal behaviour. Slowly, his guttural moans resolved into intelligible speech.

"Get him out, out, out," he snuffled. "Don't hurt me again, Dragon. Don't make me do it. I'm a sick man, so sick, I can't get him out of my head … make it stop, please, someone help me."

This speech descended into meaningless babble, before being repeated with a greater level of distress than before. After the fourth time, unable to bear his misery any longer, Lia burst out, "Who? Who's making you do it, father?"

"Him. The Dragon. Him. The–"

"Razzior?"

Ra'aba nodded, the words seemingly obstructed in his throat.

As she had guessed! Dragons could dominate and possess Human minds and bodies–nobody could know that better than her. Razzior had done the same to Ra'aba, not a simple projection as Grandion could do, but the whole Island. Body and soul. She could only imagine the opportunities for a Dragon of Razzior's skill in the art of *ruzal*. Had the Orange Dragon secretly controlled his fellows, through the vessel of Ra'aba? Mercy.

Aaaaa-ooooo-aaah! Ra'aba keened, taking up his rocking again.

After some minutes of this, he looked up between his fingers, childlike yet guileful. "He made me do it." His manner changed again, becoming furtive. "He made me. Twisted me like a hawser, see?" Licking his lips, Ra'aba said, "He made me do it to them."

"Them?" she echoed dully.

"Forty-seven of them," said Ra'aba, eyeballing her with the lustful glee of one who revelled in knowing exactly how much damage his words would wreak. "Forty-seven women. Azziala was one of many. So strong. So … worthwhile."

"Monster!" shouted the Enchantress who had lost control before.

Ra'aba only laughed. "Some, I kept captive for years. Shall I tell you how it felt, little Lia? Razzior made me. I had no choice. He lived through me."

Hualiama found herself shaking the bars, shouting incoherently, but Ra'aba simply kept laughing at her with that sickening, draconic smile lingering on his lips. "Oh, how the truth sears, sears her soul, the conundrum always grows, and here it comes–she cannot be Ra'aba's child. Devastated, little Lia? Traumatised? Better I stuck that Immadian forked dagger in your gut than hear this, eh?"

The old double puncture marks on her abdomen and the huge crescent scar on her back throbbed as though freshly opened. Ra'aba had been right. She had opened the cesspit and jumped right in, with her obstinate desire to understand her heritage. But she could not believe him. Lia shook her head repeatedly.

She insisted, "It had to be you, Ra'aba. There was no one else."

"Forty-seven, not counting the willing ones," he chuckled. "I kept track, see? Ra'aba never sired another child, not by any woman. Azziala's a liar. It must've been someone else."

"You're infertile? But there's still a chance, surely …"

"There's a much better chance, which would make the Maroon Dragoness right, at least by Dragonish logic," he said, waiting until with a gasp of horror, she made the fateful connection. He seemed quite sane, now. Lia wondered if his entire performance had been a sham. "A shame this isn't the beautiful, prophetic truth you so desired, is it, little Lia? Child of the Dragon. *Ruzal*-spawn abomination!"

His lunatic laughter chased her out of the room.

* * * *

Stripped to her underwear, Hualiama shivered uncontrollably in the biting wind as Azziala took the report. Grandion had killed two Dragon Enchanters that morning. Hysterical laughter burbled in the back of her throat. Not so easy to chain a Tourmaline Dragon, was it?

"Fools! You waited until evening to make this report?" demanded the Empress.

"Highness! We had to check the Protocols … four times did not suffice to bind the lizard." The man's voice rose to a raw squeal in the face of her wrath. "We think they mentioned her name, this lizard-lover's name, great–"

"FOOL!" Azziala's sceptre crashed into his elbow. The man turned grey with pain. "Go cast yourself into the Dragon's Pipe. I am surrounded by incompetents. Go!"

"Mercy," whispered from Hualiama's pinched lips. On the mountaintop, a flat area atop the tall volcanic cone she had first seen upon approaching the Lost Islands, the cold was a bitter beast borne on the wings of the ever-moaning wind, which rushed over the peak and down into twin holes which looked suspiciously like a Dragon's nostrils set side-by-side in the rock. Each hole was thirty feet wide and rimed by ice. From this place, Azziala had told her during their march up the mountain, the frost emanated which gave the western, Human-inhabited Lost Islands a climate like the deadly cold of the Islands north of Immadia.

This was the place of Reaving.

The Princess felt as though she had plunged into a frozen lake. Her bones hurt. Her teeth chattered uncontrollably. All twelve of Azziala's Councillors, even aged Feyzuria, had hiked up to the peak that afternoon, but none of them seemed to feel the cold. Perhaps their Dragon-golden skin was proof against freezing?

With a wail, the unfortunate man cast himself into one of the nostrils. His despairing cry echoed for many seconds before fading into nothingness. Mercy. Azziala had no need of magical commands. The power of her will had been enough to drive that soldier to his death.

How deep were those caves, Lia wondered? Her teardrops froze to her eyelashes. Instead of liquid, icicles tinkled against her cheeks.

Azziala said, "I knew about the disturbance this morning, but they waited until evening to make their report?"

"You did right, Highness," said Feyzuria. "That lizard is unusually powerful. A great feast awaits us."

The mother's eyes returned to her shivering daughter. "First, we must see what is needed to turn this one to our cause. Strategy, my dear aunt, is a game of years and the patience of a hunting snow leopard, as you taught me. But I sense the time is at hand. Prepare her for the Reaving!"

The Princess of Fra'anior briefly considered if she should unleash her magic. One against thirteen was poor odds. One against an Island-nation? She would doom Grandion as surely as she doomed herself, and Razzior would help himself to the Scroll of Binding–stolen or not–with a few less of the opposition to worry about. Better then to turn into an ice-statue upon a mountaintop as she bided her time? Part of her, perversely, welcomed one more chance to thumb her nose at fate, coupled with a feeling she recognised as a reckless craving for oblivion. Neither of her true parents wanted her. Their betrayals cut deeper than she had ever imagined.

A channel some three feet wide connected the 'nostrils'.

Either side a stone archway stood rooted as if carved from a monolithic block of stone, giving the appearance of a nose ring such as these Islanders used to tie or lead their orrican, a type of russet brown, thick-coated buffalo similar to the domesticated water buffalo of the Kingdom of Kaolili, Hualiama understood. She had a nasty suspicion she knew exactly where the ritual of Reaving was to take place.

To the west, the suns touched the horizon. The wind had dropped. Surprised, Hualiama glanced about her. If anything, the tranquillity compounded the cold, an illusion grounded in her notion that the wind's friction provided some element of warmth.

Azziala said, "Flesh of my flesh, bone of my bone, you stand at the roof of the world. This is the westernmost Isle of our Cluster. To the West, all is an ocean of Cloudlands. To the East lie the lands Dramagon promised us." Her hands upon Hualiama's shoulders swivelled her about as she spoke. "Child of my flesh, you came to us from afar with claims of blood and kinship. Yet flesh is weak, and born to die."

"Flesh is weak," intoned the twelve Enchantresses.

The ritual had begun? Lia forced herself not to resist as Shazziya fitted solid manacles to her wrists, and clamped her ankles together with a heavier, single-piece manacle. Whatever they purposed, she would survive.

"We turn our backs upon the night."

As one, the Enchantresses turned to face the eastern horizon. "We reject the night. We wait for the dawn."

Shazziya hefted Hualiama's diminutive frame with casual ease, moving along the peninsula between the nostrils of the Dragon's Pipe. For a bowel-twisting second, Lia presumed they meant to toss her in. The pipes were roughly circular and apparently depthless, as was the connecting part. Reaching up, Shazziya looped two short chains through metal rings embedded in the archway, and used a touch of unfamiliar magic to lock them in place. Without further ado, the Enchantress released her captive, causing Lia to drop slightly and dangle from the archway in the precise centre of the space between the two pipes. With the briefest of nods, Shazziya drew back four measured steps.

Crossly, the royal ward bade her churning stomach cease its misbehaviour. There would be worse to come. Her full weight depended upon her wrists, chained shoulder-width apart. Lia glanced down at her body. Girlishly slender and scarred by her experiences, it seemed too frail a vessel to cup the life that tingled in her veins, and a poor choice for the fire-gifts of the finest of friends. Love and loyalty were Flicker's gift to her. But what exquisite form of madness had possessed Amaryllion to grant a Human girl a whisper of an Ancient Dragon's soul-fire? And how could the Empress, in all her pomp and power, fail to detect these secrets?

As if echoing her thoughts, Azziala intoned, "Mighty Dramagon, we offer you one scarred by birth and life. Take her. Reave her. Let the breath of your mountain part flesh from bone, until nothing is left which has not been Reaved. May Hualiama become one of us, or may her flesh turn to ice with the coming of the dawn, and shatter upon the slopes of your mountain."

"Reave her!" cried the twelve.

"It was Dramagon himself, blessed father of our nation, who gave these Isles to us to be our winnowing ground," said Azziala, her expression growing yet grimmer. "Winter's ice for the Human realm and summer's warmth for the lizards to the East. A land of duality, suns-light and shadow, cold and warmth. Thus in duality your life is suspended between the heavens above and the Islands below, part of neither, part of both."

"Heavens above and Islands below," echoed the priestesses of her ghastly cabal.

Lia had always wondered where the common saying had originated. Could it be here, in the Lost Islands? Or had they twisted it to their own ends? Always, she had seen it as symbolic of beauty–the night's velvet darkness above, and the Islands' extraordinary beauty and variety below.

"A cupful of life's blood to symbolise what is poured out this night."

Shazziya unexpectedly flung a cupful of warm, sticky liquid

full in her face. It splattered her hair and ran down her chest and abdomen. Hualiama gasped and then gagged. Blood, she realised from the tang. Mercy! Oh, double mercy, it was blood mixed with the foul magic of these Dragon-Haters …

"The lifeblood of the Watchman who failed in his duty," said Azziala. Lia tried to spit. She wiped her face on her outstretched arms, spreading the crimson stain. "Very well, Hualiama. We will wait until the Reaving begins. Then we will abandon you to the night. Should you survive, you will be my daughter, heir to the Throne of the Lost Islands."

Should she wish to survive, only to attain such a hateful title?

Silence as profound as a Cloudlands abyss enveloped the mountaintop.

The Dragon-Haters stood motionless, waiting. The wind did not stir. Before her stretched the snow-capped peaks and icy Isles of their Cluster, seeming to groan beneath the burden of harsh, unforgiving cold. Dipping beneath the horizon, the suns threw a final halo across her thinly-clad body, and with that, it seemed to her that the mountain took a single, cavernous inhalation, and then began to exhale a stream of air so intensely cold, it turned to mist the instant it exited the Dragon's Pipe. The odours of dankness and decay prickled her nostrils, along with a faint hint of sulphur, jasmine and metallic minerals, suggesting the draconic with a medley of scents at once unfamiliar to the Human girl but curiously evocative. Pain spread up her limbs as the cold rose.

"The Reaving has begun!" cried Azziala.

"It has begun!" echoed the twelve. They began to file down the mountain, one by one, until Lia was left alone with her mother. Already, the stretching of her arms grew uncomfortable, and the manacles bit into her wrists. The cold dug into her calf muscles like frigid Dragon's talons slowly, unbearably, twisting their way beneath the muscles.

The Empress said, "There's a curious quality about this air from Dramagon's mountain. It strips away extraneous magic, leaving bare the kernel of our being. Even your *ruzal* will not work here, child."

Her slip-up in Ra'aba's cell had been duly noted.

"Do you hate me, mother?"

"Hate? Of course not." Her mother examined her as Hualiama imagined Dramagon might have examined one of his luckless specimens. "This is the Protocol of the Forbearing Mother, the Nineteenth. Twenty-one summers have I waited to usher you into your true place in this Island-World, Hualiama. This Reaving is an act of love, the best gift a mother can give her daughter."

"My true place is upon Grandion's back," Hualiama retorted, lifting her legs to try to evade the creeping chill.

"Every false belief will be Reaved out of you," Azziala asserted.

"Do you honestly imagine I'll ever become one of you?"

"Survive the Reaving, and you will be."

"Survive being frozen to death, do you mean?" Lia asked, openly sarcastic.

"If you're worthy, you'll find a way."

As she spoke, Azziala had been moving closer. Now, she reached up to tear away Lia's undergarments, and with them, came the White Dragoness' scale. Somehow, in all that had transpired, the cord had snapped and the scale had slipped beneath her right breast. Her mother did not appear to notice. She dropped the garments together with the scale into the black void beneath her daughter's feet. Another loss. Silently, Hualiama vowed she would find that scale again. The White Dragoness deserved to be remembered for her sacrifice.

"Now, all is stripped away," she said. "Thus will your inner self be stripped away. Child, even in your benighted life, you have risen–from Ianthine's paw to the Halls of the Dragons; from Gi'ishior to the royal house of Fra'anior; from Ra'aba's Dragonship to the shores of Ha'athior; from Ha'athior, home. Fate is your plaything. That's your true power. You rise where others fall."

Angrily, Lia said, "May I conclude, then, that your brand of love amounts solely to ambition?"

Azziala raised her chin in an imperious gesture that Hualiama recognised only too well–from herself. "How sorely you misjudge me. You're blind–"

"Not blind to the true face of love."

"What girl of two decades is an expert in love?" But the Empress wiped her brow in a tired gesture, as if all the burdens of a lifetime had become manifest at once. "I must feed. I leave you with this, Hualiama. I received your name in a dream, while you yet lived in my womb. It's an ancient name which means 'song of the Eastern star.' It comes with a story. In Dragon lore, there's a legendary star called Hualiama. It's the last star to glimmer when the suns rise in the East. The lizards say it can only be seen for the briefest of instants as the twin suns crest the horizon, just a flash of blue, on the night of a five-moon conjunction–as it will be, tonight."

"A blue star?"

Hualiama realised that she spoke to an empty mountaintop. Had she dreamed, or had Azziala defied her nature to speak a kind word to her daughter?

Her tears fell, but they turned into hailstones long before they reached the bottom of the Dragon's Pipe.

Chapter Thirty

The Reaving

KINDNESS FROM HER mother trembled her Island in ways Hualiama had never anticipated. The dreadful Empress had a Human soul. She was redeemable. And here was prekki-mush-hearted Lia picturing a tearful reconciliation with her baby-abandoning, murderous mother who thought freezing her offspring was a gift of love.

Madness! Anger summoned her fires as the mist billowed up toward her hips, making her appear as though she waded hip-deep through billowing clouds of white smoke. So glacial was the cold, she could see it undulating down the mountain in great streamers, like the straggling beard of an old man. Fire and ice fought for dominance in her and around her. At times the Princess of Fra'anior thought the fire should recover its ground, making the nerves of her lower body scream with pain every time they thawed out, only for the cold to return, deeper and more insidious. Even an hour was too much. She sweated with the supreme effort. The moisture froze and refroze to her body until her struggles cracked it open like a chrysalis. As promised, her *ruzal* lay dormant. She was trapped.

As the stars wheeled overhead and the moons waxed, brightening the cloudless night, the white fog spread over the nearest Islands with the air of an animate creature which purposed to smother any life, sucking the heat away until any final, sluggish movement froze into immobility. Hualiama wondered what might exist within the mountain that generated such an unnatural cold. An Ancient Dragon? The fabled ice-

Dragons of the farthest north? She realised that someone was raving, wailing, pleading for the pain to cease. It was her.

Lia clamped her jaw shut.

Chaotic visions beset her. Lia cried out for help and the white mist grew black and stormy, heralding the advent of Fra'anior, whose laughter belled over the emptiness between the Islands.

Ah, the thief is brought low. Suffering, little one? Screaming? Sweet music to the ears of one you purposed to defy!

I never … meant …

Meant or not, the deed is done. The Black Dragon's scorn poured over her, torrential.

Help me, she sobbed. *Help me, don't scorn–*

Don't what? Blow you away?

Storm winds broke over the mountaintop, making her chained body flutter like a flag in a stiff breeze and her long hair ripple behind her until she feared it should crack clean off her frozen scalp. Blood ran down her arms from where the manacles cut into her pale, icy skin. She could not breathe. He stole the breath from her lungs, but the monstrous power of his Dragon fire warmed her.

When the little one who bowed beneath his mighty Ancient-Dragon blast felt liquid fire sear her numbed senses, Fra'anior drew back with a new, vicious laugh. *Feel my minions rise!*

Dragonets materialised within the white cloud. Perfect little Dragons three feet in wingspan, they had ice-white scales and black eyes and talons. Their tiny claws began to cut the ice off her body but quickly, the scrabbling turned vicious as they quarried through skin and muscle. It seemed the dragonets became Razzior, savaging her body, burning and mauling her again and again, and each time Fra'anior resurrected her, laughing, *Dragon fires never die.* He gave her over to the Orange Dragon once more …

Hualiama woke screaming from a nightmare–or was she awake? Her mind existed in a plane of warped reality, visions layered upon dreams, meandering without understanding. Was it just the cold, or was the insidious magic of this place prising her sanity loose of its moorings? The clouds billowed up to her chest. Every inhalation brought fresh agony to her lungs. Her blood moved like gelid sap, and in that yawning space between each impossibly slow heartbeat, pain encompassed all. Fra'anior's thunder rent the skies. Chalcion struck her repeatedly, a percussive drumbeat of humiliation. The White Dragoness bellowed at her for losing the scale, yet it seemed that the place on her breast where it had rested, grew warm. Only her heart retained a hint of warmth, and even that was being Reaved from her. Was she dying?

The breath of her lungs frosted before her face, falling as minute particles down her body. Her pleas fell upon skies deaf to her cries, and echoed across barren Isles.

Dimly, Hualiama became aware of a great rumbling beneath her feet. The white exploded. Suddenly she was the centre of an upwelling storm, as though the air had erupted skyward, the moisture speedily adhering to her body, encasing the girl who would have danced with Dragons in an icy coffin. She was bound, body and magic, her mind and emotions ravaged by the fierce Reaving, yet Hualiama intuitively realised that she still had freedom of choice. Her spirit was free. She must choose to cling to that knowledge, no matter what this Dragon-Haters' ritual portended for her. Even in extremity, her spirit could dance.

And dance it did, uninhibited by the strictures of chains or cold, magic most hateful and even Fra'anior's wrath. Lia thought about Amaryllion, and danced upon his paw. She remembered Flicker, and laughter shook her ethereal being. Puny and hopeless her actions might be, yet they symbolised her defiance.

Troubling dreams assaulted her, centred on Azziala and her Enchantresses. The girl who hung beneath the heavens wondered if they sent forth their powers to mould her as they wished. Overwhelming waves of shame and horror battered her spirit. All the ghosts of her past paraded past, screaming the hatred of parents who had despised her since conception, the mockery of her abusive father and punishment for the forbidden love of a Tourmaline Dragon. 'Abomination!

Abomination!' Their cries echoed through her soul. Why not simply die? Why not yield to hatred? A creature like Hualiama deserved only death. Death itself quailed in disgust at the prospect of receiving her.

A vision of Numistar loomed out of the mists, an Ancient White Dragoness so vast that her tail was yet lost in the Cloudlands as she loomed over the archway holding Hualiama enchained. Dazzling, beautiful and deadly, her eyes blazed with a different type of white-fire–not the fire Lia knew, but the vicious breath of the uttermost North, the Dragonsong of cold-blasted fields of ice, hail and deathly frost. Numistar's mouth engulfed the mountaintop. From her throat waves of wintriness gusted over her, and then Fra'anior lunged from his own darkness and the Ancient Dragons battled, toppling Islands and lashing the Cloudlands into froth with their league-long tails …

There, in the darkest nadir of her suffering, Hualiama reached across time and space to touch the mother-presence of the White Dragoness who inhabited her egg-dreams, and yet it seemed that she saw another Dragoness beyond her, a midnight-blue female brooding over a clutch of five eggs.

Five? How could this be?

The White Dragoness said, *None can interfere, little one. You alone must find the strength to separate soul from flesh. Be the duality your mother spoke of. Afterward, seek the Maroon Dragoness. She's closer than you think.*

Be the duality? Hualiama wished the beneficent forces in her life would speak less in mystical riddles. She laughed wryly. Should she find her future written upon scrolleaf?

Seek Ianthine? she echoed. *White Dragoness, how is it that we can speak of such things? Who are you? Where … why …*

She questioned the night.

Lia looked upon the Reaving of her flesh as if from a distance, knowing the damage they sought to do, knowing that once more Azziala had betrayed her out of misguided and blind adherence to her Protocols. The Enchantresses were present in the wailing of the wind, their power clawed into her body, bringing on the visions that tormented her. Hualiama touched her body only enough to keep the heart beating, nothing more. All had been surrendered.

Only survival mattered.

* * * *

When first light touched her face, Hualiama did not feel it. She watched thirteen women approach the mountaintop, but it was not with eyes frozen into their sockets that she observed their climb. She watched in the knowledge of a five-moon conjunction, alive to the twin suns' radiance, and yearned for the dawn.

The Empress touched the pulse of Hualiama's neck, her face set like bronzed stone.

Feyzuria shook her head. "She didn't make it."

Azziala said, "Take her down."

Right between the twin suns, in a place which could never be seen by eyes of flesh, a tiny flash of blue glinted once, and speared across the intervening space to touch her spirit, at once fleeting and profound, with a peal like the distilled laughter of starlight. It sang, *Hualiama!*

Shazziya also shook her head, wondering, "How could she perish? We felt her strength. She has your heritage, o Empress."

"The father's the weakness," spat Feyzuria.

"No, he was a great Enchanter," Azziala said tonelessly, gathering Hualiama's stiff body into her arms. "This is wrong. WRONG!"

Her grieving cry shook the mountain.

Riding the turbulence of that magic-infused shout, Hualiama's spirit rejoined her body. Breath ghosted across her rimed lips.

Azziala gasped; placed her cheek close to Lia's mouth. "Breathe, little one. You must … she's alive!" For the first time, her voice was raw with emotion. She breathed, "Together at last, my beautiful daughter."

Lia's body could not shudder, but her spirit did.

* * * *

Abed, days slipped by in a delirium of recovery, characterised by fires kept blazing in a firepit until the temperature became sweltering, regular meals of mashed, spiced orrican kidney and liver–unspeakably foul–and Yinzi's massage of her frostbitten extremities. Despite the warmth and liberal application of herbal medicines and magic, each massage was a fresh agony, to say nothing of the state of her brain. Had Grandion enthusiastically stirred up her skull's contents with a talon and then chargrilled the mash to perfection, she would have felt no less abused. When lucidity returned, Hualiama tried to question the old midwife, but her probing met with fearful non-answers.

Lia learned they had housed her in Azziala's own chamber. She supposed she should be honoured, but quickly became aware she was still being strictly monitored, in particular by Feyzuria, who seemed to find something distasteful about the new heir-apparent to the throne. Most likely, the political plotting had reached a fever-pitch in the corridors of Azziala's underground lair. Hualiama would have been unsurprised to find a viper in her bed, or poison slipped into her drink, but she realised that the powers of these Enchantresses must keep at least some of the dagger sinister, to borrow the Fra'aniorian saying, at bay.

Late the fourth evening after her Reaving, the Princess learned what had kept Azziala from her bedside.

Without warning, the oval wooden door of the Empress' austere chambers banged open. Her retinue of watchers–they all seemed identical, always a pair of blue-robed women with the unnervingly intense eyes and unsmiling golden faces–did not startle, but left the room at once.

"Two days ago, the lizards razed one of our villages," Azziala announced. No preamble for her. No greetings or happiness that her daughter appeared well. "What do you know of this?"

"Er–as much as you just told me," said Lia.

"Look into my eyes when you speak, child! The eyes!"

Taken aback, Lia raised her gaze. Azziala eyed her narrowly. "Repeat that."

"Islands' sakes, what–"

The Empress' voice shook with wrath. "What do you know of this attack?"

Just then, the door banged a second time. Shazziya charged in, closely followed by Feyzuria.

"Lizard-lover!" spat Shazziya. The royal ward stared. The tall Enchantress' face glowed with an unholy radiance, as though her skin were lit from within. "Let me wring her scrawny little neck–with respect, Highness. I'll stake you out for a lizard's lunch! I'll rip the truth out of you–"

Feyzuria, in a voice crackling with power, snarled, "We all want to know, Shazziya. Now hold your tongue before the Empress and her heir, before we still its wagging with a blade. Answer the question, child!"

Lia queried, "You've outdoor villages? In this climate?"

"THE QUESTION!" Azziala's roar knocked her bed over and snuffed out the fire instantly.

"Nothing!" Hualiama wriggled out from beneath the tumbled bedclothes, stood toe to toe with her mother, and roared in her best impression of the Tourmaline Dragon, "Nothing! As in, not-one-thing! Now, can someone kindly–"

Azziala gripped her cheeks with the Dragon-pincer grip she seemed all too fond of. She glared into Hualiama's eyes, before shoving her aside with a growl, "Guiltless. Shazziya!" The Empress whirled. "Confirm this truth."

Having subjected Lia to the same treatment, Shazziya was forced to admit, "Guiltless. I could have sworn, Highness–"

The Empress cut her off effortlessly. "Councillors. Come inside. We might as well move our meeting into my private chambers." Her heavy sarcasm did not raise a single eyebrow among her dour-faced twelve, but Hualiama realised that at a stroke, battle lines had been drawn. "Feyzuria, the chalices. We must feed."

Lia watched pensively as the old woman moved over to a wooden sideboard which held a cloth-covered metal tray. She removed the blue velvet cloth and folded it reverently, revealing a pitcher and thirteen chalices of the finest etched crystal. Golden liquid. Dragon's blood, poured out thick and beautiful, its exotic spiciness igniting her nostrils with a delicious scent. Unconsciously, Hualiama licked her lips.

Observing her reaction minutely, her mother said, "This privilege is not for you, child. Not yet."

Freaking feral Dragons! Lia flinched. Since when had she developed a taste for–oh. Since the Reaving.

The Enchantresses received their chalices in solemn procession, before turning toward each other, chanting, "We drink. We feed. May our portion increase!" They quaffed their drinks with evident satisfaction.

Azziala said, "Join hands. You too, child."

Feyzuria protested, "Is she ready? The imprint cannot have … aye, Highness."

Imprint? So the Reaving had a sinister motive–or a loving one, depending on one's perspective. What did that mean? How was she expected to behave? Lia cautioned herself inwardly as she joined hands with Azziala on her right and Feyzuria on her left, completing a circle of ten, with four Enchantresses absent. An eerie force rippled around the circle, akin to Dragons' telepathic speech, she realised. But Lia had to snatch her hands away, yelping as a shock like lightning struck her palms.

"Sorry." She wrung her hands.

"Come, Hualiama," Azziala encouraged. "Feyzuria, I know what you're thinking. I suspect my heir will prove remarkably adept at this skill, as she is at much else."

Lia frowned at the threat veiled within her mother's compliment. Grasping the dry palms either side of her, she closed her eyes, and found a mental representation of the group waiting for her. At once, one of the women, Gyrthina by name, showed them the results of her investigation. Lia saw a village razed, as if massive worms had erupted out of the ground beneath the low log-built lodges, tossing them about like kindling, before Dragon fire had scorched the remains. No living thing remained.

A migraine blossomed between her temples as the narrative

deepened, adding layers of meaning to clarify her confusion. Their telepathic communication was so different to the draconic method. Less efficient, Hualiama noted privately, but multiplied to dizzying proportions by the presence of ten. One Enchantress noted that the Lost Islands had four different types of Dragons. Another put in, with accompanying images, 'Burrowers, Grunts, Overminds and the Swarm.' Information blossomed at the touch of Lia's intellect. All four Dragon types were subclasses of Lesser Dragons. Grunts were massively armoured with what one of the Enchantresses pictured as great ridges of metallic hide, virtually impenetrable. They were so heavy that a fully-grown adult could barely fly a league. New data flickered past her awareness. Tonnage. Wingspan. Lifespan. Strategies to combat … her mind leaped. Overminds controlled the other three types. They were smallish Dragons, mostly of a Jade colour with a smattering of Browns and Blues, possessing telepathic capabilities similar to the Humans' own, the goal of Dramagon's breeding experiments. The Overminds were long and serpentine in the body, with four wings rather than two, and short, stubby legs that made them appear much more lizard-like than Grandion. They shied from combat, leaving that to their minions.

Knowledge poured into her. Hualiama staggered, but Azziala squeezed her hand, steadying. "Control the flow." She barely heard, occupied with accessing population numbers and maps and invasion plans for the Eastern Archipelago and rosters of soldiers and logistical arrangements–the levels of available detail seemed endless. Each Enchantress had her specialties and responsibilities. They documented nothing, storing it all in the minds of their people, as if each Enchanter or Enchantress were a walking archive of lore and information.

The Burrowers were short, stubby Brown Dragons with massively oversized forepaws which gave them a mole-like appearance. As Gyrthina flashed up images of a different village under attack, Hualiama realised how powerful they were. Writhing Dragons exploded out of the ground, ripping half of the village off the edge of an Island and tossing it into the abyss.

Ruzal flickered beneath Hualiama's shields, rising in response to the minds surrounding her, dark, calculating minds bent on the Dragons' destruction. So much hate! The concerted labours of an Island-nation working toward the Dragons' downfall!

Unconsciously, her tone mimicked their hatred as Hualiama arrested the circle, demanding, "Why do I stand accused?"

Was this her? The new, Reaved Hualiama?

"Show her," Azziala intoned.

A single image stabilised amidst the chaos. Lia bit her lip sharply. The Dragons had left a personal note, constructed in runic script made of charred bodies and timbers from the former village. It said, 'Hand over the Dragonfriend, or perish.'

She tore away from the circle, panting, quivering as though she hung once more, naked and defenceless, in the mountain's arctic cold. Her stomach heaved. She could not prevent it, stumbling to the firepit to expurgate the remains of her last meal. Though she was not part of the circle, the Princess of Fra'anior sensed their approval. Aye, the imprint was working. She gagged again, fighting to swallow down the lurking, power-hungry *ruzal,* which sang to her spirit the ability to one day conquer these women, to seize power for herself, to rule over Dragons and Humans alike, for she had the gift and the power … desperate to distract their attention, Lia lashed out with an image of Fra'anior thundering amidst his storm. The Enchantresses threw up their hands and cried out in momentary terror.

"Leave me alone," she muttered, sickened by what she had glimpsed within herself. This was the Dragonfriend? This twisted, greedy, grasping thing?

"What light does the Dragonfriend shed upon these developments?" asked Shazziya, unmindful or uncaring of Lia's debility. Her tone made it clear that using the title 'Dragonfriend' was a personal swipe at Azziala.

"Razzior," said Lia.

Feyzuria said, "Razzior? He can't be here. None of our intelligence indicates it."

"Yet the pattern of the attack is new," said Gyrthina. "The

lizards have never acted in such a coordinated fashion before."

"Can you show me?" asked Lia.

"None lived, who observed the attack," replied the Enchantress.

The mental link touched Lia again. Judiciously, she imbibed their knowledge, noting how they could trace Dragons over vast distances–especially the movement of large numbers of Dragons, by the magical wash or disturbance they generated in the fabric of the Island-World. Feyzuria in particular was adept at tracking Dragons. She saw them as rippling lights, as if the Dragons were the aurora of the far north she had read about. But none of these Enchantresses had detected Grandion's approach, a tiny counterpoint voice pointed out in her mind. She saw two groups. One had to be Razzior and his kin, hurtling in a flat-out sprint for the Lost Islands. Behind them, Sapphurion and his Dragonwing?

"If the level of co-ordination and precision execution you posit from the evidence is true, my instinct would identify Razzior as the culprit," said the engineer within Hualiama, coolly. "Are you certain–"

"Quite," said Feyzuria. "Highness, there must be a link."

Lia growled, "I was not aware of chatting to the Dragons on that mountaintop, Feyzuria, unless those Overminds detected your little showpiece. Magic isn't as predictable as you think."

"Insolent puppy!" spat the old women.

Aye. She had learned conversational tactics from a Dragon.

The Empress' psyche jabbed them both, not gently. "We're in a war situation. The intelligence my daughter shared with us is rapidly becoming clear. Two mighty Dragonwings approach. Feyzuria, revisit our detailed preparations lest our Dragon Enchanters be overwhelmed by the sheer number of lizards as they approach. We must assume these Dragons, mortal enemies or none, will band together to overrun us–for they fear us enough."

Lia observed the ebb and flow of the mental conversation with interest. So the Dragon Enchanters could be overwhelmed? Swarmed, as the name suggested? Establishing a command-hold took time, she ascertained from another Enchantress' brain. Those minutes could be vital. Feyzuria pinged off mental commands to her subordinates to file new reports, to check the defences and disposition of the troops and to inspect the Dragon holding pens–mercy, how many Dragons did they keep, on how many Islands? At the speed of thought, Lia sourced Grandion's location. She reviewed the feedback from Enchanters tasked with long-range Dragon tracking, and had to admit, the two groups were distinct. Could Sapphurion be chasing Razzior? Or was the Orange Dragon playing a deeper game?

Azziala recaptured Lia's hand. "So, daughter. Found out all that you need to know?" The Empress' eyes glittered with magic as she skewered her daughter with the import of her question.

"Just overawed, honestly," Lia spluttered. "I had no idea–"

"How powerful we are?"

Everything, she wanted to say. Magic. Power harvested from drinking Dragons' blood. Command but a thought away. Lia was aware of the other Enchantresses focussing inward, directing the activities of the nation as if they plinked stones into a pond, the ripples spreading outward seemingly forever. Somehow, the cold calculation of this mental machine terrified her more than the sight of Shinzen's giants rampaging across an Island–they were yet to come, she reminded herself. Here were two opposed forces which could turn the Island-World upon its axis.

Time to pull no punches.

She said, "So, mother, I do know one way to advance our cause."

"Oh?"

"Why don't we consult the Maroon Dragoness?" Lia turned her most ingenuous smile on Azziala. "You were planning to tell me about Ianthine, weren't you, mother?"

She hoped to shock Azziala, but the perverse maternal pride her goading provoked was more shocking by far. The golden visage cracked into an openly avaricious grin. She said, "Oh, we're not quite the ingénue we pretend to be, are we, my little star? Very good. Let's you and I go question the Dragoness about your unexpected flair for the dark pathways of *ruzal*, shall we?"

Despair turned her hopes to ashes. Lia knew she was embroiled in a battle for her soul.

Chapter Thirty-One

A Promise Kept

WHY, AFTER ESCAPING from her prison in the Spits, would Ianthine choose to return to the Lost Islands? This question throbbed foremost in Lia's aching head as she walked with her mother to the Dragon holding pens, many levels down into the bowels of her underground stronghold. Was this Ianthine's cunning in action? It had to be deliberate. What did she stand to gain? If the Maroon Dragoness knew she would be enslaved, the reward must be commensurate with the sacrifice, according to most draconic logic–but Ianthine was no ordinary Dragoness. She was a maverick. A loner. Quite possibly insane.

Ianthine was also the only Dragon Azziala had referred to with a modicum of respect. Hualiama puzzled away at the similarities she sensed between her mother and the Dragoness as they traversed a floor of extensive Dragonship engineering works–preparations for war roaring along twenty-seven hours a day–creating a ripple of stiff, respectful bows. Lia was dressed in an old tunic top, dark leggings and a deep blue robe borrowed from Azziala's trunk of cast-offs, with her Nuyallith blade belted at her right hip. Time and again, the Islanders they encountered mistook her for the Empress, before taking in her wealth of white-blonde hair and doing a double take. Not encouraging for someone who might be planning to skulk in a few dark corners …

The ripe, spicy odour of many Dragons corralled in close quarters attacked Hualiama's nostrils as they took a cage-lift down a further eight levels to the holding pens.

"To your right, the harvesting pens," said Azziala, playing the guide.

Disguising how dizzy she felt, Lia coolly watched two Dragon Enchanters tapping into the artery of a Red Dragon's wing–a Red of the southern Archipelago Dragons, she realised, as sleek as Mizuki and half as large again. He stood by stolidly as his golden blood spurted into a large bucket.

"We ration a litre per day per Dragon Enchanter," Azziala said. "Five litres each for the Empress and her Councillors. We require no further sustenance."

Lia nodded. "And the incantation–"

"Draws out the Dragon's magic and binds it into the blood," her mother explained. "The process is key to *dorzallith* and the mainstay of our power. Aye, it weakens the Dragon and eventually kills him. We keep our stocks fresh. As you saw, my Dragonship fleet nears full readiness but there are many vessels yet to clothe in lizard-skin."

A fate worse than death for Dragons, drained of magic as though they were no better than sagging wineskins. "Aye, mother."

This test she would not fail. Raising her chin and denying her incipient tears, Lia followed in her mother's footsteps. They passed many pens, open chambers separated by iron frames and thick stone archways that gave the vast, low underground cavern an air similar to the dungeon beneath King Chalcion's palace. Lia learned that the caverns had been dug out by captured Burrowers, but Azziala dismissed their usefulness for harvesting. Too small and weak. Remembering how the Dragons had overturned the Human village, she could not agree.

"I believe you know this beast," said Azziala.

Hualiama had half-expected such a test, but assumed Azziala would not risk the fate of her two slain Dragon Enchanters. "Oh, Grandion," she said, as neutrally as possible, but she could not disguise the warmth that rushed to her cheeks at the sight of the Tourmaline Dragon, nor the sweet clenching sensation deep in her belly. "He looks well. Sleek."

"We do not name the reptiles. Names carry power," Azziala warned, watching her charge narrowly. "Watch. Beast, this is Hualiama. Do you remember her?"

Before she could blink, the Dragon's entire ninety-foot length tensed up, shuddering with pent-up power. His belly-fires roared as if thunder rolled in the distance, muted.

"DRAGON, BE STILL!" the Empress snapped, lashing out with her magic. Grandion subsided.

With all her heart, she would have run to her Dragon, but Lia caught sight of an additional posse of Dragon Enchanters observing the encounter from the shadows beneath one of the archways. They were taking no chances with Grandion. Could she conclude that he remained strong?

"Our command-hold upon these beasts is absolute," Azziala continued, her dark blue eyes unblinking. "Dragon, prepare to tear out your first heart."

Grandion unsheathed his claws and raised his forepaw to his throat.

"No," Hualiama breathed, dipping her gaze.

"What was that, daughter?"

Her voice faltered. "We'll need his strength in the upcoming war, mother."

"You seem disturbed."

"Unnecessary bloodshed always disturbs me." Hualiama hardened her jaw. "We can use this beast as leverage against his shell-father. Come. The Maroon Dragoness can offer us more. I'm convinced of it."

If she practised the ways and the language of hatred, it became easier. How could her pure white-fires coexist with the shadow of *ruzal?* That was the question she had for Ianthine. She had never learned the vile magic. It simply existed.

Hualiama preceded her mother down the hay-strewn corridor leading between the Dragon pens, listening to the conversation of dull, defeated beasts all around. Comments on the quality and quantity of meat they had consumed. Wishes for flight and fresh air, or battle. Gi'ishior's vitality of draconic community was utterly absent. These were herd animals, being milked for their lives.

At the cave's end, massive stone doors guarded egress to the frozen night and presumably, protected the caves from attack. Hualiama risked only the briefest glance at the doors' mechanisms. Azziala's regard burned the nape of her neck, making Lia picture a cobra salivating over a tasty rat.

Her mother's voice formed in her mind. "Aye. You sense the lizard, don't you?"

Wary of Azziala's telepathic powers, Lia returned, "Last cell on the left. Is she subject to a command-hold, like the others?"

"Aye."

But there were no additional Dragon Enchanters to subjugate Ianthine, if needed? Almost instantaneously, a command issued from her mother's mind, summoning a dozen Enchanters at the behest of the heir to the throne.

The Empress' depthless eyes, shadowed to the point of blackness, fixed upon Lia. "Allow me to teach you the command structures, daughter dearest. Say, 'Dragon, obey'."

"Give me the knowledge."

Her counter-challenge brought a touch of a smile to Azziala's lips. "Here." A mental touch sufficed to convey what she needed to know, although Lia might have bet half of Fra'anior's jewels that the information was incomplete. Some secrets must remain the Empress'.

Suppressing a crazy urge to dance around the final column–wishing to cast aside necessary inhibitions–Lia stepped forward to face Ianthine. Six years became as a moment. Here was the monstrous Dragoness, almost rivalling Yukari for bulk, still blighted and unsightly, powerful and … enchained? Perplexed, Hualiama took a moment to assemble the knowledge she required. What part had *ruzal* played in a Human baby's life? Was she *ruzal*-spawn, as her own father and others had accused her? Only Ianthine knew the truth. This was a Dragoness notorious for her cunning, one of a race of creatures who prized cunning and practised it with their every breath.

Instinctively, Lia moved to the commands. "Dragon, obey. Positive identifier required: Hualiama of Fra'anior."

"Princess Hualiama." Ianthine's dry whisper echoed in the chamber. "It has been too long."

From the corner of her eye, the royal ward saw Azziala's hand twitch with readiness. Aye. Her mother also knew this for a strange answer from a Dragoness subject to the command-hold. Defying the shadows that perversely seemed to collect around Ianthine's ulcerated bulk, her eye blazed darkly orange, bursting with the fires of Dragon life and power.

The Human girl wet her lips. "Dragon, answer my questions."

"Yours to command, freshly anointed heir of these accursed rocks," sneered the Dragoness.

"DRAGON, OBEY!" Azziala snapped. Was that a note of panic?

"As you command, Highness," Ianthine bowed her great muzzle in mock-subservience. Or was it? Tenuous as the magic's control over her might be, that was all they could rely upon.

"Dragon, do you still hold that Ra'aba is my father?"

"Is it still scarred?" The Dragon sniffed toward her. "Ah, it slithers within, delicious, delicate, devious *ruzal.*"

"Aye or nay, Ianthine!"

"So similar to the mother, it is." Ianthine cocked her head playfully, as a Dragon hatchling might during a game of wingtips. "Did she tell you about the twin? Which is the mother?"

"Silence, Dragon!" Azziala ordered.

"Now she won't answer anything," Hualiama pointed out, placing a quelling hand upon her mother's arm. "Dragon, obey. Is Ra'aba my father?"

"One must have a Human father." Ianthine tapped her foreclaw thrice, an ancient form of Dragonish agreement. "He scarred thee. He sired thee. One must know, who stole the seed from–"

"Silence, Dragon!"

Frustration boiled out of Lia. "Mother! Shall we ask our questions or not?" Mercy! And the implications … that was another issue. That whole stinking Dragonship-full of windroc entrails would have to wait. "Dragon, obey. Answer my questions. What became of the Scroll of Binding? Was it truly stolen, as you said?"

The fires danced in Ianthine's eye, mocking. "Aye, it was stolen."

"Stolen by whom?"

"Ianthine."

"Roaring rajals, answer my question honestly, Dragoness!" The Maroon Dragoness' chuckle, awash with malevolence, stilled the other Dragons nearby. Lia fought for calm. "Who stole it first?"

"Ianthine."

"What is the Scroll of Binding?"

"A scroll of Dragon lore said to outline the knowledge of–"

"I know that. Did you read it?"

"In part."

"Outline one of those parts for me."

"I've forgotten."

Azziala cursed unhappily, but Lia found her mind racing back over the information she knew, the conniving ways of Dragons, identifying and discarding possibilities … her mother might be stymied, but her daughter had reserves of stubbornness one could build an Island's foundations upon. "Dragon. Who wrote the Scroll of Binding?"

"It is unseen. Many generations of Dragons lived before Ianthine's time. You have power, child. Spend it wisely."

The exact phrase flung Hualiama six years back in time. Suddenly she saw herself in that stinking, faeces-smeared cavern, listening to Ianthine taunting her, Flicker and Grandion. Intuition struck her with the force of forked lightning. The Maroon Dragoness wanted to remind her of the bargain Lia had unwisely made. Did that bargain still hold? Further, Lia established the most likely source of her knowledge of *ruzal*–he whom the Lost Islanders worshipped as father, benefactor, law-giver and Human most noble.

Dramagon.

She had power. Knowledge was power. Knowledge was also peril.

Unconsciously, Lia's left forefinger wrote a rune up her belt, beside where it had come to rest upon the hilt of her sword. *It is remembered,* the simple glyph stated. The Dragoness allowed fire to fill her mouth but kept it behind her fangs, then snuffed it out and blew the smoke aside from her visitors.

"Hualiama." Azziala nudged her impatiently.

"Dragon, obey. Where is the scroll now?"

"Lost."

"Where is the knowledge of the scroll?"

Ianthine's eye-fires brightened as if Lia approached the nub of the matter at last. "The knowledge resides within the souls of all those who practice *ruzal*. You. Me. Ra'aba, Razzior …"

"Where would I find the greatest concentration of *ruzal* in this Island-World?"

Now, the brow-ridges drew down. "It is unseen."

"Unseen, but clearly present," the Fra'aniorian Islander retorted, recalling her tutelage at Grandion's paw. "Knowledge is unseen … aye! Ianthine–" Azziala hissed at her usage of the Dragoness' name "–confirm hypothesis: Ianthine stole the Scroll of Binding. She caused herself to forget its contents and even its location. When she flew to Gi'ishior with the babe, nothing could be proven during the Dragons' interrogation, because self-evidently, Ianthine had forgotten everything to do with the Scroll."

"Thus, it is forgotten," agreed the Dragoness, examining her paws.

"Can it be un-forgotten?"

"A logical fallacy," the Dragoness reproved her. "Complete forgetting implies a forgotten method of retrieval, otherwise there's no point in forgetting."

Azziala growled, "This is ridiculous double-talk! She stole the accursed Scroll before we could learn its secrets. Now she has forgotten everything? How propitious! We'll learn nothing here, daughter."

"No," said Lia. "Ianthine did steal the Scroll of Binding."

"Windroc droppings!"

Hualiama gritted her teeth. "Mother! Don't you understand–I told you Ra'aba accused me of being born of *ruzal*, of being … oh, mercy! Oh no. Tell me it isn't true. Mercy, mercy, mercy …"

She doubled over, clutching her stomach.

"Oh, stand up, child," Azziala snapped.

"Nay." The Maroon Dragoness shifted closer. "What is it? What is this terror-stench I smell upon your skin?"

Words tumbled out of her now, uncaring, as raw as a weeping wound. "Dragon. Was I born of *ruzal?* Conceived of it? Born of a Dragon?"

"How can I discern this?" asked the Dragoness.

"Dragon. The babe whom you accepted from Azziala–did she have any *ruzal* within her? Did you sense the taint that exists in me now?"

Ianthine said, "No."

The Empress scowled at them both in turn. "This makes no sense."

"It m-m-makes p-perfect sense," Lia stammered. "The Scroll of Binding was lost, but the *knowledge* exists. It is unseen. Don't you see, mother? Ianthine did steal something–me, in a manner of speaking. A babe. And she placed inside of me the knowledge contained in the Scroll of Binding. She stole the Scroll twice."

"No." More grey than gold infused Azziala's features now.

"Everything fits. Every answer the Dragoness gave is true. And you were so willing to give me up–you gave the Scroll away. You said, 'Take Ra'aba's whelp, Ianthine. Use it against him.' How else could I *know* this magic as if I had been born to it, mother? I was born of violation, but not of *ruzal*." Turning to Ianthine, she said, "You were protecting the Dragonkind, just as you claimed at Gi'ishior. Did you not say, '*All Dragons will know that Ianthine saved them from a fate worse than death*?"

Ianthine rumbled, "You mistake me for a noble Dragoness."

Yet here she was in the Lost Islands, serving the Dragonkind in her own demented way. Hualiama could not help feeling a thawing of her heart toward the strange, tormented Maroon Dragoness.

Azziala stared at Hualiama as though she had breathed Dragon fire from her nostrils. "You speak Dragonish? Did I just hear you speak–"

"Of course." Lia jutted out her chin. "I am the Dragonfriend, after–"

She never saw what struck the point of her chin with the kick of a war crossbow fired in anger.

* * * *

Hualiama could only have been unconscious for a few seconds, because she came to at the Empress' feet, with an aching jaw and an equally painful lump on the back of her head. Her mother must have punched her!

"DRAGON, OBEY!" her mother thundered. "You will obey! I command you by the strictest protocols to release the *ruzal* within my daughter. Then, she will write the Scroll of Binding afresh."

"It is forgotten."

A curse and a magical buffet punished Ianthine for her imperturbable reply. The Maroon Dragoness fell heavily upon her side, gasping with pain. Azziala screamed, "I'll do worse if you don't obey!"

"Stop. Mother …"

"You're in cahoots with this foul lizard, this–"

"Mother! I know how!"

Slowly, the Empress of the Lost Islands turned upon her heel, her visage terrible to behold. "Do you, now? I don't need to wring the knowledge out of my precious, lizard-loving daughter's head?"

"No. Mother–mercy, don't you understand? The Dragoness doesn't remember, but I know because I've seen visions of–" oh, mercy, and her stupid dragonet's tongue had just babbled another secret! Lia continued lamely "–uh, visions of the past."

For a second, Lia almost believed that another face peered out of Azziala's face, a cruel, alien thing, so brutally scarred that it appeared to possess neither nose nor left eye. However, her mother's face returned to its normal planes of arrogant golden perfection before Lia could dwell upon it. Her hands twitched as though she itched to wrap her long, powerful fingers about her daughter's neck and choke the life out of her.

"Show me," said Azziala.

The form was simple, the implications profound. Had the Maroon Dragoness been trying to warn her about unchaining the *ruzal*? Yet how could she exorcise this evil from her being if it remained bound, obeying the original command of one who had implanted the dread knowledge into an innocent?

Lia squeezed her eyelids shut. How could she bear yet more torment? If the Dragoness spoke truthfully, she was no abomination. Heartening, but her relief had been supplanted with the knowledge that she was the repository of the foulest of Dragon lore, a subject doubtless an intimate favourite of Dramagon's. The prophecy was true. She carried the seeds of draconic destruction in her flesh, as Ra'aba had once accused her–which begged the question. Why did he care?

Too many complexities! A soft scream died unvented from her lips. Instead, words formed upon the scrolleaf of her heart, a song she had composed while crossing the straits between Erigar and Archion.

For the power of love is greater than any Dragon,
Greater than magic, greater than soul-fire,
It changes the immutable,
Breaks all chains,
And stirs the Islands to dance.

Could she hope?

Speaking Dragonish, she let words fall like stars plummeting from the skies. *Let it be unbound.*

* * * *

Having spent three hours ruing her simple lie–the *ruzal* had been unbound, but her mind required time to remember more than the sketchiest detail–Hualiama collapsed into her bed-bowl with the grace of a punctured Dragonship air sack late that evening. What a day. Her mother clearly did not accept 'no' for an answer. She, Feyzuria and Shazziya had taken turns trying first to cajole and later to wrench or pound the knowledge of *ruzal* out of their unwilling subject. Unsuccessfully. Lia had the impression that the harder they tried, the deeper the magic concealed its perfidious presence.

Failure in Azziala's realm was clearly as painful as it was intolerable.

Oh, Grandion. What would the Tourmaline Dragon think of her now? Child of the prophecy, but no child of the Dragon, unless that appellation referred to the gift of Dragon fire. Lia flexed her fingers, remembering how her hands had burned, how the power of a single word had tossed Razzior across the Cloudlands. She still had to take Azziala to task over two things she had learned–one, that Azziala's twin might have been her real mother, and two, the monstrous accusation that it had been Azziala who had somehow overpowered or stolen from Razzior in order to have her baby.

Now the Empress was afoot, checking on preparations for Razzior's arrival by the eve of the morrow. War. The fortress bustled with activity. All day, Dragonships had been bringing Humans in from the outlying Islands, until the fortress threatened to burst at the seams.

Tonight might be the perfect opportunity to abscond with Grandion. Only one fly wriggled in the stinking ointment of her life–how? All Azziala had to do was *think* and she was as good as captured.

Too agitated to even lay her head down, Lia leaped out of bed, picked up her Nuyallith blade, and proceeded to dice up the air of the Empress' private chambers into the smallest chunks possible. She slew enemies and swooped upon Dragons and razed fortresses, all in quick order. Ha! Take that, Razzior … panting, the only female warrior-monk ever to disgrace the Cluster of Fra'anior glowered at her reflection in the tall mirror her mother used to polish her Empress-of-Doom impressions. Mercy, Razzior would employ this weakling to clean his gums, never mind his fangs.

Just then, her reflection stepped out of the mirror.

Hualiama dropped the blade with a clang. Flaming eyes, maroon hair–*Ianthine? How on the Islands …*

We need to talk, said the image. *You were smart today, child who presumes to style herself the Dragonfriend.*

Talking to herself had to count as one of the more mind-bending moments in her life. Hualiama pinched the skin of her wrist surreptitiously. Awake? Aye. *Talk about what, Ianthine? An old promise?*

The eyes suffused with draconic fury. *You intend to renounce our bargain?*

No. That would be … unwise. Ianthine snorted in a distinctly non-Human way as the nuances of Lia's Dragonish conveyed rather more than the royal ward wished. Flushing, she clarified, *Against my nature, I meant.*

O sweet, moral bearer of ruzal? The Maroon Dragoness, in contrast, was a master of nuance. Sarcasm, approbation and concern were only a few fragrances among the rich bouquet her Dragonish offered. *You're unsurprised by this power of projection? Ah, Grandion. Of course. A young rebel to the core. Are you two competing to tally how many secrets and oaths you can wreck in your respective lifetimes?*

Her blush developed into a bonfire. *You risked this communication merely to insult me?*

Thousands of years of history and Humans have never figured out the power of projection? Ghosts, visions, voices in the night, celestial beings, gods and goddesses–your kind are so easily manipulated! We Dragons–

Make your point, Dragoness. The Human projection's eyes swirled exactly like a Dragon's eye-fires at Lia's acerbic tone. *What do you want, Ianthine?*

Help me escape.

Dragon-direct! Hualiama caught her breath. And seal her fate with these Dragon-Haters? If she could simultaneously depart with Grandion, that would be a trick! But she needed information.

That's a big ask, Ianthine. I'd sacrifice any remaining goodwill I have–

To her surprise, the Dragoness did not blast her feeble attempt at negotiation with the verbal fireball it deserved. The Dragoness said, *We've mutual interests, Dragonfriend. I abused a helpless Human hatchling. You unwittingly helped me escape first Azziala, and later the Spits. Unlike many Dragonkind, I value transparency and brevity. Speak. I'm listening.*

You've changed from the Dragoness I remember. How did you neutralise the Dragon Enchanters' command-hold?

Ianthine countered, *What do* you *want, Hualiama?*

To escape with Grandion. And to know how to rid my life of this ruzal *power. And … any information which might help Grandion and I survive when Azziala comes for me.*

The image of herself bowed. *Bargain accepted.*

Lia inclined her head. *Likewise.*

At once, Ianthine asked, *What did you conclude about the nature of* ruzal *today, Hualiama?*

You saw my hesitation. This Dragoness was as sharp as her talons! But could she be trusted? Lia judged the proposed exchange too valuable to deny all but the most explosive of her secrets. *I believe* ruzal *is somehow connected to Dramagon's life and work. It appears to … respond, I guess, to threats of removal or discovery. It feels animate. Whatever binding you placed upon the knowledge of* ruzal *in a baby, which kept such an evil bound for twenty-one years, this magic still managed to escape, or leak, or whatever it did.*

Ianthine's lips peeled back over her fangs, indicating draconic approval. *A potent combination of intuition and logic, youngling, but the truth is grimmer yet. Think of it this way–how best to convey this to one unversed in Dragonish magic? You host a spiritual extract of Dramagon, the concentrated essence of his thought-life distilled into the constellated structures of magic we Dragons call* ruzal. *I only deduced this recently.*

A wheeze constituted her only possible reply.

Suddenly, Ianthine seemed to startle. The pace of her speech trebled.

See what became of me, Dragonfriend? I tried to transfer ruzal *from the Scroll of Binding into you, and was struck by the backlash of its power. Aye, you gasp.* Ruzal *is a living entity, the antithesis of the creative power the Ancient Dragons used to raise up these Islands. It is the ultimate negation, twisting all it touches. I fear that to exorcise a frail Human shell of Dramagon's Ancient Dragon lore will cost your very soul!* The image juddered, her voice growing faint. *You can be Grandion's anchor. The key is that Azziala's people require line-of-sight. Anytime they can see you, they can exert their psychic power upon you and try to change your thoughts or stun you or take over your Dragon. Duality, Hualiama. You must enfold Grandion's spirit within yours. That will protect him. He must protect you with his magic, using these constructs.*

Hualiama flinched as Ianthine hurled knowledge at her. White daggers speared behind her eyes, the pain however so sharp and fleeting, that her next breath brought instant relief. *What? Ianthine, please …*

They can penetrate most Blue Dragon shielding. Use the knowledge I gave you. The image wavered again, almost disappearing. *I must fly.*

How do you–

Duality. Insanity. I'm two in one, like your precious mother. Ianthine read her unspoken question effortlessly. Abruptly, her roar struck like a clap of thunder in the Human girl's mind, *That's the gift and the curse Sapphurion and his kin left me, after banishing me to the Spits! Accursed, ignorant fools!*

Lia pressed her fingers to her temples, feeling as though her veins were about to burst. *Don't, please …*

A word, Hualiama! Help me. Just a word from the Scroll …

Wait, Ianthine. How could she judge what portion of the *ruzal* knowledge she feared even to examine in the smallest iota, might be safely entrusted to the Maroon Dragoness? Fool! Never trust a Dragon.

WAIT? YOU PROMISED!

This time, Hualiama was ready for the blast. She had stood up to Grandion. Bracing herself against the stormy wash, she summoned the courage to keep her promises, no matter the consequences. She must not continue to be beholden to Ianthine. There lay the Island of a different madness. *Ruzal* knowledge budded at her tentative touch, eager to interact, quivering, guileful. Mercy. And while the power seduced her, a velveteen veil concealed a monster beneath, a Dragon-like shadow so oily-dark, it seemed the emptiness turned in upon itself to devour all that was good and real and worthy.

Finding a *ruzal* construct which allowed a Dragon to burrow through almost any shield, Lia bundled it up and flung the knowledge at the Maroon Dragoness.

Ah! With a triumphant screech, Ianthine's projection vanished, leaving Lia alone in the darkness.

Chapter Thirty-Two

Bonding

NEXT HUALIAMA KNEW, Azziala's hand shook her shoulder. She awoke, groggy from the nightmares filled with Ancient Dragons bickering and biting, thundering and fighting over her. Numistar, Fra'anior, Amaryllion and Dramagon. Four Ancient Dragons sporting eleven heads between them. Somehow, just before her mother's touch, they had merged into a single beast who ravaged the Island-World …

"Islands' greetings, daughter," chirped Azziala, so cheerily that Lia tripped over the bed's edge and measured her length on the rushes with an inelegant grunt. "Never a finer morning to start a war, wouldn't you agree?"

"Er–delightful, mother."

"I know just the medicine for you, grumpy girl. We'll have some lovely mother-daughter bonding time. Aren't I just the sweetest and loveliest parent ever to tread the Islands?"

Collecting her person and her jaw off the ground separately, Lia hastily assembled a smattering of cogent thought. What had bitten Azziala? The Enchantress quaffed a large goblet of fresh Dragon blood. She practically buzzed with energy and weird … exuberance. Mistrustful, Lia glanced about the room. No monsters of *ruzal* lurked in the corners. She felt remarkably refreshed considering the gigantic reptilian battle which had made her head its stomping ground for most of the night.

"Eat," said her mother, thrusting a dark rye bread-roll into her hand. "Council meeting first thing. Snip snap, dear daughter." What had snapped was her mother's mind. "Oh, we'll stop by and see your father first. He should know his old cronies will arrive in my realm today."

That was vintage Azziala, her words swirling with malign undercurrents.

"The Maroon Dragoness escaped last night." Lia choked on her bread roll, but a hard-handed slap between her shoulders from the Empress dislodged the offending crumbs. "Slipped away like the cold mists of a Lost Islands night. You wouldn't know anything about that, would you, my little star?" Before Lia could do more than feel cold sweat break out on her neck, Azziala laughed, "I could Reave you again and find nothing. Isn't it so? Because you're like me, aren't you?"

"A secret twin?"

Lia winced. Always, as the pressure ratcheted up, her secrets began to leak out of her. But Azziala only threw back her head and laughed coldly, making the pair of Enchantresses guarding Ra'aba's cell, stiffen in fear. They must imagine their nemesis stalked the corridor.

"No, Hualiama. I mean that in the mind-meld, you're able to share selectively. Oh, I enjoyed your carefully edited account of your doings you gave us during that first interrogation–my twelve swallowed it all, like fat lake trout guzzling down a swarm of tantalising dragonflies. Even now, you appear blameless."

"Rightly." Lia swallowed a lump the size of an Island. "I didn't free–"

"Deceit does not become you," snarled her mother. "You're exactly like me. Cold logic coupled with warm intuition. My enchantresses are all logic. No, you did nothing. Nothing detectable. But my bones ache, daughter. I *know* you're involved." She gripped Lia's upper arm with fingers as clawed as a Dragon's talons, stopping the blood. "We'll have plenty of time to get to know each other after this little war is done. You weren't planning to cross your dear mother, were you?"

"No." Fly as far as humanly possible from her power-mad mother–aye!

"Good. Because I want to show you how serious I am,

daughter. Deadly serious." Arriving at Ra'aba's cell, she snapped, "Open the door. And the inner one. Come."

To her surprise, Lia found two further Enchantresses seated within, in the section separated from Ra'aba's living area. Shazziya lifted a grim eyebrow. The other was Gyrthina, a fierce warrior and leader of the Enchantresses in battle. When the inner door opened, Gyrthina marched within, seized Ra'aba by the scruff of his neck, and cast him at the Empress' feet. Ra'aba whimpered, but said nothing.

Why the silence? Lia's gaze leaped about the cell like the fluttering of a trapped bird. What force gathered around them as though a storm-front of fate bore down upon the room? What was this tension pregnant in the smile curving Azziala's golden lips, Gyrthina's alert stance and the expectant glitter deep in Shazziya's shadowed gaze? Superimposed upon the trio, she saw dark-fires pouring from their inner beings and her own white-fire rallying in response. All about, the shadowy forms of Ancient Dragons writhed and reared in monstrous battle. Mercy! She was a mote in this draconic cosmos. The strain changed her consciousness, peeling away the layers of reality until she knew the stone beneath her feet was just the physical realm and the powers of the Ancient Dragon-Spirits she had once so glibly evoked to turn Sapphurion back to the Receiving Balcony, were real and awesome …

"Ra'aba." Azziala's brow darkened. "I suppose you fed her that lie about Razzior forcing you to do it?"

The man trembled. "Burning orange, lava in the mind …"

"You believed this wretch, Hualiama?" Azziala's scorn could not pull her away from the chaos enveloping her mind. Numbed, she simply nodded. "The truth is, Ra'aba was a powerful Enchanter discipled by Razzior, but the pupil became greater than the master. Ra'aba dominated Razzior. He filched what he needed from that lizard, and shaped Razzior into his tool. Ra'aba's mind was a tower of strength until we broke him."

Draconic mind-power. Control eerily similar to what Azziala's people achieved in their command-hold over Dragons, Hualiama realised. She said, "He possessed the Scroll of Binding."

"His father. A renegade from Fra'anior."

Ruzal twisted all it touched, Ianthine had warned her. Aye, the touch of *ruzal* upon Razzior's life had twisted the beast, were Azziala's version of the story true.

"I was a young Enchantress. Ra'aba had all the power of *ruzal* at his fingertips, all he had stolen from Razzior to make himself strong. Let this be a lesson to you, daughter. He overpowered me."

Still kneeling, Ra'aba raised his hands, imploring, "She took what she wanted from me, Hualiama. You have to believe me!"

Power was attracted to power, Sapphurion had warned her. Now she knew the truth of it. Standing over Ra'aba, Azziala's face seemed diamond-hard, carved in grief. Her hands were locked white-knuckled upon her belt. Blood-father and blood-mother faced her, equally reprehensible.

"You abused your power," Azziala hissed.

"You found no viable seed in me," Ra'aba returned, cackling his insane laugh. "Who knows how the likes of you brewed this vile whelp!"

"No." The Empress loomed over him, vengeful. "From that day, she swelled in my womb. Am I not an Enchantress? I knew the instant of conception. I recognised the new life within me. For months, I fought the desire to terminate her nascent life–for do we not say, 'created in hatred, whelped in sorrow?' After six months, I received my wish–and what a sweet relief it was. She died."

"What?" Lia's knees failed. She crashed to the stone.

"What?" gasped Ra'aba.

"You died." A tic twisted Azziala's cheek, pinching the muscles as she stared wild-eyed at Hualiama. "Four midwives and twelve Enchantresses confirmed it–your spirit had flown upon the Island-World's winds. It seemed the child but slept, yet her heart lay unmoving. After the prescribed two days, we prepared to remove the body. We made the drink we give women to bring on labour."

Hualiama felt as though she had been stabbed afresh in the gut. "Y-y-you're lying!"

"Stillbirth is not uncommon."

"I'm here. I'm your flesh, alive …"

"Are you?" The Enchantress gripped Ra'aba's wild, greasy black hair in her fist. "Bastard whelp of a windroc! What inhuman spawn of your blackest *ruzal* did you inflict on me that day?"

"Mother …" Lia's throat closed. Truth. It blazed in Azziala's eyes, a colder, more reaming fire than she had ever known. All she could do was raise her eyebrows in mute query.

"Nothing, no … you did it …" Ra'aba babbled.

"We had laid out the birthing cloths upon my bed. Singing the mourning song, the midwives dressed me in the white of death. That was when you moved. You began to *dance*."

Suddenly, the Empress' countenance seemed to melt. A new voice, a cackle like a windroc's screech, issued from her mouth. "And you call me the mad one?"

"Shut up, sister."

Hualiama gaped as though ensorcelled. Her body shook with every great, pounding drumbeat of her pulse. She wanted to clap her hands over her ears and flee, but the madness kept playing out before her, on and on as though it would never end.

The other voice said, "I always wondered if that child died of a broken heart."

"I know nothing," her father moaned.

Azziala screamed, "Stop it, stop it, stop *meeee!*"

The Enchantress' right hand blurred. Ra'aba made a sound like a stifled gurgle. Hualiama, who had blinked, saw an unaccountably peaceful expression cross her father's face. He tried to speak, but blood bubbled on his lips. Then, as though a ghastly brush-stroke had painted his neck, crimson welled in a long, thin line and spilled down his chest. Ra'aba slumped.

Crouching, Azziala cleaned her dagger-blade on Ra'aba's trousers. She said, "You were such a tiny babe. Bursting with life's fires. I had to give you to the Dragoness, don't you see? I had no choice."

Ra'aba had said exactly the same.

Now he lay in a spreading pool of blood, the hole of his

windpipe clearly visible inside his slit throat.

The Island-shaking outrage of Ancient Dragons filled her mind. Azziala was speaking, her lips moving, but Hualiama heard nothing as she pitched forward down Fra'anior's long, long throat and into a void of blackness.

* * * *

Hualiama awoke to the sight of Shazziya dipping her forefinger in Ra'aba's blood and tasting it. "So, Azziala found her courage at last. No magic left here. Shameful end for an evil man."

Azziala and Gyrthina had departed. Lia pushed to her feet. Wandering over as though dazed by her father's demise, Lia reflected that this was the first thing Shazziya had said she agreed with. Without a word, she raised her foot and kicked Shazziya squarely in the jaw.

The cobblers made Lost Islands boots square in the toe, stitched from reinforced Dragon hide. Shazziya's teeth clacked together with a horrible sound, but she remained conscious. Sickened to her stomach, Lia had to kick the groaning woman twice more before she subsided next to Ra'aba. She marched out of the unguarded cell door, then paused. One last thing.

Lia said, "I'm sorry it ended like this, father. I cannot say I feel much pity for you. Your pain is ended. May you rest in the peace you never enjoyed in life."

Words. Why should she comfort this man, either in death or in life? Or did the living speak over the dead to assuage their conscience, or conceal a wounding grief? Maybe she should tell Shazziya she had rather enjoyed kicking her in the head? That would balance the fates appropriately. Suppressing a wicked-Enchantress chuckle, Lia slipped down the empty corridor toward Azziala's chambers. She could not bear to abide among these Dragon-Haters one second longer.

Armed, re-shod and wrapped in a midnight-blue Enchantress cloak, Hualiama prepared to break out of the fortress-Isle of Chenak, Azziala's stronghold. Drawing deep from the Juyhallith and Nuyallith lore she had learned, she formulated a shield and a disguise. Midway, the *nzal* shocked her by offering a different solution–to alter her appearance. No. The path to the inferno began with just such a temptation. Easy. Small. Almost no thought required. Grim-lipped, the Princess braided her long, easily-identifiable hair, coiled it up, and tied the bundle with a leather thong. She put up her hood, and padded to the doorway. She loved these monk-slippers–soft and tacky, a silent invitation to nefarious doings.

Time to go rescue her Dragon. Again.

Hualiama had lifted the fortress' schematics from Feyzuria's mind–a vaster network of Burrower-excavated caverns and tunnels than she had ever imagined. Now, straight of back and arrogant of stride, a woman who looked much like Feyzuria slipped down through the fortress, wondering how exactly one avoided the detection of telepathic mental giants in their own territory. How long would Shazziya remain unconscious?

She received her answer within three minutes. Lia had barely descended four levels in the metal cage-lift when it ground to an abrupt halt. Her mind rang with a mental summons.

"FIND MY DAUGHTER!"

Line-of-sight, Ianthine had said. Hualiama glanced up and down the shaft. Thick rope hawsers connected the cage to a winch system above, much like a certain mine she had once burgled. There was a small gap in the centre of the platform through which the hawsers ran, allowing the trailing end of the hawser a free run. Usually, everything in this place operated to a tightly-monitored schedule. Lia had counted on the turmoil of war preparations to be her ally. Not so. Someone approached the shaft, above, to check the stalled lift. Soldiers sprinted to their posts, carrying out the checks within their remit of responsibility. Lia blocked out the chaos impinging on her mind. Go!

Thank heavens for a tiny frame. Wriggling into the platform's central hole, Hualiama wrapped her legs around the rope and swarmed downward with the skill of an adept Dragonship pilot. She hoped nobody looked up.

Two levels passed by without incident. Storage levels.

Perhaps nobody was bothered with those–they had no egress, and were used infrequently. But she had to pass through the Dragonship engineering works ahead. At the third level, a soldier peered over the edge of the tunnel, a four-foot gantry jutting out to make stepping from the cage lift safe and straightforward. His neck twizzled to look first down, and then up. From twenty feet above, Lia pinned him with her last poisoned dart. The man yelped, stiffened and tumbled off the edge. She raced by.

Now she sensed Azziala's mind, searching. Imagining herself a wind-blown mote, Hualiama ghosted through her grasp. Islands' sakes, Azziala was powerful! One more level. Lia swung herself around the hawser like an acrobat to build momentum, and launched herself over to the edge. Misjudged. A frantic grab fetched a fingertip hold on the edge. Panting, Lia swung her feet up and hid beneath the platform. Here came two soldiers, checking this level for the man who had fallen. The mental lattice strengthened under the directive of the Enchantresses, closing off possibilities, tightening the net in a frightening exhibition of co-ordination and teamwork. Grasping a metal stanchion in both hands, she swung back and forth twice, before arching her body upward with a supreme effort. She locked her legs around a soldier's neck and yanked him off the edge.

"Aaaaaahhhh!" he wailed on the way down.

Repeating the manoeuvre, Lia released her hands as she swung up onto the platform, and came within inches of suffering the same fate as the first soldier. His overzealous partner tried to charge her, but she was smaller and lower than he expected. He pitched over her legs and took a brief flight down the shaft. Nasty.

Hualiama bounced to her feet, dashed along the short connecting tunnel and dived behind the first stack of crates she found. Great. This cavern was heaving. She could not simply kill everyone in sight. Her eye fell on a furnace used by the metalworkers to forge Dragonship parts. Oh. What a nice little fire. Unattended. Hualiama had always been fond of fire, particularly when it came wrapped in gemstone-blue hide!

Seconds later, she removed a spadeful of red-hot coals from the glowing heart of the furnace, and tossed them onto a nearby stack of coiled-up ropes. One more. Sneaking around the edge of the cavern, ducking beneath ropes and gantries, Hualiama set a second location alight. Burn!

When sufficient smoke billowed from the spreading fires, she simply marched out into the open. "You! Put out those fires!"

"Aye, Enchantress!"

She marched right through the middle of the engineering works, her heart not giving her chest a second's respite from a good thrashing. Almost at the end, she paused. Ooh, meriatite. That conjured up all sorts of interesting possibilities. Lugging a sack, the Princess of perfidy–to coin a phrase which would have made her madcap brother wriggle in delight–moved steadily to the next platform. Drat. Three soldiers. No choice but to play out her arrogant, assumed station.

"You three. Take me down. I'm to check the heir isn't hiding among the lizards."

They glanced at her curiously. Perhaps Enchantresses did not explain their business so openly? One of them began a mental query. As swiftly as an angry cobra, Hualiama's *ruzal* reached out and modified his thought. Roaring rajals, it could do that? Lia stuffed the magic back where it belonged.

"I'm waiting," she snarled.

Hiding in plain sight? This could not end well.

The lift, however, operated perfectly. Hualiama arrived at the Dragon holding pens only slightly out of breath, to find hordes of Dragon Enchanters rushing about, renewing the command-holds on their captives. Way down at the cavern's end, the doors inched shut.

The real Feyzuria stood in the middle of it all, scanning the pandemonium with an experienced eye. Any moment now, she'd turn and see herself on the platform.

"You may return to level five," she said coldly, alighting.

Hualiama strolled casually past the first pen, and then ducked into the second. Right, where was Grandion? Sneaky. They were trying to move him. Out there, Feyzuria turned as if she had sensed the feather-light touch of Lia's mind as she snitched that information from the Enchantress. Perhaps she could turn this mental network to her advantage? No time to think about that.

Laying her hand on the nearest Red Dragon, Lia said, "Dragon, obey. You are my slave. You will do exactly as I command. You will listen only to me and no other voice. "

"Aye." The Red Dragon flexed his massive muscles.

Seconds later, the Red Dragon charged out into the open, smashing one of the stone columns with his tail, and launched a massive lava-fireball down the central corridor of the Dragon pens. Hualiama sprinted after him. Feyzuria was commendably quick to leap aside, but many of the Dragon Enchanters were not. They perished as their robes exploded in sticky, molten-rock fire. Feyzuria crashed into one of the columns and staggered away, clutching her forehead.

"Sorry," said Hualiama, pausing to deliver a whip-snap left hook to her jaw that felled the woman instantly. "No hard feelings." *Grandion! Come to me.*

The Dragon did not respond.

Had they deafened him with their command-hold in addition to the usual commands? Hualiama ran so fast that the cloak whipped out behind her like wings. "Red! Turn and attack any man wearing robes like these." How was she planning to break those stone doors? They had to be ten feet thick.

With her mind on other matters, Lia raced into Grandion's pen and bounced off his flank. Four Dragon Enchanters! Springing aloft, she kneed the foremost of their number in the throat. Then she unsheathed the Nuyallith blade, flickering it around her with deadly accuracy. Azziala must have had the briefest of glimpses, because a sharp, hot pain stabbed into Lia's head just before the last man fell. She finished him with a thrust to the throat.

No time to free Grandion from the command-hold. "Dragon, obey."

Grandion rushed out of his pen to attack the doors with his storm-power. Thunderclap after thunderclap deafened her, drowning out even the sound of Azziala bellowing for her daughter, for someone to report, for any view of the traitor. The doors shook as though kicked by a Dragon, but they seemed to be reinforced. Out in the pens, the Red Dragon created mayhem, pouncing upon any man standing, and the sight of blood and the Red's booming, triumphant battle-challenges made the other Dragons restive. A chorus of angry bellowing rumbled through the caves.

The doors would not yield. She could see no obvious mechanism. Lia ransacked the information she had stolen. Of course. They were operated from three levels above. Smart planning. Shouts came down the corridor, Dragon Enchanters trying to seize the rampant Red with the Empress' help. Merciless claws seized her temples. Lia fell against Grandion's left hind paw as he attacked the doors, over and over, mindlessly. She tasted blood.

"YIELD, DAUGHTER."

"Dragon, smoke," she gasped.

The pain abated as thick, choking smoke billowed around her. Whoever had seen her no longer had line-of-sight, stymieing Azziala, at least for the moment. How could she escape this? Suddenly, Lia began to laugh, but she sounded so much like Ra'aba's maniac cackling in that moment that the mirth died on her lips. Aye. A line or two of Saggaz Thunderdoom ought to throw the proverbial fresh meat to the rajals.

"Dragon, obey. Sing this with me. Use your Storm power."

Thus the Thunderdoom arose, borne on wings afire,
His mighty enemies to smite,
Clawed of heart, his purpose so dark-fire dire,
They fled, howling, into the night!

She could have done no better had she insulted their lineage, shell-mothers and the sacred First Eggs of the Dragonkind in a single breath. The caverns exploded. Huge reptilian bodies churned up the place, frenzied.

Suddenly, another Dragon loomed through the smoke. A

massive Brown. "You. What're you doing?"

He must have escaped the command-hold. *Creating chaos. I'm the Dragonfriend–*

I don't care who you are, hatchling, or that you speak our tongue with a barbarous accent. Are you trying to kill us all? The Brown's accented Dragonish was hard on her inner ear. His eyes blazed darkly. *They'll take us again.*

Free your brethren.

The Brown shook his massive muzzle. *My mind's dark-fires. How?*

Grandion had also seemed confused after exiting the command-hold. Inspiration struck. *Use your Brown powers to break down these doors.*

And find legion Dragon Enchanters on the far side?

Hualiama almost lost her nerve. How could she prevent this fate? The Dragons could make themselves deaf, but the commands were magical. The Dragon Enchanters probably didn't rely on auditory reception to work on a Dragon's mind.

Sight. Dragonsong. *Listen.* She fired thought-chunks at the Brown. *If they see you, they can formulate the command-hold, and they see with their minds so conventional shields simply don't work, not even your vaunted phased mental-metal shields. They can break through those like this, see? So you need physical shielding–clouds, smoke, anything to break that initial contact. Then, if you can't shut them out, fill your mind with Dragonsong. Tell your brethren to sing with all three hearts and concentrate only on the Dragonsong. Maybe that'll be enough to save some. I don't know how else–*

Enough, Dragonfriend. The Brown's fangs gleamed at her. *Here is my life-obligation-gift. My secret name is Jallynthallior!*

White-fires surged around her vision.

In those fires, the knowledge of how to help these Dragons burned within her. A sacrifice of self. "Dragon," she addressed Grandion. "Get your Dragon-kin singing. Storm them with Dragonsong."

Jallynthallior! I need your strength.

Aye. Call me Affurion, my common Dragon name.

Summoning the *ruzal* from the place of darkness, Hualiama bade it attack the ratchet-mechanism holding the doors in place, and the guides that held them in the channels filled with rollers that allowed movement. The dark magic rushed gleefully to its work. The four-winged Brown Dragon wrenched the doors ten feet apart.

Again, growled the Dragon.

A new sound rose above the bedlam. Dragonsong, hauntingly beautiful and infused with the unique melodic interpretations of the Lost Islands Dragonkind, poured from the long throats of two hundred Dragons. Lia gulped back unforeseen tears. Now? Amidst a battle? She lost count at over fifteen separate harmonic melodies as their song gelled, quelling the feral madness of the last few Dragons. No. *Ruzal* was not required; besides, it faltered as the Dragonsong gained strength and clarity. The Human girl searched for the white-fires. Pure and refining. Gracefully, she imbued Affurion's strength with her own unique brand of magic.

The Brown Dragon's eye-fires glowed an eggshell-yellow, almost white. At once, his massive earth-magic strength flowed into the rock, bending it to his Dragon-adamant will. The doors melted downward into the rock, leaving an opening three hundred feet wide to bathe the Dragons and the Dragonfriend in fresh, frosty air. Every Dragon scented freedom. Their Dragonsong swelled to a thrilling pitch.

Fifty Dragonships waited out there.

"HUALIAMA, STOP!"

Honestly, mother? Her daughter had fair winds and a clear sky. What more could she want?

One thing more. A beast of gemstone blue. Turning to Grandion, Hualiama said, "Dragon, obey. Let's burn the heavens together as Dragon and Rider."

Chapter Thirty-Three

The Dragon's Bell

THE TOURMALINE DRAGON charged across the short landing area and unfurled his wings to embrace the dawn above Chenak Island. To his left flank came the Brown Affurion, pumping his double-wings to take off, and then a stream of Dragons in twos and threes poured out the side of the Island. Smoke and mist billowed around them, produced primarily by the Jade Dragons.

Hualiama slapped Grandion's shoulder. "Dragon. Hear your instructions." And she taught him what Ianthine had shown her. Lia's skin prickled as the Tourmaline's magic enveloped them, and the Dragon seemed to sigh as she connected their sight. Already the Dragonwing peeled apart, racing in different directions as the individualistic instincts of their kind took over. Some turned back at once, falling under the sway of the Dragon Enchanters.

There was one sure-fire way to put a stop to that. *Affurion! Let's burn a few Dragonships. Grandion* … he was still unresponsive. What had they done to him?

"Dragon, obey. You are my …" Hualiama sighed. Dragonlove? "Let's whistle up a storm."

"DAUGHTER, YOU'LL REGRET SPITING ME."

Hualiama flipped Azziala a cheeky salute. It was unlikely to be spotted in the haze, but the intent probably communicated if her mother could sense her at all. "Have fun with Razzior, mother."

Grandion banked and powered ahead, accelerating to attack

speed.

"DRAGONS, OBEY! YOU ARE MY SLAVES."

Dozens of Dragons faltered and fell away, many already weakened by the bloodletting and enforced captivity, but the core group around Grandion and Affurion remained compact. They speared toward the Dragonships and lashed out with a hail of fire, acid and ice.

BOOM-BOOM-BOOM! Sweet music to a Dragon's ears. A detectable frisson of excitement jolted Grandion's flight as he dodged several incoming crossbow bolts, and jinked to avoid a tumbling airship cabin. Many simply vanished. Lia wrenched her neck trying to scout in all directions. What had happened? Illusions? Suddenly, more Dragonships–real Dragonships–appeared spaced apart in the air around that initial flotilla, and Hualiama knew they had been duped. Decoys. She groaned. Commands resounded around her as the Dragon Enchanters pounded their magic into the Dragons, picking off targets with gut-twisting ease.

Lia recognised Gyrthina's mind in the midst of the battle, directing her Enchanters with pinpoint accuracy. Dragon after Dragon fell away, overcome by the powerful command-holds of the Enchanters as they worked in pairs. She pressed Grandion into a tight turn, hunting airships. He seemed to have found her, for the Dragon secreted within her mind came alive to her thoughts.

Lightning flashed across the roseate dawn sky. *KAARAABOOM!* An airship imploded.

Laughing, the Brown Dragon flashed past their bow, turning two airships into crumpled balls of metal and cloth with a twist of his power. Acid splattered several others. Lia knew they had to take Gyrthina. Searching, she recoiled as the Enchantress responded with a blast of power. There. Hiding in a cluster of five dirigibles. Palming the small sack of meriatite, Hualiama almost laughed as Grandion's head twisted back over his shoulder, mouth agape. She flung the entire sack down his gullet. A touch of his mind showed her the meriatite being separated into two stomachs, one for holding and one for digestion. Gas billowed forth.

"Dragon, obey. Dragon, obey!" cried the Enchanters, with tenfold strength.

Grandion did not waver. Hualiama received the commands and rejected them, despite experiencing a compelling sucking at her own consciousness. Shock arrested her heartbeat. Could this command-hold work on Humans? She would not be surprised.

"Strike them down, my beauty!" Lia shouted.

Grandion's meriatite-fuelled Dragon fire engulfed the hovering airships as though they had haplessly sailed over an erupting volcano. Perhaps they expected the Tourmaline to succumb. Perhaps they thought their mental shields enough, but they buckled after briefly weathering the firestorm's white-hot onslaught. Gyrthina's thoughts flared, 'Empress! Help—' before her voice snuffed out as if someone had pinched the candle of her life.

Dragons to me! Affurion's joy drew them skyward.

Without Gyrthina's mind directing the battle, the Dragon Enchanters quickly became disorganised, picking overlapping targets or losing track of their charges amidst the heat and flurry of battle. As the Enchanters fell, the Dragons they controlled flew free, except for Grandion. Had Feyzuria renewed his commands? The Princess realised she may have erred by not killing Feyzuria. But she directed her Dragon grimly, striking down three more dirigibles before she sensed the exhaustion of his magic, and bade him follow the Lost Islands Dragons skyward. Safety lay in great height.

At last, as the remnants of Azziala's Dragonship fleet receded beneath them, Hualiama allowed herself a low laugh of release.

Then she saw further clusters of Dragonships rising from nearby Islands—from Dadak and Erak, and Irak just visible on the south-eastern horizon. She caught her breath. How many? None of the information she had received mentally made mention of additional fortresses and troops, but Lia knew now that Azziala and her twelve had withheld further, vital information. So much for trust. Well, Lia had burned, wrecked, destroyed and stampeded two hundred Dragons all over whatever non-existent trust she might have imagined between mother and daughter. Pensively, she observed several more Jade Dragons turning back. Affurion and his Dragonwing plunged into a cloud-bank, heading northeast at a rapid clip.

She slapped Grandion again, effervescing with joy. "Now fly East, my Dragon! Fly with all your strength to the end of the world!"

* * * *

Grandion slowly became aware of the caress of wind upon his scales. He realised he no longer dwelled in the strange roost of dark-fires and endless food, subject to the crushing bondage of the Dragon-Haters. Yet where was he now? And why did he sense a dominant mind enfolding his? Draconic cunning subdued his response. A Rider? A memory … a girl nearby, speaking in a curiously monotonous, disinterested voice. The same Human uttering the hateful words, 'Dragon, obey. You are my slave.' He was no one's lackey! He was Grandion, shell-son of Sapphurion and Qualiana, a powerful Tourmaline of the Dragonkind!

Before he knew it, the Dragon's rage erupted. *Let me out! How dare you …*

He spun away, blind. The Human girl sat stiffly on his back, making the sounds he knew were stifled sobs, furious and grieving. Regret squeezed his third heart. When would he learn she was fragile, her emotions like a Dragoness speeding up an Island's league-tall cliffs before plunging down the far side at an even more dizzying pace?

Sorry, he growled snappishly. *By my wings, you didn't deserve—*

Well then, don't apologise if you're going to sound like you've got the worst case of scale-itch in the Island-World.

The warmth of that rich, enchanting voice … *ha-ha-rrrrraargh-ha-ha-ha!* Grandion's laughter pummelled the air into submission. Three times, she had plucked him from the darkness. *I hurt you.*

Grandion, darling Dragon, I've so much to tell you. We've escaped. She switched moods faster than a speeding Dragon. *And we're heading East over the Lost Islands and I found both my mother and father there but Ra'aba's dead and will you listen and promise me, by your wings or mother's egg or whatever, that you won't hate me for what I have to say?*

Grr. My head hurts when you babble like an excitable dragonet. Heads before necks, and shoulders before wings. My sight, please.

"That's my sight," she said lightly. Grandion's anger burned, nevertheless.

His world flooded with colour. The Dragon gasped, "Look, Hualiama. The Rim-wall mountains–well, perhaps it is a mirage ... they're closer than I expected."

"Under certain optical conditions it's possible for an image to appear much closer and higher than it truly is," Lia said, breathless with wonder. "I've experienced this with seeing non-existent Dragonships off Fra'anior Cluster. They're definitely mountains, but look at how the horizon beneath them appears to waver."

The fabled mountains that reached the sky, twenty-five leagues tall. So high, the Dragon realised, that the weather within the bowl they created must be a self-contained system separate from the world beyond. Such wing-shivering vastness–was the Island-World ten thousand leagues in diameter? Twenty? Though the peaks lay far beyond the realms of snow or air, they appeared tipped with white. Diamonds, he fancied. The jewel-hoards of Ancient Dragons.

"You're the first Human to see the Rim," said Grandion.

"Congratulations, I saw an atmospheric hoax," said she, with that peculiarly Human brand of droll humour which so reliably itched his scales. "Those Islands down there are real. Remind me, Yukari said ..."

"From the last Island, summon Siiyumiel using the Dragon's Bell."

"The Dragon's–Grandion. Why didn't you tell me before, you pesky, uncommunicative ... male! What's this Bell? Where will we find it?"

"You'll know it when we get there."

"That's fighting talk coming from a Dragon recently on course to become Dragonship hide and shoe leather!"

Peace, thou beauteous crown of Fra'anior's glory, he returned.

His Rider began to make a Dragonish purr, before snapping her teeth crossly. *Well, I've a thing or three to share with you. Much of it, deeply troubling. May I, before we reach that Island?*

Aye. Levity yielded to gravity.

Rather than speaking, the girl moved immediately to opening her memories for him. The Dragon became an observer to her tribulation and triumph at the Reaving, to her mother's madness and her father's murder, and though the implications brought turmoil to his thoughts, he understood there was a greater fear that afflicted his beautiful, fierce Rider's soul. It cut to the quick of her being. Her soul cried, 'How can anyone love me? How can anyone love *this?* Even Sapphurion's betrayal had burned with a lesser fire.

The Tourmaline Dragon knew another truth. He had found the Scroll of Binding and completed the honour-quest given him by the Dragon Elders. He could restore his name. All he had to do was return the living Scroll to the Dragon Elders, or destroy Hualiama himself. His glory and fame would be celebrated forever among the Dragonkind, enshrined in legend and Dragonsong.

Did she suspect the murderous deliberations darkening his Dragon fires?

Had the great Dragon-Spirit Amaryllion foreseen all this? If so, why not simply destroy her outright? A prickle of seventh sense washed through his body, kindling the storehouses of his powers, and the fires which had seemed dammed up, suddenly coursed along new paths, physical, emotional and magical. Abuzz, the Dragon quivered with the force of his insight. He must stay the paw of retribution. A greater destiny lay as yet unclaimed. Have faith, Dragon! Show her the true fires of draconic wisdom!

As if attuned to his thoughts, the Human girl said, *Will you be my strength, Grandion?*

He replied, *Always. You'll never be alone.*

* * * *

Hualiama quailed at the reservation she sensed in Grandion's manner. The Dragon had every reason to despise her. He replied evasively to her probing, save to express his regret at her bereavement and his fiery draconic approval of her actions–so effusive in thanks was he, she blushed royally. Was he trying to divert her from his true feelings? Did he fear her new skills in being able to bind Dragons? Her heritage?

Yet he swooped gracefully, and brought them to a landing on an Island ledge overlooking the Cloudlands at the easternmost edge of the Island-World's lands, a place of extraordinary, rugged beauty that sang to his third heart. Jagged cliffs cut away upon all sides of an Island no more than a quarter-mile wide, but five miles tall, jutting like an uncompromising Dragon's talon above all of its neighbouring Islands to the west and southwest. Lia imagined the Ancient Dragons had raised up a marker to state, 'Our work ends here.'

Beyond lay the ocean of Land Dragons.

A vertical gully carved into the mountainside above the ledge. The Dragon's Bell hung in that space, a monstrous column of silvery metal ten times taller than Grandion's hundred-foot wingspan, depending from a bar above and metallic-looking hawsers as thick as her waist.

Taking the perilous route down his shoulder, dropping onto his elbow and then hopping down to the ground, Lia turned and bowed to the Dragon. "Best get ringing, mighty Tourmaline Dragon."

Using her gaze to help him aim, Grandion struck out with his tail.

BOOOOOOONNNNGGGG!

Lia had imagined a sweet chime. This was a note so deep it seemed to ripple down into the foundations of the Island, and from there, out into the vast wilderness facing them.

Grandion sang:

Arise, o brother of the deeps,
Süyumiel-ap-Yanûk-bar-Shûgan,
Hearken to our call.

"Erm, what was that ap-bar sugar bit in the middle there?" Lia asked, her voice sing-song with wing-tugging notes of amusement.

"Some form of Ancient Dragonish. Who cares if we don't understand it, as long as it works?"

Snarky Dragon. "You're so sly. Stop yanking my hawser, Dragon."

Grandion struck the bell and repeated the incantation twice more, while Lia covered her ears–uselessly–against the bone-tingling vibrations. They waited. The Human girl rubbed her neck and scanned the skies. Why had they seen no Dragons out here? Why did she sense unseen eyes, watching?

Placing a talon gently upon her shoulder, Grandion asked, "Do you remember dying?"

Hualiama shook her head, more of a shiver. "Not even Azziala's weird twin-voice scared me as much as when she said, 'I always wondered if that child died of a broken heart …' Oh, Grandion. Dragon egglings know their shell-mother's voice from so early on. I'm sure Human babies must be the same. They must know if they are loved or not, and if they're despised with such a deep, malign hatred … Grandion, how can a spirit leave a body and return days later? Surely the body decays? Perishes? Am I a freak? Some wicked spirit occupying a Human shell not her own?"

"Never. Lia, don't ever think that." As she doubled up, wheezing at the pain in her chest, the Tourmaline Dragon clasped her with his paw as his father once had, his talons folded over her chest and thighs like a cage of silvery swords. "These are your fears speaking. Your purpose is to rise above a loathsome birthright, to be greater than those who would strike you down. You'll forge a suns-fire destiny where others would only fall."

The Dragon quivered with the emotions he poured into his words. Lia gripped one of his talons in both hands, grateful beyond words. When her chest closed, it felt as though she would never breathe again.

"Besides, how Azziala can deny you're her daughter, resurrected or none, is beyond my mind-fires," grumbled the

Dragon. "What does heritage matter? Nothing."

"Everything," Hualiama countered, knowing draconic beliefs on the subject. "What's the only hour a Dragon doesn't spend debating genealogies?"

"The thirtieth." He completed the ancient saying with a snort of fire, and followed in rhetorical cadence, "Is our fate determined before we break the shell, taught us by our shell-parents, or grasped when we reach an age of understanding our true fires?"

"Predestined to be creatures of choice? Marvellous conundrum."

"Perfectly logical to a Dragon."

And a perfectly oblique way of encouraging his companion, Hualiama realised, smiling warmly at him. "Then I'll take the barest smidgen of the first, half of the second and all of the third, if you please."

"Say, rebellious Rider of a rebellious Dragon?"

"Aye, Grandion?"

"Did I ever tell you that in the seventh of the ascending fire-promises, or the seventh-sense promise, we Dragons swear by the light of *Hualiama,* the blue star?" After a moment, he added, "I can't see properly. Are you crying?"

"Happy," she sniffed. "Isn't that sacred lore?"

"Are you not the Dragonfriend?"

A silence of kindred spirits surrounded Dragon and Rider. Hualiama scanned the Cloudlands, working to shut out the inveigling voice that insisted, 'Dragon, obey. You will love me, forever.' Yet the morning shone bright and fair, and only the growing heat was their companion for nigh an hour.

The Cloudlands stirred. Rational thought fled. All Lia knew was stupefaction.

Three ranks of dark, wet mountain peaks broke through the clouds several leagues distant, sailing toward their position on an unmistakable bearing, as though one Island journeyed to meet another. Beside her, Grandion stood immobile, but she heard the accelerated pulse of his hearts, and his belly-fires, after initially falling mute, amplified to a steady roar. His claws gashed the rock. Like the most majestic Dragonship in existence, the creature surged up from the deeps, until fully seven rows of peaks became visible, crowning a turtle-like carapace Lia's gibbering mind estimated to be a mile wide and the stars alone knew how long–several times that? The Land Dragon comfortably dwarfed the Isle they stood upon, slowing as its approach trembled the ground.

"I–I thought A-Amaryllion was huge," Lia faltered.

"Courage, Dragonfriend. I never imagined a beast like this inhabited our Island-World." The Dragon bowed his muzzle and lowered his outspread wings, a draconic obeisance. "How honoured we are."

The Land Dragon ground to a halt perhaps half a mile offshore, the clouds eddying about its body, water and mud sheeting off the stellated carapace. Then, with a series of explosions that sounded like hydrogen detonating, the Dragon's foreparts began to separate like a bud breaking into full flower, the mountains tipping precipitately left and right. An unmistakably draconic head slithered forth, with skin like wrinkled lizard-hide and dozens of nose and facial horns surrounding seven blazing yellow eyes placed around the head's hemispherical crown, and a beaked canyon of a mouth which could have swallowed their Island with room to spare.

The head pushed forward until Hualiama feared they would be splattered against the mountainside like luckless bugs on a Dragonship's crysglass windows.

Sïiyumiel-ap-Yanûk-bar-Shûgan hearkens to thy summons, creatures of the heights.

Scalding, foetid air blasted over Grandion and Hualiama. The Land Dragon's voice was massive beyond comprehension, gently modulated yet so potent with condensed magical energies that it knocked them tumbling, as helpless as newborn Dragon hatchlings. Groaning, the Tourmaline Dragon pushed back to his feet, bashing Lia to her knees. She raised a hand to her nose in a mirror-image of her Dragon's motion. Both of them bled; one scarlet, one golden.

As quickly as the hurt had been caused, new magic pummelled them. Healing magic; a draconic apology. Now they were gasping, drowning, riding a torrent. The flow ceased abruptly. Lia flung out her hands to keep from pitching onto her face.

Shell-son of Sapphurion, noble-hearted son of flame, Alastior!

The voice was even further restrained, a dam-wall upon the point of breaking, vocalising its thoughts in packages that struck its listeners in great, heavy waves.

The Tourmaline bowed again, grace and fire united. *Siiyumiel, Blessed Lord of the Deeps, Guardian of Wisdom of the Shell-Clan. Thank you for aiding us in our hour of need.*

Thou I know, roared the great creature, inclining his head until four of his seven eyes burned upon them. *Thou art Dragonkind. Who is thy tiny companion? Bearer of ancient fires … ah. Much of thy nature is a paradox shrouded in time, little one. My fire-soul devotes itself to thee.*

Hualiama rubbed her eyes as the magic within Siiyumiel performed a draconic genuflection, great fire-wings spreading white-fires to the northern and southern horizons in her inner sight. She realised she saw his true draconic form, his fire-form, so different from the ponderous bottom-dweller, as beautiful and enigmatic as Amaryllion Fireborn had been in life and death.

She muttered, "Grandion, what's he doing? What's going on?"

The Dragon shook his muzzle, clearly nonplussed. *Yukari said he's the leader of the Shell-Clan Land Dragons, and the wisest Dragon loremaster in the Island-World.*

After Amaryllion, surely?

Grandion hissed briefly at her, before addressing Siiyumiel, *My gracious companion is Hualiama, Princess of Fra'anior, daughter of the Human Empress of these Isles.*

Ah. The breeze generated by Siiyumiel's exhalation continued for the full minute it took him to speak a single syllable. Could Dragons not simply say what they meant, rather than hinting at ten million enormously significant things they knew, but were never going to reveal? If there was any one trait of Amaryllion's which had vexed her … Lia peered as much as she dared up into Siiyumiel's swirling orange orbs, each a flattish oval one hundred and fifty feet wide and sixty tall, and tried not to imagine plunging into those fiery pits and burning forever. She sensed nothing malicious in his fire-eyes, but rather the gravitas of great age and authority, and an alien Dragonsong as thrilling and far beyond her understanding as the stars lay beyond the Island-World.

The Land Dragon said, *Speak thy need, Alastior.*

Give him the recipe, Hualiama.

After explaining Grandion's debility, Lia passed on the complex set of requirements Yukari had proposed. They waited. A quarter-hour later, the Land Dragon stirred.

I have analysed the molecular structure of this debility, little ones, and projected the effects of Yukari's treatment with a ninety-eight point four two seven percentage accuracy. It is like this–he showed them a vast canvas of computation, hypotheses, effects and outcomes, shaded with probability factors, magical constructs and instillations, and a dizzying breakdown of the recipe he would prepare–*ah, too much for your little minds? I shall summarise. The remedy will make you sick. Basic Dragon magic will fail you until the elements integrate fully into your physiological systems. Thereafter, you should experience a gradual return of your sight. I expect full healing within a … month, in your reckoning. I have begun to distil the necessary elements from my stores–from within my own body, little ones.*

Hualiama smiled as the Land Dragon clarified her unspoken question. *How can we thank you enough, Siiyumiel?*

Share with me the wisdom of Amaryllion, Siiyumiel replied unexpectedly.

The Island-World had never seemed a stranger place than when a Land Dragon paused to afford a Human girl his regard. He listened with such vast, wholehearted attention, that his manner drew nuances and hitherto unrealised insights out of Hualiama. She spoke with greater fluidity than she might have thought possible, and after the briefest-seeming hour of her life, paused as Siiyumiel declared his work complete.

Suddenly, the head began to withdraw. The Fra'aniorian Islander sensed the solidifying of mental and magical barriers, while alarm or at least alertness ran high in the great beast.

She began to call, *O Land Dragon …*

Take heed, he interrupted. *Receive this gift, Tourmaline. I wish a modicum of repayment, simply this: bring the Human girl back to this place when you've dealt with your enemies.*

Enemies? Hualiama yelped. Where? Who had tracked them here? How?

Just then, a silvery ball the size of her head flashed past the corner of her eye. With a dull, fleshy thud, it struck Grandion flush in the side of the head, two feet aft of his left eye. The Tourmaline Dragon collapsed in a heap of claws, wings and limp Dragon flesh.

Having felled Grandion with his medication, the faint-hearted Land Dragon vanished as though he had used invisible hooks to tear up a carpet of Cloudlands and dived beneath it. Turning to scan the skies hastily, Lia spotted a blazing Orange Dragon spearheading a large Dragonwing, screaming in from the northwest.

Razzior!

* * * *

Her intuition had struck the right Island. Azziala's intelligence had failed. Razzior had already reached the Lost Islands, perhaps days ahead of the remainder of his forces. "Get up, you stupid–" Kicking Grandion in the neck would do no good. Nor could her little arms shake his muzzle. But Lia had to try. As the Orange Dragon loomed larger and larger, she tried everything short of unleashing her *ruzal* power to force him to wake. Finally, she tried pushing into his unresponsive mind to stir him up.

Rise, o Dragon fires, she sang softly, as close an imitation of Dragonsong as she could produce. *Sing, thou glory of the skies. Dance with me. Beloved …*

Truly? When he did not return her love? Her conviction faded, but Hualiama saw herself reflected in his mind, as if a fiery angel took his soul's paw and led him step by step from the darkness to dance in the light. The Tourmaline Dragon ruffled his wings as if dislocated from a deep sleep.

"Razzior's coming. Hurry." Hualiama glanced upward again. Why did she feel those Dragons were not the only disturbance in the air this morning?

The Dragon snuffled about, sneezing when he took a whiff of her legs. "Where's my rock?"

"No. Grandion, it'll make you sick."

"Instantly? Nonsense."

Lia had a sick intuition this was a mistake, but the seething response she detected in him, probably battle-readiness coupled with exasperation, left no room for negotiation. "Here." She pushed the metal ball with her foot, but could not budge it. Roaring rajals, how many sackweight did it weigh?

"I refuse to wait upon blindness as our enemies approach," he growled, unnecessarily.

Aye, he was lizard ten times more brainless than the average ralti sheep–but not half as stubborn as his Rider! Lia's grin flashed briefly, grim and uncompromising. Let Razzior come. Grandion snaffled the metal ball with his fangs and tossed it down his gullet with a sharp grunt of effort. Perfect. So now her Dragon would fly like a windroc who had breakfasted on rocks. Stepping upon his paw, Hualiama accepted a boost up to Grandion's shoulder, landing lightly on the balls of her feet.

"Strap in, my Rider. Stormy weather expected this morning."

Lia's senses attuned to the doings of the Dragon's various stomachs and the organs which supplied his magical and physical Dragon powers. Aye, Grandion was brewing up a fine storm. The weather was clear, but had that oppressive stillness which often presaged bad weather. Where would their help come from? This morning's storm would be that of a Rider and her Dragon battling for their lives.

Chapter Thirty-Four

Lia Hunted

WITH HIS RIDER safely seated, Grandion sprang into a vertical take-off, wheeling as he flapped hard to gain strategic height. He knew it was useless to try to outfly Razzior. Four dozen Dragons could hound a lone Dragon like the painted dogs of the far Western Isles ran down their prey, persisting to the inevitable, bloody end. Better to face an enemy fresh, than exhausted.

The Tourmaline Dragon warmed up his throat with a ripping battle-challenge. *I AM GRANDION!*

Razzior's Dragonwing responded with a chorus of booming snarls, causing the Dragon's Bell to vibrate with an aftershock. Grandion powered into the clear sky, the song of battle already rampant in his hearts.

Lia asked quietly, "Will they want us alive?"

She understood they could not flee. "Razzior seeks revenge against my shell-father, and authority over all Dragons," he noted. "We cannot know which imperative holds the ascendancy in his thinking. I believe he'll seek to capture you alive. But if he calculates he can gain more by your death …"

"Do we admit–"

"We speak of the *ruzal* only if required."

"My senses are yours."

"Hualiama …" Rage, grief and gratitude filled his Dragon hearts with heavy-fire, a sensation like molten lead coursing through his veins. Despite all, she still offered herself? Lia was too ready to sacrifice. "And my powers are yours." What

Dragon would willingly abase himself like this? "All of them."

Her Haozi war bow creaked as she tested the draw. "Appreciated. Let's burn the heavens together–"

"–as Dragon and Rider," he finished in concert with her.

Grandion tuned in to Hualiama's senses. She sat straight-backed as always, in dignity and worth, far surpassing the title of Princess of Fra'anior which she often gently disparaged. Her gaze was sweeping yet concise, a warrior's habit of checking one's surrounds while focussing on the immediate threat. Incongruously, a picture of a bud came to his mind. Pure white, seven-petalled, it flowered before his startled observance. The perfume of her thoughts penetrated the Dragon's awareness. So close. So intimate.

Now he *knew* the paths of her intuition, so akin to a Dragon's seventh sense. She waited–for what? A deep-seated urging kept him spiralling above the Dragon's Bell. This was the right battleground, here at the edge of the Island-World. Here, her mental voice noted, the King of Dragons and his Princess would hold court. Grandion's fires clarified and intensified, burning at a pitch he marvelled at. Like Lia, he knew this for a crucial juncture, the fates about to avalanche over a Dragon and his Rider. Would they survive? Fragile as that chance was, Hualiama held it with the fabled grace of the legendary Star Dragoness, Istariela.

She believed for both of them.

RAZZIOR! The massive Orange's salutation pounded their ears.

Hualiama! Blue-star! Lia electrified Grandion's Storm powers as she produced an unexpected battle-challenge of her own.

Razzior's brow-ridges furrowed. *Grandion, shell-son of Sapphurion. Hualiama, child of Azziala and Ra'aba, heir to the throne of the Dragon-Haters. Hand over the* ruzal *you possess, or perish.*

Dragon-direct, the Orange Dragon stated his case, while seeking to tar her with her legacy.

Neither Dragon nor Human possesses the ruzal–Grandion punctuated his reply with a mocking, smoky snort–*o Razzior, renegade dark-wing, detritus of Gi'ishior.*

Razzior bared his fangs. *I'm in no mood to play games, youngling.*

I've a possession of yours, Human girl–a blade you dropped on Franxx. Using its powers, I've kept a Dragon's Eye on all your doings since. I know of Ra'aba's demise. I understand your shell-mother's hatred. And I, Razzior the Orange, declare it is time to put these misunderstandings to rest. But first I must thank you, Grandion, for your service to the Dragonkind.

The Tourmaline growled, *What–*

Why, you brought the Scroll of Binding to our trysting-place, as agreed. The Orange Dragon's eye-fires blazed as Hualiama gasped audibly. *Oh, didn't you tell your precious Dragon Rider of our bargain? Dragons of a colour wing together! Thank you, shell-brother. This is high service indeed.*

Grandion could find no words bar spluttering denials.

Hand the Scroll of Binding over to me, and I shall grant you this magical blade and your miserable lives.

I don't possess the ruzal. Lia's voice was a ravaged whisper. 'Betrayed!' it screamed. Razzior's accusation had no basis, but the Tourmaline Dragon knew the injury had been wrought in a flash. Now his Rider hated him. Her distrust also cut Grandion's pride, but he knew Razzior's indictment for a classically Dragonish ploy, twisting just enough of the truth to make his accusation seem plausible.

A hundred fangs gleamed in the late morning suns-light. Heavily sarcastic, Razzior replied, *How draconic an answer, little one. Of course you don't. The* ruzal *possesses you! Dragons, the legendary Scroll of Binding lives! There it sits, atop that miserable specimen of a Tourmaline Dragon. Deny the truth, Hualiama of Fra'anior. Tell me I lie.*

Grandion sensed the tiny flexion of Lia lifting her definite chin. *I do not deny it.*

Her damnable obsession with telling the truth and keeping promises! A chopped-off bugle of dismay issued from Grandion's throat. Razzior's eyes smouldered the enormity of his pleasure.

The Orange began to shout, *Fetch me the Dragonfriend! Kill the Tour–*

A grey mass materialised in the air literally in front of Razzior's nose and blurred into the Orange Dragon's shield, buffeting him and his Dragonwing backward with punishing force. Grandion blinked automatically, forgetting he was blind. Lia's eyes jumped. Ianthine! The Maroon Dragoness hurtled down like lightning from azure skies, followed by battalions of Lost Islands Dragons–a stranger, fiercer group of Dragonkind he had never imagined. Long, undulating quadruple-winged Dragons! Blocky beasts almost lost beneath their hide-armour! And a low, deadly drone on the wind that he quickly identified as the host of smaller Dragons gathered around the serpentine ones, as though each Dragonwing was a battle group reporting to a specific leader.

Oh, please can we play too, hatchlings? Ianthine's scorn lashed out. *I'll be taking the Dragonfriend, Razzior. This day, the Cloudlands will harvest your pitiful corpse.*

Hualiama's acuity noted the force which had struck Razzior–one of the ultra-heavy Dragons, who had eased to a dazed landing on the mountaintop above the Dragon's Bell. His wings felt leaden. Despite his labours, Grandion felt himself losing altitude. For a panicked second, he suspected the Land Dragon's medicine. His stomach felt queer. But he sensed this force emanated from Ianthine herself. Did she want them out of the way? Or was she forcing a landing to make her quarry vulnerable?

Is she ally or enemy? Lia responded to his concerns.

Enemy until proven otherwise. Agreed?

Aye.

The moment stretched so thin, the air itself seemed too rarefied to furnish breath for all the creatures gathered in uncompromising, expectant array.

Then Ianthine bellowed, *I AM IANTHINE!*

Two Dragon armies hurled themselves at Grandion and Hualiama.

* * * *

The Overminds opened up with a salvo of Grunts. A rising hiss of magical power preceded sounds like the deep popping of lava-lake bubbles. Impelled at a fantastic rate toward

Razzior's Dragonwing, each cumbersome armoured Dragon turned into a flying battering-ram. The instant before the strike, the grey Grunt twisted in the air to lead with their left or right shoulder. The Blue Dragons' shields kept them at bay–at least for two or three strikes. Hualiama recoiled as the rearmost Grunts of the slightly staggered barrage smashed into Razzior's massed force. Three Reds of Razzior's Dragonwing fell, two killed instantly, another with a primary wing-bone snapped a few feet from her shoulder. That Dragoness would never fly again. Two Blues appeared to have been knocked unconscious, but were saved from a fatal fall by the quick actions of their fellows.

Four Grunts plunged toward the Cloudlands, stunned or killed, but the rest shook themselves and circled the arena with slow, laboured wingbeats, returning to their Overminds.

Why do the shields fail, Grandion? she asked.

Backlash, he growled, shaking his muzzle in disbelief. *The flying Dragons' momentum transfers into the shield as energy, which is usually absorbed or bled off by a Blue Dragon. This power is unprecedented. Each strike sends a shockwave into the Blue, overwhelming some, as you saw.*

Barely had Grandion spoken, when Razzior's Dragonwing replied with an onslaught of fire, ice and acid. They decimated the foremost Overmind group. Charred reptilian bodies spiralled out of a cloud of acrid grey smoke, while the cries of the mortally wounded rose above the bellows of furious Dragons. Grunts hurtled forth. Another of Razzior's Blues fell. His force abruptly broke ranks in order to present a more dispersed target. Ianthine responded at once with a mental command to release the Swarm. Among Razzior's forces Lia recognised Yulgaz the Brown and Cerissae, Grandion's old flame, and some three hundred yards off Ianthine's left flank, Affurion the Brown Overmind, half again the size of his compatriots. Was he their leader? Or Ianthine?

That was the last moment she had for coherent thought. In a sky filled with Dragons, attack was swift and brutal. Grandion jinked and furled his port wing smartly, avoiding a shock-attack by one of Razzior's Reds, trying to ambush them from a height with an attack at terminal velocity. The Dragon hissed by, his fireball sucking the breath out of Lia's lungs, and came within inches of ploughing a furrow in the mountainside. Lia drew her Haozi bow, and pinned a Swarm Dragon in the eye.

By my wings, they're ugly! snarled the Tourmaline, biting a Purple Swarm in half. He spat to clear his mouth.

Underslung of jaw and mean of eye, the Swarm were as fast as bats and triple the size of the average dragonet, up to ten feet in wingspan. Lia yelled, *Mind their poisoned fangs–they'll paralyse you–and their tails.*

What about their tails? Grandion hissed, rolling away from a Green Dragon. His hind legs kicked out, slashing bloody furrows in the Green's flank.

The Swarm hunted in iridescent purple shoals, as if rainbow trout swarmed in the suns-shine. They mobbed individual Dragons like army ants attacking a luckless spider, trying to paralyse with multiple bites. Their tails shot grapnel-like barbs–just like the Swarm around Grandion now. Helpfully, Yulgaz's fireball crisped ten Swarm in a single shot, but the Tourmaline did not pause to thank the Brown. Thundering a challenge, Grandion slapped Yulgaz in the jaw with his tail while simultaneously encasing six Swarm in tombs of ice. The Dragons fell into the mountainside and shattered.

Lia cried, *Shot, my beauty!*

Still, thirty or forty Swarm pursued the much larger Tourmaline Dragon. He bellowed and shook his right wing as grapnels pocked its surface. Lia groaned in concert with him as the fifty-foot, silken cords attached to those grapnels snarled his wing and anchored his attackers. She began to unbuckle her straps, but Grandion stopped her with a snarl, *What're you doing?* He cleaned his wing with a brief blast of ice-shards. But the Swarm were too numerous! Lia quickly expended her stock of arrows on keeping Grandion's wings clear. He flapped hard to gain height, but the strange opposing force continued to shepherd them toward the mountaintop.

Grandion thundered his fury!

Lia snapped, *Save your strength, my Dragon. We need cunning. Do you sense any Burrowers, any of the*–she accessed Feyzuria's knowledge, flashing it across their mental link–*the Anubam?*

No … Cerissae!

The Tourmaline Dragon jolted as Cerissae's undetected attack opened a ten-foot gash in his flank. The Amber-Red Dragoness whirled, trying to force them toward Razzior's Dragons, Lia realised.

Grandion snapped at her, but the wily Dragoness side-slipped out of range. *So, Grandion, does the Human runt light your fires as I do?* Her sneer was only a smokescreen for a new attack, thick ropes of yellow fire which lashed from her throat and wrapped around Grandion's body, sizzling against his scales.

He flicked them aside with a touch of his shield. *Pathetic, you double-crossing null-brain.*

Cerissae reached out with her mind, but Lia was faster than Grandion, this time. His strength had only just begun to fade when she presented a shining, white-fire mental armour to the Dragoness, who recoiled. *No healing reversals today,* Lia growled. Could she fight like this? Could she help Grandion somehow with the magic which sang so fiercely within her, she must surely release it or die?

Caught in her inner reflections, Lia startled as she realised that Grandion battled toe-to-toe with Yulgaz and Cerrisae, while Razzior had rallied his Dragons somehow to hold off Ianthine's Lost Island forces. He wanted her. She knew it in his burning, covetous gaze. He desired her power.

Grandion traded muscular blows with Yulgaz. The Tourmaline had grown strong, no longer that juvenile the vile Brown had once trapped beneath Ha'athior Island. He clashed with the older Brown, taking punches to the chest without flinching–against his natural Blue Dragon shield, Lia realised–while his own claws-bared slap tore deep into the flight muscles of Yulgaz's left shoulder. He split the Brown's lip with a blow that shattered half a dozen fangs. Lia tossed the Haozi bow down onto the Dragon's Bell. No use for that now. She'd fetch it later. Drawing her Nuyallith blade, she hacked at Cerissae as the Amber-Red twisted by, trying to knock her off Grandion's back with a cunning paw-strike. Yulgaz seized

Grandion with his Brown Dragon power, shaking him as he would shake a mountainside, dislodging boulders and cracking open the living stone.

Keep close, Lia called, imbuing Grandion's shield with a touch of pure Hualiama laughter and Dragonsong. Yulgaz's attack faltered. Laughing his bloodlust as the Brown backed off, Grandion fired a shaped bolt of ice, spearing frozen shards ten feet or more into the bone and muscle around the Dragon's first heart. With a blast of wind, he flipped the shocked Brown into a vertical position in the air, exposing his underbelly.

BOOM! A stray Grunt smashed into Yulgaz, snapping his spine.

Lia cried out. How had Grandion seen that? Her own reactions were too slow for Dragon combat, for now Cerissae had Grandion in a death grip, four-clawed she stood atop his back. The Dragoness clawed her way forward with avaricious draconic fire-eyes fixed on the prize, strapped between Grandion's spine-spikes like a hare spitted and prepared for flame-grilling. The Tourmaline arched his neck to fire ice down the length of his body, past his Rider, but he had other problems. Swarm Dragons screamed in, shrieking their piercing, hawk-like cries, snarling Grandion and Cerissae with their ropes and biting indiscriminately.

Cerissae reached out, but her grasp was two feet short of the mark. She had Swarm hanging off her lips and nostrils. Grandion landed heavily, probably puncturing the Dragoness' belly with his spine-spikes upon landing, but she seemed undaunted. One hot breath, and Lia would be roasted. Slashing at her belts, the Human girl leaped to her feet, lithely poised upon her Dragon's back. She raised her blue blade.

Barbecued Princess is not on the menu today!

Her shout made Grandion chuckle and Lia groan inwardly. Mercy. Was that her best, scariest challenge? She sounded like Grandion in his hatchling years. No time. Dancing aside from Cerissae's lunge, Lia drank deep of the awesome presence of a Dragon in her mind, of her years of warrior-monk training and the knowledge Ja'al, bless his tattooed blue head, had poured into an undeserving vessel. The blade ignited. Blue flame wreathed her sword arm from her elbow to her hand, extending along the blade and beyond. Suddenly, she wielded an eight-foot Dragon-slayer of a weapon. The Amber-Red Dragoness' jaw cracked open in shock as Lia swung backhanded, a vicious arc from above her right shoulder toward her left leg, braced as if to anchor her power in the storehouses of the Tourmaline Dragon beneath her feet.

The fire carved a trench through Cerissae's muzzle, cuffing her head sideways in a spray of golden Dragon blood. Lia danced forward with a triple-step, and thrust the fiery blade deep into the Dragoness' chest, spearing her first heart. The sword's metal did not even touch her hide. There was no need. Lia's white-fire shone with the refining heat of a furnace, cremating the flesh and bone it passed through.

Her third raking stroke, made as she darted beneath Cerissae's swinging neck, sliced five feet deep into the area below the Dragoness' ear canals, right across the major jugulars feeding her brain. Draconic scale-armour parted with a sizzle.

The last sound the Dragoness made was a wet rattle of surprise.

* * * *

Being grounded during a Dragon-battle, while his viewpoint danced up and down his back like a demented dragonet, was a new and largely unwelcome experience for Grandion. How was he meant to protect her, or himself, against a roiling melee of Dragons bent on capture at any cost? Buffeted, braced and brazen, he and Lia defied their foes. His magical shield was their fortress. Lia's blade sang on the offence. She danced upon his shoulders as he spun, lashing his tail. She flexed with him as he cuffed a Red Dragon aside, and ducked as smartly as he to avoid a Grunt which tore an indiscriminate swathe of destruction through the confusion, crushing a dozen Swarm Dragons and breaking the wings of two of Razzior's force in a single attack.

Everywhere Hualiama looked, Dragons writhed in battle, the two forces struggling as much to keep each other from

Grandion and his Rider, as to attack them. So much Dragon blood had already been shed, a golden mist drifted over the battlefield. Maddened Dragons tore chunks out of each other. The sweet redolence of blood stoked their battle-lust. Razzior's lava attack splashed his shield. Grandion felt the severe drain on his power even as Lia rolled away from the blistering heat.

Why attack us directly? Her thoughts had a disorganised, rattled edge.

To weaken me. I can't keep shielding us forever.

Lia growled at the image in his mind, *You want me beneath your belly? I can't protect you from there.*

Who's protecting whom here?

They chuckled softly, simultaneously. Grandion shuddered at the impact of a Green Dragon acid attack, but the hissing spit slid off an invisible shield just above his spine-spikes.

Please don't sacrifice your flesh for me.

Wretchedly perceptive Dragonfriend! Grandion whirled, arching his back to deflect a Red Dragon's attack. The huge, hoary Red slewed off to the south, coming under heavy Swarm attack. Ianthine speared down, leading her Dragonwings in a sustained assault. Thunder! Growls and clashing paws! Dozens of Dragons hurled themselves at the mountaintop, seeking Hualiama's hide. Grandion cast aside Dragon fire and flying rocks and even a Glue-power attack. Successive concussions rattled them, but Lia far more so than the Dragon, for her ear canals could not close or mute sound as his did instinctively.

She gasped, *Keep me from the* ruzal, *Grandion. Razzior wants–*

Aye. It's my fault he stole your power.

Water off the Island. Hualiama darted around his paws, hacking briefly at a marauding Swarm Dragon. She rolled smoothly away as he whirled to face an incoming enemy Green, muzzle agape as a fireball formed in his throat. *No. He's in my mind … quarrying … help me, Grandion. Razzior's burning …*

The Tourmaline Dragon raged against their foes. Her sanity would crack beneath this assault. Forces as fearsome as the powers contained in the First Eggs of the Dragons, those same virtuosic powers which had raised life out of the noxious Cloudlands, had always made Hualiama's being their personal battleground. Razzior's attack was a vortex of dark pain, summoning that taint within Lia, stoking the *ruzal* into ugly exuberance. Her white-fires dwindled in response.

Straining inwardly, the Dragon bolstered her strength. *Resist.*

Grandion's sixth sense saw a wedge of maroon-coloured power slam into Razzior, ending his attack. But that was also a signal for Ianthine's forces to assault the mountain. The Dragon staggered as a posse of Browns tore into the living rock with their Stone powers. Splinters jagged into his belly and chest, but the Dragon danced the movements of his battle-song and the girl danced with him. Grandion clashed with a charging Yellow Dragoness, shoulder to shoulder, laughing horribly as he rebuffed her attack. He raked his talons across the Yellow's eyes. Blindness? What blindness? He would shield Hualiama from these burned-out worms. Then he would … deliver her intact to the Dragon Elders?

He must complete his sworn duty. Dark-fires seared the pathways of his magic as though he had swallowed a bellyful of Green Dragon acid spit. Must the price of his life be hers? His fiery bravado expired in a weak puff of smoke. She was the Scroll of Binding. He had made an oath to seek out the Scroll and bring it before the Dragon Elders. Should he fail, or the Scroll fall into the paws of Razzior or worse, the Dragon-Haters of these Isles–all Dragonkind would suffer. Could he be foresworn, and live with the dishonour? Not this Dragon. Never again.

In his mind's eye, Hualiama danced into his grasp. *My Dragon,* she laughed. *My Dragonlove.*

The lurking Orange Dragon roared at an entirely new pitch of fury. His thundering shook the morning as Grandion belatedly realised what he had revealed; what Razzior's *ruzal* had stolen from his awareness.

Blistering lava splashed over Dragon and Rider. Five Grunts struck the mountain in a perfectly-timed array. *KERRRUUUMP!* The sound rolled away with a vast echo, the Bell vibrating in sympathy.

The Tourmaline howled as an avalanche swept them away.

* * * *

Lia suddenly found herself swimming neck-deep in rubble. Brown Burrower Dragons rippled around her, shepherding the flow, laughing like monstrously overgrown trout frolicking in a waterfall. The avalanche yanked her and the Tourmaline apart. *Grandion!* She hacked ineffectually at a passing Brown. Lia groaned at the pressure of boulders grinding against her chest, before the spatulate paw of a Burrower scooped her loose and flicked her away from the torrent. She sailed free, only to scream as a monstrous power seized her body and dragged her skyward, arrow-swift toward Ianthine's waiting paw.

Ghastly, gap-toothed, the Maroon Dragoness' smile mocked the Human girl. Come suffer at my paw, she smirked. Give me the power of *ruzal* …

But the moment Hualiama thought of *ruzal*, the untameable dark power slipped free.

Razzior boomed, *Now, you're mine!*

If darkness could radiate like suns-beams from behind a cloud, that was how Hualiama perceived the Orange Dragon's attack. The instant Razzior's magic bathed her face, the thought pierced her mind that every light had its darkness, and every ordinary shadow could be banished by light–but this was a darkness that pulsed as with a diabolical heartbeat, which assumed the form of the mind directing it, a sentient entity in its own right. Strength evaporated from her body as Razzior guzzled at the font of her powers. Shuddering, Lia shut off the spigots.

Parasite! Magic-stealer! Hualiama felt her trajectory shift in the air, slinging her in a new arc that terminated in Razzior's right paw, but without wings of her own, she was powerless to resist. Lia built her layers. She buried her abilities, and drew a cocoon of light about the core of her person.

Blind to the Island-World, she felt Razzior's paw clasp her chest.

Ah, Dragonfriend, he hissed, slithering into her mind.

Hualiama! Resist! Grandion called from nearby. By the tenor of his voice, Lia knew he was under heavy attack. At least he had escaped the avalanche.

A being of draconic dark-fire entered the portals of her mental space, as dark and fearsome as Grandion's manifestation had always been a dazzle of light. Razzior. He and her father had shaped each other. They had been drawn as much to evil as to each other, and combined their Human and Dragon talents in unprecedented ways, feeding off each other in a ghastly parasitic orgy.

The creature faced her, unblinking. *Aye, I learned much from your father.*

He may be my blood-father, but I am the child of the Dragon, Hualiama countered.

A spirit-child? What a quaint, useless affectation. Did Amaryllion pretend regard for an unlovely, unloved and unlovable Human waif? Lia writhed as his words lashed her with the dark-fires of her own soul. *You pride yourself on this power of love, Dragonfriend, but your every flight generates hatred. Are these Dragonkind not gathered to war over your pathetic person? Dying for the Dragonfriend? They war to gain your magic–your foul, perverted powers, from your command of* ruzal *to your claims upon the Dragon who betrayed you from the first.*

Grandion did not–

Grandion, your Dragonlove? Razzior spat. *You make me sick! How you corrupt and blacken the peerless Dragon fires of our kind! Accept your weapon. I've no more need to turn a Dragon's Eye upon your transgressions. I'll rid this Island-World of your filthy presence after you accord me my desires.*

To her surprise, Razzior's claws unclenched. The Dragon dropped Lia onto the curve of his left paw, which held like a pin upon a Human's palm, the matching blade of her Nuyallith set. She glanced up at the Orange Dragon, guessing that he wanted her to seize the blade and ignite it. His fiery gaze dared her. In the curve of his neck and the clenched, scar-twisted muzzle, Lia read the pride and arrogance of the Dragonkind which drove him to demonstrate his dominance over her, his enemy, by granting her access to her most powerful weapons. The stronger the enemy, the greater the glory to be sung in Dragonsong. Razzior ached for glory, for recognition and status among his kind. For her, he knew only hatred. She was less than the dirt beneath his paws.

The Orange Dragon powered aloft, sliding between the serried ranks of Dragonkind with a flair which Hualiama realised had to be magical. She knelt to grasp the blade, and could not rise. Her heart laboured to shift molten-lead blood, thick with anguish. Hopeless. Beleaguered on every side. The Tourmaline roared but receded. Razzior needed no might of claw to shred her soul.

Hualiama curled inward. Where was her strength now?

Ianthine bugled, *Stay, Razzior! The Dragonfriend is mine!*

Stay? You decrepit, moth-eaten old windroc! The Orange's claws curled about his prize as the Dragoness rose to intercept them. Fire billowed from his mouth, choking Hualiama with sulphurous smoke. *Desist, or watch me destroy this puny Human.*

The Maroon Dragoness sneered, *Go roost-love a ralti sheep, hatchling. You haven't captured the Dragonfriend.*

Hualiama groaned as Razzior's claws clasped about her chest like bands of iron. He shook the fist containing his captive at Ianthine. *Haven't I? What is this?*

A bar of soap, said the Dragoness.

Bah. You–what?

Suddenly, air-pressure popped and creaked in Hualiama's ears as if she were underwater. The sounds of battle became muffled. She knew Ianthine and Razzior exchanged insults, but she could no longer hear their telepathic Dragonish. As Razzior's paw clenched, the compression seemed to shift along her body, behaving exactly like a hand grasping a wet bar of soap. She slid between his talons. He shifted his grip, voicing a disgruntled roar, only to see her slip in another direction in an invisible cocoon.

Delighted laughter burbled from Lia's lips as the Orange Dragon sweated over his prize.

"Whoops," she laughed. "Careful, Razzior."

"You … impossible …" The Orange made a convulsive swipe at her escaping body, but it seemed as slick as a Dragon hatchling breaking the eggshell. "Come here!"

His grasp only multiplied Ianthine's magic. Lia squirted out of his grasp like a boulder shot by a Brown Dragon, soaring across the void above Dragon's Bell Island.

A swift, cunning Red Dragon's paw snagged her belt midway. Talons sliced into Lia's lower back.

Two wingbeats later, the Red imploded in a cloud of golden blood.

"Morning!" bugled Mizuki.

"Hey, short shrift!" Elki screamed happily. "Keep flapping those arms, you might even fly!"

"You're mine, girl," growled Ianthine. Lia's body snapped sideways, punched by an unseen force. The tremendous acceleration caused white to crowd in around her vision, a tunnel leading only to Ianthine. Maroon talons snaked around her body, establishing the Dragoness' custody of the treasure all Dragons desired. "I've not suffered all these seasons–"

A familiar voice crashed over all the Islands of her world. "DRAGONS, OBEY!"

Chapter Thirty-Five

Medley of Dragons

TOO MUCH! LIA'S mind reeled. The Copper Dragoness had appeared from nowhere with Saori and Elki aboard. Likewise, almost in the same breath, her mother made her grand entrance on the field of battle. Dragons swung toward Azziala with ugly snarls, both the Lost Islands Dragons and Razzior's Dragonwing, while yet another Dragon army rushed up from the southwest led by none other than Sapphurion. They would arrive within minutes.

Her mother stood with haughty ease atop the head of a docile eighty-foot Blue Overmind. How? Surely crossing the Lost Islands at such a speed was impossible, unless–*Aye, daughter,* Azziala's voice trickled into her mind. *Teleportation is another of our powers. Enough minds, enough power … it's possible.*

Her mother boomed, "Dragoness. Bring me my renegade daughter."

Unbelievable cunning. Azziala must have been lying in wait while the Dragons destroyed each other. Perhaps Razzior's threat had tipped her hand. Everyone wanted Lia. Nobody wanted her dead, not yet. Not until she gave up the *ruzal.* Then she would become instantly expendable–she should not cling to any illusions in that regard. Azziala had made her intentions plain; so too Razzior.

Ianthine flapped ahead slowly, clearly fighting the Enchantress' mind-bending power. Azziala's force drifted on the wind several thousand feet above the main battle, perhaps twenty enthralled Dragons bearing dozens of her Dragon

Enchanters. Feyzuria and Shazziya flanked the Empress on her Dragon. Most of Razzior's force already displayed the slack-jawed contentment Lia had come to recognise as capitulation, but the Overminds or Dramubam resisted, especially Affurion. He rallied his Dragonwings while the Dragon-Haters worked economically, attacking the resilient Overminds in teams of up to a dozen minds and transferring control of subjugated Dragons to lesser Enchanters.

Sapphurion was about to speed into the jaws of Azziala's trap.

Hualiama reached for Grandion, but could not identify him amongst a host of stupefied minds. Thunder! Four Grunts rattled Azziala's psychic shield, the hindmost breaking through to crush one of her Dragons, instantly killing all the Dragon Enchanters aboard.

Quick. Ianthine. She had to trust the Dragoness now, for she was the only one Lia could touch. Ignore the pain. Forge past the soft-as-quicksand sensation of Azziala's command-power draining her will to oppose, Lia opened herself to the unstable Dragoness.

"Dragon, obey. You are my slave."

Never! A storm-howl protested Lia's takeover of Ianthine's mind.

Imagining herself an Island struck by a Cloudlands storm, Lia allowed the Maroon Dragoness' rage to sluice over her. In its wake, she soothed, "Ianthine. Work with me. Wake your second self."

She *saw* the Dragoness. Hers was a realm of strange voices and conflicted emotions, and a mind scarred in ways Hualiama could hardly begin to imagine. A new tone entered Ianthine's voice, with wild notes that reminded Lia of lava leaping and spitting in Fra'anior's caldera. "Traitor! Release this Command-hold."

"No. Shut your fires and listen." A talon sprang from its retractable sheath toward Lia's neck. She gasped, "Ianthine! I'm trying to help, trust me."

Only she had the power to break Azziala's hold. If she could not do it, these Dragons would fall and Sapphurion shortly thereafter.

"Trust? First, it gives me power."

"You still lust for *ruzal* after all you've suffered? Ianthine–" Lia listened to the Dragoness' stillness, which belied the internal war raging between her different personalities "–Dragoness, you must choose the right. Hatred will not win this day."

After what seemed an eternal silence, Ianthine said, "It trusts like a babe. Undraconic in innocence, my dark-fires it incites. What does it intend, o treacherous beauty, this beggar of sweetly insane oaths?" Lia shivered as the mad voice gathered strength. She knew this Ianthine, for the Dragoness had taunted her before with the knowledge of Ra'aba's identity. "Is it secretly a Hater? Seeded to doom all Dragons?"

"No. I promise–" The word throttled Hualiama momentarily. Promise a Dragoness? Had she not learned? "I promise to release you. As for my plan? What could be more draconic than to attack?"

Ianthine gurgled with pleasure as Hualiama sketched a plan in her mind. "Agreed, Dragonfriend."

Slow wingbeats brought the Maroon Dragoness up to the Empress' position above the battlefield. Ianthine kept her expression carefully blank, yet her belly-fires seethed as though a thousand hornets were trapped beneath her hide, matching Lia's trepidation. If the Dragoness could use her unique powers coupled with the word of *ruzal* Hualiama had taught her …

The raddled Dragoness appeared to swell. Hualiama's heart turned over as a new magic filtered through her broken scales, transforming the Ianthine into a radiant jewel. Enchained as they were by the Dragon Enchanters, Azziala's flotilla, to a beast, sighed and made moon-eyes at the Dragoness. The Empress frowned, clearly confused as a hum of approving Dragonsong rose about her. Lia ironed a grin off her lips. Ianthine would never openly admit to possessing the draconic power of seduction, would she?

Fifty feet from Azziala's commanding position, Ianthine broke into an eye-catching display of streamers of dazzling, coruscating magic. Behind Azziala, her Enchanters gasped as their Dragons bumped into each other and lost position in the formation, trying to keep a burning eye upon the object of their collective desire.

In that instant, the Dragoness hurled Lia at Azziala.

Mid-air, the Princess of Fra'anior unsheathed her Nuyallith blades, crossing the gap in an eye blink. A flash of Ianthine's *ruzal* sliced through the Dragon Enchanters' shield. Adjust. Slash! Azziala's eyes widened as she dived aside, flinging up her hands in reaction. Lia's left-hand blade sliced cleanly through the outer edge of her mother's hand, while the right gashed Azziala's ribs shallowly, deflecting off her body armour and piercing Shazziya's right thigh, a clean thrust. Hualiama cannoned off the tall Enchantress' hip, losing her grip on the blade jutting out of her thigh. She landed deftly, whirled on her heel and slammed her second blade down upon her mother's back. Shazziya's arm barred hers like a metal stanchion. *Crack!* Pain speared up into her elbow. The blade gashed Azziala's exposed shoulder, but caused no further damage. Lia's right forearm hung at an odd angle.

Shazziya barely blinked. "Hands off my Empress, wretch."

She had barely begun to blanch when the Enchantress blasted her off the Dragon's back.

* * * *

Grandion saw Hualiama's flight as a comet-like trail across his magical vision. He had finally worked out how to implement her ideas. High-speed pulses tracked her location amidst the chaos, sound bolstered with a touch of magic that sought out her song, the unique combination of scents, potentials, heartbeat and white-fires which had come to symbolise Hualiama to a blind Dragon.

It seemed she fell slowly. Shadows surrounded her, Dragons in a battle-frenzy, clashing with each other while she fell, buffeted but essentially unmolested, through a sky rife with slashing talons and blooms of Dragon fire. Having thrown up an optical shield the instant he heard Azziala's commands, Grandion had avoided capture. Now, he knew that the Maroon Dragoness laboured to free her fellows while Lia tumbled through the sky. The Tourmaline flexed his huge flight muscles, powering upward so strongly that his spine creaked with the effort.

A Grunt! The pressure-wave alerted him. Grandion spun mid-air, stalling with his left wing while pumping the right. The speeding Dragon clipped his tail on the way past. He lunged, talons outstretched.

"Got you!" Relief made his voice especially basso, a booming from the depths of his chest as he clutched Lia to his chest.

"Grandion. Thank the heavens."

"You attacked your mother? That was brave."

"I failed. Grandion, you heard Mizuki. Your shell-father's coming–"

He growled, "Where are you injured?"

"Split lip. Talon in my back. Broken arm. Nothing serious."

"Nothing serious?" The Tourmaline's displeasure stunned his Rider.

"Islands' sakes, next time I won't hitch a ride on a passing avalanche! Grandion, Sapphurion's coming. We need to rally the Dragons and drive off Azziala." She drew him into her mind. *Now fly, o prince of the dawn fires!*

Her shout galvanised his waning powers. There was a strength of draconic Storm that caused his words to reverberate like a thunderclap among the Dragonkind–audible and magical, he caused every muzzle to turn in his direction. *DRAGONS TOGETHER! RISE AGAINST THESE HATERS!*

Bellowing this cry many times, Grandion rallied the disparate Dragons. Lia was right. They could easily be turned against Azziala, for Humans were lower on the food chain.

"Lower on the food chain?" Lia kicked his paw. "Charming beast."

"Sit, Rider!"

The Tourmaline did not do contrition–not in the midst of a battle. But Lia only laughed at his smoke and thunder. "More war poetry, Dragon, or can I trust you to do the job properly this time?"

Hurricane-force winds preceded the Tourmaline Dragon's solo assault on Azziala's forces. Lightning jagged from his throat. Multiple branches struck the Dragon-Haters' shield, followed by a brief salvo of Grunts–those left alive. Then, Razzior rose at his left flank and Ianthine and Affurion to his right. The Dragons pummelled the Lost Island Humans with fire and ice, lava and acid, and a stream of superheated glue from the single Grey amongst Razzior's Dragonwing.

Azziala's force vanished for long seconds behind curtains of flame, but somehow they weathered that first assault at the cost of several Dragons' collapse.

"DRAGONS, OBEY!" screamed the Enchantress, every vein in her neck and forehead etched in gold. But many of the Dragonkind were beyond reason or restraint, including Grandion. These lowborn scum had turned proud Dragons into slaves. Dragon-thunder shook the morning, and with it, came Sapphurion and his Dragonwing of Gi'ishior, including the egg-siblings Zulior and Qualiana, both massive Reds, and Andarraz the Green, Brown Tarbazzan and Haaja the Yellow Dragoness.

Through the cacophony, Lia's soft inner cry reminded Grandion of the cost of what these Dragons wrought. Having just lost her father, her mother now stood on the brink of annihilation. She would lose everything.

I AM SAPPHURION! The mighty Blue leader's breath frosted the morning air, an ultra-cold blast that froze the Dragon-Haters' shield in solid sheets which gleamed like crysglass in the suns-light.

Stretching her neck like a cannon, his mate Qualiana fired a series of white-hot fireballs against the shield, so rapidly that they became a single smear of colour across Hualiama's vision. The Dragon-Haters' magic shattered. Hundreds of Dragons snarled their praise. Heat seared Grandion's throat as he joined his Dragon-kin, fire mingling with fire, and a fierce Dragonsong of joy buoyed his wings as a firestorm swept over the enemy Dragons and their detestable cargo. Beautiful fire!

The stench of sulphur and charcoal upon the air … oh, blackened bodies tumbling from the sky, a rain of judgement!

Mother, Lia breathed.

* * * *

In the wake of that stunning obliteration, the Dragons drifted on the breeze, arching their necks proudly or flicking their wings to loosen the soot and grit. Many watched the corpses falling until they were lost in the Cloudlands a league below.

Sapphurion was the first to move, winging over to greet his shell-son with a wingtip touch. *Fiery and sulphurous greetings, my shell-son. The Maroon Dragoness tells me you've found the Scroll? My happiness is unbounded.* His eyes measured Hualiama. *Well met, Dragonfriend.*

She inclined her head respectfully. *The most sulphurous greetings of Great Fra'anior to you, noble Sapphurion.*

Incongruous. Such formality–a warning?

As if drawn to a lodestone, Dragons gathered around Hualiama and Grandion in the air, and the animus in many of their fiery gazes made her shiver. Cradling her injured arm, Lia watched Ianthine and Affurion drawing together with their remaining half-dozen Overminds, while Razzior summoned his Dragonwing with an imperious flick of his tail. Sapphurion's group matched the combined strength of Razzior's kin and the Lost Islands Dragons. Balance? Could she hope? Her very presence upon Grandion's back must enrage them.

Mizuki, bearing Saori and Elki upon her back, descended to align herself with Grandion. Small mercies. Her brother nodded at her, by his bearing, acutely aware of the escalating danger.

Lightly, the wind wuthered atop the Dragon's Bell.

"My Dragon-kin, there is much work yet to be done," Sapphurion began.

"There is the matter of the Scroll of Binding," Razzior inserted smoothly. "And these young Dragons who openly flout the law. What say you to this, Sapphurion? Shall justice not prevail amongst the Dragonkind this day?"

Here it came. Lia's stomach churned as the great Dragon Elder regarded them, his manner, ineffable, the fire of his eyes bright and proud, as though he harboured not a qualm in the world. She expected him to advance a cunning reply, a draconic subterfuge.

Instead, the Dragon Elder said, "With all my hearts, I approve."

Silence rippled from his words. The very air seemed to freeze. Such was the nobility and truth of his demeanour, Sapphurion seemed unassailable. Was this payment for his betrayal of his son? Hualiama sucked in her lip.

"A new magic lives in our Island-World, my Dragon-kin," Sapphurion added softly. "This is the magic bequeathed us by Amaryllion Fireborn, last of the Ancient Dragons, and I say that this magic is the white-fires which live in Hualiama Dragonfriend–aye, fires clothed in Human flesh."

Even Ianthine flinched.

"Magic?" Razzior growled. "What is this magic but the taint of the *ruzal* corrupting her flesh, and the miasma of a Human who claims to *love* a Dragon?" He projected an image as he spoke–Hualiama, spinning into Grandion's paws, crying, 'My Dragonlove!' Every Dragon perceived, from her perspective, how she looked at the Tourmaline Dragon in that split second. "Do you condone this perversion too, Sapphurion?"

The Blue Dragon hesitated. Fatally.

The wily Orange Dragon crooked his claw. *TRAITOR!* thundered over the draconic congregation. Hualiama did not at first perceive what had happened. Andarraz the Green Elder had a hundred-fang grip upon Sapphurion's neck. Ambush! Khaki, boiling acid spurted out of his jaw as the glistening Green added to that appalling bite, the highly corrosive acid and poison that the most powerful Greens were noted for. Sapphurion's mouth gaped in agony. Tarbazzan and Haaja flung themselves at Sapphurion, now a knot of other Dragons roared in, some to support him and others to attack the enormous Dragon Elder.

As Grandion launched himself into the fray with a panicked

bugle, Lia's gaze flicked to Razzior, taking in the sardonic curve of his lip. Almost lazily, the Orange Dragon accelerated to close with Qualiana, who fought in a thundering frenzy to reach her besieged mate.

Perfidy! She should have guessed. Razzior had turned some of the Dragon Elders against Sapphurion. Perhaps it had not been difficult. Dragon egos were as oversized as their mighty frames.

Swooping at his maximum acceleration, Grandion fired shot after shot of jagged ice spears at Andarraz, peppering his flank as though dozens of crossbow bolts had struck him at once. Gobs of boiling flesh and smoke continued to pour out of Sapphurion's neck as the feral Green refused to relinquish his bite, despite Qualiana snapping around his ear-canals, her talons apparently buried halfway down his throat. Grandion's focussed thunderbolt knocked Tarbazzan out of the reckoning. The Brown fell limply toward the ledge beside the Dragons' Bell. Meantime, the Tourmaline clamped down on Andarraz's back.

Sapphurion's plight moved Hualiama's hearts to grief. Her grief spoke in fury and fire. Nothing in the Island-World could restrain her magic now. Igniting her left hand in lieu of her Nuyallith blade, Lia waded in with a vengeance. She hacked at the Green's head, severing skull-spikes and carving steaming ruts around his upper skull and muzzle. Suddenly, Razzior pounded Sapphurion with a glob of molten rock at least twenty feet across, careless of friend or foe, jarring both Grandion and Andarraz loose. Lia had a glimpse of holes in Sapphurion's neck she could have climbed inside with ease, before the Tourmaline spun on a brass dral to assault Razzior. A flurry of gigantic blows staggered even the tough-as-diamonds Orange, before Hualiama added a parting swipe that sheared the final fifth of his left wing clean off.

Razzior screeched, *You'll pay for that*–Lia did not even know the word he used in Dragonish, but it was clearly a curse.

She whirled her flaming sword about her head, yelling, *Come here and I'll trim the other wing to match!*

More Dragons peeled off the Gi'ishior Dragons' original

Dragonwing, mobbing Sapphurion and Qualiana with champing jaws and flashing fangs. Golden blood spurted from dozens of wounds. The mated pair fought with the fierceness of ten, but the tide was against them until Ianthine threw her might into the fray. Mizuki screamed past Grandion, lining up Haaja with her fearful power of Shivers, that ultra-rare draconic power which vaporised flesh or rock. The front half of the Yellow Dragoness shattered in a spray of blood.

Dragons and Dragonesses knotted together above the Dragon's Bell, slowly losing height as the tremendous expenditure of magic and Dragon fire took its inevitable toll. Sapphurion was the first to fall, crash-landing near the base of the Bell, and Qualiana, lifeless, crumpled upon the rock beside her mate. Mizuki became marooned amongst a group of Lost Islands Dragons who were steadily driven off to the west, while Razzior and his expanded force closed in on Grandion and Ianthine.

The Maroon Dragoness looked worse than ever. Razzior in particular had chewed her over, but she flung herself tirelessly against the Orange Dragon, thwarting his repeated attacks on Lia and Grandion. They clashed with their *ruzal* wiles, tearing strips of hide off each other and battling as much mind-to-mind as in the physical realm. Grandion swept a clutch Dragons off the battlefield with his Storm winds, but Andarraz rose again into the scrimmage, unleashing a spray of sticky, rope-like fluid that snarled Grandion's wings enough to stall the Tourmaline. Razzior roared over her Dragon's arched back.

Hualiama never saw the blow that knocked her loose.

Her ribs felt as though she had been struck amidships by a runaway Dragonship. Ianthine plucked up the gasping, wheezing Princess, whereupon Razzior pounced on the Maroon Dragoness, clamping his forepaws around her neck as he sought to knock Hualiama out of her paw. Lia responded with a bolt of lightning which burned a small black hole in his snout. Shouting, she repeated the attack, with even less effect.

Razzior laughed, "Having trouble, Dragonfriend?"

"What have you done?"

"Give me the Scroll of Binding, child. This battle is between Dragons."

"Dragon, obey," she spluttered.

Razzior only chortled, champing closer beneath Ianthine's neck. Without warning, he whirled in the air, crushing the Dragoness against the Bell's metal surface. Another great peal rang out. The impact jarred Lia loose. She tumbled down the near-vertical surface, faster and faster, pursued by both Ianthine and Razzior. The ground rushed upward. She flailed, but found no more fire within herself. She had burned out.

Ianthine's right wing flapped loosely, obviously snapped. But with a supreme effort, the Maroon Dragoness outpaced the younger Dragon, rescuing Hualiama from a fatal fall a split-second before they struck the ground. Lia landed beside the Dragoness' nose, feather-soft on a burst of Maroon power. Razzior thundered down, breaking Ianthine's lower spine with a monstrous kick of his hind feet.

For a second, Ianthine's fires blazed with a twin-suns fury. Then they become occluded by pain.

She gasped, *Keep the* ruzal *from him, Hualiama.*

I will, she promised.

The eye-fires guttered with appalling slowness, allowing Lia to take in both the expiration of a Dragon's fire-soul, and the triumphant pose the Orange Dragon struck atop her body.

Ianthine spluttered, *I saved you, didn't I? Didn't I, Dragon … friend?*

You burned with true-fires, Ianthine, Hualiama choked out. *May your soul fly to the eternal fires.*

The Dragoness was gone. Lia bowed her head.

Razzior stalked her, snarling, "Yield, girl, or I'll order them to execute your precious Tourmaline."

* * * *

The image of his girl, so tiny before Razzior's swirling dark power, shimmered before Grandion as he expended the last of his lightning power on the Dragons surrounding him.

Andarraz's acid burned his back. *Down, hatchling!*

They wanted to capture him? Grandion fought with all of his strength and cunning, but ten Dragons crowded his airspace, forcing him downward with merciless bites at his wings, while Andarraz and four other Dragons piled upon him from above. He was ninety feet long and stronger than any one of their number, but their combined efforts forced him to a bone-crushing landing a hundred feet from Lia's position. Grandion's left hind leg buckled upon impact. He had no chance to reflect upon the pain as the Dragons subdued him with the tonnage of their bodies, pinning his wings, tail and upper body beneath a huge pile of Dragonflesh.

Dragons landed all around them. Tens of Dragons. More than he could have imagined. How many had Razzior turned? No, some of these were Dragons who had not joined the battle, waiting to align themselves with the victorious side. Or these Dragons stood against a Dragon and his Human Rider, waiting to see how Razzior dealt with her before making the angle of their flight clear. Grandion knew he had doomed his Rider.

"Yield," snarled Razzior.

Hualiama turned. He sensed the weight of her regard.

Grandion wondered if her eye-fires still held that softness he had once observed, an expression reserved for her Dragon. Exhaustion spread through his body, but he would not give up. No, this Dragon would fight until he spilled the last drop of his fire-soul …

"I yield for his sake," she said. His muzzle slumped against the ground. "But I will die rather than give you what you want, Razzior."

The Orange was all arrogance now. "What do I want? Justice. You are the Scroll of Binding. You and your knowledge are the greatest danger ever to threaten the Dragonkind. Sapphurion was a blind fool. I will restore the rule of draconic law and the strong paw of justice. No Dragon will ever submit to a Human again!"

Snarls hailed his words.

"Dragons! This Human is the daughter of Azziala, leader of the Dragon-Haters. She came to Grandion, shell-son of

Sapphurion, and seduced him with promises of *ruzal*. She rode Dragonback." His voice throbbed with outrage, making the tall metal bell sing in response. Over the rising thunder of the watching Dragons, Razzior roared, "Now she twists other Dragons to her ways. But I say we are the masters of the air! Lords of every Island! Never will a Dragon be shackled. Our task is clear. We must immolate these Dragon-Haters with our fire, starting with this one right here! Who will speak for this Human?"

* * * *

Sapphurion groaned, "I will … speak."

As if unchained, Hualiama rushed to the Blue Dragon. "Sapphurion. Mercy …"

The great eyes darkened as his fires receded. Then, the Blue Elder appeared to rally. By his suffering, he commanded their attention. "No Dragon can know peace … while his fires … yet burn! Dragon-kin, I know this hatchling. I raised her in my roost for three years. I fed her from my own paw. There is no fire in her but the fire of Amaryllion Fireborn, the fire-gift of an Ancient Dragon!"

Hualiama bowed, weeping as the great Dragon struggled to speak his last words. "Sapphurion …"

"Warring among ourselves, we grow weak. For the future of the Dragonkind, for the sake of our shell-sons and shell-daughters, let us bind lasting peace between Dragons and Humans!"

He remembered! Long ago, Lia had begged the Dragon Elder to bind his purpose to peace; she had risked all to prevent open war between the Dragons and Humans of Fra'anior Cluster. That stage seemed tiny in comparison, now. Azziala had fallen, but Razzior and Shinzen still vied for the ultimate power.

I have third-heart-loved her as my own hatchling! Sapphurion roared, spitting his words between gouts of blood pouring from his muzzle and neck. *Truly she is named the Dragonfriend. Witness how I pass my soul-fires to my beloved shell-son, Grandion. For he is worthy! And my only blindness was not to love his fires from the first.*

With that, the great Dragon heaved one final time to his paws. A whisper-storm of fire rushed over Hualiama and poured into Grandion. Sapphurion collapsed. The rasp of his breathing slowed.

Thou my soul's fires, my guiding star, she heard Grandion whisper.

Sapphurion lay silent.

Razzior pounced! With his paw, he swatted Hualiama aside. "Away from this noble Dragon, beast!"

"What?" Lia groaned as her injured arm struck the Dragon's Bell. She stumbled to her knees, too enervated to stand. "I–"

"I'll be the first to celebrate this Dragon's passing into the eternal fires! I will raise my Dragonsong the loudest and the longest in praise of Sapphurion's noble deeds," declared Razzior. Fire leaked from his nostrils to accentuate his words. Very slowly, playing his role to the hilt, he raised his fore-talon to point at the Princess of Fra'anior. "But first, we must execute this liar."

"I'm no liar!" she shouted. "You twist Dragons to your bidding."

The Orange sneered, "Her secret gift is even deadlier than the power of these Dragon-Haters!"

"What gift?"

Across from her, Grandion's muzzle poked out from beneath a pile of Dragon bodies. She saw his fire. If she could hold Razzior's wrath for a moment longer, might he recover? What strength could oppose Razzior now? He had these Dragons eating out of his paw. She read it in their mood, in the slow, sinuous approach of Andarraz and Tarbazzan, of the Dragons slinking around her, even up the mountainside to gain a view. Razzior's long, lava-coloured body smoked with the force of his passion; that passion was what drew the Dragons to him, fire to fire. Honeyed words, they would say on Fra'anior. Words to turn Dragons feral with rage.

"She loves a Dragon," he said, stabbing a claw toward

Grandion. "That Dragon."

Hualiama saw her chance. She could destroy the *ruzal.* She had to. With its power, the living knowledge secreted inside her being by Ianthine, Razzior would be unstoppable–and the only thing which prevented her from unleashing her dark magic upon him, was that she refused to become like her father. Ra'aba had not mastered *ruzal.* The magic had used him; burned and destroyed him.

A fate worse than death.

Aye, Razzior's serpentine voice slithered into her mind. *Use your magic. Give it to me.*

Desperately she searched the storehouses of her being. Where was the white-fire now? Where was the power of laughter, of dance? Her soul rained sorrow. Only in sacrifice could the light shine, a light that would free Grandion from the taint of her presence.

To the heavens, she shouted, *Aye, I love him, heavens have mercy! But he never loved me.*

Chapter Thirty-Six

Dragonlove

ALL DRAGONS WOULD know the truth of her words.

Grandion stared, appalled. She truly believed he held no regard for her? Impressions cascaded through his mind. Her laughter. Lia's song trilling out over his back as they flew that first time together, offshore of Ha'athior. The fires of her soul. A moment of wicked desire as he admired her nudity … that had shaken him down to the paws. How could he feel that way about a Human?

The truth excoriated Grandion. Words and emotions seemed to stick to his shrivelled tongue. In all the time he had known Hualiama, he had never admitted to love. Never found the courage. Now his vaunted strength was spent. His magic, exhausted. What could he give? What could a Dragon do, but unchain his heart and bid it fly?

As he lay unspeaking, the hint of ghostly fire overlaying her being diminished. She meant to die for him. She would die to keep her powers from Razzior, who had stolen so much–and was still stealing, the Tourmaline realised. Razzior had stolen her Word; now, he fed off her power, his *ruzal* secretly siphoning off whatever draconic or magical power it found in his surrounds. The Orange Dragon was insatiable.

Razzior postured, spitting acid upon the idea of a Human loving a Dragon. He fuelled the furnaces of their rage and pride with visions of the end of draconic power in the Island-World, and promised a new reign of justice–led by himself, of course. Hualiama knelt, apparently submitting to her fate, while all around the rumbling of Dragon-fires swelled until the heat of their fury shimmered the air.

This was wrong!

The Tourmaline began to roar, *I*–but the weight above him bore down suddenly, redoubled.

Even now, Razzior fought him. The Orange Dragon feared what he could do. Grandion surged, the sorrow-rage granting him the might of many Dragons, but he could not gain his paws. A hundred Dragonkind surrounded his Rider, his peerless Human, and he lay powerless to intervene. Even his telepathic Dragonish seemed to be blocked. Razzior. His mental grip overlaid the Dragons subtly, so gargantuan yet subtle that his kin had no idea they were being manipulated. Heat rose around the draconic shadows–his vision was returning!

Amidst that draconic congregation, Hualiama knelt. Never more beautiful. Never more tragic.

* * * *

"And so, I invite all Dragons of true draconic fires to join me in burning this lawless Dragon Rider, this heinous Dragon-murderer, this child of *ruzal*, to ashes!"

Razzior's final challenge sparked a sudden hush of expectation. Fire-eyes and bared fangs surrounded Hualiama, headed by the trio of Razzior, Tarbazzan and Andarraz. To her right hand, Qualiana lay unmoving. Sapphurion's hearts still beat, occasionally, but the fires had departed from his eyes. Ianthine lay further away, surmounted by Andarraz's paws. So much death. All, as Razzior had accused her, because of the Dragonfriend. Why had fate cursed her? The Island-World would be a better place without the indwelling darkness.

Grandion seemed unable to speak. Was that an enlivening spark of fire she saw in his eyes?

Now, as Lia prepared to release her spirit, the world's freshness tantalised her nostrils. Heat stole the breath from her lungs. Streamers of white-fire burnished the sky. The Dragon-battle aloft had paused, as if alive to the knowledge that enfolded her soul in a starkly wonderful truth.

A love tested in the crucible of fate must burn, or die.

Through the oh-so-languid blossoming of fires in the multitude of muzzles encircling her, Hualiama saw as through a white tunnel, Grandion's face. Courage flowed from his spirit to hers. There was no need for speech, though the exhausted, battered Tourmaline's mouth worked to expel the Dragonsong of his soul. She knew him. He knew her.

In that final instant of silence, all she knew was her soul's longing for the unattainable, beautiful *beyond.*

The world exploded.

Hualiama knelt within the heart of a living volcano of Dragon fire. Screaming. Burning. Tormented beyond comprehension. The searing fires turned the rock beneath her knees to slag, and consumed her clothing in a millisecond. Fire lapped and boiled around her as though she soared across heavens ablaze, passing through veils of reality loosened by the all-consuming magic of Dragon fire, and through the thunder resounding in her ears, filling and somehow amplifying the vortex of fire, Grandion's shout carried to her awareness:

HUALIAMA! HUMANLOVE!

Joy vanquished her grief. Disbelief supplanted the fear. She had submitted to death's final claim upon her accursed existence, and … what? How could she be alive? Thinking? He … loved her? Her Dragonlove loved her!

Surely, she dreamed.

* * * *

Abruptly, Lia saw stars. Dazzling ribbons of stars adorned a velvet night sky. What? Was this a vision of death? She trod stairs of milky white marble up to a hexagonal colonnade made of the same ethereal stone, silhouetted against the darkness. Barefoot, noiseless, Lia stepped lightly between the columns. At the centre, close enough to touch, she found a huge bed covered in white linens, surrounded by filmy white drapes depending from a vaulting, gazebo-like bedframe.

A girl slumbered upon the bed. Midnight-blue tresses

tumbled over the pillow-roll, obscuring her face from view. The Princess of Fra'anior tilted her head quizzically. Despite its improbable colour, the girl's hair seemed oddly familiar. Apart from a slim hand embracing the pillow, it was the only splash of colour in the entire place.

Why was she here? Hadn't she been dying somewhere? Burning to cinders?

Memories flitted about in her mind, as teasing as Fra'aniorian fireflies investigating a crimson fireflower.

She felt safe. A sense of timelessness pervaded this scene. Nothing else existed. Slipping between the hangings, Hualiama perched upon the bed's edge. Did she recognise this girl?

Reaching out, she clasped the other girl's hand. "Wake up."

She woke quickly, as though woken from a daydream. She rose on her elbow, keeping hold of Hualiama's fingers, and whispered, "I've waited so long. What kept you?"

Lia gasped, "You're …"

"Don't be afraid." The girl smiled shyly. "I'm Hualiama."

"*I'm* Hualiama."

The desire to know this person trumped the fear that insisted she snatch her hand back. The connection between them was so intense, so deep and inexpressibly sweet …

"You're me." For an awkward second, Hualiama was unsure which of them had spoken. "I mean, you're perfectly me, but … *are* you me?"

The blue-haired girl chuckled, exactly the same throaty note Lia knew she made. "It's complicated. I didn't mean to scare you. I know it must be a shock–"

"I know! I mean, I've always known … right, I've no idea which Island I've landed on. Who are you?"

Reaching up, the girl tucked a strand of platinum hair behind her mirror-image's ear. "You're beautiful, Human girl."

Hualiama looked away, stammering, "O-O-Oh, that's just freaky." The girl's laughter trilled across her embarrassed explanation, "Me telling me I'm beautiful? No. I'm not vain. Am I dreaming? Is this some incipient insanity, the *ruzal* turning me into an Ianthine or–Islands' sakes–much worse, my father?"

"I'm sorry. It's just that I've waited so long, ever since you woke me–"

"I woke you? I woke me?"

Specks of starlight shone in the other girl's eyes. Impossible! Everything about her was Hualiama, from the way she held her head, to the magic suffusing those blue orbs. She said, "When you cried, '*Let it be–*'"

Unbound. Lia shuddered. "You aren't the *ruzal* taken form and life–no. I sense your goodness. I unbound you? You were my captive? But I'd never–I'm babbling like a dragonet, aren't I? My head hurts. How can you be me? Hualiama?"

"Be at peace. All will become clear."

Lia scowled at herself. "If you really are me, you'd know how much I hate it when people say that." But she could not suppress the upward curve of her lips which accompanied those less-than-heated words.

The girl wriggled into a kneeling position. Squeezing both of Lia's hands in her own, she said earnestly, *I'm you. We've been together since before you were born. I've protected us. I took this form because I thought it would help you understand. While I believe we are meant to be together, I could not* force *myself …*

The nuances of Dragonish conveyed so much. Appalling truths. The girl meant how Ra'aba had forced Azziala, how Azziala's madness had killed her unborn babe, and how the draconic way was to command without question, the way Grandion had dominated her before. Mirror-tears streaked mirrored cheeks. The fragile connection deepened, gathering strength and significance. This girl, this maybe-spirit-creature, was somehow her and not her, as if life indwelled a facet of her pre-existent personality. Understanding filled Hualiama. Conviction. This was right.

They spoke simultaneously, *I waited for you.*

Love squeezed her heart. Both of their hearts. Bizarre as it seemed, she loved herself, unselfishly and completely, yet with a freshness that touched her soul with astonishment. All the Islands of her world should quake, and they did, but she knew peace.

Blue-haired Hualiama added, through her tears, "I waited in

our dreams for you to find the way."

"Truly, I don't understand."

"I know, but if I told you …" Other-Hualiama wrinkled her nose drolly. "I think you'd believe me. But I'd prefer to show you. We love surprises."

"You're as cheeky as–me. I've so many questions! Who am I? Where did I–or you–spring from? Protecting me, how? Why have you been hiding all these years?" An enigmatic smile was her answer. "Do you have all my memories? Our memories? I don't have words … I feel as if I've known you all my life, but I don't. What do I call you? Me? Other-me?" Lia begged, "Please. Help me understand."

"You will."

"Are you an unborn twin?"

"No." Her alter-ego's blue eyes twinkled with gladness; love, even. "Surprises first. Clever guesses later."

Blonde-Lia growled, "I take it if I swat you, I'll only hurt myself?"

"Indeed. You're so me, but you need to go now."

"How will I find … me, again?"

"Sheer stubbornness?"

That final, mischievous grin exploded into a constellation of stars as an overwhelming force gripped Hualiama. She cannoned into a realm of heat and fire.

* * * *

Irrepressible laughter thundered from Grandion's throat. Seventy feet away, Razzior's fire choked off as though the Tourmaline had personally flown over and stuffed it back down his gullet.

Echo upon echo rolled away over the Cloudlands as the Dragons ceased their assault.

Hualiama's depthless blue eyes–oh, how he longed to see more than the traces teasing his scarred vision–lifted, luminous with power, and her hair shone as though inhabited by the fire which had passed over her, yet left her untouched. Her soul-fires seemed haunted, as though fragments of her life-force still roamed the Island-World.

The Tourmaline knew. His seventh sense *knew* the truth …

"You herd of feckless, overgrown ralti sheep!" Grandion snarled. "You've all the fire of a herd of woolly bleaters. Bring me some real Dragons, not pathetic null-fires and windroc hatchlings. Shall I add some lightning? Maybe you should try burning her again, with hotter fires?"

* * * *

Hualiama's scandalised cry cut through her Dragon's laughter. "Grandion!"

The Dragon was mad. *She* was mad. How could she be standing knee-deep in cooling rock? Lia gaped as Grandion taunted Razzior. He had burned her before. She should know. Her skin … was not even blistered. The heat alone should have turned her to ash. The blast should have blown those ashes over the Cloudlands. Mercy.

The Orange Dragon's talons raked trenches in the rock as he gaped slack-jawed at the impossible sight of a Human who had survived his most incendiary Dragon fires. Then, his body juddered. His scales shimmered with the fire and heat churning within him. Here it came. Immolation.

Razzior's rage shook the mountain. White-hot lava gushed from his throat, endless streams of molten rock that pinned Lia against the Dragon's Bell, swallowing her up. The other Dragons followed suit, producing an unbridled conflagration, a volcanic Cloudlands hell vented upon the lone Human. Unendurable. An orange sea boiled around her. Riven with agony, her sanity threatened to expire in Dragon fire.

She could not believe, but she must, for the torment raged unending. Even death's Isle would not have her.

Distinctly, she heard Grandion's whisper in her mind, *Dance, my beloved. Become the fire.*

What did he know that she could not grasp?

She escaped to the dance. It was the only way. Dance could lead her to the inner flame. The *Flame Cycle,* always her favourite, captivated her with its mystical depictions of a

Dragon's soul. There, in the crucible of her greatest affliction, the great Black Dragon seemed to smile upon her once more. She danced the soul-dance in honour of Amaryllion. Her bare feet tripped across molten rock, no longer feeling solid ground. She bathed in the fire, breathed it in, welcoming Dragon fire into her soul. Even the sharp pain of her broken arm seemed to diminish, for she was fading now, melding into the glorious fire-dance which had always beckoned and seduced her innermost desires.

A tranquil harbour in the inferno, she invited the other presence into her soul. *Be mine. Be me.*

All became white. All was glorious.

* * * *

It seemed that the Islands danced upon their foundations.

Starlight, so pure and penetrating that a Dragon's secondary nictitating membranes could not protect against it, bloomed before the stupefied Orange Dragon as though a bud unfurled its petals. Every Dragon present had to shield their eyes, even semi-blind Grandion. He looked with the eyes of magic. Even he could not gaze into a star's dazzling heart.

A fledgling's Dragon fire easily reached furnace temperatures. An adult Blue male could produce lightning in excess of thirty thousand degrees. The fire that burned where Hualiama had stood–he had no words. It lapped gently over Razzior and Andarraz, and they were gone. Tarbazzan had reaction speed enough to half-turn before the light engulfed him. Grandion blinked. Obliterated. Between one pulse of his hearts and the next, the Dragons surrounding Hualiama and even those crushing him beneath their flesh-mountain, evaporated into the mystical starlight. He could not even detect a vapour-trail. They had not been teleported–that mythical ability of the Ancient Dragons. Only the tip of Tarbazzan's tail remained, lopped off with surgical precision. It twitched one last time as though even dead flesh sought to convey that the impossible had just transpired.

This was magic to blast a Dragon off his paws.

Filaments threaded the receding light, tracing a design of wing-shivering beauty, now solidifying into a creature which cast no shadow. Could it be? Grandion's intuition insisted that such indescribable magic should split the skies with the peals of its thunder, or raise volcanoes from the deeps. It should hurl stars about like the fires of first creation. But this creature was *she,* the transcendent purity of starlight, and the incarnation of feminine innocence. She shone, and no evil could stand against.

His nostrils twitched. That smell–oh, a beguiling, well-remembered smell! The huge Tourmaline Dragon stumbled forward, flaring his nostrils in shock.

He purred, *Who are you, little one?*

* * * *

When her vision cleared, Hualiama found herself standing opposite the Tourmaline Dragon. He crouched ten feet away, gaping at her with quite the most befuddled expression. Her eyes blinked twice, oddly. A queer grin displayed his fangs. *Who are you?* His ardent growl flustered her senses most delightfully.

She stammered, "Grandion, w-why are y-you looking at me like that?"

He haplessly imitated a ralti sheep chewing a mouthful of grass.

Fuelled by the unexpected heat roiling in her belly, an irritable edge entered her voice. "It's only me–Hualiama, chief trouble-stirrer. Where's Razzior? What just happened?"

"Hualiama?"

Still the weird, discomfiting purr! "Grandion, who else …"

Her voice choked off as she took in the expressions of the watching Dragons, those who had not joined Razzior in trying to burn her. Her neck twizzled. Lia blinked as her strangely inflamed eyes wallowed in impossibly magnified details, or sped to a wide view that included Sapphurion to her right side, gazing at her with unguarded wonder. Her mind felt fragmented, filled with thoughts not her own. Cascades of sight and sound and smells sluiced over her senses.

She snatched at the threads of normalcy. "Sapphurion, you tell … um, aren't you dead?"

Sapphurion lowered his muzzle and raised his wings half-aloft, a gesture of the utmost draconic respect. *She is born!* he bugled, so powerfully that the sound carried beyond the mountaintop and across the Cloudlands. Hualiama froze. Frissons of Dragonsong frolicked along her spine. *She breathes! She burns!*

Movement rippled around the watching Dragons. In twos and threes they stooped and raised their wings aloft, even Grandion–even her Dragon! The Tourmaline bowed regally, causing a buzzing in her ears and a disconcerting expansion in her senses, driving inward and lapping outward simultaneously. First the Land Dragon, now the Lesser Dragons? No right-minded Dragon would dream of abasing themselves before a Human, not even Grandion. Why her? What by any of the five moons did this mean?

Here came Mizuki. The Copper Dragoness bowed aerially before putting down neatly not fifty feet from Grandion's left flank. Sapphurion, the mighty Dragon Elder, held his genuflection, his eyes more effulgent than she had ever seen.

So fragile the moment, it trembled upon the cusp of glory.

"What're you Dragons doing?" Lia's voice joined the plaintive wind. "Please, I'm not worthy. I don't understand. Grandion … help …"

Panicked, she tried to run. Hualiama tumbled over her paws and landed flat on her overlong muzzle.

Oh no!

She writhed to her feet–to her paws–with a horrified squeak. Normalcy? What Island of insanity was this? "No. I have … mercy! I'm a Dragon? I'm a Dragon!" She hissed with pain as her injured wing flared. Lia almost knotted her neck looking at herself, wild of eye. "No!" She raised a paw. Stared at a wingtip bunting her nose. "This is cosmic madness. I'm Human. No wings, definitely no scales. Islands' sakes, I'm burning." Flames licked around her muzzle. Dazed, she muttered, "Why am I burning?"

Sapphurion rumbled, "That's Dragon fire, my shell-daughter."

As one beast, the Dragons broke into glorious Dragonsong:

She breathes! She burns!
The Dragonsong of living fire.
Blessed eggling, born to fly.

Lia's heartbeat thrashed in her stomach and up in her throat and there was fire, so much fire … their song rose over the crazy-fast rushing of blood in her ears, the words changing to an ancient Dragonish dialect that spoke of the quickening of a Dragon's fire-soul, distilled from the infernos of creation … and now she was burning, burning up, until nothing remained of her but fire-soul.

Dimly, she heard the Dragon Elder add, "Your fires do the Island-World honour, Star Dragon."

* * * *

Grandion lunged forward to pluck up the hatchling Dragoness as she sagged. *Gently, little one,* he soothed. Oh, hatchling-sweetness! How protectively his paw cupped her tiny body! A Dragon-instinct made her curl up on his palm, her tail first slapping her shoulder before settling down.

The Tourmaline growled, *Lia? Is it you, Hualiama?*

D-Do you c-call dead Dragons, Star D-Dragons? Oh mercy, what's happening to me … everything feels so peculiar …

He crooned, *Fold your wings like this, little one. Gentle your fires. You need to find your paws.*

G-Grandion … I'm a … how? I'm a Dragoness, aren't I? Aren't I, Grandion?

A tremor ran the length of his long throat. *You're perfect.*

The Dragoness' hearts sped along at a terrific rate, giving her posture a quivering, kittenish appearance. Grandion wished he knew what to say to calm her. How could he express the Dragonsong thrilling his hearts? This, he could never have imagined, not in a million summers. He feared to release this treasure lest Lia disappear to wherever she had been hiding her

Dragoness before, or worse, might she return to her Human form? He yearned to twine necks with her, to fly over mountaintops and show her the wonders of the Island-World. The strength of his emotions staggered the Tourmaline Dragon. The Human girl had chosen to be cremated, to die for him. No living creature could have endured the fires Razzior had blasted at her.

His senses rode the breeze. Aye, all of Razzior's fire had been extinguished. Not even the bones remained.

Breathlessly, the Dragoness sang from his paw:

I'm scared, I burn, o Dragon please tell me,
How do you love a fire?

Every scale upon his body trumpeted its delighted recognition. He bugled back:

You become the fire.

Even his dim vision conveyed the brilliance of her eyes. Had that exchange been prophetic? Had his hearts known all along … no. Surely, the mystery of draconic magic could not transcend the bounds of belief by such a margin. Yet here she was. Dragoness. Star Dragon. He quivered, awestruck. Impulsively, Grandion dipped his muzzle to scent the little mite, missing his mark to snuffle around her haunches. Oh the beauteous, complex aroma–he snorted with laughter as Lia cuffed him across the nose, open-clawed.

G-G-Grandion, that's so inappropriate! Get off me!

Had he any doubt, it flew off the Island at her oh-so-Hualiama response.

Feisty little beauty, isn't she? Sapphurion grinned, pushing closer to Grandion to look her over. His talons curled jealously.

Her eyes were wells of the deepest blue, and her eye-fires swirled wildly as she regarded the Tourmaline Dragon with a coy tilt of her head. The Dragoness was flawless. Twelve tiny feet of draconic radiance. He stroked her spine-spikes with a gentle claw-tip. So soft, so pliable. Her scales were the blue of a late evening sky, with a slight sprinkling of white which reminded him of stardust. His free paw closed over her back, forming a womblike space in which her petite fires purred away, a vibration that transformed his belly into a trembling, molten lava-pit of passion and fiery joy.

In every respect, Hualiama surpassed his wildest imaginings. Dreams he had never believed, now stood incarnated in Dragon claw and wing, and in the embodiment of a newborn fire-soul–an undeniable, triumphant truth. A miracle.

"What have you done with my sister, you bunch of overgrown armoured Islands?" Elki shrilled nearby. The Prince of Fra'anior bowed curtly as Mizuki shouldered a space clear for him. "Thanks. Listen, I'm Elka'anor, Prince of Fra'anior and Dragon Rider. You. Blue Dragon."

Grandion and Sapphurion raised their muzzles in identically imperious gestures. "Aye?"

"Where's my sister?" He measured her height with his hand. "Human. About this tall. Cute, but has a dragonet's penchant for mischief. What was that white fire? Where'd Razzior go?"

Sapphurion began to whisper to Hualiama, but Grandion stilled him with an upraised talon. "Allow me, shell-father. Noble Prince, may I present your sister? Dragoness. About this tall." He illustrated with his talons. "Cute, but has a dragonet's penchant for mischief."

Elki's scowl mellowed as he considered the contents of Grandion's outstretched paw. "Exceptionally cute, I'll grant. But I was looking for a … a rather less scaly version of my–"

The Dragoness' smile flashed a mouthful of fangs like needles made of milky quartz. "Elki, you stork-legged excuse for a snivelling princeling, you had a pet parakeet named Flame-Head when you were eight. Don't you know a bit of short shrift when you see it?"

"No. N-N-No!" The Prince paled. "You aren't–you are–*oooh* …"

* * * *

"Catch him!" Hualiama yelped.

She sprang twenty feet past Elki in a single bound. Lia whirled, snapping and snorting, jarring her broken wing.

Grandion hulked opposite, apparently quite unaware of her brother's inelegant sprawl. He rumbled, "If you can stun a Human with a smile, you're definitely all Dragoness."

Human-Lia wanted to smack him. Dragon-Lia wanted to do things with a sexy Tourmaline Dragon that–well, she wasn't entirely sure what she wanted to do with him just yet–but they definitely weren't ideas any sane girl should have in her head as she practically dribbled fire over her Dragon. She clacked her fangs together with a dangerous snarl. Ooh, this was freaky. Two sets of feelings warred within her. A touch of Human made her begin to conceal her nudity, while the Dragoness reminded her that she was covered in armoured Dragon hide. Dragon-Lia salivated over every detail of Grandion's chunky physique. Yum. Human-Lia tried to figure out what she'd do with her blades, now that she had no waist for a sword belt.

Was this other-Hualiama's surprise? Rascally dragonet! She'd have words with herself–schizophrenic madwoman or none. Which was the real Hualiama? Both? Would she sleep as a Dragoness, and wake in her true Human form again? Her belly bubbled like an overheated cauldron at the thought.

Before the Island-World reverted to sanity and order, there was one thing she needed to do.

She purred, "Well, Grandion, just wait until I smile at you."

The Dragon stalked her with a lithe rippling of musculature, arching his wings in a way that she recognised as a draconic courtship ritual. Majestic as his pose might be, it was the song of his hearts that she ached for, that every fibre of her being willed him to reveal. How he loomed over her, tenderness enwrapped in fiery power, his nobility trembling the Islands of her world.

Barely could she breathe in anticipation of the words rising within her Dragonlove.

Hualiama of Fra'anior, you are the breath of this Dragon's fire-soul.

He wafted his flame gently against her muzzle. Cinnamon. Sulphur. She breathed in tangy notes of iron mingled with the subtle allure of jasmine and vanilla; a heady artist's palette of draconic scents which communicated the depths of his need and desire for her. *I love thee from the ends of the Island-World to the farthest stars that grace the heavens. Your greatest secret was foretold in your name, for truly you are* Hualiama, *the song of the Eastern star. May the Spirits of the Ancient Dragons bear witness to the fire-promises of my third heart.*

A draconic fire-promise! Somewhere, a Human girl was leaping and spinning, dancing and screaming with elation.

Grandion's flanks heaved, his voice grown solemn and throaty as the deepest furnaces of his feelings opened to her awareness. *I give gladly of my soul's veriest fires to thee, Star Dragoness, and may eternity smile upon us. Hualiama, thou art my Dragonlove.*

Dragon-Lia's fire caressed his muzzle. She whispered, *And thou, mine.*

Today, the enchantment over the Isles was love.

Chapter Thirty-Seven

Requiem

SLIDING A TALON beneath her chin, Sapphurion raised Lia's muzzle. "An Island's-weight of diamonds for your thoughts, melancholy Dragoness?"

"Will you be alright, shell-father? You must miss Qualiana."

"Alright? No." Sighing heavily, the huge Blue stooped to turn his burning eye upon her. "I've … it's like I lost a wing. I fear my fires will never burn again. Little one—"

"Why couldn't I heal her? Why?" The pain behind her breastbone pierced her hearts as surely as if she'd swallowed an Immadian forked dagger. Hualiama stared unseeing at Grandion, returned from negotiating with the Lost Islands Dragons. She knew he listened, even though he spoke with Mizuki as Elki worked on bandaging Saori's wounds with strips torn off his shirt. "Sapphurion, I failed you. I'm so sorry."

"Failed?" he thundered, then tempered his tone. "You did not fail. Even a Star Dragon's power cannot raise the dead. Her soul had flown, little one."

"You came back."

"Star Dragons restore balance in the Island-World. I cannot instruct you as your shell-mother could, but I know a smattering of lore. You healed me while my fire-soul yet dwelled in my flesh. There are many paths of healing. Star Dragons bring imbalance back into equilibrium. My Qualiana was a prodigy in physical healing, but her powers also extended beyond our physical realm into the treatment of magical diseases."

A Dragon could hear grief. Smell it. Taste it on her tongue. In the midst of her staggeringly expanded awareness, Hualiama still clung to her old stubbornness. "No, it can't be true," she insisted, drawing a deep, forlorn chuckle from him. "I didn't manage to heal myself, did I?"

Sapphurion touched her flank with his knuckle. Lia could but marvel at the sensations a simple touch conveyed to her Dragon senses. "You must accept the truth of what is. Healing oneself is always the hardest. I'll be grateful for every breath I take beyond this day. But I grieve, Dragonfriend. She was … so …"

"She was your Dragonlove."

"Aye." His muzzle turned to the sky, shaking slowly. He had been unable to speak as Dragon after Dragon came to welcome the Star Dragoness to the fires of draconic life, or to add a seal of their fire to Hualiama's and Grandion's fire-promises. "Ask your question lest it burn more than your tongue."

He knew? "Noble shell-father, how can I accept this truth? This … Dragoness?"

"What do you mean, little one?"

Cold winds blew over the Islands. She kept expecting to fade into morning, to wake from the dream. How could she trouble him with her paltry grief, when he had lost his soul-mate? Bitterly, Lia said, "My mother and father are dead. How can I become a *Dragon?* Dreams don't come true for girls like me. They just … don't."

"Never say that, little one," he whispered. His paw drew her against his great muzzle, although it was he who shook more than she did at the mingling of their emotions. "Never think it, for untruth is dark-fires to our kind. You're still that little sprite I held in my paw. Clothed in a different raiment of beauty, aye. But the fundamental spirit, the essence of *Hualiama*, remains unchanged. We'll help you learn to fly. We'll believe with you. Every wingbeat. One day, you'll wake to the knowledge that you've flown beyond your eggling dreams."

Kindness to cut to the living pith of a person.

"But it's all wrong!" she burst out, spitting fire

unexpectedly. "If I'm a Dragon, how come I'm so tiny? Islands' sakes, I can curl up in your paw. I must be a tenth of your size!"

"You're a hatchling. Just the right size."

"I'm not a hatchling! I'm twenty-one years old. Sapphurion, this is ridiculous. I'm a Dragon and I still can't have him." The great Blue quirked an eye-ridge at her. Of course he didn't understand. Cringing at her selfishness, Lia muttered, "I wanted to–you know, I imagined I could *be* with Grandion …"

"Oh?" One syllable, and the Blue Dragon had his shell-son's belly fires howling with embarrassment. "Give it a few years. Little Dragonesses grow into–"

"I don't want to wait."

"ENOUGH!"

Azziala! Every Dragon gasped. Elki leaped to his feet, fumbling for his sword.

"Oh, don't bother with that." Azziala surveyed them from her perch on a rock not thirty feet from Lia's left flank, her face bloodied and burned, yet her eyes still blazed with that unnerving blue. "Touching as you seem to think this revolting spectacle is–Dragon, obey! Roll over."

Mizuki flopped over on her side like a hound begging for its belly to be scratched.

A dozen Dragons swivelled, summoning their fires.

"DRAGONS, OBEY. BRING MY DAUGHTER TO ME."

Hualiama yelped as Sapphurion's claws raked her departing tail. She wriggled free, desperately trying to escape the clutch of claws from all sides, but with a wing broken beneath the secondary wing-joint, she was not about to fly anywhere. Azziala casually deflected four fireballs, and froze the attacking Dragons in their tracks with a click of her fingers, not even bothering with the command-hold structures.

The Empress' eyes glittered as she surveyed her draconic captives. Sapphurion. Grandion. Mizuki. A dozen more. "No more hiding, Hualiama."

The Dragoness shifted from beneath Grandion's belly, where she had scuttled as he batted at her with his paws. The

Tourmaline stood immobile. Bound.

Lia matched Azziala glare for glare.

Her mother said, "You see, daughter, I also possess a talent for surviving in the most adverse circumstances. There's much to admire in your spirit–how you breached a sealed underground lair, pretended to die and even concealed this disgusting lizard from my Enchantresses, despite our Reaving. You'll have to teach me that star-fire trick. I imagine a power which can fry a Dragon in his own hide will come in useful when we start our campaign to conquer the Kingdom of Kaolili."

Coiling in readiness, Hualiama spat, "Still think I'll join you? You're deluded." She'd show Azziala exactly what her Dragoness could do!

"Oh no," said her mother. "Guess again."

Hateful woman! Yet, the cold calculation in her smile gave Lia pause. What was Azziala scheming? How could she, alone, hold so many Dragons in her thrall? Had she been concealing her true power all along? Now, she had every Dragon in sight quivering at her fingertip command–save Lia. Surreptitiously, she reached for Grandion. Nothing.

Azziala said, "Silence, my daughter? Most refreshing, where you're concerned. When were the lizards going to tell me about their most devious plot–to supplant a babe in my womb with a Dragon?"

Hualiama gasped. "No." Azziala was wrong. She must be, yet Lia remembered the rage of a seven-headed Ancient Dragon unleashed upon a tiny eggling … *the third great race will emerge from the shadows.* What was she? Not the crux of a draconic plot. But Humans did not become Dragons. It was impossible.

"Aye. Let this knowledge Reave you, the knowledge of the depths Dragons will stoop to in order to grasp their objectives."

"M-Mother, that's v-vile." Lia hated that in extremity, she always stammered.

"Aye!" Azziala sounded far too cheerful. "With you, I fear, it has always been a matter of finding the right leverage. I could threaten the Tourmaline. Turn him against you. Wipe his mind of all memory of an irksome dragonet masquerading as a Human. But I've a better idea."

Hualiama gritted her fangs. "Oh please, do tell."

"You will join me and my Dragon Enchanters in a new enterprise. You'll teach me how to raise Land Dragons. You will lead these motely lizards against my enemies, turning neither to the right flank nor to the left, unswervingly obedient."

"I'll resist you to my last breath."

"You forget one important detail, child. Unlike last time, you won't have a mind left to resist." Her finger rose in an uncannily talon-like gesture, as if she intended to claw Hualiama's Dragon hearts out of her chest one by one. "You're Dragonkind, now. And I am your worst enemy."

In that instant, Hualiama knew what it was for her Dragon fires to turn to dark-fires, for despair to invade and chill even the spirit of a creature created of fire and magic. The Island-World froze in accord with her realisation. The dream was in truth a nightmare, her own nature the seed of her destruction.

The Empress of the Dragon-Haters made a mocking beckon with her forefinger. "DRAGON, OBEY."

End of Book 2

Hualiama's story continues in *Dragonsoul*, Book 3 of the Dragonfriend Series.

Appendix

Lesser Dragon Subspecies of the Lost Islands

The Lost Islands boast a unique ecosystem and four unique Dragon types–subspecies of the Lesser Dragons–developed by the Ancient Red Dragon scientist, Dramagon, to be the perfect draconic war-machine.

Tynukam: nicknamed 'Grunts'–a literal flying fortress. Deep red in colouration, the Tynukam are squat, massively armoured Dragons of relatively low intelligence. Their scales overlap like plate armour and they boast a double row of short, conical fangs in the upper and lower jaws. They supplement their diet with large quantities of metal ore. Due to their massive metallic sheets of armour, these Dragons can fly short distances at best and are more suited to ground or underground warfare than aerial combat, unless supported by an Overmind. A favourite combat technique is for Overminds to pick up Grunts and propel them at the enemy at ridiculously high speeds. Grunts, of course, are expendable.

Anubam: burrowing Dragons. Short in stature with massively oversized forepaws which make them look mole-like. Very slow fliers, they prefer to ambush their prey from beneath the earth or rock. Being Brown in colouration, Anubam possess magical capabilities to burrow through, pulverise, shape and shoot all forms of rock and earth. They have a particular love of garnet gemstones and will spend months polishing a favourite jewel. Easily distracted by a sparkly gift, but vicious when roused–which is often, as they are a rowdy, factious clan which loves nothing better than an all-claws-in brawl.

Indubam: the 'Swarm'. Small and manoeuvrable bat-like Red Dragons which grow up to ten feet in wingspan, with iridescent purple bodies and a hinged, underslung jaw capable of accommodating an unexpectedly large bite. Hunt in large shoals up to fifty strong which resemble flying piranha. Their long, curved fangs produce a paralysing sting and their ovipositor-like tails shoot a barbed hook attached to a cord, which allows them to bind their prey before eating it alive. Have no ability to breathe fire. Once a year, the Swarm drink copious quantities of highly nutritious nectar produced by their females before indulging in days-long aerial combat to determine the alpha male of the clan.

Dramubam: the 'Overmind'. Smallish Dragons usually no more than fifty feet long, Jade in colour with a smattering of Browns and Blues. Long and serpentine in the body, with four wings and short legs. Named by Dramagon in honour of his magnificent genius, Overminds are the crowning glory of his breeding programme. They possess powerful psychic gifts, but are also inveterately lazy and vain. They keep both Human and Dragon slaves and shy from combat, preferring to leave such messy labours to their minions. Nevertheless, due to high intelligence coupled with a malevolent temperament, most Overminds make dreadful friends and even more terrible enemies. The best defence is to set Overminds at each other's throats by complimenting one at the expense of others.

About the Author

Marc is the bestselling author of over a dozen fantasy books. Born in South Africa, he lives and works in Ethiopia with his wife and 4 children, 2 dogs, a rabbit, and a variable number of marabou storks that roost on the acacia trees out back. On a good night you can also hear hyenas prowling along the back fence.

When he's not writing about Africa or dragons, Marc can be found travelling to remote locations. He thinks there's nothing better than standing on a mountaintop wondering what lies over the next horizon.

If you enjoyed this story, please consider leaving a review on Amazon.com, or reading one of my other works. Every review matters and I read them all!

Where you can find me:

Email: marcsecchia@gmail.com
Twitter: @authormarc
Facebook: www.facebook.com\authormarc
Website www.marcsecchia.com

Other Books by Marc Secchia

Shapeshifter Dragons: (Young Adult and older readers) Chained to a rock and tossed off a cliff by her boyfriend, Aranya is executed for high treason against the Sylakian Empire. Falling a league into the deadly Cloudlands is not a fate she ever envisaged. But what if she did not die? What if she could spread her wings and fly?

Long ago, Dragons ruled the Island-World above the Cloudlands. But their Human slaves cast off the chains of Dragonish tyranny. Humans spread across the Islands in their flying Dragonships, colonising, building and warring. Now, the all-conquering Sylakians have defeated the last bastion of freedom–the Island-Kingdom of Immadia.

Evil has a new enemy. Aranya, Princess of Immadia. Dragon Shapeshifter.

Aranya
Shadow Dragon

Shapeshifter Dragon Legends: (Young Adult and older readers) A young Pygmy warrior is stolen from her jungle home and sold to a zoo, where she lives for seven years before being kidnapped by the Red Dragon Zardon. Now, the courage of the smallest will be tested to the utmost. For Pip is the Pygmy Dragon, and this is her tale.

The Pygmy Dragon
The Onyx Dragon

Dragon Thief: (standalone New Adult/adult fantasy)

Kal was not a thief. He certainly did not intend to steal any dragon's treasure.

Adventurer. Avid art collector. Incurable wealth adjuster and risk-taker. Kal had legendary expertise in the security arrangements of palaces and noble houses the world over. He hankered for remote, craggy mountaintops and the dragon hoards he might find hidden beneath them. Besides, what harm was there in looking? Dragon gold was so very … shiny.

Most especially, he was not planning for any treasure to steal him.

Dragon Thief

The IsleSong series: (Young Adult and older readers) A story for anyone who loves the ocean and its whales, salt water in their hair, and the gentle rasp of beach sand between their bare toes. This story will transport you to a beautiful, unspoiled ocean world where people have to rely on Whales to travel between the islands. A world where danger can, and does, lurk beneath any wave.

The Girl who Sang with Whales (IsleSong Book 1)

The Shioni of Sheba series: (Middle Grades and older readers) Unique African historical fantasy adventures set among the myths and legends of ancient Ethiopia.

Shioni of Sheba #1: The Enchanted Castle
Shioni of Sheba #2: The King's Horse
Shioni of Sheba #3: The Mad Giant
Shioni of Sheba #4: The Sacred Lake
Shioni of Sheba #5: The Fiuri Realms

Epic fantasy (New Adult and Adult readers) Epic length tales of unique worlds and powers.

Feynard
The Legend of El Shashi

The Equinox Cycle series: (Young Adult and older readers)

Trapped in a car wreck, crushed by a train. In seconds, Zaranna's world is torn apart and she must start life anew, as a survivor. A double amputee. Yet why does this promising equestrienne remember a flash of sulphurous fire, and a crimson paw hurling her mother's car onto the train tracks? Why does a tide of beguiling butterflies flood her increasingly chaotic dreams?

As Zaranna Inglewood adjusts to life minus legs, plus gorgeous Alex, the paramedic who cut her body from the wreckage, she learns the terror of being hunted. Relentless and inimical, the enemy lures her to a world where dreams shape reality. Equinox. A world of equinoctial storms; lashed by titanic forces of magic, dominated by the Pegasi and their centuries-old enmity with Human Wizards and the Dragons. This is a world where a girl can Dream her destiny. Where her soul can fly, or be chained forever.

She is Zaranna, the Horse Dreamer. Survivor. Fighter. A

girl who doesn't need legs to kick an evil fate in the teeth. All she needs is courage–the courage to Dream.

The Horse Dreamer